MW01623422

Awakenings

I Found My Heart in San Francisco
Book One

Susan X Meagher

AWAKENINGS

I FOUND MY HEART IN SAN FRANCISCO: BOOK ONE

© 2006 BY SUSAN X MEAGHER

ISBN 0-977088-51-0

THIS TRADE PAPERBACK ORIGINAL IS PUBLISHED BY BRISK PRESS, NEW YORK, NY 10011

FIRST PRINTING: FEBRUARY 2006

THIS IS A WORK OF FICTION. NAMES, CHARACTERS, PLACES, AND INCIDENTS ARE THE PRODUCT OF THE AUTHOR'S IMAGINATION OR ARE USED FICTITIOUSLY. ANY RESEMBLANCE TO ACTUAL PRESONS, LIVING OR DEAD, BUSINESS ESTABLISHMENTS, EVENTS, OR LOCALES IS ENTIRELY COINCIDENTAL.

THIS BOOK, OR PARTS THEREOF, MAY NOT BE REPRODUCED IN ANY FORM WITHOUT PERMISSION.

Acknowledgements

I began to write this story in 1998, intending to write a longish book about a budding relationship. I began posting the story on the Internet, and over time came to know a large number of wonderful people who have helped and encouraged me to expand it to its planned 26 books.

Daylene has been reading the books for 7 years now and has given me countless hours of her editing talent. I owe her a lasting debt of gratitude for her help.

Thanks to the team who helped proof this edition. It took a lot of time and effort from all: Stefanie, Edye, Judy, Karen, Laura, Lori, and Elaine. It takes a village of sharp-eyed people to reduce the number of errors that make it to print.

My partner, Carrie, is an integral part of my writing career, and neither my books nor my life would be the same without her.

Last, but never least, this series is dedicated to my dear friend and chosen sister, Anne Brisk, a true grammarian and lover of language. My world has been slightly off its axis since you left it.

By Susan X Meagher

Novels

Cherry Grove

All That Matters

Arbor Vitae

Serial Novels

I Found My Heart in San Francisco:

Awakenings

Beginnings

Coalescence

Disclosures

Entwined

Fidelity

Getaway

Anthologies

Girl Meets Girl

Tales of Travelrotica for Lesbians: Vol 2

Undercover Tales

Telltale Kisses

The Milk of Human Kindness

Infinite Pleasures

To purchase these books go to

www.briskpress.com

Chapter One

She grabbed the first shirt that caught her eye. In a casual move, she slipped it on over the tank top she wore. The small, blonde shop owner noticed that her customer didn't look in a mirror to determine her satisfaction with the garment. It seemed as though she possessed an internal mirror to gauge her appearance, and that impression gained credence as she stood for a moment or two until a look of pleasure overtook her handsome face. The shop owner met her glance and walked over to greet her beautiful customer.

"Is there something I can help you with?" she asked, hoping to engage this woman in at least a conversation.

"Yeah, I think I'll take this shirt," she indicated, passing her strong hands down her torso. Looking like she already knew the answer, she asked, "Is it me?"

The golden haired woman openly admired her statuesque visitor. "Definitely. But anything in here would look great on you,"

"That's the nicest compliment I've had all day," the brunette drawled as a smile twitched her lips.

"It's only eleven o'clock. I'll bet that you'll have more than you can handle by dark."

Wow, she really wants to play. Well, I'm always up for a game—let's see how far she'll go.

The dark haired woman showed a wolfish grin. "Wanna hang out to help me fight off all of the compliments being hurled my way?"

"I would," the shop owner said hesitantly, as she darted a glance around the store, "but I don't have any other help today. I'm stuck here until nine tonight."

"Hmm, that is late," the raven-haired beauty agreed with a regretful shake of her head. Her perfectly shaped eyebrows knit together for a moment, and then her features broke into a sly grin. "How do you stop for lunch or a break?"

"When business is slow I can lock up for a little while." She blushed a bit as the implications of this thought and the knowing grin of her pursuer hit her simultaneously.

"No one's come in since I've been here."

"I'm not sure I'd have noticed if someone had," she replied, feeling a little weak in the knees. She had never flirted this shamelessly, but something about this woman made her unable to control the responses coming from her mouth or her body.

"If you were to take a little break to nibble on something where would you go?" Blue eyes darkened with open desire.

The store owner's dry mouth squeaked out, "I have a little office with a couch in the back of the store," and she felt her hand point weakly at a door in the rear of the building.

"I'll be right back," soothed the stranger, as she made her way with confident strides to the front of the store. She glanced at the door and spotted a sign that mimicked a clock that read "Will Return In" with blue plastic clock hands. She moved the hands to noon, turned the sign around and slapped the bolt on the door in place. She was back before the shop owner could take a step in either direction. The customer gently clasped her hand and led the way to the office.

In less than the beat of a heart, the blonde found herself sprawled across the worn, dark leather of her couch, responding with ferocity to the caresses of her beautiful customer. The intensity of the touch and the powerful aura that radiated from this woman were truly overwhelming, so much so that she felt completely powerless to slow the pace or collect her scattered thoughts. She knew that this was very much unlike her, but she had no desire to stop the relentless assault to her senses. There was a fire within this woman and she needed to dive into the conflagration.

She felt her clothing being gently removed—first the deep red French-cut T-shirt, then the short black skirt. Both were tossed casually to the floor. She shivered a little at the coolness of the leather on her bare skin. The strong hands moved over her body, rubbing her breasts through the lace bra. Then they slowly glided over grinding hips to caress soft curves through silky panties. The practiced hands then removed even these barriers to the fierce blue eyes and warm, wet lips.

Lips descended on the smaller woman with a burning fire that ratcheted her desire up several notches. She desperately craved more contact as she wrapped her fingers in the onyx tresses and ground the woman's mouth to her breasts, arching into the sensation. Reluctantly, she released her grasp when she felt the dark head sliding down her abdomen. She raised her legs and slid them around the broad shoulders that paused above her for a moment. Looking beseechingly at those clear blue eyes, she uttered the only word that would tumble from her lips. "Please." She was met with a wide smile and a look of quiet pleasure from the beautiful blue orbs. The dark head dipped and tasted her passion, which flowed from her like lava, burning in its intensity. She gasped and tried to vocalize her pleasure, but was unable to utter more than a low growl. That tortured sound was met by an even lower growl that sounded like the contented murmurings of a panther over its kill.

She thrust her hips at the mouth that covered her, watching with half-closed eyes as the dark head moved slowly between her legs. Long, blissful moments passed while she allowed herself to be completely consumed. But after too short a time she felt herself go rigid for a split second, teetering on the edge of climax. One firm, wet kiss and she plummeted over, completely unable to hold back any longer. Grunting out her pleasure, she grabbed the dark head and pressed it against herself. Finally she felt the mouth slowly still. She rested for a moment and then felt delicate kisses begin to tenderly remove the traces of her ardor. Her legs relaxed and she was finally able to speak. "That was wonderful," she languidly enthused to the dark head still nestled between her legs.

The head tilted up and rested on her abdomen, and the blonde was rewarded with a full, rich smile. "You seemed to enjoy it."

"Let me return the favor," the smaller woman huskily responded, reaching up to unbutton the new shirt from her talented customer.

"I wish we had time, but it's almost noon," the stranger said with obvious regret. "I'm sure you have customers. Remember, I promised to only keep you for a little nibble."

"There are plenty of other clothing stores on Telegraph Avenue," the golden haired woman responded lazily from her still blissful languor.

"Yeah, but none of the others have such great customer service " She was rising from the floor and straightening her clothing as she responded.

"Are you really leaving? But … don't you … I want to please you too."

"You already did." She smiled again, charming the store owner thoroughly. "I'm glad I decided to buy this shirt. " She indicated the rumpled garment with the wet marks gracing the placket. "The ah … design might not appeal to all of your customers," she said, with a quirky grin that lit up her face. "But I think it'll become one of my favorites. Which reminds me, what do I owe you?"

"I should pay *you* for that little lunch break," the blonde said, blushing modestly. "Please consider it a small thank you gift."

"Okay, but next time I'll try not to damage the merchandise before I've paid for it."

The honey haired woman paused a moment, then asked tentatively, "Will there be a next time?"

She was met with a confident leer, "Count on it." The tall woman turned and started for the exit, sparing her one last dazzling grin as she hesitated at the door for a second or two, then was gone.

Straightening her clothing, the owner made herself as presentable as possible, finally floating dreamily out of the office to walk behind the counter. Resting neatly on the glass surface were two twenty-dollar bills and a note that read, "Thanks for the nibble. You made my day."

I hope I didn't make a mistake in taking this class. I'm afraid I'll stick out like a sore thumb. I wonder what I should wear? That's gonna be a tough one. I really don't want to look too straight … hmm.

"Oh, that feels really good sweetheart," Jamie murmured into Jack's ear. As soon as the words of encouragement left her lips, she regretted her statement. In his defense, Jack was nothing if not receptive to instructions. Regrettably, he took them a bit too seriously. He seemed to reason that if something felt good, he should continue to do it until he was bodily forced to stop.

"That's a little too much, Jack." Jamie did her best to keep the edge out of her voice. She sighed deeply and reflected that she was absolutely sure that she didn't have instructions printed on her stomach, but Jack acted as though he was following some kind of script. Yes, he was tender and sweet and very attentive—but he had no spontaneity—no intuitive sense of how to please her.

He went back to his usual routine, and Jamie fell back into her reverie. *I can always drop the damn class if I feel too uncomfortable with those people. It's no big deal.*

Jack was close now and she whispered words of love into his ear to hasten his climax. As she spoke she idly considered how she loved his ears—they were perfectly shaped and had a light covering of downy blond hair on them. When he was excited they glowed with an attractive blush that Jamie found irresistible.

He threw his head back as his eyes became glassy and unfocused. With a grunt, he spent his release into her as she rubbed his back and murmured into his pink ear. After a moment, as his breathing slowed, he looked at her with concern in his deep blue eyes, "You didn't finish, did you?"

"That's okay, honey, you can get me twice tomorrow," she said with a sweet smile. "You look so tired, love, put your head down here." She patted her chest, smiling gently as she could see him consider the request. He looked as though he wanted to argue, but she was gently tracing patterns on his back and he quickly lost his will to resist. With a deep sigh, he rested his sandy blonde head on her breast and was asleep in moments.

She regarded his attractive tanned face with loving eyes. *I'm so lucky to have him*, she thought. *He tries so hard to please me. Not many men would be so concerned with my pleasure. I wish I knew how to explain the way I like to be touched.* She lightly ran her fingers through the damp hair covering his forehead. *I wish I could relax about the whole thing*, she thought. *I'm only twenty years old and they say most women don't hit their sexual peak until they're in their forties*. Jack shifted a bit and nestled his head into her neck. *Well, that thought really helped*, she groused. *I'll just wait twenty years to feel hot*.

Jack had turned twenty-four just the week before, the same day he had gone back to Stanford for his third year of law school. Their relationship had reached this stage of intimacy quite recently. Jamie's friends had teasingly called her the "last attractive virgin in California," for the past four years. But when Jamie made up her mind about something, it was tough to change it.

She had decided when she was fifteen that she wouldn't have intercourse with a man she didn't love. She steadfastly stuck to that resolve, even when her hormones were on full alert. It had surprised her and shocked her friends that a guy like Jack had continued to date her for two years, given that Jamie refused to have sex. But Jack, like Jamie, knew what he wanted, and would sacrifice to get it. He felt like everything was worth it when she relented at the beginning of the summer and they had consummated their love. They had spent a lot of time together during the past three months, but Jamie continued to stay with her parents to avoid any questions about their relationship. It had been hard on Jack to see her for just a few hours a day, but he coped with the inconvenience like he did so many things.

They were both looking forward to the start of Jamie's fall semester at Berkeley as a way to have more quality time together. They'd made plans for her to come down to Palo Alto every Friday night to spend the weekend, and Jamie hoped these times together would give her some indication of what married life would be like.

As she cradled Jack's head on her chest she reflected over the last two years of their relationship. When they met Jamie had just graduated from The Oaks, a private academy on the peninsula of the San Francisco bay area. Much to her parents' displeasure, she was going to attend the University of California at Berkeley. Both of her parents were Stanford alum's, and they were very much invested in having their only child attend their alma mater. But Jamie wanted to see a different side of the Bay Area. She knew that Stanford would be like continuing in high school. The same type of rich, smart kids. The same types of parties, although now in a fraternity house. She wanted to see the grittier, more vibrant side of the city that her family home in Hillsborough insulated her from.

Thinking back, Jamie had to admit that she was taken with Jack from the onset. He had been working as a summer associate at her father's law firm, getting ready for his first year of law school. She still remembered the night her father had brought him home for dinner. She took one look at the tall, well-built young man and knew that her sparkling eyes were sending a clear message. Over dinner, he responded with a matching level of interest, and by the next weekend they went on their first date. He was tall, with broad, sloping shoulders and a runner's lean frame. He had a strong face with a perennial deep tan, and his deep blue eyes were framed by pale blond lashes. His thick, straight hair, colored a nice shade of ash blonde that lightened a bit in the summer, was worn parted on the side and relatively short in the back. There was usually a thick shock of it hanging in his eyes that gave him a cute, boyish look that Jamie loved from the start.

He was such a welcome change from the boys she had known in high school. He was mature, and confident and very interested in her. But unlike her high school boyfriends, he didn't seem only interested in her for sex. He wanted to build a relationship.

As she watched Jack sleep in her arms, she felt a fierce well of emotion build up inside of her. *I'll try to be what you need, Jack. But I need you to be patient with me while I figure some things out.*

Sunday morning dawned bright and clear. Jamie was up early, as was her custom, always enjoying the early morning solitude. When Jack made his way into the small kitchen, she was sitting at the counter drinking a large latte and reading *The New York Times*.

"Hi, sleepyhead," she teased as their eyes met.

"Wow, I didn't realize how tired I was. It's almost eight! I never sleep that late." As he shuffled over to her, she opened her arms and enveloped him in a big hug. "Maybe Dr. Jamie's sleeping potion was too strong for you," she murmured, adding a nibble to his earlobe.

He grinned down at her as he replied, "That reminds me, I need to give you a double dose of that potion today."

"It's a deal. But at the moment I'd like to get you into clothes, not out of 'em. Remember, you promised we could go to church today."

"Oh, right," he said. "Let me take a quick shower, and we can get going. Did you want to hit the nine, or the eleven o'clock service?"

"I thought nine o'clock, and then maybe we can play a round with Daddy, if he's available."

"Sounds good, sweetie," he said over his shoulder as he walked into the bathroom. "Why don't you give him a buzz?"

The day was shaping up well. Her father happily agreed to play golf, and since her mother had just returned from her month long vacation to visit her family in Rhode Island, she wanted to come along and have brunch beforehand. *Gosh, I can't believe I completely forgot that she was back this week,* Jamie thought. *I should have called her on the day she came back. I've got to get better about staying in touch. It seems like we barely speak anymore.*

The young couple settled into a pew near the front of the small Episcopal Church on the outskirts of Nob Hill in San Francisco. As the choir began the opening hymn, Jamie turned slightly to watch the procession. As the acolytes, the verger and the choir filed past, the young woman made eye contact with a gray haired, elegant looking priest. She wrinkled up her nose a bit and winked at him. He gave her a fond smile and winked back.

Charles Sloan Evans had been an Episcopal priest for nearly forty years. He and his wife had reared a son and two daughters, the eldest child being Jamie's father. Jamie had always known where her father got his sense of humor and his generally easy going nature, but as much as she loved her father, her grandfather was Jamie's ideal of what a man should be. He was kind, warm, empathetic and very funny. Jamie spent many an hour in his study just talking about life. He seemed to understand her in a way that she doubted anyone else ever would. Her grandmother had died before Jamie was born, but her grandfather never seemed lonely. He was very dedicated to his calling, and genuinely loved helping people through the trying times of their lives.

After the reading of the gospel, Rev. Evans climbed to the pulpit. His deep, clear voice warmed Jamie's heart, and she smiled to herself as she felt the familiar satisfaction that always touched her when he spoke. Today's sermon focused on love, one of his favorite themes. As she let his warm, comforting words reach her heart, she spared a moment to consider the people who chose to attend a church where the heart of the message was sin and retribution. It puzzled her that people would select that type of spiritual teaching when they could easily avail themselves of a more hopeful, forgiving tone. *I suppose it's what you're used to*, she decided.

Reverend Evans spoke of love being God's greatest gift to man, and the most visible sign of His presence among us. Through love for another, humans acknowledged this gift of love from God and expressed it in concrete form. In no other way could we feel His love for us as completely. This manifestation was a gift to be cherished—not taken frivolously. Through the loving pairing of two people, God dwells among them.

Jamie was thoughtful through the rest of the service. *Is that how I feel? Are my feelings for Jack that deep? Is this the height of my expression of God's love?*

As they filed out of the church hand in hand, Jack turned to Jamie and said, "Wasn't that a great sermon?"

"Yes," agreed Jamie, her brow still furrowed, "it really gave me something to think about."

"Your grandfather just expressed exactly how I feel about you," her fiancé said. Jamie felt her heart break at the look of love on Jack's face, and at that moment she desperately wished she felt the same way.

She pasted on a similar smile, and said, "I'm very happy that you told me that, Jack." She stretched on her tiptoes as she reached up with tears in her eyes and gave him a chaste kiss. He beamed down at her and remarked, "We're two very lucky people."

"We are," she said, sniffing away a tear. *But right now I feel like the lucky one.*

Jack enthusiastically shook Rev. Evans hand as they exited the church. Jamie gave her grandfather a big hug that was returned with gusto. "You hit another home run, Poppa," she said.

"Well, when I have such an attentive audience it inspires me to swing for the fences." After a few minutes of banter, the couple excused themselves to allow him to greet the rest of the congregants. Walking back to the car in reflective silence, they headed towards the club for brunch.

The Olympic Club was the scene of the majority of Jamie's Sundays since she was a small child. When she was young, her parents dutifully took her to church and Sunday school, but when she was old enough to drive herself, they began to find excuses for the religious part of the day. Even though the church services fell from their agenda, they still managed to spend many Sunday afternoons at the club. Her father played golf, while her mother chatted with her friends or sometimes played tennis. No matter their personal preferences, they nearly always enjoyed brunch together as a family. As they sat at their table overlooking the eighteenth green Jamie regarded them all with an appraising eye. *This is exactly where I'll be in twenty years,* she thought, shivering at the scene. *Jack and I will be with our children at a table just like this one. We'll be eating the same food—from the same china. Some of the waiters will still be here, and they'll tell the kids about me when I was a little girl. We'll be having the same topical conversation with the other members—about our golf games and our families and our busy lives. Jack and I will love each other, but I doubt that we'll share much other than the children. His real love will be his career—just like Daddy's is. Is this what I want? If not, what do I want?*

She was jolted from her musings by the crisply uniformed waiter saying, "Miss Jamie, what would you like to drink?"

"Oh, I'm sorry Harold, lemonade would be great, thank you."

"Jamie, you seem a thousand miles away this morning," said Jack. "Is anything wrong?"

"No, of course not," she replied, forcing a light tone. "I'm just thinking about school starting tomorrow. I guess I'm preoccupied."

"Do you have your pencils sharpened and a new Star Wars lunchbox?" he joked, giving her an impish smile.

"I'm partial to Malibu Barbie," she retorted, tossing her hair.

"I'm sure this will be a great year for you," he reassured her as he squeezed her hand. "And for us," he added with a confident grin.

Jamie made her way back to the home she shared with her roommates, plodding along the 101 freeway in her yellow Porsche Boxster, fighting the heavy traffic. *Why does every living soul have to leave the city for the weekend?*

I hope Mia's home tonight, she thought idly as she flipped through her CDs, trying to find something that would lift her out of her funk. *I guess I need to be sure what this mood is about, before anyone can help me get out of it*. She felt so—restless. Yes, she was restless—but for what? She truly didn't know—all she knew was that she felt unsettled—and had been since before she and Jack became engaged. One of the reasons she had accepted his proposal was that she hoped the decision would finally resolve her unease. She thought that once this part of her life was secured, she would feel more at peace. In reality, it had made things more uncomfortable. The problem was that no matter how much thought she devoted to the problem she didn't know how to rectify it. There was nothing wrong with Jack. She was sure of that. Nine tenths of the women in America would give their right arm to be with a man like him. The problem seemed to be with her. There was something missing from her life. There was a feeling of peace that she craved but couldn't conjure up when they were together. When she was honest with herself, the peaceful feeling was not something that she experienced very often, with Jack or alone. *I'm only twenty years old. Maybe I'm supposed to feel unsettled*, she thought as she drove on through the night.

When Jamie announced her decision to attend Berkeley, her parents had very reluctantly agreed, with the proviso that she not live on campus. They wanted her in an atmosphere similar to that of a real home, and they were helped in this quest by some of Jamie's prep school classmates. Mia Christopher was the daughter of Adam and Anna Lisa Christopher. Adam was a partner at a prestigious law firm in San Francisco, and a Stanford classmate of Jamie's father, Jim. The families were cordial with one another, but the girls' mothers were not particularly close. Anna Lisa was a fiery first-generation American, whose family hailed from Italy, while Jamie's mother Catherine was from a very old, very wealthy W.A.S.P. lineage. The women liked one another well enough, but they were far too different to feel truly comfortable.

Another prep school classmate, Cassie Martin, also enrolled at Cal. The situation with Cassie was just the opposite from Mia. Jamie's mother and Cassie's mother, Laura, were very good friends, but their husbands had never hit it off. Likewise, Jamie liked Cassie well enough, but she had never felt particularly close to the woman, nor had she ever truly trusted her. Their mothers' close relationship forced the girls to associate frequently, but Jamie didn't dislike Cassie enough to fight the enforced togetherness, so she went along and made the best of it.

All three sets of parents agreed that if the girls were to attend Cal it would be best if they lived together in a suitable home. So the three mothers got together and swept through Berkeley like a tsunami. They interviewed real estate agents, and found an acceptable house within walking distance of campus. It was a large, craftsman-style bungalow, built in the early 1920's. It had originally contained three bedrooms and one bath, but through the years additions had enhanced the original layout to create more generous bedrooms and add one and a half baths. All of the bedrooms and two baths were on the second floor. The first floor contained a very large, airy kitchen with a powder room and a door to a small, shaded back yard, a formal dining room, a spacious parlor and a small oak-paneled library. The house was truly beautiful with its generous deep front porch, original leaded glass windows, and beautifully restored redwood moldings throughout, and the young women were grateful to have it. Jamie loved the house from the moment she saw it, which was lucky since neither she nor her friends were consulted on the decision. Catherine Evans had made the actual purchase of the house, since she could make a purchase of that size without even noticing the dent in her bank balance. She assumed she would sell the property when the young women graduated—and given the housing market in the Bay Area, the investment would do as well, if not better, than having the money in the market.

The girls' mothers had furnished the home in a very attractive, if not luxurious, style. Jamie's mother had purchased all of the kitchen utensils, since the other girls had no interest in cooking. Her mother's investment proved beneficial to the other girls. Jamie put her hours of observing their family cook, Marta, to good use in cooking for herself and anyone else who was willing to help clean up afterward.

They got along well all through their freshman year, but during that summer both Cassie and Mia obtained steady boyfriends. Mia's new love, Jason, went to UCLA, and Cassie's boyfriend, Chris, went to Cal. This changed the dynamic between the women, and upset the balance they had created during their freshman year. While they didn't really argue, Jamie and Mia began to grow more distant from Cassie, and spend less and less time together as a threesome. Even though Jack was just down the freeway at Stanford, the fact that she didn't often see him during the week allowed Jamie and Mia to still spend quite a bit of time together.

Jamie had always liked Mia, but during the past year, their sophomore one, they had grown particularly close. They had begun to share the intimate secrets of their lives, creating a deep bond. Mia liked Jack and constantly teased Jamie about him. Jamie also liked Mia's boyfriend Jason, but she saw very little of him because he was in L.A. and didn't often travel to the Bay Area for visits.

As Jamie pulled up to the drive, she saw that Mia's car was at home, and that Cassie's was absent. By any reasonable standard, it was silly for them to have three cars in Berkeley. They didn't drive to school or use the cars much, but they came in handy for driving to the Peninsula for the occasional weekend at home.

"Hey Mia, are you here?" Jamie asked after she had opened the door.

"Yeah, I'm upstairs."

"You want anything from the kitchen?" Jamie shouted back up the stairs.

"Yeah, bring me a diet anything."

After making her brief stop in the kitchen, Jamie lugged her overnight bag and two diet Sprites up the wide oak staircase. Mia was lying on her bed, her room a total mess, as usual. She was inattentively watching television with a CD playing in the background. Jamie stood in the doorway and watched her friend for a moment, looking at her usually sunny, slightly cherubic face that was now resting in a bored grimace. Jamie sat next to her friend and handed her the soda. "Couldn't decide?" Jamie asked, pointing at both the TV and the CD player.

"I'm bored," Mia moaned, shaking her curly, mid-length, medium brown hair. "I'm so glad you're home early, James," she said as her dark brown eyes twinkled up at her friend. Jamie smiled at the nickname that Mia had bestowed on her during high school, thinking that she wouldn't allow anyone else to use it. Mia stretched languidly, pulling her five foot four inch frame to its full length. As Jamie gazed at her she acknowledged that Mia's body resembled her own in both size and weight, even though Jamie had passed Mia's height during high school. Both women were quite thin, almost painfully so at times, but there was a sturdy athleticism lurking within both that had never really been tapped.

"I'm glad I'm back too, I missed you, buddy."

"You did? Why? Did the perfect couple have a fight?"

"No, of course not. You know we don't fight. I just wanted to spend some time with you and get some girl talk in."

Mia rolled over and braced herself on her forearms so she could get a better look at her friend. "What's up, James? You do look a little down."

Jamie stared into space, the silence lasting until Mia started to grow uncomfortable. "I don't know," Jamie said, looking very frustrated. "That's my problem. I feel restless, like I want something to happen, but I don't know what." She slapped at her thighs with her open hands, the sharp sound startling Mia.

"You really seem wound up." Mia reached up and scratched between her friend's shoulders. Trying to inject a little levity, she asked, "Are things any better between the sheets with old Jack?"

"Please, don't tease me," Jamie said. She knew she shouldn't be irritable with Mia, but she was unhappy about her sex life, and she felt uncomfortable discussing it. She would never have broached the topic with Mia, but since her friend had been sexually active since she was sixteen, and was very open and cavalier about the topic, she knew she was a good resource.

"Hey, James, I didn't mean to offend you. Are you okay?" Mia asked.

"Yeah, I'm sorry. Things aren't any better and I'm getting frustrated," she admitted.

Mia sat up and moved closer to her friend. She put her arm around her shoulders and let her head drop until their temples met. "You know, James," she said, speaking softly. "I didn't start really enjoying sex for three years after I started. And it's only been since Jason that I love it consistently."

"Really?" Jamie asked, astounded at this news.

"Well, there were some parts that I always liked, but I didn't like fucking until Jason."

"But that's what's frustrating, Mia." Jamie's shoulders dropped in a gesture of defeat. "Before we actually had sex it was great. We would kiss and touch each other for hours. I felt so close to him. Honestly, I'd go home some nights and feel like I was on fire. But since we started to, well, you know," she blushed, "it feels so mechanical."

"James, I hate to break this to you but you're experiencing what every woman goes through when you go from teasing a guy to really doing it," she said, laughing wryly.

"I don't know what you mean."

"When a guy can't go all the way he has to spend all of his time doing what he thinks you want. For most women that means kissing and holding each other and touching each other. He keeps doing that until you figure, 'This guy will really know how to make love to me.' You finally give in, and then he has all the cards. He finally gets to do what he wants and it's payback time, baby! As little foreplay as possible, check for moisture content, and then it's time for the main event!"

Jamie looked at her with a completely shocked expression on her face.

"That look on your face says I've hit the penis on the head," Mia said.

"But … but why would women ever want to make love if that's all it was?" Jamie practically cried in frustration.

"Well, girlfriend, that's not all it ever is. If you find a guy who really loves to make love, it's all that and then some."

"But Mia, Jack tries so hard. It really bothers him if I don't come. He attacks me like a legal brief. He believes if he works harder and smarter it'll be great. I've tried to get him to relax. I've even considered faking an orgasm, but he watches me so closely I know he'd know I was faking, and that would really hurt him."

"Have you tried to lend a hand, so to speak?" Mia asked with a playful tone as she wiggled the fingers of her right hand.

"Yes," Jamie said, blushing again. "But he seems to think that I do that because he's failed. I've tried to tell him that I'm just helping a little, but it's hardly worth it when I see the hurt look on his face."

"I feel for you, hon," Mia said. "I've engaged in more bad sex acts than I can count, but it must be hard when it's with a man you love."

"That's what really scares me. That's the thing that wakes me up in the middle of the night. I'm gonna spend the rest of my life with Jack. If we don't enjoy sex now, why should I believe it'll be better in the future? Honestly Mia, at times I hope he comes to bed and doesn't want to do it," she said. "I mean, shouldn't we be tearing each others clothes off this early in our relationship?"

"Well, I'd think so, judging from my limited experience in doing it with guys I love. But don't worry so much, James. You have a great relationship, and Jack is a fantastic guy. Maybe he's right and more hard work will help everything to work out."

"Yeah, you're probably right," Jamie said, even though she was doubtful. "I mean we've only been doing it for three months. Maybe we have to get used to each other a little bit more." She pasted a smile onto her face and said, "Thanks for talking this over with me. You're the only one I trust enough."

"You're welcome, sweetie. I hope you know you can tell me anything."

As Jamie got ready for bed she thought over what her friend had said. *I've got the rest of my life to work on this; I guess I don't have to be in that much of a hurry. Mia's right. There's no reason to think this won't all work out in the end.*

As the class settled noisily into their seats, Professor Linda Levy scanned their faces. *Not bad*, she thought. *At least there are three men for a change.*

"May I have your attention, please?" Twenty mildly expectant faces gazed at the professor. "Welcome to Psychology 197—The Psychology of the Lesbian Experience. My name is Linda Levy. I'd like to get some housekeeping matters out of the way, and then I'll give you an overview of the class. If we have time I'd like each of you to introduce yourselves. I should warn you though, that this class is very interactive. If you're looking for a quiet spot where you can sleep in the back row for three hours a week, you've come to the wrong place."

Jamie closely regarded the professor. She was a small woman, a little shorter than Jamie. She was fit, and trim, and wore chinos with an attractive print silk blouse in shades of tan and brown. She had a warm smile and lively, sparkling eyes. Her wavy, chin-length hair was parted on the side, and there was a sprinkling of gray in it. Jamie guessed her to be somewhere in her forties, although she had to admit that she was not terribly good at guessing ages.

Linda walked from row to row and handed out three by five cards. "I'd like you to give me some personal information on these cards." Several women had an attack of the giggles. "It's not necessary to give me *that* information unless you think it's relevant," she replied with a laugh of her own. "I suppose we should tackle that issue right away." She perched on the end of the large wooden desk situated at the front of the room.

"I am now, and I always have been a practicing lesbian," she said, smiling. "However, lesbianism is not a pre-req for this course. I'm sure that will relieve you guys," she said as she pointed at the three men sitting near one another. "This class deals with the psychological issues that may be encountered by a group of people who have in many ways been marginalized by society. We will be undertaking this survey with the eyes of scholars—not participants. This is not a 'How to be a lesbian' course. You don't need to declare your sexual orientation to the rest of the class. The class usually turns out to be predominantly lesbian, but I not only welcome heterosexuals, I really encourage straight people to take the class. It's the people who aren't part of the peer group who can have the biggest impact on changing societal perceptions," she stated with conviction.

Jamie was relieved by this explanation. *I think I'm going to like this.*

Linda continued, "On the cards I'd like you to give me your names, phone numbers and a general idea of when you're available to do outside projects. I want to pair up class members based on their time availability to make it easier for everyone."

The class worked on their cards for a few minutes as Linda watched. *Well, they look less nervous now. This looks like the makings of a good group.*

Jamie worked on her card, neatly writing her relevant information on the white rectangle. She indicated her home number, and just to be thorough she included Jack's number with the words "fiancé's home number." *Well, it doesn't hurt to get that out of the way right from the start.*

Linda looked quickly at the cards as they were turned in. *Oh, that's cute*, she said to herself as she saw Jamie's card. *It always amazes me how people get those tidbits of information in*, she thought wryly as she noted that Jamie had found a way to mention that she was engaged to a man. She tried to match people's availability, and was pleased that she was able to do so fairly easily. "Okay, I'm going to write down partner names on the board. After we do our introductions you'll be able to find each other."

She strode to the board and began to write the ten pairs. Jamie saw her name go up on the board next to that of Ryan O'Flaherty. *Oh, great*, she moaned to herself, *I take a class in lesbianism, and I get paired up with a guy. Well, at least he won't assume he can hit on me. Unless he's the type who thinks lesbians are hot,* she thought suspiciously. *God, Jamie, get a grip! Yesterday you were afraid of the women, and today you're disappointed that you're paired with a man!*

Linda returned to her perch on the front corner of the desk. "Okay, let's get to work." She launched into a rather lengthy speech on how the course was developed, how long she'd been teaching it, and how it fit into the curriculum for psych majors.

Jamie was pleased with the way the course was organized. *This could really be interesting*, she thought. *I know so little about lesbians—and that's a liability in San Francisco. That's like living in L.A. and not knowing anything about the beach!*

Linda looked at her watch and noted with surprise that the seventy minutes were about up. "I apologize for going on so long," she said. "If you don't mind you can try to find each other after class to meet your partner. I'll see you all on Wednesday morning and we can discuss some of the class projects."

Well, at least I have it easy, thought Jamie—*there're only three guys*. She approached the first and tentatively asked, "Are you Ryan?"

"Nope, I'm Todd." The other two men were Demitrius and Mike, leaving Jamie at a loss. The rest of the class seemed to be more successful, and were all busily exchanging info. As people began to drift away Jamie noticed one lone figure sitting quietly. She was idly twirling a quarter on the surface of her desk, and didn't seem to be in any hurry to find her partner.

Jamie approached her from the back and asked, "Are you Ryan?" with a hint of exasperation in her voice.

The dark head turned and Jamie was nonplussed to see the most dazzling white smile she thought she had ever encountered. "Well, if I wasn't before, I am now," the beautiful woman answered with a tease in her voice, as a terribly sexy grin lit up her face.

Jamie blushed all the way to the roots of her blonde hair. The woman unfolded herself from the desk that was obviously too small for her long frame. She extended her hand, and Jamie mindlessly parroted her. "I'm Ryan O'Flaherty," she said, flashing that smile again. Jamie knew that it was her turn to speak, but for some strange reason she felt unable to. "And you're … " Ryan cast a quick look over at the chalkboard, "Jamie Evans?"

"Oh, right, I mean yes, I'm Jamie Evans," she heard her voice automatically respond.

"It's good to meet you, Jamie Evans."

Jamie knew that she should stop staring, but she was unable to control herself. Ryan was probably, no, Ryan was definitely the most beautiful woman she had even seen. She stood over six-feet-tall, with a sturdy but lean, muscular build. There was something very feminine about her body that the muscle paradoxically seemed to accentuate. Jamie guessed her jet-black hair was quite long, even though it was pulled back in a ponytail and partially hidden under a black knit driving cap—worn backwards. A tight, blinding white, thick cotton T-shirt hugged each of her ample curves, and covering that was a black and maroon paisley vest. This topped a pair of well-faded 501's that looked like they were created specifically for her long legs. A pair of shiny cordovan penny loafers worn without socks completed her ensemble, and even though it was a casual look, the clothing looked absolutely elegant on Ryan's graceful body.

Jamie realized that she was still gripping Ryan's hand, and immediately dropped it as though it were burning her. Ryan continued to smile at her, and Jamie found that it was very difficult to meet her penetrating gaze. When she finally forced herself to do so she was again shocked to discover the most dazzling pair of ice blue eyes that one could imagine. *Jesus*, she thought as she tore herself away from that intense gaze, *how does one woman get this many perfect parts*?

"Uhm, Jamie did you want to exchange phone numbers, or arrange to meet, or something?" Ryan asked gently, stooping down at bit and moving her head around as she tried to make eye contact with her new partner.

"Oh, sure, yeah, that's good, uhm … phone numbers … good," Jamie began to curse herself for her inarticulate ramblings. *I'm an English major*!

With Ryan providing most of the leadership, they finally exchanged their personal info. Ryan took down Jamie's number in a neat black organizer that Jamie noticed had a very busy schedule meticulously filled out. "When's the best time for you to get together?" Ryan asked.

"Well, I don't have a job, and my bo …" Jamie caught herself, and decided that she didn't want this woman to know about Jack. "My time's pretty open." she finally stated, without elaboration.

"Great. I'm pretty swamped, but weekday afternoons and weekend mornings are my best times. My schedule is really kind of unpredictable, but I'm sure we'll be able to get together." She smiled that impossibly dazzling smile again, and Jamie felt her brain once again begin to freeze.

"Where do you live?" Ryan asked with a small chuckle, as she unsuccessfully tried to hide a knowing grin.

Oh God, oh god! Jamie screamed to herself, *she knows!* She began to blush again and finally began to stutter, "Uhm … I … ahh …"

Ryan graciously took pity on her, and removed her piercing gaze. She looked down at her organizer and tried again. "Do you live in Berkeley?"

"Yeah," Jamie breathed out in relief. "Really close to campus."

"Oh, that's good. I live over in Noe Valley, but I'm sure we could meet here. You don't have a car do you?"

"Car?" Jamie said as though this was the first time she had ever heard the word.

"Yeah, you know, a big metal object with wheels, let's you go places that your feet can't take you," Ryan said, as she mimicked holding a steering wheel.

"Oh, yes I do! I do have a car!" Jamie was outrageously pleased with herself for being able to get a complete sentence out without stuttering. She decided against all reason that she liked being teased by Ryan and began to loosen up a bit.

"That's great," Ryan said. "I've got a bike, but some people don't like riding on it." Jamie dully wondered where on Ryan's bicycle she would ride, but banished that thought as Ryan once again extended her hand.

"I guess I'll see you on Wednesday then, okay?" Those crystal clear blue eyes locked on hers again. Jamie felt her hand being engulfed by the larger one and then gently shaken. Then felt her head bob a bit in response. Ryan dipped her head to make eye contact and winked playfully as she broke into another grin. Then she turned gracefully to stride from the room.

Jamie felt herself slide limply into a desk. She dropped her head to the cool wooden surface and sat in puzzled confusion for a moment. Finally she lifted her head and asked herself in a befuddled haze, *What in the hell was that all about?*

That night, after a quickly prepared dinner of salad and soup, Jamie and Mia sat cross-legged on Jamie's king-sized bed. The room was spotless, as always. Mia didn't understand Jamie's fixation on order, but she had to admit that it was really nice to be able to easily find things that she wanted to borrow. The room was generously sized and had a view of the small back yard. It was the biggest bedroom, and it made sense that Jamie should have it since her mother had purchased the house. There was a deep eave over the back of the house and it kept the room cool in the summer, even without air conditioning. Because the room was at the right rear corner of the home, there were windows on two sides that allowed for a great breeze most of the time.

The space was decorated in bright shades of yellow, with lots of white painted trim and a splash or two of marine blue. It gave the room a clean, almost nautical feel, and the near constant breeze enhanced that feeling. There were two doors, one to the wide hallway and another that opened to the tiled bath that Jamie shared with Cassie.

The only common wall was the one that bordered the bath. Jamie liked the sense of privacy that the layout provided her. Even though Jack had only stayed overnight once so far, it reassured her that her roommates couldn't hear any activity that might occur. Since Cassie spent most of her time with her boyfriend at his North Berkeley apartment, Jamie had gotten used to the privacy and secretly regretted the nights that Cassie did sleep in the house.

"Just back up a minute there, honeybunch," Mia said.

"What do you mean?"

"You, of all people, are taking a class called the Psychology of the Lesbian Experience?" Mia's expression was one of puzzlement mixed with shock. After a moment, she looked at Jamie with a rare somber gaze. Tentatively, she placed her hand on her friend's leg and asked, "Jamie, is there something you want to tell me?"

"Mia, you don't have to be a lesbian to take the stupid class," Jamie said, clearly exasperated by the implication.

With a face full of sweet innocence, Mia explained, "I was just asking if you were planning on switching to psychology as a major. Why would you jump to the conclusion that I think you're a lesbian?" The feigned innocence was still in place. "That's a very odd reaction, Jamie. Maybe you should look into this a little deeper."

Several heartbeats later, Jamie finally wised up. She pushed Mia's hand away and said, "Very funny. You're wasting your time in college when the stage is calling to you."

Mia laughed heartily, happy to catch her friend off-guard. "No, really, James. Why would you take that class? I've never known you to be overly interested in our more androgynous sisters."

"I'm not interested, per se, Mia. I needed an easy three-hour class. I haven't taken any other soft science so far, and this one meets early in the morning, which is my favorite time of day. There's no final, just a bunch of special projects that I have to do with a partner. I only have to write two short papers, and with the rest of my schedule being so difficult I can use all the easy classes I can get."

"Just how special are these projects?" Mia asked, a sexy leer on her face.

The blonde had taken about all of the teasing she was willing to take from her friend, so she decided to throw a little back at her. "Well, one is to participate in a bondage scene at a lesbian S and M club, and the other is to make a multi-media collage about cunnilingus—"

Her joke was interrupted as Mia spit a mouthful of Diet Coke all over her sleep shirt. "Mia!" she shouted as she jumped from the bed, trying to hold the Coke onto her shirt to keep it from dripping onto the spotless carpet. She scampered into the bathroom and emerged moments later to retrieve another oversized T-shirt from her dresser.

"Serves you right, Jamie. Don't make me laugh when I've got a mouthful of Coke. You know I have very little control over my reflexes."

"Well, it was worth it to get you like that," Jamie admitted. "Normally, I'm the brunt of jokes around here."

"Hey, did you say you have to do these projects with a partner?" Mia asked as Jamie resettled herself on the bed.

"Yeah, we got assigned partners today."

"What's she like, James? Did she bring her big rig to campus, or leave it idling out at one of the truck stops?"

Jamie rolled her eyes as it became obvious that this was going to turn into a semester long joke. "Why do you assume it's a woman? There are a few guys in the class."

"Not so fast, pal. Maybe you should order up some chromosome tests before you say that with such conviction."

Jamie glared at her friend as she shook her head. "You know, as the professor said today, it's people like you and me who can make the biggest impact on getting rid of stereotypes about gay people."

"Aw Jamie, you know I'm kidding. You've gotta admit it's kind of funny though, don't you?"

"I guess so," she finally admitted. "And for your information my partner is a woman named Ryan. We talked for a few minutes after class."

"Do you think she's gay?"

"Yeah, I'm sure she is." Jamie said this quickly, too quickly for Mia to ignore.

"Ohh, scoop, scoop, why are you so sure?"

"Well, to be honest, she flirted with me."

"Jeez, Jamie, what do you expect? You're probably the hottest woman in that class. They can all smell fresh meat. They were probably drawing straws to see who got you!"

"Mia, you're being ridiculous! If anyone in that class is gonna be in demand, it'd be Ryan."

"Ooo, is she good looking?" Mia inquired, her tone dropping into a deep register.

"Calling Ryan good looking would be an insult," Jamie said. "She's absolutely stunning. Long black hair, gorgeous blue eyes. She could model—and make a ton of money."

"Damn," the brunette drawled, "maybe it was you who was flirting with her."

"That's not funny. It really kind of made me uncomfortable," she said, although she clearly wouldn't tell Mia just how uncomfortable she had been.

Now that she saw that Jamie was bothered by the experience, Mia was, as usual, supportive. "Maybe she wasn't really flirting, maybe she's just friendly."

"No," Jamie snorted. "I've been flirted with enough to know the difference. It was like talking to a really good-looking guy. You know the type. The guy who's oozing with self confidence and hits on you without even trying."

"Well, you know, you've got three class meetings to drop it if you really don't like the vibes you're getting."

"I know. But I don't think she meant anything by it. She just seems like the kind of woman who feels really comfortable in her own skin. And when I tell her I'm straight I'm sure she'll stop."

"What! You didn't tell her you're straight?"

"No, it didn't come up, but I'm sure it will when we meet on Wednesday. Don't worry, I'll make it clear that I have a really big boyfriend right down the freeway who I think could beat her up."

"Well, I'm sure that'll be very reassuring to Jack," Mia said with a grin. "By the way, what does he think about your taking this class? I know Jason would want me to bring a cute one home for him to play with."

"Uh, we haven't really discussed my class schedule, you know how busy he is this year, what with law review and everything."

"Uh-huh, I see," said Mia slowly, eyeing her friend suspiciously.

"Knock it off, will you? I'm sure we'll discuss my schedule, and then I'll tell him. It's really no big deal." *Is it?*

Splash!! "Not yet … wait … wait …okay, fetch!" Ryan watched the curly haired black dog gambol through the surf, boldly ducking his strong head under the water as a small wave hit the shore. She kept a watchful eye on him as he paddled his way out to the large stick that she had thrown, and grabbed it with his soft mouth.

He made his way back through the waves and galloped up next to her. Waiting until he was inches away, he violently shook his coat. "Lucky for you I could use a little cooling off, Duffy boy," she said, laughing. They had been running on the beach since just after dawn, Ryan's favorite time of the day. She loved the smell of the ocean, loved to hear the gulls crying overhead, and especially loved spending time with Duffy in his true element. There was nothing her dog loved more than swimming and frolicking on the beach. "You know Duff, sometimes I think I'm more like you than I am human." Duffy looked at her with a silently understanding gaze. He was a fairly big dog, about twenty-five inches at the shoulder. He weighed in at around seventy-five pounds, and most of that was muscle. His mother was an elegant black standard poodle who had an unplanned liaison with a randy black Labrador. The poodle owners' loss of a litter of purebred pups was definitely Ryan's gain, since the owner was one of Ryan's clients. She asked Ryan for a ride home one day, and it took all of two minutes before the curly black male had a new home.

Martin O'Flaherty, Ryan's father, was not immediately happy about the addition to the family, but within a week the dog was the pride and joy of the whole clan. Duffy was really the perfect dog. He didn't shed, he loved to run and exercise, but he could tolerate being ignored for a full day if required. He almost never barked in the house, but outdoors he signaled the arrival of every person, dog or truck. He loved to be with Ryan but would gladly spend the day with anyone who had the time. Ryan secretly thought that her father was really the one most in love with Duffy—not that that was a surprise. Martin was a very big softie—although he liked to play the tough dad role.

On the walk to the car, Ryan planned her day—eight o'clock psych class, ten o'clock bio lab, lunch, one o'clock anatomy, work from four until nine. "Well, it's the start of another fun year, Duff."

Psych class sounds like it's gonna be fun. It's nice to take a class where you get to interact with humans. Living humans, she added as an afterthought as she considered her anatomy class. She thought about her psych partner, Jamie. *She really was cute with that blush she got when I teased her. But God,* she thought with a laugh. *she sure did seem nervous around me. I wonder what that was all about. It's hard to tell if she was really interested—or really nervous. I guess it could be that I'm gay, but if that bothered her why would she take a class about lesbians? I'm pretty sure she's straight, but you never know ... Now Ryan, you know you shouldn't feed or taunt the straight girls,* she reminded herself. In actuality, she had nothing against trying to change the minds of straight women. It merely seemed like an awful lot of trouble when you lived in San Francisco. Ryan was nothing if not pragmatic, and it seemed a waste of her valuable time given all of the eligible willing women she encountered. Now that it was so common for "straight" women to approach her for a brief tryst, she could maintain a steady diet of them if she so chose. *Things really have changed in the last few years,* she thought. *It's kind of nice to be the current fad.* She assumed that lesbianism would die out as a hip thing to experiment with, but she was more than willing to ride the wave while it lasted.

"Let's go Duff—I'll race you to the car!" She hoped they were home by the time her father noticed that his truck was missing, or else she'd be washing both the dog and the car that afternoon.

Jamie arrived at her psych class about five minutes early. She secretly hoped that Ryan would be there early too, and they could chat for a few minutes. *Relax Jamie, it's a long semester.* Initially she was pleased, but her pleasure turned quickly to pique, when she saw Ryan. Her long, lithe body was casually slumped in a small desk, and she was looking up at another student, female of course, who was leaning over her. The look on her partner's face was one of passive amusement. The woman flirting with her was pretty cute, too, by Jamie's assessment. About five foot six inches, dark skin, with coal black hair pulled into a braid. Ryan watched the woman with polite interest. After a few more moments, Professor Levy made her way into the room. Jamie saw Ryan take her felt tipped pen and write a phone number right on the palm of the woman's hand. The recipient of this little gift looked extremely pleased and a bit smug as she walked back to her desk. Ryan slowly turned her gaze to the left and made eye contact with Jamie. Her face broke in to that damned grin again and Jamie couldn't help but smile back with the same intensity, completely forgetting her pique.

As Ryan turned back to look at the professor, Jamie studied the younger woman critically. Today her outfit was quite a bit more casual than Monday's ensemble had been. Faded denim overalls covered a form-fitting red tank top. Red high-top basketball shoes, and a red Nike cap, backwards again, completed her look. Ryan's black hair was pulled into a ponytail again, and peeked out of the bottom of the bill of her cap. Jamie looked at her own clothes for a quick comparison. A mint green, sleeveless sweater covered by a matching long sleeved cardigan topped tight, stretch Capri chinos, and a new pair of delicate black leather sandals graced her feet. *We sure don't look like we're going to the same event!*

While she watched her classmate she felt her anger returning. Even though she knew she was being irrational, she didn't like Ryan spending her time flirting with another woman. *I wanted to use that time to arrange to get together for these projects,* she thought. *Right Jamie*, she chided herself. *It's the second class meeting and you don't even know what the projects are. Getting together is really urgent.*

The professor called them to attention during her musings. Jamie shook her head a bit and tried to focus.

"Good morning everyone. I trust you were all able to meet up with your partners on Monday. Sorry that I went a bit long and wasn't able to arrange those meetings in a more organized fashion. Let's make up for that by starting out with introductions.

"I'd like each of you to spend a few minutes describing yourself. You can talk about anything that you think is important. Remember, this doesn't have to be a coming out party, but if you want to discuss your sexual orientation I want you to feel comfortable. Why don't we start with you?" she pointed at a young man sitting near the door.

He looked like he'd pay anyone else to go first, but did as he was asked. "I'm Scott Williams. I'm a senior psych major. I plan on going to graduate school next year to become a psychologist. I'm interested in this class because I want to be comfortable working with disparate groups of people. I'm straight, but not narrow," he said, smiling.

He's really cute, thought Jamie. *I wonder if I should say I'm a psych major, too. That's at least a good reason for taking this course.*

The students continued in order. The woman Ryan had been flirting with introduced herself as Chitra Chuisapor . She was a psych major also, and she immediately dropped the "L" bomb. Jamie paid very close attention as she noticed that every person disclosed his or her sexual preference. *Oh, I don't want to do this*, she thought as her turn loomed near.

Ryan was next. "Hi, I'm Ryan O'Flaherty," she announced with her perpetual smile. "I'm a junior, majoring in biology and math, and this is my first semester at Cal. I'm interested in this class because I haven't done much reading on the lesbian experience and I think there's a lot to learn. I have done a lot of fieldwork, though," she added, waggling one expressive eyebrow.

How does she do that? Jamie wondered, trying the trick herself. *Don't most eyebrows move as a pair?* While she tried to imitate Ryan's facial gesture, she reflected on what the woman had said. *Does she have an accent? It doesn't sound strong, and I only notice it on certain words. I'll have to ask her*, she thought, as she happily considered conversing with Ryan again.

Her ears perked up when she heard four women declare that they couldn't claim any sexual orientation at all. Each of them had a variation on the statement that they were open to a wide variety of experiences, and didn't like to feel limited by a label. *Hmmm, that's interesting. It must feel strange not to feel one way or the other. I wonder if they're really gay, but don't want to be thought of that way. I can't blame them,* she thought. *That must be a very difficult life.*

Finally it was Jamie's turn. "Hi, I'm Jamie Evans," she began nervously. "I'm a junior English major. I'm engaged to a guy who's a third year at Stanford law school." She shot a glance at Ryan, hoping to see surprise, but was greeting with a calm, encouraging gaze. "I don't have a particular reason for taking the class other than the fact that I haven't taken any other psych classes. Oh. It fit my schedule really well," she admitted, pleased when some of her classmates laughed.

Well, that went okay, she thought as the next woman began to speak. *I hope I wasn't too obvious, talking about Jack like that, but I don't want anyone to get the wrong impression.*

After all twenty of them had introduced themselves, Linda spoke again. "I'm really glad to meet all of you. I think we'll have a great semester. Now let's discuss our projects. I'd like each pair to choose three of the following activities. You'll need to write a short paper on each of these projects, and I'll need each of you to do your own paper, since you'll have different reactions to the activity. The activities are as follows: you can visit a lesbian coffeehouse or bookstore, spend a day in the Castro, looking around and thinking about why the neighborhood became such a gay Mecca, attend a film during the gay and lesbian film festival, if you're straight, you can play 'gay for a day' with your partner, you can visit a lesbian bar if you're over twenty-one, or volunteer in a lesbian community organization for a day.

"Now, I'll allow you to use the last fifteen minutes of class to discuss the activities with your partner. See you all on Friday."

Jamie watched Ryan pull her long form from the small desk. She stood at her full height and gracefully began to stretch her back out. Jamie approached her from the side and gave her a small smile.

"Were these desks made for a grade school, or what?" Ryan asked as she bent over from the waist and let her fingers tickle the linoleum.

"I don't know, they seem just right to me."

Ryan looked her over from top to bottom, appraising her as if for the first time. "Well, you're about the size I was in grade school, so I've made my point."

"Hey, don't make fun of the height impaired," Jamie said with a scowl as she crossed her arms across her chest and tried to look intimidating.

"I wouldn't dream of making fun of you," Ryan said, her eyes suddenly turned serious.

"Right," Jamie said, her mouth suddenly dry. "So which of these projects do you think we should tackle?"

"Well," Ryan said, "do any of 'em particularly interest you?"

"Uhm, I guess I could do any of them. But since you said you have a busy schedule, maybe you should decide."

"Well, we live on different sides of the bay, so it might be easier to do the things that'd keep us in the East Bay most of the time. We could go to a women's bookstore in Oakland, and I know of a good lesbian community organization right here in Berkeley. You're not twenty-one yet are you?" she asked, looking uncharacteristically unsure of herself.

"Is it that obvious?" Jamie whined, petulantly stamping her foot.

"Well, yeah, a little, but I figured if you were a junior, there was a pretty good chance that you were about twenty."

Jamie was pleased that Ryan had listened to her so attentively. "You're a junior, too," she observed, "but I take it you're past the age of majority."

"Quite."

She wasn't forthcoming with any more information, and Jamie let it pass, deciding she could grill her later. "So that eliminates going to a bar. What about the film festival?"

"I might be able to squeeze some films in," Ryan said hesitantly. "But I think most of them are at night. I usually work at night, so that might be kind of tough."

"That's okay. There are still four other activities that we can do. And lucky for you I am obviously straight, so we can do the 'play gay for a day' thing."

"Do you think it's … obvious?" Ryan cocked her head and looked at Jamie very dubiously.

"Uhm … err … ah … well … yeah! Don't you?"

"Yeah, it is," Ryan said, She leaned her head back and laughed heartily, very pleased with her joke.

"You're teasing me again," Jamie said, tapping her foot and narrowing her eyes.

"Well, it's kind of fun, but I'll stop if it bothers you. I really will." She looked entirely serious, and Jamie believed her.

"No, I'm used to being the butt of jokes. I think it comes with the height thing."

"How about I make it up to you by buying you some coffee later?" Ryan offered. "Actually, if you're free we could go to Daughters of Sappho later and get one of our activities out of the way today."

"Alright, that would be fun." She had planned on going shopping with her roommate, Cassie, later, but she was sure she could put that off until next week.

"I've got a lab until two. Could you meet then?"

"Yeah, I can go get my car and pick you up. Where do you want to meet?"

"How about right in front of Cafe Roma?"

"Okay. See you at two."

The morning dragged on for Jamie. First, a long, rather rambling lecture on Wordsworth, followed by a slow walk home for lunch. She was pensive during her walk, thinking a jumble of thoughts about her psych class in general and her new partner in particular.

She really seems sweet and funny. I hope we can become friends, she mused. *She's so different from anyone else that I know. She seems so self-assured. I wonder what Jack would think of her? For that matter I wonder what Jack will think of this class? I know I should have told him, but he didn't directly ask me what I was taking. I don't have to tell him everything about my life, do I?*

Jamie knew that she was trying to convince herself of something, but she wasn't sure what that something was. She honestly didn't know what Jack's reaction to the class would be. For that matter, she had no idea what he thought of gay people in general since it wasn't a topic they'd ever discussed.

Well it's not like there has been a reason to discuss gay people. We don't know any as a couple. And all of the gay people I know are hairdressers or decorators, so that's kind of expected. Of course, I'd never have guessed that some of those women in the class were gay. For that matter, I'd never guess that Ryan was either … if she wasn't such a flirt, that is! I can't believe she was already hitting on someone from class. Of course, it looked like that woman was doing most of the hitting. Maybe Ryan was only being polite. She actually might be one of those "all talk, no action types."

After a quick lunch, Jamie settled down in one of the overstuffed chairs in the sunny living room, and did some reading for her 20th Century American Women Writers class. At 1:45 p.m. she hopped into the Porsche and took off for Cafe Roma. She had removed the car's convertible top, and her short blonde hair blew in the light breeze. She gazed at herself appraisingly in the rear view mirror. Her hair was cut in a relatively short style, about three inches long on top, tapering to about an inch at the base of her neck. She had cut her long hair when she was a freshman, not bothering to mention it to her fiancé before doing so. Jack was none too happy about that event, but she had grown tired of spending so much time keeping it looking good. Now she could wash it and not even bother to blow it dry if she was in a hurry.

Jamie was thin and in relatively good shape. A generous layer of flesh that gave her a youthful appearance covered her muscles. Jack teased her about her baby fat, but he really enjoyed being held by that soft, yet firm, body. Luckily she had never had to work out to maintain her figure. Her activity level and relatively low caloric intake saw to that. She had a good golfer's body—flexible, strong and lean, but not overly muscular.

As she maneuvered through the crowded streets of Berkeley she hoped to herself that Ryan would be on time. *Nothing worse than having to circle around the block in this mess,* she thought. Traffic was really snarled in front of her, and she could see the sign for Cafe Roma a block and a half ahead, but her progress was glacial. As she inched closer, she thought she could make out Ryan's cap-bedecked head. *Yeah, that's her. Wait a minute …* Ryan was sitting on a short concrete post that protected the sidewalk diners from errant cars. Her overall clad legs were spread wide, and between them stood Chitra from class. Her arms were around the taller woman's neck, and Ryan's hands loosely encircled her waist. Chitra was bent over slightly with her mouth firmly attached to Ryan's. Her head moved slowly as she thoroughly kissed the tanned face. *My God!* Jamie thought. *They look like they just got out of bed! I hope she's not planning on going with us,* she thought. *I only have room for two people!*

As she got close, she saw one blue eye open and catch sight of her. Ryan gently tried to remove her date from her death grip on her mouth, but she was obviously having a difficult time of it. Jamie could see the muscles of Ryan's arms tense as she firmly pushed Chitra away, giving her another little kiss as a reward. The beaming smile that she gave the banished woman was an added bonus. Chitra gave Jamie a quick wave, which she returned after forcing a smile onto her face. Ryan opened the passenger side door and settled herself comfortably. She turned and met Jamie's somewhat shocked gaze, giving her a little shoulder shrug along with a delightfully crooked grin. "We were just having lunch."

"You looked like you were lunch," Jamie replied, in a mock scolding tone.

Ryan actually blushed at that comment, and Jamie instantly felt a stab of regret at the sharp tone she had used, but Ryan didn't seem to mind. She lobbed back the banter, "I like to make friends in class. You never know when you're gonna need to copy someone's notes."

"Were her notes written on her tongue?" Jamie drawled as she cast a wry glance at her project partner.

A cocky smile settled onto Ryan's face, and she sat quietly for a moment. But then she turned and gave her partner a searching look. "That didn't bother you, did it?"

"Why would that bother me? You're my partner, not my girlfriend," Jamie replied, secretly hoping to draw another blush from those sculpted cheeks.

"I know, but I don't know how comfortable you are with the whole lesbian thing. That would've bothered some women. I want to make sure you're not one of them. I can behave ... if I have to."

She gave the playful woman a confident smile and said, "This is Berkeley, Ryan, you can't walk two feet without tripping over a lesbian! It's no big deal."

"Good. I'm glad it doesn't bother you. Now, have you ever been to a lesbian coffeehouse?"

"No, can't say that I have. But there's a first time for everything."

They drove the short distance just chatting about things. Ryan was very impressed with the little yellow Boxster that Jamie drove. She seemed to know a lot about cars and asked scads of questions about its engine and handling capabilities. Jamie didn't have answers for most of the questions, but that didn't deter Ryan from asking more. The blonde finally shook her head in frustration and pulled over. When she got out, Ryan looked at her with a puzzled expression.

"Come on, Ms. NASCAR, you drive it and answer your own questions," she said as she walked around to the passenger door and opened it. Ryan gave her a dazzling grin, protesting weakly while simultaneously grabbing the windshield and the back of the driver's seat and hoisting herself gracefully over the stick and into the seat.

Jamie began to latch the seat belt over her shoulder as Ryan carefully adjusted the rear view mirror. Seeing that the brunette couldn't find all of the proper switches,

Jamie dropped the belt and leaned over to point out the somewhat hidden switch by Ryan's left thigh which adjusted the side view mirrors. As she did so she felt her arm brush against Ryan's breasts. A little jolt of electricity shot up her arm as the contact occurred. *Yipes! Where did that come from? Next time, you'd better just tell her where things are. If that happens again you might fly out of the car!*

Ryan settled herself comfortably and smoothly pulled away from the curve. "Oh, wow!" she moaned in delight. "I have never in my life been behind the wheel of anything this delicious." She closed her eyes slightly in pleasure. Finally she turned her head a bit to lock eyes with Jamie. "I can't tell you how pleasurable this is for me."

Jamie was struck dumb for a moment, but finally got out, "I've never seen anyone enjoy anything quite so thoroughly, Ryan."

"I really love cars, as you can tell," she admitted, "but I think I love this car more than any other." Her voice took on a dreamy quality, thoroughly enchanting Jamie. "Do you know what it reminds me of?"

"Uhm, no, I can't guess," Jamie said, but she was dying to find out.

Ryan closed her eyes slightly as she gave the blonde a very satisfied smile. "A woman," she said simply.

"My Porsche looks like a woman?"

"Yep. This car not only has beautiful breasts," Ryan purred, "it has absolutely luscious hips."

Well, she is most definitely a lesbian, Jamie thought as she tried to get some moisture back into her mouth. *I've never met a straight woman who looked so sexy when she talked about breasts and hips!* "I'm not sure I see that," she replied, trying, but failing to sound off-handed.

"Really? Just look at the front fenders! Don't you see that graceful curve? It looks like a firm, young breast. See it?"

She had to admit that the fender did have a nice curve, and yes, it could look like a perky young breast. "Okay, I think I see what you mean. Now show me the hips."

Ryan had to pull over for that part of the demonstration. "Okay, turn around. See the rear fenders? They remind me of the nice, cushy hips of women in the paintings of the Renaissance. See how they curve so smoothly around to the tail lights?"

"Gee, I had no idea I was driving such a woman-centered car," she said with a laugh. "My father bought it for me, do you think that's what attracted him? "

"Subconsciously, I'm sure of it," Ryan smirked. "The designers at Porsche didn't do this by accident."

When they started up again Jamie looked over at Ryan and saw how much she was enjoying the experience of driving the car. "I don't have the heart to put an end to your joy," Jamie said. "Why don't we go for a drive up in the hills? What time do you have to be at work, anyway?"

"Uhm, four o'clock, but I work over in the city. To get there on BART I need to leave here by three." She cast a quick, sad look at the clock on the dash.

"Tell ya what," Jamie offered, "I owe my grandfather a visit," not mentioning that she had seen him three days earlier, "he's right off Nob Hill. Where do you have to go?"

"I work near the Castro, and that's not very close to Nob Hill."

"It's close enough for me. This car eats real estate faster than you can imagine."

"I really don't want to inconvenience you."

Jamie could see the hopeful look in those blue eyes and knew that she wouldn't mind walking to Castro in order to satisfy it. "It's really no bother, Ryan. I'd love to have dinner with my grandfather. I don't see him nearly enough." While she spoke she pulled her tiny cell phone from the glove box and speed-dialed the number.

He answered on the second ring. "Hi Poppa, it's Jamie. How would you like me to treat you to dinner at the Tadich Grill tonight?" After he enthusiastically agreed, the two women settled down for their drive.

They meandered through the hills of Oakland, looking at the plethora of monstrous new homes that dotted the hillside since the devastating fire that had consumed the whole area six years earlier.

"Wow, I haven't been up here since people started rebuilding," said Jamie.

"It's kind of a mess aesthetically, but that's what happens when people get a big insurance settlement. They build to the lot lines."

"You seem to know a lot about this area."

"Yeah, I guess I do," she said thoughtfully. "My father is a firefighter in the city. We used to come up here and look around after the fire. Kind of a busman's holiday."

"Oh, did your father fight this fire?"

"No, he doesn't fight fires any longer. He's the cook for a firehouse close to our house in Noe Valley." Jamie looked at her new friend and saw a look of true pride on her handsome face.

"Wow, I can't imagine cooking for all of those hungry firemen."

"Fire*fighters*," Ryan said.

"Oops, sorry."

"That's okay. Actually it's all men in his battalion. But the city has quite a number of women in the ranks now."

They continued to chat about nothing in particular until Ryan began guiding them down to the highway that would take them to the city. She was a good, careful driver, but she drove as fast as she could, given the conditions. Jamie noticed how she was able to move the car effortlessly through the growing traffic, and she found herself sliding sideways in her seat so that she could watch Ryan as she drove. Ryan still had a look of total pleasure on her face. *It's really cute how she accepted this little bit of happiness,* Jamie mused. *She doesn't seem afraid to really let herself go—even with a stranger,* she thought. *Well, clearly, she doesn't mind letting herself go with strangers after that little demonstration on the street today*, she reflected with a slight tinge of disapproval. *I wish I could be that free and unconcerned about things, though. I just can't believe she was kissing a woman right in the middle of a busy street. I don't kiss Jack like that on the street. Actually, I don't kiss Jack like that at home, anymore.*

As they crossed the Bay Bridge leading to San Francisco, Jamie let herself relax in her seat and take in the beautiful view of the city. *I feel so peaceful and happy.* She turned to look at Ryan again and was met with another charming smile from that beautiful face. Again she felt a chill roll down her whole body. *Jeez, Jamie will you please get a grip!*

Since it was only 3:40, Ryan took Market all the way to Castro. Jamie could tell that she chose the slow route to prolong her test drive, but she didn't mind a bit. *I think she's gotten more pleasure from this car in an hour than I have in two years. It's kind of nice to see things through such appreciative eyes.*

Ryan again offered to go directly to Jamie's grandfather's place and take Muni to her job, but Jamie insisted that she go directly to work. Ryan didn't offer any details on her job, and Jamie was in too relaxed a mood to do her usual cross-examination, so she just relaxed and enjoyed the next few minutes.

"So, are you still up for a visit to the coffeehouse this week?" Ryan asked as they neared the Castro.

"Absolutely."

As they pulled up to a rare empty meter, Ryan tugged her organizer out of her black nylon book bag.

Jamie noticed that they were parked in front of a Blockbuster Video store. "Is this where you work?" she asked tentatively.

"Huh? Oh, no." She pointed vaguely down the street as she continued to peruse her schedule. "A little farther down. Okay," she said. "I'm free from ten to noon and from six to nine tomorrow. On Friday my schedule is about the same as today. Are any of those times good for you?"

Jamie thought for a moment before she chose the Thursday from six to nine p.m. slot. "Do you want to get dinner before we go, or do they serve food there?"

"Yeah, dinner would be great. I have to work afterward, so that'll be the only time I have to eat. I don't think they serve anything substantial enough for me at the coffeehouse, so we should probably go somewhere else for dinner. Do you have any suggestions?"

"You start work after nine at night?" she asked in surprise.

"Yep. Open all night," Ryan said, smiling her enigmatic smile.

"How much time do you think we need to spend at the coffeehouse?" Jamie inquired, momentarily too fragmented to inquire about Ryan's job.

"Well, since we have to write a paper, we should probably hang out for a bit, you know look at the books, observe the subjects in their native environment," she teased.

"Why don't you come to my house and I'll cook dinner for us. That'll save time."

Her dark head cocked as she looked at Jamie carefully. "Are you always this nice, or do you just take pity on starving lesbians?"

"Well, I'm generally pretty nice. And you certainly don't look like you're starving," she added as she passed a gaze at Ryan's solid form.

"You've got me there. I don't miss many meals," she patted her flat stomach. "Let me get your address so I can get to work. My clients hate to be kept waiting."

Clients ... working late at night ... what in the hell does she do?

Chapter Two

On Thursday at five, Janie pulled into her driveway, fresh from a visit to her favorite market. She was stunned, and a bit dismayed, to see Jack's Honda Accord parked in front of the house. "Oh, shit, not tonight!" she moaned. "Ryan's gonna be here soon!"

She grabbed her grocery bags and made her way into the house to find Jack sitting in the kitchen with Cassie, drinking a Coke and looking very relaxed. Trying to appear glad to see him, Jamie greeted him as she put her bags down on the marble counter. "To what do I owe the unexpected honor?" She crossed the kitchen and affectionately tousled his hair.

He rose and enveloped her in a hug, then pulled back just enough to give her a quick kiss. "I had to drop off some research at the office, and I figured this would be a good place to ride out rush hour. I thought we could have dinner before I've got to head back." He walked over to the counter and began to investigate the contents of her bags. "Ooo, this looks good." He pulled out the fresh pasta and the marinara sauce and waggled them in a playful manner. "What are you making me?"

"Oh honey, I'd love to have dinner with you, but I have a classmate coming over for dinner. We're working on a special project together, and we need the time to discuss it." She found she had to exaggerate her regret to make it sound sincere, and for a change, she didn't feel guilty about it.

"What kind of projects do you have for English classes?" he asked absently, continuing to poke through the bags.

Jamie was unreasonably annoyed at his interest in her purchases, and she began to take the items out of his hands as he removed them from the bags. She put the salad ingredients on the counter by the double stainless steel sinks, and placed the pasta and sauce in the refrigerator. Snagging the chocolate gelato from him, she placed it in the freezer before he could even comment. As he looked longingly at a fresh loaf of Italian bread, she took pity on him and partially relented. "I can try to make you something before she gets here," she said unenthusiastically.

He gave her his puppy dog look and said, "I don't want to put you out."

Cassie had been watching the pair, and she finally piped up. "Jack, let me take you out to dinner. We don't get to spend much time together, what with Jamie monopolizing all of your time".

Jamie was grateful to her roommate for this unexpectedly thoughtful offer. Jack looked like he wanted to refuse, but when Jamie looked at him with a blank expression he shrugged his broad shoulders and said, "Okay, Cassie. That'd be great. But can we wait until Jamie's friend gets here? I'd like to have a few minutes with her after going this far out of my way."

The guilt trip partially worked, and Jamie spent a moment wondering if she should call Ryan and cancel. But she resisted the urge, finding an unexpected source of selfishness that surprised her. Cassie's words jolted her out of her reverie. "Sure Jack, I'll be up in my room. Call me when you're ready."

Jack sat back down and Jamie walked over to the counter to prepare dinner. She was still thinking about her unexpected supply of backbone, and had a hard time focusing on her boyfriend. He was chatting about his day, and updated her on the progress of his law review article. She tried to listen, but the intricacies of the R.I.C.O. laws as applied to the violation of restraining orders against protest groups didn't hold her attention, for some reason. She was also nervous about Jack meeting Ryan. *Why didn't I think this through more thoroughly? Now it's gonna be a whole big thing. God, I hope she doesn't look too gay tonight. That's all I need!*

Jamie handed Jack plates and silverware, followed by napkins and place mats. "You may as well make yourself useful, honey."

"I guess this is good preparation for married life. I suppose this'll be my job until I train one of our little tow-headed kids to do it."

Jamie was surprised and touched at his comment. Jack didn't often speak of his vision of their future. He usually spoke of his career, or things they'd do together, but it was rare for him to speak of having children.

"Are kids important to you Jack?"

"Well, yeah, I guess they are. I've assumed we'd have a few. Aren't they important to you?" he asked with a note of surprise as he turned to look at her.

"Oh, yeah." A genuine smile lit up her face. She walked over to him and put her arms around his waist. "I'd love to have a raft of little blonde copies of you."

He bent down and began to place several tender kisses on her lips. The softness of his kisses contrasted with the slightly rough stubble on his face. She hugged him tightly and he returned the hug enthusiastically, then increased the intensity of his kisses. *Uhn-uh*, she thought. *I'm not gonna change my mind, no matter how turned on you try to make me*. She started to pull away just when the door to the living room opened and Mia and Ryan entered. Jamie jumped in surprise, nearly hitting Jack's chin with the top of her head.

"Knock it off, lovebirds, your company's here," Mia said, stating the obvious.

Jamie stared open-mouthed at Ryan, completely nonplussed. Wind-blown black hair hung loosely around her shoulders. A black leather baseball-style jacket covered a skintight black T-shirt. Well-worn, snug black jeans topped sleek, black, low-heeled leather boots. In her right hand was a shiny, black, motorcycle helmet. *Oh, my god. She looks like the centerfold for Big Dyke Magazine!*

"Hi, Jamie," the black clad vision said.

"Hi," Jamie eventually choked out.

Jack cleared his throat as he stepped back out of Jamie's loose embrace. "Hi, I'm Jack Townsend," he said as he extended his hand, when it became clear that Jamie wasn't going to introduce him.

Jamie regained her composure, and her manners, and made proper introductions. Cassie came downstairs moments later and was included in the scene. Jamie noticed both of her roommates eyeing Ryan critically, passing raised eyebrow looks between them. *Oh shit! Mia must have told Cassie about my class. They're really giving her the once over. Not that it'd be too tough to guess that she's gay in that outfit.*

"So, what's this project you two are working on?" Jack asked Ryan, trying to make conversation to fill the completely silent room.

Ryan gave Jamie a quick glance, and allowed her to answer. "It's just a project for our psych class. I'll tell you all about it later, sweetheart. We've gotta hurry up and eat, and you two need to get going," she said to Cassie and Jack. "I'm sure you've got a ton of work to do tonight, honey."

"Okay, I know when to leave," he said with a small smile. Jamie gave him another hug and a kiss, and then he and Cassie left.

Mia, however, apparently found this all too interesting, and made no move to depart. "What's for dinner?" she asked, peeking at the pans on the stove.

Jamie came up behind her and physically removed her from her position. "Ryan and I are having pasta. You're having whatever you make for yourself after we leave. We're in a hurry."

"Okay, okay," Mia laughed as she retreated. "Can I at least get a soda? And maybe a little of that bread?"

"Yes, Mia, you may have some bread," Jamie said. "Then scram."

"You run a pretty tight ship around here, Jamie," Ryan said after Mia scampered out with her purloined bread.

"Those three would have eaten every bite," she said. "They're like vultures. Especially Jack. He eats more than the three of us combined."

"Well, I don't blame them. It smells great," Ryan said. "And I really am starving. I didn't get a proper lunch today."

"I forgot to ask you if there was anything you don't eat. I figured pasta was on almost everyone's list."

"I don't eat anything that's currently breathing," Ryan said. "Other than that, I'm game."

Ryan proved herself true to her word. Jamie had made the entire two pounds of fresh pasta, in order to have leftovers for lunch the next day. But Ryan acted as though her two massive helpings of pasta were the bare minimum required to keep her going. Jamie mused that she'd never seen a woman eat quite so much, but her thoughts were interrupted by Ryan beginning to eye the salad bowl. Jamie pushed it over to her, and Ryan bent her dark head and ate every bite, finishing off the loaf of bread along with it.

"Do you have room for gelato?" Jamie asked, knowing that her guest had to be full to bursting.

"What flavor?" Ryan narrowed her eyes and waited for the answer.

"Chocolate."

Without hesitation, the brunette said, "I've always got room for chocolate. Always."

"What flavor would you have refused?"

"I can't think of one, but you can't be too sure."

Jamie had only bought one pint of the freshly made gelato, and as Ryan finished her second bowl she regretted that she hadn't bought two. "Uhm … have you had enough?" she asked as Ryan leaned back in her chair with a satisfied smile on her lovely face.

"Why, is there more?" Ryan asked, looking around the kitchen with a hopeful expression.

"Are you teasing me again?"

"Just a little," her new friend replied. "I think you've actually filled me up for a change. Not an easy task."

"You do have a healthy appetite," Jamie observed tactfully. Healthy for a defensive end!

"Hey, I'm a growing girl."

"Don't grow too much or I'll need a stepladder to talk to you."

"That's not the direction I'd grow if all of my meals were that delicious." Ryan gifted her with one of her most dazzling smiles, and Jamie blushed at the compliment.

After they quickly cleaned the kitchen, they went to the front door and Ryan paused to ask, "Would you like me to drive?"

"Sure." Jamie handed her the keys to the Porsche.

"No, I mean would you like to ride on my bike? It's the perfect ride for a visit to a lesbian bookstore."

"I've never been on a motorcycle before," Jamie admitted with a nervous laugh. "But I've always thought they were cool …"

"My motto is 'Always give in to temptation,'" Ryan said with a sexy leer that made Jamie's knees slightly weak.

"But I don't have a helmet, wouldn't I need one?"

"That's why I brought this one in," Ryan said. "I thought we could adjust it where the light was better."

"Isn't this yours?" Jamie asked. She narrowed her eyes in concern, not wanting Ryan to give up her only helmet.

"No, mine's on the bike. This is my extra one."

"Okay, I'm game," Jamie replied with significantly less hesitation than she felt.

Ryan leaned over and placed the helmet on Jamie's head. She fidgeted with the strap for a moment, then gripped the helmet with both hands and gave it a tug. "How does that feel?" she asked, looking closely at Jamie's face for her reaction.

"Feels great. Let's go," she said with false confidence. She grabbed a butterscotch leather jacket from the coat closet and slid it on as they walked out the front door. "Wow, that's a good looking bike!" She regarded the aqua and cream-colored Harley with a critical eye. She knew absolutely nothing about motorcycles, but it was clear that this one was well loved. The leather was supple and immaculate, the chrome gleamed, and the paint was perfect.

"Yeah, I really love this one. I've had a Yamaha, a Honda and an Indian, but this one really sounds like a bike. You feel it all the way through your spine," she said, trailing her hand lovingly over the saddle.

Jamie was unsure of what that meant, but she figured she'd find out soon enough. Ryan threw her long leg over the saddle and pushed the bike off the kickstand. "Come on," she said as she held out a hand.

Jamie took her friend's left hand, and placed her right hand on Ryan's shoulder as she swung her leg over the seat. It was a stretch, but she accomplished the feat with a little hop on the planted foot. She settled down comfortably, but quickly felt her comfort evaporate when she was forced to nestle her thighs around Ryan's butt.

"Hang on tight," Ryan instructed. "Feel free to put your arms around my waist. All you've got to do is hold on and lean into the turns like I do. And don't worry, you'll have fun," she said as she patted Jamie lightly on the thigh.

Jamie privately admitted that she was already having fun. She loved sitting on the big bike, so close to Ryan. She realized that she inexplicably felt safe and protected by this near stranger. As the bike roared to life, she understood what Ryan meant about the sound. She definitely heard it, but she felt it with her body more than her ears. *Wow, this is pretty intense*. The intensity grew as the bike began to cruise down the street. Involuntarily, she threw her arms around Ryan as the bike moved through its gears. There was a small jerk with each shift, and she unconsciously held on tighter, chagrined when she felt the larger woman laughing softly.

As she become accustomed to the sensation, Jamie realized that this was truly a glorious feeling. She had never realized how insulated she was while in a car, even a small convertible like her own. This, however, was a feeling of complete freedom, letting her feel as if she were flying. She inhaled deeply as she noticed the sweet smell of the flowers, and the scent of damp grass as they passed the well tended lawns. *Why would you ever ride in a car if you had one of these?*

The trip was over much too soon, and as they pulled up in front of the bookstore Jamie regretted having to get off the bike. Ryan let her get off first, then she propped the bike on its stand and killed the engine. As Ryan turned to face her, she reflexively returned the huge grin on Jamie's face. "I take it you enjoyed your first time? I told you it was fun."

"That was awesome!" she gushed, her enthusiasm bubbling up. "I had no idea it would be so cool! Why would you ever ride in a car?"

"Well, when it's under fifty degrees and raining, cars start to look pretty good." Ryan gave her a wide smile, and slid her arm around Jamie's shoulders. She opened the door and waited for the smaller woman to enter. Placing her hand on the small of her friend's back, she guided her into the cozy store.

Jamie was very aware of how Ryan touched her. *She treats me kind of like a guy would if we were on a first date,* she mused. *But it doesn't feel like she's coming on to me today. It feels like that's just part of her personality. She's obviously used to being in charge. I wonder if lesbians really have roles when they're ... together? If so, Ryan's definitely the guy.*

But a guy with an absolutely drop dead gorgeous body!" she thought with a smirk as her friend urged her further into the store.

The place was larger than it looked from the street. It was roughly divided into two separate spaces, the one in which they were standing, which was the coffeehouse/entertainment side, and the other, which housed books and other items. As they stepped more fully into the space Jamie saw that the front of the room held a small elevated platform—obviously a stage. Near the right side of the room was a coffee bar, and behind the bar was a small window that must have led to an unseen kitchen. A woman was busily making coffee drinks for the customers who were seated at the scattered small tables. There were a few comfortable-looking, well-used sofas and overstuffed chairs. They didn't match, nor seem to be terribly clean, but they lent a comfortable familiarity to the room that appealed to Jamie.

Ryan caught her wandering gaze and quietly asked, "Would you like to sit and have a coffee, or would you rather look in the bookstore for a bit?"

"Since it's not too crowded, let's look around first, then maybe we can sit down for a while. Will there be entertainment later?"

Ryan looked up at a good-sized chalkboard near the stage. Multicolored chalk letters heralded the name of a performer and the notation "Eight p.m. Tonight." Ryan checked her enormous watch. "Yeah, in about an hour."

Jamie grasped her hand and took a look at the timepiece. "God, Ryan, what does that monster do?"

"Well, I have to time my clients so they don't overstay their hour," she replied. "And sometimes I'm doing two people at once, so I need two timers." She indicated the two timers with her index finger. "And I use it for running and swimming. See, it has two lap counters," she said, pointing them both out. "I also use it as my alarm in the morning, and every once in a while I can get a little nap in at work." She gave Jamie a conspiratorial wink and said, "Don't tell."

What in the hell does she do for a living?

Just as Jamie was forming the question, a short, pleasant-looking, middle-aged woman appeared from behind the bar. She was heading right for them, and Jamie noticed Ryan's face light up in a smile.

"Ryan O'Flaherty, as I live and breathe!" the woman gushed in a broad, theatrical Irish accent.

"Hi, Babs. It's good to see you again," Ryan said as she gave the small woman a big, friendly hug. "This is my friend, Jamie. Jamie, this is Babs Jablonski—she owns this den of ill repute."

Babs elbowed Ryan sharply in the ribs, then grasped Jamie's hand in a firm shake. "Any friend of Ryan's is still welcome here," she joked in her normal voice.

After a few more minutes of banter, Ryan showed Jamie to the bookstore. She was surprised to find the store sectioned off in categories, just like at a regular bookstore. But these categories were a bit different than the ones found at Barnes & Noble. "Coming Out," "Lesbian Sexuality," and "Lesbian Parenting," caught Jamie's eye as she glanced around the small room. She also noticed that there was a section where CD's and tapes were sold. She strolled over to that area and realized that none of the artists were familiar to her. "Are these uhm … lesbian specific singers?" She held up a CD for Ryan's inspection.

"That's a cute way to put it," Ryan said. "I'd say for the most part these artists are lesbians, but there's a good bit of generic women's music also, along with some self help and spirituality tapes. I guess God helps the lesbian who helps herself."

"How do you know so much about this place, and how do you know Babs?" Jamie found the courage to ask, hoping that she wasn't prying too much.

Ryan certainly didn't seem to think the question was invasive. "When I was a kid I couldn't get into the bars, even though I thought I looked quite mature," she said. "I read about this place in one of the lesbian newspapers I found in the Castro. I came over one day on BART, and I became such a pest that Babs took pity on me and let me hang out on the weekends and earn a few bucks helping out."

"So you've known you were gay for a long time?"

"I'll tell you the whole sordid story, but let's finish up in here first."

Jamie spent quite a few more minutes looking carefully at the titles that lined the lilac painted wooden shelves. "I must admit, this is all a bit surprising to me," she said. "I guess I've never thought that there would be a whole cottage industry catering to lesbians like this. Do you think it's necessary?"

Ryan seemed to consider her question for a moment. She gazed at her carefully and replied, "Yeah, I really do. When you think about it, gay people are the only ones who don't share minority status with their parents. When people come out, many of them are overwhelmed by the experience. Even if their parents are supportive, they don't know how to help. Places like this can be a lifesaver for people who are really struggling. I know it was for me."

"I can see that it would really help someone who was sure of her preference," Jamie stated after a moment. "But what about girls who are just confused? Don't you think this could push them into a place they don't really belong?" she asked with a look of concern on her face.

"I know you don't know all of the lingo, but most gay people really prefer to have their sexuality be considered an orientation rather than a preference."

"I'm sorry," she said quickly. "What did I say?"

"You referred to someone being sure of her preference. It's not a real big deal, but it's not a preference for me."

"Okay," she said slowly, drawing the word out while she considered this. "I don't really see the difference—"

Ryan interrupted. "I assume you consider yourself heterosexual, right?"

"Well, yeah," she laughed. "So does Jack."

"If you broke up, would you accept a date from a woman?"

"Uhm …" Jamie found herself absolutely dumbstruck at this question.

She seemed to have lost her ability to speak, so Ryan replied for her. "I'll take it that's a no," she said. "I think sexuality is like that for many, if not most, people. You focus on one gender for your sexual attraction. You don't look at the whole human race and decide which one you slightly prefer. Your orientation leads you to only look at men as sexual partners, right?"

"Right!" she finally said, as a deep blush covered her face and neck. "Right!" she said again for emphasis.

"Please don't be embarrassed, Jamie," she said gently. "You're not offending me at all." She smiled sweetly and maintained eye contact as she continued. "That's how it is for me, too. I don't *prefer* women. The thought of being with a man sexually has as much pull for me as being with my dog. And that's not a put down of dogs or men," she added, laughing. "It's just something so outside of my orientation that both of those options seem equally far-fetched to me."

"Okay," Jamie said slowly. "I think I get your point. And I can see why having it called a preference could be offensive."

"Sorry if that seemed like a lecture," Ryan said. "But I figure that you want to understand this stuff or you wouldn't have taken the class."

"Absolutely! Now do you remember the rest of my question?"

"Verbatim," she said. "I don't think a place like this can push someone into a life that isn't right for them. This type of place isn't a recruiting station. It's to help people figure out their true orientation and learn to be comfortable with it."

"But," Jamie interrupted, "what about all the girls and women who are just dabbling in lesbianism? It sure is popular now to have done it with a woman. It really seems like a fad. You have to have a piercing, a tattoo and lesbian sex just to graduate from Berkeley!"

"I doubt that those women will ever think of themselves as lesbians," Ryan said. "I think it's a right of passage for a lot of 'em. Kinda like getting drunk, or doing drugs—even if you don't really want to. But that might be a good thing—it might remove some of the stigma from being gay if more people had some experience with it. It'd be hard to be homophobic if you've slept with another woman, wouldn't it?"

"I guess you could be right," she said, looking very pensive. "But what about the long run? Don't you think it might come back to haunt them?"

"You're kind of making it sound like the Scarlet Letter, Jamie," she said with a tiny frown. "If you're just trying it out, it's just sex. It's like having a threesome. Something different that you don't want to do all the time. The women who have it rough are the true lesbians. Having sex with a woman finally confirms their feelings. Then they have to deal with all of the fallout from that realization. And that's where this place comes in."

"I guess I see your point, but this is a lot to absorb. It's kind of like visiting another culture. It takes time to get acclimated."

"Maybe some coffee would help," Ryan suggested with a smile. "Let me buy you one."

They settled down into a burgundy velour sofa, and Jamie accepted two large mugs of latte from Ryan. "Oh, this is good. I like the little sprinkle of chocolate on the top," she said as she licked a white foam mustache from her top lip. "Do you have time to tell me the story of your sordid lesbian past?" she asked playfully, reminding Ryan of her earlier promise.

"I've only got an hour," she replied as she looked at her watch, "that should get us through a year or two if I gloss over the scary parts."

"Was it really hard for you Ryan?" she asked as her face grew serious. "I mean, you seem very happy being gay now."

"Yeah, I'm perfectly content with who I am now, sexually at least," she said with a smile. "But it was really hard for me. I mean, I knew from a very early age that I was somehow different from the other girls. But I didn't understand how I was different—I just knew there was something."

"Did you have boyfriends when you were younger?"

"Nope—never had one. No dates, no crushes, nothing. I've never even kissed a guy, and I don't think I ever will at this point."

Jamie gave her a tentative smile as she shot a look up and down her rather voluptuous, but still sleek form. "I don't mean to embarrass you, but how did you avoid having boys hound you? You're pretty gorgeous, you know."

"Thanks," Ryan grinned. "But most guys don't seem to agree with you."

"Really? You don't get hit on all the time?"

"No," she said. "I never really have. I was lucky because I went to an all girls high school, so that took some of the pressure off. There weren't any guys around to make it obvious that I wasn't interested. I was really into sports, and the girls I hung out with weren't very boy crazy either. Plus I was almost five foot ten inches by the end of eighth grade. I was a head taller than the boys my age until I was sixteen or so."

"So you really had no interest in going out with guys?"

"Zip," she said decisively. "I liked boys, but I thought of them as friends. I just couldn't imagine kissing one of them. I really didn't understand what was going on with me. I mean, most of my friends talked about guys they liked, and by high school guys were the main topic of conversation for most of my classmates. But it wasn't until the end of my junior year that it all fell into place for me."

Jamie waited expectantly for Ryan to continue. But her face had clouded and she stared into her mug with a very sad look on her face.

"We don't have to talk about this, Ryan," she said softly as she placed her hand gently on Ryan's forearm.

She looked up at her with such pain in her eyes that Jamie had to resist the urge to reach out and wrap her in a hug. "It's okay," she said as her voice caught. "I knew I was gay because I finally realized that I was madly in love with my best friend." She pursed her lips as she needlessly added, "Let's just say that she didn't share my feelings."

Jamie slid her hand down and grasped Ryan's hand, then gave it a little squeeze as she caught and held her gaze. "I'm sorry."

Ryan's lips slowly curled up into a shy smile. "I don't know why, but I'm kind of embarrassed by this. I know it was a long time ago, but it still hurts me to think about it. Those early wounds don't ever seem to go away. When I think of that time, I feel just as devastated today as I did then."

She had such a forlorn look on her face that Jamie spoke without thinking. "I think it's her loss to turn down a prize like you. She must still be kicking herself."

Ryan looked at her with a large measure of surprise on her face, but she recovered to give Jamie a huge, crooked grin. "Easy for you to say now, but I was kind of a mess back then."

"I rather doubt you were ever a mess, Ryan."

They passed the next few minutes in idle chatter. Ryan stood after a bit and shrugged out of her leather jacket, folding it neatly and placing it over the arm of the sofa. Jamie had a hard time controlling her desire to stare at Ryan's sculpted body, starkly outlined by the skin-tight, French cut, T-shirt that covered her torso. To her relief Babs approached again. "Hey, Irish, are you gonna ride again this year?" she asked as she nodded her head towards a large poster promoting the 1998 California AIDS Ride.

"Yep, I'm doing it again," Ryan replied. "You should be getting a new poster soon. And don't worry Babs, I'll be hitting you up for a sponsorship sooner than you wish."

Jamie looked at her new friend and gushed, "Oh Ryan, that's so cool! Every year I watch the news coverage of the ride. But I've never known anyone who's done it!"

"Well, now you do. And don't think I won't try to wheedle money out of you too," she added as she pinched Jamie's cheek.

"No problem. I'd be honored to support you."

"Don't make it easy on her, honey," Babs said. "She can already sweet talk the silk off the corn. Make her work for it."

As Babs wandered away, Jamie continued her inquiry. "How many times have you done the ride?"

"Every year," she replied with a note of pride in her voice. "This'll be my sixth."

"I really admire your dedication. It must be quite an ordeal."

"It's not too bad if you stay in training throughout the year. I just do the same amount of riding all year, so it doesn't seem like that big a deal. There's one day of the ride that's a real bear though. It's an inland day, so there isn't much of a breeze, and it's mostly uphill all day. That's the time you just wish you could get in the SAG van and ride the whole way."

"Sag van?"

"Yeah, sag means support and gear. The ride is fully supported by teams of volunteers. There are vans to help you if you can't make a hill. Some people use the vans to get up the worst of 'em. And of course, some get injured and have no choice."

"Boy, I bet I'd be in that van all of the time," Jamie said. "Have you ever had to ride?"

"Me? In the SAG van? I'd rather lie down and die," Ryan said, a touch of indignation in her voice.

Jamie laughed at the expression on her friend's face. "I'd love to come and watch you all take off this year," she said, surprising herself at her forwardness.

"You could get a really good view, if you rode instead of watched."

"I could never do anything like that! I'm way, way too much of a wimp."

"That's what most people think. But it's not a race, it's a ride. The point is to challenge yourself."

"I've never even considered doing it. You know, I don't know anyone who's had AIDS," Jamie said as she wracked her brain. "Maybe that's why the idea seems so foreign to me."

"You're lucky," Ryan said as a flash of pain clouded her face, "You're really lucky."

At eight-thirty sharp, Ryan stood and stretched and gracefully slid her jacket back on. She held a smooth hand out to Jamie and said, "I can't be late for work, so I've gotta run."

They rode the short distance in silence, which was fine with Jamie since she needed all of her concentration to focus on the sensations of the ride. She enjoyed the experience even more on the return trip, now that she felt more comfortable being with Ryan. God, she's so easy to talk to, she thought. *It feels like we've known each other for years.*

As the bike pulled up in front of her house, Jamie struggled to get off with a little assist from her new friend. The engine was still running as Ryan retrieved Jamie's helmet and secured it. "I had a nice time, thanks for going with me."

"I really enjoyed it, too. Thanks for being such a good tour guide and for giving me my maiden motorcycle ride," she added with a grin.

Ryan reached out and gave her shoulder a squeeze. "Always happy to initiate a new convert." She grinned with that devastatingly sexy smile. "See you tomorrow," she called out as she roared away.

Jamie was so occupied in watching her ride away that she didn't see Jack glaring at her from the front door.

As Jamie turned for the door, she noted with alarm that Jack's car was still parked in the driveway. *Oh, oh, this can't be good. There's no way he stayed this long just to talk to Cassie.* She hit the first step of the wraparound porch as the front door opened.

"Hi," Jack said quietly, an unreadable expression on his face.

"Hi, yourself," Jamie replied as casually as possible. She made sure that she was smiling, and did her best to adopt a neutral expression. "I'm glad you're still here." She stood on her tiptoes to wrap her arms around his neck and give him a kiss. She noted with alarm that he didn't respond to the kiss. In fact, he seemed to move away from her touch. She stepped back slightly and placed her hands upon his broad chest as she looked up into his eyes with concern. "What's wrong, honey?"

"Where were you tonight?" He looked directly into her eyes, unblinking.

"I had to work on a class project with Ryan, like I told you," she answered with more than a touch of defensiveness in her voice. "Why?"

He backed away from the door and turned to cross the parlor. He began to climb the staircase, apparently to go to the bedroom. She noticed that he looked very tired, and his posture didn't carry its usual confident attitude.

Jamie began to follow him up the stairs. She grabbed his hand as she caught up with him and pulled him to a stop. "Jack, what's wrong?" she demanded with growing alarm.

"In private," he said wearily.

Jamie was beginning to panic, and her mind grasped wildly for an explanation for his obvious anger. In their two years together they had never had what most people would call a fight. Of course they had disagreements, differences of opinion and the like. But they agreed on most of the important issues of life, and both of them felt more comfortable keeping their relationship on an even keel. Usually, when one or the other was angry they'd think of a reason to take a short time out, until the storm had passed. Jamie also realized that she usually gave in when there was a potential trouble spot. Tonight, however, she couldn't give in, since she had no idea why he was angry.

Jack entered her room and she followed close behind. He closed the door and walked to her stereo system, where he considered her CD's for a moment before he made his selection and loaded the disk. Turning the volume louder than Jamie would have chosen, he walked over to the love seat in front of the far window. He sank into the comfortable cushions and dropped his head into his hands, looking weary and frustrated, and Jamie knew this was going to be very bad. He finally looked up and said, "I feel like you've lied to me." His eyes were sad and he was clearly confused, as well as angry.

"Lied to you? I've never lied to you Jack," she said as she walked over to the loveseat and dropped to her knees right in front of him. She tried to grasp his hands, but he shook her off roughly, astounding her.

"Why didn't you tell me about this class, or about this … woman?" he demanded as his eyes bore into her.

"What? What? What on earth are you talking about? What's the big deal?" She was becoming angry now, both at his attitude and his obvious disapproval. "I'm taking a stupid psych class. Besides, since when are you interested in my schedule? You never asked me what I was taking. You acted completely uninterested."

"This isn't a class that a normal girl should take," he explained as if talking to a slow child. "Why would someone like you want to spend her time learning about lesbians and their experiences?"

Like a jolt, a light came on in Jamie's head. She took a deep breath and asked slowly, "How did you know the name of the class?"

Now it was his turn to look defensive. "Jesus, Jamie, you're out late, on a motorcycle no less, with some big dyke, and you don't tell anyone where you're going. Cassie didn't know, Mia didn't know. I was worried about you!" he shouted.

She gave him a withering look and said, "Oh, I see. You were worried about me because I was out until almost nine, right? So you did what … look through my book bag and my organizer?"

"Yes, Jamie, I was worried about you and I did look through your stuff—but only to find out where you were. Cassie told me that woman had been hitting on you. What if you'd needed my help?"

Jamie was flabbergasted both by his behavior and by his assumptions. She stood and stared at him, her anger boiling over. "Do you think I'd spend the evening with someone who frightened me? Do you think I need your protection to get through the day? Who in the holy hell do you think I am? I'm not some little girl that you have to supervise. And what did you think would happen? Did you think she'd throw me across her bike and kidnap me? Or do you think lesbians have to rape straight women to get any action?" She was really heating up now. "I'm furious that you looked through my things. I never want you to do that again. Do you hear me?" This last was said at full volume as she stood right in front of him and looked down.

"Yes, Jamie, all of Berkeley heard you," he said bitterly. "It's obvious that you're in no place to discuss this rationally. I'll call you tomorrow." He turned and started to make his way to the door, but Jamie was on him like a panther, grabbing his arm and abruptly turning him around.

"How dare you start this and then leave!!"

He reached over to her small hand and gently began to remove her fingers, one by one. "I said I'll call you tomorrow," he said firmly as he again turned and walked out.

She stood in the center of her room, panting from the flood of emotions that raced through her brain. Her stomach churned with a mixture of anger, sadness, hurt, betrayal and fear. Hurling herself to the bed, she began to cry, remaining just like that for a long while until exhaustion overtook her. Finally, she kicked off her shoes, removed her leather jacket and flopped back onto the bed where she quickly fell into an exhausted sleep.

The next morning, Jamie waited outside of the classroom until the professor entered, loathe to make small talk with Ryan today. For that matter, she didn't want to speak to anyone but Jack. She was still terribly upset about their fight, but she didn't want to talk about it with anyone else, particularly Ryan. Even though she didn't know Ryan very well, she had a feeling that her new friend was perceptive enough to know if something was bothering her, so avoiding her seemed like the best idea.

That was so unlike Jack. I've to get to the bottom of this, but I have a very strong feeling that Cassie was involved in making this into a bigger deal than it had to be. Cassie must have said something that pushed him over the edge. He just doesn't do things like that. She wished that she could have marched into Cassie's room and confronted her last night, but Jamie tended to resolve her anger first, and then have a rational discussion later, and today was no exception.

As she took her seat, Ryan turned and smiled at her, mouthing a greeting. Jamie returned both with a look that was close to her normal demeanor in spite of her sour mood. Ryan was wearing a navy blue and cream vintage Hawaiian shirt, and a pair of well-worn khakis. Jamie looked at the Teva sandals on her feet, and hoped that she hadn't ridden her motorcycle. *Maybe her mother should worry about those things for her*, she chided herself.

Linda took her usual place on the corner of the large wooden desk. "Hello people. Today we're going to discuss social attitudes toward lesbian identity." She launched them into a fascinating discussion of the subject. Jamie paid rapt attention, running her mind on two tracks. Although she was very focused on Linda's words, she was concurrently applying those words to Jack's behavior. The discussion was lively, and most of the class participated. The hour passed much too quickly, and she was still so filled with unanswered questions that she couldn't turn off her brain at the end of class. As she sat at her desk, deep in thought, she sensed and then saw Ryan squat down next to her so they were at eye level.

"Hey, you look down today," Ryan said, her deep blue eyes filled with concern. "Are you alright?"

Jamie took a deep breath and tried to answer, but she couldn't find the words to express how she was feeling. Her head was still tilted down, causing her hair to fall into her eyes. With a tender gesture, Ryan reached up and gently brushed her bangs back to reveal troubled green eyes. "Yeah, sure," Jamie said, obviously lying. "I'm fine." Then, almost as an afterthought, she asked, "Do you have a few minutes to talk?"

Ryan glanced at her watch. "I've got nearly an hour." She held out her hand and pulled the troubled woman to her feet.

"Something happened last night, and it's really bothering me," Jamie said pensively, as she shot a glance up at Ryan.

Concern immediately clouded Ryan's face. "Was it something I did?"

"Oh no, not at all. I had a great time with you," Jamie said. "It was after you dropped me off that the shit hit the fan."

Ryan took a deep breath and let it out slowly. "Let's go sit outside. We can get a soda at the vending machines."

They walked in relative silence. Ryan glanced at Jamie occasionally, noticing that her friend seemed very deep in the problem that was bothering her. *I hope she doesn't want boyfriend advice. I'm pretty much out of my league there. For that matter, I'm pretty much out of my league giving advice on any kind of romantic relationship.*

As they approached the shaded outdoor patio, Ryan reached into her pocket and fished out a handful of change. "I'll buy—what'll you have?"

"Uhm, some kind of soda, doesn't really matter," Jamie replied absently.

Ryan nodded and started to leave, but she spent another moment looking at Jamie's face. *She really doesn't seem like herself today. I think I'll get her some juice. She could use some energy instead of empty calories.*

She took two bottles of cranberry juice and two bottles of apple juice over to the table. Jamie looked up at her in surprise. "Is that soda?"

"You looked like you could use a little energy," Ryan said. "Soda will only make you jumpy."

Jamie was charmed by this thoughtful gesture, and without stopping to censor herself, she reached out and patted Ryan's hand while giving her a sincere smile. "Thanks for caring."

Ryan looked embarrassed at this gesture, but she gamely returned the smile. "So, what's up?" She began opening bottles, waiting for Jamie to begin.

"I was thinking about our discussion of this morning," Jamie said thoughtfully. "You know, about homophobia and heterosexism?" At Ryan's nod, she continued. "I think I got a first hand example of both last night."

"What happened?"

"It seems that my roommates are overly interested in the fact that I'm taking this class." Jamie wasn't going to tell Ryan the whole context of her evening. She didn't want to hurt her new friend's feelings, so obviously she wouldn't tell her that Jack called her a big dyke. She also didn't want to reveal issues that she felt belonged to her and Jack alone, so she tiptoed around the issue as carefully as she could, while still telling enough to be able to get some advice.

She continued, "One of my roommates apparently told my boyfriend about the class, and he flipped out that I hadn't told him about it. What really has me confused is why he had such an emotional reaction to the mere fact that I was taking a silly class."

"Was he also upset that you were with me?" Ryan asked softly, lowering her eyes to the table.

Jamie didn't really want to go there, but she didn't feel comfortable lying to Ryan either. "Uhm, I guess that was part of it," she admitted. "But I think the bigger problem is that my roommate stirred up some suspicion in his mind. I guess it just surprised me that they'd all be so weird about it. You know—the class, and the topic, and, well, you." Jamie was also staring at the table by this time. She felt Ryan's reassuring hand gently grip her folded ones.

"That's exactly what Linda was talking about today," Ryan said. "Many people have a gut reaction to gay people and gay issues. I can't say I totally understand it, but I see it all the damned time. Things like this have caused me a lot of pain, Jamie, and I'm very sorry that you had to experience it too. I just hope that it won't affect our friendship. I really like you," she said shyly, as her eyes once again fell to the ground.

"Oh no, Ryan. I like you too. This is an issue that they're gonna have to get used to. I just want to understand it better so I can help them get through it."

Ryan looked at her carefully as she pursed her lips in thought. "Can I ask you a personal question?"

Jamie fidgeted in her seat as she tried to guess what her new friend wanted to know, but she replied, "Sure, what is it?"

"Why *didn't* you tell your boyfriend you were taking the class?"

Four excuses readily popped into Jamie's head. They hadn't discussed her schedule at all, Jack was too busy to be bothered with the details of her life, she didn't think it was important, she was going to tell him when she got a minute. But as she gazed into Ryan's eyes she felt drawn to be completely honest with her. As she opened her heart she realized that she hadn't been honest with herself, either. She was surprised to hear her own answer, "I didn't think he'd like it, and I was afraid that he'd either talk me out of it or somehow make me feel bad about it."

Ryan didn't say a word in response. She just slowly nodded her head as if she had expected that answer. Jamie wondered what was going on behind those ice blue eyes, but Ryan wasn't giving up her secrets today. She squeezed Jamie's shoulder and said, "I've read some really good books on homophobia and heterosexism. Call me at home this afternoon, and I'll give you the titles. I'll be home by three, and I don't leave for work until almost five. But speaking of time, I've got a bio lab in five minutes." She stood and chugged her remaining cranberry juice, then eyed Jamie's untouched apple juice as she hefted her enormous book bag onto her shoulder.

"Go ahead," she said, smiling at her. "You're a bit of a bottomless pit, aren't you?"

"My father always says I've two hollow legs."

"You get going—I'll call you later." Jamie waved as Ryan took off and began to run, scampering around slower students on the path.

I guess juice does give you extra energy!

The phone rang shrilly in the small, Victorian home in Noe Valley. It was picked up on the second ring and answered by someone with a deep, melodic male voice. "Hello?"

"Hi, this is Jamie Evans. Is Ryan at home?"

"Hold on a minute and I'll check." He dangled the phone by its cord and yelled, "Ryan! Phone!"

Ryan trotted up the stairs from her basement room to glare at her brother. "Thanks a lot Conor. Very cultured. All those years of charm school really paid off. Do you know who it is?"

"I assume it's the girlfriend du jour," he replied, using a poor French accent.

"That's helpful," Ryan said as she elbowed him out of the way. They tussled briefly before she wrenched the receiver from his hands. "Hello," she finally said into the phone.

"Jeez, what's going on over there? It sounded like the phone was being ripped from the wall."

"Well that's happened more than once. But today that was my charming older brother trying to gain some much needed attention," she said, sticking her tongue out at the brother in question.

"I didn't know you lived with your brother," Jamie said.

"Oh, yeah, I still live at home. Much to my regret, at times," she said, laughing.

"I don't know why, but you don't seem like the type to live at home," Jamie mused. "You seem very independent."

"No, that's not really what I'm like," Ryan said. "I'm really close to most of the members of my family." She giggled as her brother snuck up behind her and tickled her around the waist. "Stop it!" she shrieked as Jamie laughed at her surprisingly adolescent girlish giggle.

"It sounds kinda wild over there," Jamie said, while Ryan continued to giggle.

"It's always wild over here," she agreed, trying to control her breath. "Oh, I've got those titles for you." She reached into her pants pocket for a folded piece of paper.

"Great," Jamie said. "I'm ready."

After they conversed for a few minutes Ryan excused herself to get ready for work. As she began to walk back down the stairs to her room, her brother spoke from his place on the sofa.

"Was that today's entree, Ryan?"

"No, Conor," she explained. "Actually that one's in your camp. She's a woman from my psych class, and she's straight!" she said with mock alarm.

"Not for long if you get her in your sights, Sis," he predicted with a chuckle.

After her conversation with Ryan, Jamie drove to the bookstore they had visited the night before. She knew that the store would definitely have the titles that Ryan had told her about, and she guessed that the chain bookstores might not. After purchasing the books, she got back in her Porsche and began the long drive down to Palo Alto. Jack was due home by seven or so, and since she imagined the trip could take up to two hours, she felt she needed to brave the always heavy Friday night traffic to be there when he got home.

Much to Jamie's surprise, the trip took merely an hour, and she was in Palo Alto by a little after six. She had a key to the apartment, but after the fight she was reticent to show up without his permission. Instead, she went to her favorite coffee shop, just down the street from Jack's. She settled herself at a table with a steaming cup of latte and began to peruse her purchases. Immediately becoming engrossed in Loving Someone Gay, the time flew as she concentrated on the book. It seemed like only a few minutes had passed, but she glanced at her watch and saw that it was already seven. She retrieved her cell phone and dialed, and Jack answered on the third ring.

"Hi," she said as neutrally as possible.

"Jamie," he said, a clear tone of relief in his voice. "I just called your house, but no one knew where you were."

"I'm right down the street," she said. "If you want to see me I can be there in five minutes."

"Of course I want to see you," he said fervently. "I couldn't stop thinking about you all day."

"Okay, I'll be right there," she agreed, relief flooding her voice.

By the time she had put her purchased books in her bag and began to exit the shop she could see Jack jogging down the street. *That's better than an apology*, she thought, smiling widely when he approached.

She walked just a step or two before he was upon her. He lifted her effortlessly, his arms fully encircling her small waist. He squeezed nearly all of the air out of her lungs and nestled his head between her shoulder and neck. She leaned back a bit to regard him as he whispered, "I'm so sorry, Jamie. I acted like a total asshole, and I hope you can forgive me."

She responded with a tender kiss to his soft lips. That kiss was followed by another, slightly less tender, but with more emotion. As he gently lowered her, he grasped her cheeks with his large hands, and pulled her close for a dizzying series of kisses that left her panting. "Let's go," she rasped out as she grabbed his hand and began to lead him down the street.

The pent up emotion of the past twenty-four hours began to pulse in her veins as they covered the short distance. As they entered the apartment she grabbed him by the shirt and roughly pushed him against the wall. He gasped in surprise at this totally unexpected display of aggression from his normally demure lover. She pounced upon his mouth and kissed him thoroughly, keeping at it until she felt his knees begin to buckle. They began to slide down the wall in tandem, with Jamie frantically trying to undo his belt. He wrenched his T-shirt over his head as she bent to focus intently on her task. Finally, she loosened his belt and unzipped him. She grabbed his jeans and shorts and yanked them as far down his legs as their position would allow her.

He was sitting with his back against the wall, pants around his shins as Jamie straddled his thighs. He grabbed her golf shirt by the hem and pulled it over her compliant, outstretched arms. She threw her arms around his neck for another bout of heated kisses while he expertly removed her bra. The only barrier now was her jeans, and Jack couldn't tolerate this encumbrance to her skin for another second. He grasped her around her waist and tumbled them both onto their sides, where his nimble hands slid her zipper down with agonizing slowness, hearing the click, click, click as the metal gave way. They both gasped at the sound and at the promise of what lay ahead. Taking over to speed things up, Jamie pushed her jeans and panties down and out of the way.

She seized the opportunity the momentary distraction provided, and rolled him onto his back on the hardwood floor. Straddling him again, she grabbed his hands and placed them firmly on her breasts. Using her own hands to guide him, she pushed his hands against herself roughly. She began to grind his large hands against her aroused breasts with a brazenness and ferocity that Jack had never before seen her display.

Dropping her head to his, she began another assault to his lips. Her tongue entered his mouth, and she let out a fierce, animalistic groan. They kissed for a long time, both of them ravenous for the taste and feel of the other. They drew apart only to breathe, the kisses so intense that they were both panting.

Jack's hands never stopped grasping and squeezing her now tender breasts, and when she knew she was ready she slid back onto his lap as he raised his knees. She impaled herself on his aching member and rode him for a few short moments before she cried out her release. He followed her seconds later, his mouth seeking hers while he groaned with satisfaction.

The spent woman collapsed onto his chest, feeling it rise and fall rapidly. Their sweat-drenched bodies lay tangled together, arms, legs, jeans all entwined. "Does this mean I'm forgiven?" he finally asked with a wan smile from his languid stupor.

Even though the start of the weekend had been explosive, by Saturday morning things seemed just like usual. They had developed a very familiar pattern, and they both fell back into it.

They sat together in the sunny, small living room, focused on their studies. Jamie caught up on most of her reading for the week and completed her short paper on the visit to the bookstore. By Saturday afternoon, Jamie had gotten current on all of her classes while Jack had just started to make a dent in his.

Late in the day she began to make dinner, after a quick trip to the grocery store. She had decided to make Jack's favorite meal, chicken enchiladas, as a little peace offering. While she worked, she thought about the previous evening. They didn't discuss the fight at all, and that was fine with her. Both of them thought that the blow up was a one-time-only occurrence and neither saw the need to rehash it. That was one thing that both of them appreciated about their relationship. Neither of them needed or wanted a lot of drama to keep them entertained. But even though she wasn't a drama queen, Jamie had to admit that she had never felt as much lust for Jack as she had yesterday. *Maybe a blow up is a good idea every once in a while. God knows that was the best sex we've had in … I don't know how long!*

After dinner, Jamie watched a movie that she had rented while on her earlier errand. She watched wearing headphones, since Jack was still diligently working away. They sat on the couch together, he sitting up, she lying on her side with her head on a pillow at the other end of the couch, and her legs resting on his lap. His textbook was resting on his thighs, propped up by her legs.

Around midnight, Jack gently stroked her arm to wake her. "C'mon sleeping beauty, time for bed." He helped her sit up, but she only lasted in that position for a moment before collapsing onto his chest.

"Too tired," she grumbled sleepily.

He turned a bit and reached under her knees with one arm while the other cradled her back. He rose with her in his arms as she nestled down into his embrace. "My hero," she crooned softly.

They reached the bedroom and Jack placed her on the edge of the bed. He bent to remove her shoes, smiling when she fell to the bed in an exhausted heap. He eventually removed the rest of her clothing with not a bit of help from Jamie. He gazed at her naked body, legs hanging off the side of the bed, arms stretched out over her head, just as he had left them after removing her shirt. He took off his clothes as well, taking his just removed T-shirt and placing it over her head. Then he wrestled her arms into the garment, and moved her into a more comfortable position.

Jack slipped into a pair of cotton pajama bottoms and joined her. He had never met anyone who fell asleep so soundly or completely. It was a trait that he found undeniably cute, even when it prevented him from making love to her. He pulled her into an embrace, kissing her face and head, and then settling her against his side as they both fell into a deep sleep.

Jamie began to wake just as the dawn was beginning to break. Her first sensation was of a tender, languid touch roaming up and down her bare legs. Hands slowly moved to the front and began a slow, teasing dance on her twitching thighs. Unhurriedly, she began to gain some semblance of consciousness, and she started to respond to the touch by gently sliding into it. It was clear that she wasn't fully awake, but also clear that she wasn't asleep.

The touch moved up her body to tenderly rub her stomach, sides, breasts and arms. Her T-shirt disappeared, and the touch now encompassed her whole bare body. Jack was still lying on his side behind her, and she began to move her hips in time with his touch. As she sensually arched her back into him, he turned her so they lay face to face. He began to slowly and teasingly kiss every part of her that he could reach. After a seeming eternity she was softly moaning and grinding her hips, needing his immediate attention. He responded quickly, slipping into her as she let out a small gasp. They moved together smoothly and she was surprised to find herself once more groaning out her release, minutes later.

Jack cuddled her and spoke nonsense words of love into her ear for a few tender moments. The feeling of warmth and contentment overtook her again and she fell back into a sated sleep.

At ten, Jamie pried her eyes open and forced herself to look at the bedside clock. *Wow, I had the strangest dream*. After a quick physical inspection however, she realized that she hadn't been dreaming. *God, two times in two days! What's gotten into him? For that matter, what's gotten into me? Whatever it is, I hope it stays around!*

Jamie felt much better about her relationship with Jack when she returned to Berkeley. By Monday morning she was still in high spirits during her psychology class, and she received a good bit of teasing from Ryan after the class was over. "May I assume that things got resolved between you and your boyfriend?" she asked with a twinkle in her clear blue eyes.

Jamie gave her a smirk and replied, "We definitely made up. I'm not sure that we resolved anything, though. That behavior was so out of character for Jack that I'm just going to assume that he was momentarily possessed."

"Hey, I've got my usual hour free, can I interest you in another bottle of juice or three?"

"Yeah, that'd be nice." As they walked through the campus Ryan was pleased to notice that Jamie chattered away non-stop in her usual style. Jamie was first to reach into her book bag, and offered to pay for the drinks. Ryan agreed and picked out a table, watching Jamie struggle to carry the four bottles back.

"I'm not even going to pretend that two of these are for me."

"Actually, I could drink all four, so you'd better be careful," Ryan replied with a little eyebrow wiggle.

"How do you consume all of the calories you do and stay so thin?"

"Well," Ryan said thoughtfully, "I am really active, and then with all of the sweating I do at my job, I find I can eat whatever I want."

"What in the hell do you do for a living?" Jamie finally blurted out.

Ryan looked slightly confused as she answered. "I'm a personal trainer. I told you that."

Jamie began to laugh so hard that tears rolled down her face. She clutched at her sides as she rocked back and forth in her chair. "I've had a lot of reactions, but never that," Ryan said, clearly puzzled.

"I'm not laughing at your job. You hadn't told me what you do, and I let my fertile imagination run wild. I imagined you as some high paid lesbian prostitute."

At this revelation Ryan threw back her head and roared. After a few moments she wiped the tears from her eyes and gave Jamie a mock scowl. "Hey, it just dawned on me that might have been an insult. Are you saying I look like a prostitute?"

"No! Of course not! But I couldn't figure out why else you'd have to time your clients for an hour, potentially have two at a time, and be able to take naps in between. And, let's be honest Ryan, you're great looking, and I could see women paying for the pleasure of your company."

"Hmm," she said as if contemplating switching jobs. "I wonder how many women share that view. Nah, I'd hate to mix business with pleasure," she finally decided with a good-natured grin.

The classmates fell into a routine of spending an hour after class chatting before Ryan's biology lab. Within a few weeks the habit was so ingrained that they didn't even ask each other before they automatically began the short walk to the vending area.

Jamie had inquired once or twice about Ryan's participation in the AIDS Ride, asking how her training was going. On a crisp, clear, September morning after another such question Ryan looked at her seriously and said, "You know, if you're at all interested I could get you ready to do the ride."

Jamie was nonplussed at the mere suggestion that she could accomplish such a monumental undertaking and quickly demurred. "Ryan, I don't even own a bike. I haven't ridden at all since high school, and I wasn't very serious about it even then. The most energetic thing I do is play golf, and as I always say, if you can smoke while doing it, it isn't a sport."

"Everybody who rides has doubts about her ability. There were people on the first ride who had every type of physical and emotional disability you can think of, and the group has gotten more diverse every year since then. I've seen people participate who weigh more than 300 pounds, amputees, people with AIDS. There were two people last year that'd never been on a bike before they started training. From the looks of you," she eyed her carefully up and down, "you don't have any excuses."

"Well, I guess you're right. I don't have a good excuse. Do you really think you could get me ready to do it? It just seems like such a gargantuan task. I'm really out of shape, Ryan. I don't know if it's possible."

"Gee, could you come up with any more excuses?" Ryan teased as her eyes twinkled playfully. "I know I could get you ready if you're willing to try. I've trained people for ultra marathons, and I've trained people for triathlons and the principles are the same. Start out slowly and build. I'm not saying it's easy, because it's not. But for me it's one of the most rewarding things I do," Ryan said.

Jamie looked at her friend for a moment. "Why does it mean so much to you? Is it that big an accomplishment?"

Ryan shook her head. "No, not at all." She took a sip of her juice and looked away, lost in thought for quite a while. Finally, she said, "I lost my cousin Michael to AIDS ten years ago. He was one of the sweetest men I ever knew, and he was only twenty-seven when he died. Anything I can do to stop another family from going through that pain is worth any amount of sacrifice to me."

Jamie sat in pensive silence for a few moments, mulling over her friend's words. "Well, if you're willing to take on a hopeless case, I'm willing to give it a try. Where do we start?"

Ryan beamed a smile that Jamie had to return. "I suppose the first order of business is to get you a bike, assuming you don't have one. Can you afford to spend some money on a bike now?"

"Yeah, I can manage."

"When are you free to go shopping?"

"How about tomorrow? We'd better do it before I lose my nerve."

"It's a deal. I'm free from ten to one tomorrow. I normally study during that break, but I am amazingly caught up for a change. Is that good for you?"

"Perfect."

As agreed, Jamie picked Ryan up at ten, and they drove to Ryan's favorite bike shop in Oakland. "I've been coming here for a long time," Ryan said. "These guys really know their stuff, and they don't try to sell you things you don't need."

They entered the shop to a boisterous welcome from the gray-haired man behind the counter. "Hiya, Ryan, long time no see."

"That's only because you do such a good job on my bikes that I never have to come back. It's your own fault, Bill."

The man walked around the counter, and Ryan made introductions. "Bill, this is my friend, Jamie. I've convinced her to ride with me this year in the AIDS ride. She doesn't have a bike, so you need to fix her up."

"Excellent, Jamie," he said. "With Ryan as your guide, you'll do well. She's gotten some pretty hopeless characters to finish the ride. So what do you have in mind?"

"I know nothing about bikes. You two are the experts. What do you suggest?" she said as she looked at Ryan.

"A road bike would be the best for the ride," Ryan said thoughtfully. "The only downside is that you can't take it off road at all. But it'll let you climb hills easier, and it goes a lot faster than a mountain bike."

"Price is a big factor," Bill explained. "I can get you a road bike for $300, but you'll feel every pound on that long ride. At the other end of the spectrum, I can make you a bike that'll feel like you're riding on air—but that'll cost some serious money."

"I think I'm gonna need all the help I can get. I'd rather spend more to make this as easy as I can. What would you suggest if money wasn't a factor?"

Ryan's eyes nearly flew from her head, but Bill didn't flinch. "Not a factor at all?"

Ryan gathered her wits and interrupted, "Are you sure that you mean that? Bikes can really get up there in a hurry. I mean, Bill won't take advantage of you, but he can work with whatever budget you have."

"Well, what's the real difference between a moderately priced bike and the top of the line? Is the more expensive bike really worth more?"

"On a long ride an expensive bike can be worth it," Bill said. "The higher quality components are a lot smoother and more responsive. But the biggest factor is weight. You could easily save about seven pounds of weight by going with top quality. The higher priced bike would have much lighter components. You'd save three pounds just on wheels alone if I made you top quality rims. Now, seven pounds doesn't sound like a lot, but believe me, you'd notice it—especially on a 500 mile ride."

"Five hundred miles! I've driven to L.A, and it's under 400. What gives, Ryan?"

"Oh, didn't I mention that the route isn't real direct?" Ryan said, her attention seemingly focused on a new bike seat.

Jamie put her hands on her hips and glared at her friend while Bill laughed softly.

Slowly, Ryan raised her head and looked at Jamie with a slightly chagrined expression. "Come on! Do you really think 400 miles is easy? The difference between the two is pretty minor when you think about it. That's less than fifteen miles a day over a week."

"Well, I guess that's true. What do you think I should do, Ryan?"

"If I could afford to drop seven pounds off my bike, I'd be first in line to do so," Ryan said. "But it's not something you need to do if you can't comfortably afford it. People ride bikes that I wouldn't wish on my worst enemy, and they do just fine."

"No, no, I can afford it, and I really do want to make this as enjoyable an experience as possible."

Ryan looked at the man and said, "Looks like this is your lucky day, Bill. Show us some frames."

"Cute ones," Jamie demanded, grinning up at Ryan.

"Cute ones," Ryan agreed.

They left the bike shop a little before noon. "I'm famished," Ryan groaned, theatrically clutching at her stomach. "I've never seen anyone take longer to make a decision on anything!"

"I wanted to make sure I got what I wanted. You're the one who convinced me to have Bill make the bike, rather than buy a stock model."

"I'd have taken you to Target if I knew it was gonna take so long," Ryan said with a teasing grin.

"Okay, you big baby, I'll buy you lunch—and I know just the place."

They climbed into the Porsche and drove a short distance to a favorite deli in Oakland. "Oh, wow," Ryan enthused. "I didn't know there was one of these in the East Bay. I go to the main store in the Marina, and the one in the Mission all the time. I absolutely love this place." Her clear blue eyes lit up as she licked her lips in anticipation of her meal.

"You really are easy to please," Jamie said, marveling at her friend. While they waited in line, she reflected that one of Ryan's most appealing qualities was the joy she experienced at the little things life offered. She had an unguarded, childlike exuberance that was truly infectious, and Jamie realized that she never felt more alive than when she was with her new friend. As she watched Ryan carefully peruse the menu, she laughed to herself. The brunette read every word, and changed her mind at least six times while they waited to order. "It's almost our turn," she reminded her friend. "Are you able to stick with your decision?"

"You're referring to the highlight of my day," Ryan explained. "Lunch is my favorite meal. And since eating is my favorite activity, lunch is no laughing matter."

As Ryan spoke Jamie began looking though her wallet. "I've only got $47 on me. Do you think that'll cover it?"

"I'll go easy on you since you're new at this," Ryan said. "But next time don't be so unprepared. A trip to the ATM is always a good idea before you offer to buy me lunch."

After ordering their food, they found a table outside. The weather was starting to turn, but the table was in the bright noonday sun so they were quite comfortable even without jackets.

"So," Ryan said after they got comfortable. "That was some exhibition of buying power. I don't think I've ever seen Bill look so happy. He hasn't made that much off me in seven years."

Jamie blushed at having the spotlight on her financial status. "It made sense to buy the better bike for a ride like this."

Ryan gazed at her for a moment, as if deciding whether to ask a question. Finally she curled the corners of her mouth up in a small grin and asked, "I don't mean to ask an indelicate question, but are you loaded?"

"Gee, I'm glad that wasn't indelicate," Jamie retorted as she playfully slapped her friend's arm.

"I'm sorry if I'm prying," Ryan quickly added. "You really don't have to answer that question."

"You're not prying, and I don't mind talking about private things with you. But I get kind of embarrassed by it. I mean, oh, it's hard to explain."

"So loaded isn't a strong enough word?"

"Not really," Jamie said. "More like filthy rich."

"How filthy?"

"Obscenely."

"Wow! I've never been friends with anyone who was obscenely rich. That's really kind of cool," Ryan said. "Will you pay me to like you? For the right price I could even be your *best* friend."

"Very, very funny."

"Hey, don't be mad. I feel like I can tease you because you don't seem like a rich kid. If it wasn't for the Porsche and the bike you seem just like me," Ryan said. "But if you're sensitive about it I promise I'll never tease you about it again."

Jamie considered the question for a moment. Ryan was looking at her with that open, guileless expression that made her feel like she could trust Ryan with any of her secrets. "It's okay when you tease me. I don't know why, but your teasing never seems mean spirited. I hate to be sensitive about this, but it has been a problem for me throughout my life."

"Do you feel like talking about it?" Ryan's face bore such a friendly, accepting expression that Jamie found herself telling her the whole family story.

"My mother comes from very old money."

"I love old money," Ryan said wistfully.

Jamie rolled her eyes and continued, "Her maternal grandfather owned most of the coal mines in the country at the turn of the century. And her father's family was pretty well off, too."

"Hey, that sounds like my family's story, except both of my parent's families didn't have two nickels to rub together."

"Shall I go on?" Jamie asked, giving her friend a good-natured smile.

"I wish you would. What's stopping you?"

The blonde sighed and continued, "My maternal grandfather's people are sixth generation Californians, and they're into the whole social scene. My dad was pretty middle class, though."

"Hey, something I can relate to!"

"Maybe not," Jamie said. "My dad's father is an Episcopal priest, and his mother was a homemaker."

"No priests in our family," Ryan said. "Besides, our priests can't marry. Big drawback."

"I can imagine," Jamie said, giving her friend a smile. "We live mostly off my father's money now—and he works his tail off. My mother uses her money for trips, and she bought most of our houses, and big things like that. But my father has always stressed the value of money, and I got a very modest allowance when I was growing up. I try not to flaunt my wealth, because it really puts people off, but it's a part of my life, and I want my close friends to know about it."

"I'm glad you told me," Ryan said. "It means a lot to me that you trust me to know about your family."

"I do trust you, Ryan. I don't know how I know this, but I know you won't let this get in the way of our friendship."

"No way," she said emphatically. "After all, you haven't let my lesbianism get in the way of our relationship." She gave her friend a dazzling grin and asked, "Tell me more about your father. He must be really secure to have his wife be a lot richer than he is."

"Yeah, I respect him for it. Although now he makes a load as a partner in a big law firm. So we're rich even without mother's money. But it must have been hard for him when they were first together."

"Do you spend much time with your extended family?"

"No, we don't. My mother goes to her mother's family home in Rhode Island for at least a month in the summer, and when I was little I'd go with her. The whole extended family would be there, but I never felt like I fit in. They lived like the truly wealthy—servants everywhere, elegant dinners, spending the day sailing on huge yachts. But I never felt like I belonged."

"I can see that would be kind of hard. What about your mom's paternal side of the family. Are they local?"

"Yeah, there's tons of them around, but it's not a warm and fuzzy kind of group. They're not into spending holidays together or anything like that. My mother sees them at occasional social functions and the odd wedding and funeral. There's no animosity or anything, but there's some definite emotional distance."

Ryan looked at her quizzically and asked, "Tell me what the hardest thing about having money is."

"Mmm," Jamie said thoughtfully, "The difficult part is that my money has nothing to do with me. I got it as an accident of birth. I didn't earn it or deserve it in any way. Sometimes it really is a burden."

"I can understand that," Ryan said. "And I bet it doesn't make it any easier since so many people believe they'd be happy if only they had more money."

"Exactly!" Jamie smiled at her friend with relief. "You really do understand."

"I do. The hard parts of my life wouldn't change one bit because of money. I mean, I could work less if I earned more, but I'd probably just buy more junk!" she laughed. "People are always talking about how much better their lives would be if they had more money. I've never understood that. If you're happy, you'll be happy no matter how much or how little you have. And if you're miserable, all the money in the world won't make you happy."

"I think I'm going to consider your offer to be my best friend," Jamie said after a moment. "How much will it cost me?"

Ryan's eyes grew wide as a server delivered their heaping plates. "Consider yourself paid in full!"

After plowing through her sizeable lunch and picking over the remnants of Jamie's, Ryan said, "Now we need to work out how we'll train you for this ride."

"What are our options?"

"Saddle time is critical. There isn't much you can do to duplicate the feeling of actually riding, so we're going to have to log a lot of miles. To get the most out of your riding you've got to be in pretty good shape. I don't mean to be rude, but I don't see a lot of muscle lurking under your skin," she said as she reached for an absent bicep.

"Just 'cause I'm not rock hard like you doesn't mean I don't have any muscle," Jamie said, snatching her arm away before Ryan could get a good grip.

"I am just teasing, you know," Ryan said. "But the more muscle you've got the more you can demand of your body. So we need to increase your cardiovascular capacity, tone your muscles and ride like crazy. The easiest way to work on your lungs and your muscles is at a gym. Do you belong to a club?"

"No, I was going to join one, but I never got around to it."

"Well, now's a good time to join. We could use my club, but that's too much traveling for you. My place has a branch in Oakland. I've never been there but I'm willing to check it out for you. Is there any place you've heard about that you'd like to try?"

"Some of my friends go to a club they really like. Why don't we both do some research and compare notes?"

"Sounds good. I'll check mine out on the way home tonight. Let me know when you've checked out a few and then you can decide," Ryan said.

"Great. Now comes the hard part," Jamie said as her face grew serious. "Obviously, I'm going to pay you for your time. How can we work that out?"

Ryan's eyes grew wide, and she shook her head. "I can't charge you, Jamie. I want to do this because you're my friend. It'll be fun for me."

"I appreciate that, and I'd agree, except for one thing. I know how busy you are. I've seen that little black book of yours, you know. This is how you make your living. If you weren't working with me you'd be working with a regular client, wouldn't you?"

"Well, yeah, sometimes, I guess so." she said hesitantly. "But I can work you in without too much trouble. I've got three or four hours a week that are unscheduled, and I can work out with you sometimes, and I never do that with a client."

"What are your arrangements with your club, if you don't mind my asking?"

"I pay them a flat monthly fee, and I can work out whenever I want and train anyone who's a member. They hook me up with clients and I can bring people in myself. The member pays me directly, usually $40 per hour."

"Do you train people who aren't members?"

"Yeah, I have some private clients. There are some places that let trainers come in and pay an hourly fee. That lets me train people who don't belong to my gym. And

I've got one woman who has a gym at her house, but I didn't see any iron laying around your place when I was there for dinner."

"How much do you charge private clients?"

"$125 per hour if I like you," she said. "The price goes up as your likeability goes down."

"Is that really true?"

"Yeah, the woman with the gym in her home pays me $175 per hour. And if she complains about the price one more time it's going up to $200," she laughed. "She started out at $125 like everyone else, but she kept bitching about how expensive it was. That made me mad, so I raised her. She kept bitching, so I kept raising. Pretty soon I won't have to take any other clients. She can support me," she said, laughing.

"How about this? If I join your gym I'll pay you the standard $40. But if I choose to join somewhere where you aren't affiliated, I'll pay you $125. Unless I make you mad, of course," she chuckled. "I know you don't want to take my money but if I don't pay you I won't feel comfortable using you as often as I want. I want you to think of me as a client for this and give me your undivided attention okay?"

"I don't like charging friends, Jamie. But I do want you to feel comfortable using me when you need to. So I'll agree, with one proviso. If I work out at the same time, you don't pay at all, unless there's a daily gym fee. In that case you can pay to get us in, but that's all. Okay?"

"That's an excellent deal, Ryan. You're hired," she agreed as they clasped hands and shared a smile.

Chapter Three

During the next few days, Jamie checked out four potential gyms. All were reasonably close to her home, and each was vastly different. Her first stop was the club that Mia belonged to, but seldom visited. It was in North Berkeley and was expensive and very much in vogue with young women. Mia arranged for a visit and agreed to accompany Jamie.

After their trip, Jamie decided that the facilities were top notch, but she hated the atmosphere. It was filled with young professionals and a few members of the Junior League set. There was a juice bar that was filled with people checking each other out while trying not to be obvious about it. The locker rooms were very nicely appointed, but it reminded Jamie of the girls' rest room in high school during a dance. Women were comparing notes on which guys were there and who was dating whom. The dressing area was populated by women fixing their hair and adjusting their perfectly matched outfits prior to their workouts. Jamie realized that she might have chosen this place a few months ago, but now she really wanted to work out—not socialize.

Next she looked at a club that was very close to campus and open twenty-four hours. It was fairly nice also, but she learned that she couldn't bring her own trainer. *That rules that out.*

Next was a club that was inexpensive and populated by serious weightlifters. *Maybe later, but right now this place would intimidate me.*

Much to her surprise, her favorite club was small, a bit out of the way, and women only. Women Power was obviously for women who were serious about working out. There was a small locker room that held only that—lockers. No showers, no saunas, no Jacuzzis. But there was a dazzling assortment of free weights and well-maintained weight machines. There were also five elliptical cross trainers, seven treadmills, five stair climbers, five recumbent bikes and five upright bikes. The women seemed friendly, but most of them were very serious about their workouts. The staff was all women also, and what Jamie liked most was that she was free to bring Ryan for only ten dollars per visit. She also appreciated that there was a clear price schedule for membership. No hard sell, no "special only if you sign up today" garbage. They merely explained the price, and asked her if she wanted a one-week guest pass to try out the facilities. She happily accepted and called Ryan as soon as she got home to relay her findings.

Ryan had been unimpressed with the branch of her club in Oakland, so she agreed to meet Jamie at Women Power on Friday afternoon to try it out.

Jamie picked her friend up at their normal meeting place, and they slogged through Friday afternoon Berkeley traffic to reach the gym. They had previously arranged for Ryan to take BART to campus that morning so that Jamie could drop her off at work on the way to Palo Alto. As they muddled along, a thought occurred to Jamie. "Have you eaten today?"

"Not really," Ryan sheepishly admitted. "I had breakfast, but I haven't had any other breaks today. Why? Is my stomach grumbling?"

"Why didn't you say something?" Jamie asked with an exasperated tone.

"I know you wanted to check this place out and I didn't want to slow you down. I can get something before work. It's really no big deal."

"Oh please! The way you eat, missing a meal must be catastrophic to your system! Your poor stomach must be leading a revolt right this minute."

"It's not that bad," Ryan said as she looked at the site of the possible rebellion. "Although," she patted her stomach and leaned down to listen, "I do hear the faint signals of discord."

Jamie glanced at her watch. "It's only 2:35 now. If you're due at work by six we don't have to leave the East Bay until five-thirty. Are you gonna work out, too?"

"No. I hadn't planned on it."

"Then an hour and a half should be enough to decide if we like this place. We can easily spare an hour for you to eat."

"Gosh, it all sounds so easy when you say it like that." Ryan closed her eyes and let a pleasured smile settle on her face. "I do love lunch."

Jamie looked at the sensual smile on her friend's face, observing her for a moment. Surprised, she realized that Ryan no longer flirted with her. *That's kind of weird. She was so flirty when we met, and now she's just like any of my other friends. I wonder what changed? Maybe she got the message that I was straight and gave up. I guess I should be thankful—it's a lot more comfortable to be with her now. But still ...*

"Hey, anybody home in there?" Ryan asked, making Jamie start.

"Oh, sorry. What were you saying?"

"I just wondered where you wanted to stop. Now that you brought it up I've gotta feed the beast or there'll be trouble." She patted her belly again and grinned.

"What are you in the mood for? We can get almost anything." Jamie waved her hand at the plethora of restaurants on the surrounding streets.

"Hmm." Ryan's eyes closed in concentration. One blue eye popped open momentarily as she asked, "I can have *anything* I want?"

"Yep. Anything."

Jamie glanced at the intense look of happy concentration on Ryan's face and had to smother a laugh. She could almost see the panoply of international dishes floating through her friend's imagination.

Finally, Ryan's eyes opened fully and she said with barely contained glee, "Chinese."

"Chinese it is, and I know just the place."

Ryan sat with a steaming bowl of hot and sour soup in front of her and a blissful look on her face. "This is divine. Are you a big foodie?"

"Yeah. I like to eat. Not as much as you do, but I can hold my own. You should get me down to the Peninsula or the South Bay. I think I've been to every restaurant within twenty miles of Hillsborough, where my parents live."

"I don't think I've ever been there," Ryan said. "I actually haven't been down to the South Bay much at all."

"It's nice, but a little sedate. You'll have to come down sometime. Anyway, my dad was never home for dinner, and my mother loves to try new places, so we cut a swath though the whole area. A place can't be open for more than a week before my mother hits it."

"That's the opposite of my family. We don't go to a restaurant more than once or twice a year, and that's only under duress."

"You know, Ryan, I really don't know much about your family. Who's at home with you?"

"Well, there's my father, Martin, my oldest brother Brendan, who doesn't officially live with us, but he's always there for meals, my brothers Conor and Rory and me, I'm the baby. Oops, I almost forgot my dog, Duffy, I guess he's really the baby."

"What about your mother?"

"My mother's dead," Ryan said without explanation. She bent her head to concentrate on her soup.

"I'm sorry to hear that," Jamie said. She wasn't sure if Ryan wanted to discuss it, but she asked, "Has she been dead long?"

"Yeah."

Jamie continued to look at the top of Ryan's head. When the deep blue eyes lifted, Ryan realized that the question was still open. "Sixteen years in December."

"My God, you were just a baby!"

The previously somber face eased into a small smile and Ryan demurred, "Well, not quite a baby, but I'd just turned seven."

Jamie looked at her friend with an expression full of sympathy. "God, that must have been devastating for you."

Ryan paused for a moment, as if considering the idea. "I don't think devastating covers it, to tell you the truth. Losing your mother changes everything. I don't know if I'd be a better or worse person, but I know I'd be different if she were still alive."

"How did it happen?" Jamie asked softly.

"She had breast cancer." After a moment she looked contemplative and added, "You know, it's funny. She was only thirty years old when she was diagnosed. She had no family history, she was thin, she ate a healthy diet, she had children when she was young, and she had good medical care. And she was dead in four years." She cleared her throat and slowly lifted her chin, letting Jamie see a completely lost look in her deep blue eyes.

Jamie wasn't able to say a word. She merely reached over and tightly gripped Ryan's hand while looking into her eyes. They sat like that for a few minutes, sharing their feelings with their eyes alone. Ryan had never looked smaller, younger or more vulnerable. Jamie thought her heart would break at the feelings she could plainly see in her friend's eyes. She'd barely noticed it, but tears were sliding down her cheeks and Ryan reached over somewhat tentatively to wipe them away with a gentle touch.

"Wow, I don't know where that came from." Ryan leaned back in her chair and let out a heavy breath. "Her birthday's coming up. She's been on my mind a lot lately."

"Do you remember her well?" She was interested in her friend's history, but she was also loath not to let go of this intimate moment before she had to.

"Yeah, I do," Ryan said with a small smile gracing her lips. "She was sick from the time I can remember, but she tried so hard to be there for me. I still don't know how she did it." With a wistful smile she added, "I'm really lucky. My family talks about her a lot. Although sometimes I don't know if I really have all these memories, or if I remember her through their eyes. I guess it doesn't matter in the end though. She's still alive in my heart." She showed such an adorably sweet smile that Jamie's caught in her throat.

Fearing her expression would reveal too much, Jamie shifted the conversation back to Ryan. "Your father never remarried?"

"Remarried!" Ryan laughed. "He's never had a date that I know of. I guess he wasn't much of a catch when we were young. Who wants a man with four wild kids who's away from home for three days at a time?"

"You were left alone that much?"

"No, we weren't alone much at all until the boys were old enough to take care of me. We have a gaggle of aunts and cousins who all live in the city, all within walking distance. While my mother was sick, and for the first few years after her death, someone stayed with us when my father was at work. After a while, Brendan was old enough to be in charge. I'm sure it was hard on him, but he never complained. He was, and is, a very good brother."

"How old are your brothers?"

"Rory's twenty-five, Conor's twenty-seven and Brendan's twenty-nine. That's Irish family planning. Plan on having a baby every two years," Ryan said, trying to inject a little humor.

"Are you okay talking about all of this?" Jamie asked gently.

Ryan's head was still tilted down, something that Jamie noticed she did when she was talking about something that was difficult for her. She smiled and looked up at her friend with hooded eyes. "Yeah, I am with you. I don't talk about her much with people outside of the family, but it feels good to talk about it with someone who isn't as invested as we all are."

Jamie smiled at this admission and realized that she still gripped Ryan's hand. She felt a blush rise on her cheeks and released it, only to have Ryan reclaim hers. "Thanks for caring," she said as they locked eyes.

Their server interrupted the moment as he appeared carrying plates of pan-fried noodles, Szechwan green beans, and stir-fried broccoli with mushrooms.

Ryan rubbed her hands together, waiting for the plates to land. By the time the server had departed her chopsticks were ready for action. She dug in enthusiastically and Jamie watched in amazement, noting that Ryan didn't eat particularly quickly. But once she started, she didn't slow down for a moment. She kept up a steady cadence that wasn't interrupted by unnecessary speech. She paid attention to Jamie, but mostly nodded and shook her head as required. Jamie understood that Ryan needed her mouth to eat rather than talk, so she kept up a running monologue, mostly about school and her classes.

After Ryan had finished every bite she leaned back in her chair in a pleasant post-prandial haze. Jamie regarded her with a smirk. "Do your brothers eat as much as you do?"

"More, much more. Dinner time at our house isn't for the faint-hearted."

"I'd love to witness that," Jamie said, imagining the carnage.

"That can certainly be arranged. I'd love to have you."

Jamie was pleased with Ryan's appraisal of the gym. "This place is the bomb, Jamie," she said with a big grin on her tanned face.

"I like it too. Shall we get to work?" She was wearing an emerald and navy blue sports bra over matching, thigh-length, nylon shorts, exposing her completely to Ryan's considered gaze. The blue eyes wandered up and down Jamie's lithe form for another minute or two, until the blonde began to shift nervously. "I feel like a deer in the headlights here, Ryan."

"Oh, sorry," Ryan said with a grin. "I was just trying to get an impression of your musculature."

"It's that bad?"

"No, of course not. In fact, you really have a great body. But you can definitely use some more muscle here." She ran her long, cool fingers down both of Jamie's shoulders, stopping at her elbows, "and here," another pair of gentle tracings down the front of her thighs. "Now we haven't talked about this much, but have you thought about whether you really want to change your body?"

"What do you mean?"

"Nothing bad." Ryan giggled at her friend's wary expression. "It's just that some women don't think it's womanly to show muscle. And some men don't like it either. I wondered how your fiancé felt about your looking buff."

Jamie realized that this was the first time they had ever discussed Jack and his proprietary interest in her body, and she was quite sure she didn't like the implication. "He doesn't get a vote. My body—my choice. Besides, I think women look great with muscles. I think they enhance femininity—as long as they're natural looking." Jamie had a sudden interest in seeing Ryan exposed in the same way she was. It occurred to her that she'd never actually seen her muscles, even though it was obvious that she had them. Ryan was usually pretty well covered up—much as she was today. Jamie looked at her navy blue warm ups and wondered what was underneath them. *You'd better not go there. What was that about being glad she doesn't flirt with you any more?*

"That's great. I'm glad you're comfortable with this. Is there anything you'd like to change? I mean, if we can," Ryan added.

"I'm not sure what you mean. Are you saying I get to choose how I change?"

"Yeah, to some extent. Some areas respond more quickly to weight training. But genetic predisposition affects the final outcome."

"So are you saying you can guess where those areas would be on me?"

"Kind of. Do you mind my staring at you again?"

"Be my guest." A warm flush crawled up her cheeks, and she tried to adopt a casual pose.

Ryan stood back a step or two and crossed her arms over her chest. Once again she stared at Jamie's body, starting at the shoulders and working her way down. "Because of your height I'd guess that large leg muscles wouldn't look great," she said. "And I bet your legs and butt will get big easily—if we let them." She gently squeezed the muscles at the middle of Jamie's thighs and nodded her head. "I think your quads could get really big if you like that look, but if you didn't want that we'd want to work on elongating your muscles there rather than just making them big."

Next she placed her hands on Jamie's shoulders. "You've got a nice deltoid just waiting to come out here." She placed her fingertips loosely on the tops of Jamie's shoulders again and slowly traced her thumbs over the muscles just above her breasts, "You could develop really nice pecs, too. And if I'm not mistaken," she said as she ran the flat of her hand slowly down Jamie's bare abdomen, starting just under her bra and stopping just above her pubic bone, "you could have killer abs." She said this with a decided twinkle in her eyes.

Jamie struggled to replace the saliva in her mouth. "How can you tell that?"

"You don't have much adipose tissue there. Those muscles are just dying to pop out. Me, on the other hand," she lifted her jacket and her white nylon shirt to expose her tanned abdomen, "I've got a pretty thick layer of fat here. No matter how much I work on my abs they can't pop out like yours will." She grasped Jamie's hand and placed it on the warm body part in question. "Here, feel the difference." Now she placed the hand on Jamie's stomach. "See what I mean?"

Jamie was now fully involved in the exercise. "I do, I really do. Mine feels like just skin covering muscle, but yours is softer." She gave Ryan's stomach a little pat, "but there's some pretty hard muscle right under that … what do you call that tissue again?"

"Adipose tissue. That's trainer talk for fat." She whispered this last word right into Jamie's ear.

The smaller woman chortled. "I think your fat is in all the right places."

She received a smile and a small laugh in return. "Part of the occupational requirements. Can't have an out of shape trainer."

After the preliminaries, they worked their way from machine to machine. Ryan had a little notebook which she used to make notes about every machine. She carefully adjusted each apparatus to perfectly fit Jamie, then indicated each of these positions in her book. She then made an estimate of the weight she thought Jamie could handle, while she explained how to perform the exercise. Ryan explained that each correct movement through the exercise was called a repetition, or a rep. Ideally, Jamie would perform somewhere between twelve and fifteen reps. Ryan said that Jamie should begin to feel fatigue by the twelfth or thirteenth rep, but no sooner. If she was tired before that, the weight was too heavy. Conversely, if she felt like she could do another five or six reps without a break, then it was too light.

Ryan explained that there was no easy way to figure out the perfect weight to start with. It was all trial and error. She also said that eventually Jamie would perform three sets of each fifteen-rep exercise, with a minute rest in between sets. As for now, her goal was to get Jamie comfortable with the exercise and get a feel for her capacity.

"It's important to slowly acclimate your body to this new level of stress. Don't force yourself to do things that don't feel comfortable. I want this to be pleasurable for you," Ryan said.

"So what's this I hear about 'no pain, no gain?'" Jamie asked. "That doesn't sound like pleasure."

"That's true to a certain extent. Your muscles enlarge from stress. The stress of tearing small fibers and allowing them to heal is what makes 'em grow. But you only need to feel a slight discomfort. If you're really sore, I haven't done my job well."

"Good, I love to have someone to blame."

"You've got some responsibility too," Ryan said. "You should drink more fluid than you normally do to flush the lactic acid from your system. And eating well is critical, too."

As Jamie performed each of the exercises, Ryan paid close attention to her form. She carefully watched her face for signs of stress or too much exertion. Ryan placed one hand at the highest point that she wanted Jamie to extend, and her other hand at the lowest. On the machines where she was forced to move a lot of weight, like the reclining leg press, Ryan gripped the footplate in her strong hands and pulled it back to reduce the stress on Jamie's legs.

After an hour, they had covered all of the exercises for her legs. Ryan suggested they stop so that Jamie wasn't overwhelmed with information. The smaller woman agreed and shook her tired legs out. "Let me help with that," Ryan offered.

"Okay," Jamie agreed, giving her a skeptical look.

Ryan grabbed a floor mat and instructed her to lie down on her tummy. She grasped Jamie's foot and slowly pushed her leg toward her butt. She held that position for a few moments, and then repeated the stretch with the other foot. After instructing Jamie to turn over, she gripped her foot with both hands and pushed until Jamie's knee was near her chest. Again, she held the position before she switched to the other foot. Now she gripped behind her ankle with one hand and placed a restraining hand on her knee. She pushed her leg toward her body until Jamie's butt started to lift off the floor. "Keep your butt down," she said. "This'll give you a nice stretch in your hamstrings." After she had completed the stretch, she picked Jamie's foot up and braced it against her chest. Then she began to massage her thigh with strong, knowing hands. Jamie closed her eyes in pleasure as Ryan's hands kneaded her tired muscles deeply.

"Do you do this to everybody?" she asked as she slowly sat halfway up and rested her weight on her forearms.

"Yeah, pretty much."

"Then you don't charge nearly enough," Jamie said, and collapsed into a heap on the mat.

Ryan laughed as she offered a hand down to her, "C'mon jellyfish. They frown on sleeping on the floor." As she was pulled to her feet, Ryan said, "The only bad thing about this place is that there aren't any showers." She looked at Jamie's sweat-drenched clothing. "You really shouldn't drive all the way to Palo Alto in those clothes. I'm afraid you'll stiffen up."

"It's only four-thirty, we could go by my house so I could take a quick shower."

"I think you should do that. I could just take BART home if you don't want me to come with you," she offered, uncharacteristically hesitant.

"Why would I …" Jamie thought for a moment, then realized what Ryan was thinking. "Are you worried about my roommates?"

"No, I'm not worried about them. I just don't want them to hassle you about hanging out with me. I don't wanna make your life more difficult."

"Ryan, I'm honored to be your friend. Anyone who doesn't like you isn't worth my time. I mean that."

The tanned face broke into an adorable grin as she blushed and looked down at the floor. "Thanks. That means a lot to me."

Despite her protestations, Ryan was relieved when they entered the house and found it empty. "I'll just sit down here and read, if that's okay."

"Sure. Make yourself at home; I'll only be a minute." Jamie started to walk up the stairs and winced a little bit. "I think you were right about these babies tightening up," she said, grasping the back of her leg.

"C'mere for a second," Ryan said. "I can loosen 'em up again. They're tight because you let 'em get cold too quickly." She directed Jamie to the area rug in the middle of the parlor. Jamie removed her sweats and lay down on the rug, where Ryan once again began her strong massage. "After I get these loose, you should stay in a hot shower for a few minutes. Then they should be fine." While Ryan worked diligently on the legs, the front door opened and Cassie stared at them in surprise.

Ryan dropped the leg as if it burned her and immediately adopted a guilty look. Jamie looked from Ryan's face to Cassie's shocked expression and rolled her eyes, mentally cursing her roommate's timing.

"Hi Cassie," she said, as casually as the atmosphere allowed.

"Hi Jamie. What's going on?" she asked, her stare moving from one woman to the other.

"Ryan and I were at the gym, and my legs stiffened up. She was just loosening them up for me."

"You were at the gym?"

"Yeah, I was. Ryan's a personal trainer, and she's helping me get in shape for a bike ride."

"You need a trainer to ride a bike?" Cassie asked, her voice colored with uncertainty.

Jamie shot a quick glance at Ryan who seemed to have recovered her cool. "This isn't just any bike ride, Cassie. Ryan and I are going to do the AIDS Ride together. It's from here to L.A."

Cassie laughed hard at the mere thought. "Jamie, you've got to be kidding. You don't even own a bike."

"I will as of Monday. And I'm not kidding. I think it'll be a great learning experience for me. Plus, it'll give me a chance to really get in shape."

"Why on earth do you need to get in shape? You don't need to lose weight."

"I'm not trying to lose weight, Cassie. I'm trying to get fit. There's a difference, you know."

"Okay, why do you need to get fit?"

"Well, so I can do this ride," Jamie said, cringing at the lameness of her reasoning.

"Doesn't that logic seem just a teeny bit circular to you?" Cassie asked.

"No, it doesn't. I really want to do the ride, and I want to be in better shape. There's nothing circular about it."

"Whatever," Cassie finally said with a shake of her long blonde hair. As she began to ascend the stairs, she turned and asked, "Aren't you going to see Jack this weekend?"

"Yeah, I am. As soon as I take a shower, we're leaving."

"Oh, is your friend going?" Cassie asked, putting on a syrupy sweet tone. "I'm sure the three of you will have fun. Or is Jack bringing a boyfriend, too?"

Jamie laughed as Ryan casually picked up her leg and placed it once again on her chest. She continued the massage as if Cassie didn't exist, "No, sadly not," Jamie replied trying to match the saccharine tone.

Without further comment, Cassie turned and quietly took the stairs two at a time. When she was out of earshot Jamie mumbled, "I wish I lived alone."

When they were back in the car, Jamie gave Ryan a quick look and asked, "Why did you act so funny around Cassie?"

"What do you mean, funny?" Ryan inquired, her voice betraying a touch of nervousness.

"I don't know, kind of like you were caught doing something … wrong."

After a full minute of silence, Jamie thought that her friend was going to ignore the question. She was almost startled when the deep voice said, "Do you remember our class discussion on homophobia?"

Jamie wondered how this was the answer to her question, but she knew that Ryan's scientific mind sometimes worked in strange ways. "Yeah, I do."

"Not only straight people can be homophobic. Gay people do it, too."

"What do you mean? That's like a Jew being anti-Semitic."

"Yeah," Ryan said. "And that's possible, too." She saw the puzzled look on Jamie's face and said, "Look. I know Cassie doesn't like me. I assume that's because I'm gay, right?"

"Yeah, I guess so," Jamie admitted, "since that's the only thing she knows about you."

"I wasn't aware I was doing this, but I internalized her feelings, and when she came in I felt momentarily guilty about being gay. I was holding your leg and rubbing it in a way that probably looked awfully friendly," she said, looking uncomfortable, "and I felt like she caught me doing something wrong."

Jamie was quiet for a moment, then found the courage to ask the next question. "Do you have sexual feelings for me? Were you doing something that you felt guilty about?"

"No, I don't," she said, shaking her head forcefully. "I don't think of you in that way. Although, if I'm completely honest, I did when we first met. You were just another woman in my class then. Now we're friends."

Jamie let out the breath she'd been holding in and said, "I'm really glad you told me that. It's nice to know my instincts work with women as well as men."

Ryan's jaw went slack. "Oh, no! Could you really tell?"

Jamie nodded, a small smile on her face. "Yeah, at first I could. I really could."

Ryan's embarrassment turned to curiosity. "And that didn't bother you?"

"No," Jamie said, her tone casual. "It didn't seem aggressive or anything. You just acted like you thought I was cute."

"Oh, I was definitely interested, but when I started to get to know you, I liked you too much to put you in the potential dating category."

"You don't date people you like?" Jamie asked, entirely confused

"It's ahh … complicated. I'll tell you all about my scarred psyche someday, but not today."

"It's a deal," Jamie said, hoping that someday came soon.

Crossing the Bay Bridge, Jamie asked, "Do you like working at your current gym?"

"Not really, no."

"Why do it then?"

"When I was working as a trainer full-time, I had a really good client list but when I started back to school full-time I couldn't keep everyone. I really need the money, so I hang out and answer questions at the gym at night. It's boring as hell, but I don't have time to find more clients. Vicious cycle."

"You were out of school for a while?"

"Uh-huh. Long story," Ryan said, giving her a half smile.

"Everything about you is a long story," Jamie said. "I think you just don't like to talk about yourself."

The brunette merely gave her an enigmatic smile, not saying a word.

"Okay, Mona Lisa. I won't dig. I do have one simple question, though. Would you rather work in the East Bay?"

"Yeah, I guess I would. I've got some pretty long breaks between classes. Maybe I should check out some of the gyms over there and see what I can scare up. I really hate losing all of my evenings."

"Maybe something will turn up," Jamie said confidently.

Since she was chronically early, Ryan was usually sitting in her seat when Jamie arrived at class. However, one day during the fifth week of class, Jamie was standing in the back of the room chatting with a classmate named Rhoda when Ryan entered. The brunette made eye contact with Jamie as soon as she came in the door, flashing those incredibly white teeth in a warm grin. Jamie observed her make her way to the front of the room, giving only half of her attention to her other classmate. She observed that Ryan looked particularly good today. Her hair was shining and bounced across her back when she walked. A bright blue, crew-necked, cable-knit sweater of a very soft looking wool clung to all of her abundant curves. The sweater covered a white turtleneck that contrasted sharply with her black hair. Well-worn, button-fly jeans and shiny, black leather loafers completed the outfit. Her cheeks were rosy from the chill in the air, and she radiated good health and confidence.

Jamie watched as heads turned to regard Ryan. It was obvious from the longing glances sent her way that some of the women openly desired her. It was equally obvious that some of them had fulfilled that desire. Ryan stopped for a moment to chat with three women who looked to be in the latter category. She spoke to each of them in a casual, yet familiar way. The tall woman would grace them with a gentle touch or a small pat on the shoulder, giving the impression that she was very much interested in talking with each of them, but that pressing business was calling her away. Jamie watched in fascination as each of the women looked pleased that they had received even this small token of her affection. *God, is she going to plow through the whole class? There are nine lesbians besides Ryan. If she's gone through three already, that only leaves six. She's gotta make the other six last for eleven weeks. She might have to have a repeat … or she could also date the women who don't like to label themselves lesbians …*

Jamie was startled from her reverie when she was poked in the ribs. "Not you too!" Rhoda said, laughing at the look on Jamie's face.

"What?" the blonde asked, truly puzzled.

"You don't have O'Flaherty Fever too, do you?"

"What? Oh, no, no, *no!*" Jamie finally got out. "Ryan and I are friends—just friends. But I've never seen this … show! Does that happen every day?"

"Yep. That's why I sit in the back. It's the most entertainment I get all day," Rhoda said. "Ryan really is a player," she added with admiration in her voice.

"Yeah, I guess she is." A scowl was firmly settled on Jamie's face, and it stayed there as she watched one of the "no labels" women approach her friend. Ryan's eyes lit up when she saw the woman approach, and Jamie watched her whole body language change. Ryan drew the woman in by leaning back against the desk. She was obviously speaking softly, because the woman had to move in closer and closer to hear her. Once she had her where she wanted her, she slid to the edge of the desk and leaned dangerously close, her smile turned a bit feral. Then she leaned back and regarded her prey. The dark head nodded, she smiled broadly, then removed a business card from her back pocket. *Wasn't that handy! She must have them printed by the thousands!* Ryan scribbled something on the back, probably her pager number, and handed it to the beaming woman, then gave her hand a gentle squeeze.

The blonde shook her head, her eyes closing. *Is no woman safe?*

After class, they went outside for their morning break. Ryan noticed that Jamie wasn't her usual talkative self, but she passed it off to a bad mood. After Ryan purchased a few bottles of juice, she returned to the table to find Jamie looking at her with an expression that could only be described as a glare. "What'd I do?" she asked, sounding a bit like a child accused of a wrong she hadn't committed.

The smaller woman shook her head. "Oh, I'm sorry," she said quickly. "You didn't do anything. I'm sorry if I look as though you did."

"Are you sure there's nothing wrong?" She searched Jamie's eyes and found that her friend was having a hard time making eye contact. "C'mon, Jamie, you can tell me."

"No. It's really stupid and I feel like an idiot," she said, pouting.

"I've never seen you do anything stupid or idiotic. If something's bothering you I'd like to help, if I can."

"Okay, okay, you win." Jamie finally gave her a small smile. "Last week you told me that you didn't date people you liked. Why?"

"That's certainly not where I thought we were going," Ryan admitted. She paused for a moment as she looked at her friend. Finally, she tilted her head and locked her gaze onto Jamie's eyes. "If that's your question, why do you look angry with me?"

Jamie hated the way Ryan's mind worked. She could always see through ancillary issues and home right in on the crux of the matter. "All right, I'll confess," she said, with a large measure of frustration in her voice. "It bothered me to watch you come into class today." Ryan looked at her blankly, clearly at a loss. "You were talking to some of the women and flirting with others, well, you were flirting with all of them. It made me think about what you said the other day, and it pissed me off. You're depriving yourself of something by dating so many people," she added, hearing how lame this sounded.

"So … you're angry with me because I don't have a steady girlfriend?" Ryan asked slowly, clearly trying to understand, but not having an easy time of it.

"I told you it was stupid," Jamie said, clearly flustered. "I don't know why it bothered me, but it did. I'm sorry; I know it's none of my business. You seem perfectly happy, and it's stupid of me to want something for you that you don't want."

"Would you like me to explain why I don't have a girlfriend?" Ryan asked quietly, her eyes never leaving Jamie's.

"If you want to. But I don't want you to feel pressured."

"I'm happy to. It's really a very simple answer. I've been focused on either earning money or going to school for over four years now. My time's very valuable to me, and I don't like giving too much of it to anyone. I have to work hard to get everything done during my free time, and I can't afford the distraction that a relationship would cause. Plus, since I live at home, I can't comfortably bring women home. And I get a ton of shit from my brothers when I stay out all night." She smiled and said, "I don't mean to be crude, but I'm not interested in dating just to see a movie. If I can't spend the night—it's not worth my time."

Jamie finally got to the question that was really bothering her. "But is that fair to the women that you date?"

Ryan leaned back in her chair and considered the question for a moment. Jamie detected a momentary flash of hurt pass across her face. She pursed her lips together and blew out a breath as she softly replied, "I get it now. You think I lead them on, don't you?"

She truly didn't want to hurt her friend's feelings, but she was in too deep to stop now. "Ryan, you should have seen their faces. They all looked so hopeful," she finally blurted out.

"Jamie, I swear I've never led anyone on. I always, and I do mean always, tell women that I'm not in the market for a relationship. I'm obnoxiously up front with them."

"Maybe so," Jamie said thoughtfully. "But they all looked like they hoped they'd be the one to change your mind. Like the woman who was talking to you at your desk today," she added.

Ryan waited until Jamie raised her eyes and met hers again. While she waited, she wondered, *Why does this bother her? I could see that she'd want me to be happy, and I can understand that she doesn't want me to use people. But why be angry about it?* "You don't know the whole picture. Today was a perfect example. Blair came over and asked me if I wanted to have lunch. I know she hangs out with Lisa and Amy, so I figured she'd know something about me."

"Who are Lisa and Amy, and why would knowing them tell her anything about you?"

"They're in our class," Ryan explained patiently.

"Do you know everyone's name?"

"Well, yeah. I make it a habit to learn everyone's name. Then I figure out who knows whom. It makes things easier for me."

"Okay." Jamie took a breath. "I assume you've 'dated' Lisa or Amy?" She pronounced "dated" about the same way she would have said "molested."

Ryan shot her a look that was far from happy. Her voice took on an edge as she replied, "I tried to 'date' Amy. We went out for coffee during the first week of class. I told her that I'd love to take her out, but that I didn't have room in my life for a girlfriend. She asked me a few questions to make sure I was serious, and when she was satisfied that I was, she didn't want to go out with me. I didn't have sex with her, Jamie. I didn't touch her," she added with a scowl.

Jamie was so intent on the reasoning, that she didn't notice Ryan's expression. "Oh, I get it," she said. "You assume that Blair would know that you don't want a girlfriend since she knows Amy."

"Yeah, that seemed like a good bet. But just to make sure I'll tell her at lunch." She stared at Jamie for a long moment before she said, "You know, sometimes I come across like a real jerk. I mean, someone might just want to have lunch and talk about school, but I make it a point to tell her that I don't want to be in a relationship. It really makes me sound like I'm full of myself."

The blonde realized that she'd offended her friend. "Ryan," she said softly. "I'm sorry that I hurt your feelings. I don't know why today set me off, but I never should have spoken to you about it. It's really none of my business."

"That's okay. I want you to be able to tell me what's on your mind."

"No, I shouldn't have done that. But since we did talk about it, I'm really impressed with how honest you've been. That's really honorable."

A small smile finally graced Ryan's features. "You know, even if I wasn't honest, word travels fast in the community. And there's not one woman in the Bay Area who can honestly say that she was my girlfriend."

"Not one?" Jamie was shocked at this revelation.

"Nope. Not one."

"I find that nearly impossible to believe!" Jamie struggled with this information. "You've never met anyone that you'd like to build something with? Are you that picky?"

"I guess I am incredibly picky," Ryan admitted, a little sheepishly. "But I do occasionally find someone special. When that happens, I try to make her into a friend."

"Like me?" Jamie asked tentatively.

"Exactly."

"So do you just have uhm … one night stands?" she asked hesitantly.

"No, sometimes I have a meal or go to a movie with a woman. I like the companionship of women even when they're vertical. I'm a homophile as well as a homosexual," she said pointedly, a frown creasing her forehead.

"Homophile?"

"Yeah. Loving to be with women makes me a homophile. Having sex with women makes me a homosexual. You're a heterophile and a heterosexual. The sex part and the attraction part are two distinct things."

"That doesn't sound very elegant," Jamie said, "but I think I read something about that concept." She looked at Ryan contemplatively. "So you do see the same person more than once?"

"Sure. I'll go out with a woman until she starts to get too serious. Then I back off."

"Have you ever met anyone that you liked who didn't want to get serious?"

"Yeah, I've got a few uhm ... buddies," she said, a deep blush climbing her cheeks.

Jamie noticed the coloring, and decided she had to find out what was behind it. "What do you mean by buddies?"

"Uhm, there's kind of a term for people who just sleep together."

"What's the term?"

"Ahh ... fuck buddies?"

"Fuck buddies, huh? I must admit I've never heard that one. Do you have a fuck buddy, Ryan?" she asked with a twinkle in her eyes, taking sadistic pleasure in seeing the discomfort in her friend's posture.

"Yeah ... I've got a couple of people that I see occasionally for ..."

"Sex?" Jamie helpfully supplied.

"More or less. More if I'm lucky."

"So these are women who feel like you do about relationships?"

"Exactly. They want the same thing that I do. Occasional sex and nothing more."

"Do you see these women very often?"

"It depends. I guess I usually see each of them three or four times a year. Oh ... I see my friend Ally more than that. We might see each other three or four times in a two week period, then not for a few months. I really like her, and we get along great in bed, but we're both clear that we couldn't ever have a real emotional connection. It's strange, but we're not very close emotionally. Maybe we're too much alike."

"But you're missing so much, by never letting anyone get close Ryan," Jamie continued to argue.

"Like what?" the dark-haired woman asked, sounding truly curious.

"Like intimacy, and caring, and a depth of feeling that you can't get from casual dating." Jamie's voice was rising, and she was beginning to get frustrated again.

"There's nothing casual about the way I date," Ryan said with a little leer.

"Do you really not understand what I'm getting at?" Jamie dropped her head into her hands, moaning in frustration.

"No, I think I do. I want all those things, too. Just not now. And since I don't feel that I can commit to one woman, what would you have me do?"

"I don't know, Ryan. It just seems unfair to the women who want more of you—as well as to yourself."

"On one level you may be right," she replied thoughtfully. "But I don't feel that I'm gonna be ready for another couple of years. Are you really suggesting that I should be celibate for that long? 'Cause that's not gonna happen."

"How long have you gone?" Jamie asked dryly.

"Does it count when I had broken ribs?"

"No. I want the able-bodied record."

"Hmm, I guess about two weeks or so during finals."

"Two weeks! Do you mean to tell me you haven't gone without female companionship for more than two weeks in your adult life?"

"I love women. I *really* love women. I love meeting them. I love talking to them. I love the chase. I love it when they want to play the game as much as I do. I love pleasing them. I love having someone new all the time. I am never, ever bored," she said. "How many women can say that?"

"I agree that your sex life is exciting. But who do you confide in? Who do you feel completely comfortable with? Who do you know will always be there for you?"

With a completely open, trusting look on her lovely face, she said, "You, Jamie. I feel comfortable with you. I confide in you. I know you'll be there for me. I don't have to have sex with you to feel that, do I?" Her hand reached out to clasp her friend's.

"Oh Ryan, that's so sweet." Jamie jumped up and threw her arms around her neck and gave her a fond hug. "You never cease to surprise me."

Ryan replied with a bright smile, then affectionately tousled Jamie's hair. "You're sweet too. That's why I like you."

After her last class, Jamie walked home and grabbed a salad. She forced herself to spend a couple of hours working on the next day's classes, then rewarded herself with a trip to the bike shop to pick up her new wheels.

Bill was glad to see her, and greeted her warmly. "You're going to love this baby," he said. As he spoke, he weaved his way through the maze of bikes, finally stopping to grasp one and lift it over his head. "Here she is."

The new bike was a sleek, shocking, day-glo orange. "It even looks fast," she said with delight. The components were top quality, but not the most expensive available, and as she regarded the bike she felt very satisfied about her choices. Bill spent a good half hour going over all of the components and handing her the little instruction booklets for each. He finally had her sit on the bike while it was on a trainer, and he adjusted the seat and pedals. Next, he showed her how to clip her new racing shoes into the pedals, and had her practice unlocking them a few times.

After she was comfortable with the bike, she had to decide on what type of bike rack to buy. They discussed all of the available options before choosing a light, collapsible model that rested on the trunk and rear bumper of her car. "How can I protect my new beauty from theft?"

"Only one way I know of," he replied. "Keep your butt on the seat!"

"Don't any of those locks work?" She pointed at the array of cumbersome locks on the wall.

"They work very well if you're protecting your bike from someone who doesn't really want it."

Jamie frowned. "I really want to be able to take it to campus. The only way I'll get all my training in is to ride everywhere."

"This bike won't last a week on campus," he said. "But I might have a solution for you. I got a nice, light, mountain bike in as a trade the other day. It's a good bike, and I think it'd fit you perfectly. It cost about $1800 new, but I can let you have it for $200. It's about five years old, and the paint is scratched up, but I put new tires and brake pads on it. And," he added, "one good thing about doing some of your training on a heavier bike is that your road bike will feel like air. With a mountain bike you could also tag along on some of Ryan's night rides up on Mt. Tam."

"I didn't know she rode up there."

"Oh, it's quite a scene," he said, laughing. "You've got to get her to take you, but bring some band aids. It's a tough group."

Jamie and Bill loaded both bikes onto the new carrier. Once she got home, she immediately hopped on her road bike and took it for its maiden spin. After just a few blocks, she felt her mood brighten, and a sense of freedom enveloped her. She sped along the streets of Berkeley, humming a happy tune. I'm gonna like this!

After a pleasant hour, Jamie went home to change into her workout clothes, tossing sweats over her Lycra as she headed to the gym.

As she was checking in, she spotted the manager that she had spoken with when she first visited the place. "Hi," she said in her usual friendly manner. "Remember me?"

"Yeah, sure I do," the woman said. "Did you decide to join?"

"Yeah, I did. I really like it here. My trainer was very impressed."

"I didn't know you had your own trainer. I got the impression you were just starting out."

"Oh, no, I'm hooked up. She's working at a gym in the city now, but she's looking for a change. She's getting more women clients in the East Bay, and I think she'd prefer to work over here now." Her statement was a very generous embellishment, but she thought that was allowed when discussing business.

"Have her look me up the next time she's in," the woman replied. "Maybe we could make her an offer to join us."

"Actually, I'm her business manager," she said confidently as the embellishment switched to outright lies. "What kind of a deal would you cut her?"

They moved into the manager's office, where Jamie took a chair. "Our standard deal for independent trainers is to charge them $200 a month to be able to use the facilities. There's no additional charge when they work with a member, but when they have an outside client, they, or the client pays us $10 per hour."

"How many hours a week do most of your trainers book?"

"Not a lot, probably five. Some book up to ten."

"If my trainer booked fifteen to twenty hours a week, what could you do for her?"

She thought for a minute, and made her first offer. "I could reduce the monthly fee."

"By how much?"

"Half?" she replied, a bit tentatively.

"That's fair. But I'd like her to get some benefit from the new members she'll bring in to the club. The monthly fee for a member is $85 a month, right?"

"Right."

"And Ryan would pay you $100 to use the facilities if she worked fifteen hours a week, right?"

"Right again."

"Would you agree to waive her fee altogether if she brought in five new members?"

The manager considered the proposal, and said, "Yes, I would. We make most of our money off the monthly fee anyway, so that would help both of us."

"Do you need any more trainers on staff right now?" Jamie decided she might as well go for broke.

"Yeah, but only the worst hours, like six in the morning. Those are always hard to fill."

"How much per hour?" Jamie sensed a weakness.

"$15?" she said, a hopeful tone in her voice.

"Nope." Jamie was unmoved. "I couldn't let her work those hours for less than $25."

"How many hours is she available?"

Jamie looked at her appointment book thoughtfully. Absolutely nothing about Ryan's schedule was written there, but she thought she remembered that she was free until eight. "She's available from five-thirty to seven-thirty, Monday through Friday," she stated, hoping that was true.

"You've got a deal," the woman replied as she extended her hand, breathing a sigh of relief that Jamie wasn't selling life insurance … or swampland in Florida.

After she left the office, Jamie rubbed her hands together and scouted the gym. "Ahh, potential patsies," she said to herself. She watched each of the women carefully from her position on a treadmill. Finally she spotted one woman who looked both well-off and clueless. Hopping off the treadmill, she positioned herself next to the confused woman. "Do you need help?"

"I guess I do," the woman said. "I had someone explain this machine to me last week, but now I've forgotten how to adjust it."

"I get confused, too. That's why I've started to work with a trainer. She's helped me more than you can imagine," she said conspiratorially.

"A trainer, huh? They tried to get me to sign up with one when I first came here. But the woman who's here in the afternoons is a dunce."

"Why don't you try mine? I'm certain you'd like her. Everyone does. She's normally down on the Peninsula, but she's devoting a few days a week to her clients in the East Bay now. She's simply fabulous." She uttered this last statement as she produced Ryan's business card, which she had swiped when her friend wasn't looking.

"Is she really expensive? I don't want to spend a lot."

"Oh, she's terribly expensive!" Jamie moaned. "It's absolutely highway robbery! But she's so wonderful that she can get away with it." If there was one thing Jamie was sure of, it was that rich people loved to moan about how much things cost. But they also loved to overpay for everything that was trendy. "She charges me $125 an hour, but I heard that her rates are going up again! I'm gonna have to hock my Porsche if she charges me much more. I see her three times a week now, and it really adds up."

"Wow, that's astronomical! Do you really think it's worth it?"

Jamie leaned in and whispered, "I went to a benefit last week in a sleek little Dolce and Gabana sheath. I got more attention in that dress than I knew how to handle. My entire body has changed since I started to work with Ryan. I think she's worth three times what I pay her," she confided. "But don't tell her that!"

The woman shot a quick glance around to make sure no one was eavesdropping. "I have my fifteen year college reunion coming up this spring. If she could get me in shape for that I'd sign my life away!"

"That's the attitude! Your classmates will think you've found the fountain of youth. Give me your number, and I'll have Ryan call you," she said with a wink.

After two more visits to the club, Jamie had filled all of Ryan's afternoon time slots. Now all she had to do was tell Ryan that she had a new job.

After class on Friday, they sat at their usual spot and sipped their juice. "Uhm, Ryan," she started nervously, "I've been interfering in your personal life." She glanced down at the ground, seemingly in shame.

"You didn't find me a steady girlfriend, did you?" Ryan asked with a mock scowl.

"No, nothing like that. Remember when you said you'd rather work on this side of the Bay?"

"Yeah," Ryan slowly drawled.

"Did you mean that?"

"Yeah."

"Well, I kind of got you a job."

"You got me a what?"

"I got you a job?"

Ryan's face broke into an indulgent smile. "Do I get to learn the details, or do I just show up and get my uniform? I don't mind flipping burgers, but I hate to cook French fries. It's too hard to get the oil out of my hair."

"No silly." Jamie laughed as she slapped her lightly on the shoulder. "I got you a job at Women Power, and I think you're really going to like it."

Ryan continued to look at her with a quizzical smile on her face, so Jamie launched into her sales pitch. "They want you to work every morning before school. I know you like to get up early, and I thought that you could work the early shift to avoid traffic. That's from five-thirty to seven-thirty. They wanted to pay you fifteen dollars per hour, but I held out for twenty-five," she said, adding a proud smile. She paused a millisecond for a breath. "Then they agreed to let you train people there without having to pay a monthly fee as long as you bring in five new members." She paused for another tiny bit. "They'll charge you ten dollars an hour to train your private clients, but if it's a client that you bring in or that's already a member you don't have to pay at all." A longer pause for a bigger breath. "Oh, and I got you seven new private clients who each agree to pay you $125 per hour—that fills up all your afternoon time slots. How'd I do?" She let out all of her most recent breath and looked at Ryan's stunned face.

The silence went on for quite a while as Ryan continued to stare at her with a slightly opened mouth. Finally, she said, "Well, gosh. I was working at a place I didn't like, making no money, working bad hours when I was tired, having no social life, and it forced me to ride my bike through rush hour traffic every afternoon. You found me a job where I work half the hours for about the same money, during the hours I like, and I get my evenings back. You also save me $250 a month in fees, and find me new clients worth $875 a week." She paused for effect. "I guess you did okay," she said casually. After a moment her eyes grew playful, and she rose from her chair and stood towering over Jamie. "You know what I've got to do, don't you?"

"N … n … no?"

"This." She placed her large hands around Jamie's small waist and effortlessly lifted her to her feet. Deep blue eyes gazed at the smaller woman in wonder, as Ryan leaned close and placed chaste kisses on each cheek, followed by a very large, very expressive, full body hug. "That's the nicest thing anyone has ever done for me, Jamie," she whispered, as tears formed. "I don't know how to thank you."

Jamie's eyes drifted shut, and she relaxed completely into the tender hug. She'd have been content to stay just that way for the rest of the day, but Ryan finally released her. "I have to admit I had selfish reasons," Jamie said, a bit choked up herself. "I wanted you to be available to go on some evening bike rides with me. I heard about some hot ones on Mt. Tam."

"We'd better get to work if you want to do those, kiddo. That's where the big girls go."

"You're a big girl. Can't I go with you?"

Ryan's words contained a teasing quality, but her expression was entirely serious. "I'll take you anywhere you want to go, Jamie, anywhere at all."

On the following Monday, Jamie met Ryan at the gym at precisely four. Jamie was dressed in a navy blue tank top, which covered a gray sports bra. Her thigh-length shorts were also gray, and slouchy white socks peeked out from her high-top cross trainers. Ryan wore her new Women Power polo shirt. The black shirt was cut generously, allowing her plenty of room to move, but hiding her curves. "Women Power" was written in lavender script across her left breast, and "Personal Trainer" was printed across the back in two-inch block letters, also in lavender. Regrettably, the sleeves ended just above her elbows, effectively hiding her biceps. Black nylon warm-up pants also blocked Jamie's view of Ryan's legs. *I can't believe I go to the gym with her and I still don't get to see her muscles!*

Jamie was pleased to see that Ryan looked right at home, even though it was her first day on the job. "Hi there, boss," she said when she spotted Jamie. "Have you gotten me a raise yet? This is my third hour here, you know."

Jamie gave her a winning smile as an answer. "So today we're doing trunk and shoulders, huh, coach?"

"Yep. Did you get your ride in this afternoon? I was kind of jealous when I was in my chem lab, thinking about you out there pedaling away."

"I sure did. That trip computer you talked me into is really great. It let me keep a good cadence, just like you told me. I practiced trying to pedal in a smooth circle and trying to pull on the upstroke as well as push on the down stroke. I've got to tell you Ryan, that bike is a dream. I'd have kept riding if I had this bike then. It feels so effortless."

"I'm really glad you're happy with it," Ryan said. "I knew that Bill wouldn't steer you wrong, but I was worried that you'd be unhappy with having spent that much."

"No, not at all. I tend to think about financial decisions rather carefully, as you can attest," she said with a grin. "But once I make up my mind, I don't second guess myself."

"Well, I know you're going to love riding, and I think you'll really enjoy working out, too. You're very goal oriented, and I think this is gonna hold your interest."

Jamie was delighted that Ryan knew these details about her personality without explicitly having been told. "So, where do we start today?"

Ryan led her to a weight bench and sat her down. "Okay, we're gonna start with your shoulders. She tapped the top of the muscles. "They're called deltoids or delts. There's another group of muscles here." She touched Jamie's back just above her scapula, "called the rotator cuff. There are four muscles there that keep your arm from slipping out of the socket. They're just under your delts. We're gonna work on both sets of muscles. I usually use free weights for shoulders, since I find they're easier to control. And control is very important with your shoulders. You have to do these exercises correctly because your rotator cuffs are easily injured."

Jamie loved the verbal instruction that Ryan gave when showing her the exercises. The explanations really helped her because she processed things by understanding them verbally before she tried them physically. Ryan seemed to understand this, and was very careful to make sure that Jamie understood the underlying issues.

"Now, you should do these in the order I show you. We're gonna do a press, a lateral raise, a front raise and a back fly. You'll be able to lift the heaviest weight with the press and the lightest weight with the fly." She looked at Jamie with a serious expression, "Have you ever injured your lower back, your neck or your elbows?"

"No, I've never had any significant injuries."

"Boy, would my father like to trade for you," she laughed. "He was in the ER with me every other week."

"I bet you were a wild one."

"You don't know the half of it," Ryan said, giving Jamie one of her most charming grins.

While they worked their way through the exercises Ryan was very attentive to Jamie's posture and positioning. She encouraged her but didn't push her, like Jamie had seen some of the trainers do. Ryan knew that her friend would push herself, and she made it a point to rein Jamie in a bit so she didn't injure herself.

When they had finished with the shoulder exercises they moved on to the lower back. Ryan again launched into her explanation of the how's and why's of the exercises. After she showed Jamie how to perform a back extension and a pelvic tilt, Jamie mentioned that these were exercises she had learned when she played golf in high school.

"You were on the golf team?" Ryan asked with interest. "That's pretty cool. You know, I've never hit a golf ball."

"Well, we're just gonna have to remedy that, missy. I'd love to do something that I can beat you at."

Next they moved to the abdominal muscles. Jamie knew some of these from her golf conditioning also. Ryan showed her six different exercises and reminded her that she had a lot of potential in this area.

At the end of the hour, Jamie's mind was swimming. She sat down on a bench to dry off, and she watched Ryan making notes in a little booklet. "I made this for you," she said as she thrust the book in Jamie's direction.

Inside the leather, loose-leaf book, Jamie saw each of the exercises they had covered neatly named and described. On the leg exercises the position of the seat and the adjustment of the bars were also annotated. Under each description was a series of columns which indicated the date, time, number of reps, sets and one column where Jamie was supposed to indicate how she felt when she began to exercise on a scale of one to ten. Jamie was absolutely charmed, and her face reflected this. "Ryan, this is so thoughtful," she said, clasping the book to her chest.

"That's the very least I can do for you after all you've done for me."

"I like to take care of my friends. I didn't do anything that I wouldn't have done for anyone I care for."

"Then I'm very lucky to be counted among that number," Ryan replied. As she said this she slid behind Jamie on the bench and began to knead her shoulder muscles. She worked on her for about five minutes until Jamie was dropping her head forward in a relaxed bliss.

"God, you're good at that. Those hands should be registered with the government."

"Well, they are, kind of. I do have a license to do this."

"You're a masseuse too?"

"Yep, these babies are trained and licensed." She held up her hands with a proud smile. "When I was taking classes to be a personal trainer I just figured I might as well be as fully trained as possible. I'm glad I did it. I really learned a lot about relaxing people after a tough workout. And it's a skill that comes in handy in my private life, too." She grinned as she waggled her eyebrows.

"Well, you've certainly relaxed me. I don't think I can move, much less ride my bike home."

"I've got my bike here, let me give you a ride home," Ryan offered. "After you take a shower we could get a bite to eat and then you could drive back to get your bike."

"That sounds mighty appealing. But are you sure you're willing to risk the wrath of Cassie if she's at home?"

"Yeah, I am. She just caught me off guard last time. I'm ready for her now." She rubbed her hands together in a menacing fashion as she narrowed her eyes.

They sped back to Jamie's house and were both relieved to find only Mia at home. The curly-haired woman spoke pleasantly to Ryan for a few moments before she headed upstairs to her room, and Jamie followed her upstairs to shower and change.

Jamie stood in the shower for a good long soak, then she dried her hair quickly and was just finishing getting dressed when Mia came in. "What did you do to Ryan?"

"What do you mean?" Jamie gave her a puzzled look.

"Do you want to see something kind of cute?" At Jamie's nod, she beckoned her out to the hallway. They both looked over the railing to where Ryan had been sitting on the couch. Only now her shoes were off and she was sound asleep, her lean form stretched out on the short couch, long legs hanging over the arm. Her hands were folded peacefully across her chest, and she wore a sweet, perfectly contented expression on her face. Jamie marveled at how very young and innocent her friend looked as she slept.

The roommates walked back into Jamie's room and both burst out laughing. "I'm glad to see she feels so comfortable around here," Jamie continued to laugh.

"She seems like a nice person."

"She's nicer than you can imagine," Jamie said. "She's just an extraordinary woman."

"Does she still flirt with you?" Mia asked this with some hesitation, knowing this could be a touchy subject.

"No. Not at all," Jamie said without hesitation. "We actually talked about it, even though it was hard for me to bring up. She admitted that she had been flirting but that she was over it now that we were friends."

"God, weren't you embarrassed?" Mia cried. "I can't imagine asking her that!"

"That's what's so cool about Ryan. I can say anything to her. She never judges me or acts hurt by what I say. I really felt amazingly comfortable talking about it with her. I wish you could get to know her better," Jamie said. "I know you'd like her."

"I trust your judgment about people, James. I'm sure I'd like her. Maybe we could all have dinner some night."

"That'd be great. I want you to be comfortable with her, Mia. You know that your friendship means a lot to me." Jamie hesitated for a moment before she broached the next subject. "You know, I was really angry that you told Cassie about Ryan flirting with me."

Mia started to defend herself, but Jamie cut her off. "I'm not angry any more—really. I'm sure you didn't do it to be malicious. But Cassie really dislikes her. She got Jack all worked up about the whole situation and we had a major fight. So please don't talk to her about Ryan. It'll just make matters worse."

"Oh, shit, James. I didn't know that! I swear I won't ever bring it up with her again." She shook her head, her lips pursed. "I'm really sorry I did that, buddy. It was stupid of me to tell Cassie anything about you. I know she tries to get in the middle of stuff. Damn! Sometimes I wish she'd just move in with her boyfriend. We'd be better off without her."

"Yeah, I know, but we've been together this long, I think we can hang on," Jamie said. "At least I hope we can."

After Mia returned to her room, Jamie took her time finishing her preparations. She combed her hair carefully and put on blush, then chose an emerald green, rough wool sweater, and a soft yellow turtleneck. Then she picked out a pair of khakis and some black loafers. She checked out her image in the full-length mirror, chiding herself briefly as she did so. *It's just Ryan, you know. This isn't a date.* When she walked back down the stairs she was surprised to find that Ryan was still asleep.

She sat down in the upholstered chair next to the couch and just watched her friend for a few moments. Ryan was remarkably still as she slept. Jamie was struck by the thought that she had never seen her when she wasn't in motion. Ryan was usually very active, sometimes a little hyperactive. Even when her body wasn't moving Jamie could almost see her quick mind processing something. She again marveled at how peaceful and open her face was in repose. Ryan rarely looked severe, but she often had a cool, composed expression on her face. Jamie watched her chest raise and lower and observed her lips slightly parted in sleep. Suddenly she felt an overwhelming urge to place a kiss on those soft looking lips. She resisted the urge with a violent shake of her head. *Get a grip for god's sake! Where in the hell did that urge come from?* She sat in the chair for several more minutes mulling over the conflicting thoughts in her head. *Maybe I just feel protective over her. She has such a confident exterior, but now that I've seen her vulnerability it makes me feel so tender towards her. When she sleeps she looks like the little girl who lost her mom. And that's the part that makes me want to kiss her. She looks so sweet, just like a child,* she thought fondly. *Yeah, and how many little girls have you ever wanted to kiss?* Finally deciding that she couldn't immediately resolve this jumble of thoughts, she quietly moved over to the couch. She leaned over and gently placed her hand on Ryan's shoulder, then gave her a soft shake.

Ryan was awake immediately, and amazingly, seemed fully alert. Jamie was surprised at this response, and her face must have shown it. Ryan detected the startled look and asked, "What's wrong? Was I asleep too long?"

"No, no, I was just amazed at how quickly you woke up."

"Oh, that's from years of practice," Ryan said. "I need about eight hours of sleep, but I only get six. I've trained myself to sleep almost anywhere when I get a few minutes down time."

"That's truly amazing," Jamie marveled.

"Not really. You can train your body to do a lot of things if you really need to."

"I'm just glad you felt comfortable enough here to be able to sleep."

"Well, I do feel very comfortable around you, but truthfully, I can sleep almost anywhere. I can even sleep pretty well sitting up in a chair. And once I got a good fifteen minute nap while leaning against a wall."

"You certainly do have many skills, Ryan," she admitted as she leaned over and ruffled her bangs.

"And you haven't seen half of 'em."

After they finished their dinner of falafel and Greek salads they discussed the workout schedule for the week. Jamie decided that she'd take her bike to Jack's and do her long ride on Saturday afternoon while he studied.

"Ooo, Saturday," Ryan said with pleasure. "I haven't had a Saturday free in years. This is gonna take some getting used to," she said with a happy expression on her face. "I've worked on weekends since I was sixteen, but now that I'm making so much money, I don't have to. This is the happiest quandary I've had in years."

"Why don't you come down and ride with me on Saturday?" Jamie offered. "You could see the Peninsula and maybe help me pick out some good rides."

"Is that really a good idea, Jamie?" she asked slowly. "I mean, wouldn't Jack mind?"

"Why would he mind?" she asked, a little confused. "He'll be studying, and he doesn't ride a bike anyway."

"No, uhm, I mean … I thought he wasn't very happy about having me around … at all."

"No, Ryan, that's not true. He was mad at me for not telling him things that he thought were important. I don't think it had anything to do with you, personally."

"If you're sure," she said, "I'd enjoy coming down. It might be nice to see a different part of the bay. And I've heard about some really great rides down there."

"Then it's settled. Oh, but how will you get your bike down there? Should I pick it up from you on Friday?"

"No, I can get it down there. I can borrow my father's truck if I need to. When do you want to meet?" she asked as she grabbed her ever-present organizer.

Chapter Four

"Castro Fitness Center, this is Ally speaking."

Ryan smiled at the familiar sound of the deep, alto voice. "Hi, Ally, guess who?"

"I'll bite. Actually, I'm pretty good at this." She paused for a few moments, and Ryan could hear her take a breath. "I'm gonna guess that this is a really hot brunette, six feet plus, legs for days … How am I doin'?" she asked, her voice growing even lower and a sexy timbre coloring it.

"Excellent," Ryan purred. "You are good at this."

"I must not be," the woman laughed, "'cause I don't know anybody like that. Who the heck are you?"

"I'm just a lonely woman looking for a little companionship. Do you know anyone who could keep me company on Friday night?"

"Friday night? You actually want to see me on a Friday night? I thought you were only allowed out of the house in the afternoons."

"I've had a change of schedule," she said, her happiness obvious. "My weekends are now my own."

"Really? You haven't had a weekend off in all the time I've known you. Do you have any idea how to fill a weekend?"

"I hoped you could help me out with that. What do you say to Friday night?"

"Best offer I've had all day," Ally replied. "Do you want to go out or stay in?"

"I can go out with anyone," Ryan purred in a dangerously low tone. "I wanna stay in with you."

"I'll be home by six. Bring dinner with you, hot stuff, 'cause you're not leaving 'til Saturday."

Ryan buzzed over to the Castro on Friday night, thinking about Ally. They'd met shortly after Ryan graduated from high school. She had started to take classes to become certified as a personal trainer, and had lucked into a job at Castro Fitness.

Ryan was sure that Ally had barely noticed her, and she was surprised when the near-stranger approached her one day and brought up the topic of safer sex. Ryan had spent the previous year engaged in some fairly risky behavior, and to her shock the slightly older woman seemed to know this. "Listen Ryan," she'd said, "you just can't run around and be wild with everyone you meet. You've got to use safer sex practices every time you have sex."

The dark-haired young woman blinked in surprise and tried to defend her actions. "The risk of contracting HIV isn't very high for lesbians," Ryan said, thinking that her argument was sound.

"No, it's not very high, but any chance is too high. You're seventeen years old. Don't risk cutting your life short just to get a little action. Besides, HIV isn't the only thing to worry about. I guarantee you'll contract a venereal disease within six months—if you haven't already. Herpes and vaginal warts are permanent. And no matter how attractive you are, your popularity will hit the skids if you've got warts on your fun parts."

"Okay, let's say you're right," Ryan said. "No one I've ever been with has mentioned safe sex, and I don't uhm ..." She trailed off, looking embarrassed.

"You're a smart girl; you can do some research and figure out what you need. But I'll make you a deal. Come over tonight after eight, and I'll show you everything you need to know."

Ryan laughed when she thought about how easily she had succumbed to Ally's charms. They had spent that first night at Good Vibrations, a woman-oriented sex toy shop in the Mission district. While at the store, Ally explained how to use sex toys and latex barriers so that Ryan could protect herself. Then, just to make sure that her student understood everything perfectly, they had gone back to Ally's apartment and tried out every item Ryan had purchased. By the next day, Ryan was terribly sore but very well trained in the art and the science of safer sex.

The pair had hit it off immediately. They both enjoyed working out, riding bikes, and having sex—lots of sex—with lots of women. To her surprise, Ryan found herself falling for her new friend. But Ally made it clear that she wasn't in the market for a girlfriend. She continued to date anyone who caught her eye, and she never made an attempt to hide her lovers from Ryan. After a while, Ryan got the message that Ally really wasn't going to return her affections, and she forced herself to think of her as nothing more than an occasional sex partner. As long as she kept it very casual, Ally was always willing to spend a day or two with her.

Their normal pattern was to see each other quite a few times in a two or three week period. But as soon as things started to get too intense Ally would stop calling, let three or four months pass, and then start up for another round.

When Ryan was being totally honest, she had to admit that it was always Ally who called a halt to their little flings. That was hard on her ego, since no one she'd ever been truly interested in had refused her. But she didn't let the rejection stop her—she always made time for Ally, and when she hadn't heard from her for a few months, Ryan called her for a date.

They sometimes went to a club or a bar, and one year they went to Gay Pride weekend together, but they generally just got together for incredibly good sex. Ryan had never met anyone who had her number quite like Ally did. Maybe it was because they had slept together so many times, but there was something about Ally that drove her wild.

Physically, Ally wasn't Ryan's type. She was the only woman that Ryan had ever been with who could pick her up—and she did it a lot, sometimes just to show her who was boss. Ally was just a little taller, but she was incredibly strong. She competed in body building competitions and usually did pretty well, as long as they were chemically free. Ally was very antagonistic about steroids and she refused to compete if the athletes weren't tested for their use.

Ally had a very androgynous look, a look that Ryan had never before gravitated towards. She wore her medium brown hair very short, about one and a half inches all over her head. Half the time it stuck straight up like a crew cut, which Ryan loved, delighting in the bristly little hairs as they rubbed over her naked body. Her eyes were somewhere between blue and gray depending on the light, but there was a fire in them that Ryan was always attracted to.

She stopped to pick up burgers and malts, Ally's favorite junk food. They both tried to eat healthy most of the time, but when she wasn't getting in shape for a competition Ally was pretty flexible. Ryan was easily tempted to treat herself to some junk food, and hamburgers were one of her favorite indulgences.

As she parked her bike about a block from Ally's building, she felt her pulse begin to pick up. She didn't often get nervous when she went on a date, having learned a long time ago that a lot of great looking women were absolute duds when you had to spend an evening with them. But she knew Ally well, and she knew what to expect—as much sex as she could handle. Ryan had always fancied herself as the dominant partner in almost every liaison that she had. She liked—she needed—to control the action. But she never got to do that with Ally. Even though she was only two years older, Ally had always treated Ryan like she was young and inexperienced. She controlled the entire evening, and Ryan had learned that if she wanted to keep their connection going, she had to allow her friend to be in charge.

Ryan trotted up the stairs to Ally's third floor unit, buzzed the door and waited patiently, hearing her friend walking around inside. The taller woman opened the door with her portable phone in her hand, and smiled broadly as she indicated that Ryan should go into the kitchen and get dinner organized.

As she finished putting everything on plates Ally snuck up behind her and enveloped her in a big bear-hug. She snuggled her head down against Ryan's neck, and held her tightly around the waist. "I've missed you, sugar," she whispered in her ear.

Ryan felt a chill start at that lucky ear and travel all the way down to her toes, giggling a little as the warm breath tickled her skin. She loved the soft Southern accent that her friend hadn't shaken, even though she had moved to San Francisco from Chapel Hill, North Carolina over eight years ago. She was ready to be released from the hug, but as usual, Ally held on just a bit longer to let her know she was still on top. Ryan turned in her embrace, and lifted her head just an inch to brush her lips against Ally's silky soft mouth.

One of the things that Ryan loved best about the woman was the contrast between Ally's external demeanor and appearance, and the soft, warm, womanly curves that were usually hidden under her workout clothes. Ally had large breasts for her size, and a delightful curve to her hips that Ryan loved to run her hands over. Ryan found that Ally's external toughness accentuated the hidden treasures that she loved to indulge in. "I've missed you too, Ally."

"How long has it been?" Ally stepped out of Ryan's embrace, and reached around to pick up a French fry and toss it in her mouth.

"I was thinking about that on the way over," she said. "I think it was right after the AIDS Ride. I remember that my legs were stiff when I came over and that they stayed that way for another week thanks to you!"

"You know I never guarantee not to bruise the merchandise," she purred as she backed Ryan up against the table. Ryan slid her arms around Ally's neck and allowed herself to be thoroughly kissed. Those big, strong, hands held her tightly around the waist as Ally worked on her mouth with a methodical intensity. She pulled back slowly and chuckled a bit as Ryan kept her arms twined around her neck, eyes tightly closed. "Aren't you hungry, sweet pea?" the larger woman asked softly.

Ryan mutely nodded, eyes still closed.

"You look like you're hungry for some love." Ally bent to lavish another round of heated kisses on Ryan's hungry mouth.

Ryan couldn't stop a low groan from escaping as her mouth was claimed by her friend. She often felt powerless when she was with Ally, and she had to admit that she absolutely loved it. There was something reassuring about feeling that someone else was in charge once in a while that really appealed to her. She didn't think she'd like to feel this way all of the time, but it was a welcome change that she had come to rely on and actually yearn for during the past five years.

"Come on, sugar baby," Ally said softly, as she pulled away from the embrace. "I need to keep my strength up to handle you all night long." She picked up the plates and carried them into the living room, while Ryan handled the malts and a fistful of napkins. They sat in the cozy living room, Ryan on the low futon/couch, Ally on a butterscotch leather club chair. They chatted about Ally's most recent weight lifting competition that had just been held in San Jose. Ryan knew some of the competitors, and one or two of the judges, and Ally filled her in on who was in particularly good shape. As they chatted companionably, Ryan reflected that their conversations centered almost entirely on working out, weight training and acquaintances that they had in common. Ally usually asked her a few questions about school, but it was clear that she did so to be polite. They didn't share an interest in hardly anything, Ryan mused. A Wynona Judd CD was playing quietly in the background, to highlight one area of disagreement. Ryan liked to listen to World Music, with a particular fondness for Afro-pop and contemporary Irish artists, while Ally never varied from Wynona, Shania, Reba, and Faith. Her apartment was devoid of books, the only reading material being fitness magazines.

Ally came from a big family, but she had left home almost immediately upon graduating from high school. She had been having sex with women since she was fifteen, but an older brother caught her with another girl during her senior year, and her family made life unbearable for her that last year. After she left North Carolina she maintained a relationship with one of her sisters who had also left home for good, but that was it. She had never been back home, and she had no contact whatsoever with her parents. Ryan wasn't even sure if her parents knew where she lived. She knew that there must be a lot of pain hidden behind her friend's sunny demeanor, but they never talked about it. Ally preferred to concentrate on current issues, and Ryan had decided long ago that she needed to honor her need for privacy if she wanted to maintain the relationship. Perhaps because of her family situation Ally also never inquired very deeply into Ryan's home life. She knew that Ryan lived at home, since they could never go there for a date, but she rarely asked after the rest of the O'Flaherty clan. Their relationship almost seemed to exist outside of their normal lives. It was untainted by any of the day-to-day issues that caused tension between most couples. There was clearly only one focus, and both of them seemed to like it that way.

"So tell me about this new schedule," Ally said as she picked up Ryan's now empty plate and carried it into the kitchen.

"I got a new job," Ryan began as Ally came back into the room and sat down right next to her on the couch. Her friend casually draped an arm around her shoulders and pulled her close, and Ryan smiled demurely as she automatically snuggled up against Ally's side. She rested her hand on Ally's flat stomach and began to draw random patterns there as she spoke. "Actually, a friend got me a new job," she said, just to be accurate.

"You're leaving Castro?"

"Pretty much," Ryan said. "My new place is over in Berkeley. It's really cool, Ally. It's women only, and it's filled with people who want to work, not pose. I've got two clients who don't want to move with me, and I think I'm gonna have to let 'em go. It's just not worth it to pay $250 a month and have to come back over here to make $375. That just knocks my hourly down too low. Would you like to take 'em?"

"When do you see them?"

"I see Mark on Wednesday at nine and Sunday at noon, and Vanessa at four on Sunday. I think they'd actually prefer to come on a weekday, though. Mark's a writer, so he can make his own schedule, and I think Vanessa is either a sex worker or a dancer. We've never talked about it, but she's got a lot more silicone than I think you need for normal purposes," she said with a laugh.

"I'd love another couple of steady clients," Ally said. "Do you want to hand them off, or should I call them?"

"I'm paid up at Castro through October, so I was planning on finishing out the month with them. Wanna come over on Sunday and meet them?"

"Sure. Why don't you come over tomorrow night and we can have brunch on Sunday morning before we go over?"

Ryan gave her a lopsided grin as she made a small plea. "That works for me, but you've got to promise not to wear me out too badly tonight. I've got a long bike ride scheduled for tomorrow, and I can't do it standing up. Plus I need to reserve a little energy if you want me to come back tomorrow night."

"Okay." Ally leaned over and started to kiss Ryan's neck. "I'll go easy on you tonight, but tomorrow all bets are off." She nipped her neck rather sharply in anticipation.

Ryan gulped audibly as she considered what she was in for. Ally never hurt her or really tried to dominate her physically, but she seemed to take great pleasure in wringing every bit of desire from Ryan's body. She didn't use any elaborate bondage paraphernalia, but she did like to restrain Ryan, usually with her hands or sometimes just with her personality. Ryan knew exactly what it was like to be in Ally's shoes, since she behaved just like her when she was with other women. But it was a very big turn on for her to be the object of desire when they were together. When Ally said all bets were off that meant that she'd be up all night, giving herself over totally to her friend. Ally could rarely stand to let her off with just one orgasm, and since Ryan wasn't multi-orgasmic she needed to rest for an hour or so between bouts. So some of their dates turned into very long marathon sessions, with short naps or even a run out to a twenty-four hour diner for a little sustenance to keep them going.

Ryan leaned her head back as she closed her eyes and gave her friend total access to her sensitive neck. Ally liked for Ryan to look butch on the outside, so the brunette had worn a tight, black, v-necked T-shirt, with the short sleeves rolled up a little, and carpenter's-style canvas jeans. But she also satisfied her friend's desire for sexy underwear. Under her tough girl outfit, Ryan wore a nearly transparent black lace bra, and some tiny black bikinis. Ally started to work her shirt out of her pants and Ryan reflected that she had never undressed herself when they were together. Ally had a need to control the entire scene from start to finish, and undressing her partner was a very important part in setting the stage.

After she had pulled Ryan's shirt free, she returned to her neck and started kissing down the v of her collar. She didn't like the angle she was working at, so she slid her arms behind Ryan's back and knees and effortlessly pulled her onto her lap. Ryan smiled serenely as she felt herself being lifted so easily. She was always the one to cradle a woman in her lap, and she loved the role reversal. There was something so freeing to let herself go and allow Ally to make all the decisions. She briefly wondered if Ally had anyone to switch roles with, but all such thoughts flew from her mind as she felt her shirt being lifted from her body. "Oh, I love this." Ally's voice burred against her ear as she ran her powerful hands all over Ryan's breasts.

She felt her nipples snap to attention as they were teased through the somewhat rough lace. She hadn't warned Ally to go easy on her breasts, and she shivered as she imagined how thoroughly they'd be loved. Ally was decidedly a breast woman, and it seemed that most of her arousal came from fondling that part of Ryan's anatomy, returning to them again and again as they made love.

Ryan leaned languidly against Ally's neck as she continued to massage her breasts through her bra. A small moan escaped from her lips as she felt those big strong hands grasp and play with her increasingly aroused mounds, but she knew that Ally would go at her own pace, no matter how aroused she was. Ally clearly wanted to please Ryan, but her own pleasure was the focus of their interactions. She waited until she was ready to move on in their lovemaking, and Ryan knew that she might as well relax and enjoy the ride. Ally was driving, and she had no control over the route or the destination.

She slid her hand down to grasp Ally's full breast, but she felt her hand being gripped firmly as her friend whispered, "Focus, sugar. Just feel what I'm doing to you." Ryan submissively complied with her instructions as she wondered whether she'd be allowed to touch Ally this time. She was usually allowed to please her friend, but she normally had to wait until Ally had made love to her at least twice. There seemed to be a barrier that they had to cross in order for her to be receptive. Sometimes they'd be together for two days with Ryan never being allowed to even kiss her breasts. But Ally clearly didn't want to talk about her desires or her needs. Ryan assumed that she had been molested as a child, since there were certain ways that she couldn't tolerate being touched. There were also certain positions that Ryan had learned never put her in—for instance, Ally couldn't tolerate being on her back with Ryan on top of her. The one time she had tried that she found herself nearly thrown from the bed, so she was careful never to repeat that move. But sometimes, rarely, they reached a level of intimacy that allowed Ally to shove down her barriers and welcome Ryan's touch without restriction. Ryan loved those times best of all. As much as she loved being touched, touching Ally seemed like a gift. She'd focus all of her energies on pleasing her friend and sometimes they'd fly into a frenzy of lovemaking that was overpowering for both of them. But every time that happened Ally would withdraw the next day and be unavailable for three or four months. Ryan reflected that the last time they had seen each other they had gotten very intimate. Ally had been more vulnerable than she could ever remember her being, and had in fact softly wept after Ryan had made love to her. But the experience had obviously been uncomfortable since she hadn't heard from her friend since June.

It was clear tonight that Ally didn't want Ryan's hands to wander into restricted space. She slowly unbuckled Ryan's belt, while keeping her gaze locked on her. She pulled it from the loops and quickly wrapped it around Ryan's hands and gripped it tight, completely restricting her ability to move her hands. She gently tossed her onto her back and tied the belt over the wooden arm of the sofa, causing Ryan's arms to fully extend over her head.

Ryan sighed deeply as she felt her hands being removed from her control. She was completely confident in Ally's concern for her, and she knew that she'd stop anything she was doing if Ryan asked her to. She didn't restrict Ryan for her own pleasure as much as she did to remind her to relax and give up any desire for control. And Ryan had to admit that it worked perfectly. She opened herself up to Ally's desires and let her friend use her body to bring both of them the pleasure that they sought.

Ally moved down to remove Ryan's big, black, lineman's boots, and her thick, white socks. She spent a long time massaging her feet, sending waves of pleasure up and down Ryan's spine. Ryan was so relaxed that her limbs felt heavy and weak. Ally decided to crank her back up a bit, so she raised Ryan's foot up and began to sensually suck on her clean, pink toes. The feel of that terribly soft, warm mouth on

Ryan's foot brought her right back up to her previous level of arousal. She started to slowly twitch her hips as she waited for her friend to make her next move. She sincerely hoped that it would involve her vulva, but she had a feeling that she was a long way from getting any release. Much to her surprise, Ally began to slowly unzip her jeans. She slid her hand in and tickled the mound with just the tips of her fingers. Ryan's hips shot off the sofa and tried to increase the pressure, but Ally knew all of her tricks. She lightened up her touch every time Ryan thrust at her until she was touching only her panties.

She leaned over and whispered into Ryan's flushed ear, "Are you ready for me, sweetness?"

Ryan closed her eyes and ground her hips around in a little circle as she slowly nodded her head.

"Talk to me, sugar. Tell me what you want."

Ryan took several deep breaths before she had the ability to express her needs. "I want you to touch me, Ally. I want to feel your hands on me, and I want your fingers deep inside of me."

"Mmm, I want that too, sugar," she whispered as she captured Ryan's swollen bottom lip and gently sucked it into her mouth. She nibbled on the tender flesh for a moment before she moved on to explore Ryan's mouth with her tongue. After a few achingly long moments, she pulled away and gazed into Ryan's desire-filled eyes. "I promise you'll get all you can handle, sweetness. But I don't think you're ready yet." Her voice held a note of regret, and Ryan knew that her perception was accurate. Ally didn't want to wait, either, but she would never rush a scene. "When you're ready, you'll beg for my touch."

She climbed on top of Ryan and started to kiss her again. Ryan's mouth opened and welcomed Ally's warm tongue as it began to explore every surface. As the kissing intensified, Ryan had an overpowering desire to wrap her arms around Ally's back and toss her over. She wanted to satisfy her primal urge to be on top, but her bound hands constantly reminded her that she was a bottom today, and would remain so for the duration of the evening.

After she had kissed her friend so thoroughly that her lips felt bruised, Ally moved down again. She went to the end of the sofa and grabbed the hems of Ryan's pant legs and gave a powerful yank. The jeans flew from her body, and were quickly tossed aside. Her panties were pulled down inadvertently, so Ally gently pulled them back up and softly patted Ryan's belly. Then she climbed on top again and began to kiss Ryan's nipples through her bra. The pressure of her firm tongue made the material feel quite rough on Ryan's delicate skin, and her nipples puckered so forcefully that her areolas almost disappeared. Ally's hands were never still as her mouth worked away. She ran her hands up and down Ryan's torso, touching her lightly, teasingly.

After a long while, she sat up and gazed at Ryan for a moment. She reached up and untied her hands, swiftly pulling her into a sitting position. "Dance with me," she said, extending a hand. Ryan obediently grasped it and was pulled to her feet. Ally was still fully clothed, wearing black jeans and a white cropped T-shirt that bore a logo that read "girl." Ryan guessed that she also wore a sports bra since she had no cleavage tonight. She simply hoped that she'd be allowed to find out what was under those clothes before the night was over.

A slow, emotion-laden song was playing, and Ally wrapped her arm around Ryan's waist as she grasped her hand and held it to her breast. She began to move her slowly around the wooden floor, keeping perfect time to the music. Ryan felt more naked than she'd have felt if she was, in fact, naked. Something about dancing in lacy underwear when your partner was fully dressed could do that, she reasoned.

Ally's black Doc Martin's added to her height advantage to make her at least three inches taller than her partner, but the height difference allowed Ryan to get close by tucking her breasts just under Ally's. Ryan let her head drop to rest on the strong shoulder, and she sighed as she felt her partner's head drop to gently rest against hers. There was something so intimate about this tender dance that Ryan felt a burst of emotion well up in her throat. They continued to move with and against each other until the entire CD was finished. As the music stopped they stood and swayed together for a few long minutes, with Ally finally lifting her head to kiss Ryan tenderly, just barely brushing their lips together. Her hand lifted from Ryan's back and gently held the back of her head as she slowly increased the intensity of the kiss until she could feel her partner's knees begin to weaken.

With one powerful move, she swept Ryan into her arms and started to carry her towards the bedroom. Ryan raised her hands to clasp behind Ally's neck, then leaned back and enjoyed the ride. She hadn't been carried to bed since she was a small child, and she smiled knowingly as she thought of all of the women she had done this to. When they arrived, Ally laid her gently onto the neatly made bed and started to undress. Ryan stared at her with her heavy lidded eyes filled with open desire. It was clear that she appreciated Ally's sculpted body, and she did her best to show that appreciation with her eyes. Her gaze was met with a knowing smirk as Ally showed off a bit. She removed her T-shirt and pulled her bra over her head. Standing there in her jeans, she stretched and arched her back languidly. Ryan took in all of the rippling muscles in her back and shoulders, and felt her mouth go dry with the insistent craving that pounded in her body.

Ally turned around to remove her jeans. Her only motivation was to show off her back a little bit more, but Ryan loved this exhibitionistic part of her friend. She appreciated great bodies, and she thought it only fair that the owner would appreciate her own body as well. The muscular woman shucked her jeans slowly, and displayed herself completely to Ryan's appreciative eyes. Next she slid her gray panties down her rock-hard legs, and stepped out of them. Another few stretches for Ryan's benefit, and she climbed onto the bed.

"God, you look good," Ryan breathed as she ran her fingers up Ally's legs. "I've never seen your legs look so big." Ally didn't stop her, so she continued to trail her hands over the starkly defined muscles. "Uhm, your quads are like iron," she said in wonder, as she pushed her thumbs into the big muscles. She was just about to move her hands to feel the backs of Ally's legs when she abruptly found herself on her back again.

"Break's over, sweetie, back to work." Ally had with a wild look in her eyes as she climbed on top of her again. She returned her attentions to Ryan's now-aching breasts. Once again her nipples popped up quickly, and Ally let out a little chuckle. "Somebody seems to like me." She blew a cool breath across the tender nubs, making Ryan shiver.

"Uhm, they like you a lot," the brunette purred, feeling the sensation begin to radiate out from her breasts. Ally continued to tease the taut nipples through the lacy bra until Ryan once again started to roll her hips in a very beguiling fashion.

Ally rolled her onto her side, unclasped the lace bra, and lifted it from her body. Placing her on her back again, she leaned over ruby red nipples and spoke to them as if they were sentient. "You look so red and swollen," she said sympathetically. "I bet you'd love someone to sooth you with a nice warm mouth, wouldn't you?"

Ryan answered for her nipples, grabbing Ally's head and pulling it onto one of the inflamed tips, but Ally was far too quick for her. She got a firm grip on both of Ryan's hands, and placed them upon two of the spindles in her wooden headboard, then leaned over until her nose was nearly touching Ryan's. "Keep them there."

With a heavy sigh, Ryan complied. She despised having to control herself, and even though she had never revealed this fact to Ally, she had a feeling that the larger woman knew it and forced her to do so just to make her point. It was much easier for her if Ally just tied her hands, but Ally seemed to get a lot of pleasure from Ryan's internal struggle to obey this one simple command. She gripped the spindles firmly and closed her eyes as Ally dipped her head and covered one of Ryan's aching nipples with her mouth. The warm, wet tongue was very soothing and Ryan luxuriated in the sensation. Ally blew on them again, and the brunette felt some of the heat leave the tender nubs as the cool air passed over.

She felt her hips begin to thrust as her friend began to suck more and more of her breast into her mouth. She wanted to reach down and hold Ally's head and push her mouth more firmly against her breast, but she was unable to because of her restrained hands. The fact that she was the one restraining herself made the sensation all the more deliciously frustrating. She wished that Ally would slide one of those rock-hard thighs between her legs so she could have some pressure on her vulva. It was so maddening to have her hips thrusting against nothing but air, but she couldn't keep them still, no matter how hard she tried.

Ally tossed her leg over Ryan's hips and sat up, straddling her thighs. Ryan smiled to herself as she felt those brown curls leave a moist trail as they passed over her leg. Ally opened her arms and beckoned, "Come here, sugar."

Ryan relinquished her hold of the spindles and sat up quickly, feeling herself enveloped in her friend's strong embrace. "I swear you're more beautiful every time I see you," Ally whispered into her ear and squeezed her tightly. Ryan lifted her head and Ally began to kiss her again, this time with a tender, soft, emotion-filled touch. She brought her hands around to cup Ryan's breasts and gently squeezed them as her kisses deepened. Ryan brought her hands up to rest on top of Ally's, and she pressed them harder against herself as they began to move around in a circle. "You have the most perfect breasts I've ever touched," she murmured reverently as she continued to move the tortured flesh around slowly in her hands.

She finally pulled one hand away and moved it to the back of Ryan's head, then lifted her own breast in her hand and raised it to Ryan's willing mouth. "Please," she begged with a tremulous voice. Ryan thankfully opened her mouth and sucked Ally in. They let out concurrent moans as they both felt a jolt of pleasure from the contact. Ryan's arousal shot off the scale as she sucked on Ally's breasts with a ravenous hunger. Her clit throbbed, and she squeezed her thighs together as tightly as she could manage. She was rewarded by Ally's soft moans as she worked on her generous mounds with her hands and her mouth. But after all too brief a time Ally pulled her breast away and bent to kiss Ryan again.

Ryan's head was spinning from her unquenched desire as she felt Ally roll off of her. The larger woman gave her a wicked grin as she slowly pulled Ryan's bikinis off. Ally rolled her onto her stomach, and Ryan felt her shift to get something from the nightstand. Suddenly she felt something cold and wet being poured onto her butt, Ally's second favorite body part. Her strong hands began to massage the cool gel into her skin, and Ryan purred as her cheeks were firmly manipulated. As the gel disappeared, Ryan was surprised to feel the heat begin to build as Ally blew across her cheeks. The heat continued to grow until Ryan felt like she had been spanked, but as quickly as it developed it began to dissipate until it felt cool once more.

Now Ally squeezed the gel all over Ryan, from the tops of her shoulders, down her back, across her hips and down each leg. She used her hands to spread it around until it coated every inch of skin, but she didn't rub it in. Instead, Ryan felt her climb on top of her and begin to glide across her body with an incredibly sensual tempo. Every time Ally lifted a particular body part away from Ryan the cool breeze that was blowing across the room heated up her skin until she squirmed. Ryan was quickly becoming so aroused that she was on the verge of slipping her hand between her legs and bringing herself off, but Ally seemed to sense this and she grabbed Ryan's hands and spread them out under her own powerful arms. She continued to grind against Ryan's hypersensitive skin, as Ryan pounded her hips against the mattress.

Finally, Ryan couldn't take another minute of frustration. She moaned into the mattress and begged for release. "Please, Ally, please touch me. I need you now."

"Are you sure you're ready?" she whispered into her ear.

"Yes! *Please!* I'm begging you, Ally, please let me come!"

"Okay, sugar, you've been very good tonight." She picked up a small towel and quickly wiped the excess of the gel from Ryan's back and her own chest and legs. They both shivered a bit as the air blew cool and then hot across their sensitized skin. She turned Ryan onto her back and the long legs immediately shot open as she placed her feet on the bed, waiting for Ally's touch.

Ally climbed onto her waist, facing the foot of the bed. She was so wet that Ryan could feel her friend's moisture spreading all across her belly. Ryan clearly had enough of her own lubrication, but Ally couldn't resist putting just a dab of the cinnamon flavored gel right onto her clitoris. Ryan nearly leapt from the bed when she felt the cool liquid hit her overheated clit. But when Ally leaned over her and began to blow on it she nearly hit the ceiling. Her hips flew from the bed so violently that she almost hit Ally in the face with her pelvis, then called out indecipherable words as she impotently humped the air. Ally scooted down lower to hold her still, and slid her fingers across Ryan's throbbing flesh. She had barely begun to move her fingers up and down against the inner lips when Ryan screamed out her climax. Her body bucked and jerked so violently that Ally had to steady herself with her hands to stay on top of her. But since she was bent over a bit she decided that one more good blow couldn't hurt. She watched Ryan's flesh spasm for a moment, and just when she began to still, Ally blew out a long breath that traveled up and down Ryan's over sensitized center.

"Ahh!" she yelled, as the heat began to build again. She snapped her legs shut and rolled over until she could dislodge her tormentor, then she threw her arms around Ally and they began to wrestle on the bed. "Are you trying to kill me?" she panted as she pinned her temporarily.

Ally easily shrugged out of her hold, and tossed her onto her back once again. She covered the writhing body with her own and leaned down to kiss Ryan several times. "I'm just trying to please you, sugar," she purred. "How'd I do?"

Ryan beamed back at her as she wrapped her arms around her neck. "You did great," she said sincerely as she began to kiss her. She was surprised to feel Ally begin to submit to her so she rapidly increased her attack. Her kisses intensified quickly as she squeezed the delectable mounds that hovered above her.

"Touch me now," Ally pleaded and Ryan immediately complied. Ally had never asked for what she needed, and Ryan was certainly not going to refuse this first request. She rolled her onto her back while she carefully cuddled up next to her. Just for paybacks, she squeezed some of the gel onto her fingers before she slid them into Ally's drenched vulva. The strong legs flew open, and she grasped Ryan's hand and pushed it against herself roughly. Just a few seconds of firm pressure and she began to shake as her climax hit her hard. She continued to shiver as she held onto Ryan's hand, pushing it against herself for a few more seconds. Then she lay very still for a few moments, finally looking at Ryan with a crooked grin. "Race you to the shower," she said as she vaulted from the bed and dashed in front of her laughing partner. They pushed and elbowed each other for a few moments but Ally won, as usual.

Next they fought over the hand held shower for a few minutes to remove the residue of the gel. "What is this stuff?" Ryan asked as a look of bliss crossed her features when the last traces were washed from her vulva.

"It's cinnamon flavored motion lotion," Ally said. "It tastes just like Red Hots."

"You're truly diabolical." Ryan leaned over to give her another kiss.

"You really know how to turn a girl's head."

By the time they dried off and stopped in the kitchen to feed each other ice cream, it was nearly ten o'clock. They crawled back into bed and cuddled up together to sleep. Ryan was always amazed at how snuggly and affectionate Ally was when they slept together. She had every part of herself touching some part of her partner as they settled down into a comfortable position. "G'night, Ryan," she whispered as Ryan felt herself begin to relax in her warm embrace.

"Good night, Ally," she replied as she turned her head to give her one final kiss. Moments later she could feel her relax and lean against her heavily. Ryan sighed deeply and joined her in sleep minutes later.

Jack walked into his apartment on Friday evening, and smiled as his senses took in the smell of chicken roasting in the kitchen. *There's nothing better than coming home and having Jamie here making dinner for us*, he thought. He stopped in his tracks when he came upon an obviously new, bright orange, bike leaning against the wall in the hallway.

"Jamie?"

"Yeah, honey. I'm in here," she replied from the kitchen. "C'mon in."

"Whose bike is that?" he asked when he entered the room.

"It's mine, silly," she said, walking over to give him a proper greeting. "Whose else would it be?"

"I don't know. I didn't know you liked to ride, and I didn't know you had a bike, sooo …"

"Well, I do and I do." She wrapped her arms around his neck, and silenced any potential response by keeping his lips busy for several long moments.

He wasn't to be deterred. When she pulled away, he walked back into the hall and looked more closely at the bike. "Sure seems like a nice one. Is it new?"

"Yeah, I just got it this week."

"How come?" he inquired as he returned to the kitchen, carrying his mail.

"How come what?" she replied, although she understood the question perfectly well.

"How come you bought an expensive new bike?"

"I want to get into riding," she said, as if this explained everything.

But Jack was his usual tenacious self, and he sensed there was more beneath the surface. "Why?" he asked, as he locked his gaze onto hers, giving her a clear signal that he wanted a complete answer.

"I've decided that I'm going to ride in this year's AIDS Ride in June." *That should satisfy him.*

"Why would you want to do that?" he asked, with his voice rising just a bit. "And why are you avoiding my questions?"

"What's so odd about wanting to do something to support a worthy cause, Jack? We've both been lucky enough to be unaffected by the disease. The least I can do is show my support by doing this ride."

"Jamie, we both know that if you wanted to support this cause you could write them a check that would make them faint. That can't be the reason for doing something this stupid." As soon as it was out he truly wanted to pull that last word back into his mouth. That urge got stronger when he saw the hurt look in her eyes. "I'm sorry. I didn't mean to say that." He approached her and tried to put his arms around her.

Jamie was having none of it. She turned her back on him and struggled to keep the tears from flowing. She shrugged off his repeated attempts to touch her, going into the corner to be alone for a moment. Finally, she turned around and regarded him with a hurt look. "Why would you say something like that? Are you trying to hurt me?"

"No, of course not!" He was again rebuffed in his attempt to touch her. "It's just that it seems there's more and more stuff you don't tell me. I guess I just feel left out," he grumbled with a dejected look on his handsome face.

Jamie couldn't resist the hurt puppy look, and she had to admit that he was right. She was leaving him out of some of her decisions, so she relented and took him into her arms. "I'm sorry. I don't want you to feel left out. This is just something I decided to do recently. It's important to me, and I want your support. I guess I have forgotten to tell you some things. I'll try to keep you more involved."

He wrapped her in a fierce hug, and held on for several minutes. As he nuzzled his head into her neck he broke the ice by asking, "Do you want to make up like we did last time?"

She laughed as she leaned her head back and gave him a tender kiss. "I'd love to, but dinner's about ready. Let's eat and then go to bed early, okay?"

Over dinner she explained the ride more thoroughly. She was reticent to explain how intrinsically Ryan was involved, but she was resolved to try to keep her promise to Jack. Her friend's name hadn't been mentioned since their fight, and she felt guilty about developing such a close relationship without Jack's knowledge. The first time she mentioned Ryan's name Jack paused mid-bite, but he didn't comment. Jamie dutifully told him everything. She told him about deciding to do the ride, about buying the bike, about training at the gym. She was chagrined to hear herself mention Ryan every five seconds, but she was determined to be completely honest.

Jack asked a few questions, but generally let her talk. When she was finished, he sat back in his chair and regarded her for a long moment. "I'd like to get to know this woman. She's obviously become a very good friend, and you're sure spending a lot of time with her, so I'd like to spend some time with her, too."

"How about tomorrow?" she asked with a little grin, pleased that he was making the effort. "She's bringing her bike down here and we're going on a ride."

"Tomorrow it is."

They lay in bed together late that night. Jack was sound asleep, and Jamie watched him as he lay in peaceful exhaustion. They had made love, and while Jamie wasn't physically satiated, she felt very peaceful lying next to her fiancé. She reflected that she most loved the closeness and the warmth their lovemaking provided. The physical sensations were sometimes marvelous, sometimes merely tolerable, but the closeness always made it seem worthwhile. She often thought that her favorite time was after Jack had finished and he lay collapsed in her arms. She felt so close to him, kissing his forehead and holding him tight as she whispered loving words into his ear. She snuggled up behind him and rested her head against his back as she rolled him onto his side, then she drifted off to sleep.

Jamie donned her new bike shorts and a lightweight, long-sleeved T-shirt that was designed to wick away sweat. She clomped around the living room in her bike shoes, and did a few light stretches to loosen her hamstrings and quads. Ryan was due in a few minutes, and she knew she'd be on time, as usual. Jamie was a bit nervous, and Jack seemed unnaturally quiet. *I hope this goes well. I know he'll like her if he can just give her a chance.*

Just then the doorbell rang, and she went to let her guest in. *Well, I finally got my wish*, she sighed to herself as she took in Ryan's body. *I've been dying to see her muscles, and she had to show them to me when Jack's here.* But even though she was a bit chagrined, she was glad to finally be able to check her friend out thoroughly. As she gazed at her long body she had to admit that the wait was well worth it. This woman was truly an amazing sight. She wore black ankle-length bike pants that highlighted every muscle of her legs, and a tight, red, short-sleeved bicycling jersey covered with advertising logos. Her large, red bicycle was casually slung over her broad shoulder, and a shiny, black helmet dangled from the handlebar. Her black hair was slicked back off her face and captured in a ponytail, and her face was flushed from obvious exertion—which obviously included carrying the bike up three flights of stairs. She wore a bright smile on her beautiful face as she grinned down at Jamie. "Hi."

"Di … Di … Did you ride here?" Jamie asked incredulously as she struggled to resist the urge to catch the drop of sweat that was trailing down the side of Ryan's cheek.

"Yep. I figured that since I need to put in a hundred or so miles on the weekend, this would be an easy way to do it."

"C'mon in and I'll get you something to drink. You look like you could use it," she laughed. "Honey, Ryan's here," she said, turning her head toward Jack's small office.

He emerged with a quizzical look on his face. He took in the figure before him and shook his head a bit, "Did you ride here?" he asked with a smile, as he extended his hand.

Ryan struggled to remove her padded glove, but finally got it off and took his still extended hand. "Sorry, I'm sweaty," she said as she shook Jack's hand. "That last hill was a killer."

Jamie emerged from the kitchen with a cold bottle of water, which was gratefully accepted. Ryan tore open the cap and tilted the bottle up to her mouth. As she leaned her head back to chug the cold water Jack stole a long glance. *Wow*, he marveled, *she could be a model or something. Well, maybe a model for a fitness magazine. She couldn't pull off the waif thing at all.*

Ryan dropped the now empty bottle to her thigh and breathed out a satisfied sigh. "Boy, that really hit the spot. Thanks."

"You're welcome. I'm surprised you didn't bring some along for the trip."

"Oh, I did. But I drank it all half way down. Sometimes I don't pay attention to the weather change from the city to the Peninsula. It was cold and foggy when I left home this morning, and I forgot how much warmer it would be inland. It must be twenty degrees warmer here than at home."

"Give me your water bottles, and I'll fill them for you," Jamie offered.

From the cages on her bike, Ryan handed over her two spent bottles. "Can I make a pit stop before we take off again?"

"Sure. It's right down the hall, next to the office," Jack replied.

Jamie retreated to the kitchen to complete her chore, and Jack followed on her heels. "God, Jamie, I didn't notice before how gorgeous she is," he whispered into her ear as she leaned over the sink.

"Maybe you just like the sweaty look." *I know I do*, she thought wryly. "Do you feel the standard male urge to convert her to your team?" she asked with a giggle, right back into his ear.

"No, not me, but a lot of guys sure would."

"Why not you?" she inquired as her brow furrowed.

"One—because she's not my type. Two—because I've got my hands full with you. I can't take on any side work." He bent slightly to kiss her smiling mouth. Jamie was a bit taken by surprise as he really began to get into the kiss. One hand moved up her torso as the other slipped down and palmed her Lycra-encased butt. She was about to push him away when she caught a fleeting glimpse of Ryan in the doorway.

Jamie thought about the kiss for a moment as she finished filling up the bottles, and Jack returned to the living room to chat with Ryan. *That was odd. He's normally so reserved around other people. It almost seemed like he wanted her to see that, like he was laying claim to me*. She briefly chastised herself, *You don't have to analyze everything. Maybe he just felt like kissing you at that moment. And trying to cop a feel in front of your lesbian friend,* her suspicious side warned.

Ryan hoisted her bike onto her broad shoulder while Jack did the same with Jamie's. "Jack, I brought it up here myself," she argued, "I'm sure I can get it down the same way."

"I'm sure you can. But I'm here, and I want to help."

When they reached the street, Jamie situated herself on the bike and Jack kissed her goodbye. "I really might need your help when I get home," she admitted. "If I ring the buzzer will you come down?"

"Absolutely. Now you two be safe. There's lot of traffic on Saturday."

"Okay, Dad," Jamie teased.

"I'll take care of her, Jack," Ryan said in the same teasing tone.

Jamie thought she saw the smallest flicker of irritation cross his handsome face, but she decided to ignore it.

They took off and began their short trek to the Stanford campus. "Have you been down here much?" she asked Ryan.

"No, not really. I've been to a few athletic events, but that's it. I'm actually not sure that I've ever been here during daylight hours."

"Well you're in luck, because I know this place like the back of my hand," Jamie said. As she set her trip computer to zero, she asked, "We're doing fifteen miles today, right?"

"If you feel up to it. I know I tortured your legs yesterday, and I want you to pay careful attention to how they feel."

"Well, my butt feels fine, and if we stay on this level terrain I think I'll be fine."

"Good. This is exactly the type of ride I want you to do on Saturdays. It's a good thing you come down to the Peninsula on the weekends. It's the ideal place to do your long, slow, distance ride. Berkeley is really too hilly unless you stay around campus, and that's like sucking on an exhaust pipe."

"That's a sweet image. I'm sure I'll have that in mind when I ride to class on Monday."

They rode through the palm-lined streets of the campus, which was strangely quiet. There was never a lot of activity on a Saturday when the Cardinal football team was playing, and since today's game was at U.C.L.A., it appeared that a substantial portion of the undergraduates had either taken a road trip to L.A. or were watching the game in their dorm rooms. Thinking about the team, Ryan mused that she had always thought it overly precious that the Stanford mascot was a color. But she supposed that was part of the Stanford mystique.

"So why are you so familiar with Stanford?" Ryan quizzed as they rode along.

"Well, both of my parents went here, and my mother's family has a strong connection."

"Hmm," Ryan said with a knowing grin. "Given what you've told me about your family, I assume that means some big buildings are named after you."

Jamie shot her a glance, then laughed a bit as she admitted, "Surprisingly not. My family was more into sponsoring chairs in various disciplines. I think they felt that having a building named after them would be nice, but only people on campus would know the name. But when a professor is the recipient of the 'Putnam Barrett Smith Chair of Humanities,' he or she uses that title on all of their professional publications. Lots more notoriety," she said, rolling her eyes.

"Smith, huh?" Ryan asked as she rode close. "Could you be any Waspier?"

"Don't think so."

"Don't you have any Stepnoski's or Liebowitzes or Hudek's or Antonioni's or even an odd Murphy in your family?"

"Nope. Mother's family came from England around 1650, and they've stuck to their own kind almost exclusively, near as I can tell. My father's family also came from England not long after the Revolutionary War."

"That's remarkable," Ryan said with interest. "How do you know so much about your family?"

"Wasps love to research their genealogy," she said with a laugh. "My mother's mother hired someone to research their family tree. It's all in a nicely bound leather book."

"That's pretty neat," Ryan said. "There has to be something around here with your family name on it. Some little plaque or something."

"Okay," she admitted. "I know of one thing." They pedaled over to the main quad, and hopped off their bikes. Walking over to an impressive stone archway, Jamie led her inquisitive friend to a large plaque that had been placed on the interior of the arcade. "There you go," she said as she pointed with a flourish.

The legend read that the archway was substantially retrofitted and repaired after the Loma Prieta earthquake by the generous contributions of the listed benefactors. Ryan scanned the names for a Smith and pointed to a "Roger B. Smith." "Is that your family?"

"Yeah. That's a cousin. But that's not what I wanted to show you." Ryan gave her a puzzled glance, so she pointed to the beginning of the alphabet. After a few seconds of scanning, Ryan turned to her with a cute little grin. "Are those your parents?"

"Yep."

"Why are they listed separately?" Ryan inquired as she considered the entries for both James S. Evans and Catherine D.S. Evans.

"Hmm, I'm not sure. I assume they each made a contribution from their separate funds, and they didn't want to share the glory."

Ryan shot her a glance to see if she was kidding, but it was obvious that not only was her friend serious, she didn't seem to think this behavior odd. It was a struggle not to impart her own family's sense of propriety onto the Evans family, but Ryan couldn't understand why you wouldn't want to have your name listed along with your spouse. It seemed terribly odd to her but she didn't want to make a big deal out of it, so she kept her opinion to herself. "This is quite a pretty arch," she said as she looked around.

"Yeah, it is. Do you know much about how Stanford came to be?"

"Nope. I just assumed a bunch of wealthy smart people got together and started a university," she said, grinning.

"Nope. Wrong again. It was founded as an alternative to Cal, which, at the time, was for the people with old money. Leland Stanford and his wife, Jane Lathrop Stanford, donated their own land, and used their fortune to create it. They had just one child, Leland Junior. He died just a few months before his sixteenth birthday, and they decided to create and dedicate the university to him. The actual name is the Leland Stanford Junior University."

"I didn't know that," Ryan said. "That's some memorial."

"Yeah. Mrs. Stanford was quite the impressive woman. This arch was one of her personal touches." Jamie led her friend around to the front of the structure. She pointed up at the stone carvings that lined the arch, and pointed out that each one bore a tiny heart right in the center. "She dedicated the rest of her life to making this university one of the finest in the country. She must have missed her son terribly, but I really admire her for doing something positive in his name, rather than just quietly mourning him."

Ryan was studying the arch, and Jamie watched as her elegant fingers softly stroked one of the carved hearts. Her companion was very quiet as she contemplated the structure. Finally she said, "As hard as it was to lose my mother, it's the natural order of things, you know?" she asked as she turned to face Jamie. "A child is supposed to outlive her parents. I can't imagine how devastating it would be to lose your only child at such a young age."

The sad longing in those clear blue eyes made Jamie unconsciously place her hand in the small of Ryan's back, in an attempt to comfort her. Ryan draped an arm around her shoulders and gave her a gentle hug. "Thanks for showing me this," she said quietly.

"Would you like to see the Memorial Church? It's one of my favorite places down here."

"Sure," Ryan said. "I love churches."

"It's right in the back of this interior quadrangle," Jamie informed her as they walked along. Moments later they were standing in the beautiful, non-denominational church. Ryan's head was thrown back as she gazed at the magnificent stained glass windows that surrounded her.

"These are outstanding!" she whispered as Jamie approached.

"Yeah, this place is pretty special," she said quietly, even though they were the only people in the structure. "The inscriptions on the walls are from Mrs. Stanford's writings. Some of them are quite beautiful."

Ryan was obviously fascinated by the church, and Jamie left her to her wanderings. She sat down in a pew to rest her legs, but found herself slyly watching Ryan as she stopped before each inscription. When she spotted her friend staring at one particular inscription for a long while, Jamie finally walked over to her and read it.

Ryan turned to her slowly and said, "Those are the words of someone who has known sorrow—but refused to let it own her."

Jamie gave her a small smile and pondered the words:

> *There are but few on earth free from cares, none but carry burdens of sorrow. And if all were asked to make a package of their troubles, and throw this package on a common pile, and then were asked to go and choose a package that they were willing to bear, all would select their own package again.*
>
> *Your heartaches may be great, burdens heavy, but look around you and with whom would you change?*

She was deep in thought when she felt Ryan's warm hand on her shoulder. "You okay?" she asked gently.

"Yeah, yeah," she said as she shook her head. "I was just thinking of how lucky I've been. I mean, I just feel like I haven't experienced any terrible sorrows, or known any serious troubles."

Ryan turned her and gave her a gentle hug, as she leaned over and whispered, "Don't rush it, Jamie. Live long enough and you'll know your share." The smaller woman looked up at her friend and rested her head against her broad shoulder for a second. In a flash it hit her—she wasn't commenting so much about her charmed life—she was fervently wishing that she could remove the sad, haunted look that came over her friend's blue eyes when she thought about her own losses. But she didn't feel comfortable sharing this thought with Ryan, so she just gave her a little squeeze and released her.

When they returned to the bright sunshine and got back on their bikes, Jamie pointed out some markers of her family history, including the spot under a beautiful redwood where her father had proposed to her mother. "That's really neat, Jamie! How old were your parents when they married?"

"Mother was only twenty when she had me, so I guess she was still nineteen when they married. I think Daddy was twenty-four."

"How old is Jack?" Ryan asked.

"He's twenty-four. Four years older than I am. Just like my parents. It's funny, but we met when I was a freshman and he was starting law school—just like my parents did."

"That is funny. When's your wedding set for?"

"The summer after I graduate," Jamie replied. "I want to have the whole college experience as a single woman. And I want Jack to have a year's work out of the way."

"Does he know where he's going to work?"

"Yeah, pretty much. He wants to clerk for a federal judge after he graduates this summer. That could take him anywhere, though. He can't be too picky about the location, although he wants the Ninth Circuit Federal Court of Appeals. That would have him in the western region, but it could be Montana or even Hawaii. That's why I didn't want to get married right after he graduates."

"Wow, won't that be hard if he's that far away?"

Seemingly for the first time, Jamie considered that. "Uhm, I guess it will, but it's what he wants, and it'll help his long-term career prospects."

For the second time that day Ryan bit her tongue rather than comment on the strange ways of these people of the Peninsula. "What are his plans after the clerkship is over?"

"It's pretty obvious that he'll get an offer from Morris, Foster."

"What firm does your father work for?"

"That would be Morris, Foster," Jamie admitted, blushing.

"I'm not prying, am I?" Ryan asked, with a hint of concern in her voice.

"No, not at all. I know that Jack's really talented. It just seems like an ideal opportunity for nepotism, even though I know it's not. I guess I'm just sensitive to being perceived in a certain way."

"I certainly don't perceive of you as anything other than a hard working woman, who I'm certain would never marry anyone other than a hard working, talented man," Ryan said confidently. "Besides, the mere fact that your father works for the firm isn't that big a deal. I mean, it's a huge place, isn't it?"

Jamie rolled her eyes a bit as she revealed, "Yeah, it's huge all right … but my dad doesn't just work there. He's the managing partner. That's something like being the CEO of a business."

"Oh … well, I bet in a way that'll make it harder for Jack. The last thing your dad wants is to hire some dolt and have everyone think it's mere nepotism."

"Thanks, Ryan," Jamie replied, a bit relieved. "It's just that I know people think that everything comes so easily for me, and that my parents get me everything I want. I worry that people will think that Jack got his job because I demanded it."

"I know that's not true," Ryan said. "Money can't buy everything. It can't buy you big quadriceps!" This last sentence came from over her shoulder as she put on a terrific burst of speed and left Jamie in her dust, a mellow laugh trailing after her.

"I thought the key for this ride was long slow distance!" Jamie huffed as she finally caught up to Ryan's slowing form.

"It is. Why, do you want to go fast?" she asked with the most cherubic of faces.

"It's obvious that you were raised with brothers, Ryan O'Flaherty."

"Yeah, sometimes it's painfully obvious!" Ryan teased, as she burst into another flash of blinding speed.

They completed the scheduled fifteen miles with just a few more sprints. By the time they returned to the apartment, Jamie was definitely beginning to tighten up. "I don't think I could go another mile," she moaned. Ryan looked fresh as a daisy, of course, and this slightly irritated Jamie. "You know, you could at least try not to look like you've been lying on the beach for the afternoon."

Ryan laughed and did her best to put on a tired and bedraggled expression. She dragged herself over to the buzzer and rang it several times. "I guess Jack went out," she finally said after three tries.

"And I was going to bribe him to carry me upstairs."

"Well, you're way too heavy for a poor tired woman like me," Ryan teased. "But I could help you out with this." At that she leaned over and grabbed Jamie's bike frame with one powerful arm, and hefted it onto her shoulder. She grabbed the wheel with her hand to steady it, and then repeated the series of motions to pick up her own bike. She turned and grinned at a startled Jamie, "Lead on, princess."

Jamie climbed the stairs quickly, extracting her key from a small hidden pocket in her bike shorts. She held the door open for Ryan to enter with her cargo. As the brunette carefully squatted and placed all four wheels on the ground, Jamie stood in front of her and steadied both sets of handlebars.

"Thank you, Oh Powerful One," she intoned as she bent in praise.

"Oh, that's nothing," Ryan replied casually. "I probably could have left you on the darn thing, but it would have upset my center of gravity."

"Yeah, right!" Jamie teased along with a little poke in the gut. "Hey," she said seriously as she poked again and was met with a very firm resistance, "I thought you said your tummy was flabby."

"I'm quite sure I never said that," Ryan assured her with a chuckle. "I said that I've got a thicker layer of abdominal fat than you have, but my abs are in great shape, if I do say so myself. Keeping them built up really helps with bike riding."

Jamie reached over to pat her again. "They're like iron," she admitted, wishing that Ryan would lift her shirt for a peek. "How do you get them so firm? Do you do the same crunches you showed me?"

"Yeah, sometimes," she said. "But I like to challenge myself so I've devised some little tortures that I don't think you'd like."

Jamie crossed her arms across her chest and glared at her friend. "Like what, tough stuff?"

"Well, my new favorite is to lie on a declining bench and do some crunches."

"That doesn't sound so hard."

"No, that part isn't hard. But I have someone toss a medicine ball at my gut while I'm doing them."

"What? One of those heavy, sand filled, leather balls?"

"Uh-huh," she said, as she blithely refastened her ponytail, trying to suppress a grin at Jamie's shocked expression.

"I don't think I believe you."

Ryan could never resist a challenge. She stood tall and gazed at her friend with a daring look and said, "Hit me."

"What?"

"Hit me," she repeated. "Hit me in the gut—hard as you can."

"Ryan! I wouldn't do that! I'd hurt you!"

Ryan gave her a slight smirk as she scoffed, "Don't think so."

"You don't think I could hurt you?" she asked incredulously. "I'm not as weak as I look!"

"Prove it," she demanded, her blue eyes sparking fire.

"Fine!" Jamie fumed, quite insulted that her friend treated her like a weakling. Ryan tensed her abs and jutted out her chin defiantly while Jamie pulled her arm back and popped her right in the gut at about fifty percent of her capacity. She had closed her eyes as she swung, since she didn't want to see the pain in her friend's face, but when she opened her eyes Ryan was not only not in pain—she was laughing at her.

"Is that all you've got?" she scoffed.

"You want more? I'll give you more!" This time she kept her eyes wide open as she reared back and slammed her fist into Ryan's midsection with as much force as she could generate. But at impact it felt like she had slammed her hand into a brick wall. Only this wall was smirking at her.

"That was better," Ryan advised. "Wanna switch?"

"You're truly mad!" Jamie fumed, rather outraged that she had been unable to hurt Ryan's body, or her attitude. But just as that thought hit her she slapped herself in the head. "You made me want to hurt you!" she gasped. "I've never hit someone before!"

Ryan slung an arm around her shoulders and gave her a sound hug. "Boy, you missed a lot not growing up with brothers! If one of us wasn't bleeding or crying at the end of the day we just felt incomplete!"

"Well I've had enough," she grumbled. "I don't ever want you to taunt me into hitting you again! Are you sure I didn't hurt you?"

"Nope," she declared. She reached out and grasped Jamie's right hand and closely examined the wrist. "You didn't hurt yourself did you?"

The smaller woman shook her hand roughly a few times. "No, but it does sting a little. How on earth do you make your abs that hard?"

"Nothing but years of hard work, pal." Ryan cast a glance at the slight quiver in Jamie's thighs, "Time for a little rub down, Buffy."

"Ohh, my favorite part of any exercise."

Jack walked in to the apartment as Ryan was finishing her massage of Jamie's hamstrings. His face was friendly, but impassive to Jamie's eyes. Please don't let this bother him. "Hi, honey. Where did you go?" she asked brightly.

"I had to run down to the bookstore for a few minutes. I'm sorry I wasn't here to help you bring the bike up."

"You should be, I really needed a hand," she lied. She glanced at Ryan to see if her lie would get a reaction, but Ryan's head was bent in concentration at her task. "Ryan's a massage therapist," Jamie added, even though Jack hadn't commented on their activities.

He forced himself to banish the thought of Ryan giving a woman an intimate, all nude massage, and said weakly, "Oh, that's nice."

Jamie was pleased that the rather intimate contact with Ryan didn't seem to bother Jack. *Maybe he's really getting used to her.*

Late that night as Jack hovered over her, claiming her with a need that was foreign to their lovemaking, Jamie wondered if Ryan was the cause. *Whatever the cause*, she thought, *this is a very good thing*.

Early the next morning, as Ryan lay quivering in Ally's arms, she thanked the gods that she had the foresight to request gentle treatment on Friday night. *My God, if she had done me like this on Friday I'd have had to cancel our bike ride. I'm not even sure I'll be able to ride my Harley home. Oh well*, she thought as she drifted off to sleep, *I sure couldn't choose which of those orgasms to give back, so I guess I'll keep them all!*

The pair was so exhausted from their lovemaking, they not only didn't have time for brunch before their appointment with Ryan's client, Mark, they barely made it to the gym by noon. Ryan did her job on autopilot, and by the end of the hour she wasn't sure if Mark liked Ally or not. But he happily agreed to switch, and he gave Ryan a big kiss goodbye and wished her luck.

Ryan looked at Ally through her bloodshot eyes and moaned, "If I don't get some food into this poor abused body I'm gonna faint!"

"We've got three hours until our next appointment. I'll buy you some lunch, sweetness. What would you like to eat?"

"Anything, as long as it's fast."

Ally didn't take her seriously. She knew that Ryan needed some nutrients to get her through the day, so she took her to a nice little café right on Market that specialized in low-fat vegetarian food. Ryan scanned the menu and found everything so delicious sounding that she tried to find something that didn't appeal to her. She was unsuccessful, so she ordered a cheese and mushroom frittata and a fruit salad, a large orange juice and some coffee. Ally got an egg white omelet and oatmeal, her normal breakfast fare.

Ally dashed off to use the restroom, and Ryan whiled away the time thinking about their relationship. It dawned on her that they hadn't shared a meal in a restaurant in years. *Ally suggested having brunch together*, she mused. *And both nights she let me touch her much earlier than normal. I wonder what's up with that? And she just seemed to assume that I'd stay with her all weekend. Normally she doesn't extend that kind of invitation. Could she be changing the rules? Do I want her to?*

She was pulled from her reverie by Ally's light kiss on her cheek as she passed by to take her seat. "Miss me?" she asked with a twinkle in her eye.

Ryan gave her a sweet smile and reached out to lightly grasp her hand as she honestly replied, "Often."

Ally cocked her head and looked like she was going to ask what that meant, but she obviously decided not to pursue the issue. "So tell me more about this new job."

Ryan gave her more info on Women Power, and filled her in on how the opportunity came up.

"Is that the same woman you went on your bike ride with?" she asked.

Ryan was surprised that she had caught that detail. "Yeah, it is. She's a woman from my Lesbian Sexuality class at school."

Ally just shook her head at that. "Do you think they offer that class at normal schools, or just Berserkely?" she asked, using a playful moniker for the ultra-liberal campus.

"I think it's probably common at the big, liberal universities, but I don't think it's the norm by any means."

"Sounds like a great way to pick up women," she said with a wink. "Had any luck besides this Jamie?"

"Yeah, I've had a couple of nice evenings with my classmates, but not Jamie. She's actually straight. She's engaged to a guy who goes to Stanford. That's why we were riding in Palo Alto. She goes down there on the weekends to stay with him."

"Uh-huh," Ally said with a knowing smirk. "All the straight girls take a class in Lesbian Sexuality. And even more of them want to hang out with you."

"No really, Ally, she's straight," Ryan patiently explained.

"How many straight women are you friends with, Ryan?"

"Uhm …" Ryan furrowed her brow as she ran through her list of friends. With a chagrined look she finally admitted, "None."

"Exactly. And I'm guessing that it's not because you don't like straight women. In my experience, most straight women feel uncomfortable being really close with a lesbian unless they want to flip—at least temporarily. I guarantee she wants more from you than just friendship."

"Hmm, I don't know how I'd feel about that," Ryan reflected. "I think I like her too much to have a fling with her. I think it would screw up our friendship."

"Is she cute?"

"Oh, yeah," Ryan said with a playful chuckle. "She's totally cute. About five foot five or six, slim, but with some nice muscles beginning to develop, blonde hair, sea green eyes, pouty little mouth …"

"Okay, okay," Ally said with a laugh as she held up her hands, "I get it!" She looked at Ryan for another minute as she added, "If she ever gets kidnapped I hope the cops ask you for her description."

Ryan flushed at the implication. "I'm just observant," she said rather defensively.

"Hey, you don't have to convince me. But if I were her boyfriend I'd keep her away from you," she said, patting Ryan's hand. "Mother Teresa would flip for you, sugar," she said fondly.

"She's dead, Ally."

"Wouldn't matter, baby. You could bring the dead to life!"

Monday morning found Ryan lying beneath Ally's sprawled out body. After their four o'clock appointment, Ryan had gone home for dinner, but as soon as the dishes were clean she packed up her things in her backpack and headed back to Ally's. They spent the night making love with nearly as much passion as they had on Saturday night, and Ryan was almost ready to shut off her watch alarm and just stay cuddled up.

The insistent alarm woke them both, and Ally crawled off of her to go to the bathroom while Ryan waged a small war with her well-hidden lazy side. When Ally returned, she reached for Ryan and started to stroke her belly in a very friendly manner. Ryan knew if they got started again she'd lose the whole day, so she gave her a kiss and softly patted her cheek. "Gotta go, babe," she murmured softly, forcing herself to slip out of bed to avoid Ally's reaching hands. She stumbled into the shower and when she came out her friend was sound asleep again. Ryan checked the alarm clock to make sure it was set for eight, since she assumed Ally had to be at work by nine, and then she walked over to the kitchen table and left her a note.

Thanks for the marvelous lesson in how to fill up a weekend. I'll think of you all day—especially every time I have to sit down!

Love,
Ryan

She hopped on her Harley with a grimace, and rode directly to the MUNI station to catch a ride to school. *I'll be much better off standing the whole way,* she thought. *Why did we have to try out every new toy she's bought since I saw her last? Will I never learn?*

She barreled into class about five minutes late and took a seat near the door. Jamie caught sight of the wince as the brunette sat down, and wondered if Ryan had hurt herself on their bike ride. But when she looked at her again she noticed how terrible she looked. She was pale, and her eyes looked dull and bloodshot. Her hair was pulled back into a ponytail, and shoved haphazardly under a baseball cap. As Jamie cast another glance at her, Ryan's head hit her chest and she jerked in her seat as she startled herself awake. *She looks injured alright*, she smirked. *But not from biking.*

After class, Ryan waited for her outside the door. She was leaning against the wall and looked like she might fall asleep right where she stood. "I don't want to belabor an obvious point, but you look like you could use some coffee," Jamie teased when Ryan forced her eyes open.

"I don't think coffee will help," she moaned. "I think I'm gonna find a nice shady spot and take a nap until I've got to go to work."

"Don't you have your bio lab?"

"Yeah, but there's no way I could safely perform any experiments today. I could ruin a whole semester's worth of work."

"Come on," she said as she slipped her arm around Ryan's waist. "I can help you out."

After a relatively slow and silent walk, they climbed the stairs to Jamie's house. "I take it that you figured out how to fill your weekend?" Jamie asked as she led her friend up to her bed to allow her to crash.

"Oh, it got filled all right," Ryan said, thinking to herself, *Along with every other orifice.*

Chapter Five

Jamie and Ryan worked together to come up with a schedule that would allow her to train her body while getting enough saddle time. Ryan closely supervised Jamie's workouts in the gym, but she wanted to spend time riding with her, too. There were a lot of technical tips that she had to share, and since Jamie went to Palo Alto every weekend, they had to find time during the week. Ryan decided to leave her mountain bike at Jamie's house so they could ride on Monday and Wednesday afternoons.

But Ryan needed to log more miles, so she began to ride her motorcycle to Jamie's and leave it in her driveway. Then she'd fetch her bicycle and ride to work, and later to class. Cassie wasn't very happy to be roused from sleep every morning at five by the thrumming engine of the Harley, but she eventually stopped complaining when Ryan agreed to turn off the engine at the curb and walk the bike down the drive.

It was when Cassie learned that Ryan had a key to the house that she hit the roof. "Jamie, I don't want that woman to be able to barge in here whenever she pleases."

Jamie had little patience for her roommate's small-mindedness. "Fine. She needs to come in to change out of her boots and heavy jacket before she can ride her bike, so I'll tell her to ring the bell every morning. You're a really light sleeper, so would you run down and let her in?" she inquired, batting her eyes sweetly.

Cassie made a sour face. "Great, just give all the sex-crazed lesbians in town a key to our house," she fumed. "You know, I talked to some people who know her, and they say she's a real slut. I can't believe you're hanging around with her. Don't you care about your reputation?"

Not even trying to control what she knew was a scowl; Jamie pursed her lips and regarded her roommate for a long moment. "If all of my friends were as kind and generous and honorable as Ryan, I'd be one happy woman. But they're not." She turned on her heel and stalked away, hoping the other woman got the thinly-veiled message.

As the term progressed, the demands on Jamie's time increased until she felt like she didn't have a moment to herself. Her classes demanded a massive amount of preparation, and she often kicked herself mentally for taking four classes that required so much reading. When her face wasn't actually buried in a book, she was either at the gym or riding in the hills. But she found that no matter how much time she dedicated to her workouts she didn't regret her decision to do the ride. When she was on her bike she was able to free her mind of concern about her classes and her future. She didn't worry about her relationship with Jack, or think about their life together. She merely put her mind on hold and let the wind fly past as she pedaled along the steep hills of Berkeley. Having been away from bike riding for so many years she realized that she had forgotten the freedom that two wheels afforded. No matter how bad traffic was she could scoot right past the stalled cars and be home in a matter of minutes.

But as much as she enjoyed riding her bide, the workouts with Ryan were the highlights of her week. Even though they spent lots of time together, often having coffee or a quick meal, workouts were the times when Jamie felt truly special.

When she took the time to reflect, Jamie had to acknowledge that she was the one who usually spent her time making other people feel special. Sometimes it seemed that her entire relationship with Jack was spent making sure that his needs were met—making him lunch and dinner, being with him while he studied, never making demands to go out to dinner or a movie, and being an always willing sex partner. But for three hours a week, Jamie was able to put herself in Ryan's capable hands and feel as if the world revolved around her.

One of the things she had grown to appreciate about Ryan was her ability to focus completely on a task. As the weeks passed, she realized that focus was never more welcome than when it centered around her.

Jamie had observed many other trainers during her weeks at the gym, but she had never observed anyone who concentrated so fiercely on her clients. Without a word from Jamie, Ryan would automatically remove five pounds from the weight stack if it was a tiny bit too heavy; she'd order her to stop at nine reps instead of ten if she detected too much fatigue; she'd skip a certain exercise if a related one was too difficult on a given day. All in all, she was so highly attuned to Jamie and her body, that after a while they spoke very little during the sessions. But even though they didn't talk much, they communicated constantly.

After most sessions, they rode to Jamie's. Ryan was always vigilant to make sure that Jamie's muscles were warm enough to handle the short trek, and once they arrived she'd invariably order her client into the shower. Ryan would wait patiently for Jamie to finish in the bath and then she'd give her a thorough massage on whatever body part they had stressed. During the massage Ryan would usually spend at least ten minutes praising her performance in the weight room.

Jamie knew that part of the reason Ryan did this was to keep her motivated. Nonetheless, she ate it up greedily. She felt special when they spent this time together, so special that she began to wake up in a very happy mood on every workout day.

On a cool and overcast Wednesday, Jamie arrived at the gym for their usual four o'clock appointment. She looked around for Ryan, but didn't see her hanging around the front desk as she usually did. Jamie dropped her things off in a locker, and entered the main part of the gym, looking for her friend. She was about to give up and have her paged when she spotted her in the far corner of the gym.

Jamie had never even noticed the boxing equipment located on a slightly raised platform in the corner. But she noticed it today. Ryan was standing in front of a heavy, leather-covered bag, banging the stuffing out of it with her hands, which were encased in bright red boxing gloves. Jamie stood for a second and observed her friend, watching the sweat fly from her face as she delivered one strong blow after another. Jamie decided that if she were the one hitting the bag she wouldn't follow Ryan's example. But when she watched carefully, she could see that Ryan's technique was the proper one. She punched from her shoulder, getting the force of her entire torso behind each blow. Jamie noted that she was nearly standing on her toes while she punched the bag, and that her body followed her arm, with even her hips helping provide thrust. It truly amazed her that she could stand and watch her friend for such a long time without the always-aware woman noticing her, but Ryan was so intent that she was unaware of anything except her furious assault on the heavy bag. "Uhm … mad at someone?" Jamie finally asked to break the spell.

Ryan whirled to face her, sweat flying from her hair and hitting Jamie with a light spray. "When did you get … what time is it?" she asked, looking at her watch. "My God! It's four-fifteen!"

"I know," Jamie said with a smile. "I've been watching you for fifteen minutes."

Ryan looked perplexed. "You have?"

Jamie realized how odd it sounded to have been watching her friend for so long. She tried to cover by saying, "I've never seen anyone work on a bag like that. I've always been fascinated by boxing."

"Really?" Ryan asked, looking suspicious. She grabbed a small towel from a stack and wiped her face and neck down.

"Yeah, I have. That was pretty impressive, by the way."

"Thanks. My three o'clock cancelled and I wanted to do something aerobic for a few minutes. I thought this would be something that I could do and not sweat too much." She looked down at herself rather helplessly. Sweat was still running down her face, and tiny rivulets ran down her arms.

"I'd say you were wrong," Jamie said. "Very wrong."

"Well, I started out just playing around with the speed bag," Ryan said. "But when I was finished I still felt kind of twitchy, and I thought the heavy bag would tire me out."

"Twitchy?"

"Yeah," she said as a blush covered her face and neck. "Sometimes I just need to … I don't know … let off some steam."

"I think you were successful," Jamie observed wryly.

"I didn't look too bad after the speed bag," Ryan insisted. "Really."

"Well as long as you're doing a demo let me see you on that for a minute," she said, truly interested in seeing her friend work her magic again.

Ryan graced her with a quirky grin. "You sure?"

"Positive."

Ryan shrugged her broad shoulders and stuck out her hands. After a second Jamie realized that she couldn't take the gloves off herself. "Wow, these would have been a good way for my parents to make me stop sucking my thumb at night," she said, laughing.

"Hmm, I didn't suck my thumb, but I could have used these as a substitute for self control when I got a little older."

Jamie slapped her firmly in the stomach. "Some of your dates probably wish you had them now."

"Ooo, that's cold," Ryan muttered. She pulled off the gloves that Jamie had unlaced, and put on a pair of very lightweight hand protectors. Facing the bag, she centered her weight and raised her fists almost to eye level. "My brother Conor put up a speed bag in the garage when I was about ten." She started to slowly tap the bag with each hand in sequence. "I had to stand on a box to hit the darn thing, but I was much more dedicated than he was. Of course he was fourteen and just starting to get into girls, so his attention was diverted. Anyway, I loved working on that bag, and it really helped me enormously with my hand-eye coordination as well as my concentration. I was so skinny the bag would have knocked me right off that box if I didn't pay attention."

By the time she was finished recounting this insight into her youth, her speed had picked up to such an extent that the bag was a mere blur. But her motion was so effortless, and seemed so easy that her fists barely moved. It was mesmerizing to watch, and Jamie knew that she could stand here all day and watch Ryan flail away. But after a few minutes, the brunette slowed and eventually stopped the bag by grabbing it with both hands. "Look like fun?" she asked with a twinkle in her eyes.

"Yeah, when you do it," Jamie said. "Why doesn't anybody ever use this stuff?"

"Well, it's a lot harder than it looks, and most women don't know their way around the equipment, so they don't know where to start. But I'd love to show you how if you want. It'd be good for your upper body."

"Let's stick with the machines for awhile, pal. I don't wanna bite off more than I can chew." She regarded her friend for a moment and asked, "Do you have another shirt? That one's a mess."

"Good point," Ryan agreed as she plucked at the limp garment. "I think I can grab another from the office. Be right back."

A few minutes later she trotted back over in a tiny shirt. Jamie guessed that she normally wore an extra large, and this one couldn't have been more than a medium. But she didn't have any complaints, and neither did the two women on the stair climbers who followed Ryan's progress across the gym. "The only one they had was from someone who quit earlier this year," she said with a scowl. "She must have been a nine-year-old."

"You look fine," Jamie assured her. "Now let's get busy, coach. I've got my work cut out for me if I'm gonna keep up with you!"

"Dream on," Ryan said, smiling her biggest grin. "Fantasy is good for the soul."

After their very strenuous workout, Jamie asked, "Do you have time for dinner? I could whip something up."

Ryan appeared to consider the offer for a moment, but finally said, "I'd love to, but I can't squeeze it in. My father made a brown bag dinner for me, so I'm gonna have my dinner, then go study."

"Okay," Jamie said, trying not to sound like she cared, even though she cared a great deal. As much as she enjoyed the workouts, she equally enjoyed the post-shower massage and praise session. But she didn't feel comfortable admitting how much that special time meant to her, so she tried to shrug it off.

Ryan caught the look of disappointment on her face. "If you need some company tonight, I'll make time for you."

Jamie felt busted, and tried to cover it up with a careless reply. "No, I should study, too. I'm just looking for a reason not to."

"If you're sure," Ryan said with an intense gaze as she leaned over a bit to make eye contact.

"Positive," Jamie said, immensely glad that Ryan cared enough to meet her needs.

Four hours later, Jamie was hard at work on a short paper for The Lesbian Experience when she realized that she didn't have an important book. *Darn, I must have left it at Jack's.* The paper wasn't due until Friday, but she had plans to study for a Romantic Poets class the next day. This was the best night to write the paper, but it was nine o'clock, and she wasn't sure where to buy the book. She called around and found that the lesbian bookstore she'd visited with Ryan had the only copy in the area, so she hopped in the Porsche and drove to Oakland.

She circled the block, looking for parking, and noticed an unmistakable vehicle—a turquoise and cream Harley. *Hmmm, what's she doing here, "Little Miss I Have To Study?"* She was a trifle annoyed when she entered the bookstore side of the business. She looked around furtively, but didn't see Ryan anywhere. *Well, I guess there could be two of those bikes. That's within the realm of possibilities.* She found her book, stopped at the counter to pay for it, and was getting ready to leave when she paused to take a quick look around the coffeehouse.

The room was quite a bit darker than the last time she had visited. A woman was on the small stage singing some contemporary ballads in an adequate fashion. Jamie scanned the crowd in the dim light and noticed that only three of the small tables were occupied—none of them by Ryan. As she turned her head slowly, trying to adjust for the differences in brightness between the two rooms, she noted what looked like a familiar form in the farthest corner of the establishment. Two women occupied a small loveseat in the very dark corner. Sitting wasn't the proper term, because neither of them was upright. An attractive black woman with very close-cropped hair was half reclining on the loveseat, and Ryan was practically lying on top of her.

Jamie stood slack-jawed in the bright light of the bookstore, staring in shock at the pair. Ryan was kissing the woman deeply and moving against her whole body as she did. Jamie didn't think she'd ever seen anything more erotic, but every fiber of her being wanted to run out of the store and never think about the sight again. She watched as Ryan gripped the woman's face and kissed her even more passionately. Jamie found herself completely unable to move and equally unable to stop watching.

Ryan began to sit up, and the woman came right with her, latched onto her mouth. When they were both upright, Ryan put one arm around her shoulders and another under her knees and pulled the woman onto her lap. Jamie saw those strong tanned hands begin to caress the woman's body. She knew she'd faint if she didn't look away, but she felt rooted in place. She watched as Ryan's hands again moved to either side of the woman's head and held her still, beginning another round of deep kisses. Jamie saw tongues passing between mouths as they drew back an inch or two and then fell right back into each other. The woman's hands slowly slid up Ryan's torso, and Jamie had to grasp for something to steady herself as she saw one small, dark, hand grasp Ryan's left breast and begin to knead it. Ryan's head rose slowly and dropped back against the loveseat while a look of absolute pleasure crossed her beautiful face.

As the book slid from her now nerveless fingers, Jamie heard a voice ask, "How ya doing kid?" The question, which came from directly behind her right shoulder, nearly caused her to scream. She used all of her composure to focus her attention in the direction of the voice. Babs, the owner of the shop, and Ryan's friend, looked at her in sympathy. "Don't be mad at her, hon," she said. "Ryan's not a bad kid, but she can't get tied down to any one woman. She's just not the type."

"What?" Jamie looked at her in total confusion. "Why would I be m …? What?" Never in her twenty years had she felt so completely inarticulate.

"It's okay, kid. You aren't the first and you won't be the last. Don't let it get to ya."

"B … b … but, we're not … she's not … *I'm not* … I didn't …" Jamie truly wanted to sink to the floor and cry. She was so frustrated with her inability to form a coherent sentence and her chaotic feelings about Ryan that she was truly at a loss.

"All's I'm saying is that there're plenty of women who'd love to date a good lookin' girl like you. And most of 'em wouldn't give you up so easy as Ryan did. I love that girl to death, but she's a dog, honey." She patted Jamie on the back, and walked back in to the coffeehouse.

Jamie was even more stunned now. As if in a trance, her eyes traveled on their own accord back to the dark corner. She watched as Ryan and her date disentangled themselves from each other and stood on wobbly legs. The woman had her arm wrapped around Ryan's waist and Ryan's arm was draped across her shoulders. Their heads were very close together as they stumbled out into the darkness.

In order to give herself time to collect her feelings, Jamie picked up her book and sat down at one of the small tables. She sat motionless and dazed for at least fifteen minutes, with her mind a complete jumble. She was angry, puzzled and curious, and although she hated to admit it … totally aroused.

Finally, she felt as though she had enough control to drive. She walked outside and was puzzled to see the Harley still in its space. She walked around the corner and saw Ryan and the woman leaning up against a car, continuing their torrid make-out session. The problem was that the car they were leaning on was right in front of Jamie's.

Now Jamie was able to sort out her feelings—she was angry. *I want to leave, for god's sake! And I don't want her to see me! She'll think I'm stalking her!*

Her quandary was solved a moment later when the woman opened the rear door, crouched down and slid across the seat. Ryan dove in and their heads dropped below the windows.

Jamie ran to her car and got in quickly. After a moment of fumbling with her keys, she started the engine and roared off as fast as her little German wheels would take her.

Once at home and safe in her room, she pondered her reactions to the evening. *It's not like I didn't know she was with a lot of women. It's just that actually seeing her with a woman was such a shock. But why did I feel so turned on?* She considered that question for long minutes. *It must just be the shock and the thrill of seeing someone do something that's kind of forbidden. I'd probably get turned on from watching Mia and Jason really go at it, too.* She could feel her body flush as she considered just how passionate Ryan had looked with her date. *God, she was so powerful and strong. Her hands owned that woman. She kissed her with a ferocity that I've never experienced. God, I wonder what they're doing now?* Her mind only paused a second before it delivered the obvious message. *What do you think they're doing? They're having hot sex in the back seat of that car! Oh god, why didn't I take abnormal psychology like everybody else?*

Jamie decided that speaking to Ryan about seeing her at the coffeehouse would serve no useful purpose. She was perturbed that her friend had been less than honest about studying that night, but she was more than happy to forget her own reactions to the event. She used her well-honed powers of denial, and pushed the affair into the back of her mind. She and Ryan didn't speak on Thursday, but after class on Friday they stopped for their customary juice break. Jamie was bemused to see Ryan pull a brown bag from her book bag and begin to eat her snack.

"Uhm, Ryan?"

"Mmrmfh?"

"Why are you eating cold, dry pancakes?"

The brunette swallowed. "They're cold because they were made last night, and I don't have access to a microwave. They're dry because syrup doesn't travel well." After delivering her logical answer she gazed at Jamie with an open, placid look on her face. This was one of Ryan's idiosyncrasies that Jamie both loved and hated. The woman invariably answered your question—she just answered it exactly as it was asked. The thought passed through Jamie's mind that everyone she knew thought like a lawyer.

"You know that's not my real question," Jamie said as she gave her arm a slap.

"Okay, I'll confess. I didn't call home by three to tell my father that I wouldn't be home for dinner. This," she said as she shook her snack, "is my punishment."

"I guess that clears it up," she replied with a confused look.

"Here's the deal," Ryan said. "My father expects each of us to be home for dinner at 6:00 p.m. sharp. It's no big deal if we can't make it. But if you don't opt out by three, he cooks for you. If he cooks for you, you damn well better eat it. So, if you miss a meal, you get it for lunch the next day."

"But you don't have to eat it, Ryan," Jamie laughed. "He wouldn't know if you threw it away and bought a hot lunch."

Ryan looked at her for a moment, her expression sober. "I have to eat it. It's important to my father."

"What do you mean?"

"When my mother died, my father did his best to keep us functioning as a real family. Having meals together is a big part of what makes that work. When I break one of the family rules, there should be a price to pay. It's all about respect." Her deep blue eyes were serious as she gazed steadily at Jamie.

"I'd love to meet the man who you respect so much," Jamie said as she covered Ryan's hand with one of her own.

Ryan gave Jamie a big smile. "Why don't you come for Sunday dinner and meet everyone?"

"I'd love to."

"Sunday at three. Don't be late," she threatened ominously as she gave her cold pancake another shake right in Jamie's face.

Jamie left Palo Alto extra early to insure that she'd be on time for Sunday dinner. She followed Ryan's neatly written directions as she moved along U.S. 101 and exited at Cesar Chavez Boulevard. She mused to herself that she had never been in this section of the city. She often took 101, but usually only to see her grandfather up near Nob Hill. As she drove along Chavez it became clear why she had never been to this neighborhood. Her family was interested in high culture, fine restaurants and major sporting events. This modest neighborhood looked like a fine place to get a good Nicaraguan meal, but that was about it. The neighborhood wasn't run down, but it strongly reflected the culture of its recent immigrants from Central America. *Is this Ryan's neighborhood? I know she doesn't have much money, but this seems awfully modest.*

After a couple of miles she crossed Dolores Street, a broad, divided street with a large greensward down the center. At that imaginary dividing line the neighborhood began to change dramatically. Now the houses were very neatly tended, and the shops looked decidedly more upscale. *This is really cute*, she thought as she regarded the plethora of narrow, two and three story Victorians that graced every block.

She arrived at the stated address at 2:40 and found a parking space rather easily. As she walked up to the neat little Victorian, she heard music playing from the attached garage, and decided to check there before climbing the exterior staircase to approach the front door. Two dark figures were lying on the floor flanking a turquoise and cream Harley as she approached.

Walking into the garage, she tentatively asked, "Ryan?" still not positive that one of the figures was her friend.

"Hey, Jamie," replied her friendly voice. "Did you bring your overalls?" Ryan scooted out from beneath the bike and rose to her full six-foot plus height. She wore her black hair in a neat braid that stuck out from beneath the bill of her backwards, red baseball cap. A tight, white, ribbed tank top showed every one of the many assets of her torso. Very old, very faded 501's covered her long legs, large rips at each knee and small ones beneath the soft curves of her butt. As she stood, Jamie could make out gray underwear through the rear rips that seemed to extend well past the norm. *What does she have on under those jeans? Does she wear boxers?* Big brown lineman's boots covered her feet.

Jamie could almost feel her chin hit her chest when the next figure stood. She was fairly certain that Ryan didn't have a twin, but the tall man who now stood beside Ryan was clearly a testosterone-laden clone. Looking at them together, Jamie marveled at the likeness, but where Ryan had smooth curves, the man had tight muscle. He was at least three inches taller, and a lot broader in the shoulders, and his hips were narrow. He didn't have an ounce of fat anywhere it didn't belong. His hair was identical in color and texture, but he wore it short around the sides of his head and a little long on top. His eyes were the same deep blue, and they had the same intensity as Ryan's. But Jamie quickly noticed that they lacked the gentleness that Ryan's often bore. His gaze seemed intimidating, almost predatory, while Ryan's usually seemed open and interested. He was dressed in a similar manner, but his T-shirt covered his shoulders, and his jeans had fewer holes.

Ryan looked amused at the expression on Jamie's face. "Kinda creepy, huh?" she teased.

"Yeah," she admitted. "You aren't twins, are you?"

The man was busy wiping his hands on a towel. As he finished, he extended his right one in greeting. "She should be so lucky to share my chromosomes," he said, laughing.

Jamie laughed as Ryan punched him rather hard in his bicep. "This is my sweet, charming brother Conor. Conor, this is my friend, Jamie."

"I'm pleased to meet you, Conor," Jamie finally got out, aware that she was still staring, but unable to stop.

"It's only gonna get worse, Jamie. Prepare yourself," Ryan warned.

The grungy siblings spent a few moments putting their tools away and neatening up the work area. Jamie watched them work, still unable to get over the astounding similarity. After they had finished they all exited the front of the garage to walk up the narrow staircase that led to the front entrance. When they reached the landing, she noticed a very nice flower-rimmed deck that obviously covered the two-car garage. "Nice," she said appreciatively, taking in the neat space.

"Yeah, we've got the only deck on the block. Actually, one of the few in the whole neighborhood. It's a great place to sit out and get a fog tan," she chuckled, acknowledging the few clear days that the city was blessed with. Giving a quick glance at the surrounding houses, Jamie noticed that they were all of a similar type. They were all quite narrow and spaced very closely together, so close that most of them seemed to touch each other on both sides.

Conor held the door for her and she stepped in before the siblings. "Your home is charming, Ryan," she enthused. As Jamie looked around she thought to herself that part of the charm was the near Lilliputian size of the rooms. The house was two rooms wide and two rooms long. The small entryway led to an equally small, but attractive, living room. The living room opened into a formal dining room that was identical in size to the living room.

The living room held two love seats and a comfortable looking, leather, wing-back chair. A full sized sofa would never have fit, and the room was cramped with the current seating arrangement. There was a small fireplace topped by a mantel that was filled with pictures of the family. Small leaded glass windows bracketed the fireplace. Additional photos and diplomas lined the walls under the windows. The wall to the left of the fireplace held a floor to ceiling bookcase that was lined with books and more photos. The opposite wall revealed a door, but Jamie couldn't figure out what room would open off the front of the living room.

As she looked around, she noticed that the most attractive feature of the room was the exquisitely detailed woodwork. The ceiling was bordered by a deep crown molding, with a wide picture molding right underneath. Each window and door was trimmed out, as was the fireplace. "I love all of the moldings in here," she said to Ryan.

Conor gave her a big grin as he offered a slight bow. "Thank you, Jamie," he said.

Ryan explained, "Conor's a finish carpenter. After he got out of trade school he used the house as his little project. We've got every kind of molding and trim that you can imagine."

She ran her hand over the elaborate woodwork of the mantel. "You certainly do nice work, Conor."

"Don't encourage him too much," Ryan warned. "He'll pull out his pictures and monopolize you all night."

"Some people are interested in craftsmanship," he sniffed. "Jamie certainly seems to be able to recognize quality."

"My mother's into home decorating," Jamie explained. "We did a major remodel a couple of years ago and we had a lot of trim installed, so I learned a lot about your craft, Conor."

The cozy dining room held a very large oak table, rectangular in shape. It had room for ten, but only six places were set today. As Jamie finished surveying the room, she was greeted by yet another of Ryan's clones. This one looked a bit older, and while he was also well built, he didn't leave the impression of raw power waiting to burst out of his skin that his siblings had. "Oh, Brendan, when did you show up?" Ryan asked as she crossed the room to give him a big hug and a kiss on the cheek.

"I came over about a half hour ago, but I've got good clothes on and I wasn't going to let you grease monkeys talk me into ruining another pair of pants."

"Brendan, this is my friend, Jamie." Ryan began the introductions, and was forced to add another, "and this is Rory," she said as the last brother entered the room.

Well at least he's not a clone, Jamie thought. Rory was shorter than Ryan by two or three inches. His hair was also lighter, and Jamie guessed that it would be a deep red in the sunlight. His eyes were a soft green and they twinkled when he smiled. His skin was fairer than his siblings, but his features were quite similar.

"I'm pleased to meet you both," Jamie said as she shook hands with each in turn.

A voice rang out from the kitchen, "Dinner will be served in exactly one half hour. Anyone with a spot of grease won't be served."

Conor and Ryan stole guilty glances at each other. "Flip you for the shower," Ryan said. She produced a dime from her jeans, but Conor lucked out. "Please leave some hot water for me, Conor," she begged.

"What's it worth to ya?"

"Well, it's you who has the most to gain since I sit next to you at the table."

"Good point, stinky," he relented, "I'll hurry."

The voice boomed from the kitchen yet again. "Shi' vawn", the man called, "Use some manners and bring your guest in here."

"Shi' vawn?" Jamie mouthed to her friend.

Ryan looked sheepish. "It's my real name," she admitted. "I changed it when I was a kid, but my father doesn't acknowledge it."

They walked through the dining room, and turned into a very large kitchen. The room was rectangular in shape and ran about fifteen feet to a screened door at the rear. It was about ten feet in width, but the high ceilings and bright tile made it look much bigger. The kitchen wasn't what mesmerized Jamie, however. That distinction fell to the older male clone stirring a pot on the stove.

Gee, I guess they're not adopted. Martin O'Flaherty was clearly the original from whom the little O'Flaherty copies sprang. He was a good three or four inches taller than Ryan, with a bit of gray at his temples. His physique matched Brendan's, and from a distance he could have been thirty years old. But up close his face had the small lines and weathered skin that befitted a man who worked at a dangerous profession. His eyes, however, were exact copies of Ryan's, deep blue, warm and friendly.

"Da, this is my friend, Jamie."

"Ahh, Jamie," he said warmly with a more than a hint of an Irish accent. "My daughter speaks of you well and often. I'm very pleased to make your acquaintance, but I wish it'd been weeks earlier." As he said this, he shot a glare at his smirking daughter.

"If she speaks half as well of me as she does of you, Mr. O'Flaherty, then I'm a lucky woman."

"Are you certain you don't hail from the old sod?" he said with a laugh. "You seem to have kissed the Blarney Stone rather recently. But there's no Mr. O'Flaherty here, darlin'. You may call me Martin or Marty, whichever you choose."

"What do you prefer?"

"Pay attention, love," he said to Ryan, with a grin identical to the one Jamie had seen hundreds of times on her friend. "The girl has manners." He turned to Jamie and looked a bit pensive as he finally said, "I suppose I prefer Martin. It's the name my parents gave me, and I can't think of a reason to change it." This statement was also directed at an amused looking Ryan. "Another lesson you could take from this one is how to dress for dinner," he said as he regarded Jamie's outfit. She wore a forest green, cashmere, crew-neck sweater, and a pair of wide-wale, corduroy slacks in a buttery cream color. Shiny, brown, faux alligator loafers completed the outfit.

"I'll try, Da, but I don't think even Jamie could do much for my sense of style." She cocked her head in concentration. "I think Conor's out of the shower. Wanna come to my room to give me some pointers, Jamie?"

"Sure," she replied hesitantly. Even though she was very interested in seeing what was under those jeans, she knew it wasn't the wisest course of action. But she put her cautions aside and followed right on Ryan's heels. They walked back to the small entryway, turned to the left and descended a low staircase that caused Ryan to duck her head severely. It seemed to Jamie that they were in a room that would be located right behind the garages. The room was surprisingly bright, as it was partially above ground. A large, casement, double-hung window loomed over the bed and faced the small neat backyard. Jamie could see a large, black, dog peering through the window with a quizzical look on its face.

"Hi, Duffy," Ryan said as she knelt on her large bed and opened the window. "Duff, this is Jamie. She's my very good friend, and I want you to greet her gently." The dog cocked his big black head and gave her a stern expression that seemed to imply agreement. "We'll be out soon, so you go practice." She closed the window, and the dog trotted away.

"He's awfully cute, Ryan," Jamie said. "What kind of dog is he?"

"He's half black lab and half standard poodle. I got him from a client three years ago. Best tip I ever got."

Ryan rose from the bed and crossed the room to a well-built set of drawers and doors that lined an entire wall of her room. She began to open the doors to look at her wardrobe. Jamie walked up next to her and marveled at the way everything was organized. Each drawer was labeled neatly. Long-sleeved T-shirts, short-sleeved T-shirts, sleeveless T-shirts, sweats, sweatshirts, socks and underwear.

"Got enough T-shirts?" Jamie asked, opening a drawer to confirm that indeed the shirts stored inside didn't have sleeves.

"Hey, I'm a dyke," she said defensively. "T-shirts are part of the uniform."

"Do you need help picking out an outfit, Shivawn?" Jamie asked innocently.

"Don't start," she warned with a smile.

"God, Ryan, I think I know you so well, but I don't even know your real name."

"I haven't used that name since I was seven," Ryan said. "Only Da and my grandparents use it. The boys even stopped when I beat them up. And you do know me, Jamie," she said sincerely. "You know me very well. I wouldn't have invited you here otherwise."

Jamie remembered that Ryan's mother had died when she was seven. Thinking there might be a connection, she chose not to pursue the matter. "I'm sure I know all the important parts," she said. "Besides, a touch of mystery becomes you."

Ryan laughed and resumed her task. "My big problem is that I don't have any nice pants. Every time I decide to buy something nice, I find some new bike pants or a new warm-up suit that I know I'll wear ten times more often, and I buy that instead."

She pulled out a perfectly acceptable pair of navy blue, wool slacks and a cream-colored, cable knit sweater. She laid her selections out on the bed and sat down to unlace her boots. Jamie chickened out as she considered watching her undress. "I think I'll offer to help your father while you get ready."

"He won't let you help, but he'll appreciate the offer."

As she turned to leave she remembered something that had puzzled her. "Why do you call him Da?"

"It's the Irish equivalent of Dad. Many kids call their parents Ma and Da rather than Mom and Dad."

"It's kind of cute," Jamie said, quickly turning and scuttling away when Ryan started to unbutton her jeans.

As Ryan predicted, Jamie's offer to help was rebuffed by Martin. "You go play with the children," he said, directing her to the now-open door off the living room. The relatively big bedroom was filled by a king-sized bed, a well-worn, upholstered chair and three men lounging in various positions as they watched the Forty-niners battle the St. Louis Rams.

Refusing the offer of a chair, Jamie sat on the floor and quickly joined in the discussion of the Niners' lack of a good tight end. Ryan joined them, freshly scrubbed and shockingly beautiful to Jamie's eyes. Ryan looked older and more sophisticated in her dress up clothes, and when she sat next to Jamie the smaller woman smiled when she smelled the clean, fragrant aroma of her soap.

Ryan quietly watched a challenge that Conor had obviously just made with Jamie. They were each putting five dollars up, and Rory was acting as judge. Jamie scrunched her face up, deep in thought. "Well, there has to be an 'S', she said, "and an 'H'?"

"Two for two!" said Rory.

"How about an 'A'?"

"Three for three!"

"A 'W'?"

"Nope, one wrong," he replied.

"S-I-O-B-H-A-N," Ryan enunciated, returning the money to the players.

"No fair, Ryan," said Conor, perturbed.

"I don't like people to play games with the spelling of my name. You know I'm sensitive about it," she said, looking at the floor with a wounded expression.

"I'm sorry, Ryan." Conor rose from the bed and squatted down to give her a kiss on the cheek. "I wouldn't have done it if I knew it'd bother you."

"Well," she admitted, "it doesn't bother me much, but it did get you off the bed and into my evil hands." She laughed gleefully, and tickled his sides unmercifully. He quickly lost his ability to remain upright, but she stuck right with him, the pair rolling around on the floor.

"Please, please, no more, I can't take it," he pleaded as he giggled hysterically. "You win, you win!"

She stopped the torture, and helped him sit up. "I always win," she said proudly. "I'm the little sister."

"Just our luck, boys," Conor said, addressing his laughing brothers. "We get a little sister who can kick all of our butts."

The football game began again just as Martin called them to dinner. Brendan rose and hit the record button on the VCR, and they all walked into the dining room without a word of complaint.

Jamie couldn't remember ever having a better time at the dinner table. Meals at her home were always pleasant enough, but there was never much spark. The O'Flaherty clan however, spent their mealtimes in a boisterous game of one-upmanship. They tried to top each other by telling funny stories and jokes and both were accompanied by constant teasing. Jamie was pleased that they seemed to welcome her into the group seamlessly. They teased her unmercifully but gently, and she noticed that they did the same to each other.

By the end of the meal Jamie had formed some tentative impressions of each of the O'Flaherty men. Martin was clearly in charge. All of the children seemed to respect and admire him, but she didn't detect even a glimmer of fear in their interactions. When he told one of them to stop a tease that was becoming too sharp, he or she did so immediately. He had quite a flair for storytelling, and Jamie noticed that each of the kids listened to him raptly even though she imagined they had heard his stories many times. The number of repetitions was obvious when he finished one and all of the children complained that he had changed the ending. "How else can I keep the lot of you on your toes?" he explained with a laugh.

Brendan was the most serious of the group. He was a lawyer with a small public interest law firm, working to secure the rights of people with disabilities. The other boys and Ryan looked to him as a bit of an arbiter also. He was quite adept at keeping the rest of them in line, with his wit and easy laughter, but his teasing was very gentle and sweet.

Conor was clearly the troublemaker of the boys. He seemed to love to get under everyone else's skin. Jamie could just imagine the practical jokes he must play on his siblings. She wasn't surprised when Martin told of the number of times he had to leave work to bail young Conor out of the principal's office.

Conor worked as a carpenter, a trade that he loved and was obviously very good at. He had built Ryan's wall-to-wall closet and Martin's bookcase, and the work was immaculate. He worked for a firm that did renovation work in the city, and he took obvious pride in talking about the historically accurate work his firm did on the city's many Victorian homes.

Rory was very boyish and shy. He was a musician, and played in a band that often performed at various pubs and clubs in the city. Ryan explained that his group primarily played traditional Irish music. Jamie wasn't sure what that meant, but she hoped to find out. He traveled quite a bit when his band toured with bigger name acts, but he was at home for several months this winter, playing around the city. He'd occasionally lapse into a soft Irish brogue that one of the others would call him on. Ryan explained that he spent most of the summer in Ireland every year, playing all over the country, and that the accent sometimes came home with him. Ryan seemed particularly fond of Rory, and she boasted to Jamie about his considerable talents as a musician. He blushed and shook his head at the compliments, but it was clear that he appreciated them.

When dinner was over, Jamie was amazed at the next development. With nary a word from Martin, or to each other, each child got up and began to perform a particular task.

Brendan went into the kitchen, rolled up his sleeves and put on an apron. He began to run water in the big double sink as he cleared off the surrounding counters. Conor began to clear the table in a quick, efficient manner. Rory joined Brendan and prepared to dry the dishes. Ryan was in charge of removing and folding the linen tablecloth and napkins. Jamie offered to help, but Ryan refused her offer saying, "Once we get going, you could get hurt if you tried to step in."

Conor moved to Rory's right and began to place each washed and dried item in its' proper home. Ryan grabbed a broom and began to sweep the entire dining room floor. She had to shoo Martin and Jamie away from the table in order to place the chairs upside down by their seats on the wooden surface. Jamie moved to the doorway of the kitchen to watch the precision event unfold.

Brendan was finished washing by now, and he moved to wash each counter in the kitchen with a mild bleach solution that he had prepared in the sink. Rory and Conor finished up and moved back into the dining room to set the table for the next meal. They used a pretty everyday tablecloth and some ironstone dishes, setting the table for five. Brendan cleaned the tops and fronts of all of the appliances while Ryan swept the kitchen. After she had finished, she got out a mop and bucket and mopped the entire room. She backed out of the room to the outside landing and disappeared, reemerging a few minutes later, via the front door, accompanied by Duffy.

Duffy tried his best, but gentle wasn't the term for his initial greeting. He placed his big, black paws on her waist and whimpered until she lowered her face enough to be thoroughly licked. "I guess I should have asked if you like dogs," Ryan drawled.

"Lucky for you, I love them," Jamie said. "We never had one, but my grandfather had an adorable longhaired Chihuahua when I was little. I used to beg to go see him."

"Why couldn't you have a dog?" Ryan asked.

Jamie looked thoughtful. "I'm not sure. It was one of those 'Don't even bother to ask' things."

"I got that reaction when I asked for a chimpanzee," Ryan said, chuckling.

"You were a chimpanzee, sweetheart," Martin deadpanned. "I just didn't want two."

Ryan smiled at her father, then sat down on a love seat. Duffy climbed right up next to her and dropped his head in her lap. "Duffy, we've got company," she reminded him. "You know there are only enough seats for the humans."

He looked up at her with plaintive, sad eyes, begging for a reprieve. He was rescued by Brendan, who reminded everyone that the game was probably over. When the door to the bedroom opened Duffy bounded off the couch and headed right for the middle of the bed. Brendan checked the TV to make sure the game was over, and when everyone else was assured they wouldn't inadvertently hear the score, they all entered the room.

Jamie was surprised to see Ryan, Duffy, Conor and Rory all fit on the bed. Ryan had dashed downstairs to put on a pair of jeans and a navy blue hooded "Cal" sweatshirt, and Duffy cuddled next to her from her horizontal position at the foot of the bed. Conor and Rory each sat against the headboard, easily able to see over Ryan and Duffy's dark heads. Brendan brought in a dining room chair for himself after Jamie refused his offer to bring one for her. She sat on the floor at the foot of the bed, close to Ryan's head. Martin sat in his well-used, upholstered chair and acted as though he were reading the newspaper.

The game was a close one, way too close for the assembled Niners' fans. Everyone complained and cajoled the team to improve their execution. Every mouth however, dropped open in shock when Jamie shouted in frustration, "Oh, please! My grandmother could have read that blitzing linebacker. Hit the slot! Hit the slot!" She slapped her thighs in frustration, mumbling. "How can you make it to this level and not know to dump it off when you read a blitz?"

After a moment's pause, she realized that all eyes were on her. "I watch a lot of football," she admitted with a small blush.

"How much is a lot?" Ryan inquired. "Do you hang out in sports bars down in Palo Alto?"

"No," she said, laughing. "But I've gone to every Stanford home game since I was born, and we go to almost every Niners' game."

"You've got tickets?" Conor and Rory shouted at once.

"Yeah, my father's firm has tickets."

"What's your father's firm?" asked Brendan.

"Morris, Foster," she said, hoping Brendan didn't have an aversion to the large, corporate firm.

"Oh," was all he said.

No one else seemed interested in talking about law firms after the quarterback threw a perfect spiral to the young running back to cap a beautiful, game-ending, forty-five yard scoring drive.

They chatted about the game for a few more minutes, until Brendan excused himself to go home and get caught up on some work. Ryan caught Jamie's eye and indicated that she wanted to go downstairs. Jamie got up and followed her out the door and down the stairs.

"So, what do you think?" Ryan asked, as she flopped down on her big bed. Jamie sat on Ryan's desk chair, pulling it next to the bed and putting her stocking feet up on the comforter.

"About what?" she asked innocently.

"You know what—what did you think of my family?"

Jamie gave her a big smile as she admitted, "I don't remember when I've met a nicer group of people."

"You must not get out much," Ryan drawled, but she was obviously pleased by the compliment.

"I get out plenty, Ryan, and believe me, you're one lucky woman. Your brothers clearly adore you, and your father's face lights up every time he looks at you."

Ryan gazed at her in contemplative silence for a few minutes. "I really do know how lucky I am," she said softly. "I spent a couple of years feeling sorry for myself during puberty. I missed my mother so much, and it was hard going through that with a bunch of clueless men. But once I got older and saw how few people share the love we have for each other ..." she let out a sigh, "I thank God every day for all that I have".

"Do you really?" Jamie asked, interested in this unexplored facet to her friend. "You've never talked about your beliefs. Are you religious?"

"No, I wouldn't say so, but I'm pretty spiritual." She pointed to a corner of her room. A board was elevated on a few bricks, and draped with a colorful cloth. It was an extremely simple altar, holding a bible, a few other books and a golden cross. A square pillow lay on the floor, and Ryan said, "I sit down and spend a few minutes meditating and praying every morning and most nights. Unless I fall asleep while I'm studying," she adding, smiling. "How about you?"

"I pray, too," Jamie said. "But I'm also pretty religious."

"What's your religion?" Ryan asked.

"I'm an Episcopalian."

"Rebel," Ryan said, teasing her friend.

"Yeah, we were pretty wild to break away from the Catholics. But ya gotta do what ya gotta do when the Pope won't let you remarry."

"I've always wondered why the king didn't name it Henryism," Ryan said. "When you start your own sect you should be able to name it after yourself."

"Thank God," Jamie laughed. "I wouldn't want to be a Henryist. That sounds too goofy."

"I'm not very religious now, but I was when I was young," Ryan said. She looked thoughtful for a moment, then said, "I wanna tell you something that I've only told Da." She locked her clear eyes on Jamie, obviously waiting for permission.

Jamie returned her look and gave her an encouraging smile, "Okay."

Ryan cleared her throat nervously as she began. "I told you my mother died when I was seven. I was just starting first grade when it happened, and we were beginning to receive religious instruction. The nuns told us about letting Jesus into our hearts and all of the standard religious stuff they think seven-year-olds can comprehend. But what struck me the most was when they talked about the Virgin Mary. Sister Kevin explained that we could talk to Jesus directly, but we could also get a message to him through his mother. She said that Mary would always watch over us just like our own mothers would." Ryan looked down at her folded hands and wiped a tear from her eye. Jamie took this opportunity to get up and sit down right next to her, reassuring her by her presence.

"I figured that since my mother was already with God, I didn't have to go through the Virgin Mary. I had an insider to listen to my prayers and direct them to the proper party." She laughed at the memory of her childish self. "So from then on I prayed to my mother instead of God or Jesus. I knew that no one would ever care more for me than she did, and I knew she'd always be there to watch over me. I still do that every night," she admitted. Her voice caught, and the tears began to flow in earnest. Jamie scooted even closer and wrapped her arms tightly around Ryan's shaking shoulders.

"Shhh, shhh," Jamie cooed into her ear as she rocked her gently and caressed her head.

They sat like that for a few long minutes, Ryan seemingly at ease revealing herself so totally, Jamie touched beyond words at the trust that Ryan showed by her actions. After a bit Ryan leaned away to grope for a box of Kleenex on her bedside table. She took several for herself and wiped her eyes and blew her nose, then watched as Jamie did the same.

"Does it always upset you to talk about her, Ryan?"

"No, not with you or my family," Ryan replied. "I miss her more than I can express, but she loved me so well that I can still feel her love. Of course, I'd give anything to have her back, but I had her so totally when she was alive, that I'm forever grateful for the short time we had together. I really love talking about her with people who understand what she means to me. It makes her come alive for me again."

Jamie was pleased at this revelation of Ryan's feelings for their friendship. She leaned over and gently kissed both of her friend's moist, pink cheeks. "I'm sure she'd be proud of the woman that you've become."

Ryan looked at her with the most adorable grin that Jamie had ever seen on a human being. Her eyes were hooded, and she looked just a bit embarrassed as she said, "Thanks. That means a lot, coming from you."

After they sat in companionable silence for a few more moments, Jamie got up from the bed and walked around the room, examining it closely. The room looked very much like its owner. Clean, neat, organized and fairly utilitarian, but with a little color here and there. A large built-in bookshelf covered the wall opposite the closet and it was filled with science texts, magazines, awards, trophies for various sports and photos. Jamie was struck by one such photo, and after staring at it for a few moments she turned back to Ryan with tears in her eyes again. "You knew, didn't you?" she inquired. Ryan rose and came to stand next to her. She put an arm around Jamie's shoulders and looked at the very familiar picture.

The photo in the simple frame showed a very ill woman holding a small, melancholy child. Ryan's big blue eyes stared up at the camera and revealed all of her fears. The woman, whom Jamie guessed was quite beautiful before her illness ravaged her, also stared directly into the lens. She had a stoic, calm look in her green eyes and it was clear that she still possessed a fiery spirit. Little Ryan was holding on to her tightly, her small arms wrapped around the woman's neck. Ryan's head was resting on a bony shoulder, and a painfully thin hand held the back of her small head.

"Yeah, I knew how sick she was. This was my seventh birthday," she said wistfully. "I didn't understand what death was, but I knew that she was going to leave soon—and I knew she wasn't coming back. She died about a month after this picture was taken."

"Oh, Ryan, I'm so sorry you had to feel all of that pain," Jamie said as she turned and was enveloped by Ryan's strong arms.

"Everybody feels pain like that if they really love someone," Ryan whispered. "No one gets out of here alive, you know."

"I know, but you were such a baby. Look at that precious little face," she lamented as she looked at the photo again.

"I'm not saying that I didn't have a tough time. I know I did. It was incredibly hard for a little girl not to have her mother. There were times that I felt so lost I didn't think I could survive. The pain was just so great. But I got through it and it made me stronger and it deepened the connection that I have with my brothers and my father. That's what I'm most grateful for. Death tears many families apart, but it made ours stronger."

"You don't have to answer this if you don't want to," Jamie said as she pulled away from their embrace, "but why did you change your name?"

"Well, it was because of my mother, as you've probably guessed. She loved the name Siobhán, and Da said she was ready with the name for each of the three boys. I liked it too, mainly because it was different. I got through first grade okay because everybody was just getting used to each other, and having an odd name was hardly noticed. But when I came back to school after my mother died, a little boy started making fun of my name. We were just learning to spell using phonics, and as you found out today, that's one name where phonics doesn't apply. The other kids kind of picked up on his teasing, and I just flipped out. It was probably too soon for me to be back at school, but there I was, and I had kind of an 'episode.' In retrospect, it must have been a panic attack. But from that day forward, every time a person outside of my family called me Siobhán I flipped out and got hysterical. Nobody knew what to do with me. It was only a couple of weeks after my mother died, and everybody in the family had their own issues they were trying to deal with. Luckily, Sister Kevin sat me down and asked me what I'd rather be called. Most of my ideas were unacceptable. I was particularly fond of Tigger as I recall," she said with a gentle laugh.

Jamie let out a little laugh of her own as she continued to look at the picture.

"Finally, and with a lot of prompting from Sister Kevin, we settled on Ryan. It was my middle name and my mother's maiden name, and Sister Kevin pointed out how that would keep her with me every time someone spoke my name. That was just about the only time that Da just wasn't able to support me," she admitted sadly. "He was really invested in the name since my mother had loved it so. But he didn't put up too much of a fuss after Sister Kevin explained it all to him. The side benefit, of course, is that I don't have to spell Siobhán several times a day," she said with a smile.

"Wow, Sister Kevin sounds like a neat lady."

"Yeah, she really was. I lost touch with her when her order left our parish, but I still think of her often."

"I do have one more question," Jamie finally said. "That balletic performance of cleaning the kitchen was something to behold. How did that come about?"

"That's another effect of my mother's illness. When she was too ill to cook or do housework we were all assigned jobs. I was so little that I had to do the jobs closest to the floor. Brendan helped me with the moping for years, but I think it was important that they made me feel a part of it," she smiled at the memory. "After my mother died, we just kept to the same tasks. Da transferred from active fire fighting and became a cook. He did it mostly because he just wasn't willing to risk his life anymore. We couldn't afford to lose him, too. He became a good cook and we just drifted into him doing all the cooking and us doing all the cleaning. It's a little militaristic, but that's how a firehouse is run."

Jamie spent a few more minutes looking at the photos placed all over the room. She found one of Ryan's mother when she was about Ryan's age. "Wow, she was a great looking woman."

Ryan grasped the picture in her hand and looked at it for a few moments. "Yeah, she was," she said softly. "I used to wish I looked more like her. She was small and delicate, fair-skinned, with auburn hair and vivid green eyes. She had a lovely, soprano singing voice and the gentlest touch you could imagine. When I was going through puberty I felt so big and awkward that I wished I had inherited her bone structure. But it all worked out in the end," she admitted.

"Yeah," Jamie agreed with a chuckle. "I don't think you'd get much sympathy complaining about your looks, Ms. O'Flaherty."

Ryan blushed deeply as she changed the subject quickly. "Let's go see what the boys are doing." They returned to the second floor, and Conor came out of the bedroom and asked with a hopeful grin, "Jamie, Ryan said you've a Boxster. Could I take a look at it?"

"Sure, Conor, you can drive it if you want."

"Can I really?" he asked. "I've never driven a Porsche. Cars are kind of my passion, but I have to drive a truck for work."

"Here's the keys," she replied, tossing them to him.

"Aren't you gonna go with me?"

"I will if you want me to, but it's okay if you want to go alone."

He gave her a boyish grin, showing even, white teeth. "I don't want to hurt anything. You can show me where all the buttons are."

As they walked to the stairs, Ryan grabbed Jamie's arm and whispered, "Be careful. He thinks he's God's gift to women."

Jamie wrinkled up her nose and whispered back, "And you don't?"

Conor wore a look of childlike exuberance as they walked down the street to the waiting Porsche. "Thanks a lot for letting me do this. I keep threatening to dress up and go to the Porsche dealer, acting like I'm interested in buying, but everyone tells me they keep a tight leash on you."

"I think everyone's right," Jamie said, laughing. "But you can go wild tonight. If your love of cars is anything like your sister's, it'd be a crime to deprive you of a drive."

"I think I've got the car bug more than Ryan does," he said. "But she's got the motorcycle bug a lot worse than I do. We used to drive Da crazy. We were always in the garage working on some engine. I got my license when she was only twelve, and from that time on you couldn't keep the grease off of her."

"So she gets it from you?"

"I guess she does. Brendan and Rory don't care much about cars, and Da just sees them as transportation. I got my license at a time when Ryan idolized me a little, and I think she acted interested to be able to spend more time with me."

"That's so cute," Jamie laughed. "But didn't it bother you to have your little sister hanging around all the time?"

He looked at her quizzically as he opened the driver door. "Why would it bother me? You know Ryan. She was always pretty much like she is now. She never was a pest. She picked things up really quickly and was always eager to do the grunt work. She had a lot of patience for a little kid, and her small hands fit into a lot of spots that mine wouldn't."

Jamie was charmed by this open expression of affection. "You all seem so close, Conor. It's really nice."

"Yeah, we are. I guess we're lucky that way, huh?"

He was now firmly ensconced in the driver's seat, carefully noting all of the gauges and switches. He adjusted the side view mirrors, and brought the engine to life. "Oh, this is sweet", he said as he closed his eyes and let a satisfied smile cross his lips.

"That's exactly how Ryan looked when she turned the car on!"

He looked at her with a leer. "I bet she didn't punch it like this!" He hit the accelerator hard, and they flew away from the curb, leaving a little bit of rubber to commemorate their journey.

Conor drove much faster than Jamie thought prudent, but the streets of Noe Valley were deserted on this early Sunday evening, so she allowed him to conduct his test drive as he chose. She also noticed that he seemed to get great satisfaction from making her squeal as they crested a rise in a hill. I bet that's not the only way he likes to make women squeal.

"Can I drop the top?" he asked after they reached a more congested neighborhood.

"Sure, as long as you keep it under forty or so. I'll freeze if you go as fast as you have been."

"Scout's honor," he promised, as he raised three fingers in pledge.

They glided down Market for a while, Conor keeping his promise about the speed. They had crossed nearly the entire city when he noticed that Jamie looked cold. "How about a hot drink? There's a Starbucks right up ahead."

"I'd love a latte, but we'll never find a place to park."

He pulled into a bus stop and said, "Here's $20. Go on in and order me a latte, too. I'll wait here and put the top back up."

"Will you call Ryan and tell her we'll be gone for a while? I don't want her to worry."

"Sure," he said, giving her his friendliest smile.

Jamie hopped out and he dialed his home. Ryan answered on the first ring. "Hi, Sis, it's me."

"Where are you?" she said crossly. "You've been gone forever."

"You sound a bit possessive, Ryan. I thought this one was on my team." He laughed, irritating Ryan all the more.

"She's on your team, but she's somebody else's starting pitcher—so keep your mitts off her."

"I have no intention of touching her … unless she wants me to, of course. We're stopping for coffee to warm up. We'll be home soon. Don't wait up if you get tired. I'll make sure she's well taken care of."

"Conor, if you harm one hair on her head I'll kick your butt all the way across town."

"How can I hurt her getting a cup of coffee?" he asked innocently.

"Just bring her back in one piece—and still engaged!" The phone was slammed down, making him flinch.

"Gotcha!" he crowed as he shut the phone off.

The car a few spaces behind him left, so Conor threw the car into reverse and claimed the spot before anyone else could. He went inside and found Jamie retrieving their coffees. "Hi," he said. "I found a parking spot, so I thought we could sit down and warm up."

"Okay," she said. "Did you call Ryan?"

"Yep. She's cool." He held a chair out for his guest, then slid into another. "So, Jamie," he said as he gazed at her with those intent blue eyes, "tell me about yourself."

"What would you like to know?" she inquired, as she tried to avoid his penetrating gaze.

"Well, you know all about my family, tell me about yours."

"I'm an only child. We live down in Hillsborough. My dad's an attorney, and my mom stays at home. We don't have a dog. There—now we're even," she said, giving him a wink.

"Gee, could you be more succinct? You were rambling so much I think I missed something."

"I'm just teasing you. What do you really want to know?"

"Oh, the usual. What do you do for fun?"

"When I'm alone or with my fiancé?" she asked, batting her eyes innocently.

He gave her a charming smile as he drawled, "Oh yeah, Ryan mentioned something about a boyfriend. Isn't he getting out of San Quentin soon?"

"Something like that. He's graduating from Stanford law school this year."

"Right. I knew it had something to do with law … or prison," he added as he looked confused.

"His name's Jack, and we're getting married a year from June."

"How old are you?" He made a face, then said, "I don't mean to be rude, but you don't look old enough to get married."

"I'm twenty. I'll be twenty-two when we get married."

"Damn! I'm twenty-seven and I can hardly decide what to have for lunch. There are so many choices on the menu and they all look so good," he drawled, giving her a look that skittered up and down her body.

"Yeah, but when you find that perfect, one of a kind sandwich, you'd better order it before someone else does."

"With my luck, there'd be some hidden ingredient that I was allergic to," he said, laughing.

"Well, I'm really happy with what I've ordered. I'm not looking at the menu."

"If you ever get hungry for a little Irish fare," he said with a heavy brogue, "don't forget me."

"Between you and your sister, no woman in San Francisco is safe," she said as she laughed heartily.

"You're telling me," he agreed, his predatory smile replaced with a friendly one. "I'm just glad she's a lesbian. If she were a guy, there wouldn't be any straight women left unsullied."

"Huh. I never thought of it that way, but she'd be a player if she were a man, too." She laughed at the image of a male Ryan, then turned thoughtful. "Does her, uhm, sexual orientation bother you, Conor?"

"No, not a bit."

"Did it ever?"

He thought about her question for a moment, then said, "She and I spent a lot of time together, Jamie, and it was obvious from very early on that she was never gonna be swooning over guys. She never did any of that teenaged girl stuff. It actually pissed her off when her friends would cancel plans because they had dates. I mean, Ryan never had a crush on a guy, and it's not like she wasn't good-looking or anything," he added.

"Did you ever think she just wasn't sexually mature?"

"Well, I might have," he said, laughing again. "But she was always very, very willing to hang around when I had a girl over. A few times I caught her looking at my girlfriends like they were big, juicy steaks, and she was a hungry wolf."

Jamie threw her head back and laughed. "Oh, Conor, I can just see it!"

"The only problem I had was that when she was thirteen or fourteen I had eighteen-year-old friends who wanted to go out with her! Rory had to stop bringing guys over because they all wanted to hang around until Ryan came home. She finally told us she was gay when she was seventeen, and we were all like, 'What took you so long?'" He laughed at the memory. "I'm sure it helps that we live around a lot of gay people and we had a gay cousin that we all loved, so it never seemed like a big deal."

"I'm sure my family wouldn't be as accepting as yours was," she said, shaking her head.

He leaned over a little bit, and his blue eyes bore into her. "Well, lucky for you, you'll never have to find out, will you?"

She knew her mouth was hanging open, so she tried to look outraged. She slapped Conor on the shoulder and said, "You are such a devil!"

He didn't reply. He just gave her a grin that she couldn't quite read, and took a sip of his coffee.

The next day Ryan's head was swimming from the plethora of questions that Jamie threw at her. They were sitting outside having their usual juice break. It was a clear sunny day, in keeping with the usual Bay Area phenomena of the best weather of the year being in the fall. Ryan was wearing a black warm up suit made of a fabric that looked like washable silk, and a bright white T-shirt peeked out from beneath the jacket. Ryan looked carefully at Jamie as she spoke. She was wearing a sleeveless, golden yellow sweater that just covered the belt of her green khaki pants. A matching cardigan was loosely tied around her shoulders. Ryan thought about how much she liked Jamie's style. *She always wears something that compliments her. Like that sweater. It's just a shade or two darker than her hair. I wonder who taught her how to dress? Probably her mother, unless her mother hired someone to do that!*

"So what instruments does Rory play?" Jamie persisted, asking her fiftieth question of the morning.

"Keyboards and accordion mainly, but he can play a lot of instruments in a pinch."

"Do the rest of you play anything?"

"Yes," Ryan answered patiently. "We can all play something. And the answer to your next question is that I play clarinet, flute and the Irish whistle. I can muddle along on keyboards, and I was rabidly interested in the guitar for a few years, but my ardor has cooled recently."

"I can just see you playing the guitar," Jamie said, smiling at her friend. "You probably wanted to be a rock star and have women throwing themselves at you."

"Hey! Stay out of my fantasy life!" Ryan said, giving her a mock scowl.

Jamie wrinkled up her nose, a gesture Ryan found adorable. "Tell me about the kind of music Rory's band plays. I don't know much about Irish music."

"I can see there's only one way to satisfy your curiosity," Ryan said, "The next time he plays locally, I'll take you to hear him. Then all of your questions will be answered."

On Thursday night, Jamie was riding her bike home after a long session at the library. It was about nine o'clock, and the wafting scent from her favorite coffee bar called to her. She locked up her bike and walked in to the warm space. As she stood at the counter waiting for her latte, she spied Ryan sitting in the corner, her head bent in conversation with a young woman. A very young woman. A very, *very* young woman. *Boy, she doesn't fit the mold.* But as Jamie thought about it, she realized that the only common thing about the women she'd seen Ryan with was the lack of a Y chromosome. This woman had a shaved head and a riot of piercings on her ears and eyebrows. *I bet she's got some that are hidden, too.* That bet was quickly resolved when the woman got up to go to the restroom. She walked right by Jamie, and her thin tank top didn't hide the large rings that hung from her nipples. Jamie stared at her in shock. *She couldn't be out of high school!* She turned her gaze to Ryan who was staring at her with an amused expression on her face. Jamie marched right over to her, her pique growing with each step.

"Gee, Ryan, isn't it a school night?" she asked with sarcastic sweetness. "You don't want your date to be late for the bus."

"What do you mean?" Ryan had a look of pure innocence on her face.

"That woman doesn't look like she's even out of high school!"

"Don't be ridiculous," she said with a big grin. "Jennie isn't in high school."

"Well, you could have fooled me—" she began, but was cut off by the woman's return.

"Hey, Jen. My friend Jamie thought you were in high school."

Jennie laughed too, and mumbled, "I wish."

"Jennie's in grade school," Ryan explained with a virtuous tone that matched Jamie's earlier one. "She just turned thirteen."

Jamie felt as though her head would burst. She knew her face was bright red, and she felt completely unable to form a word or a thought.

Ryan turned to Jennie, "You don't mind if I tell my friend about how we know each other, do you?"

"Nope," Jennie replied easily as she smiled at Jamie.

"I work with Jennie though a group called Gay Teens in Crisis. She's currently living in a group home here in Berkeley. She's kind of my little sister," she added, as Jennie beamed at her.

Jamie felt all of the color drain out of her face. She struggled to pull out a chair and sit down before she fell down. As soon as she looked up at Ryan's sweet smile, she felt her color rise again, this time in shame.

"Did you order something, Jamie?" Jennie asked looking at the empty space in front of Jamie.

"Uh-huh, a latte," she mumbled.

"I'll get it for you. Then I gotta take off. Got a nine-thirty curfew." She got up, leaving the two women alone.

Jamie stared at Ryan who looked back at her placidly. They sat that way until Jennie returned. She kissed Ryan on the cheek, then picked up her book bag and her bike helmet. "Put it on," Ryan ordered.

"It's so rank! Ruins my image."

"Well, I happen to like your brain." Ryan stood and plunked the helmet on the stubbly head, "and since you don't even have hair to cushion it, you've gotta wear this."

"Okay, you win." Jennie gave Ryan a quick hug. "Good to meet you, Jamie," she said over her shoulder, as she hiked up her huge khaki pants and left the shop.

Jamie dropped her head to the table with an audible thunk. "I am such a jerk!" she moaned into the wood.

"It's okay," Ryan replied as she patted her back. "It's not like it's outside of the realm of possibility that I'd be with a younger woman. Although thirteen is a little young, even for me. I like my women to at least be able to go to a PG-13 movie with me."

"I am such a jerk!" Jamie repeated, still not lifting her head from the table.

"You're no jerk! I was taunting you a little. I made it worse, and I'm sorry." After a moment she added, "As long as you've got your head down there, can I ask you something?"

"Sure," Jamie mumbled from her new tabletop home.

"Were you at the bookstore last Wednesday night?"

"Oh, God," she moaned, and sunk even lower in her chair. "Is there no end to my humiliation?"

"What did you see?" Ryan asked gently as she again placed her hand on Jamie's back and gave it a reassuring scratch.

"I saw you … uhm … talking to someone," she said as she lifted her head, hoping that Ryan didn't know what she had seen. "How did you know I was there?"

"I saw your car when I went outside. I figured you were there, but I was kind of a ... occupied," she said, blushing. Now Jamie felt much better. She was beginning to get her normal color back, and had risen to sit upright in her chair. "Plus, Babs told me she thought she saw you."

As Jamie's color rose, her body sunk until she was again face down on the table. "Shoot me now, please," she moaned. "What did she tell you?"

"She was under the impression that we'd been ... dating. And she said that you looked kind of upset." Ryan paused a bit. "I wasn't going to say anything, but I thought that might be why seeing me with Jennie bothered you."

"Yeah, that's probably true," she said with her muffled voice.

"Why didn't you say something? I hate to think that I upset you. Tell me what happened?" she said gently as she lifted Jamie's head with both hands.

Jamie lifted her head the entire way and sat up straight. "I had to pick up a book for that report we were doing. I went and was just leaving when I saw you. It was like watching a train wreck!"

"Uhm ... I don't think I get the analogy."

"You know, when something happens that you know you shouldn't see, but you can't help it. I saw you getting kind of frisky, and Babs came up behind me. I felt like I'd been caught doing something wrong. She jumped to all sorts of conclusions, but I was too embarrassed to set her straight. I just stood there unable to explain a darn thing."

"Go on," Ryan reassured her.

"Well, I was mortified to have her make those assumptions, and to have been caught staring at you, so I went out to my car, and you were uhm ... occupied, right in front of me. I felt like I was stuck there, because I certainly wasn't going to interrupt you at that point," she blushed fiercely as she shook her head. "But you got in her car, and I was able to leave."

"So ... does it bother you to see me with a woman?"

"No, I don't think so. I saw you with Chitra from class that time, and it didn't bother me at all."

"That's true," she mused. "But you didn't know me very well then. Do you think that made a difference?"

"That might be part of it," she admitted. "But I think the bigger issue this time was that you didn't know you were being watched. I felt like voyeur," she confessed. "I'm really sorry I saw you and that I didn't turn away immediately."

"And I'm sorry that I made you uncomfortable. Robin lives at home, too, so we don't have anywhere to go to be alone. I don't usually let myself get carried away like that in public, but it's been kind of a while, and I just lost my head. Like I said at the gym, I was feeling twitchy," she said, looking embarrassed.

"Not having any privacy must be difficult for you."

Ryan grinned broadly, "You don't know what difficult is until you try to do it in the back seat of a Corolla when you're over six feet tall."

"Well, I hope it all worked out in the end."

"Yeah, we reached our destination," she said, "but my neck's still stiff." She rubbed the part in question. "I've got to start inquiring about living arrangements before I accept dates."

Jamie smiled as she forced herself not to consider exactly how that neck got so stiff.

After class on Friday, Ryan was bubbling with energy. She had recently decided that she no longer needed to work the early shift at the gym since Jamie had gotten her fifteen hours of private training a week, and that was more than enough to support her. The gym was sorry to see her cut back, but they were happy with the new members she'd brought in, so they felt they had gotten a good deal.

Now her first appointment was her eight o'clock class. This allowed her to sleep an extra two and a half hours, or even go out at night, something that hadn't been possible for years. She was using some of her excess energy rapping out a tune on a concrete table, amusing her break partner. "You know Jamie, I've got a quality of life that I didn't ever imagine I could have. I'm more rested than I've been in years."

Jamie regarded her friend carefully. Ryan did look better than she'd ever seen her. *Not that she ever looked truly bad,* she thought with a laugh. But she now looked completely relaxed, and was childlike and very playful the vast majority of the time. The little lines of tension that sometimes nestled between her eyebrows were completely gone, and Jamie also noticed that Ryan's chronic habit of rubbing her eyes had almost stopped.

"Did you hear Linda say that we didn't have class on Monday?" she asked, in an apparent non sequitur.

"I've never missed hearing a teacher canceling a class," Ryan said. "I could sleep 'til noon if I wanted to. I'm all caught up on my lab work, so I'm free until that afternoon."

"I have a little idea about how to occupy your morning, if you're up to getting your butt kicked."

"I guess that depends on who's doing the kicking."

"How about me?"

"How are you planning on kicking my butt? What's your weapon of choice?"

"Golf clubs," Jamie replied, a fiendish grin on her face.

"I think my butt's in big trouble," Ryan said, grimacing.

Jamie pulled up in front of her friend's home at six sharp. She was driving an enormous, claret red Range Rover. Ryan popped out of the front door looking absolutely perfect for a day on the links. She wore a navy blue turtleneck under a navy blue, emerald and white argyle cardigan. Navy blue poplin slacks covered her long legs, and her hair was in a neat braid that hung down her back. She looked at

Jamie with a quizzical grin. "Uhm, Jamie," she said across the roof of the big vehicle, "something ate your car."

"As much as I love my little car, golf clubs don't fit. My father has an apartment in the city, and he keeps this car there. He wasn't planning on using it, so here we are."

"Pretty nice spare," Ryan replied as she looked the car over thoroughly.

Jamie tossed the keys to her without a word. Ryan gave her a winning grin and trotted around to the driver's side. "You know me too well. I've got to learn to keep some secrets from you."

"I don't think you can ever learn to keep that grin off your face," she said, giving her friend a fond gaze.

Ryan looked like she belonged in the big car. The scale fit her perfectly, unlike Jamie, who looked a bit lost in it. "Where to? I hope it's far," she added, gripping the wheel with a devilish look in her eyes.

"We're going to the Olympic Club."

"The Olympic Club?" Ryan nearly shouted. "I've never been on a golf course before. They play the U.S. Open there!"

"I'm well aware of that, pal. My mother's family has belonged for generations. But don't worry your pretty little head. We'll get warmed up on the driving range, then we'll get a cart and you can caddy for me if you don't feel comfortable."

"Do I get to drive the cart?" she asked. "I've always wanted to drive one of those little things."

"Yes, you can drive the cart," she replied indulgently as she smiled at Ryan's hopeful look.

"Okay, let's go!"

As she glanced into the rear of the car, Ryan noticed only one set of clubs. "Did you bring some clubs for me?"

"Yep, those are for you. If you can play with right-handed clubs, that is. My father keeps a spare set at the apartment for guests or when he wants to play another course. He's about your height, and you're easily as strong as he is, so I thought they'd fit you."

"Well, since I've never struck a golf ball I guess I can do it equally poorly from either side, so right-handed clubs should be fine."

"Well, it's more complex than that, Ryan. Is your right hand dexterous?"

A waggling right eyebrow was her devilish response.

"Come on, silly. Be honest with me. I'm sure we can rent a set of left-handed clubs at the course if we need to."

"No, right-handed ones are fine. I'm a natural lefty, but I switch-hit when I play softball, and I can throw with either hand."

"You're quite the jock, aren't you?" She cast a sly glance at Ryan's athletic body.

"I do all right." Jamie noted the touch of smugness her friend was unable to hide.

A few minutes later, Ryan pulled up to the clubhouse as an attendant in a white shirt and pants dashed out to greet them. "Good morning Miss Evans," he greeted Jamie cheerfully. "Are you joining Mr. Evans this morning?"

"No, my friend and I are going to play alone today," Jamie replied as another attendant ran to open Ryan's door. The first young man jogged around to the trunk and lifted the gate. "Will you be having breakfast first?"

"No, but I'd like a large hot chocolate." She rubbed her hands together against the morning chill. "How about you, Ryan?"

"Sounds great. I'd love one."

"We'll be over at the range, Charlie," she said as she led Ryan into the clubhouse.

Jamie guided her friend through the ornate clubhouse, finally wending their way to the ladies locker room. She walked over to a wooden locker which bore a neat plaque labeled "J. Evans." Jamie opened the door, and Ryan watched as she removed a pair of white golf shoes. As she watched her, Ryan mused that Jamie looked particularly at home in this setting. She wore a sea-foam green turtleneck with a cream-colored, sleeveless cardigan. Her cream-colored, lightweight wool slacks were held up by a thin black belt, giving her a casual, yet elegant look. After she had tied her spikes, she pulled a navy blue, nylon anorak out of her locker and stood to leave.

"What size shoes do you wear?"

"It depends on the shoes," Ryan replied. "My gym shoes are usually eleven's, but some of my loafers are ten and a half's. Why?"

"Come with me."

A few minutes later, they walked into the opulent pro shop, where Ryan gazed around the overstocked shelves, a bit in awe. "Hi, Jason," Jamie called out.

"Morning, Miss Evans," he replied. "What can I do for you today?"

"My friend needs a couple of things. Hold up your left hand," she instructed as Ryan obediently complied.

"Hmm," Jason said. "Looks like a men's small. What color?"

Jamie replied for her. "Navy."

He handed Ryan a navy glove, which she slipped onto her left hand. "Seems perfect." She got the idea, and held up her hand for Jason's inspection.

"Looks great. What else?" Jason asked.

"A pair of Foot-Joys, size ten and a half, leather soles, this style." She lifted her own foot for him to see. This got her a wide-eyed look from Ryan, but Jamie just winked at her and said, "Trust me."

Jason brought the shoes out and Ryan sat down and removed her gym shoes. "Would you like to wear two pairs of socks, ma'am?"

Ryan looked to Jamie who again replied for her. "Yeah, can you get her a pair of white Foot Joys?"

As he left to find the proper socks, Ryan said in a whisper, "What are you doing? I can't afford this, and I certainly don't want you buying this for me."

"You can't judge if you like the game if you don't have the right equipment. Now be quiet or I'll buy you golf clubs!" she teased. Ryan closed her mouth abruptly and kept it closed. With two pairs of socks she needed the size eleven shoes, but she nodded her assent when Jason asked about her comfort.

They clomped out of the pro shop and walked in silence to the rear of the building. Exiting, they walked the short distance to the driving range where their clubs were set up neatly on bag stands. Large buckets of clean white balls stood near each set of clubs. A golf cart sat about five feet behind the clubs, and Ryan could see two large insulated mugs in the drink holders.

"So this is how the other one half of one percent lives," she observed dryly.

"Yeah. Tough life, huh?"

Ryan held her friend's gaze and said, "I don't wanna be an ingrate, but I wouldn't have accepted this invitation if I'd known you were gonna spend this much money on me."

"Why do you think I didn't tell you beforehand?" Jamie asked, tilting her head.

"I'm not teasing," Ryan said. "It really does make me uncomfortable."

"Hey," Jamie said, "I didn't mean to offend you."

"I'm not offended," Ryan said. "I'm ... well, I don't know what I am. This has never happened to me before."

Jamie sat in the cart and patted the seat next to her. "We should talk about this." Ryan gamely joined her, and met her eyes. "One day I'll have so much money that I don't think I could spend it all in my lifetime, unless I started buying military aircraft."

"But that's your money. I shouldn't benefit from being your friend."

"I wanted to come here to play today. It's much more fun for me to have you with me. You'll enjoy the day more if you have the proper shoes. You won't get a blister on your hand if you wear a glove. The membership here belongs to my father. He's happy that I brought you here. He figures that if I have a friend to play with, I'll play more. If I play more I get better. When I play well it gives him enormous pleasure. So, really, you've made my whole family happy by being my guest." Her mouth curled into a cute little grin that Ryan had no defenses against.

"Well, if it makes the whole family happy, I guess I can't turn it down," she grumbled.

"Ryan, you're the last person who'd want to be my friend because of my money. But it gives me pleasure to spend just a tiny bit of it on you. Will you let me do that once in a while?"

She took a deep breath, gazing into Jamie's eyes and found herself saying, "Yeah, I will. I promise I won't bring it up the rest of the day. I'll sink into the lap of luxury and enjoy."

"That's a girl."

She gave Ryan's shoulder a squeeze as they hopped out of the cart and walked over to their clubs. Jamie briefly explained all of the rudiments of grip, stance and swing mechanics. Ryan watched her studiously, and seemed to absorb all of the important points. Jamie picked up a three-iron and instructed, "Stand behind me and watch for a few minutes. Then go around and watch from the front."

Ryan did as she was told. She noticed that Jamie began her swing with a small downward and forward movement of her hands. The next move was a pronounced cock of her wrists, followed by a pulling of her right arm as the club moved behind her back. Her torso was fully coiled at the top of her back swing, and Ryan noted a counterbalancing tension in her legs. When she reached the apex of her swing it almost looked as though her upper body was ready to be thrust forward by her lower body. A millisecond later that was exactly what happened. Her arms paused at the top of the swing. Her left shoulder was tucked firmly under her chin, her hands were behind her head and her body was fully coiled. She exploded out of the stance by striking her left heel to the ground. Her knees shifted laterally as her hips opened toward her target. At impact it appeared that all of her momentum was taking her in the same direction the ball was traveling. The ball clicked sharply and flew into the cool air, landing a good 200 yards away. Jamie finished her swing with almost all of her weight on her firm left leg, her torso turned toward the flight of the ball, her chest pointing slightly upward, and her hands pausing high above her left shoulder.

"Wow," Ryan said, "that's a very complex move. There must be fifty different elements to that swing."

"That's the biggest problem most golfers have. The swing really is complex. I'd guess it's harder to hit a baseball because it's moving, but this is really tough to do well. That's why it annoys me when people say golf doesn't require much skill." She shrugged slightly and added, "I mean it's not as much of a sport as baseball or football, but just because you don't get tackled, doesn't mean it isn't hard."

"Well, it certainly looks hard to me. I've got no idea where to start."

"Let me get you set up right so you can see how your body should feel when you address the ball," she suggested. "Move your feet about shoulder width apart. Flex your knees a little so you feel like your weight is over your butt and on the balls of your feet." Ryan did as instructed, and Jamie watched her carefully. "Good. Now keep your back straight, but not rigid. You want a firm stance, but you also have to stay fluid—if that makes any sense."

"Sure it does," Ryan said. "Just like my batting stance when I play softball."

"Yeah, I guess that's true. Do you mind if I stand behind you to take a practice swing?"

"I don't mind a bit, but I don't think you can accomplish it," she teased. "I'm probably ten inches taller than you are."

"More like seven or eight, but that's just one thing you're wrong about. It's easier to do when you're smaller than your student." She stood so close that the toes of her shoes touched the heels of Ryan's. "Bend your knees a little more," she said. "You should almost be sitting on my lap."

"I don't get to sit on many women's laps," Ryan said, chuckling softly.

"You can only sit on mine when we're standing up," Jamie said. Her own knees touched the backs of Ryan's, and she realized that she was speaking right into her friend's pink ear. "That's much better," she said softly, feeling very intimate. *Maybe this wasn't such a good idea*, she thought when she began to lose her concentration. Ryan smelled so good that she felt herself trying to sniff her neck. Her breasts were pressed against Ryan's back, and their legs touched from their pelvises down to their knees. *Concentrate!*

She wrapped her arms around Ryan's, and loosely placed her hands atop her friend's. "Okay, just stay loose and let me move you," she said, hoping she'd be able to do it. Ryan complied with her instructions, and Jamie began the swing. "Okay, start with a good flex of your left knee … good … now here come the hands … feel your hips turn … good, now feel the stretch in your torso when we really extend at the top … excellent!" At the top of the swing they were completely entwined. Jamie felt her mouth go dry as jolts of sensation shot up and down her body everywhere that it came in direct contact with Ryan. She knew that they had been in position long enough, but she was having trouble making herself move. She took a deep breath to clear her head, but that just made matters worse when she got another good whiff of Ryan's sweet scent. She finally forced herself to move through sheer willpower. "Okay, now plant your left heel firmly and uncoil your hips," she said as she pressed her hips against Ryan's. "Here go the arms … just let them follow … good … now a big follow through … excellent!" She pulled away regretfully and said, "You're very easy to work with. Very coachable."

Ryan turned around and regarded her thoughtfully for a moment. "This really is your sport, isn't it?"

"What do you mean?"

"You just seem to understand the swing at a fundamental level. When you can explain it as well as you do, it must be something that really resonates with you."

Jamie thought about that for a moment. "I guess you're right. I feel really comfortable when I play. It makes me feel calm … like I'm in a kind of Zen state."

"I feel like that when I run. It's an altered state," she said. "But this golf swing is mighty intriguing. There are so many elements, I don't know where to start."

"My suggestion is to put one simple swing thought in your head. Imagine that marker," she said, pointing at a 100-yard marker, "is an open window in a big wall. Now imagine that you have to stand laterally to that wall and heave a heavy weight through it. Try that without holding a club."

"Okay," Ryan replied, a little doubtful. She did as she was told, and felt herself approximate Jamie's swing. "Hey, that works!"

"Don't think about the club, don't think about hitting the ball. Just concentrate on tossing that big weight," Jamie instructed. She handed Ryan a five-iron, and showed her how to sole the club. She bent over and placed a ball in front of the club. "Give it a whack."

Ryan did so, and made very acceptable contact with the little white ball. The ball shot out past the marker, and she looked up with a big grin, flashing those perfect white teeth. "That was fun!" she said gleefully. "Should I stop while I'm ahead?"

"Nope, we're gonna hit all of these babies," she said as she poked the bucket of balls with her club.

Ryan got to work, and did an admirable job of dispatching each of the little orbs. When she'd whiff one or two, Jamie stood behind her and gave her a few simple tips. After watching her for a while she commented, "You'll do a lot better if you loosen your grip on the club. Think about caressing it rather than gripping it." Ryan gave her a cute little smirk, but applied her tip and found the results to be quite successful. By the time she was finished, her sweater was off and her cheeks were flushed bright pink. She put her five-iron back in the bag and stood a few feet behind Jamie, where she spent a good deal of time just watching, finding herself very impressed with her friend's skill. She seemed very comfortable, very much in control of her body. *She's really a good little athlete.*

Jamie used all of the clubs in her bag to warm up, but she instructed Ryan to stick with the irons for the time being. "Are you ready to hit the links?" Jamie asked brightly, when she had finished her bucket.

"If you've got the nerve to play with me, I'm ready."

"My guess is you'd be beating me like a drum in six months if you played regularly," Jamie said. "I think I'd better take advantage of you while you're a neophyte."

They hopped in the cart, with Ryan at the wheel as promised. Ryan drove carefully over to the starter. "Hi, Miss Evans," he said. "Would you like me to pair you up, or go off alone?"

"We'd like to play alone, Donald. Can we tee off now?"

"Yep. You're cleared for takeoff. Have a good round, ladies."

Jamie was very impressed with how easily Ryan took to the game. She was strong and tall and her balance was very good. She concentrated during her swing, and was still and quiet when Jamie was at work, but was relaxed and playful when one of them wasn't actually addressing the ball. She had no idea what to do with her pitching or sand wedges, and they spent no time at all on putting, so her short game was non-existent. But her iron play was admirable for a rank beginner. Of course, she hit her share of clinkers, but that was to be expected, and it didn't seem to bother her a bit. She didn't keep score, since Jamie told her not to focus on scoring, but instead to focus on feel.

Jamie kept score, and seemed quite pleased with her game. Ryan enjoyed the look of intense concentration on her face before she hit a shot. When Jamie missed a shot she didn't get angry, but Ryan could tell that she went over her swing in her head, trying to figure out what she had done wrong.

The course was truly a marvel, and Ryan was tremendously impressed with the quiet and the peacefulness she felt walking around the wide expanse of perfectly groomed grass. Much of the time it felt like they were all alone on the course, and Ryan treasured the solitude—something she didn't get to experience often enough. Besides the serenity and the peacefulness, some of the views were breathtaking, and Ryan felt extremely lucky to have been invited.

It was nearly noon when they finished, and Jamie gave her friend a hopeful look and asked, "Lunch?"

"I'm famished," Ryan said, "but I have a two o'clock gym appointment."

"You were supposed to see me at four. We could skip today if you could move your two o'clock."

"You're the devil, aren't you?" Ryan picked up the offered cell phone and checked her ever-present organizer for the number.

Her client was flexible, so the pair went to the locker room to freshen up before they went to the grill.

Ryan was impressed by the understated opulence of the room. Every server knew Jamie by name, and Ryan was pleased to discover that Jamie had taken the time to learn their names also. Martin had always told Ryan that the easiest way to judge a person was to see how she treated food servers, and Jamie passed that test with a very high score.

After a delicious lunch, Jamie signed for the bill, as she had all day. Ryan pondered how she'd repay her, and finally reached a decision. "Jamie, I can't tell you how much I've enjoyed today. You wouldn't have brought me here and paid for shoes and a glove and my lunch if you didn't feel like I was a good friend."

"You are," Jamie said, smiling. "A very good friend."

"I feel the same about you. That's why I can't let you pay me for training anymore." She held up her hand to stop Jamie's imminent protest. "Yes, I know that I'm a professional trainer, and that I'd be able to work with a paying customer if I wasn't working with you. But I want to give you my time because you're my friend."

"But Ryan," she protested. "That's $375 a week!"

"I'm well aware of that," she said as she gazed into her friend's sea green eyes. "But money isn't an issue between us. If we weren't working out together I'd still want to be with you, just hanging out. I really enjoy our workouts—I look forward to them. So please don't ask me to accept money for spending time with you. At this point in our relationship, I just can't accept it."

"Okay," Jamie agreed reluctantly as she gazed back into those mesmerizing eyes. "I can tell that you've made up your mind. But can I bring you to play golf every once in a while?"

"Deal," Ryan replied as they shook hands on the agreement.

Ryan had just enough time for Jamie to drop her off at home. As the Range Rover pulled up to the house, Conor was maneuvering his big, black, Dodge Ram into a nearby parking space. *Boy, he looks good in that.* He came over to the Range Rover as Ryan got out and dashed in the house to change. "Do you have a different car for every day of the week?" he asked.

"No, only one. This is my father's. We borrowed it so we could play golf this morning."

"Golf? Ryan played golf?" he asked in amazement. "I started playing about five years ago, and she hasn't stopped teasing me about it since. Thanks for the ammo," he said, his eyes sparkling with mischief. "So where did you play? Tilden?"

"No, we played at my father's club," she replied, hoping he wouldn't pursue the point.

"Which is ...?"

"Olympic," she said without embellishment.

"You took Ryan to play at The Olympic Club?" His mouth hung open in shock. "Are you still a member, or did they throw you out?"

"She did very, very well, I'll have you know. I've been playing since I was six, and I bet she could beat me within the year if she worked at it. She's such a gifted athlete."

"Oh, she'll work at it, all right. She owes me at least twenty rounds after all the teasing I've put up with. That gives me an idea for her birthday, though."

"Her birthday? When is it?"

"It's Friday. She's gonna be twenty-three."

"I had no idea, the little rat!"

"Well, you've really helped me out. I didn't have any ideas for a present for her until now. Hey, it would be fun if Brendan and I could play as a foursome with you two sometime."

"I'd like that."

Ryan was barreling down the stairs to fetch her motorcycle, when she spotted Conor still at the driver's door of the Range Rover. "You can't drive that one, Conor. It's her father's," she stated authoritatively.

"Did you drive it?"

"Yeah, but I'm trustworthy," she stated, winking at Jamie.

Jamie laughed and said, "Sorry, Conor, I've got to get back to Berkeley before traffic gets bad. But next time, I'll let you drive it."

Ryan grabbed her bike from the garage and walked it up next to Conor. "What were you two talking about?" she asked.

"Oh nothing, nothing at all," Conor said. He waved goodbye to Jamie and sauntered into the house.

Ryan smiled up at Jamie and said, "I had a fabulous day." After a beat she asked, "Have we ever had a bad time together?"

"Nope. But I'm sure I'll wear on your nerves over time."

"Don't count on it, buddy," Ryan said. She gave her friend an affectionate smile and gently patted her cheek.

Chapter Six

One of the class projects that Jamie and Ryan had signed up for was to spend a day volunteering at a lesbian community organization. Ryan had a long association with one such outfit, and she agreed to arrange for two evening volunteer sessions at the Gay and Lesbian Teen Talk Line. They checked with their professor, and even though she had wanted them to work with a lesbian organization, she approved their plan when Ryan promised she could arrange to deal with young women only.

The day arrived, and Jamie picked Ryan up from the biology building at six-thirty. They generally didn't see each other on Tuesdays, but Jamie knew that it was Ryan's busiest day. She also knew that her friend had a tendency to ignore her own needs in order to be early for her appointments. "Have you eaten?" she inquired.

"Yep," Ryan replied as she patted her flat belly. "Da fixed me a delicious spaghetti dinner which I ate with gusto."

"Good. Then let's get over there so we can get set up." Jamie always felt more comfortable when she was early for an appointment, and she knew that Ryan had the same quirk.

They drove through the streets of Berkeley, and crossed over into Oakland. When they reached a rather seedy neighborhood, Ryan pointed out the building, and Jamie pulled up in front. A small sign read "G.L.T.T.L." "That's certainly unobtrusive enough," Jamie remarked. "Do you think they get harassed?"

"Not that I've ever heard of," Ryan said. "It's not a bad idea to be cautious, though."

As they went into the small building, Jamie noticed a series of tall cubicles, jammed into a long room. She could hear soft voices wafting over the tops, but the voices were indistinct. Ryan led the way, and they walked into a small office near the rear of the building. A large redheaded woman rose to greet Ryan, a big smile on her expressive face. "Ryan, I've missed you!

Ryan enveloped the woman in a hug. "I've missed you too, Yvonne. I wish I had more time to come help out. The school year is pretty tough for me."

"Honey, you still hold the honor of logging the most hours of any volunteer we've ever had. Your name is still up on the plaque," she reminded her, indicating a wooden sign that listed the most loyal volunteers. "We're just glad to see you again," she said as she patted Ryan's back.

"Oh, Yvonne, this is my friend, Jamie." Jamie nodded at Yvonne, and Ryan continued, "I thought I could take calls and have Jamie listen in. If she wants to handle some, we can do that on Thursday after she feels more comfortable. Does that sound okay to you?"

"That sounds fine, Ryan. You know the drill. You can use Marsha's office to give yourselves more room."

Ryan thanked her and escorted Jamie to a second small office. There was a cluttered desk, and it took Ryan a minute to find the phone. Once she did, she searched for a pair of headphones for Jamie. She came back with the headset, and hooked it into the side of the device.

"All of the calls come in and are answered by one person. She logs them in and sets them into a cue. It's not always easy, but she tries to match the calls to the abilities of the volunteers. I requested calls from lesbians, and she'll make that happen. Now, the operator knows that I have a lot of experience, and that I'm older than most of the other volunteers, so she'll probably send some tough ones our way."

"But you're going to actually talk to the callers, right? And I just listen?"

"No, not just listen. I want you to help me. There are a lot of resources here, and I want you to get comfortable with them. I'll probably need some things, and you can help me look up information to make the calls go faster." She gestured at the disarray that surrounded her, and then gave her friend a sheepish smile. "I don't know if I can work in all this mess. Sometimes my neatness fetish gets in the way."

Ryan set to work to locate all of the pertinent reference materials. While she looked around she said, "Now, the callers can't hear you, but you can hear them. I can mute my voice so we can talk about a call if we need to. If you have any questions, or want me to tell the caller something you can write on the white board."

"I'm sure you'll think of everything."

"No I won't." She looked at Jamie for a few seconds with a very serious expression. "The calls can cover anything. I've had people ask me how to use a microwave oven. But some of the calls are really serious. I do my best to make appropriate referrals, but sometimes the kids' stories are heartbreaking. If any of 'em bother you just let me know, and we'll stop for a while to decompress, okay?"

Jamie was touched by Ryan's concern for her. "Thanks for looking out for me," she said with a smile. "I'll let you know if anything gets to me."

When Ryan was organized, she pressed a button and told the operator she was ready. Less than a second later, the phone rang. "Gay and Lesbian Teen Talk Line, this is Ryan. How can I help you?"

The calls came in so quickly that Jamie hardly had time to grab the appropriate books to give Ryan reference numbers. She was amazed at the astounding variety of issues that kids called about. And most of the callers were kids. They took calls from girls as young as twelve, and nearly every question involved sexual behavior, which truly shocked her. One young girl had kissed another girl at a party and she wanted to know if that made her gay, a sixteen-year-old was sure she was gay, but her

Orthodox Jewish parents prohibited her from going out without being chaperoned, a nineteen-year-old wanted help with a paper she was doing for school. Ryan didn't spend a lot of time with that call, but she suggested some web sites that would help with the research.

Not surprisingly, Ryan handled each call with professionalism and an amazing amount of empathy. She dispatched the calls as quickly as possible, but let kids ramble on if she thought they needed to. *God, she has an amazing amount of patience.* A particularly non-verbal young woman couldn't spit out her question, but Ryan hung in with her and coached her to be able to spit it out. Jamie jumped to her feet several times to write questions on the board, and each time Ryan incorporated them into the call. She'd generally mouth a thank you or give Jamie a grin when this happened. After about an hour Ryan buzzed the operator to let her know she was going to take a break.

Ryan stood and stretched thoroughly. After a minute she lay down on the floor and performed a series of stretches that worked her back even more systematically. Jamie did the same, but with much less efficiency. Ryan gave her a smile and asked if her back was hurting her. When she nodded, Ryan said, "Come here and put yours arms around my neck." Jamie gave her a puzzled look, but did exactly what she was told. She got close and placed her hands around her friend's neck as the taller woman leaned over to accommodate Jamie's height. "Now lock your hands together tightly," Ryan said from mere millimeters away. Jamie again followed her instructions, and was surprised to feel Ryan rise to her full height, each vertebra seeming to slip back into place when her feet left the ground.

"Oh, God, this feels good."

Ryan smiled at her with a satisfied grin. "All better?"

"Pretty much," Jamie said, twisting around a little bit. "Except for one spot right in the middle. There's a spot there that's not right."

"I've got another one for that," Ryan said. "This time put your elbows around my neck." Jamie felt her mouth go dry as she contemplated the request. She stood so close, and Ryan leaned over so far, that they were breathing the same air. The warmth of Ryan's breath on her cheek caused her heart to pick up its beat, but she gamely stood her ground and placed her arms just as Ryan instructed. This time when Ryan rose, Jamie was draped along her body and her chin rested right on her broad chest. She turned slightly so that her cheek lay on Ryan's clean-smelling, white T-shirt. They both heard an audible snap, and Ryan's low laugh rumbled right through her entire body. "Ready?" Ryan asked.

"For what?" Jamie replied into the strong pectoral muscle.

"For me to put you down."

"If you must," she heard herself reply after a deep sigh.

Ryan wore an amused grin, watching as Jamie got her legs functioning. "You really are a pleasure hound, aren't you?"

"Uhm … I can't say that I knew that about myself, but I guess I am."

"Lucky for you that pleasure hounds are my favorite animals," Ryan said, while tweaking her nose.

I'm gonna have to sit on uncomfortable chairs more often.

After their break, the first really tough call of the evening came in. It was from a fourteen-year-old girl who had been raped by her mother's boyfriend, apparently because he thought she was gay. The girl, Karen, related that the man had been with her mother for about a year and had been harassing her because she didn't have a boyfriend yet. She claimed that he drank a lot and that his abuse got worse when he was drunk. Her mother worked nights as a waitress and Karen was often left at home with the boyfriend.

She said that he had come into her room on Sunday night and demanded to know why she never had boys calling. She tried to get rid of him with a flippant answer by telling him that she was a lesbian. But her plan backfired when he flew into a rage and beat her severely, then raped her, telling her that he wasn't going to have a queer living in his house.

She was terrified to tell her mother, because she was afraid that her mother would believe him rather than her. During the call she was periodically hysterical, which was absolutely normal. But the hysteria was followed by long periods of silence, which frightened both women. Ryan asked her directly, "Have you had any thoughts of death or of killing yourself, Karen?"

Jamie looked at her with wide eyes. She thought it was a very bad idea to suggest such a thing to the girl, afraid that it would give her an idea that she didn't currently have. But after a long pause Karen finally answered. "Yes," she said softly.

"Tell me about them. Tell me everything."

The girl sniffled and paused again, then she said, "I keep thinking about my funeral. I think about how sorry my mom's gonna be for having him in the house. And I think about the kids from my school finally understanding how much this hurts."

Ryan placed the call on mute and said, "I hate to do this, but we've got to trace this call. I think she may have already taken something. Go talk to Yvonne and tell her what's going on."

Jamie dashed in to Yvonne's office, told her about the call and what Ryan had said. She ran back in after Yvonne immediately agreed to call the phone company to trace the call. During one particularly long period of silence, Ryan caught a look at Jamie's terrified face and grabbed her hand, holding it tight while she continued to talk in quiet, reassuring tones, hoping to draw Karen out again. At least ten more minutes passed and now Jamie agreed with Ryan's take on the girl's mental state. Her voice was becoming slow and dreamy when she wasn't crying uncontrollably, which happened time and again. Ryan had been letting her lapse into silence for a few minutes, but after another interminable silence Jamie could see the tension in Ryan's face and felt the pressure of her hand becoming more intense.

Several minutes passed, and the pressure in the room was unbearable. Ryan finally stood up and started to pace in a small circle. She spoke in a louder voice, "Come on, Karen, talk to me. Please talk to me!" Finally she couldn't take the silence anymore and she yelled in a frustrated plea, "Karen for god's sake, please talk to me!"

Every muscle in Jamie's body was coiled with tension. Ryan was pale and rigid as she stood in place with her eyes tightly shut. Just when Jamie was sure they had lost her, an older female voice picked up the phone and identified herself as an Oakland Fire Department paramedic. She had to hang up immediately to begin resuscitation, but she promised that someone from the department would call back when they got the girl stabilized.

Ryan hit the disconnect button and sank into her chair. Her head dropped into her hands and she sat motionless for many long moments. Jamie was shaking all over, and felt like she was freezing to death. When Ryan finally looked up, she saw the pallor on Jamie's face. Jumping to her feet, she guided her friend into the chair and shoved Jamie's head between her knees. Then she grabbed a paperweight from the desk and flung it against the wall. Yvonne came running, and Ryan instructed her to get a cold cloth. The older woman returned seconds later with the requested item, and Ryan told her she could leave, thinking that Jamie would respond better to her alone. She placed the cloth on the back of her clammy neck and slowly massaged her tense muscles. After a few minutes she felt her begin to stir and helped her sit up.

Jamie was still stark white, but she was shaking less and Ryan guessed that she was in no danger of passing out. She helped her to her feet and guided her out of the small office. As they passed Yvonne's office, Ryan said quietly, "I'll call in an hour to see how the girl is." Yvonne mouthed a thank you and Ryan nodded her acknowledgement.

As they got to the curb, Ryan propped her up against the car and searched through Jamie's bag for the car keys. When she found them, she turned off the alarm and opened the passenger door. Jamie's color hadn't improved, and Ryan began to worry that she shouldn't have moved her. She appeared to be in shock, and Ryan hoped that being in familiar surroundings would calm her down. She had a rather vacant look in her eyes, but she seemed cognizant of where they were.

Ryan maneuvered her into the seat and belted her in securely, then ran around the car to get into the drivers seat. As she started the engine, Jamie moaned loudly and started to struggle to free herself from the seat belt. Ryan unhooked her own belt and once again ran around to the other side. When she opened the door, Jamie leaned over dangerously close to the sidewalk and began to vomit. There wasn't much Ryan could do at this point, so she knelt down and placed her hand on the back of her neck for comfort, then grabbed some tissues from the box on the floor and gently wiped her mouth. Then she lifted her back into the car and checked her vital signs. Her pulse seemed a little quick, but Ryan expected that. She reclined the seat as much as possible, and placed her limp form back against the seat.

Jamie was beginning to stir by the time they approached her house. She moaned slightly and shifted a bit when Ryan pulled into the drive. "Please let no one be home," Ryan prayed aloud. She trotted to the passenger side, opened the door and removed the seat belt, then squatted down and made eye contact. "Are you going to be sick again?"

A small nod and a lurching movement were the only warning that Jamie provided. Regrettably, Ryan's reflexes weren't fast enough, and the remaining contents of

Jamie's stomach caught her right in the crotch of her jeans. She swallowed the bile that was rushing up her own throat, and did her best to comfort her friend. When she was finished gagging, Ryan slid one strong arm behind Jamie's shoulders, and the other under her knees. She grunted deeply from the strain as she rose to a standing position. *Boy, I wish we had the Range Rover tonight. That squat was a killer!*

She struggled to carry her friend up the walk and shot a concerned look at her as she moaned softly. Her diverted attention caused her to stumble just a bit on one of the stairs. *Please don't drop her,* she pleaded with herself as she hoisted her burden higher on her chest to free her right arm. She managed to get the key in the lock and turned the knob, where she was overjoyed to find the house dark and still. They crossed the threshold and Ryan went to the sofa and lay her down. "Jamie?" she said quietly. When she got no response, she lightly slapped her face. *Great! Now she's unconscious!* After making sure that she wouldn't tumble off the small sofa, she dashed into the kitchen to fetch a dishtowel, which she wet and filled with a few handfuls of ice, flicking on the overhead lights as she returned to the sofa.

She sat Jamie up again and gave her a brisk ice massage on the back of her neck. The smaller woman began to respond and finally muttered, "What happened?"

"You almost passed out at the help line. You're in your living room now. How do you feel?" Ryan dropped to her knees and held on to her shoulders to steady her and looked closely at her eyes.

"Okay, I guess. Sick to my stomach, though. How long was I out?"

"Not long." Ryan exhaled deeply and rubbed her eyes in her familiar gesture of fatigue. "But a lot longer than I'm comfortable with. Has this happened to you before?"

"Yeah. I …" she began, but Ryan saw the green tinge return to her face. She scooped her up and began to climb the stairs quickly, feeling beads of sweat pop out on her forehead as she struggled with her weight.

She carried her into the bathroom, and let her kneel on the floor and rest her head on her folded arms crossed upon the toilet seat. Another round of gagging followed, and after a few quiet minutes Ryan helped her to her feet and guided her into her room.

"What did you have to eat today?" Ryan asked.

Jamie thought for a minute, trying to order her muddled brain. "I don't remember. Didn't we eat together?"

"No, that was yesterday." Another worried look crossed her face. "Jamie, I want you to think about today. This is Tuesday. Tell me about what you did today."

"Uhm, did we have psych today?"

"No, that's on Monday. This is Tuesday. You have your romantic poets class on Tuesday. Did you go?"

Jamie concentrated hard, and after a few minutes her memory came back. "Yeah, I did. After that I went to the library and then I got some lunch."

"What did you have?"

"Uhm, I felt funny, so I just had some soup and a couple of crackers."

"No breakfast?"

"I don't think so. Oh, no, I was running late, so I just had a diet coke."

"Okay, what did you do after lunch?"

"I had my next two English classes, back to back. Then I went back to the library and got really engrossed in reading for my class. My watch alarm went off at six, and I rode my bike home and got my car. I drove back and picked you up at six-thirty." She gave Ryan a wan smile, proud of her accomplishment of remembering her day.

"So, you asked if I had eaten, but you didn't tell me that you hadn't," she chided her gently. "I guess you need someone to look after you, too," she said as she ruffled Jamie's hair. "I'm going to call your parents to let them know about this. I think you should see your doctor."

"No!" she cried. "Don't call them, Ryan! Please!" she begged with a note of panic in her voice.

"Okay, okay," Ryan said as she gently caressed her cheek. "But we've got to get something into your tummy. Do you think you have any 7-up or ginger ale?"

"Probably, but I'm not sure."

"Do you feel like I can leave you for a minute or two?"

"Yeah. My stomach's still bad but I don't think I'll pass out again."

When Ryan returned with a glass of ginger ale, she resumed her questioning. "Tell me about when you passed out before."

"It's kind of embarrassing, but I tend to pass out when I'm under stress. My blood pressure's kind of low and I tend to go out."

"Do you get any warning?"

"Yeah, like tonight I could tell that as soon as you disconnected the phone ..." Her voice got fainter and she began to lose her color again. Ryan reached over quickly and removed the glass from her weak hand.

"I'm gonna get you into bed. Then we're gonna talk about this. What do you wear to bed?"

"A T-shirt," Jamie said. Ryan pushed her down on the bed and lifted her legs, placing them on the bed also. She walked over to the dresser and picked out a very large, light blue T-shirt, obviously one of Jack's. She returned to the bed holding the shirt up for Jamie's approval. Her questioning look received a nod in return.

Ryan stood at the foot of the bed, and began to unlace Jamie's brown, leather, ankle-length boots. She dropped each boot to the carpet and touched a sock as she asked, "On or off?"

"Off," was the faint reply.

She walked around to the side of the bed and began to unbuckle the brown leather belt which held up the khaki chinos. "I can do that, Ryan," Jamie insisted, trying to sit up.

Ryan let her give it a try, but she flopped back down again in seconds. "God, why am I so dizzy?"

"Because you've been vomiting and you had almost no food in your stomach to start with. You're probably dehydrated. Let me get you undressed, then we'll try to get some fluids down you, okay?"

"I feel embarrassed," she admitted with a small voice.

Ryan gave her a hurt look and sat down next to her on the bed. "Jamie," she said softly. "I … I'm not trying to … I mean I don't want to …"

It hit Jamie that Ryan assumed she was afraid of her, and she hastened to reassure her friend. "No, no, please don't think I'm worried about your seeing me naked because you're a lesbian. I'm just shy … around everyone," she insisted. "I don't even like Mia to see me naked, and she runs around here like it's a nudist camp."

Ryan nodded her head, feeling reassured that Jamie wasn't afraid of her in particular, but she didn't want her friend to lie in bed with her stained and smelly clothes on. She looked rather helpless until Jamie sighed and said, "I'm being silly. Please help me."

Hesitating only a minute, the taller woman unbuttoned and unzipped her friend's pants. "Pick your butt up a little." Jamie did as she was told, and the chinos were removed and neatly folded.

Ryan began to unbutton the multicolor pastel plaid flannel shirt. She worked the buttons of the sleeves open and removed one arm, then she turned Jamie over onto her side and removed the shirt completely. Next she tugged the pale yellow T-shirt up her torso and over her head.

Ryan pulled her up into a sitting position, braced against her own body. "Are you okay?" she asked gently.

"Yeah," she said, but it was clear that she was feeling queasy again. Putting her arms around Jamie's torso, Ryan unclasped her peach-colored bra. Sliding it off her shoulders, she tossed it away, being careful to avert her eyes as much as possible. She got her into the sleep shirt, then wrangled her into the bed, drawing the sheet over her and resting her head on a pair of fluffy pillows.

Jamie's color was much better, and Ryan felt she could leave her for a moment. She checked her watch and noticed that it was almost eleven, so she walked over to the phone and called the help line. Yvonne answered the main number and Ryan asked if they had received word on Karen yet.

"Yes, the paramedics called about ten minutes ago. They pumped her stomach and have her stabilized. They were confident that she'll be okay. Physically, at least," she added. "How's your friend?"

"She'll be fine. She's fainted before. Probably has low blood pressure."

"Send her my best," Yvonne said. "And if she wants to cancel for Thursday, I'll understand."

"We'll let you know," Ryan said. "Keep us posted if you hear any more about Karen, okay?"

"I will, Ryan. Talk to you soon."

Ryan hung up and walked back to the bed. She looked down at her friend, shaking her head in sympathy when she saw her quietly crying. Sitting down, Ryan put her hand on her knee and said, "Come on now, it's all over. Karen's gonna be fine."

Jamie raised a hand while mumbling something that Ryan couldn't quiet understand. But she got the impression that her friend wanted to be left alone for a while. She'd already decided that she was going to stay overnight to keep an eye on Jamie, so she took the time to change into something more comfortable.

She found some thin, cotton, flannel pajama bottoms that must have been Jack's. Her own T-shirt was clean, so she shucked her shoes and her wet, smelly jeans, then put on the pajama bottoms. She was flexible enough to wriggle out of her bra without taking off her shirt, so she didn't even bother to go to the bathroom for privacy.

Jamie was still crying, so Ryan spent another minute calling her father to let him know she wouldn't be home. She dialed the familiar number of the firehouse, and heard her father's strong voice answer. "Hi, Da. It's me."

"What's wrong, Siobhán?" he asked, his tone showing his concern.

"Nothing big. Jamie and I went to the teen talk line tonight, and we had a really stressful call. A young girl overdosed and we got to her just in time. Jamie hadn't eaten, and she passed out. None of her roommates are here, so I'm gonna stay over to watch her."

"Oh, the poor lass. You take good care of her, Siobhán, she's a lovely little thing."

"Thanks Da, will you let the boys know I won't be home?"

"Sure thing, sweetheart. I love you, Siobhán," he said softly. "And I'm proud of you for helping that child tonight."

"I love you too, Da. See you tomorrow."

She hung up and looked over at Jamie. The smaller woman was sitting up with her knees raised and her arms wrapped around them. "I feel better now. Are you gonna stay?"

"Yeah. I want to make sure someone keeps an eye on you, and since your roommates aren't home … "

"I'm sure I'll be fine, but I'd love some company." She began to shake, and Ryan crossed over to the bed.

"Can I give you a hug? You look like you need one."

"Please," she said, her voice a mere whisper.

Ryan sat down, then scooted right next to Jamie and pulled her into the crook of her shoulder. Jamie's head dropped onto Ryan's breast, and she shook with quiet sobs for a long while. "How could someone be so cruel to a child?" Jamie finally gasped out. "How could you rape a little girl because you think she's gay?"

"I can't answer that. I can't imagine abusing someone so vulnerable. The really awful thing is that Karen's innocence is destroyed. She might get through the trauma, but she can't reclaim her childhood. That's gone forever."

"I'm so proud of you Ryan," she murmured. "You saved her life. You really saved her life."

"No, the paramedic did that. I just knew enough to call them."

"I didn't realize how bad it was until the end. She would have died if I'd been there alone." She began to sob again, crying so hard that Ryan misted up, too.

"You don't know what you'd have done if you were alone. Don't speculate about things like that," Ryan said into her ear as she held her close.

Jamie began to calm down after a few more minutes of sobbing. The stress of the evening began to claim her, and she was sound asleep within moments. After Ryan was sure she was in a deep slumber, she rolled her onto her back, drew the comforter up to cover her breasts, and pulled her arms out of the covers.

The brunette slipped off the bed and looked around for a good place to crash. She found a small quilt lying on a chair, then tried to get comfortable on the loveseat. She tossed and turned, finally giving up. *I can't afford to lose a night's sleep, so I hope Jamie doesn't mind a buddy.* She flipped off the lights and got onto the bed, lying outside of the covers as she placed the quilt around herself. She lay in that position for a long time, unable to relax enough to sleep, her mind replaying the incident over and over. But she was exhausted too, and eventually she drifted off for a few restless hours of sleep.

Just after dawn Ryan awoke with a start. She rubbed her weary eyes and carefully rolled out of bed. When she bent to pick up her shoes, she heard Jamie stir.

"What time is it?"

"It's just six," Ryan replied. "You can go back to sleep. You could use the rest." She walked over to Jamie's side of the bed, and sat on the edge to check her out. "I'm gonna take a shower and go downstairs to fix some breakfast. You stay in bed, and I'll come check on you at seven. If you're better, you can come down and have some breakfast before school, okay?"

"Okay. Gimme a hug." She extended her arms, and Ryan dutifully complied, giving her a small kiss on the top of her head for good measure.

By the time Ryan reached the door to the bathroom, she heard Jamie's breathing fall into a steady pattern. She smiled wearily at her sleeping friend and closed the door.

After a partially rejuvenating shower, Ryan ambled downstairs to find something for breakfast. She did a reasonably decent job of washing her jeans out, and tossed them in the dryer while she searched the kitchen for acceptable food. The closest she could come was some instant oatmeal. The pantry held every type of spice and herb, but the only real food was microwave popcorn, fat-free cookies and diet soda. *This is disgusting. Every one of those three is underweight, and I bet they're all malnourished. I can't do much about the other two, but Jamie is gonna start eating better if I've got to move in here to cook for her.* There was no fruit in the house, but she did find some milk that had a day left before it went bad. So she put the instant oatmeal in the microwave, and grumbled to herself as it cooked.

She extracted the bowl and added the milk and some brown sugar, finding herself on the verge of gagging as soon as she took her first bite. *What a terrible thing to do to a poor little oat. Every bit of flavor and texture has been removed!*

Her stomach was queasy as it was, and the wallpaper paste that claimed to be oatmeal was making matters worse. *I can't do it. I'll grab something on the way to class. Anything would be better than that!*

She was pleased to hear Jamie stomping around upstairs, but she thought she should give her some privacy, so she climbed up on the marble counter to wait for her pants to dry. Just a few minutes after seven Jamie came down the stairs, clean, pressed and very pale.

Ryan hopped off the counter and walked over to her. "You don't look much better. How do you feel?"

"About like I look," she said. "I'm still sick to my stomach, and I feel pretty shaky."

"I think this is a perfect day to skip school," Ryan said. "Why don't you go back upstairs and hop into bed. I'll go to the store and buy you some human food for breakfast."

Jamie looked at her blankly while Ryan turned her around and steered her back up the stairs. "Scoot," she commanded.

Without a word she climbed the stairs, unbuttoning her blouse as she went. Ryan pulled her still-damp jeans from the dryer and struggled into them. *Nothing better than hot, wet jeans that still smell like vomit,* she thought cheerily. She picked up the keys to the Porsche, and was just locking up when Cassie pulled into the driveway.

"What a surprise," she said dryly as Ryan passed her on the walk. "Do you have keys to the house *and* the car now?"

Ryan bit her lip to stop herself from snapping at her. "No, I don't. Jamie's ill, and I'm taking her car to get her something for her stomach. Is that all right with you?" she added with a false smile.

"What's wrong with her?" Cassie asked sharply.

"She got upset last night, and hadn't had much to eat. I think her stomach is just raw from throwing up."

"Why was she upset?"

"She and I were volunteering at a help line and we had a really stressful call. A young girl had been raped and she tried to kill herself." Ryan didn't want to give her all of this information, but she didn't want to lie either.

"That's ridiculous!"

Ryan thought that was an odd term to use, but she agreed "Yeah, it's really upsetting to think of what people can do to kids."

"No, it's ridiculous that Jamie was put in that position. She's not used to that type of person."

There wasn't one thing in the world Ryan could have said that wouldn't have involved profanity, so she shut her mouth and turned on her heel. Cassie was left standing on the sidewalk, mouth open in shock at being treated so rudely by Jamie's uncouth friend.

After a $50 trip to the market, Ryan returned to the house to start breakfast. Luckily, Cassie had obviously just stopped in before class because she was gone when Ryan returned. After spending a few minutes organizing all of the supplies in the pantry, Ryan started her own meal started. She assumed that Jamie wouldn't be up for some time, but she could hardly wait another minute to eat. She decided she wanted French toast and ham, so she mixed up the batter for the crusty brioche that she had purchased. She got everything together quickly, and within minutes had it all cooking. When everything was ready she heated her very large latte in the microwave, then sat down to enjoy her repast. She pulled out one of her textbooks so she could study while she ate, and the time flew by. Looking up to see that it was ten o'clock, she realized she'd already allowed some decisions to be made about her day. *I guess I'm skipping my bio lab. Good thing I'm pretty well caught up.*

Moments later, she heard Jamie get out of bed. She gave her a few minutes to go to the bathroom, and when the noises stopped she walked back up the stairs to see how she was.

"Come on in," Jamie replied when Ryan knocked softly. She had crawled back into bed, but she looked a lot better than she had earlier in the morning.

"Are you going back to sleep, or are you ready for some food?"

Jamie recoiled at the mere thought. She scrunched up her face in distaste and moaned, "I'm never gonna eat again."

"Oh, yes you are," Ryan insisted. "Your stomach won't feel better until you get something in there. You can have tea and toast or cereal or oatmeal or French toast or pancakes or scrambled eggs. But you're putting something in there if I have to hold you down." She put her hands on her hips and gave her friend a stern look.

Jamie had to laugh at her fierce demeanor. "Joke's on you, Ryan. We don't have anything to eat around here except popcorn."

"You do now. I went to the store." She waited a beat before she added, "And I ran into Cassie. We had a little chat, and I'm pretty sure she's mad at me."

Jamie rolled her eyes and pulled the pillow over her head. "I'm not up to hearing about it right now. Will you tell me after my stomach has calmed down?"

"I don't need to tell you at all," Ryan said. "I just wanted to let you know so you were in the loop. Now what can I make you?"

"I tend to like sweet things when I'm sick. Do you think I could keep French toast down?"

"I think you could if you don't put too much syrup or butter on it. Stay in bed until I'm ready for you, okay?"

"Okay," she said, letting out a massive yawn. "I'm still tired."

Ryan went down stairs and made three pieces of French toast, then put the plate on a tray and added a small pitcher of syrup, a mug of sweetened tea, silverware, a linen napkin and a bud vase with a bright yellow Gerber daisy that she had purchased at the market. She expertly balanced the tray as she opened the door to Jamie's room. "Breakfast is served," she said cheerily as she entered.

Jamie struggled to sit up, her face curled into a delighted grin. "That's so sweet! I can't believe how thoughtful you're being."

"You were really in a bad way last night. And I feel responsible for it. I feel like I should have better prepared you for the types of calls we got, or at least asked them to give us easier ones."

"No way, Ryan," she said as she shook her head. "This is just me. There's no way you could have known that I had a tendency to pass out under stress. I should have warned you." She took a bite of the toast and closed her eyes in pleasure. "Thanks for making this. It's just perfect for my sad little tummy."

Ryan was still quite concerned about her friend, and peppered Jamie with questions about her health, as the now ravenous woman diligently worked away at her breakfast. "How many times have you passed out?"

"I'd say it's happened to me four or five times."

"How old were you when it first happened?"

"I don't know, but I think I was in high school. I do remember that I'd been studying for a big test, and I felt sick to my stomach and I just went out."

"Have you ever mentioned this to your physician?"

"Yeah. I had to have a physical before I was admitted here and she asked me if I had ever fainted. She didn't think it was a big deal."

"When it happened before did it last as long?" Ryan asked, still concerned.

"I'm not sure how long I was out. I think it's usually just a few seconds."

"I'd say you were out cold for a total of ten minutes. I was really worried about you. I was seriously considering taking you to the hospital."

"I'm sure I've never been out that long. Maybe I should call my doctor."

"You said that you felt funny at lunch yesterday. What did you mean?" Ryan asked.

"I just felt queasy all morning. Actually I've been feeling off for a while. Maybe I'm not getting enough sleep or something."

Ryan looked at her for a minute, and forced herself to ask a question that had been niggling at her all morning. "Uhm … I don't want to upset you, but is there a chance that you might be pregnant?"

Jamie's face drained of all color in less than a second. Ryan could see her hands grip the edges of the tray so tightly that her knuckles turned white. Her eyes were wide and Ryan was very concerned that she'd pass out or throw up again. After she sat for a minute in shocked silence, she tried to answer, but couldn't find her voice.

"I'm gonna take that as a yes," Ryan said. She raised her hand to gently stroke Jamie's cheek. "I'm sorry I've upset you, but if it's a possibility you really should be seen by your doctor."

Jamie pushed the now empty tray away from her lap, and let her head fall back against the pillows. "Please God, make it not be true," she whimpered. "I don't know what I'll do if I'm pregnant."

Ryan sat closer and wrapped her arms around her tightly. "Don't worry about it. You're just speculating, right? Let's get you dressed and go to your doctor. They can give you the results in just a few minutes—then you can put your mind at ease. Do you want to call Jack and have him go with you?"

"No, no, I really don't. Won't you go with me?" she asked, looking like a frightened child.

"Of course I will. I'll call the doctor and make sure they can see you. Do you have the number handy?"

"Yeah, I have her business card in my wallet."

Ryan found the number, and instructed Jamie to get dressed while she went downstairs to make the call. She didn't want Jamie to hear her cancel her one and two o'clock clients, or to hear what she said to the doctor, so she hoped it took her friend a few minutes to get ready.

"Hi," she said when the receptionist answered. "I'm calling for Jamie Evans. She had an episode last night where she was unconscious for almost ten minutes. She also vomited numerous times, and she can't rule out that she's pregnant, so she'd like to come in for a pregnancy test and to have the doctor look at her."

"Well, the doctor is only in the office for another hour today. She's at the hospital all afternoon. Could she get here quickly?"

"Yes," Ryan said confidently. "We can be there in a half hour."

Jamie came down just as Ryan was canceling all of her clients for the afternoon. "We've got to rush," she told her. "I promised we'd be there in a half hour."

They dashed out of the house and quickly got onto the relatively clear freeway. Luckily they were on the road right between the morning rush hour and the heavy traffic that occurred around lunchtime. They didn't talk at all on the way over to Palo Alto. Jamie was going over every possible scenario that could occur if she was pregnant; Ryan was concentrating on driving fast enough to get there, but slow enough to avoid a ticket or an accident.

When they pulled up to the charming, two-story brick building that held the physician's office, Ryan pulled over to the curb to let her out. "I'll park and be right in." Jamie looked hesitant, but Ryan insisted that she get in before the doctor left.

Ryan found a spot only two blocks away, and after loading the meter she ran all the way back to the office. The waiting room was empty, and she started to sit down to read a magazine when the door opened and a nurse beckoned her in. "Jamie's in room three," she said as she pointed Ryan toward the room.

"Does she want me with her?"

The nurse looked at her like she was slow. "How else would I have known to come get you?"

"Good point." Ryan walked down the hall to the examining room, finding that Jamie had already taken off her clothes and put on a green paper gown. She looked small and scared and very cold. Ryan immediately stood right next to the table and wrapped her in her arms, not caring who saw them. Jamie seemed very grateful for the comfort, and she nestled her head right into Ryan's neck. "I already gave them a urine sample," she mumbled. "They're doing the test now."

After a perfunctory knock, the door opened and a very young-looking doctor entered. She gave Ryan a puzzled glance, but recovered quickly. "Hi Jamie," she said with a friendly smile. "I hear you've had a tough day."

"Yeah, pretty tough. This is my friend, Ryan. She was with me last night, so she can answer any questions, since I was so out of it."

"Hi, Ryan," the doctor said as she extended her hand. "I'm Alison Atkins."

Ryan shook her hand and stepped back out of the way as Alison started to examine Jamie. The brunette positioned herself so she was close to Jamie's head, but far enough away so that she couldn't see the more intimate part of the exam. Alison checked Jamie's blood pressure and took her temperature and then she drew a vial of blood to run some tests. Next she asked Jamie to lie down so she could perform a pelvic exam. Ryan felt uncomfortable, but Jamie clearly wanted her here, so she stayed right where she was, holding the shaken woman's hand.

"Have you had any adverse reactions to the new pill, Jamie?" Alison asked.

"No, I haven't had any side effects from it. But I haven't been on it for a full month, so it might be too soon to tell."

"Have you been using condoms?"

Jamie blushed deeply as she admitted, "Usually. But there were two times where I had sex without one. Both times were on the same weekend, about three weeks ago."

"The date of your last period was ..." she looked on Jamie's chart and checked her watch to confirm the date, "thirty days ago."

"Yeah, I should have gotten my period two days ago, but I thought the new pill could have messed me up a little."

"Hmm," Alison said as she stripped off her latex glove and tossed it away. "You can scoot up now. Everything seems normal. But it's too early for me to use a physical exam to tell if you're pregnant. Tell me about your symptoms."

"I've felt lethargic for a month or so. My sleep has been off a little bit too. And I've been queasy in the mornings for about a week."

Alison was staring at her intently as she listened to her description of her symptoms. "Are you urinating more than normal?"

"No, no difference."

"How do your breasts feel? Any tenderness?" She stood close and lightly palpated them, watching Jamie's face for signs of pain.

"Yeah, they're tender but they always are before my period."

"Tell me about last night."

"We were volunteering at a crisis line, and we got a call from a young girl who had been raped, and tried to commit suicide. The call went on for at least a half hour and I was tenser than I've ever been in my life. The paramedics got there in time, but as soon as we finished the call I started to pass out. Ryan got my head between my knees and I felt better. But as soon as we got in the car I started to throw up. I'm not sure how long I threw up, but eventually we got home. I'm not sure about anything after that," she admitted.

Ryan piped up to continue the story. "She passed out briefly in the car, but she came to pretty quickly. She vomited several more times before I could get her out of the car, and as soon as we got in the house she fainted again. She was out a long time—much longer than I was comfortable with—I'd say a total of ten minutes."

"Hmm, that's a long time." the doctor mused. "Any other symptoms? Have you changed your eating habits or your activity level?"

Jamie started to say no, but Ryan butted in. "Yes, she has. She's decided to ride in the AIDS Ride this year and I'm training her. She rides fifty to seventy-five miles a week, and she works out three days a week with weights. She also does strenuous aerobic work three times a week."

"I'm concerned about your weight, Jamie. I notice that you're ten pounds lighter than the last time you were in. How have you changed your diet to accommodate your increased activity?"

"Uhm, I haven't?" she admitted weakly.

Ryan butted in again. "Could you recommend a sports nutritionist for Jamie? I don't think she has very good eating habits."

"Yes, I know someone in the East Bay who could help you change your diet. Let me run some tests on your blood. I'll have the results by Friday, okay?"

"Okay."

"I'll be right back," Alison said as she opened the door. "You can get dressed, Jamie."

As Ryan handed her the neatly folded garments, she said, "I should have my certificate revoked!"

"What?"

"It's criminal that I didn't notice that you'd lost ten pounds! That's my responsibility. I'm really sorry that I let you down."

"You didn't let me down, Ryan. It's all my fault. I knew I was losing weight, but I didn't say anything or make any adjustments to my eating. I liked being underweight for a change. I usually gain weight around the holidays, so I figured it would all even out."

"I guess it's not as obvious with you because I see you so often. It's hard to detect a change when it comes on so gradually, but I'm still really mad at myself for not noticing it."

"Ryan, you don't see me naked, and I've been wearing looser clothes to work out in. I didn't want you to see that I was losing weight. It's really my fault and I'm sorry."

The doctor knocked as she came in again. "You didn't want to be pregnant did you?" she asked with a smile.

"God no!" Jamie shouted.

"Then I've good news," she said. "You're officially not pregnant."

Jamie threw her arms around Ryan's neck as she broke into tears. Alison just nodded to Ryan and backed out of the room quietly. Jamie cried for a few minutes as Ryan rubbed her back. She finally lifted her head and said, "Thank you so much for being with me today. I don't know what I'd have done without you."

"I'm glad I was able to be with you. That's what friends are for."

When they were back in the car, Jamie looked embarrassed as she said, "Was it okay to be in the examining room with me? I mean, I know I should have asked you first, but I couldn't bear to be alone."

"Of course it's okay. I'm honored that you trust me enough to want me to be with you. But I was surprised," she admitted. "You seemed so embarrassed last night."

"Oh, I'm just a big baby sometimes. I slapped some sense into myself last night, though. I'm gonna try to be more relaxed about my body. Although it was kinda weird when she was asking me about having sex."

Ryan patted her now relaxed hand and said, "It's okay. It's perfectly natural to have sex with your fiancé."

"I know. It's just embarrassing to talk about it."

"Now you know how I felt when you saw me practically having sex in public," Ryan teased.

"There was nothing practical about it Ryan, you were having sex."

Ryan shot her a little grin as she quickly changed the subject. "Tell me about your typical daily caloric intake."

"I have no idea what I take in," she said. "I just try to eat when I'm hungry."

"What do you usually have for breakfast?"

"Usually a latte, sometimes a biscotti."

"Okay, what about lunch?"

"I usually get a salad from the Student Union."

"Do you eat anything between breakfast and lunch?"

"No, I almost never eat between meals. And before you ask I usually make soup and a salad for dinner."

"That sounds like you're eating less than 1,000 calories a day!" Ryan nearly shouted.

"Ryan, you told me at the beginning that I needed to eat right. I guess I just ignored you."

"Well, you're not going to ignore me anymore. I'm going to watch you like a hawk. And I'm going to weigh you at the gym every week. If you lose another pound you're moving in to my house. Da will fatten you up in no time!"

"Speaking of eating, do you want to have dinner together on Friday?"

"Uhm, sure," Ryan said as she shook her head slightly at the abrupt change of topic. "I don't have any dinner plans. Where do you want to go?"

"My house. I want to cook for you to thank you for taking such good care of me last night. What's your favorite food?"

"You don't have to do that, Jamie. You're my friend—and my duty as your friend means that I take care of you when you need my help."

"I know that Ryan, but I want to do this. Now spill it!"

"My favorite food—no restrictions?" she asked with a familiar look of satisfied contemplation on her beautiful face. She leaned her head back and closed her eyes, cocking her head just a little as she met Jamie's amused gaze, "Lasagna," she said with finality.

"Lasagna it is."

When they reached the O'Flaherty home, Jamie gave Ryan a broad smile as she said, "Thanks again for being there for me. I just realized that today's Wednesday and you missed all of your clients. Can I pay you back for that?"

"Yes," Ryan said quickly, surprising Jamie a bit. "You can go home and make yourself a nice dinner with the things I bought from the store this morning. Then you can call the nutritionist and make an appointment. After that you can take a long nap and pamper yourself for the rest of the day. If you do all of that we're even," she grinned.

"You're the best friend I have, Ryan," she said softly as she gave her a gentle smile.

After she left the city, Jamie stopped at her favorite gourmet grocery store to buy the ingredients for Bolognese sauce to make Ryan's birthday lasagna. Luckily the store carried her favorite Italian cookbook so she could double-check the ingredients. Once home, she began to make the sauce. She spent a good hour prepping the vegetables and then began to cook. The sauce took her three hours to make, but it was delicious. She cooked spaghetti for her dinner, along with a basil, tomato and montrachet salad that she sprinkled with olive oil and balsamic vinegar. *Is this good enough for you Dr. O'Flaherty?* At around nine-thirty the phone rang. Ryan's deep voice asked, "Did you speak to the nutritionist?"

"Hi, Ryan, yes I dutifully followed your instructions. I'm meeting with him on Monday. And I've eaten so much today I could burst," she laughed.

With uncharacteristic unease Ryan asked, "Uhm … was this your first pregnancy scare?"

"Yeah, it was," Jamie said. "And I certainly hope it's my last."

"One more reason to be thankful I'm a lesbian," Ryan teased. "I'd probably have ten kids by now if I were straight."

"Well, you do seem to have a few things in common with bunnies."

"You're just lucky I can't reach you from here," Ryan replied threateningly.

"Where are you anyway? It sounds loud."

"I'm at a bar in Oakland. I've kinda got a date waiting for me, so I'd better go."

"Okay, you little rabbit. Don't do anything I wouldn't do."

"Don't count on that! They don't call it the luck of the Irish for nothing."

"Are you sure you're up to this?" Ryan asked for the third time. "Yes, Ryan, I'm sure. Tuesday was just an anomaly. I'm much better prepared for the types of calls we can get, I've eaten, and I feel perfectly fine."

Ryan was still concerned, but she trusted Jamie to be able to assess how she felt. As a precaution, she had already decided to tell the operator not to give them any really rough calls if possible.

When they arrived, Yvonne greeted them with concern. "Are you feeling alright, hon?"

"Yeah, I'm fine," Jamie assured her. "That was just a series of factors that combined to knock me out. I'll be fine tonight."

After an hour of fielding mostly routine inquiries, Ryan insisted that they take a break. As they stood outside in the cool night air, Ryan asked Jamie she wanted to take some calls. "Oh, I don't know. I'm still freaked from Tuesday, "she admitted.

"If you want to, I'll talk to the operator and ask her to give you some easy calls. She'll do that if we ask."

Jamie stood in the cool night air, trying to summon the courage to face the unknown. "I'm willing to try, but will you promise to take over if I ask you to?"

"Absolutely," Ryan replied without hesitation, giving her friend an encouraging smile.

"Gay and Lesbian Teen Talk Line, this is Jamie. How can I help you?" she asked nervously.

"Hi, this is Carrie. I've got a problem that I can't figure out. Can you help me?"

"I'll certainly try, Carrie. Tell me about it."

Carrie was sixteen years old and was attracted to her best friend. She knew her friend had been sexual with another girl, but Carrie didn't know if she should pursue her friend, mainly because she wasn't sure what it would do to their friendship. Jamie finally got her to admit that she was also afraid of being labeled gay.

"Tell me about your friend," Jamie asked.

"She's my age and we go to school together. She's real cute and really nice to me," Carrie sighed. "Normally she goes out with boys, but she told me about one time when she went down on a girl."

Jamie blushed as Ryan caught her eye and gave her a little eyebrow wiggle. "We do almost everything together. She's a lot of fun and she makes me laugh all the time," Carrie explained.

"How do you feel when you're with her?"

"It's kinda hard to explain. I guess things just feel right when we're together. My stomach gets all tingly when I know she's coming over."

"Have you had any boyfriends?" Jamie asked.

"Not really boyfriends, but I've gone out with guys."

"Did you ever really, really like a guy?" Jamie asked patiently.

"Yeah, one guy at school, last year. We went out a couple of times, but he dumped me."

"How did you feel about him? Did it feel anything like you feel for your friend?"

"No, not really. I liked him and everything, but it didn't feel like it does with Lori."

"Have you had sex with any guys yet?" Jamie asked.

"No, I haven't had sex. I don't want to until I'm sure about a guy."

Wow, I'm really impressed! Jamie thought. *I was beginning to think that every sixteen-year-old girl had lost her virginity.*

"I've given guys blow jobs, but that's all," Carrie said proudly.

Oh brother! Jamie turned to Ryan who was grinning broadly and trying not to laugh out loud. Sticking her tongue out at her friend, Jamie continued on gamely, "Do you think about having sex with your friend?"

"Oh yeah," she said dreamily. "I think about it all the time. I think about how she'd feel and what it would be like to kiss her and stuff."

"Hmmm," Jamie thought for a moment, and finally replied, "You know Carrie, it's possible to have very complex feelings for your friends. Some of those feelings might be sexual. But just because you have that feeling doesn't make you a lesbian. Actually, sometimes it's hard to tell if your feelings are really sexual or just a desire for closeness. It's possible that you just want to feel even closer to Lori and you think that sex is the way to do that."

"I don't know," Carrie replied suspiciously, "I think I really wanna have sex with her."

Another glance at Ryan earned another lascivious wink.

"Has she given you any indication that she'd like to have sex with you?" Jamie asked.

"No, not really. We hug and stuff but that's about all."

"Imagine that she came over to your house tonight and you had sex. How do you think you'd feel tomorrow?"

"I think I'd feel good ..." she replied, "But I'm afraid that I'd feel gay."

"What does that mean to you, 'to feel gay'?" Jamie asked. "Do you think your friends or your parents would be different to you if they thought you were gay? Or is it how you feel about yourself?"

"I guess I'm afraid of what the other kids at school would say if they found out."

"Do you think that Lori is someone you can trust? How many people did she tell that she had sex with another girl?" Jamie asked.

"I think I'm the only one who knows. None of our other friends have ever mentioned it."

"Okay, I think I've got enough information to give you my opinion," Jamie said after a moment. "It sounds like you really care a lot for Lori. And it also sounds like you're really interested in pursuing a sexual dimension to your relationship. But your privacy is very important too, and you're afraid that your friends will give you a hard time if they found out."

"Yeah, that's all true."

"Do you really feel that you need to make a decision right now?" Jamie asked.

"Uhm, no I guess I don't."

"One option is to continue to play with your fantasies. You could be more open with Lori about your feelings in general. Then if she feels the same way, she may approach you. That might take some of the pressure off," Jamie said.

"Okay, I think I could do that," she said tentatively.

"Another option is to tell her that you're confused by your feelings for her. You can tell her that you feel that things are changing in your relationship and ask if she feels them too. If she says no, you're not as vulnerable as you'd be if you made some physical overture that she didn't like."

"Yeah, I like that idea a lot. That one feels right" Carrie said confidently.

"But there's one thing I want you to remember," Jamie said. "Are you listening?"

"Yeah, I'm listening."

"Having feelings for another woman doesn't make you a lesbian. Acting on those feelings with one woman, or several women doesn't make you a lesbian. Your sexual orientation might not be clear to you until you're in your twenties, or even later. Nothing that you do now has to be permanent. You're still developing your sexuality; so let yourself develop at your own pace. Got it?"

"Got it. Thanks a lot!"

Jamie hung up and looked over at a beaming Ryan. "Jamie," she asked ingenuously, batting her eyes the whole time, "do you think I'm a lesbian?"

"No, I think you're a brat!"

They took another short break for Ryan to heap compliments on her friend. "I can't believe what a good job you did!" she enthused. "You were right there with her. I know you reached her, and your advice was so perfect!"

Jamie beamed at these heartfelt compliments. "I must admit, our class has really helped me see sexuality in much broader terms than I did before. When I was her age I'd have thought that having feelings for a woman would brand me forever. Now I know it doesn't."

Ryan looked right into Jamie's green eyes with a quizzical expression as she cocked her head slightly. Feeling completely exposed, Jamie imagined that her friend saw every one of her secrets. As the silence stretched on, Ryan looked like she wanted to ask a question, but Jamie quickly looked away and said brightly, "Let's go do another!"

"Gay and Lesbian Teen Talk Line, this is Jamie. How can I help you?"

"Hi, this is Star. I've started having sex with my boyfriend and another chick and I don't know how to make sure we have safe sex. Is it okay to go down on her after he comes inside her?"

Jamie sat with her mouth slightly open and a completely stunned expression on her face. She felt the phone being taken from her hand and heard Ryan answer smoothly, "No, Star. You can't safely do that. HIV and other sexually transmitted diseases can infect his semen. Whether it's in his penis or her vagina, it's just as dangerous."

"Well, what can I do to her?" she asked, with a touch of petulance in her voice.

"HIV is found in semen and blood and vaginal secretions. The safest thing to do is to use a barrier between her vagina and your mouth. You can get free latex barriers called dental dams at the Free Clinic. If you get caught in a bind and can't get a dental dam you can cut open a condom. A lot of women really like how it feels, too."

"Yeah, right," she scoffed.

Ryan's brow knit as she insisted. "That really is true, Star. I've been having sex with women for almost six years, and I practice safer sex every single time. And I've got to tell you, I've a great time even with dental dams."

"But how great is the risk?" she demanded.

"It's impossible to say, Star. You'd have to know someone's complete sexual history and the sexual histories of all of their partners to know if you're safe. I've had a lot of great sex, and I've never had an STD. I figure that a little inconvenience isn't as much trouble as sitting in a four-hour line at the Free Clinic for penicillin shots."

"Okay," she relented. "That covers going down on her. What else can I do?"

Isn't that enough? Jamie shouted to herself in indignation.

"Do you ever use sex toys inside each other?" Ryan asked.

"Yeah, sometimes. Is that cool?"

"Not unless you put a condom on each toy every time you use it. If you insert something into anyone take the condom off and put on a new one before you insert it into someone else. And never move a toy from your anus to your vagina without changing the condom. I assume you know that your boyfriend should be using a condom every time you put his penis inside your body."

"Even for blow jobs?"

"Even for blow jobs," Ryan replied gravely. "I know that guys don't want to do it, but it really can be dangerous not to. If you put just a dab of water based lubricant in the condom before you roll it on, it makes it feel better."

"What can I do without latex?" she muttered.

"You don't need latex to touch each other with your hands and there are some great vibrators out there."

"What about kissing?" Star asked, clearly afraid that nothing was safe.

"Go for it," Ryan said. "There's a very small risk, but a girl's gotta have some fun," she said with a twinkle in her eye.

After the call, Jamie hung her head. "I feel like Mary Poppins in a leather bar," she moaned. "I can't believe how little I know, or how little I've experienced."

"There's nothing wrong with taking sex seriously. I think it's really great that you found someone to be monogamous with. Don't be ashamed of that."

"I'm not ashamed. I just feel so naive. These kids are four or five years younger than me, and they've done tons more than I have."

"So, the guys you've been with have been a little conservative. What's wrong with that?"

"Guy," Jamie corrected her.

"What do you mean?"

"I've only had sex with one guy—just Jack. And I mean my definition of sex, not Carrie's," she said, laughing.

"I think that's adorable, Jamie," Ryan replied sincerely. "He must feel special that you felt he was the one you wanted to share your sexuality with."

"I don't know if he feels special. He wasn't particularly happy that I made him wait for so long. I think at times he'd have preferred it if I were the town strumpet."

"How long did you make him wait, if I can ask?"

"Till this past summer," she said, giving Ryan a slight shoulder shrug. "June the fifteenth to be exact."

Ryan nodded her head and looked like she was at a loss for words. Finally she uttered one, "Wow."

As the night wore on, Jamie began to get over her hesitancy and was even able to get through most of the calls without blushing. On the way back to her house, she asked, "Latte for the road?"

"Sure," Ryan replied. They stopped at the local coffee bar and found a small table near the window. "So," Ryan began, "tell me how you're feeling."

"I feel pretty good. I've really cranked up the calories, and I think it's helping already. My stomach is back to normal, so I think I'm ready to start working out again."

"I still want you to take tomorrow off," Ryan said. "You need a few days to get your strength back after being as sick as you were."

"Okay, doc, I'll stay home and get your dinner ready," she said with a smile.

"Can I ask you something pretty personal?" Ryan asked, a tentative expression on her face.

"Sure, I don't have any secrets from you."

"Why were you so devastated when you thought you might be pregnant? I mean, I could see why if you weren't in love with the guy, but you are. And you're getting married in a year and a half. So what's up?"

Jamie sat in silence for a few minutes. She was obviously thinking, so Ryan didn't interrupt. She finally looked up and said, "I'm not sure I know. But it felt absolutely horrible. I felt exactly like I would have when I was sixteen."

"That's kind of odd, don't you think?" Ryan continued. "I also wondered why you wouldn't tell Jack. Shouldn't he have been involved?"

"I don't know," Jamie said. "It just didn't feel like something he could be helpful with. I mean, I know he loves me, but he's not very good at the emotional comfort thing. I think he'd have been upset—probably with me—that we had sex without a condom."

Ryan gave her a wry smile. "Are you in charge of birth control for both of you."

"Welcome to the world of the heterosexual woman," Jamie said. "We're all in charge of birth control—for ourselves and our partners. I can't imagine a guy volunteering to wear a condom."

"Are you on the pill now?"

"Yeah. But I had trouble with the first two types I took. I got breakthrough bleeding with one and the other made me terribly nauseous. So I had to wait a month before I started this new one. Alison told me to use a condom during the transition, but we got carried away once and he snuck up on me early in the morning the other time." She looked down at the table in embarrassment at revealing this intimacy.

Ryan slid her hand over and patted Jamie's. "I'm sorry if I'm prying. I'm just worried about you."

She gave her a broad smile and replied, "It's okay. I know I've got some issues that I have to work out with Jack. I guess I just want to make sure that we don't start our family until we get them resolved. I think we've got quite a few years of growing up before we're ready."

"I think you're awfully mature for a twenty-year-old," Ryan said. "But having kids is a whole new world."

Chapter Seven

Jamie rushed home after her morning classes and dove into her work. She didn't cook elaborate meals very often, but she enjoyed doing so when she got the chance. She actually had more fun making something difficult than cooking an ordinary dinner, especially when she was feeding someone who really enjoyed food—and she didn't know a soul who enjoyed eating more than Ryan. The dish she decided to make was from a tiny little restaurant in Bologna where she had the most extraordinary lasagna imaginable a few years earlier. She was pleased to find the exact recipe in an Italian cookbook, and it was now the only kind of lasagna she'd eat.

Methodically, she assembled all of the ingredients that she'd need, placed them neatly on the counter and then organized all of her utensils and her stainless steel pasta machine.

The first order of business was to make dough. She wanted spinach noodles, so she first had to blanch some fresh spinach. Getting the dough ready was simple, but messy. Mixing eggs and flour together was an easy enough task, but she'd never found a better way than doing it with her hands. When the dough held together she got to her favorite part. Sprinkling flour on the marble, she began to knead the dough. Kneading always reminded her of the fun she had playing with modeling clay when she was young, and she was also able to work out any frustrations when she put her muscles into the job. After about eight minutes of steady work, the dough felt as smooth and supple as a baby's bottom.

Satisfied that the dough was perfect, she clamped the heavy pasta machine to another part of the counter and began to run small sections of the dough through it. She ran the dough through again and again, closing the rollers one notch at a time until all of it was at the proper thickness.

Now came the hard part. She stuck each strip into a large pot of boiling water for mere seconds, then scooped it out and dropped it into a bowl of ice water. After several strips were in the ice bath, she removed them one at a time and ran cold water over them. Then she delicately wrung them dry, treating them rather like fine lingerie, then laid each strip back onto its respective towel to dry.

Well, that was a quick two hours, she thought as she looked at her watch. Ryan was coming over at five, and she felt like she just had enough time to finish the lasagna and the desert and wrap a few little presents. But first, she ate an apple and a few pieces of cheddar cheese, just to satisfy Dr. O'Flaherty. Jamie quickly prepared a béchamel sauce, then she was ready to assemble. She put a thin layer of béchamel sauce on the bottom, then a single layer of green noodles, and a mixture of the warmed Bolognese meat sauce that she had prepared on Wednesday combined with the rest of the béchamel. A bit of freshly grated Reggiano Parmesan completed the first layer.

She repeated this process until she had nine thin layers of pasta and sauce, finding she had just enough sauce left to spread a thin layer on the topmost noodles. She again sprinkled Parmesan on the top and added a few thin pats of butter at various strategic locations. *Not bad for a WASP,* she thought as she stepped back to regard her creation with pride. *Now comes the true test of my prowess.* The dessert she had planned was tricky, but she thought it made the perfect compliment to the lasagna, and she wanted the meal to be very, very special.

She mixed egg yolks with sugar, beating the mixture until it was a beautiful, pale yellow and formed soft ribbons. Fresh orange peel and milk were brought to a simmer, and then added to the eggs. She stopped periodically to run the mixer again, being careful to thoroughly beat the mixture together. Finally, she added a tablespoon of Grand Marnier and stirred it well. She put the whole mixture into a saucepan set on a medium flame, and beat it with a whisk for a couple of minutes, making sure not to let it reach a boil, then she took it off the heat and set it to chill in the refrigerator.

Her next task was to clean the enormous mess she had created. When she had done most of the dishes, the custard was chilled, so she put it into her electric ice cream maker to freeze and let the machine do all the work.

By now it was 4:45 and she knew Ryan would be on time, so she flew around the house and assembled her wrapping paper, tape and scissors. The last gift was just finished when the bell rang at five o'clock on the dot. As she dashed to the door, she quickly hid the small presents, and ran her hands through her hair to order it.

She was greeted by a broadly smiling Ryan who leaned over to give her a hug, a habit they had recently begun when they hadn't seen each other for a few days. Jamie felt very comfortable with the increased intimacy, and found that she missed the contact on the rare occasions Ryan didn't offer it. She was a bit surprised to be hugged today, but only because they had seen each other earlier at class. "You certainly look happy," Jamie said, taking in Ryan's beaming face.

"You're cooking, aren't you?"

"Yes, I most certainly am," Jamie said, unable to keep a silly grin off her face.

"Then I am most certainly happy." She leaned over again and gently brushed her thumb across Jamie's cheek a few times. Holding her hand up close to her eyes, she nodded her head and said, "Flour."

"I get wild when I cook. Who knows what's hiding in my hair!" *God, one smile from her and I'd cook like this every day. The world is lucky that she uses that smile for good, not evil.*

"It smells very good in here," Ryan said, twitching her nose reflectively. "I smell something sweet. Do I get dessert, too?"

"Yes, of course you get dessert. I don't believe in making a partial thank you dinner."

"You don't owe me any thanks, Jamie. We're friends, and I take my friendships very seriously. You were really out of it on Tuesday, and I felt responsible for you. I know you'd do the same for me."

"Well, conceptually you're right, Ryan. But I was thinking about that night, and I don't remember walking on my own volition at any time after that phone call."

"You walked to the car," she said, "but I had to carry you into the house."

"And up that huge staircase?" Jamie asked, already knowing the answer.

"Yeah. You were about to go out again, and I couldn't leave you on that little sofa."

"Okay, now let's switch roles. Where would we be if you had passed out that night?"

"Uhm, still lying on the floor of the building, I guess," she admitted with a smile. "It'd take two men and a strong boy to pick me up."

"My point exactly. My spirit would be willing, but my flesh is weak. So the bottom line is that I'm very thankful not only for your friendship, but your big muscles are awfully nice to have around too."

"So you're just replenishing all of the calories I expended, huh? I guess that does seem fair. But I'll admit that I wished we had the Range Rover that night."

"Why's that?"

"I had to power you up from a deep squat to get you out of the car. I'm gonna have to do some more work on my quads if I'm going to continue to pick you up off the floor." She slapped her ample thigh muscles while grinning at her friend.

The smaller woman laughed and said, "Maybe you shouldn't try to get my weight back up. It might be to your detriment."

"I think I'd rather make sure you don't get that stressed out that badly again," Ryan decided as she slipped her arm around Jamie and they wandered into the kitchen together.

Ryan offered to help with the last of the dinner preparations, so Jamie set her to work on setting the table and choosing some music. Ryan bustled around the large kitchen, discovering on her own where everything was kept.

She was just about finished when Jamie asked, "How do you feel about anchovies?"

"I feel very kindly towards them, as long as they lie still while they're being eaten." She walked up behind Jamie and enthused, "Oh, Caesar salad, my favorite."

"Ryan, I swear that almost everything you eat is your favorite!"

"Well it is," Ryan said, defending herself. "I have tons of favorites, but what I choose to eat at any particular time becomes my favorite right then. Caesar salad is my favorite Italian style salad, particularly when served with anchovies and followed by lasagna."

Jamie smiled at her, loving to hear Ryan explain her reasoning process.

"How much time do you spend thinking about food?"

"A lot. Okay, a whole lot," she amended when she caught Jamie's dubious glance. "Food really is the highlight of most of my days. An hour or so before lunch I start thinking about what I'll have. I do the same at dinner. It gives me a lot of pleasure."

"I guess the pressure is on to perform, huh?" Jamie asked.

"Nope. Not at all. You get tons of points for the effort, even if the execution isn't perfect. Where do you get your recipe for lasagna, anyway? Is it a family secret?"

"I come from a family of diners, not cooks," Jamie said, laughing. "My mother could probably make a peanut butter sandwich, but I've never actually seen her do it. And come to think of it, I'm certain she'd never eat peanut butter, so it really would be a lost exercise."

"Are you being serious?" Ryan asked as she stopped in the middle of the kitchen and stared, absolutely dumbfounded.

"Completely. I've never eaten a meal that my mother prepared for me. Come to think of it," she said, a thoughtful expression on her face, "I wasn't even breast fed."

"Not even tea and toast when you were sick?" Ryan asked, her mouth gaping open.

"Nope. I had a nanny who took care of me when I was sick. My mother didn't get involved in the day-to-day caretaker stuff."

"God, Jamie, I find that so hard to believe!"

"Well, it's true. Our relationship has always been friendly and pleasant enough, but distant. She traveled and spent time on her hobbies, but child rearing wasn't really one of them."

Friendly? Pleasant? What kind of words are those to use for your relationship with your mother? "So how did you learn to cook?" Ryan asked, trying to change the depressing subject.

"We had a great cook named Marta. She's still with us, as a matter of fact. She's from Spain, but she can cook anything. She does a lot of Northern Italian cuisine because that's my mother's favorite, but she can also do classical French and some great spicy Spanish dishes for my father and me."

"Did you just watch and learn?"

"No, she was a really good teacher. She knew I was interested, and she spent a lot of time with me, teaching me the fundamentals. My mother found it odd that I wanted to spend my time chopping vegetables into julienne, but she didn't mind much as long as I was entertained. Actually, Marta was one of the best teachers I ever had. She didn't have any children, and we spent a ton of time together just talking and hanging out."

Ryan was enormously saddened to hear her friend speak of this emotionless upbringing. The thought of young Jamie having to get her parenting from the hired help was just too much to consider. She tried to change the subject again. "So, you know my favorite food, what's yours?"

Jamie turned thoughtful as she finished tossing the Caesar salad. "I think my favorite is a good steak and pomes frites from a French bistro. I've had some extraordinary meals at Chez Laurent," she said. "Have you been there?"

"No, but Conor has. He said he liked it, but the portions weren't big enough. Not that that's surprising," she said. "He's used to getting seconds."

"I think we're ready to eat. Hungry?"

"I was hungry when I got here. But smelling that lasagna cook has put me into a whole new classification of hunger. It's beyond famished … bordering on starvation, I think."

"Then have a seat and get ready. I'll take the lasagna out so it can cool for a minute." She went to the oven and pulled out the pan, finding that Ryan didn't sit down as instructed, but walked right behind her, looking over her shoulder, mouth watering.

"God, Ryan, you look like a hungry wolf with a wounded animal in its sights."

"That's exactly how I feel at the moment," she said, never taking her eyes from their bubbling target. "I think I'm willing to risk burns to my mouth to eat that right now."

Jamie grabbed her by the shoulders and turned her firmly around to face the kitchen table, giving her a little push as she said, "Sit. Now."

Ryan complied, grumbling the whole time.

"Would a Caesar salad placate you for a few minutes?"

"I suppose," she moaned as she let out an aggrieved sigh.

Jamie filled two salad bowls and deposited them on the table. Ryan dug in, and in moments her face became a study of various levels of pleasure. She started at mere happiness and by the fourth bite had progressed to ecstasy. "My God, this is good," she moaned. "You've ruined me for life. All other Caesar salads will be pale imitations. I'll never be satisfied with another!"

"Then you'll just have to come here when you need a fix," Jamie replied, terribly pleased at the effusive compliments.

Ryan mopped up every bit of dressing with a piece of crunchy Italian bread. "Is it rude to lick the salad bowl?"

"There's just a tiny bit left, but be careful that you don't ruin you appetite. We've got a lot of lasagna waiting for us."

"My physiology is just like a cow's. I've got six stomachs, all in different stages of digestion. I'll just put the entree in another stomach." She was already on her feet, moving toward the salad bowl. As she passed the cooling lasagna, she leaned down and gave it a hearty sniff. "You're next," she growled.

Jamie laughed heartily at her antics. Ryan was so full of life, so immersed in the pleasure of whatever she was involved in, that it was impossible not to enjoy being with her. Jamie thought of all the women that Ryan had been with and felt a little sorry for them. She knew how much they must crave further contact, and how few of them got their wish. She considered herself very lucky to be able to be close to Ryan and receive so much of her time.

Ryan was polishing off the remnants of the salad right from the serving bowl. She used more bread to capture every bit of dressing and every tiny green leaf that tried in vain to escape.

"I don't think I've ever met anyone who enjoys food as much as you do. You seem so immersed in the whole experience. It's fun to watch!"

Ryan's face grew serious. "Honestly, that's my whole philosophy of life. I try to be fully involved in whatever I'm doing. The simplest task is beautiful if I'm fully into it. When I eat I try to feel it with every sense. That's why I love to eat with my hands. I love the feel and the texture of food. I love to look at food before I eat it. I love the colors and variety of textures. I even enjoyed the crunch the croutons in the salad made." She grinned at her friend with a slightly embarrassed smile. "I know that sounds kinda nutty, but that's how I approach life."

"That's the least nutty thing I've ever heard," Jamie replied. "You're really teaching me a lot about savoring life, Ryan, and I want you to know how grateful I am for that."

Ryan gave her a full, warm smile, looking pleased. "I didn't realize that, but I'm glad it's helpful for you. I made up my mind when I was a teenager that I wasn't going to let life pass me by. I knew that every day we have is a gift, and I try to make the most of every one."

"Speaking of gifts," Jamie said as she rose and walked to the counter, "happy birthday, Ryan." She lit the candle that she had placed in the lasagna and carried the large pan to the table, leaning over her shoulder to give her a kiss on the cheek.

"How did you know?" she asked, her voice betraying her delight as well as her surprise. "I'm sure I didn't tell."

"No you didn't, you big dope. I had to find out from Conor."

"You know, you're right. I should have told you. I usually spend the day with my family, and sometimes I forget to include other people. I kind of hate to have a big deal made out of it, but I should have included you. I'm really glad that Conor told you."

Jamie served up a steaming plate of the lasagna, and Ryan took a hearty bite. She was silent as she closed her eyes, deep in concentration. Jamie could just imagine each of her senses kicking in, feeling and tasting and smelling the delectable bite.

"If I didn't believe in God before today, I would now. This," she said while she waved another forkful of the dish at Jamie, "is a clear sign that God loves us and wants us to be happy."

"I'm glad I could make you something that you enjoy so much," Jamie said, trying unsuccessfully to control her beaming smile.

"I've eaten lasagna at least two hundred times in my life. I order it every time it's on the menu. But I can truly say I've never tasted lasagna before today."

Jamie just grinned in response.

They ate in silence for a few minutes to allow Ryan to concentrate. Finally, she looked up from her plate. "I have to know how you made this. There's nothing about this that I recognize, not the noodles, not the sauce, nothing! Most of the time lasagna is heavy and kinda oily. This is so light and delicate."

Jamie explained the entire process, with Ryan watching her in rapt fascination. Finally she shook her head and locked her clear blue eyes on her friend. "You did that all for me?"

"Yep. And I'd do it again in a minute to see you enjoy yourself so much."

"Do you cook like this for Jack?" Ryan asked after a moment, a bit off topic.

"I do cook for him, but I don't think I've ever done anything very elaborate. He doesn't care about food a lot. He thanks me for cooking, but in the same way he thanks me for vacuuming. I think he eats to live, and that's about it."

"Well, anytime you need an enthusiastic taste tester, you know where to find me."

"I'll keep your name on file," Jamie replied with a grin.

After Ryan had eaten much more than Jamie thought wise, they sat together in the living room with large cups of cappuccino. "Is there anything you don't cook well?" Ryan asked as she sipped her coffee.

"I'm sure I've screwed up my share of meals. I just had a good day," she said. "But I must admit, cooking for an appreciative audience is part of the fun."

"If I were any more appreciative I'd be on the phone to the Vatican petitioning you for early sainthood."

"I was thinking about the teen talk line," Jamie said after a few moments. "Yvonne said you were the volunteer who logged the most hours. When did you put in all of that time?"

Ryan was silent for a few moments. She looked down at the floor, and finally said, "It's a long, sad story. Are you sure you want to hear it?"

"Only if you want to talk about it."

"Yeah. I like to reflect on my life on my birthday. It's a good way to appreciate all of the gifts I've been given. So I don't mind. But I guess I've got to go back to high school to have it make sense. Did I ever tell you about Sara?" When Jamie shook her head, Ryan continued. "She was my best friend all through grammar and high school. Remember the caller you helped the other night—the girl who was in love with her best friend?"

Jamie nodded.

"It was like that for me. I was totally in love with Sara. She was my whole world. I've never felt like that about anyone—before or since," she admitted, her hooded eyes dark. "I went to an all-girls, Catholic high school. I knew that I was different from my friends, but it didn't bother me. I thought I was just unique," she said as she gave Jamie a crooked grin. "I didn't ever have a crush on a guy or have any desire to go out with one. Luckily, we didn't have the pressure of having guys around all the time, so the issue was never forced. I honestly never considered that I might be gay, though. I just thought I was … me. I thought everyone had crushes on her girlfriends and teachers. I honestly thought everyone scheduled her week around *Cagney and Lacey*," Ryan said with a small laugh at the memory.

Jamie didn't understand the reference, but she nodded to encourage Ryan to continue.

"Anyway, as the years passed, I began to feel more than close to Sara. I wanted to be with her, even though I didn't really know what that meant or how to go about it. I was really naive when it came to sex. That was one area where Da did a crummy job. And the boys were certainly no help. It might have been different if I had been worldlier, but my whole universe was sports and Sara. I didn't watch TV very often or go to many movies or participate much in community events so I was just not clued into lesbianism."

"You must have been so confused," Jamie empathized.

"In a way I was, but in another way I assumed Sara felt like I did. We were so close it was like we shared a soul." Ryan dropped her head a little, but continued. "I was finding the temptation overwhelming just to touch or kiss her. She was all that I thought about, Jamie. I wanted to let her know how I felt, but I was so confused about what this thing was, that I didn't feel able to."

Jamie nodded to encourage Ryan to continue.

"One night I was staying over at Sara's. We did that a lot. It was the end of my junior year. She was a year older, and had already decided to accept a soccer scholarship at Cal. Her graduation was in a couple of weeks, and she was going to go to a soccer camp in San Diego as soon as school was over. I was panicked at the thought of her going away, and I let my fear of losing her override my fear of expressing myself."

Jamie cringed, knowing right where this was heading.

"We got into bed and I started talking. I told her that I didn't think I could live without her. I told her everything—how much I wanted her, how I dreamed about her, how she meant everything to me. She was kind of quiet, but I thought she agreed. After a minute, I reached for her and I kissed her. I had never kissed another person in my life and it was kind of overwhelming." She shook her head and stared at the floor. "I was shaking so hard she must have heard my teeth chattering, and I could tell she was nervous, too. But God, Jamie," she took a deep breath and let her head drop back against her shoulders, "nothing in this whole world has ever felt that good to me."

"What happened, Ryan?" the smaller woman asked softly, her stomach in knots as she guessed the outcome.

"I thought she was enjoying it as much as I was," Ryan said with a rasp in her voice. "No, I know she was enjoying it. I know it," she said firmly, her eyes tightly closed.

Jamie moved closer, drawn to comfort her friend. She didn't touch her, but she was so close she could feel the heat radiating off her body.

"In my fumbling, terrified way I kept going. I don't know where I got the courage, but I got more and more bold. I explored every inch of her body with my hands. After a long time of tender touches we began to get more passionate. And it wasn't just me. She didn't touch me like I touched her, but she kissed me with so much emotion …" Ryan closed her eyes again and stared up at the ceiling. "I can still taste her lips," she whispered as she shook her head and took in a deep breath. She seemed on the verge of tears, but she gathered herself and continued. "Eventually, I discovered what she liked and brought her to orgasm. I cannot tell you how that made me feel. I can honestly say that was the happiest moment of my young life. I felt closer to her than I thought possible. I'd used my hands and my body to give her such pleasure. She seemed so satisfied, and a few moments later she kissed me with such love in her eyes. She fell asleep in my arms, and I held onto her like she was a treasure that I had to protect."

Ryan blew out a big breath, and Jamie steeled herself for the inevitable.

"I didn't sleep much that night. It felt so wonderful to be that close to her. I can't describe it as anything other than feeling like I was finally home. I watched her sleep and occasionally would kiss her forehead or brush her hair back from her eyes. Through that long night my mind was a blur … I was planning our lives together," she said wistfully. "I decided that night that when I followed her to Cal we'd live together and start our lives together." She smiled sadly at the memory.

"In the morning, Mrs. Andrews came to wake us up. Sara acted very flustered when her mom was there, and I figured she was nervous about us getting caught. She came up with some lame excuse and told me she had to go somewhere with her mother. I felt funny about it, but I wasn't really worried." Ryan shook her head slowly, then allowed it to drop until her chin practically hit her chest. In a voice raspy with emotion, she concluded, "I should have been worried. That was the last conversation we ever had."

Jamie sat in the still room with her hand on Ryan's knee. She knew the depth of the hurt—could see it on Ryan's face—hear it in her voice. But she had no words to heal the old pain. Instead, she just patted Ryan's knee in sympathy and understanding.

"She wouldn't return my phone calls. On Monday at school she wouldn't even make eye contact with me. I honestly almost lost my mind that day. After school I went to her house. Her mom told me that she didn't want to see me anymore. She asked me to never call their house again."

"How unspeakably cruel!" Jamie shouted in indignation. "How could she do that to you?"

"You know, that's one of the things that made it worse, if that's even possible. I was really close to her mom. She was one of my primary mother substitutes, but I never saw her again after that day. But I don't blame her." She gave Jamie a small grin as she admitted; "I can't say the same for Da or the boys though. Sara was obviously really upset, and I guess her mom didn't want it to get any worse. Sara must have told her what had happened, because her mom told me that she hoped things worked out for me, but that Sara wasn't like I was. I don't know," she said softly. "If my daughter were in the same situation I might have done the same thing."

"I don't believe that for a minute, Ryan," Jamie said firmly. "If you were her mother you'd find a way to be supportive of a child that was going through a very difficult time. You wouldn't turn your back on a girl who needed you!" Jamie continued to stroke and pat her leg, and Ryan finally gave her a smile.

"It was a terrible time. After the loss of my mother, this was the worst thing that ever happened to me. It screwed up the way I felt about myself for a very long time. It was the only time in my life that I felt bad about being gay. I believed every bad thing I had ever heard about gay people. If someone as wonderful as Sara and as great as her mother thought I was sick, I assumed that I must be. I started doing some crazy stuff—hanging out in the Castro, and going to bed with older women. I was almost seventeen, but I looked older, and I'd be with anyone who wanted me. It's funny," she said thoughtfully, "but even though I had a lot of sex, I didn't really get anything out of it for a long time. I just wanted the contact. I wanted to be with other freaks like me."

"Oh, Ryan, you're not a freak." Jamie was unable to contain herself any longer. She wrapped her arms around her friend and hugged her close, saying again and again, "You're such a wonderful woman … I'm so sorry you had to go through that."

Ryan nodded, deeply touched by how much her friend empathized with her. "You know, that's what's so hard for so many gay kids. We don't get a chance to develop like straight kids do. Not many of us get to have normal dating relationships. A lot of us go from a crush to having sex. And I realize now how harmful that is for kids. It's too overwhelming to have your first kiss followed by your first time making love."

"How did you come out of it?" the smaller woman asked.

"It took a while. The next school year things got quite a bit worse. I'll save the details on that fiasco for another day. Sara obviously told some people about what I did to her, and everyone started to treat me like a pariah. I spent the whole year just trying to survive. It was an unbelievably tough year."

"Didn't you talk to anyone?" Jamie inquired gently as she continued to run her hand up and down Ryan's leg.

"Yeah, I did, but it took me a while. My first semester grades came out over Christmas break, and Brendan sat me down and said he was worried about me. The boys didn't know what I was doing, but they knew that I'd changed. I never came home drunk when Da was home, but he was gone three nights out of the week. Brendan was away at school, and Conor and Rory had their own things going on, so they didn't keep a very close eye on me. When we talked, Brendan told me that I could tell him anything, and after a good bit of prodding he pulled it out of me. He was so wonderful, Jamie." Ryan smiled at the memory. "He was so completely understanding. He reassured me that there was nothing wrong with me. He said that as I got older I'd find lots of women who wanted to be with me. A little while after we talked I made myself tell Da and the other boys. I've never asked Brendan, but I think he told them first so they'd be prepared. They were all super. Da told me that I was precious to him no matter who I loved."

"I'm so glad they were all supportive of you, Ryan. That must have really helped."

"More than I could have imagined. I didn't feel like I was bad for being this way any more. My self-image got a lot better, and I stopped being with people just because they wanted me. Brendan did some research, and he hooked me up with the teen talk line. I talked to someone really nice who was very supportive. She told me about the coffee house and some other places where young women could go. After a while I went to the talk line and got trained as a peer counselor. Talking to other kids helped me realize how good things were for me. By second semester my grades were back up, but I had screwed up at the worst time. My scholarship to Cal was withdrawn and I had to come up with another plan."

"What did you do?" Jamie asked.

"Conor started taking me to the gym with him, and I really got into it. After I graduated, I spent the summer taking classes to become a trainer, and I worked every possible minute that I could. I had been accepted at the University of San Francisco as my fallback school, but it was really expensive, so I had to work full time to be able to afford the tuition."

"But why go somewhere so expensive? Couldn't you have gotten in somewhere else?"

"Getting in places wasn't a problem," Ryan assured her. "But I had such a hard time during my senior year that I couldn't bear to live away from home. I really needed emotional support. Besides, after all of the problems I had in school, taking a couple of years off seemed really appealing. So I worked for two years and I really enjoyed it. I could focus on what was important to me. In retrospect, it was a foolish decision to waste two years and have to pay my own way, but I was so heartbroken over not being given my scholarship that I just couldn't bear to attend Cal. And the thought of seeing Sara around campus was something I couldn't risk. After I completed two years at USF, I decided that I had sulked long enough and I transferred. Cal's where I'd always dreamed of going, and I finally decided that I was only hurting myself by not going there."

Jamie patted her back, her mind reeling with thoughts of how her friend had struggled because of her sexuality. "I can't fathom how hard things must have been for you."

"Yeah, but I got through it. And I feel pretty darned good about myself now. I mean, I must be doing something right to merit a friend like you.' She looked over at Jamie with those clear blue eyes, her mouth quirked into a warm grin.

Jamie just soaked in the words of friendship that Ryan offered with such ease. *I don't understand why she isn't in a relationship! It seems so easy for her to open up and show her feelings. Is she really that different when sex is involved?*

After Ryan had digested enough of her dinner to allow for dessert, Jamie led her back into the kitchen. "I hope you like this," she said, concern showing through. "I know you say you like everything, but this is a little different." Ryan's interested expression led her to continue. "The last time my mother and I were in Bologna, we had this at the same restaurant that made this style of lasagna. It's really the prototypical dessert of the region, and I thought it would be a perfect compliment to dinner."

Ryan watched as Jamie took the frozen insert of the ice cream maker from the freezer and removed two pale green milk glass bowls from the cabinet, scooping the frozen concoction into the bowls. Then she artfully arranged some delicate orange and chocolate flavored cookies on a matching plate. She shot a look at Ryan, and saw her eyes go wide.

"You *made* ice cream?" she asked dubiously. "I thought you had to be Ben or Jerry to make ice cream."

"No, it's not hard if you have a good ice cream maker."

"You know, you're the last person in the world who should be underweight. You obviously don't cook much for yourself." Ryan playfully tried to pinch her friend's waist.

"No, I really don't," she giggled as she tried to dance out of the way. "I like to cook for other people."

"If you don't stop saying that you're gonna find me on your door step every evening," Ryan playfully threatened. Her attention was focused on her bowl as she took her first big bite of the custard. Her eyes closed, and she dropped her head to her chest. Both hands came up and balled into fists, and she lightly pounded on the table for a few beats, then looked up at Jamie in wonder. Her hands opened and rose halfway to her face, then she shook her hands lightly as she wagged her head from side to side.

Not a word had been spoken, but Jamie knew that she was being lavishly complimented. After every bite Ryan would look at her with a delighted expression of amazement. Finally, when her bowl was clean, Ryan finally muttered, "I have no words." She shook her head again and looked rather helpless as she said, "If I could have another bowl, I'd be forever grateful."

As her second bowl was presented, Ryan predicted, "I'm sure I'll be more erudite after my second helping." She dug in again, but was once more totally silent. Her brows knit in concentration, and she looked very reflective a couple of times, as if she had a point to make, but she'd again shake her head lightly and shrug her shoulders in a sign of defeat. She regarded her friend once again, and admitted, "I just can't form a cogent thought. I want to do justice to that ambrosia, but I'm unable to come up with a compliment that's representative of my feelings."

"None needed," Jamie replied as she gently patted her cheek. "Just watching you eat is the supreme compliment." As she spoke, she rose and crossed the room to retrieve the hidden presents. She brought the small pile over to a dumbstruck Ryan who finally gave her a delighted smile.

"Jamie, you certainly didn't have to buy me presents after all this!"

"I know I didn't have to. But I wanted to. It really gave me a lot of enjoyment to be able to buy you a few things."

"Okay, you win. If you get pleasure out of doing this, then I'm going to shut up and let myself enjoy it," she decided as she grabbed the first box.

Jamie watched her face take on a childlike glee as she shook each box in turn. "I like to guess. Can I?"

"Of course, birthday girl. You can do anything you want."

"What I want is for you to be my personal chef," she said with a grin. "But I'll settle for opening my presents." She shook a box that was about nine inches square, noticing that it gave a funny little rumble. "Hmm," she mused. The next box was even smaller, about two by three inches. As she shook this one, a muffled, wooden, clicking sound emanated from it. The last gift was about seven inches long and four inches wide. It was no more than a quarter inch thick and made no sound when shaken. "I think I'm ready," she finally pronounced. "I believe there's a common theme?"

"Yep, there certainly is."

"So one box will lead me to guess the others?"

"Most likely."

"Okay," she said as she waved the long, thin package. "I think this one is a golf glove."

"How did you do that?" Jamie inquired, quite amazed.

"Well, you did just buy me one. I remember the shape of the package it came in. And I can detect a leather aroma. See?" she offered the package up to Jamie's nose.

"Wow, how good is your sense of smell?"

"It's pretty good, I guess. I don't realize how good it is until I can catch a scent several moments before anyone else. Sometimes I even beat Duffy," she said proudly. "And I'm the official smeller of anything suspect in the refrigerator." She quickly tore open the little package. "Oh, a white one. Now I won't clash when I wear another color." She opened the cardboard cover and slipped the glove on. "You remembered my size!" she said with delight. "Thanks, Jamie." She half got out of her seat and leaned over to kiss her on the cheek.

Jamie knew that she shouldn't feel a flash of pleasure tear up her spine, but she quickly convinced herself that the excitement of watching her friend's joy had become contagious.

Ryan tore through the rest of the neatly wrapped presents, correctly guessing the two dozen golf balls and the little box of tees. She hadn't guessed that the tees were personalized however, and this detail delighted her to no end. "These are the bomb, Jamie," she said as she shook the box. She hopped up once again to kiss the other cheek, and Jamie briefly wished that she had wrapped each of the tees separately. "I'm gonna feel like a pro with all my cool stuff."

Her glee continued when she opened the last box. It was a gleaming, golden set of ball markers and a divot tool. Each was neatly monogrammed with "S.R.O." Ryan jumped up and came over to Jamie's side of the table, grabbing her hands as she pulled her to her feet. "This is all so nice," she enthused. "I can't thank you enough." They stood toe-to-toe, Ryan's hands on Jamie's shoulders, smiling faces locked onto each other. Ryan bent to kiss her cheek just as Jamie turned her head slightly, thinking she heard a noise in the parlor. The edges of their lips brushed just a tiny bit, no more than a quarter inch, the chaste kiss causing a jolt of feeling that suffused Jamie's entire body. She stood in shocked silence, her mind desperately trying to explain her feelings away.

Ryan didn't seem to notice her reaction, as she wrapped her in her powerful arms for a generous hug. Jamie felt the larger body noticeably stiffen in the middle of the embrace. She pulled back and watched Ryan's face close as she backed away. Moments later, the kitchen door opened and Mia walked in.

"Wow, what smells so good?" she inquired brightly. "Hi Ryan, Jamie".

"Hi, Mia," they both replied, nearly in unison.

Mia walked over to the pan of the now cooled lasagna, grabbed a knife from the drawer and carved off a piece. She stuck the whole big bite in her mouth and mumbled around it, "This is great. Did you make this?"

"Yeah, I did," Jamie replied.

"What gives?" Mia asked as she looked at the gift laden table. "Is it your birthday or something, Ryan?"

"Yep, it sure is."

"That's cool. Happy birthday," she said as she surprised Ryan by walking over to her and giving her a hug.

"Thanks. It's been a very happy birthday so far," she said, grinning at Jamie.

"Oh, that reminds me," Mia added. "Jamie tells me that you've got available time on Monday, Wednesday and Friday afternoons. I think she's started to look great, and I don't want her to get too far ahead of me in the looks department." She shot Jamie a playful grin. "Would you be willing to work with me?"

"Absolutely. Do you know what my rates are?"

"Yeah, Jamie told me. That's not a problem. Can we start on Monday? I want to look good for this summer when I go to L.A."

Ryan marveled at the financial freedom these women had. Dropping $375 a week on a whim wasn't something she could ever imagine doing, but she was glad that Mia was able to do it.

After Mia left, Ryan gave Jamie another winning grin as they sat back down at the kitchen table. "You couldn't stand not to have me get paid for those hours could you?"

"Nope. You're gonna be swimming in dough when I get through with you," she laughed. "Hey, I forgot to ask why you were available today. I figured you'd be with your family."

"Da had to work tonight, so a bunch of my relatives are coming over for a barbecue tomorrow." After a moment she looked at Jamie and asked, "Would you like to come? I'd love for you to meet the rest of my family."

Jamie was very tempted to immerse herself in a whole sea of O'Flahertys, but since Jack had been none too happy about her absence this evening, she thought she'd better not. "I wish I could, but I need to go down to Palo Alto."

"No big deal. You'll have plenty of opportunities. Actually, I was surprised that you were available tonight. You've never stayed in Berkeley on a Friday evening, have you?"

"No. You've never had a birthday on a Friday evening, silly," she said as she grinned over at her friend.

"Did you really stay in town just for me?"

"Well, yeah," Jamie replied as if the answer should be obvious. "I was going to have you over next week to celebrate, but when I found out you were free on your actual birthday I decided I had to move it up."

Ryan gazed at her for several minutes, her intense sapphire eyes never wavering from their hold on Jamie's. "You're so thoughtful and so giving … I hope … I hope

Jack appreciates you like he should." She took Jamie's hand in both of her own, and idly traced the tendons visible just under the skin.

"I … I … think he does," she stuttered as she tried to appear casual, her heart thumping rapidly in her chest at the feel of Ryan's hands. "My birthday wish for you is that you find someone who truly appreciates how special you are."

"Thanks," she said as she continued to hold her gaze. "I hope so too."

"So what are the rest of your plans for the evening?" Jamie inquired, trying to lighten the mood. "Surely you won't be without female companionship?"

"I guess I could be wrong, but you certainly seem like a female to me," Ryan replied dryly, running her eyes up and down her friend's torso to double check.

Gulping audibly, Jamie said, "That's not the type of companionship I meant, and you know it."

"Okay, okay. I do have plans to meet someone later."

"Anyone special?"

"No, not really." She shrugged her shoulders, giving Jamie a blank look.

"Gee, that must make her feel good."

"That's not what I meant," Ryan said, clearly embarrassed. "I just meant, well, you know what I meant." She looked to Jamie for understanding, but found a blank face. "I'm still seeing that woman you saw me with at the coffeehouse. I like her, I really do. I don't sleep with people I don't like," she said, defending herself. "But I don't see this progressing very far. It's just fun."

"Why?" Jamie asked, cocking her head a little.

"Why?"

"Yeah, why won't this last?"

"One big reason—and I think it's a good one," she replied with a chuckle. "She doesn't think she's gay."

"Really?" Jamie asked, rather shocked.

"Really. Robin has a boyfriend who goes to the University of Washington. He's actually on the football team, so I hope he never finds out about me!" she said with a crooked smile. "I don't think I'd look good with two black eyes and a few broken bones!"

"Uhm … doesn't that bother you?"

"What? That she's bi-sexual, or that I'm cheating with some guy's girlfriend?"

"Uhm … either, I guess."

"Well, it doesn't bother me a bit that she's bi-sexual. I think we're way too caught up on labels for our behavior. And two—she claims that they both date others during the school year. They're just monogamous when they're in the same city"

"Would it bother you if she *were* cheating?" Jamie asked, knowing that she was treading in waters where she didn't belong.

"Uhm … I guess it depends. I'd never try to get someone to cheat, and I'd never seek out someone I knew was in a relationship, but I've slept with women who were involved with someone else, and it didn't really bother me. It's their relationship, and if they want to screw it up I feel like it's not my business. But I'll admit I could never be serious about anyone who cheated. If they do it to someone else, they'll probably do it to me."

"Yeah, I can see that would prevent you from trusting someone. So it doesn't bother you a bit that she has a boyfriend?"

Ryan pursed her lips and gave the question some serious thought. "Well, I guess if I'm completely honest there's one thing that bothers me. I don't mind that she has a boyfriend, but it does bother me that she doesn't really want to be seen in public with me."

"*What?* She's ashamed of dating you?"

Ryan gave her a delightfully crooked grin and said, "That outraged tone was a very nice compliment, Jamie. Thanks for the props."

"Well, really, Ryan," she scoffed. "What kind of idiot wouldn't want to be seen with you?"

"She doesn't want her boyfriend to find out about me. He doesn't know that she dates women."

"Oh," Jamie replied with a slight head nod. "So *he* doesn't know she's bisexual."

"Correct." Ryan stood and extended her hand to Jamie. "Enough of this serious talk," she said with a wide smile. "I think it's time we went to our respective lovers and had some fun!" As they walked to the door, Ryan started to soulfully sing the chorus of an old song, throwing her head back as she belted out, "We are strangers by day, lovers by night. Knowing it's so wrong—but feeling so right!"

Jamie gave her a hard bump with her hip as they neared the door. "You get a lot of pleasure out of being bad, don't you?"

"Go with your strengths!"

"You're incorrigible, Ryan."

"I do my best," she replied with a grin.

When Jamie walked into Jack's apartment a little before ten, the look on his face told her more about his mood than she wanted to know. "Hi, honey," she called out in greeting, trying to act like she didn't know he was upset.

"Hi," he replied, barely looking up from his book.

"Did you have dinner? I brought you some lasagna."

"Yeah, I made myself a sandwich."

"Is everything okay, Jack?" she asked, even though she didn't want to open what she knew would be a nasty can or worms.

"Sure, why wouldn't it be?" he coolly replied, again not lifting his head to look at her.

She was already sick of his attitude, so she turned the tables on him. "No reason that I can think of," she said with a sweet tone. "I'm going to get ready for bed. Be back in a minute." She could feel his eyes burning into her as she walked down the hallway, but she refused to beg him to talk if he didn't want to.

She brushed her teeth and washed her face, both at a leisurely pace. Stripping off her clothes, she put on one of Jack's T-shirts, then picked up a novel by Djuna Barnes that she had to finish by Monday.

As she walked back into the living room, she asked if he needed anything while she was up. He muttered something under his breath, and it sounded like "a full time fiancée," but she acted as though she hadn't heard a word. Inwardly she was seething, and the smile she gave him was obviously fake. Sitting down on the end of the couch, she put her feet up on his lap and refused to let his cold disregard penetrate her outer demeanor. Luckily, her novel was mesmerizing, and she was fully engrossed for almost two hours. True to his always-stubborn form, Jack didn't loosen up one bit, not touching her in any way—completely ignoring her presence in the room.

At around midnight, he stretched and announced, "I'm going to bed."

She waited until he was about halfway up, then gave him an "inadvertent" push with her foot. He grumbled a bit, but still said nothing. The rigors of the day caught up with her and she decided to turn in also.

As she turned off the lights and followed him into bed, she expected the tension to remain, but much to her shock, as soon as he got into bed he started to make sexual overtures. *Oh, please! You can't say a civil word to me but now you want to screw me?* She was angry … angrier than she had ever been with him. She was shocked at the words that came out of her mouth, but she was bound and determined not to have sex with him. So, for first time in their relationship, she found herself intentionally trying to hurt him. "Jack, I have something to tell you."

He lifted his head from her breast with a quizzical look, but still said nothing.

"I had a pregnancy scare this week." She didn't have a lot of experience in this area, but she honestly thought he might have just set the speed record for deflating penises. He shot up into a sitting position, and stared at her with a look of pure horror of his face.

"What happened? Why? What …"

"I haven't been feeling well for over a month, and I've been queasy in the mornings. But on Tuesday I passed out, and that made me take action," she related, leaving out every pertinent piece of information that might have actually helped him to understand the whole situation.

"What … Where …?"

"I went to my doctor on Wednesday, and she gave me a pregnancy test. Obviously it was negative," she said without further elaboration.

"Where's your doctor?" he finally got out.

"Palo Alto," she said with a small smile, knowing that he'd be hurt to find out that her doctor was three minutes from his campus.

He gave her a look of total disgust and said, "Since you didn't call me to go with you, I guess I don't have to ask who did."

"Maybe if you tried really, really hard you could be more self centered," she said, with yet another false smile. "I was feeling sick for a month, unable to eat in the mornings because of nausea. I faint twice in one night, and vomit all over greater

Berkeley. I have to skip a day of school to go to the doctor. I find out I've lost ten pounds without wanting to or trying to. The doctor takes my blood and runs a bunch of tests to find God knows what. But I can see that your most pressing concern would be who took me to the doctor!"

"You have the nerve, the unmitigated gall to bust my chops and try to make me feel sorry for you!" he shouted. "How the fuck can I feel sorry for you when I don't know any of this! I'm your fucking fiancé, Jamie! You didn't tell me that you've been sick, you didn't tell me that you've lost weight and you didn't tell me that you passed out! How in the fuck can I feel bad for you?"

He leapt from the bed and started pacing in a straight line, back and forth across the carpet. His agitation was growing by the minute, and Jamie was almost afraid of him. In three years she had never even heard him raise his voice, much less curse at her, and she hoped it would be a very long time until it happened again.

"I can guess why you didn't tell me about your pregnancy scare," he growled. "You and your buddy would just decide what to do about it. You two could have gone behind my back to abort my child!" He stopped abruptly and stared at Jamie with cold fury, but when he saw the frightened look on her face every bit of his anger evaporated. He looked like he had been punched in the solar plexus as his shoulders dropped along with his head. All of the fire, all of the spark were just … gone. He came back to the bed and sat on the edge, facing the wall.

For a few moments the room was filled with silence, the loudest silence she had ever heard. Forcing herself to look at the situation from his perspective, she allowed herself to feel some empathy for him. He looked like a thoroughly defeated man, and she cursed herself for intentionally trying to hurt him. She crawled over to him and put her arms around him from behind, and he stiffened at first, but as she murmured into his ear, he began to relax.

"I'd never do that, Jack. I'd never, ever abort a child, especially yours. I love you; I don't want to hurt you," she whispered.

He pulled her arms from his neck and got fully onto the bed. His last words were, "No matter what your intent is, you're hurting our relationship, Jamie. You need to make some choices."

They kept a very cool distance in bed. She was dismayed to wake up at seven and find him gone. There was a note on the kitchen counter that read, "Law Review deadline on Monday. Be back late, Jack." *Well, that says it all*, she thought glumly. *No, "Love, Jack," no "I'm sorry," no "I'll call you later."* Jamie booted up his computer and his printer, then sat down to compose her thoughts.

Dear Jack,

I'm sorry that I hurt you last night. I know that I should have told you what was going on with me, but I didn't. I don't know why I didn't, but I'll try to figure it out.

Something is bothering me, and I need some time to work it out. If I stay here this weekend I know I'll be angry that you're gone. So for both of our sakes I'm going home.. Feel free to call me at home or on my cell phone. If you don't feel like talking today, or even for a few days, it's okay.

I'm not angry with you, Jack. I know you're really busy and I don't want to make things any harder for you. Whatever is bothering me is about me, so don't worry. I'm sure I'll feel better soon.

I love you.

She printed off the note and signed it. After a few minutes of staring into space, she picked up the phone and dialed Ryan's pager. When she didn't get an immediate return call she got in the shower and spent a long time letting the hot water clear her mind. She was just finishing drying her hair when her cell phone rang.

"Jamie?" asked the deep voice.

"Hi, Ryan. I didn't wake you up, did I?"

"Heck no, Duffy and I were running on the beach. He won, of course, but we still had fun. What's up with you at this time of day?"

"Is that invitation to your party still open? I'm unexpectedly free today."

"Absolutely. I'd love to have you," she replied. "Are you okay? You sound kind of down."

"I am, but just a little. Jack's tied up all day, but I didn't learn about it until this morning. I just don't wanna sit here alone all day."

"Well, you're never alone at the O'Flaherty's. Not even when you want to be."

Ryan gave her all the details of the party and steadfastly refused her offer to bring anything. Jamie signed off, and realized that the two-minute conversation had already brightened her spirits. *I've known her for two and a half months. She can tell in two sentences that something is bothering me. I've been dating Jack for two and a half years and he couldn't tell if I were having a seizure! Do I just need more than he's able to give me? Can any guy make me feel understood like Ryan does? Maybe I just want things I can't have.*

She drove onto Ryan's street at two sharp, having a difficult time finding a parking spot. Ryan answered the door and gave her a delighted smile, showing those incredibly white teeth. *Wow!* Jamie marveled, *she looks absolutely fantastic*. She mused that she didn't often step back and just look at Ryan objectively anymore. They had grown so close that she saw her inner self more than her package. But occasionally she just looked at her and enjoyed the wrapper, and this was one such day.

Her friend was wearing a black, knit, silk T-shirt which clung to every curve. Black linen, pleated slacks and soft black loafers completed her monochromatic outfit. She looked exactly like Ryan should look, tall, sleek, graceful, athletic, and terribly, terribly sexy. "Hi, I'm really glad you decided to come," Ryan said enthusiastically, giving Jamie a big hug.

"You did say two, didn't you?" Jamie asked as she looked around the house which was bursting with people.

"Yeah, that was the announced time. But in this family they show up when they want to. We've had people show up at nine in the morning for Thanksgiving dinner." As Ryan guided her into the teeming mass of people, Conor swooped down from his place on the staircase. "My, my, my, don't you look lovely today," he said as he looked Jamie up and down. "Isn't that a gorgeous outfit?" he said to Ryan as he continued to appraise Jamie like a new Ferrari. She was wearing a very slim-fitting, sleeveless shell of nubby silk in tangerine and gold that just brushed her waistline. Slim-fitting slacks of the same material showed off her trim legs, with a silk knit sweater in the same tangerine draped around her shoulders.

Jamie blushed as the two siblings conferred. "Yes, Conor, I'd agree that Jamie looks marvelous today," Ryan said with a big smile, "but I've yet to see her look less than lovely," she added with a twinkle in her deep blue eyes.

Conor boosted the wattage of his smile and asked, "Have you been given a proper tour of our home?"

"Uhm, not really," she said, giving Ryan a quick glance. "I just saw this floor and Ryan's room."

"Ryan's manners are so atrocious, sometimes," he scoffed as he gave his sister an aggrieved shake of his dark head. "Please allow me to make up for her faux paux," he stated as he held out his arm to escort her. She giggled at his exaggerated gallantry and gamely took his arm. As he led her off she turned to give his sister a wave, meeting a pair of blue eyes narrowed in mock anger. Jamie's eyes widened at the scowl, which immediately turned into a bright grin. Conor escorted Jamie up the staircase at the rear of the small living room. He didn't stop to introduce her to the many people that they climbed over, and she noted with a smile that they all continued their conversations as though they didn't notice the interruption.

When they reached the first of two rooms, he indicated the instrument cases, open luggage and clothes strewn about.

"Rory's getting ready to go on a short tour," he explained. "He and the band are leaving tomorrow for a month."

"Really? Where's he going?"

"I believe they'll just be on the west coast," he replied. "He doesn't tour much in the winter, but he's gone all summer long."

"I'd really love to hear him play," Jamie said. "By the way, Ryan says you all play an instrument. What's your specialty?"

"I spent most of my youth playing the fiddle and the bouzouki," he replied. "But now I spend most of my practice time playing the mandolin."

"I've no idea what a bouzouki is," she admitted, "but I know a mandolin when I see one. Do you practice often?" she inquired as she turned from Rory's room to face him.

"I play for fun now. I don't care if I ever improve. I usually play for a while before I go to bed. It really relaxes me after a day pounding a hammer." He touched her arm lightly at the elbow to lead her into his room. "Would you like to hear a bit?"

"I'd love to," she enthused as she sat down on the edge of his bed and gave him an expectant look. Conor picked up the carved wooden instrument and tuned it for just a minute, adjusted it against his body and began to play a lovely, haunting melody. Jamie wasn't familiar with the piece, but it was eerily beautiful. Conor's eyes were closed, and he played his mandolin with a depth of emotion that truly astounded Jamie.

When he was finished, Jamie sat transfixed for just a moment, then slowly said, "I can't tell you how beautiful that was, Conor. Thank you." She stood and touched his arm in a friendly gesture, looking up at him with emotion-filled green eyes.

Come to Papa, he grinned to himself. *I'm not gonna let you have this one Ryan. She's staying on my side of the river.*

After the short tour was complete, they began to make their way down the stairs. Ryan was sitting on the third step, leaning casually against the wall with her long legs effectively blocking their path. "Did our house just get a lot bigger or did you show Jamie the roof?" she asked sweetly.

"No, the house is the same. Jamie was just interested in my mandolin, and I played a bit for her."

"Hmm," she replied suspiciously. "Well, I've been working on my atrocious manners while you were gone, and I realized that Jamie hasn't been properly introduced to the rest of the clan." She removed Jamie's hand from Conor's arm and placed it on her own. "I plan to rectify my error immediately." She gave Conor a twitch of her long, black hair and moved off with her friend firmly in tow.

"You two never stop do you?" Jamie asked her with a giggle.

"No, we don't," she admitted with an embarrassed grin. "We've always been competitive. I guess you just stick with familiar patterns as you grow up. It's funny," she reflected. "We all played together growing up, but only Conor and I were ever competitive with each other. It really doesn't make sense, but that's the way it worked out."

As they moved through the house, Jamie mused that when she was with Ryan and Conor the siblings treated her like some prize they were fighting over. *Ryan seems much more aggressive when Conor's around. And it feels a lot more like she's flirting with me*, she thought. *No, that's not it, she corrected herself. She's not flirting—she acts like she's already won! She actually acts like I'm her little prize. It would piss me off if Jack did that. I wonder why it doesn't bother me in the least when Ryan does it?*

They maneuvered through the small house, and eventually broke through the crowd in the kitchen to reach the tiny porch that overlooked the small back yard.

There were about a dozen men in the yard, all gathered around two big Weber kettles. "I thought I'd give you an overview before I boggle your mind with introductions," Ryan explained. "This is the male side of Da's family. That's my Uncle Patrick," she said, indicating a man slightly smaller than Martin, but just as handsome. "That's my Uncle Francis." She pointed to an equally handsome, but slightly older looking man who was very muscular and brawny looking. "And that's my Uncle Malachy." She indicated the youngest and best looking one of the bunch. He looked like a slightly older Conor, although he wasn't quite as tall as the younger man.

"Wow!" was all that Jamie could say.

"Now for the next generation." She ticked off her cousins one by one. "Uncle Patrick has Niall, Kieran, Colm and Donal." She indicated each of the dark-haired men in turn. "Declan, Dermot, Liam and Padraig belong to Malachy, and Frank, Sean, Seamus and Brian are Uncle Francis' boys."

"Is anyone in your family less than gorgeous?" Jamie finally uttered as she shook her head in amazement.

"Uhm, what do you mean?" Ryan responded, her face a blank mask.

"Do you mean to tell me that you don't know how beautiful everyone in your family is?" she asked in bewilderment.

"Uhm, well, no, not really. I guess I never thought about it," she said as she fidgeted a bit in obvious discomfort.

"You never thought about the fact that your uncles and cousins and brothers all look like Calvin Klein underwear models?" Jamie had to laugh at Ryan's perplexed expression.

"No, I never did. Looks aren't a big deal in my family. I mean, I know that we're not exactly ugly," she said with a grin, "but we were never encouraged to feel good about ourselves because of how we looked." She looked thoughtful for a moment before she continued. "Da always told us to never feel proud or ashamed of our gifts or liabilities. He said that what you did with those gifts, and how you overcame your liabilities was all that mattered. Everything else was just genetics." She shrugged her broad shoulders slightly and looked to Jamie for comprehension. "He also told me to be very suspicious of people who spent a lot of time complimenting my looks. He said if someone was very focused on the outside of me, they wouldn't have any time to look at the inside."

Jamie cocked her head and considered her friend's words. "That's a wonderful view of the world. It's very different from how I was raised, but I like it a lot better."

"Were looks a big deal in your family?" Ryan asked.

"Not just looks, although that was important, but appearances were the big thing for us," she replied. "You know, wearing the right clothes, being seen with the right people, driving the right car. That sort of thing." She grew thoughtful for a long moment. "I'm going to try to adopt your philosophy for my children," she told Ryan.

"You can thank Da for that bit of philosophy," she replied. "Speaking of Da, I know he wants to see you," she said as she guided Jamie down the stairs to the gaggle of O'Flaherty men. Ryan's immediate family had joined the outdoor crowd, and

Jamie was warmly welcomed by each man. After lengthy introductions, she knew that she'd never remember the difficult names, but she appreciated the hospitality nonetheless.

The return trip was more difficult than the outbound had been. Rather than try to negotiate the interior staircase, Ryan led her out the front door, down the stairs and past the two-car garage to a door on the ground floor. "This way is easier today," she announced as she produced her key chain and unlocked the frosted, glass-paneled door. Jamie's head was spinning when they entered Ryan's room after a short trip down a narrow hallway that took them past the length of the garage. "I don't think I can remember one person's name," she moaned. "There were so many of them. And they look so much alike!"

"Well, there are two sets of twins," Ryan said, matter-of-factly.

"Two?"

"Yeah. Sean and Seamus and Declan and Dermot are twins."

"At least I'm not totally losing my mind," she laughed.

"Do you really want to remember them all?"

"Yeah, of course I do. Will you go over them again and quiz me?"

They knelt at the head of Ryan's bed and looked out the big windows at all of the assembled men. After four or five tries Jamie had them all pretty well sorted out. "Okay, Ryan. I want you to quiz me all day. That's the only way I'll learn, but it might help if you wrote them down for me, too. I remember things better when I see them."

"I'm not sure that'll help you," she said. "Take Padraig, for example. How would you spell that?"

"I guess it would be P-o-r-i-c?"

"Nope. P-a-d-r-a-i-g." She smiled as Jamie tried to get her mind around the odd spelling.

"Are they all that bad?"

"No. I'd say Kieran, Padraig, Niall and Siobhán are the worst of the bunch."

"I don't believe you've told me your mother's name."

"Fionnuala," Ryan replied quietly.

Jamie placed her hand on Ryan's shoulder, and forced eye contact. "It's beautiful. Really lovely."

Ryan was totally charmed and touched by how interested Jamie was in her family. After they completed a few more rounds of "guess the cousins" she pronounced Jamie ready to meet the rest of the family. "You need to meet the O'Flaherty aunts and the Ryans. "But don't worry," she reassured her, "there are far fewer of them, and their names are all American."

"If there are fewer of them, why's your house so crowded?" Jamie asked in amazement.

"Oh, there's people from our parish here, some of my aunts' families are here, and even a few neighbors. But I'm not even going to introduce you to any of the ancillary people. It's hard enough just to get the key players memorized—especially given the difficult names."

"I must admit, I've never heard so many Irish names in one place." She paused a moment to reflect. "You've never told me about how your family came to America. I mean, were your parents born here?"

"Not hardly," Ryan replied with a laugh. "As a matter of fact, I wasn't born here."

"Are you serious?" Jamie was frankly shocked. She assumed that most Irish people were third or fourth generation Americans, even though she had to admit that Martin's accent was far from American.

"Quite," Ryan replied. "But that was a bit of a fluke. My mother came to this country in about 1965 or so. She met my father, and they married a couple of years later. The boys were all born here, but when she was seven months pregnant with me, her mother in Ireland became very ill. She felt like she had to go home even though it must have been hell on Da to be left with three little boys. And I suppose it was pretty bad for her, too, having to travel that far when she was huge with me. After she was there for a month, I surprised everyone by arriving almost a month early."

"So are you an Irish citizen?" Jamie asked, not sure of citizenship requirements.

"Yeah. I have dual citizenship. They boys could have it too, and Rory went through the process, but Conor and Brendan don't have much interest."

"So your father was born here?" Jamie asked.

"Correct, but with an explanation," she said. "He and all of his brothers were born here. Their parents had immigrated during World War II. But after the war, my grandfather couldn't keep a job because of all the returning vets, so they eventually went back home. I think they left here in 1950."

"So is your father a citizen?" Jamie asked, still confused.

"Yeah, he is. But my mother was illegal. She was just here on a tourist visa when she met my father. The lure of his company was obviously more appealing than her fear of the INS," Ryan chuckled, "and she overstayed her visa. His brothers still tease him that she married him only for his citizenship status."

"I never thought of Irish people being illegal aliens," Jamie mused.

"Last time I checked we were the second largest group of illegal aliens in this country," Ryan said. "But we look like Americans, and people are charmed by Irish accents, so there's very little prejudice against us anymore."

"That's pretty neat that you're an Irish citizen. Could you move there if you wanted to?"

"Yeah, but I don't see that happening. I feel American," she said as she gave a little salute. "Even though I've spent a ton of time in Ireland, I'm always ready to come home."

"What happened with your grandmother? Did she die?" Jamie asked tentatively.

"Nope. She's still kicking—along with my grandfather. She'll be eighty next year and my grandfather will be eighty-five. They're both pretty spry," she said affectionately.

"Do you have many other relatives there?"

"Yeah, my father has tons of cousins and a few uncles and aunts still living around Tralee. And my mother's younger sister Moira still lives in the town they grew up in.

Aunt Moira and her husband Eamon have four kids, Aisling, Cait, Brenna and Cormac."

"More Irish names and I bet I couldn't spell one of them," Jamie teased.

"Yes, you could use a good course in Gaelic just to hang out with my family," she admitted. "But speaking of family, let's go meet the rest of them."

It took nearly twenty minutes for Ryan to introduce Jamie to her Aunts Eileen, Deirdre and Peggy. Each woman attentively asked Jamie about herself and her family, but something caught Ryan's eye and she pulled her friend away from the small group of women. "You must meet my favorite relative," she said as she wiggled an eyebrow and led Jamie through the growing mass of people to find the prize that Ryan had been seeking. "There she is!" Ryan said with delight as her eyes locked onto the object of her affection, a pair of equally vivid, but green, eyes.

Ryan held out her strong arms and a tiny face looked up at her rather blankly. The cutest baby that Jamie had ever seen was squealing, and the woman holding her handed her over to Ryan without a word of protest. The baby was too young to register much in the way of emotion, but Ryan's beautiful face wore a broad smile that made Jamie's heart melt.

"Isn't this the most perfect child you've ever seen?" Ryan asked in a tone that brooked no dissent. Jamie studied the little person. She was very small, maybe a month old, fair skinned with a shock of blond hair. Beautiful light green eyes were framed with long blonde eyelashes, but the child hadn't yet learned to use her eyes to express herself like her older cousin had. The baby nestled her little head in the crook of Ryan's broad shoulder and yawned, exposing dark pink gums.

"I'd have to agree with you on that one, Ryan. What's this little beauty's name?" she asked as she tickled a perfect little foot.

"This is Caitlin," Ryan said, giving the precious bundle a kiss on the cheek. "She's my cousin Tommy's baby." She looked around the room for the proud parents. "That's Tommy there, and his wife Annie is right there," she pointed in one direction, then the other, as Jamie confirmed the sightings. "But when they're here, they never get to see Caitlin. We're always fighting over who gets to hold her. Ryan wins, huh Caitlin?" she whispered conspiratorially into the tiny ear. Jamie was delighted to see Ryan interact so lovingly with this tiny child. *Boy, she'd be a good mother. I wonder if she plans on having children?* "You know, Jamie," the brunette said as she held Caitlin up next to Jamie's face. "She looks more like you that anyone else here." Jamie looked at the tiny face and then gave another long look at each of the child's parents. There were little pieces of Caitlin on each face, but neither matched the child quite as well as she did. *She looks just like my baby pictures*, she marveled. Various members of the Ryan clan agreed with the assessment. As Jamie was paraded around, Ryan would hold the baby next to her face and ask for an opinion. But when she was introduced to the baby's grandmother, Ryan's aunt Maeve, the agreement was beyond enthusiastic. Maeve made over Jamie as if she were sent directly from heaven. She looked at her from every angle and finally wrapped her in a big hug and said that Caitlin would be lucky indeed to continue to resemble Jamie as she got older.

To get away from the crowds, they decided to go downstairs to play with the baby. She was far too young to be able to do much, but she loved to be talked to and held. They took all of Ryan's pillows and made a safe nest for Caitlin. When they got her settled, Ryan lay face down on the bed and rested on her arms as she held up a rattle. She worked hard trying to entertain the baby by holding it up and quickly hiding it in her large hand for several moments. Despite her best efforts, Jamie was quite sure the child had no idea what her cousin was doing. After five minutes, she started to slump over even with the generous support, so Ryan picked her up to cuddle her again. Ryan continued to gently bounce the tiny baby up and down, and after a few moments her little head dropped to Ryan's shoulder as she grasped tiny handfuls of black T-shirt material rhythmically. The dark-haired woman smiled down at the still form and kissed her gently on the head.

"Do you want to put her down on the bed?" Jamie asked.

"No. She's not heavy at all," Ryan said. "She's clearly a Ryan. She went to the doctor the other day and Annie said she's only in the twentieth percentile in weight and the twenty-fifth in height. Besides, I really like holding her," she replied sheepishly. "I see her a lot, but still, she's different every time. She's growing so fast; I won't be able to do this for long. I really want to enjoy it while I can."

"This baby couldn't weigh more than ten pounds," Jamie said, laughing. "You'll be able to pick her up for another ten years."

"Only ten years? Ten years?" Ryan stared at her friend with mock horror. "I'll never let her go!"

Jamie approached and patted Ryan gently on the shoulder. "You're such a sweet person. You're just a mass of contradictions," she said with a smile. "You look all strong and confident, like a real loner, but you're such a tender person when you're with people you trust."

Ryan replied with a sweetly crooked grin, looking just a little embarrassed.

"So little Caitlin is a Ryan?"

"Well, technically she's a Driscoll," she corrected. "My aunt Maeve was married to Charlie Driscoll and they had three sons. The oldest was my cousin Michael. After Michael got sick, Charlie just went off the deep end. They wound up separated, and they stayed apart until he died about a year ago. It was really hard for Maeve and the boys, but he hated Michael for being gay," she said, the sadness showing in her eyes.

After a few moments of watching Caitlin sleep, Jamie asked quietly, "Do you want to have children?"

"Yeah, I do," she said. "I actually can't imagine not having them." She paused for a moment, looking pensive "I'm not sure how I'll do it, though."

"Do you mean technically?" Jamie asked tentatively.

"No, I mean whether I'd physically have them or adopt or just co-parent with another woman."

"How would you do it, uhm, physically."

"Lesbians have the same parts that you do, Jamie," she teased.

"That's not what I mean, and you know it!" she said as she gave her a little slap on the head. "I mean would you use somebody that you know? Would you do it the old fashioned way or what?"

"I don't have any desire to experience that particular union," she said with an involuntary shudder. "I'd probably either be inseminated from a known donor or use a sperm bank."

"Would you want the uhm … donor to have a role in raising the child?"

"That's where it becomes tricky for me," Ryan said. "I wouldn't want to deprive my child of having a wonderful father like mine. But I'm not sure how to do that in a way that makes everyone happy. That's the only part of being straight that I envy," she teased. "Well, that and the marriage laws."

"That's one of the perks. But the downside is that you have to use birth control." Jamie made a sour face.

"I guess having kids is a big deal for everyone. What about you? I assume you and Jack are planning to reproduce, although you made it clear you're not ready yet."

"Yeah, I think we both want a few kids, but I want to be a lot older before I do that."

"What do you want to do before you have kids?" Ryan asked.

"I'm not sure. But I want to do something for myself, like graduate school. Who knows, maybe I'll write for a while."

"I don't know, Jamie. A little one of these," she tipped the sleeping baby toward her friend, "can be awfully tempting."

After a few minutes, Ryan offered to go upstairs and fetch some drinks and something to snack on. To avoid waking Caitlin, Jamie sat down on the bed as Ryan transferred the precious cargo to her lap. Caitlin stirred as she adjusted to her new home. Her little blonde head was comfortably resting on Jamie's breast as she slowly moved a perfect little thumb into her mouth. "I see your point about the temptation, Ryan," she admitted as she gazed down at the baby. "I can feel my ovaries aching already."

Ryan smiled fondly at the pair as she took in the scene. "I think motherhood would suit you, Jamie. You two look perfect together."

Ryan had been gone just a minute or two when there was a quiet knock on the door. Caitlin's grandmother poked her head in and said, "I just wanted to check to make sure you didn't need anything."

"Nope. Everything's just perfect," Jamie said as she smiled up at the proud grandmother. "I must say, this is one lucky baby."

"Well, I do know that she's loved beyond words," Maeve said, retrieving a clean diaper from the bag she carried. She placed the cloth on Jamie's shoulder to protect her blouse, as she casually asked, "How long have you and Ryan been seeing each other?"

Jamie knew that her blush was rapidly traveling up to her hairline. "Uhm, Maeve," she finally said, "Ryan and I aren't together … in that way. We're just close friends."

"Oh dear, I hope I didn't embarrass you. I'm sorry for making assumptions." She patted Jamie's arm reassuringly. "It's probably just wishful thinking on my part," she admitted.

"What do you mean?" Jamie asked.

"I was so pleased that Ryan had brought someone home to meet the family," she explained. "She's never done so before, and I just assumed you were someone special to her."

"She is," came the quiet voice from across the room. "She's very special to me." Ryan was crossing the room now, with a small smile on her face. "Regrettably she's not my girlfriend," she stated as she shot a grin at Jamie.

Jamie was terribly pleased at this expression of their growing bond. She grinned up at Ryan broadly. "You're pretty special yourself, kiddo."

"I'm sorry for jumping to conclusions, Ryan," Maeve said sincerely. "I just hope that when you do bring someone home, she's as special as young Jamie here."

"The odds of that aren't good," Ryan intoned seriously. "Jamie is truly one of a kind."

After Caitlin woke, Ryan changed her diaper and the three of them went back upstairs. Jamie was charmed at how Ryan claimed the small child as her own. The baby was very content to be carried around all day, and Jamie found it cute that most of the cousins teased Ryan about when she'd have a child of her own. *They certainly seem comfortable with her sexual orientation. But maybe that's because she seems so sure of herself. It's hard to be uncomfortable around someone who seems so comfortable in her own skin.*

Dinner was ready at around five o'clock. A huge turkey and a ham accompanied the dishes Ryan's aunts had brought, the food completely covering the dining room table. As everyone gathered around the table, Jamie felt her cell phone vibrate from its place on her waistband. *Uh oh, that's gotta be Jack.* She briefly debated just letting it ring, but she thought better of it and stepped outside through the front door. She could still hear the muffled din coming from the house, but she fervently hoped that Jack could not.

"Hello?" she said as she answered on the fifth ring.

"Hi," Jack replied, sounding small and hesitant.

"How are you sweetheart?" she asked, trying to sound as warm and loving as possible.

"I'm okay. Where are you?"

"I'm back in the city, honey." She was intentionally misleading him, but she didn't have any intention of continuing the fight. "Are we okay, or are you still mad at me?"

"I'm not mad, Jamie. You've just been so different lately, I'm just really confused."

Jamie was dismayed to hear him sounding so sad. "Do you want to be alone, or would you like me to come back down?"

"Would you do that?" he asked hopefully. "I really do want to see you. I miss you, sweetheart."

"I'll be there by eight o'clock," she promised. "What would you like me to bring for dinner?"

"I don't care about dinner. I just want you."

Jamie didn't eat much of the celebratory feast, too busy working over in her mind how she was going to avoid Jack's questions about why she was dressed up. *I know, I'll stop at the Nordstrom's on Market and buy a new outfit. My pants are all falling off anyway. I could use another pair of jeans until I gain the weight back.*

From their perch at the top of the staircase, Ryan watched her friend pick at her food. Ryan still held the baby in one arm while she tried to get a bite or two of dinner into her mouth. "Was that Jack on the phone?" she eventually asked.

"Oh, yeah, it was. I think I'm gonna go back down to Palo Alto."

Ryan waited a moment, hoping that Jamie would continue, but she didn't. Finally she asked, "Are you two having trouble?"

Looking up at her, Jamie spent a moment trying to decide how forthcoming to be. "Yeah, we are," she sighed. "Things haven't been great for awhile now."

Ryan looked at her with sympathy and said, "If you need someone to listen, I'm always here for you."

"Thanks, Ryan. I appreciate that more than I can say." She removed Ryan's plate from her hand and said, "If I don't help you out here, you're going to starve." Balancing Ryan's sturdy paper plate on her knees, she cut up her turkey into small pieces, then speared bites of turkey and vegetables and fed them to her friend, one at a time.

"I guess this is why it's so hard to be a single parent," Ryan said wryly as she removed Caitlin's little hand from her hair.

Conor and Rory sat on the other side of the room with a few cousins. Conor leaned over and quietly asked his brother, "So what do you think about Jamie?"

"I like her a lot. She seems like a good friend for Ryan."

"No, I mean do you think Ryan's gonna make a play for her?"

"Why do you want to know?" Rory asked suspiciously.

Conor smiled smugly. "Because I think she'd be perfect for me."

"I'll make you a friendly little wager on that," Rory said. "If young Jamie is swayed by any O'Flaherty, I'm putting my money on Ryan."

"You're on. Let's make it interesting, say $50?" They shook hands to seal the bet. Rory cast a glance at the pair and watched Jamie carefully feeding his sister. *It would be a lot easier for Jamie to just hold the baby while Ryan fed herself. I think my money is as good as won.*

Jamie checked her watch one last time, finally deciding that she had to leave to get to Jack's. Caitlin was asleep on Ryan's chest again, and Jamie leaned over to kiss her sweet-smelling head. "I had a great time, Ryan. Thanks for letting me meet your family."

Sapphire blue eyes regarded the blonde woman for a moment, then Ryan pulled Jamie back down by gently placing her hand behind her neck. She kissed her cheek lightly as she said, "Thanks for coming. You made the day special for me."

The mantra began on the short drive to Nordstrom's. *It's perfectly normal to feel affectionate towards your female friends. Women kiss each other all the time. I kiss Mia … it's no big deal.* She was doing pretty well with the positive feedback, but a tiny voice kept trying to make itself heard. Finally, as she turned off her car in the parking lot, it broke through. *You've kissed Mia plenty of times … but you've never felt tingles shoot down your spine when she kissed your cheek. Explain that one away, Jamie.*

Pushing the thought to the deepest recesses of her mind, she dashed into the store and purchased a new pair of jeans and a long-sleeved shirt. She asked the sales clerk to remove the tags, and while the clerk rang up the purchase she went back into the dressing room and changed into the new clothes. Giving her a slightly puzzled look, the clerk neatly folded her other outfit and put it in a bag, privately wondering what the young woman was trying to hide.

Arriving at Jack's neighborhood just before eight, she stopped and bought dinner from a favorite deli. Jack was very glad to see her, and he wrapped her in a big hug, holding her so tightly that she was afraid they'd stay like that all night. He had his face pressed against her neck, repeatedly breathing in her scent. Finally he released her and asked, "Do you still love me, Jamie?"

"Of course I do," she said with feeling. "I'm unsure about a lot of things, but I know that I do love you." She wrapped her arms around his neck as he bent to kiss her. They progressed in their intimacy, finally stumbling towards the bedroom, dinner left to cool on the counter.

Chapter Eight

Jamie's cell phone rang just after eight. She scrambled out of bed, pushing her hair from her eyes as she searched for the phone. She grabbed it on the sixth ring. "Jamie?" asked the deep, familiar voice.

"Oh, hi Daddy," she said, trying to sound awake.

"Did I wake you, sweetheart?"

"No, not at all," she lied, walking through the apartment, trying to find Jack.

Sitting at his computer, Jack gave her a wave and a lecherous grin as he gazed up and down her naked body, finding her disordered hair and shyness a turn-on. Even though they had been intimate for almost five months, she still felt uncomfortable walking around the apartment naked. *I don't know if I'll ever get over my shyness,* she thought, knowing that her cheeks had already turned pink. They had made love for a long time the previous evening, with Jack revealing a neediness that was very uncharacteristic. He caressed her like he was trying to absorb her through his touch. Jamie had enjoyed the tactile sensations, but she had to admit that she was turned off by his insecurities. He had begun to touch her again before dawn, but she had feigned sleep to avoid another needy encounter.

"How about a round of golf this afternoon?" her father asked.

"Hold on and let me ask Jack." She was still uncomfortable having her father know that she stayed at Jack's on the weekends, but he had never commented on their physical relationship, so it obviously didn't bother him.

She placed the phone on mute and asked, "Do you want to play golf with Daddy this afternoon?"

"Yeah, that'd be fun. I feel like I haven't been outside in weeks. I have to work until noon or so, though. Is that too late?"

"I'll see." She spoke into the phone again. "How about one o'clock?"

"That's great, honey, I'll call and make a tee off time. See you at the club."

After she hung up, Jamie walked over to Jack and gave him a kiss. "I'm going back to bed," she said with a smile, fondly patting his cheek. "You really wore me out last night."

"Would you like me to help you relax?" He slipped his hands around her small waist and drew her close. When he rubbed his face against her breasts, she giggled as his unshaved cheeks tickled her bare skin.

"I'd love to, but I won't be able to walk if we make love again," she said, blushing as she kissed him again.

He didn't release her, holding onto her waist with his large hands. "You know, I really like the way you look lately." He stroked her concave stomach with the back of his hand. "Working out has really improved your body. But you're getting awfully thin. Are you going to try to put some weight back on?"

"Yeah, I'm going to start working with a nutritionist so I can learn to eat right. I'm using a lot more energy, and I need to be able to fuel my body more efficiently."

Jack didn't comment on her plans or her goals, merely placing his hands under her breasts and lifting them slightly. "I just don't want you to lose any more weight here," he said with a wicked grin. "These are just perfect." He pulled her forward and latched onto her nipple, sucking the already-tender flesh into his mouth.

Jamie flinched, and Jack looked into her eyes, seeing her discomfort. "I guess I was a little rough last night, wasn't I?" But before she could reply he was at it again, now working on her other, equally sore nipple. She let out a little moan, born of pain rather than pleasure, and he looked up, his mouth still attached. He was sucking so aggressively that he made a popping sound when he pulled away. He turned his face so that his cheek rested on one breast. His voice was soft, and his breath warm. "It turns me on to have sex when we're both a little sore. Your breasts are so damned sexy when your nipples are swollen."

She smiled stiffly and moved back so he couldn't reach her again. "I wish I had your stamina, but I'm still pretty new at this. I have to build up my tolerance."

"You'll get there," he said, playfully swatting her butt when she turned around.

She walked back into the bedroom, fell to the bed and stared at the ceiling for a long time, not really tired, but feeling too depressed to do anything else.

I can't believe that we still haven't talked about our fight. He honestly thinks that making love solves all of our problems! He didn't even ask me about my doctor visit. I told him she was running tests; doesn't he even care if I'm ill? I guess it doesn't matter as long as my breasts don't get smaller! After stewing for a long while, she finally drifted off into a fitful slumber.

Jamie was glad to see her father, and even happier to have a break from Jack's attention. He had woken her at around ten, once again trying to interest her in lovemaking. She put him off again, claiming that she needed more sleep. Even though she was perfectly well rested, she faked sleep for a long time, lying quietly, hoping that he'd get the hint. Finally opening her eyes again a half hour later, she was dismayed to find him sitting in a chair in the bedroom, obviously watching for the moment she woke. With a heavy sigh, she relented, tossing back the covers to welcome him back to bed.

His clothes were off before she could even think of changing her mind, and it was clear that he had been ready for quite some time. As he moved over her she had to bite her lip to stop from crying as she thought, *I told him I was too sore to do this. But he doesn't even seem to hear me. I'd never ask him to do something that was uncomfortable just for my pleasure.* He began to forcefully thrust into her, his chest rubbing against her sore nipples. Suddenly, she began to fantasize about turning the tables on him. *Maybe I'll get one of those sex toys that caller mentioned the other night. I'd like to see how he feels about having something shoved into him. It turns him on to have me in pain, but I'd guarantee he wouldn't feel the same way if it was his ass!*

They teed off at around one-thirty, after spending a few minutes warming up on the driving range. Jamie hadn't played since that day with Ryan, but it had been a lot longer for Jack. She was beating him handily, and by the sixteenth hole she was ahead by eight strokes. As usual, he didn't care how he played, a trait that she'd always admired. Jamie was a better player, and Jack took a certain pride in her ability to best him.

"Have you been playing much, Jamie?" Jim asked, beaming with pride over her skills. "You look very sharp today."

"No, not really. I've been too busy lately."

"I was pleased when you called to say you were bringing a friend out to play," he said, just making conversation.

Oh, please, Daddy, don't bring this up today!

Jack was facing away from Jamie, but she saw him visibly tense at this comment. He turned to her and asked neutrally, "You didn't tell me you played here. Who'd you bring?"

"I brought Ryan," she said without elaboration. She forced herself to concentrate, and hit an impressive drive. When she turned to Jack, she saw that his expression had turned into a sour scowl. She gave him a thin little smile. "Your turn, honey," she said as she passed by him.

"Who's Ryan?" Her father had noticed that something was going on between the two of them, and he was now interested in finding out what it was.

"Just a friend of mine from school," Jamie replied after Jack hit a powerful slice that landed on the third fairway.

"A guy?" Jim asked hesitantly.

"Only partially," Jack growled as he climbed into the cart and drove off to find his ball.

Jim and Jamie watched Jack flying across the fairway—shock registering on both of their faces. "What in the hell is wrong with him?" Jim asked.

"He's just been in a mood for a while," Jamie said. "I think he's got too much stress with law review and his class work."

"What did he mean by that comment?" Jim persisted. After Jamie hit her second shot, a nice five iron that landed softly on the green, she replied, "She's a friend from school that Jack doesn't like."

Never one to let a topic drop until he understood it completely, Jim followed-up, "What did he mean when he said she was partially a guy? That was a very odd thing to say."

Jamie sighed and decided to be honest. "Ryan's a lesbian. And for some reason Jack feels threatened by that."

"Hmm, that seems strange," he finally said.

At least he's on my side, Jamie thought as Jack finally reached the green. They finished the hole in silence, not another word passing among them until they finished up on eighteen. Jim looked at them both and said, "Let's go into The Grill. I don't want you two to leave like this."

Jack looked guilty about his belligerent attitude, and Jamie had no reason to refuse, so they agreed. After they were settled with drinks, Jim broke the silence again. "Do you mind talking about what's going on?"

"It's not a big deal, Daddy," Jamie said. "Jack's been unhappy about my friendship with Ryan, but I'm sure he'll feel better when he gets to know her a little." She omitted most of the facts, since she really didn't want her father to know how childish Jack was being about this.

"I don't want to get to know her, Jamie," Jack said, through gritted teeth. "If you respected my opinion, you'd stop spending all of your free time with her."

"I *don't* spend all of my free time with her."

He let her comment hover in the air for a moment, then asked, "How many times did you see her this week?"

"This week?" she asked weakly, knowing this was a very bad week to pick.

"Yeah. This week. Why don't you tell your father how often you see your friend. I think he'd be interested." He looked at Jim and said, "Ryan's not your typical lesbian. She's gorgeous and single and apparently has women climbing over obstacle courses just to sleep with her."

"That's not true ..." Jamie began, but her voice trailed off once she considered his statement. Every word was true, and she knew that Jack wouldn't let her get away with contradicting him.

Jim's eyebrows rose, and he looked at her with a puzzled frown. "How often *do* you see this woman?"

"Well," she hesitated, "Uhm ... we played golf on Monday because we didn't have class that day. Then I saw her in psych class on Wednesday and Friday, but that's no big deal."

"Did you spend time with her after class?" Jack asked, making Jamie angry with herself for telling him about their juice breaks.

"Yes." She looked at her father and said, "We both have a free period after psych class, and we usually get a bottle of juice and talk about class."

"Go on," her father said, his frown growing.

"We have a class project that we have to do together, so we volunteered at a community organization on Tuesday and Thursday nights."

"There's more," Jack said, looking like a prosecutor who has a witness on the ropes.

Jamie sighed, then continued, "She's my personal trainer, and we worked together at the gym twice."

"Any bike rides?" Jack asked, crossing his arms over his chest.

"Two," she admitted.

"Don't forget dinner on Friday night," he said, giving her a false smile.

"I didn't," she said, shooting him a lethal look. "It was her birthday, and I made dinner for her."

Jack didn't say a word in response to her admission. He merely raised one dark blonde eyebrow and narrowed his eyes a bit in obvious triumph.

"But I don't see her that much all of the time," she said defensively. "This week was an anomaly."

"That's not what Cassie says," he said, pulling out his trump card.

Jamie's face had been relatively composed through this interchange, but now it grew bright pink with anger. "Do you have any others spies keeping track of me, or only Cassie?" she said, her teeth nearly clamped together.

"Jack, Jamie" her father finally said, trying to calm them down "It's obvious that this is a big issue between you two." Jamie continued to glare at Jack, who was glaring right back at her. "Jamie," he said as he turned to her, "I think the solution is obvious."

"I don't know if I can wait for Jack to grow up, Daddy," she said, dripping sarcasm as she turned to look at her father.

"No, no," he said firmly, "that's not the problem." He sighed as he tried to think of the best way to get his point across. "When you're engaged, you can't put your friendships ahead of your commitment to your fiancé. Friends will come and go, but your spouse is with you for life. His opinions have to come first, honey."

Jamie felt all of the color drain from her face. She turned from her father to Jack and then back again, her mind reeling from the betrayal she felt from both of them. "So that's what makes a good marriage? Giving in to every irrational request that your partner makes? Or is it only the woman who has to give in?" she added, her voice filled with anger.

The looks she was regarded with were identical. Neither man had ever seen her stand her ground so forcefully, and neither liked it. Rather than cause a bigger scene, she stood and regarded both of them. Her head shook forcefully as she fought to control the tears that desperately wanted to come. But rather than cry, she turned and left the room.

After a half hour in the Jacuzzi, she found an attendant in the locker room and handed her a note, which the woman assured her would be delivered to her father immediately.

Jim and Jack were patiently waiting on a pair of overstuffed chairs within view of the women's locker room. The attendant recognized Jim, and handed him the note. It read,

I've arranged for a ride home. Please respect my wishes and give me some time alone.

"Well, Jack, welcome to married life," Jim said as he handed Jack the note and stood to leave.

After Jamie had written the note, she tried to figure out how to get home. First she called Mia, but no one was home. Next she tried Mia's pager, but got no return call. *Oh, right, she's in L.A. this weekend. I don't think she'll be home until tomorrow morning.* Next she tried her grandfather, but no one was home at either his house or his office. *I shouldn't do this, but I don't have enough cash for a cab.* She dialed Ryan's pager number, and waited just a few minutes for the return call.

"Hi," Ryan's voice called out brightly. "Are you calling to get a piece of birthday cake?"

"No," Jamie said as she started to cry.

Her voice filled with alarm, Ryan asked, "What's wrong?"

"I need a very big favor. I wouldn't ask you to do this, but I don't have any choice."

"Anything. Name it."

Jamie gave her a short version of her plight, and Ryan immediately agreed to come get her. *How does she do that? Two minutes of talking to her, and I feel that everything will be okay.*

Jamie showered and dried her hair mechanically, just to give herself something to do while she waited. Rummaging in her locker, she found a heavy, lined, warm-up suit that she sometimes wore on rainy days, knowing that she could use all the layers she had for the bike ride. She pulled her slacks and sweater back on, and then put the warm ups on over her clothes. Leaving the locker room, she glancing around carefully, hoping that her father and Jack had heeded her wishes, knowing there would be massive trouble if they saw her get on Ryan's Harley. She walked out to the circular drive, and was very pleased to hear the Harley roar up the long entryway just a few moments later.

The attendant looked puzzled when Jamie came over to the bike, since he had helped her out of Jack's car just a few hours earlier. He was unsure of how to help, so he just let Ryan pull her on to the big machine. Sparing the young man a look, Jamie settled the spare helmet on her head and they pulled away.

When they got to the street, Ryan pulled over to the side of the road and killed the engine. She turned around as much as possible, and gently asked, "Where do you want to go?"

"I'm not sure," she said as the tears overtook her again.

Ryan gave her a very sympathetic look, then tossed her leg over the bike and faced the distraught woman. Jamie stayed on the bike, but she leaned heavily against the sturdy woman, allowing her warm embrace to help right her world, which seemed dangerously out of control. After a long while she felt able to speak again, and she explained, "My car's in Palo Alto, so I guess I have to go there."

"I can drive you down there tomorrow," Ryan said. "You're too upset to drive back all that way by yourself. Why don't I just take you home?"

"I guess that's my only option," she said, a pathetically sad look on her face. "I'm just afraid that Jack might be there waiting for me. And if I see Cassie, I might actually kill her."

"I've got a better idea," Ryan said as she got back on and kicked the big bike to life.

More relieved than she cared to admit, Jamie gladly let Ryan control the situation, trusting her to do what was best. She knows what to do to calm me down, she thought dreamily as she rested her face between Ryan's shoulder blades to cut the wind. Her arms were wrapped tightly against her trim waist, and she felt safe for the first time all day.

Once they were in San Francisco Ryan turned around at a stoplight and asked, "Do you need anything for the night? I have some sweats and stuff, but nothing will fit you right."

"Are we going to your house?" she asked, hoping that they were.

"Yeah. No one knows my number, or my address. You can have the night to calm down without worrying about seeing Jack or Cassie."

"Is there someplace that I could buy a few things? I also need a bookstore to buy a novel that I have to read by tomorrow."

"Sure. We'll head over to 24th Street."

They did just that and stopped at The Gap, where Jamie purchased yet another pair of jeans and a bright blue shirt, along with a pale yellow T-shirt. Another stop at a small lingerie boutique added panties, a pair of cotton boxers, another bra and a pair of socks to her pile of purchases.

Luckily, a used bookstore had a copy of her Barnes novel, so she was set for the night.

They pulled up in front of the home in Noe Valley just after six. It was fully dark, and she could see that the house was dark also. "Where is everyone?"

"Conor is helping my cousin Niall work on his new house over in the Sunset district. I assume they'll go out for a drink afterwards, so he won't be home tonight. Da had to fill in for someone at work, so he's gone all night. Rory left on his tour today, so we have the place to ourselves for a change."

As they hopped of the bike, Jamie regarded her thoughtfully, "You didn't have plans tonight did you?" she asked suspiciously.

"No, not really,"

"I thought that this could be a good opportunity to see your friend," she replied. When Ryan's face showed no recognition, she continued, "You know … the one who lives at home."

"Oh, no, no. I'm not seeing her anymore," Ryan said, laughing. "I've sworn off all women who live at home—especially if they're in the closet. We were supposed to go to her house on Friday, but her younger brother showed up with a bunch of friends, and I didn't even get a kiss."

"So what were you going to do?" Jamie asked. "I know you had something in mind."

"Well … I was thinking about calling my friend Ally," she said with a waggling eyebrow. "But it's never in my best interests to see her on a school night."

"How come?"

"Remember the day you had to let me sleep in your house?"

"Yeah."

"That was all due to Ally. Moderation isn't her middle name," she said. "You have no idea how much my body will thank you for saving me from going over there."

Jamie felt herself shiver at the thought of what that really meant, but just gave her a playful poke in the ribs as they climbed the stairs. They were greeted enthusiastically by Duffy, who acted as though Jamie was his long lost best friend.

"Boy, I've forgotten how much better a friendly greeting can make you feel."

"Hey, Duffy isn't the only one who's friendly," Ryan said as she approached her and offered her arms for a hug.

Jamie gratefully accepted, sighing deeply as the warm, strong arms circled her. Her body sucked up the comfort like a dry sponge, letting herself relax in the embrace and begin to let go again. She began to sob as Ryan rubbed her back in a calming, reassuring gesture. After a few minutes, Ryan pulled away and said, "You feel really warm. Why don't you take your jacket off?"

Jamie numbly complied, as Ryan did likewise. Next she removed her warm up pants, and folded both items neatly. Ryan placed an arm across her shoulders and guided her to the sofa, where she gently pushed her down and leaned over to look at her face closely. "Do you drink alcohol?"

"Uhm, yeah," she said, unsure of where this was headed.

"I'm going to make you a warm drink to relax you a bit."

Ryan ambled into the kitchen. Duffy looked from Ryan's retreating form, to Jamie, and back again. Making up his doggie mind, he scrambled onto the sofa and lay his big black head on Jamie's lap, uttering a heavy sigh as he did so.

When Ryan returned, Jamie was stroking Duffy's head and murmuring sweet nothings. "I can tell who his favorite is," Ryan stated as she gave him a mock glare. She placed a mug on the table and said, "C'mon Duff, I saw her first." The dog leapt from the couch and settled onto the floor, looking depressed. "He'd steal all of my friends if I let him," she whispered conspiratorially as she handed Jamie a steaming mug.

Jamie took a sip and purred with contentment, "What's in this? It's delicious."

"Hot cocoa and Bailey's Irish cream," she replied as she sipped her own mug. "The Bailey's counteracts the caffeine in the cocoa, so it really relaxes you."

Ryan turned as she put her mug on the table, then leaned over and grasped Jamie's legs, pulling them onto her lap. She unlaced her boots, and tossed them to the floor when she finished. "I want to know everything that happened since I last saw you," she said soothingly, as she began to massage her feet.

Sinking down into the cushions, Jamie felt herself immediately begin to relax. "I went down to Palo Alto after I left here last night. The evening went okay," she said, deciding to gloss over the sexual aspects. But something about the day was bothering her too much to ignore. "Can I ask you a really, really personal question?"

"Sure. Anything."

Jamie pursed her lips as she thought about how to frame her question. "Have you ever tried to ..." she struggled as she tried to adjust the question for Ryan's sexual orientation. "Have you ever tried to get your partner to do something that was painful for her?"

Ryan looked at her with a slightly cocked head as she tried to think of how to answer. "That's a tough one. I'm not sure what you're getting at, but there have been lots of times where I've pushed just farther than was probably wise. Sometimes it's hard to tell if a sound means 'Do that harder' or 'Ouch!' Is that what you mean?"

Now Jamie shot her a confused look. "I don't know what you mean."

"Do you want me to be graphic? I don't mind giving you a blunt answer, but I don't want to tell you more than you want to know about my sexual habits,"

A myriad of images flew through Jamie's fertile imagination. She shook her head to clear it and realized that she had to be the one to be more graphic. "Here's the issue. Jack was insatiable last night. He really seemed needy, and sometimes he seems to express himself only through sex. I think it's his way of feeling close again after a fight."

Ryan nodded in complete understanding. "That's a common reaction to a fight."

"Right. And even though his insecurities don't appeal to me, I didn't complain. But he tried to make love to me three separate times this morning. I told him that I was too sore, but he wouldn't stop. I finally gave in just to get him off my back, but I was really resentful. It upset me that he wanted to have sex even when he knew it was causing me pain. And it pissed me off that he could enjoy himself when I was just lying there like a dead fish!"

Ryan was unsure of how to comment on this. She had never in her life tried to talk any woman into having sex when she didn't want to. And she could no more enjoy sex with an unwilling partner than she could fly. But she didn't want to reveal how insensitive she thought Jack was being. Jamie was engaged to this guy, and even if he was sometimes a jerk, she didn't think it was wise to be the one to point that out.

"I don't think it's fair to compare how people react to things that are really emotionally loaded," she said. "What's really important is how that made you feel. Tell me about that."

"I don't think there's any lonelier feeling than lying in bed with someone who's using your body for his own pleasure," she murmured as she began to cry softly.

Ryan quickly got up and went to the other end of the loveseat. She lifted Jamie's torso and sat down, lowering her back down until her head was in her lap. Then she started to run her fingers through her hair in a gentle, calming fashion. After a few minutes she said softly, "I'm so sorry, Jamie. I can't stand to see you hurt so badly. I wish I could do something to help."

"You are, Ryan. You're doing more than you know," she reassured her as she patted her hand. "But I've got lots more to bitch about, so I may as well get it over with."

As she took a deep, slow, breath and furrowed her brow in concentration, Ryan's soft voice wafted over her. "Is this okay?" She lifted a good portion of Jamie's shiny blonde hair, and gave her scalp a little scratch to indicate the nature of her request.

Sea green eyes lifted and gazed at her, deep gratitude reflected back. "This is the best I've felt all day," she replied with a sad smile, as she covered Ryan's warm hand with her own. "Actually," she amended, "it's the best I've felt in weeks." She looking into Ryan's eyes and added, "It's more than all right. It's keeping me sane."

Ryan gave her a gentle, sweet smile as her hand drifted lower, and she began to trace the smooth planes of Jamie's face with her fingertips. It was difficult for the prone woman to keep her train of thought, but she struggled to get through her story. "We played golf with my father this afternoon." She paused briefly to concentrate. "My father made a comment about bringing you to play on Monday, and Jack flipped out," she said. "He gets angry so rarely, and never, ever, in front of my parents."

Ryan's fingers grew more determined in their efforts to remove the stress from her friend's face. She worked at the tense lines with both of her thumbs, smiling to herself as she could see Jamie begin to relax a bit. "Then what?" Ryan softly inquired.

Jamie decided not to reveal the slur that Jack had made toward Ryan, since it wasn't vital to the story. "After the round we went to have a drink, and my father really wanted us to talk about it. Jack said that he didn't want me to see you anymore," she said as she began to cry in earnest. Ryan nudged her friend upright and sat down behind her as she put her arms around her shaking body. "That's not the worst part, though," Jamie sobbed.

Ryan continued to smooth her hair and stroke her back. "It's okay, Jamie. It will all be okay."

"The really bad part was when my father agreed with him," she finally got out through the raking sobs.

Ryan could hardly believe how much this revelation hurt her. She felt as though she'd been kicked in the chest, but she didn't want to make matters worse for her friend. She just held her tighter as she murmured reassuring words to her. After a long while the sobs turned to whimpers. Ryan said very softly, right into her ear, "I don't want to cause problems with your boyfriend and your family. I understand if you need to stop seeing me so much."

Jamie sat bolt upright and got to her knees, turning to face Ryan with a look of abject panic on her face. "Not you too!" she shouted as she grabbed Ryan roughly by the shoulders and gave her a forceful shake. "Don't you understand?"

"Jamie, Jamie, it's okay," Ryan said calmly as she removed Jamie's fingers from their death grip. "I just want you to know that I support you in whatever you choose to do. It would hurt me terribly to stop being your friend, but if you need to see me less I want you to know that I'll understand. I'd do anything to make this easier for you, Jamie," she said with tears in her eyes. "Anything!"

"Oh Ryan," she cried as she slumped against her friend's strong chest, sobbing once again, "you scared me."

"How did I scare you?" she murmured as she wrapped the smaller woman in her arms and began to slowly rock her.

"I thought you were treating me like they were. Like I'm too stupid to make up my own mind about what I do and who I see," she said as she continued to cry softly.

"I'll never do that to you Jamie," she replied solemnly as she stroked her hair. "Never. I see you as a mature woman who's very competent to make her own life decisions."

"I know one thing for sure, Ryan," she said with her determination shining through her tears. "If Jack Townsend thinks he can control me, he's in for a very nasty surprise."

After Jamie had composed herself, Ryan went into the kitchen to make dinner. "We've got turkey and some mashed potatoes left over from yesterday," she called into the living room. "Is that okay?"

"That sounds great." She sat on the loveseat with Duffy, and when Ryan came back a while later, Duffy immediately jumped off and took his place on the floor.

Ryan ate in her normal hearty manner, but Jamie just picked at her plate. "I know I'm not a great cook, but it's not that bad is it?" she asked as Jamie moved the same piece of turkey around in circles.

"No, it's delicious, really," Jamie said as she popped the piece in her mouth. "I just get an upset stomach when I'm tense. I'm always afraid I'll throw up, so I don't like to eat much."

"You don't feel like you did at the help line do you?"

"No, I don't feel faint. I'm just nauseous."

"I guarantee that you won't throw up. Would you humor me and eat just a little? I bet you haven't had much today, have you?"

"No, not really."

"And you didn't eat much yesterday either, did you?" she asked.

"No," she admitted as she looked down at the floor.

"Come on then," Ryan said as she took her fork and loaded it up. "Here comes the airplane into the hangar." She did a few loop-the-loops with the turkey-laden fork.

Jamie gave her a shy grin as she opened up and accepted the turkey, deciding that it really did taste a lot better now that Ryan was urging her on. They continued their little game until the plate was clean. "Good girl!" Ryan enthused as she rubbed her head, messing her blonde locks haphazardly. "Now you can have some cake for dessert."

After they had cleaned the kitchen, they went down to Ryan's room to study. Ryan sat at her desk and wrestled with some problems that looked so complex that Jamie was unable to tell what subject they covered. She sat on the big bed and read her book until she fell asleep sitting up.

When Ryan noticed that she was sound asleep, she walked over to the bed and woke her with a light touch on her cheek. Jamie slowly batted her eyes and Ryan felt a catch in her throat at how terribly beautiful and completely vulnerable she looked. *Damn you, Jack,* she thought. *How can you not realize what you have here? She trusts you, and you kick her again and again! Your stupid insecurities are ruining your relationship, you jerk!*

"I think you'd be more comfortable in Da's room. Then you'll have your own bath." She stood and pulled Jamie up with her. "I'll go change the sheets and get it ready for you. And you go get ready for bed," she said as she gave her a little push towards the bathroom.

Ryan brought her a new toothbrush and showed her where the towels were. "You like to wear a T-shirt to bed, right?" Jamie nodded her assent as she brushed her teeth. Ryan walked back over with two T-shirts, "You can have long or short sleeved."

"I think I'll take the long," she replied thoughtfully as she removed the garment from Ryan's hand. "Is it okay if I just wear the shirt and the boxers I bought? I don't want to scandalize Conor when he comes home."

"I'm sure Conor will think you're seriously overdressed," she said with a smirk. "But I think it sounds appropriately modest. Do you need anything else?"

"No, I'm fine."

Ryan left, and a few minutes later Jamie walked into the room in her sleep clothes. "I'm just gonna hop in bed and try to forget about this whole day."

"I think that's a great idea," Ryan agreed as she pulled the crisp sheet back for her. "I'll be up for a while doing some homework. Just yell downstairs if you think of anything you need." When Jamie was situated, Ryan pulled the sheet up and tucked her in. She sat on the edge of the bed and leaned over to plant a kiss on her cheek. "You sleep tight tonight, okay?"

The fond regard that flowed from Ryan's expression made Jamie's heart clench in her chest. "I'll try. Thanks for being there for me."

"I'm always here for you. I'm really glad you called me today." She kissed her cheek again, and ruffled her hair, making the blonde smile in response.

Around ten o'clock Ryan heard Jamie get up. She listened for a minute and decided that she must just be going to the bathroom, quickly returning to her chemistry problem. She was sitting at her desk wearing her standard study outfit—her underwear. Her hair was pulled straight back into a tight ponytail with just a wisp or two sneaking out of the band and framing her face. Small, round, silver wire-rimmed glasses were perched upon her nose, giving her a very serious, almost professorial look that even the underwear didn't diminish.

She was slightly startled when she heard Jamie's soft voice right behind her. "Ryan?"

"Hi, what's up?" she replied as she turned around in her chair. "Having trouble sleeping?"

"Yeah, I guess I am." She looked down at the floor, clearly avoiding looked at Ryan.

"Tell me what's wrong." Ryan stood and faced her.

You mean besides the fact that you're in your underwear? "I woke up a while ago, and I can't get back to sleep. I saw your light on, so I came down." The floor was still holding her interest. "But I don't want to disturb you. I mean you're in your ... pajamas and all," she said to the carpet.

"You're not disturbing me. I was just studying." She lifted Jamie's chin and looked into her eyes, "I'm planning on being up for another couple of hours. Would you like to stay down here with me?"

"I don't want to invade your privacy," she said as she shot a quick glance at Ryan's outfit.

The brunette finally caught on. "Does it bother you that I'm in my underwear?"

"Uhm, that's underwear?" she asked sheepishly.

"Yeah. Haven't you ever seen these?" Jamie studied her outfit closely. Ryan was wearing a gray, ribbed, tank-top that fit like second skin. The tank top just covered the waistband of matching, cotton knit, mid-thigh, gray boxers. *Boxers?*

"These are regulation women's underwear, I'll have you know. I don't borrow my brothers' or anything," she teased as she made her way over to her built in dresser. "When I started working out at the gym, I began to wear Lycra shorts. I really liked them and got used to not having elastic around my upper legs. I found these Calvin Klein women's boxers a short time later, and I never plan on going back. They never ride up and you don't get the dreaded VPL."

"VPL?"

"Visible panty line, of course. It's the scourge of womankind." She laughed as she pulled a pair of navy blue sweat pants out of a drawer and slipped them on. Next she found the T-shirt she'd been wearing earlier, and pulled that over her head.

"You don't have to get dressed just because of me."

"It's okay. I want you to feel comfortable around me." Ryan gave her a reassuring pat. "Now, what would you like to do? Do you feel like talking, or do you want to lie down while I study?"

"I think I'll just lie down here if you don't mind." She flopped down on the bed. "I'm really tired, but I just can't relax."

"Why don't you let me help you relax?" Ryan sat down next to her, opened a bedside drawer and pulled out a bottle of herbal scented massage lotion. She held it up invitingly in front of Jamie. "Can I tempt you?"

Jamie flopped over onto her stomach with her arms stretched straight out at her sides. "If you must," she said with mock resignation.

"Do you mind taking this off?" Ryan tugged on the hem of the oversized T-shirt.

Jamie felt more than a touch of embarrassment, but she sat up slightly and pulled the shirt over her head, then lay back down.

Ryan swung her legs up on the bed, and scooted over until she was right next to her friend. Deciding that the angle was wrong, she swung one knee over and straddled her slim hips. *Thank you Jesus, for making her put on sweats.*

Ryan poured a generous amount of lotion onto her hands and rubbed them together briskly to warm it. She placed those strong hands gently on Jamie's shoulders and softly asked, "Ready?"

For anything, Jamie thought dreamily as she struggled to stay lucid. Ryan's hands were works of art as they worked over her tense muscles. *There's no way those hands have ever forced a woman to do anything against her will. Although, anyone who would be crazy enough to refuse this touch is beyond me.* The hands pushed and pulled and prodded each muscle in turn until Jamie was a quivering mass of relaxed flesh. She could feel Ryan's powerful thighs flex and move against her as her friend leaned over to reach more distant muscles, could feel the heat radiating from Ryan's body as the massage grew more strenuous.

After a few minutes of very deep muscle work, Jamie felt the intensity begin to wane. Her body grew heavy and sluggish, and as Ryan continued to work she struggled to remain awake. Ryan obviously felt this too, as she continued to stroke her lightly, finally ending with a feather light touch all over her neck, shoulders and back.

Jamie was vaguely aware of Ryan's efforts to place her T-shirt over her head again and pull her arms through the long sleeves. Then she felt a soft blanket settle over her and a tender kiss brushed her cheek. With great effort, she struggled to stay awake to savor the sensations, but the peace that had settled into her flesh compelled her to fall asleep deeply and soundly.

When Ryan was certain that Jamie was asleep, she got up gingerly from the bed and returned to her desk. *I cannot study with clothes on,* she decided as she shucked her pants and T-shirt and settled down with her chemistry problems.

After another two hours of struggling with her studies, Ryan heard Conor come home. She checked on Jamie to be sure she was warm, turned off the computer and put her pants back on. She caught Conor just as he was about to go up to his room.

"Hey," he said when he spied her emerge from the staircase. "What are you still doing up?"

"I've been studying," she said through a yawn. "Oh, Jamie's downstairs. She had some boyfriend trouble, and she's gonna sleep in my room. I'll take Da's."

"Is she okay? Anything serious?"

"She'll be fine. She just had a really tough day. You know how it is."

"Yeah, I do," he said, frowning a little. "What do you think of this boyfriend, anyway?"

"I don't know him very well. Part of the problem is that he doesn't care for me much, and he's been trying to stop Jamie from spending time with me."

"Why wouldn't he like you?" Conor asked with a sharp tone.

"He doesn't think Jamie should spend so much of her time with a lesbian," she said. "I guess he feels threatened."

"Oh, please!" Conor said, truly annoyed. "What does he think you'll do to her? I'd like to give that jerk a piece of my mind."

"I guess he thinks I'll seduce her. That's the only reason that makes sense."

"Riiight." He tossed his head back and laughed. "What this jag-off doesn't get is that if you wanted to seduce her—she'd already be seduced." He wrapped his elbow around his sister's neck and gave her a gentle tap on the chin with his fist. "No woman is safe when my baby sister sets her trap."

"That's the stupid thing, Conor. I don't feel that way about Jamie. She's my friend, and it infuriates me that he can't recognize that. Plus, it's a terrible insult to her. She's totally faithful to him, and to assume she'd have sex with me just because I'm gay is just rude."

"You really don't want her?" Conor asked. "You could do a lot worse, you know."

"No, I don't have those kinds of thoughts about her. I feel very close to her, and kind of protective, but not sexual." She shrugged her shoulders and gave him a decidedly lecherous look. "But if she were single and interested–that would change. She's just my type."

"We're in complete agreement, little sister," he said as he placed an arm around her shoulders and escorted her to their father's room.

Jamie woke with a start when she felt a warm tongue lap her face. She blinked her eyes open, and saw a smiling Ryan and a panting Duffy watching her. Ryan was obviously just back from a morning workout. She wore a gold turtleneck covered by a navy blue, short-sleeved T-shirt. Her legs were covered by black Lycra pants, and black and electric blue roller blades were strapped to her feet. Her hair was styled in a loose braid, and the few wispy bangs she normally wore were soaked with perspiration. Her cheeks were very pink, and her blue eyes were bright and mischievous.

"Duffy insisted on seeing you this morning, and I couldn't refuse," she said as she shrugged her shoulders helplessly.

"Can he get on the bed?"

"If you don't mind, I don't mind."

"C'mon, Duffy boy," Jamie said as she patted the mattress. Duffy didn't need to be asked twice. He jumped up and began to lick every exposed inch of skin that was available to his bubblegum-pink tongue. Jamie giggled helplessly as she ineffectually tried to protect her mouth and eyes from the assault.

"I'm going to jump in the shower while you two cuddle," Ryan said as she stripped off her skates. She stopped at the dresser and picked out her clothes for the day, then went into the bathroom.

Jamie heard the shower start up, and after a minute Duffy calmed down and nestled up alongside her. After a few moments spent idly rubbing his head, she heard a light knock on the door. "Come in," she called out.

Conor's dark head poked in the door. "Are you ladies decent?"

"Ryan's in the shower, but I'm pretty decent."

He entered the room and shook his finger at Duffy. "Why do you always get to sleep with the pretty girls?" He sat on the edge of the bed and ruffled Duffy's curly, black coat.

Jamie looked Conor over as he played with the dog. He was dressed in a white T-shirt covered by a deep red and black flannel shirt. The sleeves were rolled up to expose his very muscular forearms that were surprisingly covered with very light blonde down. Faded jeans and heavy work boots completed his outfit. His hair was still damp from the shower, and he smelled great. *He smells just the way I like a man to smell*, she thought as she sniffed reflectively, *nothing but soap.*

"Ryan says you had a tough day yesterday" he said. "Are you feeling better?"

"Yeah, I am. Thanks for caring."

"You've been adopted by the whole clan. We all care about you." He stood to leave. "If that ex-con gives you any more trouble, he's gonna have to answer to me," he said with a mock glower.

"I'll keep that in mind." She smiled impishly. "Boy, would that be an unfair fight. I wasn't sure he could beat up Ryan. He wouldn't last a second with you."

"That's where you're wrong. Ryan's the one you need to be careful of in this family." Jamie was just about to ask what he meant by that when the door to the bathroom opened and Ryan called out, "Quit harassing the half naked women, Conor."

"Now you tell me she's half naked," he whined. "I never have any luck." He gave Jamie a wave and left the room.

"He's the sweetest man," Jamie said as she walked over to the bathroom.

"No, Brendan and Rory are both sweet. Conor is the most charming."

"Well, I think he's sweet and charming," she said as she folded her arms in a defiant stance.

"No, that's me," Ryan said with a twinkle in her eyes. Her hair was very damp and combed straight back. Every strong plane of the lovely face was emphasized by the style, and Jamie realized again how incredibly beautiful her friend was.

"I can't argue with that," she said fondly as she surprised Ryan with a very fierce hug. "I'm feeling a lot better today, and I think a marvelous massage has a lot to do with it."

"I was happy to help out. I don't give a lot of massages anymore, and I kind of miss it."

"I'll gratefully accept any time you feel the need. Remember, I am a certified pleasure hound," she grinned as she stepped into the warm bathroom to get ready for the day.

The trip to Berkeley was quick even in the heavy traffic. Jamie loved the freedom of being able to sail along between the slow moving lanes on the big bike. They were even allowed to use the express lane on the bridge, which carved fifteen minutes off the trip. As they approached Jamie's house, Ryan slowed and pulled to the curb. "Do you want me to let you off here in case your roommates are home?"

The smaller woman thought for a minute, and finally nodded her head. "No sense in making matters worse than they already are." She hopped off and handed Ryan the helmet, then leaned over and gave her a hug and a kiss on the cheek. "This meant an awful lot to me, Ryan. I just want you to know how thankful I am that you're my friend."

Ryan returned the hug, holding her friend close for a few moments. "It's my pleasure."

The answering machine yielded ten messages from Jack, two from her father and one from Mia. Jamie had turned off her cell phone to avoid speaking to Jack, and this was the obvious result. She dialed her father's office and left a message on his private line. "Hi, Daddy. Don't worry about me. I'm sure this will all blow over. Sorry about yesterday. I'll call later."

The next call was harder to make. She dialed the number and closed her eyes, hoping that he wasn't home, but her luck wasn't with her. Jack answered on the first ring, clearly agitated. "Jamie! Where have you been? I've been looking for you all night!" Jamie was shocked. She knew that he'd be anxious, but she was unprepared for the frantic tone to his voice. For the first time in their relationship, she thought that he might actually cry.

"I told you I wanted to be alone, Jack. I'm sorry you were worried about me, but I wasn't able to talk to you."

"I feel like you're slipping away from me. I don't know how to hold on to you!" He really was crying now, and she was amazed by how much he was affected by her absence.

"Jack, the only way to hold on to me is to let me live my life," she said gently. "I can't stand to have you or anyone else try to control me."

"Are you still in love with me? Do you still want to marry me?"

"I still love you, Jack. But I don't like you when you treat me like your property. We've got a lot to talk about, but I've got to get to class. When will you be home tonight?"

"The earliest I can promise is eight tonight. I've got a meeting for law review at five, but I'll make sure I'm home by eight if you'll come down."

"I'll be there. Now don't worry, honey. We can work this out, but it's gonna take some effort."

Ryan agreed to drive her down to Palo Alto, as long as they could leave after rush hour. Jamie got through her day in a contemplative fog, and was sitting in her living room when Ryan and Mia came in just after four.

"Hi, guys," she said as she looked up from her book. "I forgot you were going to start working together today. How'd it go?"

"She killed me!" Mia moaned. "I thought I was in pretty good shape from going to my gym, but I've obviously been wasting my time."

"You're the one who kept saying, 'More weight!'" Ryan laughed.

"Let Ryan massage your legs if they're sore, she has great hands." Jamie blinked when she heard the words come out of her mouth, and she hoped that Mia didn't jump on the suggestive implication.

"Either massage them or cut them off!" Mia dropped to the floor and offered her legs to Ryan.

With a smirk, Ryan gamely worked on the stressed appendages while Jamie tried to continue reading. But she was strangely jealous of Ryan lavishing her attention on Mia, and she had to remind herself that it had been her idea to set them up. The front door opened just as Ryan was finishing up the right leg. Cassie strode into the room and observed, "Am I the only one in this house who hasn't fallen prey to your charms, Ryan?"

Jamie heard the muttered, "You're the only one they haven't been offered to," but she was fairly sure that Cassie didn't.

"Does anyone want a cold drink?" Jamie asked as she rose to go to the kitchen. Both Ryan and Mia answered in the affirmative.

Cassie entered the kitchen right behind Jamie, who did her best to ignore her former friend, grabbing three bottles of water and brushing past her on the way out. She handed the bottles to Mia and Ryan and said, "Come on up to my room when you're done."

Cassie exited the kitchen, and stared at Jamie's retreating form, finally placing her hands on her hips and asking no one in particular, "What in the hell has gotten into her?"

Neither Mia nor Ryan responded to this rhetorical question. Ryan was finished and she said, "Take a long, hot shower to keep your legs loose, Mia. I'll see you on Wednesday, okay?" She playfully squeezed the curly-haired woman's foot, and winked at her, then started to climb the stairs.

Mia turned to a still-fuming Cassie and shrugged her shoulders. "What can I say? She's got great hands."

Jamie was lying on her bed with her hands knit behind her head when Ryan knocked lightly, then entered. "I'm glad you're here," the blonde said as she looked at her friend. "You're the only person who might be able to pull me off her if I try to strangle her."

"I'm out of the loop," Ryan said. "Why are you mad at Cassie?"

"I found out that she's been fanning the flames with Jack again. He said that she told him I spent every free minute of my time with you."

"I should be so lucky," Ryan said, grinning a quirky smile. She was curled up on the loveseat under the window, looking very relaxed.

"You sure do know how to make a girl feel good."

"That comes in handy in my line of work." Ryan waggled an eyebrow, then ducked a forcefully thrown pillow.

After a few minutes spent chatting about their respective days, Jamie grew pensive. "Would you mind if I wanted to talk about Jack for a while?"

"Nope. I'm all ears."

"Do you think I'm crazy to be getting married so soon?" Jamie surprised herself with the question. *Where did that come from?*

"Thanks for starting with something simple," Ryan said, smiling sardonically. After a moment she answered, "I wasn't ready to make that kind of commitment when I was your age. But you're a lot more mature than I was then. Actually, you're more mature than I am now, so I might not be the right person to ask."

"But you know me, Ryan. Do you think I'm ready to be married?"

"Before I can render my expert opinion, I have to ask you some questions."

"Ask away."

"Why get married? Why's marriage better than the set-up you have now?"

She considered this for a long time. "Conor asked me the same thing a while ago, and I think what I told him is the main reason."

"Which was?"

"I don't want to date a bunch of guys just because I can. I know what I want in a partner, and when I found it I didn't want to let it get away."

"That makes sense," Ryan said. "But can't you have the same thing just living together?"

"No, I don't think you can," Jamie said. "I want to make a lifetime commitment to Jack. I want to share all of my life with him. I want to share my deepest thoughts and feelings with him. I want to share my body with him alone. And I want to do everything I can to make his life more complete."

"If you can do all of that, you'll have a great marriage," Ryan said. "As long as he can do the same." She raised an eyebrow, locking her eyes on Jamie's.

"That's a big question, isn't it? It obviously isn't a partnership if he doesn't feel the same way about me. And I'm no longer sure that he wants me to be myself." Jamie got up from the bed and came over to sit next to Ryan. "I used to be certain that he felt the same way. But this whole argument about you has made me question a lot of things."

"Like what?"

"He seems to feel like he can tell me how to spend my time. I could see his being upset if my plans interfered with our time together, but they don't." Ryan nodded her understanding. "I'm really into the AIDS Ride, and my training, and it disappoints me that he doesn't seem to support me at all. He doesn't ever ask how it's going." After a moment she added, "Although he has been complimenting me on my body. That's the only thing that's registered."

"Well at least he's not blind," Ryan joked, then started to blush when Jamie looked startled. Getting back to the topic, she asked, "Did he used to be interested in your life?"

"I think so, but I'm not really sure. I mean, I've changed since I've known you. I want more from him than I used to want."

"Why's that? What have I done?"

"You're interested in me. You make me feel like I'm important. You ask me about what I do, and what I like. It's made me wish for that from him. I shouldn't have to get that from my girlfriends. My lover should care more about me than my friends."

"You might be right, but I'm not sure. It's a rare man who can make you feel connected like a woman can. And believe me, I'm not knocking men. I just think there are things you can get from women that are hard for men to give."

"I suppose you're right," she sighed. "Like when we fight he doesn't want to talk about it or work it out. He just wants to uhm … be intimate. But that doesn't settle things for me. I don't get over my emotional pains through sex."

"I know that a lot of men express their feelings through sex. Maybe you just need to spend more time explaining what your needs are. There's a good chance he'll try to meet your needs if he knows what they are."

"I suppose that's true. I haven't been very forceful in making him realize what I want from him. I've just been hoping that he'd know."

"That doesn't seem fair to him," Ryan said. "I know from dealing with my brothers that they're clueless about emotional issues. They really need to be guided."

"You seem to know a lot about men. I guess being raised with all those brothers really gave you an advantage," Jamie said.

"All I know is that it's really different being in a relationship with a man versus a woman. With a woman I feel like I can use shorthand and she'll be able to understand. You need to be much clearer with men."

"It sounds like it's so much easier being with a woman," Jamie lamented.

Ryan looked at her thoughtfully for a long time. "In a way it is, but there's a tendency for women to identify with each other too much and become too interdependent. In an opposite sex couple there's a push-pull, yin-yang kind of thing that creates a lot of tension. And tension can make for really hot sex," she said with a smile.

"Oh great! I get all the tension and none of the hot sex!"

"Uhm … you don't want to talk about that too do you?" Ryan asked, a wary tone to her voice.

"No, I'll spare you those gruesome details."

"Whew," was all that Ryan said.

Ryan dropped Jamie off in front of Jack's apartment just before eight. When Jamie got off the bike, she leaned over and planted a kiss on her cheek. "You're the best, and I'm so glad you're my friend."

"I think you're the best," Ryan said, "so there!" She revved her engine loudly, and wrinkled her nose, peeling out with a spray of dust.

"Brat!" Jamie called after her, even though she knew that Ryan couldn't hear a word on the noisy Harley.

Jack was sitting on the couch waiting for her. He got up when she entered, but he didn't make a move to come to her. She felt very awkward, and she knew that her body language showed how she felt.

"Do you mind if I kiss you hello?" he asked.

"Of course not." She opened her arms to him, and he nearly ran across the room. He wrapped his arms around her tightly and nuzzled his head into her neck.

"I'm sorry, Jamie. I'm so sorry," he mumbled, over and over.

Almost immediately, Jamie forgot about the fight and just gave herself over to his embrace. But as soon as he felt her begin to relax, he leaned his head down and began to kiss her, slowly and tentatively at first, but then increasing in intensity and confidence. She felt him begin to get aroused and she gently pushed him away. "We need to talk," she said as she locked onto his passion filled eyes.

He gave her a hurt look as he moved back, but he respected her wishes and went back to sit on the couch. He looked up at her and tentatively patted the couch cushion next to him. She smiled and sat down next to him, allowing him to wrap his arm around her.

"I know I was wrong, but I'm so jealous of that woman I can't see straight," he said, his lips pursed together.

"Jack, what on earth do you have to be jealous about?"

"What do I have to be jealous about? How would you feel if my law review partner was a gorgeous woman with a reputation for seducing every guy she could get her hands on?" He cut her off with a raised hand when she tried to interrupt. "And what if I spent a lot of my free time with her, not doing school work, but just hanging out?" He cocked his head at her. "Wouldn't that bother you?"

"That's not a good analogy, Jack," she explained patiently. "A better one would be if your partner was a very good looking gay guy who had a reputation for dating lots of other gay men." He began to scowl at this analogy. "It wouldn't bother me one bit if you became friends with a gay man."

"That's not the same thing," he replied confidently, concurrently trying to figure out why it wasn't.

"Tell me why it isn't?" she said, knowing he could not.

"I don't know, but it's not."

"Okay, let's start over. Tell me why you're jealous of her."

"I'm afraid she's acting like your friend to seduce you," he admitted with an embarrassed look.

"Well, I'm not sure who that insults more, but go on."

"I don't see how hanging out with her is any different than hanging out with a guy who's after you."

She shook her head slowly, astounded that he was unable to see the obvious differences. "Well, it's simple, really. One—she isn't after me. Two—she isn't a guy; she's a woman. Three—I'm committed to be married to you. I wouldn't cheat on you with a man or a woman."

"How do you know she isn't after you?" he asked, getting back to his biggest fear.

"Because I asked her."

"You what?" he shouted.

"I had heard the rumors about her, and I'd seen her flirting with the other women in class, so I asked her if she was interested in me," she said. "I had no interest in developing a friendship with her if she was going to be flirting with me all the time."

"What did she say?" he asked, perplexed by this development.

"She said she knew I was straight, and that she didn't like to date straight women. She also said that she thought I was cute and that she had been interested, but that she didn't like to date her friends."

"And you believed her?" he asked as though Jamie was slightly slow.

"Yes, I did, and I still do. We spend a lot of time together. She tells me all about her life and the women she sees. I know her family. I know what kind of person she is. She's loyal and honest, very forthright, funny, bright and interesting. And I trust her completely." Just to tweak him a bit she added, "She's got three older brothers and about a dozen cousins who are just as good looking as she is. And the best looking one of the bunch is always flirting with me. That's who you should be jealous of," she said with a smirk.

"Oh, now I feel better," he grumbled. He stretched his body out, trying to remove some of the tension that had settled in his muscles. "Look, I know you don't have a lot of experience with guys, but we tell girls anything to get them into bed. A guy will spend years being your friend just in the hopes of one day sleeping with you."

"I may not have slept with other men, Jack, but I do have some experience," she replied. "I know many guys are like that. But in my limited experience lesbians aren't. You seem to think she's a man without a penis—but she's a woman." She fished around in her head for an example. "How many women do you know who work really hard to get a guy to sleep with them?"

"If they're good looking, they don't have to," he said, slightly perplexed.

"Exactly. Women generally don't go to great lengths to hit on guys. The lesbians I know are more like that than they are like guys." He looked suspicious. "Oh, they flirt with each other, but they don't come on like guys do. It's much more subtle."

"That favors my point!" he said. "It's harder to tell when she's coming on to you. It's more invasive than aggressive."

"Ryan's great looking, right?" He gave a slight nod. "She can have her pick of women at school. And believe me, they practically throw themselves at her. She certainly wouldn't be wasting her time trying to turn me into a lesbian when she has so many to choose from. That just doesn't make sense."

"So you're saying that she treats you just the same as any of your other friends, right?" he finally asked.

She thought about this for a long while. She didn't want to prolong this, but she wasn't going to lie. "No, that's not true," she admitted. "The dynamic is different with her. She's very comfortable touching other women, and that makes her a bit more physically close than my other friends." She gathered her courage, "And she's very comfortable in her own body. She's a massage therapist, as well as a trainer, and she's very comfortable with physical affection."

"Like what?"

"Like rubbing my legs after a workout, or giving me a hug when I've had a bad day."

"And you truly don't think that she gets aroused when she touches you?" he asked, clearly not buying it.

"I'm certain that she doesn't," she replied firmly. *Thank you—thank you for not asking the inverse question!*

After another hour or so of discussion, Jack agreed that he'd try harder to accept Ryan as a part of Jamie's life. He also agreed that he'd do his best to not interfere in her choice of friends or activities. By the time they were finished, it was nearly ten o'clock, and Jamie had an early class in the morning.

"Can you stay over tonight?" he asked as he began to nuzzle her ear and neck.

"I've got an eight o'clock class honey. I'd have to get up before six to make it." He wasn't to be dissuaded however, and within minutes she found herself half naked on the couch. She decided that this intimacy was something that he really needed, so she let him continue his quest. She felt gentle and loving towards him as he touched her body reverently. He pushed a bit faster than she would have liked, but all in all it was a pleasant experience.

His head rested on her breast as she rubbed his back and rocked him slightly. "I love you, Jack," she murmured into his ear. "I love you."

Chapter Nine

When Jamie arrived home just before one in the morning there was a message on her machine from Ryan. "Hi. Call me if you need to talk. It doesn't matter how late it is."

She's so sweet to me. I don't know what I've done to deserve her friendship, but I'm really happy I have it. She didn't feel the need to take Ryan up on her offer, and she didn't have any intention of waking her up needlessly, so she refrained from calling.

She barely made it to her eight o'clock class. After a rather tedious discussion, she stumbled sleepily out of the classroom, bumping directly into a grinning Ryan.

"Somebody didn't have her latte yet," the brunette teased.

"Is it that obvious? I was up so late I barely made it to class. Speaking of class, what are you doing here?"

"My lab was canceled, so I had some free time. I thought I'd come see how you were."

"I didn't know you even knew what classes I had on Tuesday, much less where they were."

"Of course I know," Ryan said, a bit puzzled. "Don't you know my class schedule?"

Jamie paused, then smiled. "Yeah, I guess I do. Is this what you meant about women being more connected than men?"

"Precisely," Ryan said as she guided her through the building in search of caffeine.

Jamie spent a few minutes updating Ryan on her evening with Jack. "It sounds like it went pretty well," Ryan said thoughtfully. "His assumptions about me aren't uncommon. A lot of guys don't like their girlfriends to have lesbian friends. With any luck he'll realize that all I want from you is friendship ... and lasagna," she grinned. "But he really does sound like he wants to make you happy, and that's good news. It just seems like he's not sure how to do that."

"I know he does," she said. "I think your advice was right on point. I need to spend more time letting him know what I need, rather than expecting him to guess."

"I really hope it works out for you. You deserve the best."

The following Tuesday, Jamie showed up at the gym hoping to get a little cardiovascular work in. She looked around for her friend, and found her in the rear corner of the gym chatting with a woman. Trying to be unobtrusive, she hopped on a stairclimber to get warmed up, but the slightly elevated machine gave her an even clearer view of the action, and she couldn't help but watch.

Ryan was leaning up against one of the chest press machines. The woman was seated on the integrated stool of the machine, and she gazed up at Ryan with a very flirtatious look. Jamie was pretty sure that she wasn't a client, and as she looked more closely she noticed that the woman was considerably older than Ryan *She's old enough to be my mother!* The woman looked about forty-five or so, and in great shape. She looked very well taken care of, and the thought occurred to Jamie that this could be any one of her mother's friends.

Ryan had adopted a very casual pose. She had one of her long arms extended above her head to hang over the top bar of the machine, leaning against the bulk of it so that the woman had to crane her neck to make eye contact. But even though her pose was casual, there was that barely concealed force that just begged to be released from her body. Jamie had often seen her friend look completely relaxed and casual, but every time Ryan was sizing someone up she adopted this predatory posture. Jamie had to admit that it was very appealing, and for one brief instant she was jealous of the seated woman. But she quickly brushed that troublesome thought from her brain as she tried to watch—while appearing not to.

After a few minutes the woman tried to stand, but Ryan was directly in her path. The tall woman didn't budge one inch, and her prey was forced to alter her path. Since Ryan had a good six inches on her, the woman still had to look up to meet her gaze, but she seemed unable to look away from Ryan's penetrating stare. They were standing terribly close to one another and Ryan was clearly not going to move. To get past her the woman placed her hands on Ryan's waist and gently guided her out of her path. *Gotcha!* Jamie thought. *Once you touch her, there's no escape!*

Ryan leaned over to hear a question, and when she lifted her head she had the confident smirk that she so often wore when she was hitting on someone. She nodded her head slowly and leaned back on her heels to watch the woman walk to the locker room. Ryan walked over to another trainer and spoke to her for a moment or two, and then she went to the front desk and chatted with the woman on duty Next, she walked over to the coat hooks and picked up her leather jacket and walked out the front door with a definite swagger.

A minute or two later, the older woman emerged from the locker room. She left quickly, and Jamie spent a moment wondering if they were meeting up in the parking lot.

Knowing Ryan they don't even have to leave the lot if that woman has a big enough sports utility vehicle, she thought as a shudder rolled down her body.

Ryan stood by her bike, grinning wickedly at the woman. "Wanna go for a ride?" she teased in her deep rumbling voice.

"Ah, I don't think that's such a good idea. I really can't afford to be seen on the back of a motorcycle."

"Are you a spy, or a fugitive from justice?"

"Nooo, but I'm fairly well known around the East Bay, and my …"

"Husband?" Ryan supplied.

"Yes, my husband is well known too," she admitted. "Does that bother you?"

"It depends. Is this the first time you've …"

"Hardly," she scoffed. "We've been married for twen … a long while. We have an … arrangement."

"Will this be the last time you do this?"

"Doubtful, unless you can keep me faithful to you," she purred as she moved to stand even closer.

"Doubtful," Ryan acknowledged with a smirk. "Any kids?"

"Yes, but not at home. They're grow … uhm … they're away … at school."

Ryan gave her a slow, sexy smile. "So you'd say that spending the afternoon with me won't alter your world in any significant way?"

"Well," she said, as she brushed up against her. "I hope it will. But I promise it won't have a negative impact on my life. Or that of my family."

"One last question. And please don't think I'm as full of myself as this sounds. Do you have any interest in having an ongoing relationship with me?"

The woman's eyes grew wide with surprise. She shook her head briskly and said, "Honey, my life is nearly perfect. The only thing I don't get enough of is good sex. I have no interest in losing my husband, or the tenuous respect of my children, so if that's what you want, let's stop right now."

"You're my kinda woman, Laura," Ryan said with a grin. "Where to?"

Laura hopped into the driver's seat of a new, black Mercedes S class sedan. "Nice ride," Ryan said as she looked around.

"Thanks. I just got it a week ago. I like it pretty well, but it's a little sedate, don't you think?"

"A little, but I'm sure you have other outlets for your wild side."

That earned her a smirk and a gentle pat on the leg. "Do you prefer the Mark Hopkins or the Fairmont?" Laura asked as she got on the freeway leading back to the city.

"Never been in either, so it's your choice."

Laura shot her quizzical look but continued the planning. "Okay, I'll drop you off a block away. Then you go in and get us a room. I'll pay you back, of course. I'll meet you by the elevator. Please don't talk to me or acknowledge me in any way, though. Okay?"

Ryan looked a bit askance as she admitted, "I don't have a charge card. Can you stop at an ATM?"

"Jesus! You're over twenty-one aren't you?"

"Yes, I am," Ryan replied with a smile. "I'm still in school at Cal. The personal training is just part time."

"How do you manage without a charge card?"

"Well, I live at home, I don't have a car, I don't buy groceries, I never go on vacation, and I don't buy things over the Internet. Why *would* I need one?"

"Good point, I guess," she admitted, giving Ryan another quick glance. "No one's going to come looking for you if you're not home for dinner, are they? I don't want to see your picture on the back of a milk carton."

Ryan gave her a sweet smile. "Nope. I don't even have a curfew."

Laura pulled up in front of an ATM and handed Ryan her card along with her security code. Ryan gave her a small scowl for being so trusting, but she got out and withdrew the requested $600. When she hopped back in she remarked, "It's not a very good idea to trust a stranger with your ATM card and your access number."

"It's only money," she said lightly. As Ryan tried to hand the card and the money over. Laura took the card but instructed Ryan to keep the money. "You don't want to look like you don't have a little extra."

Ryan had been to hotels with women, but always cheap little places when neither she nor her date could find a better place. She had also been with older women, but they were always lesbians. This was a first for her, and the thought of having sex with a married woman old enough to be her mother was both titillating and frightening. This woman had obviously been around the block a few hundred times, and Ryan was afraid that Laura's experience would upset Ryan's own natural dominance. And even though she was attracted to her, she didn't want to submit to a stranger. "So, do you usually go out with women?" she asked to flesh out the issue.

"No, not usually. But you just look like too much fun to pass up."

"But you've been with women before, haven't you?"

"Yes, dear, I have. Will you stop worrying? I promise I won't fall in love with you," she said with a hint of exasperation. "Why are you so careful anyway? You're not the daughter of a famous politician are you?"

"Hardly. My dad's a firefighter. I just don't like to cause trouble or hurt anyone's feelings."

They paused at a long red light, and Laura turned to look at her closely, "You really are cute, you know." She reached over and cupped Ryan's cheek and trailed her thumb across her lips. "Why's a beautiful young woman doing something like this, anyway? Why not find someone to love?"

"I don't have time for that right now. I've got too much to handle as it is. After I'm finished with school I'll start thinking about settling down. But until then, I'm only interested in good, clean, fun," she said with a leer. "And the clean part is optional."

Laura dropped her off about a block away from the hilltop hotel. "Get a nice room, honey. I hate to feel cramped."

Ryan dutifully climbed the hill, smirking to herself that when Laura called her honey, it reminded her of her aunts. In her blue jean and leather jacket she didn't fit in very well in the opulent surroundings, but she carried herself with so much confidence that she received only appreciative glances. She walked up to the front desk and requested a room for one night.

"Very good, ma'am," the obviously gay clerk replied.

"What do you have available?"

He looked down his computer screen and informed her, "I have a single for $135. That's in the back of the hotel, no view. The only other rooms I have are suites. That's two bedrooms and a sitting area. Those rooms are $450."

"Is that really the best rate you can give me?" she asked with a friendly, but determined look.

"Well," he said, "I could give you a discount on the suite. We still have, uhm … six of them left. Just one night, right?"

"I only need it for an hour," she said with a wiggling eyebrow.

"Oh … ohhh," he said as he saw the light. "How about three hundred dollars?"

"Sold," she said, as she peeled off three fifty to cover room tax. He handed her the access card and gave her a wink. "I assume I can just fill in the name and address with any old thing that comes to mind?"

"Knock yourself out," Ryan grinned.

"Have fun."

"Oh, I will," she promised. She walked over to the gift shop and purchased two toothbrushes and some paste, then strode confidently over to the elevator. She looked straight ahead and pushed the up button, while seemingly from nowhere, Laura appeared a few feet away. They both got on along with a few other passengers. Their room was on the top floor, and by the time they reached it they were alone. Ryan continued to ignore Laura, assuming that she'd break the silence if she chose to. When the doors opened, Ryan turned to the right but Laura hung a left. The taller woman walked to the end of the long hallway and opened the door to the suite, leaving it ajar when she entered. A few minutes later Laura came strolling in, and looked around with appreciation.

"You didn't skimp. Good for you," she said, obviously happy with Ryan's choice.

"You look like you're used to first class. But I got you a deal. I talked the clerk down from four fifty to three hundred."

Laura looked at her very quizzically, but didn't comment. Ryan pulled the toothbrushes from her inner pocket and said, "My contribution to our little endeavor. It's not much, but I didn't have time to shop."

Laura walked over and stood toe to toe with her. She draped her arms around her neck and purred, "How would you like to wash my back?"

"I thought you'd never ask," she growled as she began to gently, but determinedly, remove her date's clothing.

Two hours later Ryan fought through the haze of her exhaustion, as Laura slid out of the tangle of sheets and went into the bathroom. She heard the shower running as she lazily thought, *she sure is clean*. But then she remembered that Laura was probably going home to her husband, and he might not appreciate "Eau de O'Flaherty."

She reflected on the nearly two-hour-long marathon. Laura had been insatiable in her appetite for Ryan. She had pleased her in every way imaginable, and Ryan once again considered that experience was a very good thing to have in a lover. She had surprised herself to find that she had really liked being with an older woman. It had been a while, and she reflected that there was something very sexy about an older woman's approach to sex. Laura was a very sensual and deliberate lover She knew what she liked, and she knew how to get it in a very efficient way. She seemed to have a lot of fun exploring Ryan's body, and she brought her to orgasm as though they'd been lovers for years.

Ryan reflected that Laura had obviously been telling the truth about having had other quick flings. When Ryan insisted on safer sex practices, she went to her purse and pulled out a handful of condoms, and they had managed to use every one of them. It wasn't the safest way, but a cut open condom was better than nothing for oral sex, and Laura wasn't to be denied in her quest to please Ryan in that way.

She dozed off while she was ruminating, and the next thing she knew Laura was placing a gentle kiss on her forehead. "I've got to go, honey." Ryan started to hop up but she put her hand on her shoulder to hold her steady. "I can't afford to be seen going back to the gym with you. I have some friends who sometimes go there in the evening."

"That's okay. I can take BART back. Your change is on the table over there," she said as she pointed to the sitting room.

That got her another puzzled look, but Laura just leaned over and gave her a very friendly kiss. "You could definitely become habit forming," she whispered "I can see why you offer so many disclaimers."

Ryan blushed at the compliment. The sexy, yet shy look on her face was too much for the older woman, and she sat back down next to her and took her in her arms. A few more kisses started the fires burning again, and it was very difficult for Laura to disengage, but she finally tore herself away from the lovely young woman and whispered, "Stay right there and let me see you spread out like that when I leave." She got up and walked over to the table, then turned and said, "I'm leaving you money for a cab, honey. I don't think it's safe to take BART after dark. Actually, why not stay over and go back in the morning?"

"Hmm, not a bad idea," Ryan replied as she rolled over and stretched languorously. She was on her belly, lying in the rumpled bed with the sheet half covering her thighs. Her legs were bent at the knee with her clean pink feet pointing at the ceiling. Her hair was completely ruffled, but with that "I've just had great sex look." She brought herself up onto her elbows and rested her head on her hands as she gave Laura one last sultry smile. "I had a marvelous afternoon. I hope you did, too."

"If you look at me like that for one more minute you're going to have a marvelous evening, too," she said with a mock glower. "I've got to get back to my so called normal life, but you're making it very difficult to leave."

"Just trying to keep the customer satisfied."

Laura blew her a kiss and departed as she said, "You were completely successful, honey."

Funny, Ryan thought. *After two hours of having her munching on me she doesn't remind me of my aunts anymore.* She stretched out and rested for a few minutes, but she couldn't fall asleep. Looking at her watch, she noticed that it was only six o'clock. She picked up the phone and dialed the familiar pager, putting in the full number of the hotel with her room number added at the end. A few minutes later she answered with a perky, "Hi, Conor, watcha doing?"

"Where are you?" he asked suspiciously.

"I'm playing grown up. Whatcha doing tonight?"

"Nothing. Da's at work, so I was trying to decide what to do for dinner."

"Come over and play grown up with me."

"Where the heck are you?"

"I'm at the Mark Hopkins. Room 2350. Bring your toothbrush and a change of clothes. Oh, and bring me some clean underwear and a T-shirt," she instructed, as she hung up before he could ask any more questions.

A half hour later, she was sitting on the big bed in her room watching cartoons. She had showered, and was wearing the fluffy, terry cloth robe that the hotel provided. She responded to the tentative knock on the main door, calling out, "Be right there," as she scrambled off the bed. She threw open the door to find a very confused looking Conor.

"Why are we staying at the Mark Hopkins Hotel?"

"I had a little date earlier, and she had to leave. It seemed an awful waste to let this neat two-bedroom suite sit idle all night, so I thought we should enjoy it."

"Hmm." Referring to Ally, he said, "Why not call your little friend from the gym?"

"You know her name, Conor," she reminded him.

"Yeah? Well I've never been introduced."

"I know," she admitted. "She's not my girlfriend, you know. We just fool around together."

"So why not call her?"

"Because the last thing I want is more sex," she said with a small grimace. "I had a great time, but enough is enough!"

"Wow," he enthused as he looked around the spacious dwelling. "Two bedrooms and a sitting room? What did this place cost you?"

"They tried to get four hundred fifty dollars for it, but they settled for three hundred," she said, proud of her negotiating skills.

"Where'd you get three hundred bucks for a hotel?" he scoffed as he investigated every nook and cranny.

"Are you nuts? I wouldn't pop for Motel Six! My date paid for the room; all I bought were the toothbrushes," she said with a little eyebrow wiggle.

"Gee, what kind of dough does she have? And why did you get a hotel room?"

"Well, she has a … uhm …" she stammered as a deep blush covered her face and neck.

"Girlfriend?"

"Nope. She's normally on your team, but she likes to switch hit once in a while."

"Husband?" he asked, rather incredulously.

"Yep. I'm not terribly proud of that part, but she does this all the time so I figured I wasn't a home wrecker."

"Wow, why would someone your age get married and then cheat with women?"

"When did I say she was my age?"

"How old was she?"

"Let's just say she'd be a much more appropriate date for Da."

"Gee, Sis, your moral code is just going down the toilet. Congratulations!"

"Thanks, Conor, you really know how to brighten my day. Now go look at the room service menu, and I'll buy you dinner."

"Cool!" he said as he walked over to the table to look for the menu. "Hey, where'd you get all the money?"

"Oh, my date said she was going to leave me cab fare. She must have put it there."

He walked back into the bedroom flapping the wad of cash. "Where did you tell her you lived? Napa?"

"Shit!" she cried as she jumped off the bed and ran to grab the money. "I can't believe she left me …" she started counting the money, "$250!"

"Don't forget to declare this on your taxes," he teased as he grabbed it back and slapped her with the wad of bills. "I think there's a code on the tax forms for self-employed prostitute."

She sank down in the nearest chair and dropped her head into her hands. "Conor, I swear if you tell Da any of this …"

"Yeah, sure, that's just what I'm gonna do. 'Hey, Da, Ryan had sex with a fifty-year-old married woman at the Mark Hopkins, and she got a $250 dollar tip! Cool huh?' He'd beat me just for telling him!"

"I think I need to do a little soul searching," she admitted. "This is getting out of hand."

"Before you change your evil ways, let's call room service and spend your ill gotten money. Then, if the vice squad comes, we'll have eaten the evidence!"

After her workout, Jamie left the gym, noticing that Ryan's bike was still in its place. *Gee, I wonder where she went?* she thought wryly.

Several hours later, she drove by the gym again, on her way to a movie with Mia. She cast a quick glance and noticed the bike still sitting in the parking lot. *Hmm, that's strange. I hope she's okay.*

When they drove by on their return trip, the gym was closed but the Harley was still sitting there. Jamie really was worried about her friend, but she didn't want to call and disturb her if she was still with the woman. *I guess it's possible that they went to her house and just didn't want to go out again.*

The next morning after class, Ryan was her usual bubbly self. Jamie casually asked, "What did you do yesterday?"

"Uhm … I had a date."

"Anyone I know?"

"Don't think so," she said quickly.

"Someone from school?"

"Ahh, no."

"Did you do anything fun?"

"Yeah, yeah, we had fun."

"Think you'll see her again?"

Ryan looked at her for a moment, than asked, "What are you getting at?"

"Who, me? Getting at something? Oh, do you need a ride to pick up your bike from the gym? I saw it there at midnight last night."

Ryan nodded to herself, and said in more of a statement than a question, "And that bothered you."

Jamie looked flustered as she said, "No, it didn't bother me. But I was worried about you. It's not like you to leave your bike like that, and I was worried that something had happened to you."

Ryan asked the obvious question, "Why didn't you page me?"

"Good question. I'm not sure. But it's no big deal. You left your bike there all night. You had a date. You had a good time. Case closed."

"You saw me leave with Laura, didn't you?" she asked as she fixed her blue eyes firmly on Jamie.

She looked very guilty as she admitted, "Yeah, I kinda did. I saw you leave, then I saw her leave, and then I saw that your bike was still there."

"What bothers you?" she continued. "Her age?"

Jamie looked like she didn't want to answer, but she finally nodded. "Partly. She could be one of my mother's friends!"

"Yes, and your point is that women over forty shouldn't have fun?"

"No, that's not my point at all. It just bothered me, but I'm not sure why. Do you have to make a big deal out of it?" she asked crossly.

"Nope. I wasn't aware that I started this. But I can stop it. See you later." Ryan turned and quickly walked away.

"Shit! Shit! Shit!" She cried, as she watched Ryan stride down the curving path leading to the biology building.

That afternoon, Jamie showed up early for their training session. She had a healthy suspicion that Ryan would just blow her off, so she wanted to get there while she was still with her pervious client. But as soon as she finished, Ryan made a beeline over to Jamie. "I am so sorry for snapping at you today. You hit a raw nerve and I let you have it."

"It's okay," Jamie reassured her. "I shouldn't have been butting into your business."

"Jamie, I love it when you're involved in my life. Please butt in as much as you want." She put her arm around her and gave her a small squeeze.

"So … why were you upset? If you don't mind my butting in."

Ryan looked quite contemplative as she stuck her hands into the slash pockets of her warm up pants and rocked back on her heels for a moment. "It's hard to explain. I guess I just feel like I … I don't know. I'm disappointed in myself," she said softly. "This isn't who I expected to be." She had such an open, vulnerable look on her face that Jamie truly wanted to toss her arms around her friend and take all of her pain away.

Instead, she merely gripped her shoulder and assured her, "I think the person you are is absolutely fantastic. If you could see yourself through my eyes, you wouldn't have any doubts about the person that you've become."

Ryan's mouth curled up into a crooked grin, and she returned the pressure on Jamie's shoulder. "That was a nice thing to say. Thanks for the vote of confidence."

"I'd vote early and often for you."

Jamie drove through the thick fog early one Sunday morning in mid-November. Traffic was light, but the pace was slow due to the poor visibility. She was dressed in a pair of pressed khakis, a gold turtleneck and a dark green, cashmere, v-necked sweater. Ryan had told her to dress casually, but she had also brought along dressier clothes for later in the day.

She was a bit apprehensive about their plans for the day. *Not that people haven't already thought that Ryan was my lover,* she reflected. *Her own aunt thought so, for goodness sake*. This experience was going to be a bit different, however. They had discussed all of the options available to them for their "Gay for a Day" project. It made sense to both of them to do something of a spiritual nature, so they agreed on this morning's destination, The Metropolitan Community Church. Jamie was surprised to learn that this denomination had been in existence for over twenty-five years, having been founded to serve the needs of disenfranchised gay and lesbian Christians.

Ryan jogged down the stairs just seconds after Jamie pulled up in front of the house. She was dressed in a similar manner, wearing a light blue, turtleneck sweater with a fisherman's-knit, cable, crew-neck over the top. She eschewed khakis for her usual blue jeans, but this pair was a little less faded than usual.

"Jeans for church, Miss O'Flaherty?" Jamie asked with an arched eyebrow.

"It's gay church, Jamie. No dress code."

The church was close to the Noe Valley, but Ryan had never attended a service. It was rather small; Jamie guessed it would hold about three hundred people, but it was obviously lovingly cared for. It was less traditional than most churches she had been to, but very familiar, nonetheless. There was a large, raised sanctuary containing a pulpit and a large altar, with a beautiful stained glass window rising majestically from behind the sanctuary.

Three gregarious people were at the door to greet them. A tall, bearded man welcomed them and directed them to printed worship aids, and they each took one of the little booklets and settled themselves into a pew not far from the front of the church. The church was about half full, and most of the people seemed to know one another, with many hugs and kisses and handshakes being passed around. She guessed that the majority of people were gay, but she was fairly certain that she detected a few traditional family units as well.

After a few minutes, the organ began to ring out a hymn that Jamie recognized. A large procession began down the center aisle with the entire choir and various other acolytes and ministers following. Several people, both men and women, were dressed as ministers.

The choir gathered in the sanctuary as the ministers took their places behind the altar. Both women were surprised to find that the service echoed the traditional Eucharist that both were familiar with. The main difference was that the service was concelebrated among five different ministers. An impressive looking black woman seemed to be the main celebrant, but a short, pudgy, Asian man read the Gospel and two Caucasian men read various scripture passages. The music varied between traditional Protestant hymns, and very joyous African inspired melodies, with a Caribbean themed Hallelujah sung before the Gospel that had everyone swaying to the beat.

After the consecration, the minister urged everyone to come forward and receive the Eucharist. Jamie and Ryan rose with everyone else and stepped forward. Ryan followed her, but as they reached the front of the line the minister reached out and pulled Ryan forward until they stood shoulder to shoulder. After she handed each of them a host, she placed her arms around them and pulled their heads together, offering a prayer over them and solemnly blessing their relationship. She leaned over and kissed each of them on the cheek saying, "God loves you!"

As they returned to the pew, Jamie realized just how shaken she was by the experience. She cast a sidelong glance at Ryan who was kneeling down with her eyes closed. Not detecting anything out of the ordinary with her, she sat quietly and reflected; *Why did she assume we were a couple? Do we act like the other couples here?* She looked carefully at the people approaching the communion rail. It was fairly easy to pick out who was together, since some people just seemed to fit. For some it was obvious, as they held hands or touched gently. For others it was their similar styles of dress. For still others there was just a clear bond between them that was obvious even to a casual observer. It was the way they stood next to one another, or perhaps an unconscious look or a smile. Whatever it was, she wondered whether she and Ryan had it. *We're dressed very similarly. We look about the same age, about the same socio-economic strata. But still … there's something more.* Just then, Ryan leaned over and whispered, "That was sweet, wasn't it?"

She found herself smiling at Ryan in the same way she had seen the other couples do. *There's something about us that just fits. And I think it's obvious to others. Maybe that's what Cassie and Jack have picked up on.* She worried about this for the remainder of the service. As they filed out, the minister who had given them communion stopped them to shake their hands and offer a welcome. "Are you natives or from out of town?"

"We're locals," Ryan said. "But we've never attended services here before. It's a very impressive ceremony."

"I hope you enjoyed it, and that you'll come again. It's nice to have younger couples attend church. How long have you been together?"

Jamie was completely tongue-tied, but Ryan was clearly in charge so she answered for her. "Gosh, honey, how long have we known each other?" She counted off the months on her fingers. "It's been nearly four months," she said proudly, sparing a warm glance at her companion.

"Oh, newlyweds! That's very sweet. We perform a very nice service for members of the congregation who want their union blessed. You two should think about it."

Ryan grasped Jamie's hand, and said decisively, "We'll do that, won't we, sweetheart?"

Jamie mutely nodded her assent, as Ryan dragged her down the stairs and led her to the car. "Work with me here, Jamie," she said teasingly. "You're gay today, remember?"

"I … I … I'm sorry," she stammered. "That just caught me by surprise."

Ryan looked at her carefully as she hopped into the Boxster and started the engine. "Maybe we should have talked about this a little bit more. You look like that bothered you, and I don't want you to be uncomfortable." She paused and gave Jamie a small smile, "Especially just before going into enemy territory."

Jamie managed a smile in return. "No, it's nothing, really. I guess I just don't think I look gay, and it surprises me when people think we're a couple."

"Surprises you or bothers you?" Ryan asked as gently as possible.

"Maybe both," she admitted truthfully. "I just had so many preconceived notions about lesbians before I took this class. It makes me look more carefully at some of my stereotypes."

Ryan gave her a long, appraising look and asked, "Do you feel comfortable enough to go to our next destination?"

"Yeah, I do." After a bit she continued on with the earlier topic. "I think what bothers me the most is that it bothers me," she said looking at Ryan quizzically. "Do you know what I mean?"

"I think so. Do you mean that you don't like the fact that you react to having people assume you're gay?"

"Yeah. It really bothers me that it bothers me. How am I different from Cassie or Jack or my parents if it bothers me when people assume I'm with you? I give them these big lectures about how normal it all is. Do I really believe that?"

"Jamie, don't be so hard on yourself. You've gotten negative images about lesbians for a long time. You've been seeing a more balanced portrait for only four months." She smiled, and took her hand, "I've got to tell you, I'm very sensitive to negative vibes. And I've never gotten any from you. I feel perfectly at ease touching you and hugging you. I wouldn't feel that way if I thought that it made you uncomfortable."

"You know, Jack asked me about how we interact," she admitted. "I told him that you touched me more than my other friends, but that I felt very comfortable with it."

"Do I really touch you more than your straight friends?" she asked with a touch of surprise.

"Yeah, you do. I told him that I thought it was because you're so comfortable touching women in general, and you just treated me the same way."

"I don't always initiate it, do I?"

"No, I do it a lot of the time. I just feel more physically comfortable around you than I do my other friends." She paused for a moment, "What about you?"

"I think you're right. I'm very touch positive. I really believe you need a minimum daily requirement of hugs to sustain life. But because I'm so comfortable with women I guess I do just let that comfort flow to women that I'm not sexual with." After a bit she continued with a concerned glance, "You never feel I'm coming on to you, do you?"

"No, Ryan, I never have," she said firmly. *But sometimes … sometimes I wish you did …*

When they had discussed their options for the day, they agreed that they needed to go at least one place where they might encounter some disapproval. Jamie suggested that they go to a lovely little tearoom right in the heart of the Peninsula. "If there's a straighter place on earth, I'd hate to see it," she said at the time.

Now Ryan was concerned. She was afraid that Jamie might run into someone she knew, perhaps even her mother. But Jamie was firm in her resolve. They went downstairs to change, with Jamie taking the bathroom where she could hear Ryan rummaging through her closet, softly cursing. "Having trouble out there?" she asked.

"I've got one acceptable outfit to wear. And I don't wanna wear it," she grumbled.

Jamie emerged from the bathroom looking every bit the young Hillsborough debutante. She wore a short, dark tan skirt, in a fine, washable silk. Atop the skirt, she wore a long silk jacket in a tan, black and cream paisley. The jacket was made to be worn without a blouse, as the stand up collar buttoned all the way up to her throat. Large gold knots graced her ears, and a heavy gold chain hung from her neck, resting just under her collarbone.

Jamie gasped slightly at she took her friend in. She might not like her outfit, but it liked her very, very much. A pastel pink cashmere sweater-set covered a simple, short, black shirt. A black velvet headband held her bangs back, and a simple pair of pearl earrings nestled against her earlobes. She wore plain stockings and simple, black, low-heeled pumps that didn't look like they'd seen the light of day very often. The short skirt and heels managed to make her legs look tantalizingly long, and her smoothly curved calves were very attractively displayed.

"Why on earth don't you like this outfit?" Jamie marveled. "You look beautiful."

"I hate, loath and despise skirts. Next to skirts, I hate heels." She held up her foot to display the offending footwear. "They both change the way you walk, and the way you sit. I'm sure they're both an evil plot to subjugate women and render us unable to protect ourselves." After a pause, she continued with a smile, "But thank you for the compliment."

She walked around Jamie slowly, examining her wardrobe. "This kind of thing looks like it was made for you," she said, as she pulled the jacket up to look for a label. "But knowing your family, it might have been."

"No, I bought this off the rack with the rest of you mortals," she replied haughtily. "But I did buy it in Milan, if that makes you feel better."

"My Aunt Maeve gave me this outfit five years ago for Christmas. This is only the second time I've worn it," Ryan said proudly.

As they walked back upstairs, they met Conor coming down from his room. "Wow!" he said. "Where are you two going?"

"We're going to the Peninsula for tea," Ryan replied with an elegant accent.

"I don't know how you did it, Jamie, but keep up the good work." He eyed his sisters' legs. "I forgot she was a girl," he said as he tried unsuccessfully to tickle his obviously feminine sibling.

As they drove along in the lifting fog, Ryan did her best to prepare Jamie for the encounter. "The only way you'll get a taste of what being gay is like is if we really act like girlfriends, but I want to be sure that isn't going to bother you."

"What do you plan on doing?" Jamie asked, somewhat nervously.

"Nothing graphic," she laughed and slapped her arm.

"I was afraid you were going to act like you did that night I saw you at the bookstore."

"That would get us arrested in the Peninsula," she said, somewhat seriously. "No, I just plan on acting like I would with anyone I was seriously dating. I just want to be sure you won't be uncomfortable if I touch you or hold your hand."

"I guess that depends on where you touch me," she said with a mock leer. "No, I'm certain I'll be fine. I really do want to see the reactions you get when straight people realize you're gay."

The shop was located on a main business street, and they were forced to park several blocks away. Jamie was amazed at the physical transformation of her friend. Ryan acted completely comfortable and natural in her outfit. Her gait was shorter and her hips moved noticeably more, as Jamie was all too happy to observe as she walked slightly behind her. Her posture was significantly less aggressive, and she gave off an almost demure aura. She looked physically smaller and more feminine, and Jamie was unable to stop herself from staring. Ryan noticed her stare and teased, "I like to keep 'em guessing. I think I do a pretty good straight girl imitation, don't I?"

"It's … it's amazing," Jamie stuttered. "How do you do that?"

"I just try to look less imposing. I try to look less like a jock, too," she added with a grin. "Wearing a skirt and heels helps because they really don't let you take a normal gait."

"But your demeanor is so different."

"Having three brothers helps. I know what they like in a woman, so I try to be like that."

"Truly remarkable," Jamie remarked. "I don't think I've ever noticed before, but you really are different from my straight friends."

"Aren't you observant?" Ryan smirked. "What was your first clue?"

Jamie gave her a pretty good elbow right in the ribs. "Not that difference, silly. It just dawned on me what's different about you. You don't look like you're trying to please or appeal to men. You just look like yourself."

"Exactly! It's not that I don't like men, I just don't go out of my way to appeal to them."

"Right. You relate to men as an equal. I noticed that when you met Jack. When I see someone like Cassie around him she's always batting her eyes at him or acting kind of helpless. To be honest, I do that too," she admitted. "I always let him do things for me that I could easily do for myself—mainly because he seems to enjoy showing that he's stronger than I am."

Ryan mused thoughtfully, "I think a lot of that's very unconscious, almost like it's hard wired into people. I don't consciously try to intimidate men, but I do a really good job at it. Guys notice me, but their interest only lasts for a few seconds. Once they interact with me they almost invariably back off. Funny, huh?"

"Yeah, you just give off a vibe that says, 'Not interested.' But when I see you flirting with a woman the energy coming off you is almost visible."

"Really?" she asked as she blushed a little. "I don't think I realized that."

"Oh, yeah," Jamie drawled. "Every ounce of your considerable charisma comes right to the surface. It's fascinating to watch."

"I've got to be more discrete," she moaned as Jamie laughed at her discomfort.

They walked into the tiny shop a few minutes later. The room was rather stuffy and proper, just as Ryan expected. They were greeted at the door by an elegantly dressed woman who graciously showed them to a center table. After they were handed menus, Ryan asked Jamie if she had noticed the admiring glances from the other diners when they had entered. Jamie admitted that she had not "Pay closer attention," Ryan instructed. "People are definitely looking at us."

Jamie casually glanced around the room and noticed that people were still looking at them with approval. She looked back at Ryan and said, "Yeah, people have noticed us, but I get that a lot. Don't you?"

"Why do you think people do that?" Ryan asked, ignoring the question.

"I guess because we're attractive and we're dressed well. We look like we fit in, I suppose."

"Precisely. Now continue to pay attention to the other diners." Jamie watched in fascination as the real Ryan returned. She slid her hand across the table and gently grasped Jamie's. Her eyes softened and she stared deeply into Jamie's eyes. After a moment, she tenderly lifted Jamie's hand and kissed her palm, closing her eyes in pleasure, and then softly placed Jamie's hand on her cheek, cradling it there for a moment. As she released her, she whispered, "Still paying attention?"

"Huh?" she asked vacantly. But she mentally slapped herself back into consciousness, and looked around the room again. The formerly friendly faces had uniformly grown dark and disapproving. People were discreetly pointing them out to others who hadn't noticed. Jamie nodded her head to show that she was still doing her job.

"Want to make it worse?" Ryan asked with one raised eyebrow. A small nod caused Ryan to pick up her chair and move very close. She took a roll from the basket, broke it apart and put butter on it, then held up the morsel in front of Jamie and raised an eyebrow seductively. Not getting an immediate response, she cocked her head a little and raised the eyebrow again. Jamie mutely nodded as her mouth fell open. Ryan placed the bread in her mouth, tipping it in with her index finger. Giving Jamie an extremely sexy smile, she grasped her hand again.

After a few moments of trying to make her mouth work again, Jamie looked around. Now no one was looking at them. Every other diner had obviously decided to make them invisible. They continued to chat and observe the other patrons, but as the time passed Jamie began to grow impatient. They had been at the restaurant for a good fifteen minutes, but no one had come to take their order. After another few minutes passed Jamie signaled to the hostess, but she blithely ignored her. The young woman wasn't used to being ignored, and she found that she didn't handle the brush-off well. Getting up from her chair, she stormed over to the woman, ready for a fight. "Why haven't we been served?" she demanded rather loudly.

"We're very busy today," was the arch reply.

"Every table that entered after we did has been served. I'm asking you again, why haven't we been served?"

"Why can't you people stay in the city?" she asked with an aggrieved sigh, as she brushed past Jamie and into the kitchen.

Jamie stood in shocked silence for several minutes. Every other diner in the restaurant was looking at her, either blatantly or surreptitiously. She finally walked back over to Ryan with a very angry look on her face. "For two cents I'd throw you right down on this table and ravish you in front of these idiots!"

As Ryan trotted out the door after her she said somberly, "That's why I hate to wear skirts."

Jamie turned to look at her with a puzzled look on her face. "What?"

"No pockets for change. I don't have two cents."

Jamie backhanded her right in her firm belly. "Wiseass," she muttered, as they walked to the car, laughing.

Ryan patiently listened as Jamie vented her anger all the way back to the Noe Valley. She was just about out of steam as they neared the house. "Ryan, why aren't you angry?" she finally asked out of frustration.

Ryan considered the question for a long while. Finally she replied, "Anger's not productive for me. I figure that if people are put off by me it's only because they aren't used to seeing lesbians be authentic with each other." With a little shrug she added, "I try not to take it too personally."

"But how can you not?" Jamie insisted.

"Hey, my feelings get hurt just like everyone else's. I wish that people could get over making gayness such a big deal. But that's not going to happen very soon, and I can't afford to waste my energies caring about what strangers think of me."

"Does it ever bother you?"

"Of course it does. Every once in a while if I'm feeling vulnerable, or I have PMS, I'm tempted to really lash out when it happens. You saw how it bothered me when Cassie was giving me a hard time. It also bothers me when Jack or your parents do it, but I still try not to get angry. Anger doesn't work well for me."

Jamie looked at her friend thoughtfully, "You know, you're incredibly well adjusted."

Ryan grinned. "A lot of people wouldn't agree with that, but thank you anyway."

As Jamie pulled up in front of the house, Ryan asked, "Did you bring gay clothes?"

"I wasn't sure what to wear to a lesbian sex emporium." Adopting a very affected style she said, "My charm class didn't cover that occasion."

"Did you bring some jeans?"

"Yeah, some old 501's."

"I can take care of the rest."

After watching a few minutes of the 49ers game with Martin and Conor, they went downstairs and Ryan said, "Okay, let's see what you have."

Jamie pulled out a very old pair of 501's, and a pair of black, high-top, Converse basketball shoes. "Is this a good start?" she asked hopefully.

Ryan's eyes narrowed suspiciously. "What size are these jeans?" She searched for the inside tag. "Jamie, this is a twenty-four inch waist. How old are these?"

"Uhm, freshman year, I think."

Seeing through the attempt at deceiving her, Ryan asked, "Freshman year of what?"

"High school?"

"It's been obvious that you haven't been able to gain any weight, but it's starting to look like you're still losing. You are, aren't you?"

"Yeah, a little, I guess," Jamie admitted. "I know what I should be eating, but I just can't do it when I'm tense. I'm kinda surprised you haven't been giving me a hard time about it. I was afraid you were going to really be on me."

"I reconsidered my threat to watch you like a hawk. The last thing I want to do is increase your anxiety. I want to be supportive of you, but I don't want to be another person who tries to control you. You've got enough of that already."

Jamie gave her a delighted smile as she slid her arms around her for a hug. "Thanks. I appreciate your concern, but I really am glad that you haven't tried to supervise me."

"I'm confident that you know what you should be eating. I assume the nutritionist can do her job, and the rest is up to you. If you need any help, I hope you'll ask, but other than that I just want to support you. Is your energy level okay?"

"Yeah, it's pretty good. I know I've got to eat more, but given that, I feel good."

"Okay, you're the boss. If you feel good we can keep your workouts pretty intense even with your weight dropping. But I want you to promise me that you'll tell me if you start to feel tired or fatigued."

"It's a deal, Coach."

After several attempts, Ryan was finally satisfied with her choices for Jamie's lesbian look. She wore the smallest T-shirt that Ryan owned, a yellow, cotton, baby-tee that was supposed to fit snugly. On Ryan it stopped about four inches above her waistband, but it fell just below the waistband of Jamie's jeans. Over the tee she wore a light blue bowling shirt that proclaimed "Holten's Mortuary" across the back in black script. Her own jeans and high tops completed the outfit, and Ryan was quite satisfied that she could pass for a lesbian anywhere in town.

Ryan, of course, never had a problem looking gay. She wore one of Jamie's favorite outfits. A snug, black, French-cut T-shirt, tucked into amazingly well fitted faded jeans, a black belt, big, heavy black boots, and her favorite hat, the backwards black driving cap.

They walked back upstairs so Jamie could watch a bit of the game while Ryan made lunch. Conor jumped up from his prone position on the bed, his face wide open in shock. "Ryan, what have you done to her? I thought she was rubbing off on you, and now this?" He waved his hand towards Jamie's outfit while he glared at his sister.

"Relax, Conor. It's just an experiment for our class."

"You'd better bring her back to her normal gorgeous self. This is too precious a commodity to hide under bowling shirts," he said distastefully.

Ryan decided that she wanted another breakfast for lunch, and Jamie readily agreed. Martin and Conor had already eaten, so it was just the two of them at the kitchen counter. Ryan had made fabulous banana pancakes, along with Irish bacon, and big glasses of orange juice. "This is beyond delicious, Ryan. You're quite the little cook."

"I'd say that breakfast is my favorite meal to cook. You get quick feedback, too. I don't really have the patience to cook dinner. Everything takes so long."

While they munched away, Ryan asked her again if she was comfortable with their next stop. "We could just go and look around like normal," she offered. "You don't have to make people believe we're together."

"No, we set it up this way for a reason. I want to get a flavor for all of the different facets of life as a lesbian. We had a little spirituality, we had a little homophobia and now we get a little sex." She waggled an eyebrow seductively.

"Have you ever been to a place like this for straight people?"

"No. I've never had much of an interest. It all seems so lurid," she said as she made a face. "I just don't get most porn. It's all so objectifying of women. I fail to understand how you can say you love women when you make different parts of them a fetish."

"So why do you want to go to the lesbian sex shop if you're turned off by them?"

"I didn't know there was an erotic-themed store made for women. I guess I want to see if women are interested in the same things men are. Have you been there before?"

"Uhm … yeah."

They arrived at the little store just after three o'clock, being able to walk there from Ryan's home. Jamie was duly impressed with the set up, noticing that it looked just like a regular bookstore. Shelves were arranged along the outside walls. Books, videos and paraphernalia were neatly displayed in an open manner. There was nothing clandestine or lurid about the place. There were big windows that were whitewashed to keep out casual observers, and the windows combined with the open shelving to make the store look clean and spacious and inviting. "Hi, Ryan," said a young woman shelving books. Ryan greeted her in a friendly manner as they continued to look around the store.

"Oh, hi, Ryan," said the woman at the counter as they passed.

Jamie leaned in close and whispered, "Did you say you've been here or that you lived here?"

Ryan blushed all the way up to her hat. "Maybe I just have a memorable name?" she weakly replied.

A prominently displayed video caught Jamie's eye. The title was Bend Over Boyfriend, and it was advertised as an instructional video for straight women who want to penetrate their male partners with sex toys. Jamie stood in front of the display with her mouth hanging open, and Ryan couldn't help but lean over and ask, "Getting ideas?"

She turned her head and made eye contact with her but couldn't reply. She shook her head numbly as Ryan led her away. "I ... I ... I'd never have guessed that women wanted to do that!" she gasped out. After a second she started to chuckle just a little bit under her breath, and soon she was laughing out loud at her private joke.

"What's so funny?" Ryan finally asked.

"Even though I didn't know that people actually did that, I had a very pleasant fantasy the other night about impaling Jack on something. I just didn't know that it was an approved form of sexual expression!"

"Hey, sexual expression is pretty fluid. People seem less role oriented now."

"Jack would have me committed if I brought that home!"

"Hi, Ryan. How have you been?" cooed a customer as she eyed Ryan with unconcealed interest.

"She's been busy!" said Jamie curtly as she grabbed Ryan's hand and dragged her away.

Ryan nearly doubled over with laughter. "What was that about?" she finally choked out.

"I'm supposed to be with you. She was hitting on you right in front of me. I can't tolerate someone dissin' me like that."

"You're a piece of work, Jamie. A real piece of work. So you want to play for real, huh?" she asked with a glimmer of danger in her blue eyes.

"Yeah," Jamie said with more confidence than she felt.

"Come with me," Ryan purred, as she took her hand. They walked over to the counter where yet another woman greeted Ryan by name. "Hi, J.C.," Ryan said with a friendly smile. "Got anything new in the try-on rooms?"

"Yeah, we got some things in this week. But remember, Ryan, you break it—you buy it," she said seriously. "And don't forget to put a condom on!" she said rather loudly as Jamie felt herself being led to a small dressing room in the back of the store.

Her eyes were wide with alarm as Ryan opened the door to the small room. Before she closed the door she turned a sign that read 'occupied' around to face outward. On a table lay the most unique and mysterious sex toys that Jamie had ever seen.

Actually, Jamie had never seen a sex toy, but there was little doubt that was what they were. "Yipes!" was all she could get out as she tried to avert her eyes.

Ryan laughed gently at her discomfort, then she sat down in one of the two chairs in the small room. "Do you want to continue the game, or are you uncomfortable?"

"W … w … what do I have to do?" she asked with wide eyes.

"Nothing, nothing at all," Ryan reassured her. "I was just going to show you some of the toys if you want me to."

"Uhm … okay," she replied gamely. "What did that woman at the counter mean?"

Ryan blushed again as she answered, "I brought someone here last year, and she got a little enthusiastic and broke one of these." She laughed as she held up what Jamie guessed was a vibrator. "I thought she should pay for it, since she broke it, but she didn't have any money, so I got stuck paying $40 for a vibrator I didn't use. It seemed quite unfair to me."

"What was that about a condom? That confused the heck out of me."

"They're very careful about safer sex here. They clean everything with bleach between customers, but they still want you to put a condom on before you insert anything." Now Jamie blushed as Ryan continued. "The same woman who broke the vibrator wanted to play with one of these." She held up a lavender, latex object shaped like a dolphin, "and she refused to put a condom on. So when we left I ratted her out," she said proudly. "So now they think they have to remind me to use a condom, when it was me who told on her." She shook her head, "I don't get it. I'm entirely innocent."

"Of all the adjectives in the world, innocent would be the last one I'd use for you," Jamie said as she patted Ryan's pink cheek. "Do you bring dates here a lot?"

"Well, you've gotta remember that I live at home …" she trailed off.

"And sometimes the cars are too small, right?" Jamie offered helpfully.

"Yeeeah, that's about it."

Jamie was fascinated by the assortment of devices that the room held. There was one vibrator that interested her in particular. It was a rather normal looking red plastic from the cord until about four inches up. But a clear, flexible rubber piece above that was filled with multicolor beads. When the vibrator was turned on, that rubber piece began to twist, extend and retract in a rhythmic fashion. It looked much more like a child's toy than a sex object.

There was an assortment of dildos in pretty pastel colors. Some were shaped like women, some like animals, and some were just plain cylinders. Jamie noted that none were made to resemble an actual penis.

A large bowl of various styles of condoms was centered on the table, along with a box of baby wipes. Three or four bottles of lubricant were also available for use. Jamie shuddered a bit to think of Ryan using these toys, especially with another woman, right here in public. She was very curious to find out if Ryan used things like this on a regular basis, but she realized that was too invasive a question, so she refrained.

"Do you think most lesbians use things like this?" she heard herself asking just a moment later as her curiosity got the best of her.

"I can't speak for most lesbians," Ryan replied with a smirk.

"What about the thousands of women you can speak for?" she asked sweetly.

Ryan reached out and tweaked her friend's nose. "I think most women like to play around with toys once in a while. It spices things up a bit. But I don't think that most women need things like this to be satisfied." She reflected for a moment, "My philosophy is that sex should be fun. If playing with toys makes it more fun for both of you, why not?"

"That's a philosophy that I'd like to be able to copy. Maybe someday," she said wistfully.

"You know, you could introduce some of these toys into your relationship. Some guys are really thankful to have a woman be able to assure her own satisfaction." She picked up a vibrator that looked like a stretched-out snail and turned it on. The little antennae on the top of its head vibrated against her other hand as she illustrated how it worked.

Jamie extended her hand and Ryan ran the whirring head all over her hand. "I can't imagine the discussion we'd have if I brought something like this home," she said as she shook her head. "But I bet it'd work," she said with an impish grin.

"Oh, they work all right," Ryan assured her. "I can go from zero to sixty in less than a minute with one of these babies." She had such a frankly sexual look on her face that Jamie was certain her legs were going to give out. Images of Ryan pleasuring herself flooded her mind, and she closed her eyes briefly, trying to dispel them.

"Are you about ready to leave?" Ryan's deep voice broke her reverie.

"Yeah, I guess we made a statement of some sort by the amount of time we spent in here," she said, laughing nervously.

As Ryan opened the door she wrapped her strong arm around Jamie's waist and whispered into her ear, "Look satisfied." Jamie was very glad that arm was where it was as her knees turned to rubber at the thought.

The next stop was back to the O'Flaherty house for their last change. They both got into workout clothes and covered their outfits with sweats. Jamie loaded all of her previously worn clothes into her garment bag, and they took off for the gym.

They had decided to work out together since the day didn't allow for their normal bike ride. Jamie realized that in the nearly two months that she had worked with Ryan, she had never actually seen her lift weights. They arrived at the gym around five o'clock. There was almost no one else in attendance on this cool fall day. The 49ers were locked in a big game for the lead in their conference, and the game was obviously keeping people at home or at a sports bar.

Jamie was wearing a pair of navy blue leggings with a matching sports bra, covered by a lemon yellow, oversized tank-top. Ryan had on a bright red Lycra unitard. The garment was sleeveless, and the legs stopped just at the largest point of Ryan's muscular thighs. *I am so glad that she doesn't work out with me on a regular basis,* Jamie thought with a shudder. *It's just not fair for any one woman to look that good.*

They moved out into the gym and each spent a few minutes on the stair climber to loosen up and raise their heart rates. After ten minutes, Ryan hopped off and went to the first machine. They had agreed that Jamie would do a very light intensity workout of all six of the major muscle groups, partly because Ryan was afraid of overstressing her already taxed system.

Ryan had been varying her routine just to keep things interesting. She had done a lot of rollerblading and a good bit of running to keep fresh. She hadn't worked out in the gym for over a week, but now it was time to get serious, so she decided she needed a fairly high intensity session.

Jamie sat down on the seat of the chest press machine as Ryan adjusted the weight. She went through her reps in the usual manner, but Ryan advised against doing two sets.

After she rose, Ryan adjusted the seat and the weights for herself. Jamie noticed with a bit of envy that her friend lifted over three times the amount of weight that she could handle. Ryan had been relaxed and chatty as she usually was when Jamie worked out, but the minute she sat down on that seat her entire demeanor changed. Jamie watched in fascination as the dramatic change came over her friend.

Ryan was a study of total focus. She didn't look at herself, nor did she glance in the mirror. She kept her eyes unfocused, staring out into space. Her face was unlined, but there was a level of concentration that Jamie had rarely seen before. She began to move the weight with a smooth cadence, with each rep exactly matching the one before. The plates barely touched down lightly before they were pulled into motion again. Ryan didn't appear to strain, nor did she make any sound. It was truly as though Ryan had become the machine—honestly not looking like she was lifting anything. She was just moving gracefully, and the huge stack of weight moved right along with her.

After her first set, she paused for less than a minute. She was still in a deep state of concentration, but it was clear that her breathing was slightly elevated as she began the next set. By the time she had finished her third set Jamie could see the perspiration begin to pop out at her hairline. Amazingly, she increased the weight ten pounds and sat back down for another set. She was obviously having trouble with this one, but she kept at it. Jamie could see that she struggled to make the reps perfect, and she smiled when she saw Ryan's right foot begin to tap rather impatiently on the floor as she pushed. The exertion was making her veins bulge, and Jamie couldn't help but notice that Ryan's nipples popped out as she strained with the heavy weight. When she was finished, she sat still for a moment, then got up. "Ooh, that felt good," she purred.

It was all Jamie could do not to swoon as she followed Ryan around from machine to machine. Her friend followed the same routine for each exercise, but Jamie found each to be a thing of beauty. Ryan was a study of power, grace and fluidity. She reverted to her normal demeanor when Jamie was lifting, then effortlessly shifted back into the intense concentration that she obviously needed to work.

When Ryan had adjusted the leg press machine, Jamie watched in rapt amazement at the amount of weight that she could push. Every muscle in those tanned legs stood out in stark relief, and Jamie could see the strands of muscle jump and flex from the strain. The massive weight moved smoothly through all three sets, and by the end of the third set Jamie had to fight to make herself stop staring before Ryan looked up. She was only partially successful, but just received a grin in response. "Would you like to have quads like these when you grow up, little girl?" she said with a flourish as she slapped her pumped thighs.

Jamie could only nod her head as she struggled to shut her gaping mouth. The rest of the workout went smoothly and they were finished in a little over an hour. Jamie was sweating freely when they finished, but Ryan had been dripping onto the floor for some time now. "Do you always sweat so much?" Jamie asked in amazement.

"Yeah, I do," she said. "Your output of perspiration follows your fitness level. I worry when I don't sweat," she said as she chugged a liter of water.

"How much water do you drink in a day?"

"A lot," she replied. "And even more if I'm doing something strenuous."

"Uhm, this wasn't strenuous?" she regarded Ryan's dripping clothing.

"I mean aerobically strenuous, like running or riding my bike on hills. You won't believe how much I'll drink on the ride," she said. "You haven't lived until you've tried to find your tent in a dark campground in the middle of the night when you've got to get up to pee three times."

"You know, I've never even asked you what the accommodations were for the ride. We sleep in big tents?"

"Nope. Little tents. Little two person tents."

"We each get one?"

"Nope. Two per tent. There's barely room to change your mind," she laughed. "I thought we'd bunk together, if that's okay with you."

After a short internal struggle to move her mouth, Jamie croaked out, "Sure. Fine," as she was assaulted with images of sharing a tiny little space with her friend for a whole week.

After they had returned to the locker room, Ryan began to shuck every stitch of her wet clothing. Jamie turned her back as she put her sweats back on over her own damp gear. Ryan was grumbling as she looked through her gym bag. "You don't have any extra clothes do you?" she inquired.

"No, why do you ask?"

"I guess I'm going commando," she grumbled as she dried off and put her sweats back on.

"What's commando?" Jamie inquired as she turned around to face her friend.

"That's what the boys call it when they don't wear underwear. I forgot to bring any, and I can't go out in this weather with wet clothes on."

Why does she have to tell me everything? Jamie moaned as she followed behind Ryan, eyes cast downward in an attempt to avoid an independent investigation.

As she dropped Ryan off, Jamie declined her offer of a warm shower. "I think I'm gonna go down to Palo Alto and try to make nice with Jack," she said. "I think he'd appreciate it if I went down to make him dinner."

Ryan nodded and gave her a kiss on the cheek. "I had a fantastic day. Thanks for making it so much fun."

"I'm the one who should be thanking you, Ryan. It was really cool to be let into the inner sanctum," she said with a laugh.

"Well, you didn't really see the inner sanctum. You have to take the oath before we let you in there. More importantly, you have to learn the secret handshake," she said with a definite leer.

As Jamie headed back to the expressway, thoughts about the day drifted across her mind. Images of the workout continued to flood her, and by the time she reached Jack's, her entire body was flushed with excitement and desire. She buzzed his apartment on her way up the stairs, taking them two at a time. He opened the door in surprise, as she pushed him back in to the apartment.

"I don't want to talk, I just want to do this!" she growled as she grasped his head and kissed him thoroughly. He didn't utter a word as she began to strip off her still sweaty clothes. When she was naked, she performed the same service for him. He was instantly aroused, and as she pushed him back against the couch he finally muttered, "I missed you today, Jamie."

She cut off all attempts at further conversation as she straddled his seated form and locked his lips with hers, never letting go until they were both collapsed in a post coital haze.

I guess I just need a gym in our house when we get married, she mused as they stumbled to the bedroom for another round.

She awoke at around ten. Jack was lying behind her with his arms wrapped tightly around her naked body. His head was snuggled against her back, and she felt content for the first time in a long while. *We get along fine when we don't talk,* she thought disgustedly as she extricated herself from his arms. *I wonder how many years we can stay married if the only way we communicate is with moans and grunts?* She stumbled into her sweats to make the long drive home.

Chapter Ten

Ryan and Jamie sat outside in the warm, fall sun, chatting about their psych class and their plans for the upcoming Thanksgiving break.

"You don't want to drive to Berkeley on Friday for our session, do you?" Ryan asked.

"Yeah, I do want to," Jamie said. "But I'd better stay close to home. Since we only get Thursday and Friday, I hate to commit to spend the whole afternoon up here."

"You don't sound like you're looking forward to it," Ryan said. "Don't you like turkey?"

"Sure, I like turkey," Jamie said, knowing her friend was teasing her, "but I'm not looking forward to a four day weekend with either my parents, or Jack. Lately we all get along best when we don't see each other."

Ryan nodded, knowing that there wasn't much she could say to cheer Jamie up.

"Are you busy on Friday?"

"Not really," Ryan said. "I have my morning free. Why?"

"I thought you might like to come down for a ride. I'm sure I could steal away for a couple of hours without committing a capital offense."

"It's a deal," Ryan said. "Riding down to The Peninsula is a great way for me to get a long, tough ride in. Call me on Thursday and tell me what time you want to meet."

"I hate to be so pessimistic," Jamie said, "but I think my Thanksgiving is gonna be on Sunday—when I can come back to school!"

On Thanksgiving morning, Jamie and her father sat in the sunny library, enjoying a cup of coffee. "I've been worried about you, honey. How are things between you and Jack?"

"They're okay. We've made some progress on some points." She smiled at her father and said, "Thanks for asking."

"I got the impression that things had been difficult for a while. Do you want to talk about it?"

"No, not really. I think we're just going through a phase. He doesn't like some of the changes I've been making, but I think he'll get used to my being more independent."

"I must admit that I was concerned when Jack mentioned that your new friend is a lesbian," he said thoughtfully. Jamie felt her hackles start to rise, and she looked out the window, hoping he'd drop the matter. When she didn't respond, he persisted, "Well?"

"Well, what?" she asked.

"Why are you spending your time with her? Choosing a friend like that hardly seems appropriate for a young woman like you."

"What do you mean by 'a young woman like me'? Ryan is a perfectly lovely young woman, too."

"But you're a young woman who's engaged to be married. Do you think it's wise to spend your time cultivating friendships that can't carry over into your married life? You two need to build some relationships with other couples."

"Ryan is my friend. I enjoy her company, Daddy. The fact that she's a lesbian doesn't factor into our relationship. And, yes, I think it would be nice to have some friends who were a couple, but since we never leave Jack's apartment, that's hard to do."

"Well, Jack certainly didn't seem to think that Ryan's sexual preferences were immaterial, and it sounds like Cassie doesn't either." He paused for a moment as he regarded her carefully. "Is your new friend more important than Jack's feelings?"

"Yes," she said, staring him right in the eyes. "If his feelings are based on bigoted, stereotypical notions of what a lesbian is, I have no interest in his feelings." She looked at him for a moment, wondering why he was so invested in this issue. "It upsets me that you're siding with Jack on this. I really thought you were more open-minded."

"I am profoundly open-minded, Jamie. And I don't like being referred to as otherwise," he said with a good deal of pique.

"Then why do you assume that Jack and Cassie's opinions are more valid than mine?" she asked. "I'm the one who knows Ryan. They've spent less than ten minutes with her."

"I'm not implying that their opinions are more valid. I am saying that I don't feel it's appropriate for you to spend an inordinate amount of time with someone like that. You've known Jack for three years and Cassie for almost your entire life. They know you very well, much better than some girl you just met. Why would they feel the way they do if there wasn't something about this woman that was troubling?"

"Because they've let their prejudice take over. Jack admitted that he's jealous of her because he assumes she'll try to get me into bed!"

"And why do you assume she won't?" he asked, his expression one of intense frustration.

"Well, it's nice to know you're not narrow-minded." She deposited her coffee cup on the table, and stormed out.

Dinner was a very tense affair. Not even Reverend Evans could add much spark to the occasion. He realized that something was seriously wrong between his son and his granddaughter, but he didn't have the opportunity to speak with Jamie alone to determine what it was.

Before Jamie left, he embraced her and said into her ear, "Call me tomorrow." She pulled back after kissing his cheek and quietly agreed.

On the drive to the Townsend's, Jack finally asked the obvious question. "What's going on between you and your father? You two were shooting daggers at each other all day."

She gave him a thoughtful look as she debated how much to tell him. Finally deciding that it was better to know, she asked, "Did you talk to him about our problems?"

He shot her a perturbed glance. "No, I haven't. Frankly, I'd be embarrassed to admit to him how little you respect my opinion."

"Pull the car over, Jack," she said in a tone that didn't allow for discussion. He pulled over onto a lovely, tree-lined street on the outskirts of Hillsborough, killed the engine and rolled down his window to let some of the crisp fall air into the tension-filled car. He turned towards her, and faced his fiancée with a look of quiet resignation on his face. "Yes?" he asked, in a weary tone.

"It's obvious that both you and Daddy are unhappy with the changes that I've been making. But even though I love both of you very much, neither of you are going to control me." She took a deep breath and continued. "We can have a good life together, Jack, but it has to be a life where both of us get to be who we really are."

He sat in silence for a few minutes, his shoulders still slumped. Finally, he took a deep breath and slowly let it out. "Look. I know you're used to getting everything you want. I know you've been spoiled with material things and by always having things done your way." He ignored her look of outrage, and blithely continued. "But that's part of you, and I'm willing to accept that most of the time. You ve just got to learn that there are some things that you're going to have to give in on. It can't be me who has to give in all of the time."

She was silent for a long time, her head dropped back against the vinyl seat. Her voice was shaking with both anger and sorrow. "Is that how you think of me? As a spoiled little rich girl who gets everything she demands?"

"Well, yes," he said. "I feel like I'm supposed to make the sacrifices in our relationship, and I've got to admit that I'm getting tired of it."

Her anger had been bubbling up throughout his explanation, and when he finished she felt the words begin to fly from her mouth. "What sacrifices have you made, Jack? I'm dying to hear them," she said bitterly. "Tell me about how you have to leave your house in rush hour traffic every Friday night. Tell me how you no sooner arrive than you have to start dinner, alone, while I sit in the living room and read. Tell me how you feel when I barely comment on what you've made. Tell me how you do the dishes alone while I continue to read. Tell me about how you sit in the living room and watch me study every Friday, Saturday and Sunday. Tell me about how you feel when the only time I pay attention to you is when we have sex. Tell me how you lie in bed and get so damned frus…" She yanked herself back from the abyss just before she told him exactly how unhappy she was with their sex life. The tension in the car was so thick that it was nearly visible, but she was afraid to look at him. Long minutes passed before he finally spoke.

"I didn't realize you were so miserable," he got out, as tears started to escape down his face.

"I'm not miserable!" she said fervently. "I'm not!" She lifted her hand to his face and softly stroked his cheek. "I'm not," she whispered as she began to cry, too. "Are you miserable, Jack?" she asked softly.

"No," he said through his tears. "But I was so much happier before. You seemed happy, too. Now you just seem tense around me. I know you're not happy and it's driving me crazy!" he choked out as he began to sob. She continued to stroke his cheek and run her fingers through his hair for a long time. As he got control of his voice, he added, "I know you don't like what we do in bed, but I don't know how to please you. I swear I've never had this problem with any other woman. I just don't know what to do." He leaned forward and bumped his head against the steering wheel. His shoulders were shaking, and Jamie felt like her heart would break, seeing him in so much pain.

She scooted over as far as she could and ran her hand up and down his back. "It's okay, Jack. I swear I'm not unhappy with you. It's just that I'm changing and growing up. I love to come down here on the weekends, and I love to cook for you. But when you give me such a hard time about what I do when we're not together it drives me insane! I think that's why it's been hard for me in bed," she said. "I need to feel totally connected with you to be able to enjoy sex. When we have this ongoing tension I can't relax. But that's all it is, honey, I'm sure of it."

He turned his head and looked at her with an expression that was equal parts fear and trust. The sadness in his sweet blue eyes felt like a weight resting on her chest. "Can we get out for a moment?" she asked.

He looked unsure, but he complied, coming around to stand on the sidewalk next to the car. She got out and stood right next to him and put her arms around his waist. He slid his arms around her back and held her close for a long time. Bending his head, he filled his lungs with the scent of her hair, and felt some of the tension ebb. Jamie felt the same way, and she looked up into his eyes and said, "I feel so good when you hold me. It feels so right to be close to you."

He squeezed her tightly, feeling the emotion well up in his chest again. "I'll try harder, Jamie. I swear I will."

The evening spent with the Townsends was more jovial than the tension-filled afternoon at the Evanses. Jack came from a large extended family, and a raft of aunts, uncles, cousins and their children were in attendance. Jamie spent some time playing with the assorted children, and that lifted her spirits substantially. She took a little break to go into the kitchen and offer to help. Every adult woman was in the kitchen chatting about their kids and their husbands. The conversation was fairly interesting, but it seemed a bit alien to her. After her offer of help was rebuffed she went into the living room to watch a bit of the Dallas-Philadelphia game on TV. She paid close attention to the conversation, and noted that not one man mentioned his spouse or his kids. They talked exclusively about the game, politics and their jobs. *Are we really so different? How can we ever expect to get along for fifty years if we aren't interested in the same things?*

She wasn't included in this conversation either, and she realized that Jack didn't even seem happy to have her in with the men. Even though she knew more about football than half of them, she felt like her comments wouldn't be appreciated, so she eventually went back to play with the kids.

It's odd how I feel so out of place here. When I'm at the O'Flaherty's, I never feel like a woman, I just feel like me. The boys treat me like one of them, not like I'm different. But here it feels like there are two different camps, and I'm not in either one. The women don't accept me because I'm not a mother yet, and the men never will. Where do I belong?

Jack's cousin Stephanie had a six-month-old boy named Ethan that Jamie was drawn to. She whisked him away and carried him around the house as she spoke into his ear. Stephanie was at least ten years older, but she was the cousin closest in age to Jamie. "You can get one of these for yourself," she teased as she came up from behind.

"Not for a long while," Jamie said. "I'm sure I won't have a child before I'm thirty." She hadn't noticed, but Jack was standing next to Stephanie, and as Jamie turned she caught the shadow that passed over his face. *Now what did I do?*

"So you want to keep her all to yourself for a while, huh Jack?" Stephanie asked.

"Jamie's the boss," he said with a thin smile. He turned and headed back to the safety of the football game.

Well that answers that question. They left her alone with the baby, and her thoughts immediately turned to her friend. *I wonder if Ryan has commandeered Caitlin by now? I'd give anything to be with the O'Flahertys today. I wonder if Jack will mind if I spend all of the holidays with Ryan after we're married?* She let out a disgusted sigh at the mere thought. *You'll be lucky if he lets her come to the wedding.*

After Jack dropped Jamie off at her parent's home the next morning, she spent a long time getting ready for her bike ride. The park she and Ryan had agreed on was a good ten miles away, but she decided to ride there just so she could leave earlier. As she came downstairs, her mother regarded her with alarm. "Where are you going in that outfit?" she asked, staring at the skintight, black shorts and the equally snug emerald green jersey.

"I'm going on a bike ride."

Her mother continued to stare at her, so Jamie didn't even stop to get a bottle of water. She nearly jogged to the front door, grabbed her bike from the open garage, and took off. *Ah, freedom.*

When she finally met up with Ryan, she was already tired. She told her friend the bare outline of the conversation with her father, but she elaborated on the two dinners that she had endured, and included the low points of her argument with Jack. Ryan listened carefully, but couldn't offer much solace.

As expected, the O'Flahertys had a lively Thanksgiving. "It was exactly like the party for my birthday, except we had cranberry sauce and dressing, but no cake. I stole Caitlin right at the start, and I didn't have to give her up all day," she related. "You should hurry up and get married so I can commandeer your kids."

As soon as those words registered, Jamie was struck by a bolt of panic. She realized with perfect acuity that Ryan wouldn't be a part of her future. Jack would never allow Ryan to attend their family dinners and carry their children around the house. Her father would never warmly welcome Ryan into his home, either. Marrying Jack would permanently destroy her friendship with Ryan.

"Jamie, what's wrong?" Ryan asked in alarm as she got a look at her friend's face.

"I think I have a cramp in my thigh," she said as she stopped her bike and hopped off. Ryan did the same and bent down to examine the affected part. While Ryan was bent over, Jamie did her best to compose her expression, determined not to share her revelation with her friend. Ryan began to knead the muscles while she gazed up at Jamie's face. After a moment she asked, "Is it better now?"

"Much," Jamie replied, forcing a smile. She gazed at her friend as she worked on the leg for another minute. *I can't lose you Ryan. I am not going to let them take your friendship from me. No matter what!*

After they had ridden for a good ten miles, Jamie pled exhaustion, so they found a nice grove of trees and sat at a picnic table to rest. Ryan gave her a sly smile, patted the top of the concrete table, and instructed, "Come on. You know you want it."

Jamie hopped up without a second invitation, always ready for a leg massage. Ryan removed her friend's shoes so her feet wouldn't slide on the slick, painted surface. Strong hands started at her feet and slowly worked up her leg. By the time she reached her groin, Jamie was tingling with sensation. It took her a second, but the realization hit her that this was nothing less than pure sexual arousal. She reassured herself that it wasn't odd to become aroused when anyone touched her in such an intimate way, but she knew she had to put a stop to this. "Could you concentrate on my calf where I had the cramp?" she asked in order to keep those talented hands away from her crotch.

"The cramp was up here," Ryan said confusedly as she trailed her fingers along the inside of Jamie's thigh, mere inches from her throbbing vulva.

"Oh, right. Well, I must have a new one because my calf is sore now."

Ryan gave her a puzzled look, but set to work on the illusory cramp. After a few minutes, Jamie called a halt to the entire endeavor, unable to have Ryan touch her for another moment. "Thanks," she said as she sat up and started to put her shoes back on.

"But I didn't get to the sore spot," Ryan complained.

No, and we'll get arrested if you do, she thought wryly. "Feels fine," she said even though she knew she'd feel much better if she let her continue.

Ryan hopped up on the table and sat next to her. "You seem awfully tense. Are things as bad as you thought they'd be?"

"Yeah, they really are," she said. "I just don't know what to do about Jack."

"Are you sure you still want to see me as much? I feel so guilty that at least some of your arguments are about me."

"No way," Jamie said. "You're most definitely not the cause of our problems. We've got plenty of issues besides who I hang out with. Just last night we had another fight about sex."

"Ah, wanna talk about it?"

"I don't want to make you uncomfortable," Jamie said, hoping that Ryan would insist.

"I'm not uncomfortable talking about sex. You've heard me at the talk line. I just don't want you to be embarrassed."

"So if I can stand being embarrassed, you wouldn't mind my talking about something really personal?"

"I guarantee you won't shock me. Remember that I have the most hours logged at the talk line."

"I know, I know, but you never talk about really personal things, so I guess I feel like you must not want to."

"No, that's not it at all. I just haven't had many things that have been bugging me. Remember, I've been sexually active since I was seventeen. I've had a lot of time to work out my issues."

"Does every couple have sexual problems?" Jamie asked thoughtfully.

"I've never been with anyone for an extended period where some things didn't come up," Ryan admitted. "I mean, how could they not? You're never more open and naked emotionally than you are with your sexual partner. All of your issues come bubbling up to the surface when you expose yourself like that."

"I guess that does make sense," Jamie said. "I just don't know how to get anywhere on my issue."

"Tell me about it," Ryan said.

"Well, I know I've hinted that we don't get along great in bed."

Ryan nodded her assent, maintaining her neutral expression.

"Well, last night I decided that I was tired of being frustrated. So I got more aggressive. I asked him to please me first."

Ryan tried to keep her face composed, but she was frankly astounded that her friend was so passive with her fiancé. "Is that the first time you've done that?"

"Yeah, it is," she admitted. "I usually just let him do his thing and hope for the best."

"Go on," Ryan urged.

"I thought it went well. He got me there pretty easily when I gave him a few extra pointers," she said, blushing deeply. "But when he actually entered me, he didn't seem very excited. He finally finished, but it took him forever! He likes to go to sleep as soon as he's finished, but right before he fell asleep I asked him why he didn't seem excited. He was tired enough that he didn't censor himself. He said he didn't enjoy sex as much when I went first, because I wasn't as responsive. He said I move more and act more excited before I've had an orgasm."

Ryan nodded, trying to remain impassive even though she could feel her anger start to rise.

"So the bottom line is that he'd rather I was frustrated so he can have a better orgasm!"

Ryan guessed it was her turn, so she jumped in. She was determined to stay impartial, so she didn't offer an opinion, instead trying to offer suggestions. "What about pleasing you after he has an orgasm?"

"No, I don't think so. I'm usually too sensitive right afterward, and his hand causes too much friction. He tries, but either his fingers are too big, or he doesn't know how to be gentle enough. I get all tense, and that makes him do it harder, which is the worst thing he could do."

"Okay, I have another suggestion," she said. "What about touching yourself while he's inside of you? I know the equipment isn't the same, but when a woman has her fingers inside me I have to have some stimulation on my clit to come."

Jamie wasn't sure why, but the thought of Ryan lying on her back with a woman's fingers in her was enough to make her pass out. And just hearing her say "clit" made her pulse throb. She fought with herself to stay focused on her issues with Jack, but the image kept flying through her mind. "I guess I can try that too," she finally got out. "But I don't really enjoy the penetration all that much, so I'm not sure I could get there. Besides," she added, "he seems to think it's a personal affront if I can't come from intercourse. It's like it's a personal victory for him."

Ryan's head was swirling, completely puzzled by the thought of sex being more about scorecards than emotion. "Uhm … what about oral sex after he's finished?"

"You're serious, right? He'd rather poke his eye out than do that after intercourse. I offered that suggestion once, and he acted like I was insane!"

"Too messy?"

"Yeah. But it's his mess!" she said defensively.

"Remind me to count my blessings again today," Ryan said. She ducked Jamie's swat as she continued in a more serious vein, "What about mutual oral sex?"

"Uhm … do you mean …?"

"Yeah. Could you give him a blow job while he goes down on you? That way you could both have an orgasm at around the same time."

All of a sudden Jamie regretted having brought this entire topic up. She squirmed on the tabletop for a moment before she said, "I can't do that."

"You can't do what?" Ryan asked gently, sensing Jamie's growing discomfort.

"I can't give him a blow job," she said as a deep pink flush infused her cheeks. "I don't know why, but it makes me sick to my stomach."

Now Ryan was stumped. She felt that oral sex was one of the most glorious practices ever devised, and she had a hard time understanding why Jamie would be so opposed to it. "Have you tried it?" she finally asked.

"Yes. I've tried it," she admitted softly. "But he kept hitting that thing in the back of my throat, and I truly almost threw up in his lap."

"Uvula," Ryan helpfully supplied.

"Pardon?"

"That thing in the back of your throat is your uvula." To herself she thought, *any idiot would know not to shove his dick so far down your throat as to make you gag,* but she said, "It sounds like he got carried away. Maybe you should try it again, but make sure you control how deep he goes. If you stayed on top of him you have a better chance of controlling things."

"I guess I have to try it again," she conceded, but she looked so glum that Ryan felt sorry for her.

"You're going to be with him for a very long time," she reminded her. "You don't have to have all of your sexual issues worked out before you get married, but if you close the door to a lot of experiences I'm afraid you'll never try to open the door again."

Jamie pursed her lips and nodded her head slowly. "I know I need to be more open, and that I'm being selfish. But Jack won't use his mouth on me when I need him to, and I'm unwilling to get over my fears if he isn't willing to do the same. I'm afraid it'll be my pleasing him without him trying to please me."

"Jamie," she said gently. "Please don't take this as criticism, but it puzzles me that you seem to begrudge doing things to make him happy. I mean, I've never been with a man, but if men turned me on I think I'd be playing with their penises all day long. Like when I'm with a woman," she said softly as her voice became gentler and rather sensual. "It's her breasts and her vulva that turn me on. I can't keep my hands or my mouth off them," she said, laughing gently. "Don't you feel that way about his penis?"

Oh God, why did you've to say that! Her mind locked on the image of Ryan's hands on her breasts, and it didn't want to let the image go. "Uhm, well … no, I don't think like that about his penis," she admitted. She placed her hands behind herself and leaned back on her locked arms. "I've never thought about it this way, Ryan," she had to admit, "but I don't think of his penis as a toy for both of us to play with. It seems more like the little dictator," she said with a wry laugh.

"Huh?"

"Our sex life is all about his penis," Jamie said. "When he's hard, he wants to have intercourse. It's really simple for him. Once he's inside me it doesn't take him long at all to be satisfied. It doesn't really make much difference if I'm into it or not. But it doesn't work like that for me," she explained. "I mean …" She looked at Ryan for a moment and tried to translate her frustration to fit Ryan's sexual orientation. "Remember those dildos we saw at Good Vibrations?"

"Yes, I have a working knowledge of those," she said with an impish look.

Jamie gave her a playful swat, and continued. "How would you like it if you were dating someone for a long while, and every time she pulled that dildo out you were supposed to be turned on just by looking at it?"

"Uhm ... just by looking at it?"

"Yeah. And most mornings you felt it jabbing you in the back, and you knew that she just wanted you to turn over so she could put it in you." Now Jamie was getting into the topic, and the words just flew from her lips. "And every time you made any serious romantic gesture the dildo popped up again. If you kissed her with any passion, or rubbed your hand on her thigh, the dildo would come out and you'd be on your back."

"No other foreplay?" Ryan asked weakly.

"Sometimes," Jamie admitted. "But the dildo is where all the focus is. Your partner gets almost all of her satisfaction from putting that dildo inside of you, no matter how turned on you are. And once she's thrust it in you enough, she pulls it out and looks at you with an expectant smile and asks, 'Did you come?'" Ryan nodded her head briefly and gave the obvious answer. "I'd take the damn dildo and throw it away," she said. "I wouldn't allow her to use sex toys on me if she couldn't be more connected to my body."

"That's how I feel sometimes," Jamie said. "I don't agree with Lorena Bobbit's tactics, but I have empathy for her," she said with a chuckle. "His penis dictates everything, and when he has an orgasm he seems to lose all motivation to continue to please me. I mean, he makes the gesture, but I can tell he wants me to cuddle him and let him go to sleep."

"Damn, that's really is a tough one," Ryan said. "It seems to me that the only way to approach this is to tell him what you need and make sure he does it. You're going to have to set the ground rules, because it doesn't sound like he understands how to please you."

The blonde blew out a frustrated breath and nodded slowly. "I know that's what I have to do, but I want him to want to please me. Do you know what I mean?" she asked.

"I do," Ryan soothed as she rubbed her back gently. "But maybe if you told him, he'd eventually get to know you well enough that he'd have some ideas of his own. You're going to be with this man for the rest of your life," she said solemnly. "You can't just hope for the best. I think you need to talk this through. You have to trust that each of you wants the same thing or you're in real trouble."

Jamie looked up through half hooded eyes and asked, "You've been in his position; do you enjoy performing oral sex on another woman?"

"I told you about being with Sara," Ryan said.

At Jamie's nod, she continued, "Not long after everything went down with her, I met a woman when I was rollerblading in Golden Gate Park. I was still very fragile, and I felt unattractive and totally undesirable. Katie was an intern working at the park with a program that Berkeley runs through their landscape architecture program. She was just three years older than I was, but that seems like a lot when you're not quite seventeen. She was taking a break, and came over to sit next to me on a bench. We started talking, and before I knew it she asked for my phone number. I'd never been picked up before, and I didn't have a clue what to do, so I stuck to the phone like glue until she called. Luckily for everyone in the house it only took her a day!"

Jamie laughed at her friend's self-effacing recounting of this youthful encounter.

"She had a little apartment in Berkeley that she shared with two other women. I hopped on BART, and went over for my first date with a woman. It was a Saturday afternoon in late May, and I was so nervous I practically barfed on the train. I didn't know what I was supposed to do, or what she expected of me. For all I knew we'd just sit and talk or go to a movie." Ryan's face curled into a smile as she recalled, "She had something more intense in mind."

"You must have been terrified!"

"Yeah, I guess I was. Her roommates each had jobs, and they were only going to be gone for a couple of hours, so we got down to business right away. My hands were shaking so badly that she had to go first," she said with a laugh. "She kissed and touched me until I thought my head would explode." Ryan smiled to herself at the memory. "But when she started to move down my body I just about freaked!"

Jamie joined in her laughter, completely amused by her friend's animated facial gestures. "I was sooo naïve! I knew that girls gave guys head, but I'd never stopped to think about the converse. But from the first touch of her tongue I was a convert! Wow," she mused dreamily. "I can still feel it." She shook her head, and looked over at Jamie, laughing when she caught sight of the look on her face. Her friend was intensely interested in the story at this point—sitting right on the edge of the table, hanging on to every word.

"So?" Jamie asked eagerly.

"So …"

"So what was it like?" she demanded.

Ryan turned serious and regarded her carefully. "Do you really not know, Jamie?"

She shook her head rather violently. "If the half hearted attempts that Jack's made are all there is, then you're very, very easily pleased."

"Well," Ryan mused. "I'm not sure how to describe it. To be honest, even though I still enjoy it a lot, it's lost a lot of allure since I practice safe sex all the time. Honestly, that's one of the reasons I'd like a steady girlfriend. I'd like both of us to get tested for STD's and then stay monogamous. I am so sick of barriers!"

Jamie was still staring at her intently, obviously waiting for a response to her earlier question. "Okay!" Ryan laughed at her expression. "I'll do my best. Oral sex with someone you care about is the most intimate touch that you can imagine. I mean, it's using one of your most sensitive organs to give pleasure to her through her most sensitive organ. It's exposing yourself fully to your partner's touch. You're so vulnerable in that position, but the vulnerability is very erotic for me. There's no greater sign that you care for someone than allowing her to touch you in that way. It's such a special thing—I really wish that you could experience it for yourself." She caught the questioning look that hadn't changed, and asked, "Didn't I describe it well enough?"

Her friend shook her head briskly. "You described your emotional reaction really nicely. But what's it like physically?"

"Hmm, that's even tougher," she mused as she let her head fall back against her shoulders. "I don't think I've ever tried to describe this before." She spent another few minutes deep in thought, and finally said, "I guess it's the combination of the vulnerability, the intimacy and the slightly naughty nature of the act, but all of that comes together for a real wallop on the old central nervous system," she said thoughtfully. "It's a jolt of sensation when she first touches you. It starts in your vulva but radiates out until your whole body tingles. Her tongue feels so warm and wet and soft, it's absolutely amazing. And if you're turned on enough, it feels like someone pouring aloe on a sunburn. It's really very soothing at first. But within seconds that fire is burning hotter than ever, and you just want to jump in and let it burn you alive." Ryan's eyes were half closed and her mouth was curled up into an adorable little grin as she softly described the act. She had a dreamy expression on her face that perfectly matched her soft, sensual voice. Jamie knew that she had stopped talking, and she sensed that it was now her turn. But she couldn't make her mouth move. She tried gamely, but the signal couldn't get to her mouth, since all of the other neurons were sending signals to her vulva.

Ryan turned her head to look at her friend's open-mouthed stare, and finally asked, "Too much information?"

Jamie shook her head roughly to snap herself back into reality. "No, no, not at all," she insisted. "I just … I've never … I mean …"

"I know," Ryan said gently as she patted her knee. "But you can, Jamie. I know you've got a ton of passion that just hasn't been tapped." She smiled at the still stunned looking woman and said, "I think you're gonna surprise yourself someday. I guarantee your best sexual experiences are in front of you."

"I certainly hope so! I couldn't go on if I thought they were behind me. But back to your story. Wasn't it hard to touch her that way the first time?"

"No, not really. What she had done to me felt so utterly fabulous that I had to do it to her, just as a way of thanking her!"

Jamie laughed again at Ryan's guileless face. "So, did you like it?"

"Like isn't even in the ball park," she said wistfully. "I felt like we were merged into one big, throbbing, pulsing body. I was completely, totally, helplessly in love with Katie no more than two seconds after my tongue touched her. Of course, she was more realistic about the experience," she said sardonically.

"What happened?" Jamie asked as she placed her hand on Ryan's shoulder.

"About what you'd expect," she said. "She was from Iowa, and since the term was over, she was going home. She didn't want me to write to her, and a few weeks later she sent me a note and said, 'Thanks but no thanks.'"

"You poor baby," Jamie said with a face full of empathy.

"No, no, Jamie, this isn't a sad story. I didn't know a thing about Katie. I wasn't in love with her. But she showed me how totally wonderful oral sex can be, and for that I'm forever grateful. I don't have any idea where she is today, but wherever she is I hope she's gotten as much out of it as I have."

"So is Jack being a baby because he won't try it with more enthusiasm?" Jamie asked.

"No, not really. I had someone who showed me how to do it, and how it felt to have it done to me. It's not quite the same for you, but I bet if one of you was more experimental the other might follow."

"I guess that's about the only other option I have at this point," Jamie said. "If I ever want to have an orgasm I guess I'll have to try one of your suggestions. I'm sure he won't like it though. He views every orgasm as inferior if it doesn't come from penetration."

"That's ridiculous!" Ryan shouted before she could catch herself. "I'd never try to dictate how my partner had an orgasm. Jesus! I do everything in my power to please my partner, and these are women I hardly know!" She was immediately chagrined to have allowed herself to vent like that, but she was getting so sick of this guy. She hated to see Jamie saddled with an insecure jerk like this, but she knew that it wasn't her business. She vowed immediately to keep her opinions to herself, but she was amazed by the smile that lit up Jamie's face.

"Thanks. I really mean that," she said softly. "You've really made me feel better. I've been so afraid that what I wanted wasn't reasonable. But you've helped me see that not everyone is like Jack."

"Jamie," she said as she took her hand. "Sex is an important part of a relationship. You've got a right to your own pleasure. You just need to figure out how to best please yourself, and then you need to ask for it. You can't spend the rest of your life with this man and only focus on his satisfaction."

"I know you're right. But it's just another area that isn't going to go smoothly," she predicted.

The rest of the weekend passed at a snail's pace. The restless boredom that had been tugging at her guts grew worse as the hours passed. She spent time with her mother, going shopping and trying out three new restaurants, but she felt like she was sleepwalking through the experience. *Did I used to enjoy this?* After spending yet another lunch listening to her mother talk about absolutely nothing of interest, Jamie thought that she'd scream. *I've been here for four days and neither she nor Daddy has asked about me. I know they don't know what classes I'm taking. They know nothing about my life. They don't even ask about Jack. Have I gotten so used to their disinterest that I didn't notice it before?*

After Sunday dinner with her parents, she decided to go spend the night with Jack. He was glad to see her, but within an hour he was engrossed in his schoolwork. Jamie pulled out her own books and spent the evening reading while sitting on the couch with her legs in Jack's lap.

Before bed she went into the kitchen to get a drink. He came into the kitchen just as she was finishing and sat down at the kitchen table. "I love having you here," he said with a smile as he took her hand. "It just doesn't feel like home when you're not around."

Warning bells were sounding, but she ignored them and asked the question that had popped into her head. "Why do you love me, Jack?"

He looked completely dumbfounded. "You know why I love you."

"No, I really don't. You tell me you love me, but you never tell me why." She grasped his hand and looked at him with pleading eyes. "Please tell me."

He stared at her for a long time before he finally answered. "I guess I love how I feel when I'm with you," he said thoughtfully. "You make me feel whole."

Is that all? She continued to stare at him without saying a word. Silently she prayed that he'd continue with something—anything—about her.

"I'm really attracted to you," he continued hesitantly. "I love the way you look, and I love the way I feel when I touch you," he smiled shyly as he began to do just that.

She concentrated with every fiber of her being and finally found the strength to shut down the voice that was screaming for her attention. She repeated the mantra, *He does love you, he just doesn't know how to express it. He does love you, he does.*

On Monday, Jamie got to the gym just as Mia and Ryan were finishing up.

Ryan's mood was ebullient when she greeted her friend. "Hiya," she said with a big grin, giving Jamie a hug.

"You certainly look happy," Jamie said as she caught some of the infectious mood.

"What's not to be happy about?"

"Good point," Jamie replied, thinking that she could spew for an hour about her unhappiness with Jack.

Mia was still at the gym working on the stair climber when they had finished their session. Jamie approached her and asked, "Would you like to go grab a bite with Ryan and me?"

"I'd love to, as long as I can go shower first. I'd scare the livestock the way I smell right now."

"I think we could both use a little freshening up. Let's go home so we can take a shower, then we'll decide where to go."

Mia called dibs as soon as they walked into the house, running up the stairs with the promise that she'd be quick. Ryan and Jamie walked up to her room to wait.

They discussed all of their menu choices, and when Mia was done Ryan went back downstairs to allow Jamie to get ready.

"So, how do you like working with Ryan?" Jamie asked after Mia came into her room.

"I like it a lot, James. You were right; she's really good at what she does. And she's a lot of fun too. The hour passes so quickly that it doesn't even feel like work. I guess I should just accept your view of people and save myself some trouble."

"I'm really glad you like her. I knew that you two would get along, being that you're my two favorite people." Mia smiled at her friend, pleased by the confirmation of their long friendship.

After they were presentable, they settled on a Thai restaurant within walking distance. During dinner Jamie grew pensive and finally asked, "Do you guys think it's odd that Jack can't tell me why he loves me?"

Mia looked at Ryan who returned the gaze. They mouthed "Oh-oh," in unison, as they laughed. Mia spoke first, "Guys aren't great at that kind of thing." She paused for a minute, "Let me guess—his answer was either 'Gee, I don't know, I just do,' or it was about how you make him feel."

"Ding, ding, ding, we have a winner," Jamie replied. "His answer, and I quote, was 'I love how you make me feel when we're together'." She let out an aggrieved sigh. "It makes me feel like I have to guess how he feels, and just assume I'm right."

"Well, that's the safest course," Mia agreed with a slight chuckle.

Jamie noticed that Ryan hadn't responded, and was in fact gazing down at her meal, deep in thought. She decided to drop the subject, and they began to discuss their workouts and the ride and other topics of mutual interest. At about seven-thirty Mia announced that she was meeting some friends for a movie. Both Ryan and Jamie declined the invitation to join the crowd, and Mia took off after hugging both of them goodbye.

After they had settled the bill, they began to walk down Telegraph. The street was still filled with the merchants who set up tables along the sidewalk, and they browsed for a long time. After they had turned down a quieter street Jamie suggested they stop for a coffee, finding themselves at their favorite coffee shop. They received their respective lattes and settled at a table.

Jamie noticed that Ryan was still reserved, so she finally asked, "What's bothering you? You were so up before dinner, and now you seem a little sad."

Ryan looked down at her coffee and shrugged her shoulders. "I don't know if I should talk about it."

"Should or want to?" Jamie asked. "If something's bothering you, I want to know about it, unless you don't want to talk about it."

Ryan looked up with those deep blue eyes and stared at her intently for a long minute. "It's about what you said about Jack," she finally said. "It hurts me that he isn't able to make you feel better. I want you to have a great relationship. I really want you to be happy and fulfilled," she said as their eyes locked again.

"I appreciate that more than I can say," Jamie said as she patted her friend's folded hands. "I know I shouldn't be so hard on him. Maybe I just didn't give him time to think."

Ryan shook her head a little. "That's what I was doing in the restaurant. It only took me a moment to think of what I love about you." The corner of her mouth curved into a smile, and she looked slightly embarrassed.

"Tell me," Jamie said. She grasped her hands as they continued to stare into each other's eyes.

"Okay," Ryan began hesitantly. "I love how you treat other people. You have a lot of empathy, and I can tell it's very genuine. You're thoughtful and kind and very considerate. I've never heard you make a derogatory comment about anyone—not even Cassie, who certainly deserves a few," she laughed. "I love your intelligence and your sense of humor. You have a really quick mind, and I love to see you work on a problem. I appreciate how much you love language and literature, and how deep your knowledge is of the topic. You make me laugh more than anyone I know, and that's saying a lot." She showed Jamie her most luminous grin, and Jamie found her own smile growing to match. "I love how interested you are in other people and topics that you aren't familiar with. You have a real love of life, and you're always open to new experiences." She thought for a minute then continued, "The bottom line though, is your heart. Your compassion and love for other people constantly impresses me. It's what I love the most about you." As she finished, she looked up to see tears forming in Jamie's eyes. She pulled one of her hands from Jamie's grasp and laid it on top of hers as she smiled tenderly at her.

"That was the most amazing thing anyone has ever said to me. But do you know what the funny thing is?"

Ryan shook her head as she cocked it in a question.

"As you spoke, I was thinking that every trait you mentioned was exactly how I'd describe you. I've never met anyone who's as connected to her feelings as you are. That's such a gift. I hope you find someone to share it with who really appreciates it."

Ryan looked surprised, but finally replied, "That's part of the reason I'm so happy tonight."

"What do you mean?" Jamie asked, a bit confused.

"I've been thinking a lot about love and relationships lately." She looked thoughtful as she said, "I was bothered by having a quickie with that older woman. That's why I snapped at you when you called me on it," she admitted. "I had some time to really reflect while we were on break. And I think you're right. I've been avoiding real intimacy. I'm worried that if I keep avoiding it I won't be able to be intimate when I feel I'm ready. So I'm going to try to find a real girlfriend and stop my serial dating."

"Anyone in mind?" Jamie inquired lightly, feeling a stab of panic in her chest.

"Yeah, as a matter of fact. It's someone you know."

"Who?"

"Tracy Stuart, from class. You know her, right?"

"Yeah, I know her." *Boy do I ever know her.* From the first day of class Jamie had been impressed with the tall, lean brunette. It was a toss-up between Ryan and Tracy for who was more beautiful. Tracy had a sleek, smooth feminine grace that was mesmerizing, and Jamie had often thought that Ryan and Tracy would make a knock out couple. To her surprise, the woman had never seemed interested in Ryan, clearly avoiding being a member of Ryan's fan club. "How did you make a connection with her?"

"I tried to talk to her one day just after school started, but she shot me down fast," she said with a grin. "She was dating another woman, so I didn't approach her again. A couple of weeks ago I heard that they had broken up, and I tried to talk to her again." She looked embarrassed as she related, "She told me that she had no intention of being just a stop on the O'Flaherty Express." Ryan blushed at being called at her game. "I thought about that a lot the last couple of weeks. But after that encounter with the woman from the gym I just decided that I had to stop sleeping with everyone who caught my eye. I called Tracy on Saturday and she agreed to have coffee with me," she said, smiling. "You know, Jamie, this is the first woman I've pursued in years."

"So what happened?" Jamie asked, beginning to get more nervous.

"We talked for a long time. I confessed that she really had my number." She paused for a moment. "But then I asked her if she'd go out with me if I promised not to see anyone else and be open to having a real relationship." She looked up at Jamie. "I had no idea I was going to offer that, but she really is something. I don't remember the last time I was this attracted to a woman."

"So did she agree right then?"

"Nope," she said. "She made me wait until today. She called me this afternoon and agreed to go out with me tomorrow evening." She laughed a little, "She also told me in no uncertain terms that when she said 'go out' she meant 'go out.'" She let out a chuckle as she drawled, "I don't think I'm going to have my way with this one for quite a while."

"Are you okay with that?" Jamie asked, breaking out with a laugh. "I know you have needs that you're used to having filled."

"To be honest, I think my overactive libido could use a rest," she reflected.

"This could give you a chance to get to know yourself and discover what's really important to you in a relationship."

"Oh, believe me, if she makes me wait too long, knowing myself won't be a problem," she said as she laughed at Jamie's deep blush.

On the first Friday after Thanksgiving break, Jamie walked into Jack's apartment and was astounded to find him setting the table for dinner. She smelled something cooking but was too shocked to even try to guess what it was. "Hi," he said brightly when he saw her.

"Uhm, hi," she managed to get out. "What's up?"

He walked over to her and wrapped his arms around her tightly. "I've been giving a lot of thought to what you said on Thanksgiving, and I'm going to do something about it. I don't want to have a marriage like my parents, Jamie, but I've been falling into their patterns. I'm sorry that you were so frustrated, but I'm glad you told me eventually."

"I had no idea that you even took me seriously," she said in wonder. "I can't tell you how good it makes me feel to know that you care enough to try to change."

"Jamie," he said softly as he lifted her chin with his fingers, "The way you feel about me matters tremendously. You're the most important person in my life. Don't you know that?"

She rested her head on his chest and let herself sink into his embrace. His strong arms completely enveloped her, and she felt warm and loved for the first time in weeks. "Thank you," she said softly. "Thank you for everything."

The following Monday morning Ryan walked up to Jamie after class and asked, "Juice?"

"Sure," Jamie agreed, very thankful that Ryan didn't stop their little breaks together even though she was getting close to Tracy. Out of the corner of her eye she saw the good-looking brunette talking to a group of women. "Would you like to ask Tracy to join us?" she asked with just a moment of hesitation.

"Uhm … I guess I could. But I like having time alone with you," she said. "So I wouldn't mind asking her once in a while, but I don't want to make a habit of it."

Jamie smiled up at her friend as she shook her head. "You're such a sensitive woman, Ryan O'Flaherty," she said fondly. "I really like having time with just you too, but I'd like to get to know her a little. Is it okay?"

"Sure. I'll ask her," she said with a winning smile as she sauntered over and gently placed her hand on Tracy's back. The dark head turned to regard her, and Jamie watched as Tracy's face broke into a big smile. Seconds later, both women were walking her way. "Ms. Stuart has accepted our invitation," Ryan said with mock formality. "Our usual?"

"Perfect," Jamie said.

After a few minutes of topical conversation, Jamie hopped up from the table to buy another round of juice for her always-thirsty friend. Ryan had whipped through her two bottles, and was eyeing Jamie's rather hungrily so Jamie strolled over to the vending machines to purchase another cranberry juice. *I'm amazed by how natural Ryan seems with her, she mused during her short walk. I thought she'd have the predator persona but she doesn't at all. Hmm, maybe she puts that on only when she has a woman alone.* She considered this idea but reminded herself, *No, she was very predatory with the women she picked up during class. Having an audience sure didn't seem to stop her then.* She inserted her dollar bill in the juice machine and made her selection. After removing the bottle from the tray she turned to return to the table. A smile crossed her lips as she watched Ryan gently flirting with Tracy. She wasn't up to her usual tricks, however. She was just smiling at something the gorgeous brunette said. Her eyes were half lidded, and reflected rather innocent shyness. Tracy obviously appreciated this new attitude, as she playfully touched the tip of Ryan's nose. But there was still a little predator left as Jamie watched a feral grin come over her friend's features just before her mouth snapped open to grab Tracy's index finger between her perfect white teeth.

Jamie set the bottle down on the table, admonishing her friend, "I've brought more calories, buddy. You don't have to resort to cannibalism."

Ryan just gave her a rakish look as she tamely released her prey. Tracy leaned over and patted her gently on the cheek, murmuring, "Good girl."

Tracy turned to Jamie and twitched her head in Ryan's direction and asked, "How long have you and blue eyes here known each other?"

"Just since class started."

Tracy blinked at that bit of information. "Gosh, I thought you'd known each other for years. You seem so close."

"We are," Ryan said, locking her eyes onto Jamie's. "Jamie's the best friend I've ever had."

The misty green eyes didn't waver as Jamie echoed her thoughts. "Best class I've ever taken," she said with a smile. "I've learned a lot and got a best friend in the bargain."

Tracy gave each woman a long appraising look as they grinned at each other, seemingly unaware of her presence.

After class on Wednesday, Ryan sidled up to Jamie and asked, "Do you know how to bowl?"

"Bowl? Like in a bowling alley?"

A delightfully quirky grin crossed Ryan's face as she asked, "What other kind is there?"

"Well, there's lawn bowling, but I guess they do that mostly in England."

Ryan cocked her dark head and repeated her question. "Do you know how?"

"I'd say I'd be more proficient at lawn bowling," she mused. "I went bowling once, in grade school, and the manager of the alley asked me to stop before I hurt myself," she said with a wry laugh.

"Perfect," Ryan pronounced with a very satisfied grin. "We're going bowling—tonight!"

After their workout, and a stop for a quick shower and a mini-rubdown, they got into the Porsche for the drive to the city. After some dogged questioning Jamie finally got the story out of her recalcitrant friend. "So all of your brothers and cousins are in a bowling league, right?"

"Right."

"And you fill in when someone can't make it?"

"Right."

"So tonight Brendan can't make it and for some obscure reason, you want me to be on your team to take his place."

"Almost right," she said with a smile. "Brendan is on Conor's team. I'm filling in for Rory, and he's on another team." Her waggling eyebrows indicated her extreme pleasure with her plan, and after a few minutes the reason dawned on Jamie.

"You asked me because you knew I'd suck!!" she cried in outrage as she slapped Ryan hard on the thigh.

"Hey! That hurt!" she winced, rubbing the affected part as she shot a glare at her friend. "And I asked you because Conor suggested you," she sniffed. "I thought we'd have fun together." Her eyes were dark and a tiny little pout was forming on her lovely face.

"Ryan, I'm sorry," she said quickly as she gently rubbed her hand on the still stinging thigh. "I didn't mean to hurt your feelings."

Her friend gave her a rakish grin as she admitted, "You didn't. I really did ask you because I thought you'd suck."

At the smaller woman's outraged squawk, she added, "Plus I wanted to spend the evening with you. Tracy would suck too," she reassured her, "but I didn't ask her. I just thought it would be fun because you fit in so well."

"Okay," Jamie said suspiciously. "Who would you've asked if your team needed another player?"

"Ally," she said quickly as she tried to cover up from her laughing friend's pinch.

They arrived at the Japantown Bowl just as the rest of the clan got there. Looking around, Jamie observed that they were the only women in the entire building. "Is this the Testosterone League, or what?" she whispered to Ryan.

"Pretty much. You're on the Carpenter's Local 751 team. I'm on the International Brotherhood of Electrical Workers Local 128." Her playful grin caused Jamie to smile back at her, ignoring her pique at being tricked into playing.

Conor arrived moments later, and claimed Jamie as his charge for the evening. "Finally, a teammate who I'll enjoy looking at," he said with obvious pleasure. "I'm so sick of looking at sweaty men all day—this is a treat."

"Just remember that she has her own sweaty man that she likes to look at, Conor," Ryan reminded him as she playfully patted her brother's cheek.

"Oh, I'm well aware of Jamie's marital status," he said sweetly. Turning to the blushing woman he inquired, "You're still single, but with some vague plans on marrying some unemployed guy in the distant future, right?"

"I suppose that's about right," Jamie admitted with a grin.

"Perfect," Conor said with a sexy grin that nearly matched the one Jamie had seen on his sister whenever she spotted a fresh face. "Let's get you set up." He took her hand to lead her over to the racks of balls.

Conor spent quite a few minutes helping Jamie choose a ball that fit her hand, and proved light enough for her to roll effectively. After she secured a lovely pair of tan and red rental shoes he took her up to the line and spent a good ten minutes instructing her on his philosophy of bowling. She kept looking at him with a puzzled glance and finally Ryan could take no more. She stomped over to their lane and demanded, "Are you teaching her how to build a bowling alley, or throw the damn ball?"

"Ryan," he explained. "Bowling is a difficult sport. It helps to understand the angles and the percentages of the different approaches."

"Oh, for God's sake." She placed her hands on Jamie's shoulders and said, "See the center arrow on the lane?"

Jamie nodded.

"Stand just to the right of it, take four steps, staring with your right foot. Bring the ball back to about here," she instructed as she pulled her arm back. "Release it smoothly, while looking at the matching arrow right up there." She pointed to a mark on the lane about ten feet away.

Jamie nodded once and mimicked Ryan's instructions perfectly. They watched the ball as it slowly but determinedly made it's way right to the pocket where it knocked every pin down, one at a time.

Jamie turned and threw her arms around Ryan, who was grinning like the Cheshire cat at her scowling brother. "Keep it simple, stupid," she instructed as she backhanded him sharply in the stomach on her way back to her own lane.

Ryan quickly became engrossed in her own play. She didn't own her own ball, and she sometimes had trouble finding one that fit her long, slender fingers. Her strength allowed her to effortlessly roll a sixteen-pound ball, but she had never been able to find a heavy ball that didn't fall off her hand. So she usually had to settle for a fourteen-pounder just to keep some control. But tonight she found the perfect ball. It was a sixteen-pound dark red ball, and the finger holes were nearly perfect. The initials JWB were stamped into the plastic, and she made a note in her organizer for the next time she had to fill in so that she could find the darned thing again.

The proper equipment allowed her to have the game of her life. Her first game was a 225, the second 215 and she was already at 230 in the ninth frame of the last game. Even though she was concentrating on her match, she shot glances over at Jamie every time her friend went to the line. *Not bad for a rank beginner*, she thought with a small smile. Her eyes wandered to her brother and her assembled cousins as Jamie went to roll her second ball of the frame. *Perverts!* she scoffed when she saw five pairs of eyes firmly glued to her friend's butt. But she admitted to herself that Jamie did indeed have a very watchable butt, so she really couldn't blame the lads. The second ball gave Jamie a spare for the frame and Ryan smiled broadly as the smaller woman jumped gleefully into the air and gave a whoop of delight. All of the members of her team were smiling and congratulating her, but Ryan noted with her own delighted smile that those misty green eyes immediately found her, seeking Ryan out to share her enthusiasm. She did so with pleasure, giving Jamie both a broad smile and a wink of approval.

As Ryan rolled her next frame she turned and caught Jamie gazing at her intently. They locked eyes, and for just one split second the din of the alley died down and became a very faint muted rumble. The other bowlers faded from her view. Only one face remained, and Ryan could nearly feel her breathing—so intent was their connection for that one instant. But as soon as it began it was gone—as Ryan walked into the ball return and nearly took a header. "Yipes!" she cried as only her excellent balance kept her upright. All of the cousins laughed at her completely unexpected clumsiness. She felt a deep blush cover her face as she sat down and tried to gather her scrambled thoughts. But just when she was nearly back to normal she felt a warm hand on her shoulder. She turned and saw those green eyes just inches away, this time filled with concern. "You didn't hurt yourself, did you?"

"No, no, not at all," she said. "There must have been something on the floor," she explained, trying to cover.

"You sure you're alright?" she persisted.

"Perfect," Ryan insisted, smiling to herself when Jamie's small hand gently squeezed her shoulder as she returned to her lane.

Wow, I don't know what's going on tonight, but I'm actually feeling lightheaded. I must be having sex withdrawal. Yeah, that must be it, she decided, as she focused intently on Jamie's cute little butt as her friend once again approached the line.

"Are you aware of her marital status?" a deep voice breathed in her ear. Her blush climbed her face so fast that she almost passed out from the rush.

She gathered herself with as much grace as possible, and shrugged her older brother off. "Get a grip, Conor," she snapped as she went to the line and rolled the first gutter ball of her adult life.

Unbeknownst to Ryan, Conor and the boys had been buying Jamie rounds of beers, and she had gamely tried to keep up with the much larger men. By the time the match was over her small friend was toast. "Thanks, Conor," Ryan grumbled as a giggling Jamie came over and plopped down on her lap. "Tell Da I had to take Jamie home. I'll just stay at her house so I don't have to come back across the bridge."

"No problem, Sis," he said with a smile. "But I could take her home if you want."

The giggles had stopped and now Jamie was sound asleep against Ryan's chest. "Yeah, sure," she scoffed. "Like I'd trust you with her in this condition."

"Are you sure you're entirely trustworthy?" he challenged. "I can read you like a book, Sis, and you've got it bad." He was smirking widely with his arms crossed against his broad chest.

"You're delusional, Conor," she snapped. "Now help me get her to the car, you big dope."

As they pulled up in front of the house, Ryan noted with dismay that the lights were on in both roommates' rooms. *Oh boy, another fun night with Cassie.*

It took a lot longer than Ryan would have predicted, but she finally got Jamie's half-awake body out of the tiny, low-slung car. The blonde was able to walk with assistance, but when they got to the door she couldn't produce her house key. "None of these keys work," Ryan complained as she tried each of the three keys on the ring.

"Those'r for the car," Jamie mumbled.

"Where are your house keys?" Ryan enunciated clearly.

"Pocket," she mumbled back.

"Can you get them?"

"Uhn-uh," she said as she shook her head and nearly fell over. Ryan rolled her eyes as she began to pat her down. The key was in the small inside pocket of her 501's and Ryan gamely snuck two fingers down into the tiny space. She got her fingers around it, but had a tough time actually getting it out. Jamie picked that moment to lose the ability to support herself. Her knees buckled and Ryan had to grab her with one strong arm just under her breasts. She dug into the pocket more forcefully and extricated the house key on its tiny silver ring. A minute fumbling with the lock while trying to balance the limp woman eventually allowed them to stumble into the house.

I've gotta get lighter friends, she grumbled as she stooped and swept her friend into her arms and steeled herself for the long climb up the steep staircase. She was nearly at the top when the ever pleasant Cassie Martin emerged from her room and glared at Ryan in outrage. "What have you done to her?"

"I haven't done anything to her, Cassie," she said with as much patience as she could gather. "I'm trying to keep her from getting hurt. You can help or you can get out of the way." She glared right back at the tall, thin blonde.

She won this round, for Cassie's expression mellowed and she asked, "What can I do to help?"

"Well, I've got to get her undressed and then into bed."

"I'll undress her," Cassie said firmly.

"Fine," Ryan snapped, unable to tolerate this annoying woman any longer than necessary. "If you can handle this, I'll take off." She placed Jamie on the bed and started down the stairs only to be stopped by Cassie's startled voice.

"I can't lift her!" she cried.

Ryan rolled her eyes, and trudged back upstairs. She stood next to the exasperated woman and asked, "What do you want me to do?"

"Uhm …" she mumbled as she assessed the situation. "Can you pick her up so I can get her jeans off?"

"Yes, but aren't you afraid I'll rape her if I see her in her underwear?" she snapped, unable to control herself.

"Look, Ryan, I'm sorry I said that. I just …"

"It's okay," Ryan said, her own voice gentling. "Let's just get her undressed." They worked together, awkwardly but effectively getting her into a pair of flannel pajamas. Ryan carried her into the bath and stepped outside while Cassie guided her to the toilet. When she was finished relieving herself, Ryan came back in and carried her to the neatly turned down bed as Cassie hovered.

"I'm afraid to leave her here alone," the blonde mused.

"Why don't you sleep with her?" Ryan asked, thinking the solution was obvious.

"My boyfriend is here," she said, as though Ryan could have known that.

"Why didn't you have him help you get her into bed?"

"I don't want him to see other women naked," Cassie snapped back. "It's inappropriate!"

"Great. So should I sleep with her or with your boyfriend?" she asked wryly. "I can assure you he'd be safe with me."

"You're hardly his type."

"That's a relief," Ryan muttered, just loud enough to be heard.

"Do what you want," Cassie fumed. "Besides, I think you're just what Jamie's looking for, anyway!" She stormed from the room, slamming the door and startling the half-unconscious woman awake.

"Wha … what happen'd?" Jamie muttered.

"Nothing," Ryan murmured softly as she sat on the bed and soothed her friend. "Nothing at all. You just go to sleep. I'll be right here," she promised.

"Are you stayin' with me?" she asked shyly. "I'm a little drunk."

"You're more than a little drunk, pal," she chuckled. "I'm gonna stay right here to make sure you're okay."

"'Kay," she said happily. She pushed the covers back and demanded, "Get in."

Ryan shook her head firmly, remembering the earlier flush of feeling she had at the bowling alley. "I'll just curl up on the love seat or the floor."

"Don't you trust me?" Jamie asked with her face contorted into a sad little pout.

"Of course I trust you," Ryan soothed as she sat on the bed and ran her fingers through her friend's pale hair.

"Well?" she demanded, not verbalizing the obvious unasked question.

Ryan just nodded as she kicked off her running shoes and unbuttoned her jeans. She noticed that Jamie was staring at her intently as she did so, and she briefly missed the unconscious phase of the evening. She shucked her pants and slid into bed, still in her salmon colored polo shirt and sports bra.

But even through her drunken haze Jamie was still able to make her uncomfortable. "Don't you have to wear that shirt tomorrow?" she asked lazily.

"Uhm … yeah, I guess I do."

"Why don't you put on one of my T-shirts?"

Knowing that the idea was sound, Ryan got to her feet and went to the dresser. A small voice floated over to her. "You don't have to keep your bra on, Ryan. I want you to be comfortable."

"I think I'd be more comfortable on that floor, fully clothed," she mumbled to herself, but did as her friend asked. She found a T-shirt that looked like it wouldn't be skin tight, stripped off her polo, and then yanked her sports bra over her head, demurely turning her back to Jamie as she did so.

That soft voice again commented, "You have a really nice back. Really nice."

Great! Just great! Every one of my senses are on full alert, I'm unreasonably attracted to my best friend, and she's watching me undress like a guy at a topless bar!

She gingerly approached the bed and slid in to the small space her friend had left for her. "Can I have a little more room?" she asked in a voice that hardly sounded like her own.

"Sure," Jamie mumbled as she scooted even closer and curled up against Ryan's side. She snuggled her head up against her friend's broad shoulder and let out a deep sigh. "This doesn't bother you, does it?"

"No, no, it's fine," she squeaked as Jamie's arm curled around her waist.

"Good," came the mumbled response. "I need to be close tonight."

Oh God! Ryan cried to herself. *Please, please, don't want to be any closer, 'cause I don't think I can resist!*

She lay still as a statue for a few minutes until she felt a gentle bump against her side. "Relax," Jamie mumbled. "It's okay, Ryan. I want this."

Want what?

As though she could hear that voice, Jamie replied, "I want to snuggle a little. No big deal between friends, huh?"

A small smile curled the edges of her mouth, as Ryan felt her own body begin to relax. She indulgently replied, "No big deal at all, pal." She brought her right arm around to tenderly rub her friend's back, slowly and smoothly urging her into sleep.

Just before first light Ryan slowly blinked her eyes open and tried to order her thoughts. *Where am I? And who's this?* Her face was burrowed up against a very soft, very warm back. Her right arm was wrapped around a small waist, and an arm rested upon her own with a soft hand covering hers. Suddenly, all of her senses shot to full alert. *My God! I'm wrapped around Jamie! Shit! Shit! SHIT!* She fought with her mind to think clearly and help her extricate herself from this predicament. *Okay, okay, just calm down, she soothed herself. She wanted to cuddle, remember? This was her idea. It's okay if she wakes up and you're touching.* But her rational mind reminded her, She wanted to cuddle you, but she didn't ask you to plaster yourself up against her like a wall to wall carpet! She took a deep breath to speed the flow of oxygen to her brain. *You've got to pull away before she wakes up, but you don't want to wake her when you do it, she instructed her body. You've got to be smooth and gentle!* She took a few more calming breaths and let her mind wander for just another moment. *I wonder if Tracy will feel*

this good when we sleep together? A deep sigh sprang from her chest as she thought, *I wish I could have this with Jamie. I just feel so comfortable with her. Yeah, yeah,* her conscience interjected. *You feel comfortable with Duffy too, and it would be just as morally wrong to sleep with him! Get up, you lazy bum, and stop trying to cop a feel from your best straight friend.*

She began to remove her arm as slowly as possible, but she was pulling Jamie's hand right along with it. Going for another tactic, she moved back to her original position and lifted her head until it was hovering over Jamie's shoulder. She pursed her lips and blew a forceful stream of air right onto the mussed locks of hair trailing over her forehead. Jamie's face scrunched up into an adorable frown and finally her right hand lifted to brush against her hair, freeing Ryan's arm in the process. A satisfied smile came over Ryan's face as she checked her watch alarm and reset it for seven. *No clothes to run in anyway*, she thought to herself as she rolled over onto her side, back to back with her deeply sleeping friend.

"You awake?" a soft voice tickled her ear.

"I am now," Ryan's sleep roughened voice replied. She turned onto her back and gazed up at the surprisingly bright green eyes that faced her. "You look pretty peppy for a drunkard."

"Oh God, was I really bad?" her blushing friend choked out.

"No, not at all, but Cassie and I had to undress you."

"Cassie? Did you need help?"

"No, but she thought I'd molest you, so she wanted to supervise."

Jamie flopped onto her back and draped her forearm over her eyes. "I've got to get rid of her," she grumbled. "I cannot have her insulting my friends like that. It's just not acceptable."

"It's okay. She generally doesn't bother me, and now that I know you don't care if I'm rude I'm perfectly capable of defending myself."

"You have my permission to deck her." She rolled over and got to her feet.

"How do you feel?"

"Fine," she replied easily. "Why shouldn't I?"

"Don't you have a hangover?"

"Unh-uh," she replied with a shake of her head. "I don't think I ever have."

"Do you do this often?"

"Of course not! I must just have a strong constitution."

Ryan's gentle smile beamed back at her from across the bed. "That's not how I'd describe you," she teased. "I feel like I'm carrying you up those stairs every third day!"

Jamie sat down on the bed and gently trailed the tips of her fingers down Ryan's arm, starting at her shoulder and continuing on to her fingertips. "Lucky for me that my best friend is stronger than Atlas, huh?"

Idly watching her friend's fingers meander down her arm, Ryan reminded her, "You're always unconscious. You don't hear me gasping for breath by the third stair."

"Not a chance, Buffy," she admonished her with a playful tweak of her nose. "You've got muscles for days."

"I've also got an eight o'clock class that I can't be late for," Ryan reminded her. "Let's get shakin'."

"Hey," Ryan said as she responded to Jamie's page on the following Tuesday. "What's up?"

"My father offered me four tickets to the Warriors tonight. Wanna go and bring a couple of brothers?"

"Ooo, I'd love to," she said. "But I've got a date."

"That's okay," Jamie said, a little disappointed.

"I could ask Tracy to go too, if it's important to you."

But the thought of sharing Ryan's attention made the evening seem much less attractive. "No, she doesn't look like a basketball kind of girl."

"No, she doesn't, does she? Tennis, maybe, or even the LPGA, but probably not basketball."

"That's okay. Maybe I'll call Conor and see if he'd like all four."

"He'd love to have you go too, Jamie," she reminded her. "He thinks you're fine."

"Yeah, he thinks I'm too fine," she admitted with a little chuckle. "I'm having a hard enough time with Jack. Going to a game with Conor probably isn't in my best interests."

"Well, let me give you his pager. I'm sure he'd be happy to take the tickets if you don't want to use them."

"Okay," she said when Ryan had related the number. She knew she should hang up, but she just didn't want to. "Where are you going tonight?"

Ryan laughed. "Tracy's having me over for dinner. But I have a feeling that someone else is doing the cooking. She's not very domestic."

"Where does she live?" Jamie asked, just trying to prolong the contact.

"The Marina. She has a nice little apartment—and no roommates," she added with a deep chuckle.

"The perfect woman," Jamie said, trying to get the image of Ryan and Tracy locked in a passionate embrace out of her mind.

"Yeah, so far so good. It's still too early to tell, but she's pretty special."

"She'd better be. You deserve the best."

"Thanks. I've got to run, but thanks again for the offer. Ask me again, okay?"

"Count on it."

On Thursday afternoon, Jamie went to the gym to get in a little cardio. Ryan was just finishing up her last client of the day. "Hey," she said by way of greeting when she spotted Jamie on the stairclimber.

"What's up?"

"Not much. I just finished for the day."

"Wanna hang around for a few? I could make you dinner?"

"Oh, no can do. I'm going to the opera," she said as she rolled her eyes rather dramatically.

"The opera? I didn't figure you for the type."

"I'm not, but apparently Tracy is. The things we do for love," she said with a shudder as she considered how long the evening would probably be. "I'd rather be eating your delicious food, but I've got to make some sacrifices I suppose."

"Well, have fun," Jamie said in a much lighter tone than she truly felt.

"You okay?" Ryan asked as she came closer and gave her a penetrating gaze.

"Fine! Just trying to keep up a conversation when I'm laboring on this machine," she said, slightly out of breath.

"Okay, take it easy, buddy," Ryan said as she gave her a sweet smile and took off for her date.

"I liked her better when she was a slut," Jamie grumbled to no one in particular.

Chapter Eleven

She's turned you down twice. Twice ... in a week. Of all the times you've asked to see her, she's turned you down four or five times. Total! Don't be such a baby. She has a girlfriend now. She can't be sitting by the phone waiting for your call. Tracy is everything that you say you want for her. She's smart, she's sweet, and she's very funny. Ryan seems awfully cute with her. Do you want her to be happy or not?

At least Tracy is going home to visit her parents for a couple of weeks during winter break, she thought. *That's nice ... very generous of you. Do you think Ryan would wish the same for you? She's been totally supportive of your relationship. Now you have to do the same for her.*

She knew that her conscience was correct but she really didn't want to share Ryan with another woman. But her honest reaction made her feel ashamed of herself. *Do you really want Ryan to be fulfilled, or do you just want her to be available to you when you call? You can't have it both ways. Either be her friend or admit that you're just using her to satisfy your own needs!*

After class on Friday, Ryan popped over and asked, "What's the earliest you can be free today?"

"Ahh, I'm free after two, why?"

"Let's have some fun before you have to go down to Palo Alto. I thought we could take our workout outdoors for a change of pace."

"Okay," Jamie said cautiously. "Where should we go?"

"Let's meet at the football stadium at two-fifteen. But first let's get some juice. I've gotta tell you all about this opera thing!"

At two-fifteen sharp, Ryan climbed out of the small set of bleachers next to the track, and jogged over to meet her friend. "Been waiting long?" Jamie asked, jogging to meet her halfway.

"Nope. Just got here."

She carried a small nylon gym bag that Jamie eyed suspiciously. "We're gonna duplicate our workout with the things you have in that little bag?" Jamie pointed at the kelly green bag that read, *Lady Dons*. "And what in the heck is a Lady Don?"

"Oh," Ryan said rather absently, "That's my old school, U.S.F. And to answer your question, yes, we can duplicate your workout with even less than I have in here. I'm gonna work too, and I bet I use less of this stuff than you do."

"Okay, Ms. Magic, let's see what you've got."

"First, let's do some warm-ups. Since it's cool out we need to make sure we get loose before we try anything strenuous." Ryan walked over to the infield and sat down on the closely cropped grass. "Let's do some hamstring stretches and loosen up our adductors and abductors." When they were warmed up to Ryan's satisfaction she suggested, "Let's jog a little to get our blood moving." The track was completely deserted on this cool, but sunny afternoon since it was too early in the season for the track or field athletes to be working outdoors. They moved together briskly down the brick red, pebbled, rubberized surface, increasing their pace slightly after the first quarter mile. Soon they were sufficiently warm, but Jamie was already a little winded.

"Wow," she said. "I've never run on a real track before. You move so easily on that surface!"

"Yeah, this surface is pretty new. They're always coming up with something better in the lab. When you put on a pair of track spikes, you can really fly on this."

"Have you run track?"

"Yeah, I fooled around with it in high school. I liked it pretty well, but team sports have always been my favorites."

"I bet you were fast," Jamie said, looking at her friend's lean, lithe form.

"Good guess. I was pretty quick," she said with a proud grin.

"Showoff," Jamie slapped her on the stomach.

"Wanna see me in action? I'll challenge you to a little race." Her waggling eyebrows attested to her confidence in her abilities. Jamie knew that no matter how the race was structured she'd lose, but she was interested to see her friend perform.

"Okay, how am I going to be humiliated?"

"You're not gonna be humiliated. I'll give you a very, very big advantage." Ryan walked over to her bag and extracted a well-worn pair of spikes. She sat down on the infield and quickly laced them up, then jumped up and down a few times to settle them on her feet.

"You've even got the right shoes!"

"Yeah, but I'll need them," Ryan assured her. "I'll probably break my neck as it is. Don't make it harder for me."

"Break your neck?"

"Yeah, you're going to run the track, but I'm going to do the hurdles," Ryan said as she pointed at the low hurdles set up around the track.

"When was the last time you did this?"

"Uhm, seven years ago, I guess."

"Are you nuts? You'd better practice or something before we do this for real!"

"Nah, I'll be fine," Ryan said her. "It's really not that hard. Besides, I'm a couple of inches taller than I was the last time I did this. My crotch is even higher off the ground." She said this with that terribly adorable crooked grin that Jamie had discovered that she was both addicted to and powerless to refuse.

"Do you have your health insurance card on you?" the blonde asked as they walked over to the starting line.

"Not to worry," Ryan said. "I've fallen dozens of times and lived to tell the tale." They stood together on the bright track, Jamie shooting worried glances at her friend. "They've got the hurdles set up for the 440," Ryan said. "So let's run a 440 meter sprint. You run on the outside here," she pointed at the lane next to the hurdles. She got down in a modified sprinters crouch and asked, "Ready?"

"I guess so," Jamie replied, truly reluctant to encourage her daredevil friend.

"You call the start."

"Ready … set … go!" And they were off, flying down the track as fast as their legs would take them. Jamie was concentrating so hard on her own race that she didn't even pay attention to Ryan. She heard several of the hurdles fall to the ground, and she shot a quick glance over when the first hit, but Ryan seemed fine, so she focused again and gave it her all. She dug into the track for any extra speed she could get, but she saw Ryan's dark blue clad body streak by her about five meters from the finish line.

"Excellent!" Ryan's voice rang out as she continued on for another twenty-five meters to cool down.

"But I didn't get to see anything!" Jamie said. "Show me how you do that!"

Ryan bent over and placed her hands on her knees and sucked in a few deep breaths. "Boy, I really had to haul ass to take you. You're pretty quick yourself, you little sand bagger!"

"Yeah, I'm sure I was a real threat," she laughed, secretly proud that she had at least made Ryan go all out.

After they got their wind back, Ryan stripped out of her sweats, revealing a pair of shiny, electric-blue, Lycra leggings and a skintight, white nylon, tank top. "If I'm gonna do that again I need to cool down."

Walking back to the start, she explained, "Hurdles are more about timing than anything else. It's really not that hard to stick one leg out and tuck the other one up. But you have to practice a lot to be able to always start with the same foot and keep your stride length the same. You try to take the same number of steps between each hurdle, and that's impossible to do if you vary your stride too much."

"That makes sense. I didn't realize that timing would be so important. It looks like the hard part is getting that leg up."

"Well, it takes a while to build up your legs when you're a kid. That's actually how I got my big thighs," Ryan said as she slapped her powerful quads. "You've got to have strong muscles to be able to sprint and pop that leg out."

"Show me how you do it."

"Okay," Ryan said as she got into position. "I start on my left leg. I take twelve steps between each hurdle, which is kind of a lot. I used to use ten steps, but I pulled my hamstrings a lot. So I shortened up my stride and adopted the twelve step routine. It didn't slow me down much, but it sure helped with the injuries." She leaned over and squatted down a bit before she took off, moving slowly this time so she could explain what she was doing.

She counted her steps aloud, and when she reached eleven she called out, "Watch!" as her left leg shot out straight in front of her and her right leg tucked up just like a gazelle's. She leaned in to the hurdle a little bit as she went over, almost touching her chest with her thigh. Rather than go on to the next hurdle, she made a half circle and came back to stand by Jamie. "Get it?"

"Yeah. When my father took me to Africa we saw gazelles in the wild. I swear that their back legs look just like yours."

"I'm sure they're more graceful. But thanks for the compliment."

"Will you do the whole thing for me again?" Jamie asked. "I'd really like to see you."

"Sure. But you might have to carry me home."

"Doubtful," Jamie said, watching her friend trot back over to the start. Ryan adopted her most focused gaze. Jamie could almost see the world fading from her friend's deep blue eyes. Her face became a mask of concentration, and after a few seconds she nodded briefly and took off. Now that she knew the drill, Jamie counted with her and smiled to herself as she watched her friend make exactly twelve strides between each hurdle, always starting with her left foot and always sticking that same leg out to take the hurdle. She noticed that this time Ryan knocked down every single hurdle, and she thought, *She must be a little rusty. Not that she shouldn't be after seven years!*

When Ryan came jogging back, winded but very happy, Jamie enthusiastically complimented her. "You were great!"

"Yeah, it felt pretty smooth," she admitted with a satisfied grin. "And I did a great job on the hurdles if I do say so myself."

"But … you knocked them over."

"I know," she replied with her crooked grin. "I tried to, silly. The lower you go, the less time you waste. You try to be so low that your trailing foot just ticks the hurdle enough to knock it down, but not so low that you catch your foot."

"Well, then you did even better than I thought!" she laughed as she wrapped her arm around Ryan and gave her a squeeze. "Get that sweatshirt back on, young lady. You're drenched!"

After she had dried off and put her regular shoes back on, Ryan produced several lengths of rubber tubing in various colors. The attached handles made them look like a short, rubber jump rope. "What are those?" Jamie asked as she examined one length.

"These are your weights."

"These little things? How can they duplicate what we do at the gym?"

"Oh, you'd be surprised," Ryan said. "I believe this is leg day?"

"Yep."

"Okay. On your back," she ordered producing a very thin foam pad for Jamie to lie on. Once she was down, Ryan showed her how to use the bands to provide resistance to her quads. She had her using the strongest band, and after ten reps of the exercise Jamie's legs dropped to the ground and she moaned, "Enough!"

"Not so easy, is it?" Ryan laughed. "I'll knock you down one level for your next set."

"You'd better, if you want me to do more than four reps! That was killer!"

"Well, it isn't just the tension in the band. When you use these you don't have the machine guiding you. Every bit of force and energy has to come solely from you, and that takes a lot more effort."

"I'll say," she agreed as she started her next set with the lighter tubing.

The next exercise called for her to tie one of the ends around each ankle and slowly pull one leg away while balancing on one foot. This motion also had her calling for mercy after only nine reps. "Geez! Am I that weak?"

"Not at all. This is much harder than what you're used to. This makes you use your legs to hold your balance at the same time, and that makes it very tough. But it's important that your balance be very good, especially for a long bike ride. I work on my balance all the time."

"With these?" Jamie asked.

"Sometimes, but I've got lots of things I do to keep myself entertained."

"Show me some of them if you can."

"Well," she said, digging into her bag. "I jump rope sometimes That helps a lot." She produced a professional quality jump rope with wooden handles and little ball bearings in them to allow the rope to turn smoothly. She began to slowly jump, increasing her speed gradually until the rope was just a blur. When she was at full speed, she lifted one leg slightly and jumped on one foot alone. "I try to jump on each leg for ten minutes or so," she said as she proceeded to do just that while Jamie did another set of her own exercises.

"God, doesn't that hurt?" Jamie finally asked with a grimace.

"It starts to burn a bit, but it's not too bad." When she was finished, she got a little gleam in her eye and said, "Another thing I do is run up and down the stadium."

"I can see that would stress your legs, but how does that help balance?"

"Watch," she said with a grin. She took off and started to run not up and down the steps, as Jamie expected, but down the narrow metal seats. The slick benches were spaced significantly further apart than the stairs, and their surface didn't allow for much traction. Once Ryan started flying down the steep seats it was obvious that her balance was the only thing that kept her from coming down headfirst. After she had completed three loops she started to run across the narrow benches. Each bench was only about a foot wide, but she flew across the surface like it was an airport runway. When she reached the end of a section she leapt across the aisle to the next section, never touching down on the concrete steps. The fact that she chose the uppermost bench didn't in any way relieve the knot in Jamie's stomach as she watched her dart around the stadium. When she returned to the section that she started at, she once again flew down the seats, completely at ease. Jamie was waiting for her at the bottom, wide eyed with mouth agape.

"You amaze me," she said solemnly.

Even the normally indefatigable Ryan O'Flaherty needed a breather after that demonstration. She took the exercise pad and spread it out on the infield, and then she stretched out on it like she was sunning herself at the beach. Ten minutes of rest found her ready for more. "Now what?"

"Uhm … I think I need an exercise for my calves, and then I'm done. Whatcha got?"

"Hmm, I can think of a few," Ryan said. "But the easiest is just to do calf raises. You can use the first bench here in the bleachers."

"I normally do calf raises with weight," Jamie reminded her. "I'm up to forty-five pounds now."

"We can duplicate that," Ryan said. "Actually, I could sit on your shoulders and give you a real workout." Her eyes were shining in the late afternoon sun, and her bronzed skin seemed to glow in the fading light. Jamie's appreciative eyes took her in and just for a moment she thought that having Ryan atop her was a terribly good idea. But her conscious mind reminded her that Ryan outweighed her by a lot, so it was best that she refuse.

She gave her friend a smile and got up to do her calf raises. Ryan assisted by placing her hands on her shoulders and pressing down, actually doing a good job of duplicating the feel of a fifty-pound weight on the machine. "How did you figure out all of these ways to exercise without equipment?" Jamie asked after she'd completed her three sets.

Ryan thought about that for a minute. "I don't really plan this stuff," she admitted. "But I was such an active kid that I was in fabulous shape just from playing. As I got older and started to work out with equipment I found that the structure would bore me after a while. One day it dawned on me that I was in better shape from playing than I was from working out. So I decided to stay childish!"

"Why not play all the time?"

"Well, it's easier to chart my progress in the gym, and sometimes it's too hot or wet to be outside for long. But I'd say I play once or twice a week through most of the year. I run sprints on the beach with Duffy, or I push Caitlin around in her stroller. Just simple things."

"I feel like I'm done, how about you?"

"I can do more if you don't mind hanging around."

"Mind? It's absorbing to watch you. What else do you want to do?"

"I need to work on my core balance a little, and I haven't done anything for my upper body balance."

"Upper body balance? What's that?"

"I work on keeping my balance no matter what plane I'm on. I've got an exercise I haven't done in a while that would let me show off a little," she said with a childlike grin. "Wanna see?"

"Absolutely."

"Okay, I need something about waist high that I can curl my fingers around." It was about a half hour from dusk, and she squinted into the bright light, finally finding what she was looking for. They strolled over to where trucks could drive in and out of the complex. A series of concrete filled, yellow metal sleeves were locked in place vertically across the entryway. Each was about twelve inches in diameter and very sturdy looking. It was clear that they were removable when a truck needed to enter, but they were very stable in their locked positions.

Ryan grabbed one with both hands and gave it a very firm yank. It didn't budge an inch since it was obviously sunk into the ground several feet. "This one's perfect," she declared as she took off her sweatshirt again. "I need to loosen up my biceps a little first." She hit the ground and did about twenty-five quick push-ups. "Here goes nothing," she said as she backed up about ten yards and took off in a brisk trot. Jamie's eyes grew wide as Ryan neared the post. *What in the hell is she going to do?* She had her answer a moment later as Ryan slapped her hands down on the post and executed a perfect vault, landing neatly on her flexed legs, adding a quick little hop to maintain her balance. "Okay, I think I'm ready."

When she heard no response, she turned to find Jamie once again slack jawed. "You okay over there?" she asked with a chuckle.

"That was the warm up? My God, what's the exercise?"

One waggling eyebrow was Ryan's only response. She walked back to the post and faced it, then placed both of her hands flat on the top. The heels of her hands were touching and her fingers were spread wide, obviously to give her a strong platform. A very quick movement flexed her biceps, and in the next instant her feet were off the ground and she was holding herself parallel to the earth, held up by her powerful upper arms . Her arms straightened slowly, and she rotated into a handstand. Now she was absolutely perpendicular to the ground, her entire body braced on her two hands.

Jamie was awestruck, unable to do anything but watch in wonder as her friend performed. After a few moments in the vertical position Ryan did a few push ups, obviously just showing off. Now she bent her body once more, this time rotating until her arms were rigid and her body was again horizontal. After holding the position for a few seconds, she removed one of her hands and held up her entire body by one powerful arm. She held the position for a few seconds, although Jamie could see the immense strain the move was putting on her shaky arm. Then she switched arms and held the position for an even longer time with her left arm. She placed both hands back onto the post and pushed up forcefully, landing next to it with another little hop. Just for effect, she stood ramrod straight and affixed a very theatrical smile onto her face, raised her right arm and waved dramatically as she turned slowly, acknowledging the massive crowd that filled the stadium to watch her record setting performance.

Jamie jogged the few feet that separated them and gazed up at her beaming friend. "Are you sure that both of your parents are humans? 'Cause that wasn't of this world!"

"Sure it is. It's pretty basic gymnastics."

"I took gymnastics, buddy, and I never got close to doing anything like that! I spent my years on the damn balance beam!"

"Yeah, well I took gymnastics for boys," she said proudly. "You weren't in the cool class."

"You took boys gymnastics?"

"Yep. I thought it was cool when I saw it in the Olympics. Brendan took me down to sign me up. It was pretty funny," she said as she laughed in remembrance. "He practically had to fight the guy to get him to let me in, but after they gave me a few tests they pretty readily agreed."

"I just bet they did," Jamie smirked.

Jamie was still smiling at her friend's theatrics while they walked back across the stadium. Something caught Ryan's eye as they moved along and she zipped over to the interior of the stadium and yelled, "Hey, Jamie, come over here."

With a smile and a small shake of her head she trotted over to the underside of the stadium. Near the end zone of the football field, the school had erected relatively modern bleachers to make the stadium homier for the normally small crowds that Cal drew for football. The back of the bleachers was a series of interconnecting metal supports that ran through the underside like a maze. Ryan was staring at the interlocking braces with a very studious look on her face. "Doesn't this remind you of a great big jungle gym?"

"Ahh, yeah, I guess it does," she admitted. "Boy, I used to like the one we had at a park near our house. But they decided that too many kids got hurt on it so they removed it, and the slide, and the swings, and replaced them with a really lame bunch of horses on springs. I never wanted to go again," she said somewhat wistfully.

"Well, you've got to admit that they can be a little dangerous," Ryan said with a gleam in her eye. "Especially when they're really, really tall." She said her last sentence while leaping to her full reach and grabbing one of the supports with both of her hands. She was only off the ground about eighteen inches, but she looked pretty comical, nonetheless.

"Okay, Tarzana, let's go."

"Go? You want to go?" Ryan said with an even bigger gleam. "Race you to the other end!" she cried as she started to propel herself along the undercarriage of the structure. Jamie not only didn't race her, she was stuck in place as she stared at her daredevil friend. Ryan was motoring at an unbelievable clip, but she had to follow the supports to get where she was going. In order to do so, she climbed higher and higher until she was at the very top of the very tall structure, dangling like a chimp. A wildly laughing chimp that is, who was having the time of her life.

Jamie started to jog just to keep up, but Ryan was moving much too fast for her. She looked like some breed of beautiful simian as she swung up and down the supports, gracefully propelling herself along with ease. She was standing on the ground, looking rather bored when her panting friend caught up to her moments later. "Are you insane?" she shrieked as she ran up and slapped Ryan hard on the chest with both of her open hands.

"You said you wanted to go," she said innocently, blinking down at her. "I assumed you wanted to go fast."

"I can't imagine what I'd say to your father if you'd fallen!"

"You could have said, 'You were finally right, Martin. She did fall and break her neck!'"

They walked the rest of the way in silence, with Jamie reflecting on all that she had seen. "Do you know that you can do things like that?" she finally asked with a very thoughtful look on her face.

"What do you mean?"

"I guess I want to know if you're certain that you can do something dangerous before you try it."

"Oh, heck no," Ryan admitted. "Where's the fun in that?"

"Ryan!" she said as she stopped and grabbed onto the back of her tank top. "You mean to tell me that you might have not been able to do that safely, but you tried it anyway?"

"Well, yeah. That's what makes it fun. I mean, I know I'm strong, and that my grip is really good. I know I'm flexible, and that I've got good balance. There's no reason to assume I can't do something like that, so I try it. Once I get into a situation, I'm certainly not going to back out, so I have to figure out a way to finish without breaking my neck. But I've never done that particular thing before, and if I had I probably wouldn't be interested in trying it again. Once I've done something it loses its allure," she admitted with a toothy grin.

Like your women, Jamie thought with an internal smirk as she stole another glance at the grinning, sweaty, gorgeous hunk of woman that blithely strolled along beside her.

When they reached their gear, Ryan checked the position of the sun. "Time to go, pal."

"I don't wanna go," Jamie pouted. "I'm having too much fun!"

"Come on." Ryan bent to pick up her keys and her gym bag.

Jamie was too quick for her, and her hand snaked out and grabbed the keys. "You can't leave without your bike!" she declared defiantly as she dangled them in front of Ryan's darting eyes.

One quick swipe of Ryan's left hand left her grasping nothing but air as Jamie laughed wildly and took off. Ryan joined her laugh and doggedly began to pursue her. In reality she could have caught the smaller, slower woman within three strides. But Ryan felt guilty about turning down her last two invitations, and she had planned this afternoon to give them a chance to reconnect and have fun. She had a date with Tracy, but it wasn't for another two hours so she had plenty of time to play. *Jamie seems so childlike and free*, she thought. *She hasn't been this way very often lately. We've got to get outside and play more. She really needs some cheering up on a routine basis, given how things are going with Jack.* So even though she was happy to be forced into staying longer, she couldn't *let* Jamie win—she couldn't *let* anybody win.

Jamie darted around the infield, using various track paraphernalia as a shield to keep Ryan away. She scurried around hurdles, the long jump pit, even the huge cushion that the pole-vaulters landed on. But Ryan was dangerously close, never more than two body lengths away, no matter what Jamie tried. About twenty-five yards away, she saw what she hoped would be her salvation. A large, bright blue, square cushion that protected the high jumpers was beckoning to her. She latched onto an idea and scampered aboard, crawling frantically on all fours just before Ryan grabbed her feet. The cushion stood about four feet high, clearly no barrier for her chimp-like pursuer. But as Jamie coyly reminded her, "Wherever you start to climb, I can run to the other side and jump down before you get up!"

Ryan pursed her lips and reviewed the situation. Jamie did have a point, her analytical mind agreed. It wouldn't do to just try to climb aboard. She needed to get up there, but not from the ground. A sly smile crossed her lips and Jamie looked around suspiciously, recognizing the gleam in those deep blue eyes. "There's more than one way to skin a cat," Ryan declared as she walked back to her gym bag at a leisurely pace and sat down to lace her spikes up again. When she was finished, she walked back to the cushion and turned her back to it as she appeared to be measuring off a distance in her head. She was obviously satisfied because she turned and started to run, gaining speed as she approached the bag. Jamie didn't try to run because she still didn't know what Ryan was going to do—she just stood stock still and watched in amazement as Ryan continued to barrel towards her.

When her momentum was satisfactory, she actually slowed down appreciably and turned her back just as she flexed her knees deeply and propelled herself into the air, landing rather forcefully and inelegantly onto the cushion. Her momentum carried her on her back quite a few feet across the surface, but she eventually skidded to a halt right at Jamie's feet.

She looked up at her with dancing blue eyes and put on her sexiest smile, saying, "Hi there."

"Yikes!" Jamie cried and tried to run. But this time Ryan's cat-like reflexes halted her progress abruptly. The brunette firmly grasped an ankle, and Jamie crashed into the cushion face first. She quickly rolled onto her back just as Ryan began to crawl up her body like a panther, first her right hand, then her left knee, left hand, right knee. Then she hovered over the supine woman, staring at her intently while she said, "I believe you have something of mine?"

"Can't have it!" Jamie insisted, still not willing to give up. In an impetuous move, she took the keys and shoved them into her cleavage, safe within her tight, navy blue, sports bra.

"That isn't much of a barrier," Ryan purred, locking eyes with her prey. She was panting from the exertion of her leap, and the smaller woman could actually watch the progress of a few individual drops of sweat as they rolled down her hairline, past her strong jaw, down her chin and onto her own chest.

"No, but I fight dirty," Jamie vowed. "When you reach for the keys, I've got two hands free to cause all sorts of mayhem." Her misty green eyes had grown fiery in the last rays of sunlight, and Ryan noticed that she could see flecks of gold and amber and even a bit of orange in the shining orbs. She shook her head, spattering Jamie with drops of sweat as she did. "Hey, cut that out!"

"Hmm, that's an idea," Ryan mused aloud. "When my brothers would have me pinned, they'd invariably spit in my face to gross me out enough to give up whatever prize I had. I bet that would work with you, too."

Jamie gave her a slightly suspicious gaze, but she didn't think Ryan had the nerve to spit on her.

"Nah, that's too easy," she finally decided, causing Jamie to let out the breath she didn't know she had been holding. "But this might work," she said as she quickly spread her hands out to the sides, and clamped vise-like grips on each of her captive's wrists. "That'll keep you docile," she mused, still surveying her options.

Jamie felt a deep sigh leave her chest as she looked up at the gorgeous woman holding her prisoner. *I've been in worse situations,* she decided, watching the deep blue eyes dart around in thought. "How does it help you to have both of my hands if you have to use both of yours to hold 'em down?" As soon as the words were out of her mouth she knew she had made a fatal tactical error. Almost before the end of the sentence, Ryan pushed Jamie's hands together, placing one atop the other. Her much larger, and stronger, left hand easily grasped both of Jamie's wrists, holding them above her head firmly.

"Got any more bright ideas?" Ryan growled as she wiggled her free right hand directly in front of Jamie's face. That determined hand moved slowly toward her target, a fiendish look in her eyes that showed she wasn't afraid to claim her prize.

"You wouldn't dare," Jamie croaked out nervously.

Ryan leaned down until their noses were touching. Her wet skin smelled like the earth: like rich, warm soil, just turned over after the spring rains. Jamie had never smelled another person who shared the rich scent. It was intoxicating, and she wanted to lie there beneath the weight of her friend and breathe in that heady aroma. Ryan's voice startled her back into her senses. "I never … ever … ever refuse a dare." Her right hand was less than an inch from Jamie's heaving chest, and the captive knew that she had to put a stop to this. But something deep inside wanted Ryan's hand to snake inside her bra and stay there for a very, very long time. Her conscience finally woke up and forced her to utter the only appropriate response. "Uncle!"

A few minutes later, they were standing in the deep dusk, once again clad in their sweats. "I had a fantastic time today, Ryan."

"I had a great time, myself," Ryan said, grinning. "But that's not a surprise when I'm with you." She raised her left hand and touched Jamie lightly on the nose, giving her an affectionate smile to go with it. "You bring out my wild side."

"I think you do all right bringing it out on your own," she scoffed, but secretly hoped that Ryan's statement was true.

She leaned in for a hug, but Ryan complained, "I'm all sweaty. I must smell terrible."

Jamie didn't argue with her, but ignored the warning. She held her in a fierce embrace for a few moments, wishing to imprint that distinctive scent onto her memory forever.

Christmas break was looming ahead of Jamie like a trip to the slaughterhouse. Her dread was mostly due to the fact that she was planning on spending the nearly four-week break at her parent's home. Intense anxiety would have been an appropriate term for her mental state as she prepared for the visit. The Thanksgiving visit had gone so poorly that she couldn't help but assume this one would be worse, given that Thanksgiving had only been four days.

Her last final was on December 17th, and school didn't start again until January 19th. Her only planned respite was a short visit to Ryan's on Christmas Eve afternoon. She wasn't sure how she was going to explain that little trip, but she was going to go no matter what.

She had also decided that she was going to meet Ryan at the gym for their three afternoon weekly meetings. Ryan had offered to do them earlier in the day, but Jamie wanted an excuse to hang around to avoid rush hour, so she kept their normal four o'clock time.

It just kills me that Ryan's going to be alone for most of the time, and I won't be able to spend evenings with her, she groused to herself when they met for their last workout before the break. "So what do you have planned for your time off?" she asked as their hour wound down.

"Not a lot, thankfully. I've got to do some things around the house that I've been putting off, but I think I'll spend most of my time with Caitlin. She's really turning into a little person now. Every time I see her she's picked up something new."

"Wanna have dinner tonight?" Jamie asked hesitantly, truly not wanting to be rebuffed.

Ryan gave her a luminous grin as she said, "I can't think of a better way to start my winter break!"

Jamie drove down to Hillsborough on Thursday evening, and was pleased to learn that Marta had prepared a lovely meal for her homecoming. Jamie sat in the kitchen with the cook for a long while talking about school and the training she was doing for the ride. Marta was fascinated by the changes in her body, and she teased her about her new muscles and asked if she could pick Jack up. Jamie realized after a while that Marta was the only one in the house who had asked her a personal question.

They ate dinner after her father arrived home from work. It was late, around eight-fifteen and dinner was a bit overdone, but the meal was still relatively pleasant. Even though they hadn't resolved the issue that caused it, the tension between Jim and Jamie seemed to be gone. He was in a very good mood, having just come from his office Christmas Party, always seeming to enjoy spending a few hours socializing with the other attorneys. A much more elaborate party was scheduled for the next week for the entire firm, this small event being just for the partners and their spouses. She wondered briefly why her mother hadn't gone into the city for the affair, but she realized that her mother only attended large parties—where her absence would be questioned.

During dinner, Jim talked about the little party and how enjoyable it was to get to know some of the younger partners. "I did have to stop and wonder at one point, though. One of those young men brought another man to the party. What on earth do you think came over him?" he directed his question at his wife.

"I'm sure I don't know, dear." Her voice was flat, and she didn't even look up from her plate.

"They seem to have taken leave of their senses," he continued. "Why can't they realize how uncomfortable that sort of display makes everyone else?"

Jamie knew that her color was rising, but this was the first evening of a thirty-two-day stay and she knew she couldn't afford to blow up now. She fought with every bit of her self-control to refrain from speaking.

"I guess you're used to that type of thing at Berkeley, Jamie," he said as he regarded his daughter. "But it just isn't done in the business world."

Jamie stared at her soup until she could see the individual molecules bumping into one another. She fought for composure before she finally replied, "I need some more spice in my soup. Does anyone else?" She rose from the table, soup bowl held by a shaking hand.

Once in the kitchen, she leaned against the door, willing her knees to stop shaking. Marta came over to see what was wrong, but Jamie just shook her head and went to the sink for a glass of water. "Marta, could you please get me a small glass of Scotch?" When Marta returned, Jamie thanked her and downed the two fingers of amber liquid in one burning gulp. "Thank you," she politely replied as she stepped back into the dining room, leaving the cook staring at her in disbelief.

On Christmas Eve, Jamie spent most of the day with Jack. He studied all morning, but after lunch he took an hour break and convinced her to make love. As she got in the shower after their lovemaking, she devised her plan. She had called Ryan earlier, and had been issued a blanket invitation to come any time and stay as long as she liked. A number of cousins and aunts and uncles would be there, and most of them were going to midnight Mass.

Jamie put her casual clothes back on and announced, "I'm going to Berkeley to take care of a few things. Would you mind just meeting me at church before the service?"

'Gee, Jamie, that's awfully late."

"I know, honey, but there are a couple of little things that didn't arrive before I left. I want to go to my house and wrap them. Then I need to go shopping for one teeny thing for my outfit. Rather than come back here I thought I could just go home and take a nap before Mass. I want to be rested for the service tonight," she batted her eyes. *Or: I'm leaving now so I can spend as much time with Ryan as possible, and I like her family so much better than mine. One of these two stories is the truth. Oops, wrong choice,* she thought when he gamely agreed.

Well, things are really going well. I have to drink Scotch to get through dinner with my parents, and I'm making up bold-faced lies to avoid being with Jack all day. Have yourself a Merry Fucking Christmas!

Nonetheless, she dashed home and dressed carefully. She donned a pure white, heavy silk jacquard blouse, embroidered with an Asian inspired design. The banded collar was held together by a tiny black pearl button. A trim, black velvet, square-cut vest just brushed the waistband of her black velvet pleated slacks, and black velvet slippers covered her feet. By five o'clock she was satisfied with her look, and on her way. She called Ryan from her car to inquire if she needed anything, laughing at her wry response, "Yeah, a bigger house or fewer relatives."

Ryan answered the door, looking lovelier than Jamie had ever seen her. Her black hair was combed straight back, held off her face by a black velvet headband. She wore a crimson-colored angora turtleneck sweater that gently hugged her smooth curves. Simple pearl earrings graced the ears that Jamie had never noticed were pierced, and a gold chain hung just above the swell of her breasts. Black silk pants covered her long, shapely legs, and simple black leather shoes completed the ensemble. "Wow!" was all that Jamie could get out.

"Wow, yourself," Ryan said as she ran her blue eyes up and down Jamie's small form. "You look positively lovely," she said. "C'mon in and let the men pretend not to stare at you." When she saw Conor making a beeline for them she whispered, "All except one who has no shame, of course."

Conor complimented Jamie until she blushed to the roots of her hair. He looked fabulous also, wearing a well-made, navy blue, double-breasted suit with a crisp white shirt and a green and red rep tie. His hair looked jet black and very shiny, as it was neatly combed for a change. "Are you going to stay and go to Mass with us?"

"No, I can't. I'm meeting my fiancé for services at my Grandfather's church."

"Your grandfather's a minister?"

"Actually, he's a priest." When she saw the shocked look on his face she added, "Episcopal."

"Oh, I thought maybe I'd been away from church too long and I missed something important," he laughed.

Maeve came up behind him at that moment and stated, "You have been away from church too long, sweetheart. The last time I saw you there was Easter."

Ryan took Jamie by the arm and whispered, "Let's get out of here before she starts on me." They squeezed through the mass of relatives until Ryan spied her prize. She snatched Caitlin from her Aunt Peggy and eventually found the path to her room.

Duffy followed them down the stairs, eagerly sniffing at the bundle in Ryan's arms. When they got downstairs, she sat down on the bed and allowed Duffy to lick the baby's giggling face clean.

"Duffy sure is good with her," Jamie observed. "He seems to know he has to be very gentle."

"Yeah, he loves kids more than I do. Luckily Caitlin is crazy about him too," she replied as the big dog started to clean the tiny hands one at a time. "Okay Duff, you've had enough baby kissing." She scooped the baby off her lap and placed her over her shoulder. She went to her dresser and took out a clean T-shirt, which she placed over her shoulder and chest. "Can't be too careful," she said from experience. "She just had dinner, and there's always a chance of rejection."

They all sat on the bed as Ryan propped the baby up against her legs. "So what have you been up to this week?" Jamie asked.

"Not a lot during the week but I had a great weekend!"

"What did you do?"

"Conor has a friend with a condo up near Tahoe and we went up to ski and snowboard for the weekend. It was absolutely fantastic," she said with a very happy grin covering her lovely face.

"I can't imagine what a hellion you must be on the slopes," Jamie said. "Do you ski a lot?"

"Every chance I get. If I had just a little less work ethic I could really be a ski bum."

"That would be a pretty sweet job for you. You could live in Aspen or St. Moritz, and have the wealthy women support you in the style you deserve."

"Hmm, maybe this work ethic thing isn't such a good idea," she purred as she considered the suggestion. "Well, that's enough about me. I really want to know how it's going for you so far."

Jamie considered how much to reveal, finally deciding that she needed to talk. "I had to chug a glass of Scotch to get through dinner one night, and I told Jack a blatant lie today. All in all, not great."

Ryan thought about this for a moment. "Did you use to enjoy being with your family? Or is this a new development?"

Jamie knew the answer, but was embarrassed to admit it. "I didn't mind before because I thought that was what families were supposed to be like. But after spending time with you and your family, I see how stilted and formal mine is. I swear, Ryan, your family shows much more interest in me than my own does."

Ryan smiled at her sympathetically. "We love having you here, Jamie. I think of you as a part of my family. You're always welcome." She shook her head briefly, "I feel sorry for your parents. They don't know what a treasure they have in you."

As she blushed shyly at the compliment, Jamie replied, "In their defense, it's me who's changed. I want more from them, and I want more from Jack. In a way it's a bit unfair of me, I'm the one who's changed the rules."

"It's never unfair to expect the people closest to you to love and honor and cherish you." She got up from the bed and went to her dresser. "I certainly do." She reached out and handed her friend a small package.

Jamie looked up, a wide smile lighting up her whole face. "I really love getting presents, you know. But I feel the time I spend with you is a gift. I don't need anything tangible to know how you feel about our friendship." After a pause, she added with a giggle, "But I still love presents."

She carefully removed the red and green striped paper from the little box. Inside was a small, black leather book, about the size of a paperback. She opened the pages to find a small map of each of the major bike routes in the Bay Area. The maps had obviously been meticulously removed from another book, and each one was carefully glued to a strong piece of heavy white paper. Underneath each map was a legend in Ryan's hand, detailing the options for each route, and the difficulty of each. On the page opposite each map was a space for Jamie to mark the date she completed the ride, what the weather was like, and how she felt during the ride. Every fourth or fifth page carried a small handwritten message meant to inspire or motivate. Some were funny, some spiritual, and some practical. Jamie was touched beyond words at the time and effort that Ryan had obviously expended in making this journal. She fought back a tear as she wrapped her arms around her friend in silence. After a moment she simply whispered, "Thank you."

After Jamie pulled back, Ryan gave her a grin, "I'm glad you like it." After a moment she added, "You know I don't think I tell you enough how much it means to me that you're doing this ride. I know that AIDS hasn't had a big impact on your life, and I appreciate how willing you were to take this on. I think part of the reason you agreed was because you knew it was important to me. I really thank you for that."

"That's the biggest reason I agreed to do it. I knew that you wouldn't give so much of your time to something that wasn't worthwhile."

Caitlin was getting tired of being confined to the bed, so Jamie placed the shirt over her shoulder and picked her up. She carried her around the room, letting her touch all the books and the small items on the shelves. She pointed out the pictures of Ryan and the rest of the family and explained who each person was, even though Caitlin had no idea what she was talking about. Ryan lay back on the bed and watched her friend charm her little cousin. After a while Jamie announced, "I have a gift for you too, Ryan. It's in my purse. Would you mind getting it out?"

Ryan gamely retrieved Jamie's purse and began look through it. She found a card with her name on it and held it up questioningly. "Yes, that's it," Jamie replied.

Ryan sat back down on the bed with a look of anticipation on her face. "I like presents, too," she admitted. She tore open the card, and several pieces of paper fell out and landed on her lap. She began to gather them up as she pulled the card fully out of the envelope. After she had organized all of the papers, she began to look at them carefully, her face lighting up with childlike glee as she read off each ticket. "Oh wow, the Exploratorium, the Children's Museum, Marineland!" she shouted with delight. She came over to Jamie and held up the tickets, "There's two adults and one child for each of these. Where will we ever get a child?" She dangled the tickets in front of the baby and said, "We're going to play, sweetie!"

Jamie laughed at Ryan's obvious delight. "There's a few more in there, sport." Ryan grabbed the envelope, and after a thorough audit, found that Jamie had purchased tickets for nearly every baby-friendly event in the Bay area. Finally she read the card, "Thank you for giving me a second chance at a happy childhood."

Ryan hugged her friend soundly, catching the laughing baby in the embrace for good measure. "This was a terribly thoughtful gift. Caitlin and I thank you very much."

"I've never seen you happier than you are with her. Being around you two is so healing for me. It allows me to experience some of those childhood pleasures that I didn't get to have."

"It really surprises me that you didn't do these things as a kid. I mean," Ryan struggled a bit with her thoughts, "I thought that people with money did all these things, especially for an only child." She blushed a bit, "I just assumed you were spoiled."

"I was spoiled with things," Jamie admitted. "I had every toy and stuffed animal known to mankind. But my father didn't have time to do kid stuff, and my mother wasn't interested. Besides, she thought that kid stuff was a waste of my time. We traveled a lot, and she took me to the symphony and to plays and the opera and great restaurants when I was three and four years old. So it's not that I didn't go places, I just didn't go to kid places."

"Did you enjoy going to plays when you were little?"

Jamie gave her a sardonic look, "You're kidding, right?"

"Didn't you have friends or cousins to do things with?" Ryan continued to probe, unable to believe that Jamie's life had been so barren.

"I don't have very many cousins that we socialize with. My father's oldest sister lives in Indiana, but she doesn't have kids. His other sister lives in Chicago and she has two kids, but we almost never saw them. My mother is an only child, and the maternal side of her extended family just gets together in Rhode Island in the summer. We're not a real close group," she said, stating the obvious. "I didn't start making friends until I was in Montessori school when I was four, and I was never encouraged to have those kids over. I basically played with Marta, our cook, or the maids."

"So you've been a little adult your whole life, haven't you?"

"Yeah, I guess I have."

"Well, Caitlin and I are going to change that pretty darn quick. You'll have regressed to infancy when we get through with you," she said confidently as she put her arm around her friend.

"I have one more thing to give you, but it's not a gift," Jamie said tentatively.

Ryan cocked her head and waited.

Jamie walked back over to her purse and extracted another envelope, as she balanced the baby on her knee. This one wasn't marked and she withdrew a white form and a check. "I was sending in my check for the AIDS Ride because I wanted to make some charitable donations before year-end. I decided to donate $25,000, and it dawned on me that I should make a donation in your name of at least that much. I wouldn't be doing this ride without your support, Ryan. It's become much more to me than an athletic goal. It's helping me to change my life in a fundamental manner. And it's all because of you," she said sincerely. "I know you like to secure your own pledges, but I also know how busy you've been. I just want you to know that if you're running short, you don't have to worry."

Ryan closed her eyes tightly as she struggled to hold back the tears. She bit her lip to control her shaking chin and took in a few deep breaths. Finally, she was able to open her eyes. She gazed at Jamie with her unwavering blue eyes and opened her arms. Jamie walked right into the embrace, cuddling Caitlin between them. Ryan didn't say a word, but she leaned over and kissed each of Jamie's cheeks. She had so much emotion threatening to spill out that she didn't trust herself to say a thing, but she maintained the hug for a very long while, kissing Jamie's head and cheek repeatedly.

The rest of the evening was spent laughing and eating and joking with the whole O'Flaherty clan. Small gifts were given to Caitlin by everyone in attendance, and by the time Jamie was ready to leave, the baby was once again fast asleep in Ryan's arms.

The two friends walked to Jamie's car together. "I think this was the best Christmas I've ever had," Jamie said softly when they reached the little car.

"You made it more special for me than I'll ever be able to say," Ryan replied as she gave her friend a one-armed hug, being careful of the sleeping infant. "If your family gets to be too much, I want you to call me. I've got a lot of free time before school starts, so don't be shy."

"I won't, and thanks again for everything," Jamie said as she pulled the Boxster onto the small quiet street for the short ride to Nob Hill.

On the Wednesday after Christmas, Jamie had to get away for a while. Jack was obviously trying hard, but his attempts at being closer were driving her absolutely crazy. The message that he had gotten was that she didn't like to make meals and clean up alone—so he gamely hung around in the kitchen while she tried to work. But he really was inept, whether through design or inability she wasn't sure. He was in her way so badly that she finally released him to go back to his work. So the pattern returned to their previous one. He studied, she read. He studied, she cooked. He studied, she watched a movie. The routine was getting so monotonous that she wanted to scream. *We never do anything,* she whined to herself. *We don't go out for dinner; we don't even go for walks any more. I know he has a lot on his mind, but I feel like we're setting up a schedule that might never vary. He'll just replace school with work and be just as unavailable to me.*

She realized that the main outside activity they had was brunch and golf at the club. *I've been doing that since I was born. I want some excitement in my life!*

She dialed Ryan's pager, and waited just a few minutes for her call. "Hi, what's up?" Ryan asked cheerfully.

"What's your schedule today?"

"I'm at the gym right now. I've got clients until eleven, then I don't have anything scheduled, except your workout at four. Why, do you want to play?"

"I need to do something fun," she said. "I feel like my life is so routine! If I don't get my blood pumping a little bit I swear I'll go mad!"

"When do you have to be back home?"

"I don't care if I ever go home," she sulked.

"Okay, meet me at my house at eleven-thirty. Dress warmly and wear boots if you have them. We'll go burn the carbon off your sparkplugs."

"You want to take a drive in my car?"

"Nope. Just be there."

At eleven-thirty on the dot, Ryan was sitting on her front porch. She walked over to the Porsche and inspected Jamie's outfit. The blonde was wearing a distressed, brown leather, fleece-lined, bomber jacket, taupe colored turtleneck and faded jeans. As she got out of the car, Ryan nodded approval at her ankle length, brown boots.

Ryan was wearing her usual jeans, a crew-necked, wool, marine blue sweater and her black leather jacket, along with low heeled black boots. She gave Jamie a sly look, "I know just the prescription for boredom. Come with me, little girl."

She led Jamie over to the Harley, and handed her the spare helmet. After her own was secured, she got on and helped her friend hop on. Jamie immediately slid her arms around Ryan's waist and got ready to take off.

Moments later they were heading over to Highway One. Even though she had been on the bike several times, they had never gone very far or very fast, and she found that she loved the excitement of the higher speed. Ryan drove the bike just like she drove a car—going as fast as possible, while being as careful as she could. When traffic slowed, she'd straddle the line between the number one and two lanes and slide right between the stalled cars.

Jamie knew that she should feel some level of fear or trepidation to be so exposed at such a high rate of speed, but she had never felt calmer or safer. Every bit of anxiety left her body as they flew down the highway. She forgot all about her fights with Jack, and her unhappiness with her parents. All she felt was warm and protected and safe. The wind was really quite intense, and she found herself tucking her head down and nestling it into Ryan's broad back. From her little cocoon she truly felt impervious to the outside world. Her world was just Ryan's protective body, the bike thrumming between her legs and the freedom of the open road.

She wasn't at all sure where they were going, but eventually she saw the Golden Gate bridge looming in the distance. They crossed the structure and continued on, staying on Highway One. The scenery was absolutely beautiful at this time of year, and there were very few cars on the road as they passed the forested acres around Muir Woods. They kept going, and eventually the road wound down to Stinson Beach. Jamie had to look up at this point, since the road was so curvy she felt a little sick to her stomach. When they reached the sea, Ryan pulled the bike off the road and hopped off. "Let's go for a walk," she said as she held out her hand.

After Ryan had secured their helmets, they crossed over to the sea side of the road and began to walk along on the hard-packed sand. Even though the day was beautiful, there wasn't another soul on the beach. The sun was bright, although the wind was stiff and cold as it blew in from the ocean. "I'm glad you told me to dress warmly," Jamie said as a chill shot down her spine.

Of course, Ryan noticed this, and held her arm out in an inviting gesture. Jamie shot her a shy grin, but snuggled up against her anyway. They walked along in companionable silence for at least a mile before Ryan turned around and guided her back. *I'd feel odd talking so little with anyone else. But with Ryan the silence is never uncomfortable. Even when we don't speak, I feel like we're communicating. Like now, she wants me to feel free. She brought me here so I could feel how huge the world is, and maybe that would make me feel less confined.*

When they were almost back to their starting place, Ryan broke the silence. "Are you ready?"

"To leave?" she replied with a winsome look on her face. "I guess so," she said, even though that was the last thing in the world she wanted to do.

"No," Ryan said, her eyes twinkling. "Are you ready to get started?"

"Get started doing what?"

"Having your first lesson, of course."

"In what?" Jamie asked, even though she'd gladly take a lesson in breathing or walking from Ryan.

"Your first lesson on how to ride a motorcycle."

"What?"

"I don't know of a better way to get your blood pumping than to put eighty cubic inches of power between your legs," Ryan purred.

"Uh … uh …" Jamie stuttered as she tried to decide what was more stimulating, the thought of driving the bike or considering the clear sexual tone of Ryan's invitation.

"Come on," she urged as Jamie's feet seemed unable to propel her forward. "Once you've ridden on a Fat Boy you'll never be the same."

"Fat Boy?" she gulped as she thought, *Is there a sexual allusion to every part of motorcycle riding?*

"That's the style of bike I have, it's a Harley Softail Fat Boy."

"And you want me to drive it," she finally got out.

"Yep. Your blood is going to pump so hard you might have to open a vein."

"Or several," she squeaked out, picturing her broken body strewn across the pavement.

"I guarantee you'll enjoy this. And I've never lost a student."

"Okay. But you're gonna have to call my parents after the ambulance takes me away."

They crossed the road and approached the bike while Ryan pointed to a small paved road that gently led up into the hills. "I thought that would be a good place to start," she said. "I haven't seen a car come down that road the entire time we've been here. I'll move her over there and we can get started." She started the engine, and rolled the big bike onto the blacktop. The road was relatively flat for a long while, but there was a hairpin turn about one half mile out. It then began a rapid ascent up into the hills.

Jamie jogged behind her and waited patiently as Ryan slapped the helmet on her head. "Buckle up tight," she warned. When she was ready, Ryan began the lesson. "Do you know anything at all about motorcycles?"

"Just that they're fun to ride on," she admitted with a grin.

"That's the most important factor. But there are a few more little details. Have you ever watched me shift?"

"Yeah, I think you use your left foot. Oh, and I know that you brake with your hands, kind of like on a regular bike, and I know the throttle is on the right hand thingy."

"Excellent! It really is quite a lot like being on a regular bike. Just like on your bike, it's important to stay balanced with your center of gravity right over the seat. It's important to brake with both hands and not hit the front brake too hard. There's a lean angle on both types of bikes. If you stay above the angle you won't tip over. On this bike the angle is twenty eight degrees. Can you picture that?"

"Yeah. That's really low. I have a hard time imagining going that low."

"Wanna see?" Ryan asked with a devilish gleam in her big blue eyes.

"Not just because I dared you," Jamie said quickly. "I know you can't resist a challenge."

"No, I feel really comfortable on my bike. I'll just show you how low you can go. It might reassure you."

"Okay … but I doubt it."

"Don't worry," Ryan said. "Just watch me."

She put her helmet on and brought the beast to life. She took it up the flat part of the road and went about another one half mile, and then she turned around and began to roar down the hill. When Ryan got to the hairpin turn she leaned the bike over so far that Jamie's heart flew to her throat. Ryan's knee was nearly touching the pavement, but she made the corner and straightened up easily. She skidded to a quick halt right in front of her open-mouthed student. "That was awesome. But you're out of your mind if you think I'm ever gonna do that!"

"You never know," Ryan drawled.

"Oh, I know, Ryan, I know. But I'd like to go for a nice, safe, smooth little ride."

"Okay. The first step is making sure you can hold her up. I bought this bike from a woman who had the suspension lowered about two and a half inches. She wasn't much taller than you, so I think you'll be able to handle it."

"How much does it weigh?"

"With the stuff I have on it, she goes about 640."

"Six hundred and forty pounds!!" Jamie shrieked. "I can't hold up six hundred and forty pounds!"

"You don't hold it up, silly. The wheels do that. You just have to help it balance. I couldn't hold it up if it got below a forty-degree angle while it was stationary. Let's give it a try," she urged. "I'll scoot back, you come up here and sit in front." She patted the seat in front of her as she beamed an encouraging grin at her tentative friend. "Come on, she won't bite."

Jamie struggled to throw her leg over since it was cramped with Ryan sitting in the back. She finally got up with a great deal of assistance from her friend. "Whoa!" she said, the air flying from her lungs. "This is sweet!" She placed her hands on the handgrips, and shifted around in the seat to get comfortable, feeling like she was sitting on one of the mechanical horses out in front of the grocery store that she had enjoyed as a child. It was particularly comforting to have Ryan nestled up against her back, and she realized that it felt really good sitting in front.

"Okay, I'm going to stand up and let you feel what it's like to hold her up. I'll be right here if you have any trouble. I promise," she said as she began to stand.

Jamie's heart began to thump in her chest but she concentrated and held on tight. She found to her amazement that it wasn't really that hard to balance such a huge weight if she stayed centered. "I feel okay," she said slowly.

"Great! Now I'll show you how to shift." Ryan provided a basic lesson in shifting and let her student practice a few times, going through all of the gears one at a time. "Why don't we go for a little spin? I'll keep my hands on yours and guide you up and down the hill. All you have to do is shift when I tell you."

"That's all? You're sure?"

"Yep. Believe me, Jamie. I won't trick you into doing something you're uncomfortable with. I'll tell you what you need to do, and I swear I won't expect you to do one thing more than that. Okay?" she asked leaning over to make eye contact.

"Okay."

Ryan brought the bike to life, and sat back while Jamie got comfortable. "Are you ready?" she asked as she glued herself to her back. A small nod was the blonde's answer. "Okay, put her into first gear." As Jamie did, Ryan's large hands covered hers, gripping the brakes firmly. "Now I'm going to let the brakes off, so the bike might move a little, then I'm going to give it a little gas. Just relax and let me guide you."

Jamie's stomach leapt to her throat, but she did her best to stay relaxed as the bike began to move. Ryan really was driving, but sitting in the front was a very heady experience. And the experience was made even headier by having her friend's body covering her back. Ryan's chin was hanging over her shoulder, and her chest was pressed tight against Jamie's jacket. Her warm pelvis was snuggled up against

Jamie's butt, sending jolts of feeling down and between her legs. *Ohh. I hope I don't have to walk anytime soon. I know my legs are completely useless.*

As they slowly climbed the small grade, Ryan called out when she wanted her to shift. By the time they reached the turnaround point the bike was up in third gear, and Jamie felt proud of that small accomplishment. Ryan was very enthusiastic in her praise, and Jamie was excited about the trip back down. She paid rapt attention to how Ryan's hands worked the throttle and the brakes, and by the time they reached the bottom she was ready to go up again. They made the little one-mile loop three more times. Jamie was having a ball, and was more than happy to keep her knowledge right at this level, but Ryan raised the stakes when she said, "I think you're ready to move on."

"What do you mean?" she asked suspiciously.

"This time, you take the throttle and the brakes. I'll scoot up and shift for you so you don't have too many things to think about."

"I don't know, Ryan. I'm not sure I'm ready."

"I have total confidence in you, Jamie. I know you can do this … easily."

Somehow, Ryan's confidence was enough to bolster her own, and she agreed. Ryan had to scoot even closer to comfortably reach the shifter, but Jamie wasn't about to complain. She rested her hands on the grips and prepared herself mentally, and then nodded to show her readiness.

Ryan kept her feet on the ground until the last moment to help balance the big bike. Jamie slowly turned the throttle, and the bike began to roll smoothly. Ryan kept her promise and rested her hands on Jamie's waist—letting Jamie have complete control. Jamie could feel Ryan's warm body pressed against her, and was reassured by the relaxed posture that her friend maintained. *If she's relaxed I should be*. Within seconds, they were at the turnaround and she performed her next little test very well, slowly squeezing the brakes to bring the bike to a smooth halt.

Ryan's arms circled her waist for a quick hug as Jamie turned and beamed at her. "More!" she demanded, making Ryan laughed heartily.

"It's addictive, isn't it?"

An enthusiastic nod was her clear reply. Ryan took the controls to negotiate the sharp turn, but quickly turned it over. They made three more complete circuits before Ryan's deep voice rumbled through her back, "Wanna go all the way?"

God, how does any woman refuse her? Oh, that's right, no one does refuse her!

"O … o … okay."

Ryan sat back an inch or two, and let Jamie have full control. She put the bike into first and let her go one more time. The increase in sensation was small, but significant. Now she was really in charge. If she hit the accelerator too hard or grabbed only the front brake they could easily be on the ground. But the responsibility didn't frighten her at this point. The slow buildup had reassured her at every step of the way and now she felt confident. They did three more circuits just the same way, but before they began the fourth Ryan said, "This time, you negotiate the turn on your own."

Jamie gulped noticeably, but she nodded and started up again. Her heart was pounding when she neared the top, but she smoothly downshifted just like she had seen Ryan do. When the bike was going nice and slow, she turned the wheel and leaned over just a tiny bit, turning the bike perfectly. When they reached the bottom, Ryan squeezed her until she had trouble getting a breath. "I'm so proud of you! You were so smooth and controlled. I really think you could do more if you're up to it."

"Like what?" Jamie asked, flushed with accomplishment.

"Let's go further up this hill. You can practice leaning into turns a little bit."

"Okay," she said with only a moment's hesitation. As they climbed past their previous stopping point she could hear Ryan begin to hum over the drone of the engine. After a few moments she learned the tune and began to hum along with her. They rode for at least two more miles, humming the whole way. After they had begun the song for the second time Ryan began to sing. Jamie didn't know the words, so she let that rich, deep voice rumble against her back.

She didn't start at the beginning of the song, instead picking it up right where they had left it.

Wrap your legs around me, baby.
Wrap your legs around my thighs.
Once you sit behind me, baby.
You're gonna get a sweet surprise.

Ryan then began to hum the instrumental part of the song and Jamie happily joined her. Moments later they reached a wide point that looked like a perfect place to turn around, without even waiting for permission she smoothly downshifted and glided the big bike in a perfectly executed turn. Ryan signaled her pleasure by squeezing her thighs and patting her on the leg as she began to sing again.

She was signing at full voice by the time they neared their starting point. Jamie had never heard the song, but she decided that it was a fabulous one, especially when someone was singing it to her while astride a motorcycle. Particularly a very sexy woman with strong thighs wrapped tightly around her body. Between the intense concentration needed to ride the bike and the focus needed to ignore Ryan's body, she hardly heard a word. But Ryan had timed the song perfectly and as they pulled up she wailed out,

This Harley's gonna shake your molars,
This bike is gonna be your friend.
When you sit behind me, baby,
You're gonna wish the ride would never end.

Ryan dropped her feet to hold the bike up while she performed an impromptu drum solo/congratulations on Jamie's back. "That was so awesome, Jamie! You're a total natural!"

Jamie couldn't help but catch the enthusiasm of her friend. She jumped off as Ryan tipped the bike a bit to give her better egress. She threw her arms straight into the air and ran around like a two-year-old. "I am so pumped!"

Ryan secured the bike on its stand, and she threw her arms around Jamie's small waist and picked her up as she began to twirl her in a tight circle. "Wasn't that the most wonderful feeling?" Ryan demanded as the world flew by.

It took all of Jamie's willpower not to shout. *No, this is!*

An hour later they were negotiating dinner. "Look, Ryan, you took me all the way out here just because I was bored. I'd really like to buy you dinner to show my appreciation."

"But you don't seem to get my point," Ryan explained for the third time. "I do things for you and with you because I enjoy them. I can't tell you how much fun it was to teach you to ride. It was like learning all over again. I got to experience the thrill through your eyes. That was an awesome gift!"

"Okay," Jamie said as she changed tactics. "It's just five o'clock and there's no way we want to be crossing the bridge at rush hour. I'm starving because I didn't have lunch, and I bet you didn't either. We need to waste about two hours. We can either do that at a fast food joint, or we can go someplace that I really love. It's a lot more expensive than you like to go for, so why not let me treat us to a great meal just because I can?"

"So this isn't a payback dinner?" Ryan asked suspiciously.

"Nope. It's just a 'Hey, I want to go to the Sparrow Run Inn Oh, look, there it is! Oh, Ryan's with me. That's okay, it's more fun if I have someone to dine with' kind of thing."

"I'm sold. But are you sure we're dressed up enough?"

"Yep. We can sit in the bar and watch basketball on TV while we eat. It's really casual."

"Let's go," she agreed as they made their way along the tiny streets of Larkspur to the restaurant.

It was nearly nine when they reached the city. Dinner had indeed been wonderful, and Ryan was glad that she had let herself be talked into it. As they approached the Marina district, Ryan pulled over and turned in her seat. "Do you mind if I stop by Tracy's apartment for a second? She was supposed to fly in this afternoon, and I told her I might come by tonight."

"Geez, Ryan, we didn't have to stay at the restaurant so long! I don't want Tracy to be upset with you."

As she turned even more fully in her seat, Ryan locked her eyes onto Jamie's. "There's not one minute of this day that I'd cut out. Don't demean our relationship like that. My friendships are just as important to me as my relationship with Tracy."

"I'm sorry," Jamie said quickly. "Our relationship is incredibly important to me."

"I just can't stand people who immediately drop their friends when they get into a serious relationship," Ryan said. "I like to nurture my friendships just as much as I do a sexual relationship." She allowed her face to curve into a crooked grin as she started over. "Do you mind if I stop by Tracy's for a second?"

"Not at all."

A few moments later Ryan was buzzing the apartment. They walked up to the third floor unit together, even though Jamie felt a bit uncomfortable. Tracy was surprised to see Jamie, but she greeted her warmly. "Well, well," she said as she looked them over. "What do we have here?" She wrapped her arms around Ryan for a very friendly kiss. "You've already had dinner," she said as she narrowed her eyes a bit. She leaned in for another kiss, which they held for so long that Jamie began to itch. "And dessert," she added.

If Tracy starts looking for what kind of toothpaste Ryan uses, I'm outta here!

"So where were you little scamps all day?" Tracy asked. "I called your house and your pager, Ms. O'Flaherty."

"Did you really?" Ryan pulled the device from her waistband to check it. "I didn't get a page, Tracy . Did you need something?"

"No. I called to tell you I wouldn't be home until about nine. I actually got in right before you got here."

"Good. I hate to inconvenience you. But the answer to your previous question is that we were up in Marin by Stinson Beach. I taught Jamie how to ride my bike," she said proudly. "And she was an excellent student."

"Oh, tell me all about it," she pushed Ryan into a chair. "Let me get you both a drink first. Do you want a beer or some wine?"

"I'll take some wine," Jamie said.

"Water for me," Ryan added.

A few moments later Tracy came back to the living room with wine for she and Jamie, along with Ryan's usual water. There was seating for seven in the spacious, well decorated apartment but Tracy chose to sit on Ryan's lap. "I've missed you," she said quietly. She placed another kiss on Ryan's lips while sliding her fingertips through her dark hair and massaging her scalp.

Ryan gazed up at her with a sweet, shy smile. "I missed you too." She sat up for another warm kiss, pulling Tracy against her body. They were obviously used to sitting in this position, because Ryan looked completely comfortable. She was sitting on a deep, overstuffed, upholstered chair and Tracy was leaning against her chest with her legs draped over the arm. She had her arm behind Ryan's neck, and Ryan's arm cradled her back. All in all, they looked contented and relaxed with each other, and it didn't seem to bother either of them that Jamie was there.

The couple had only been dating a little over a month, but they were already finishing each other's sentences, and other girlfriend-type things. Tracy would occasionally brush Ryan's bangs from her forehead, or push a lock of hair behind her ear. Ryan teased Tracy quite a bit, and seemed to know exactly where each of her most ticklish spots was. She seemed to delight in holding the woman down with her strong right arm while her left hand got in under her ribs or just behind her knee.

When Tracy spoke, Ryan would look up at her with barely disguised fascination. She'd cock her head and focus intently on her, as though she had some vitally important information to impart. *They really are cute together,* Jamie thought. *If I care for her as much as I think I do, I'll be happy for her. Even though Tracy takes her away from me sometimes, it's important for Ryan to have this. I get my needs fulfilled by Jack—or at least I should,* she thought disparagingly. *Ryan has needs too, and her needs aren't limited to sex. She needs intimacy and romance and tenderness and it looks like she's getting that from Tracy.*

At around ten, Ryan decided that it was time to go. Jamie wanted the couple to have a few moments alone, so she excused herself to use the restroom. She was gone as long as she thought was polite, but when she walked into the hallway it was clear that they were a long way from completing their goodnights. Ryan had Tracy backed up against the wall, and Tracy's arms were draped languidly around the taller woman's neck. Neither of Ryan's hands was visible, and Jamie could only guess that they were palming Tracy's firm butt.

It was obvious that Ryan was pulling Tracy's shapely hips forward, and equally obvious that the woman didn't mind one little bit. Both of them were uttering soft moans as they frantically devoured each other's mouths.

Oh boy, now what? I guess I can go back into the bathroom, but other than shaving my legs I can't think of anything else to do in there. But just as she was beginning to turn to go back in, Ryan pulled away with a few loud, wet kisses. "Gotta go, baby," she whispered. Jamie was afraid that Tracy was going to collapse right where she stood. Her legs looked a bit rubbery, and she still held her eyes closed. She pulled Ryan toward her and whispered something into her ear that caused Ryan to say, "I know, I'm sure I will, too." Then Tracy grasped Ryan's head, and placed several more searing kisses on her lips before she let her go. Ryan leaned her forehead against her girlfriend's and murmured, "Now I know I will," as she gave her one last tender kiss. "See you tomorrow, baby," she said as she patted her cheek in a loving fashion.

"Bye, Jamie," Tracy breathed, as the wide-eyed woman followed Ryan out.

"See you, Tracy, thanks for the wine."

"Anytime." She weakly waved a hand.

Ryan slid her arm around Jamie's shoulders as they walked back down the stairs. "Are you okay?" the smaller woman asked tentatively.

"Yeah, why wouldn't I be?"

"I thought you might need to … uhm … stay over. I could easily grab a cab back to your house."

"Nope. I want to go home."

God, I'm so turned on I ache, and all I did was watch for a moment!

When they got to the bike Ryan teasingly asked, "Wanna drive?"

"I think I'll stick to less populated areas if you don't mind," Jamie replied as she gave her a little pat.

Fifteen minutes later, they pulled up in front of Ryan's house. As they both got off, Jamie gave her a big hug and a kiss on both cheeks. "I had one of the most delightful days of my life. Thanks so much for sharing it with me."

"You're welcome. I had a great time, too. Do you want to come in for some cocoa before your drive?"

"No, I'm sure you need to get to bed."

"Well, I do have a date," she admitted with a rakish grin.

"A date!"

"Yeah," she replied as she held up her left hand and wiggled her fingers. "I'm so turned on I could scream!"

That makes two of us, buddy.

Chapter Twelve

Morris, Foster traditionally held a very large, very elegant New Year's Eve party for all attorneys, their spouses or dates. Jamie had never been invited, and she had never regretted the oversight. But this year her father had broached the subject just after Thanksgiving. After the disagreement they had she was more amenable to doing small things to please him, but she wasn't excited at the prospect of attending this party. She had nothing against lawyers in general, and she enjoyed being with one or two at a time, but an entire ballroom full of them seemed like overkill. Besides, she knew Jack wouldn't want to go, since he seemed almost agoraphobic lately, but she decided to ask him just so she could tell her father that she had brought it up.

She was as surprised as she had ever been when Jack's reaction turned out to be not only favorable, but downright enthusiastic. "I think that'd be a lot of fun," he said with more excitement than she'd heard from him all year. "It'll give us a chance to get dressed up for a change. I'd love to be able to dance with you when you're all sexy looking," he said.

Dance? He dances?

As the day approached, Jamie spent an enjoyable afternoon shopping for dresses with her mother. Even though they differed from each other in many ways, they were both inveterate shoppers, and cutting a swath through a bevy of boutiques gave both of them a thrill.

Catherine had enough formalwear to clothe a small fashion-deprived country, but she hated to be seen in the same dress twice, so she purchased a new dress for most of the formal affairs she attended. At her current weight Jamie could have easily worn one of her mother's dresses, but Catherine wouldn't hear of it. "My things are far too mature for you, dear. You need something that fits your age and your style."

The recent glut of Internet and software millionaires in the Silicon Valley had created a new market for formalwear, and Jamie was surprised at how many shops now dotted the tree-lined streets of the small towns from Hillsborough down through San Jose. Since many of the nouveau millionaires were young, many of the things she saw were very much to Jamie's taste. She finally decided on a navy blue velvet cocktail dress that Catherine wholeheartedly approved of.

On the day of the party, she waited until she was alone in the house to page Ryan. She had seen her the day before, but she hadn't remembered to ask her about her plans for the night, and she couldn't let such an oversight pass.

"You rang?" Ryan asked when Jamie picked up.

"I forgot to wish you a Happy New Year," she said. "That could've ruined my evening."

"Your evening? Ha! What about my evening? You could've ruined a whole year for me! I hope you're more careful in the future."

"Maybe I should just call you every day. Then I won't ever forget."

"Now that's the best idea you've had in weeks," Ryan said. "I'll expect your call from here on in. So what're you up to tonight?"

"We're going to a formal party at The Fairmont. A Morris, Foster thing," she said without much enthusiasm.

"Well that sounds pretty cool. At least you're doing something. I was afraid to ask when you didn't mention any plans. Do you have a new dress?"

"Yep. Navy blue velvet. I look pretty good in it if I do say so myself."

"I've known you since August and you've looked fabulous every day we've been together," Ryan said. "But I'd bet navy blue velvet would be perfect for you given your hair color and skin tone. Every guy there is gonna be jealous of Jack."

"So what are you two up to?" Jamie asked, momentarily nonplussed and more than a little pleased that Ryan had obviously spent some time assessing her physical attributes.

"We're going to a big party at The Mark Hopkins."

"Really? That surprises me. I thought you didn't like big parties."

"I don't. But you have to make some sacrifices for a relationship. Or so I'm told," Ryan added, laughing. "I'm gonna be pissed if I find out I'm making sacrifices when I don't have to."

I wish Jack would be as willing to compromise as you are, she thought, but decided to keep her gripes to herself. "Is this for girls only?"

"Yep. It's put on by one of the promoters who stages big weekend parties in the city. I told Tracy I'd take her anywhere she wanted to go, and this is what she chose."

"Do you have a new dress? I'm sure Tracy would like to see a little thigh."

"She can see my thighs when I wear shorts," Ryan said, laughing. "And yes, I have my version of a new dress."

"And what might that be? Did you find formal jeans?"

"No, but now I wish I had. Maybe I should've spent more than ten minutes shopping."

"Come on, tell me what you bought. I'm not familiar with formal lesbian attire."

"Well, the dress code is pretty darned flexible. I guarantee the diversity of my group will surpass yours."

"Spill it, O'Flaherty."

"Okay, I bought some black leather pants and a white pleated shirt—kind of a woman's tuxedo shirt. It's got little bitty black studs rather than buttons." She paused for a moment and asked, "Jamie, are you still there?"

Jamie literally slapped her head to make her brain start to work again. "My cell phone must have blanked out for a second," she said. "Your outfit sounds … cute. I'd like to see it someday." *Yeah, like tonight*, she thought dejectedly. *I'd rather tag along on Ryan's date than hang out with a bunch of lawyers. I can't imagine a person who'd look better in leather pants. And she looks so fresh and scrubbed when she wears a white shirt. Her hair looks so dark it's almost—*

"I hope you have a very good time tonight, buddy," Ryan said, interrupting her daydream. "I send you every good wish for the New Year – but you'll have to wait for your kiss."

"Happy New Year to you too, Ryan. I hope you and Tracy have a wonderful evening. Blow a kiss across the street at midnight, since my event is so close to yours. And make sure you pay attention so you can tell me all about the unique outfits."

"Will do. I'll call you tomorrow."

Jim and Catherine had arranged for the firm's limo to pick them up, and when Jamie learned this she asked if they could all ride together. Jim was happy to make it a family affair, and he chilled a bottle of champagne to begin the celebration in the limo.

Jamie came down the stairs to the appreciative gazes of both her father and Jack. "Wow," was all that Jack could get out. His eyes wandered up and down Jamie's body, making her blush under his frankly appreciative gaze.

"You look wonderful, honey," Jim gushed as he walked to the stairs to kiss her cheek.

"Thank you both," she said as she waited for Jack's kiss. "You look pretty wonderful yourself," she said softly as she leaned towards him. He had purchased a tuxedo for himself, figuring that he'd need one once he started his full-time job. He asked his law review partner to help him pick it out, and Jamie had to admit that Natalie's taste was exquisite.

The suit was quite traditional, and it had a shawl collar, which set his broad shoulders off attractively. It was impeccably tailored, and Jamie knew that it had cost more than he could comfortably afford. But he looked fabulous in it, and he'd be able to wear it for years, so she was sure he wouldn't regret buying it

His wing-collar white shirt and black tie complemented his new suit, making him look traditional, but certainly not stodgy. Jamie thought that Jack had never looked more handsome and she began to feel a little more excited about the evening. *If he cares enough to dress this carefully he must really want to do this*, she thought. *Maybe he really does want to cut loose for a change.*

Catherine made her entrance a short time later and gracefully accepted the compliments of the small crowd. She also looked particularly lovely this evening. A deep emerald green silk cocktail dress showed off both her figure and her pale blonde hair, making her look young, sexy and vibrant.

"Shall we?" Jim asked as he took Catherine's arm to lead her to the waiting limo.

Dinner was the standard hotel banquet room fare: nothing special except the prices. They sat at a table with the other senior members of the firm, but the ambient noise forced them to speak mostly to each other. As soon as dinner was finished, Jim invited Jack to join him and the other senior partners down in the bar to have a cigar. Jamie watched in horror as Jack immediately agreed. He doesn't smoke! she thought in alarm. *That's such a disgusting habit! He'll reek of the smell all night long.*

She was in a funk when Catherine leaned over and said, "You may as well get used to it. These events aren't made for us. It's just an extension of the office. Our job is to look good and not get drunk enough to cause a scene." She laughed wryly at her own joke but Jamie caught the bitter edge to her voice. "I'm having vodka tonight. How about you?"

"I think I'll stick with champagne," she said since they'd already had some in the limo.

Catherine called the waiter over and signaled for him to come closer, "I'd like your best vodka on the rocks and a bottle of decent champagne."

"We're serving Le Coq Rouge tonight, Ma'am," he informed her politely.

"I know what you're serving, but that's not what we're drinking. I'd like a good bottle." When he didn't react immediately, she clarified. "I'll pay for it myself."

"Yes, Ma'am," he said as he snapped to it. A few minutes later Jamie was sipping excellent champagne while various wives and fellow partners paid homage to her mother.

When they were alone for a moment, Jamie asked, "Do you really know all of these people?"

"A few. We've been friends with some of them since we were your age," she said. "But many of them are complete strangers. I've no idea why they insist on talking to me. It's not like your father quizzes me at the end of the evening, 'So, Catherine, did all of the partners and their wives kiss your ring?'"

Jamie laughed at her mother's usually hidden sense of humor. *She's so much more fun when Daddy's not around.*

After a while, a well-dressed woman who looked a little older than Catherine came up and asked, "Could I have a word with you in private, dear?"

Catherine looked like she wanted to refuse, but she got up and followed the woman to the side of the room. A little while later the men returned. They reeked of cigar smoke and Jamie felt a little nauseous when Jack sat next to her and spoke in her direction, but she had no interest in making a big deal about it, so she tried to ignore the strong odor. After a few minutes, he asked her to dance and she accepted—mostly to see if he really knew how. They had never been in a situation that required them to dance, and she hoped that he had some idea of what to do since she didn't think it would be wise to lead.

Her mouth nearly hit her chest as he gracefully placed one hand behind her back and grasped her other hand in his. As the music started, he led her around the floor as though he'd been dancing for years. He seemed so self-assured and elegant that she had to question her long held perceptions of him. They didn't speak as they danced, but that didn't bother her one bit. She just let him lead her with his calm but determined manner.

They remained on the dance floor for several more songs, and when they returned to their table he looked at her with his normal boyish expression and whispered, "How'd I do?"

She sat back in her chair to regard him for a moment. He looked like nothing but a young boy seeking approval from his teacher for a well-written essay. "You dance beautifully, Jack. I had no idea that you knew how."

"I didn't," he said, sitting up in his chair and looking proud of himself.

"But how …?"

"When you invited me, I knew I couldn't stumble around looking stupid, so I signed up for lessons."

"You … you took dance lessons?"

"Yeah. It's important to look like you belong," he explained.

"I think I get that," she said, trying to hold the edge from her voice. "But when did you have time to take lessons?"

"Natalie and I took a course together. She didn't know how, either, so it seemed like a good way to learn. I thought it would be a nice surprise."

"You took dance lessons?" she asked for the second time, still unable to get her mind around the concept.

"Yes, of course I did. This evening is important to me," he said as he gave her a little squeeze.

She'd never considered herself slow. As a matter of fact she usually thought that she caught on rather quickly. That's why this revelation hit her with such force. *How stupid am I? I honestly believed he wanted to come to this party to be with me!* She silently berated herself for a few minutes and shortly thereafter her father whisked Jack away for 'face time' with some of the other important people at the party.

She had to force herself to adopt a pleasant countenance after Jack departed. But even though she had a smile on her face, she had never felt so completely alone. The walls of the huge banquet room seemed to be closing in on her, and she fervently wished she was at home watching "Dick Clark's New Years Rockin' Eve," never one of her favorite shows, but supremely more enjoyable than this debacle. Turning to her mother, she caught a look of unguarded despair on the older woman's normally placid face. The look was so heart-rending that she quickly averted her gaze to avoid making her uncomfortable. "You'll never survive a lifetime of these events if you don't learn how to drink, Jamie," her mother's voice floated past her ear a few minutes later. "You've barely had a full glass."

Just then the waiter ambled past. Jamie looked up at him and asked in a clear voice, "Morphine and soda please."

Ryan was dressed and ready to roll at nine o'clock. Martin had insisted that she take his truck for the evening. "It's not wise to be gallivanting around on New Year's Eve on a motorcycle," he decreed.

She felt pretty good in her new outfit, finding that she liked dressing up as long as she didn't have to wear a dress. She had taken the time to polish her boots and she gazed at her bleary reflection in the black leather while she waited for Tracy to buzz her up.

As the door to the apartment opened Tracy pulled her in and spent a moment looking her up and down. Ryan patiently waited for her to finish, and was eventually rewarded with a low whistle. "You look so totally hot," she purred as she placed the first kiss of the night on Ryan's lips.

When she broke free, the taller woman stood back and regarded her date. Tracy looked more beautiful than Ryan had ever seen her, and that was saying a lot. She wore a white silk tank top and a very short, very tight black velvet skirt. Shimmery black stockings showed off every inch of her long legs, and her two-inch heels brought her up much closer to Ryan's hungry mouth. Her shoulder length chestnut hair was swept up off her face in a tight chignon, and the attractive style highlighted the delicate planes of her lovely face. "You look so beautiful," Ryan murmured softly as they came together in another series of slow, deep kisses. Ryan wasn't sure if it was Tracy's luminous beauty or her mesmerizing perfume, but something was ratcheting her desire out of control. She knew that if they didn't leave soon they'd see the New Year in from a horizontal position. "We'd better go," she said softly as she finally pulled her mouth from Tracy's voracious one.

"Maybe we should just watch the countdown on TV," she suggested. "It's dangerous to be out on New Year's Eve."

"It's more dangerous in here," Ryan decided. "Let's go, babe," she said as she held out a matching collarless black velvet jacket for Tracy to slip into.

By the time Jack returned to ask for another dance Jamie could hardly feel her feet, but she wasn't in the mood for a lecture, so she sucked it up and gamely followed him out to the dance floor. She was a bit surprised to see her mother being led out seconds later, and she thought, *Now being displayed for your viewing pleasure, Catherine and Jamie Evans. They walk, they talk, they dance!*

Ryan had been to many lesbian dances and parties, but this was by far the most elegant event that she had ever attended. The room was decorated beautifully, and for a change, the music wasn't ear-splittingly loud. People were drinking, but it was nearly ten o'clock, and she didn't detect any obviously drunk women yet, in contrast to most of the clubs she'd been to.

Almost as soon as they entered the room Tracy led her to the dance floor and they spent a good half hour moving against each other so sensually that Ryan felt her temperature start to rise. Even though they'd agreed they wouldn't sleep together until they were certain they were in love with each other, she began to suspect that Tracy was changing the rules.

At first she wasn't sure if she was reading her signals correctly, but the sultry glances were a good first clue. Even if she hadn't noticed the glances, the torrid kisses would have been another indication. Finally, no matter how oblivious Ryan was, she couldn't ignore the bare thigh that kept sliding between her legs on the dance floor. Tracy had the most arousing dance style that Ryan had ever seen. She danced so close that their breasts continually rubbed against one another, but the kicker for Ryan was the way Tracy insinuated her leg right between Ryan's legs and thrust her hips in time to the music. After a few such numbers Ryan's head was throbbing from her unquenched desire and her will was way past weak.

They were both thirsty from the workout, so Tracy led her by the hand to one of the small bars set up around the large ballroom. Ryan knew the last thing she needed was alcohol, so she stuck to her usual sparkling water. But Tracy seemed to want to lower her inhibitions, drinking Scotch instead of wine, her usual drink. Ryan watched her slug her drink down rapidly, then Tracy put the glass on the bar and gazed at her like a panther stalking prey. The wild look in Tracy's eyes caused Ryan to move back a few steps, but that was right where she wanted her. She pushed the taller woman against the rear wall and began to work on her mouth again. By the time Ryan came up for breath she was all in favor of seeing if she could snag another good deal on a room upstairs.

But just as she was about to suggest that they head home, Tracy pulled her back onto the dance floor and began to sway to the music once again. "Give me strength," Ryan moaned to whatever saint was in the neighborhood.

At 11:50 Jamie tried to focus on the blurred vision of her mother. "Will they come back at midnight, or do we kiss each other?"

"Oh, they'll be back," Catherine replied. "It wouldn't look right to leave us alone then, and looks are the only thing that matters."

Even from her fog Jamie could tell that her mother didn't look very drunk at all. *How in the hell does she do that?* she marveled. *She's had as many as I've had, and she's drinking vodka. That's three times as much alcohol as champagne.* But as she regarded her for a moment, she really let herself see the vacant, almost desolate look in her mother's eyes. *Why's she so unhappy? Is it her life or her self or is it just physiological? Maybe she's genetically prone to unhappiness, 'cause she sure doesn't have much to complain about!*

Jack and Jim flew up with three minutes to spare. "Miss me?" he whispered into Jamie's ear as he pulled her to the dance floor to join with all the other couples as they welcomed in the New Year.

"Desperately," she replied in the same flat monotone her mother used with her father.

"Good," he said as he wrapped her in his arms and kissed her with enough intensity to shock her out of her fog.

Oh right, she said to herself as she caught her breath. *He has to look like he's passionate.*

The stroke of midnight found Tracy looking up into Ryan's deep blue eyes and murmuring in a soft voice, "I love you, Ryan," as she pulled her head down for a tender, emotion-filled kiss.

Ryan was shocked by this declaration, but she realized that she was very close to declaring her love for Tracy, too. But since her mouth was very happily occupied, she decided to wait a bit to commit herself.

When she considered her feelings she had to admit that Tracy was exactly what she'd been seeking in a woman. She was a lot of fun, smart, sexy, very passionate, and probably great in bed. As Ryan's mouth was invaded by Tracy's searching tongue she rethought that statement. *No, she's definitely gonna be great in bed. That tongue knows how to move!*

By twelve-thirty the Morris, Foster party was winding down. The younger partners and their spouses were still on the dance floor, but the more senior members of the firm were starting to drift away. Jim approached and asked, "A few of the managing committee members want to have a nightcap over at the Top of the Mark. Will you two join us, or would you rather stay here and dance?"

Jamie knew the answer before the question was fully out of her father's mouth. "We'd love to join you," Jack answered without even looking at her.

As they waited for the elevator to the top floor of the Mark Hopkins, Jamie turned to scan the sign that listed the location of every event. *Hmm, Ryan's party is on the lower level.* "I'm going to use the rest room down here, Jack. I'll be up in a few minutes. Will you just order me some sparkling water?" He looked like he knew he should wait with her, but all of the big kids were going to play and he didn't want to be left out. "Go on," she urged. "I'll be up in a few minutes." His smile of relief was actually kind of funny, and she patted his cheek and stood on her tiptoes for a kiss. "See you soon," she promised as she started off in the direction of the rest rooms.

After a quick stop to check her makeup, she made her way down to the lower level. It didn't take long to figure out which party was Ryan's. Women of every shape, size and color were streaming in and out of the largest room on the floor. Jamie noted with relief that no one was checking tickets, so she slid right in and looked around for a few minutes.

She was just about to give up when she felt a warm presence behind her. A deep voice floated past her ear, "Are you here to learn the secret handshake?"

Jamie's entire face broke into a delighted grin as she turned to greet her friend. Ryan's arms enveloped her in a hug, and she relaxed into the embrace, feeling all of the tension leave her body. "Mmm, you smell good," Jamie said as she pulled away. "And you look fabulous," she enthused as she stood back and got a good look.

"Actually it's Tracy who smells good. I just smell like her," she said. "Boy, Jack must be unconscious somewhere to let you get away tonight. You look as good as your lasagna tastes."

Jamie playfully slapped her on the shoulder as she looked around. "Speaking of dates, where's yours?"

"I just left her in a ridiculously long line for the rest room. Where's Jack?"

"He's with the other fascinating conversationalists from Morris, Foster. They're having a drink while they try to bore each other to death."

"Oh-oh," Ryan said. "Is somebody grouchy?"

"I shouldn't be," she said with an embarrassed smirk. "But I had the crazy notion that Jack wanted to be with me tonight."

"And he doesn't?"

"Nope. It's just business."

"I'm sorry," Ryan said as she squeezed her shoulder. "I wish you were having more fun."

"That's okay. I need to get used to this since it's gonna be my life for the next several hundred years."

Mainly to lighten the mood, Ryan revealed, "I think I'm going steady."

"Are you, now?" Jamie placed her hands on her hips and regarded Ryan carefully.

"I think so. Tracy told me she loves me. I think that means we're at least going steady, right?"

"That's so sweet," she said as she gave her friend a hug. "That woman has excellent taste!" After a beat she asked, "Do you feel the same?"

"I think so," Ryan said, her delivery slow and thoughtful. "I'm not quite ready to commit yet, but I'm close."

"I'm really happy for you," she said as she hugged her again. "She's one lucky woman." As Ryan released her she said, "I've got to get back. Within an hour or two they'll miss me."

Ryan considered how little Jack must pay attention to her when she realized that Jamie's party was next door at the Fairmont. *God, he doesn't even know when she leaves the building for a half hour!* "I really wish you were having a better time. You deserve so much more." But as soon as the words were out of her mouth she wished she could pull them back in. She was always careful not to criticize Jack, but it had just slipped out this time. Thankfully, Jamie didn't seem offended in the least. She slid her arms around Ryan and hugged her tenderly as she rested her head against her chest.

"Thank you," she whispered as she pulled away. "It really helps to know that someone thinks I'm special."

"I do and I always will," Ryan pledged as she tilted Jamie's head up with her fingers. "Happy New Year," she said as she bent and placed a soft kiss on her lips. Even though the kiss was just a friendly one, the hairs on the back of Ryan's neck rose and she had to force herself to pull away.

Jamie looked up at her, trying to stifle the tears than threatened to flow. She was happy for her friend, but suddenly she felt more depressed than she had all evening. "Congratulations," she said. "I hope you and Tracy have a wonderful year together." Another quick hug and she was gone.

Minutes later Tracy was back. As she wrapped her arms around Ryan for another deep kiss she could feel the passion flare up again. "Let's go somewhere where we can talk quietly," Ryan suggested.

"Why don't we get a room?" Tracy purred. "That'd be quiet—for a while."

Ryan looked down into her sultry dark eyes and wrestled with her conscience. Tracy was definitely a little drunk, but Ryan thought that she was still able to make thoughtful decisions. Ryan was completely ready to take her upstairs and ravage her all night long, but she felt that she needed to discuss a few things first. So rather than jump into bed she suggested an alternative. "Let's have a drink first. Where would you like to go?"

"Let's stay right here," she said as she took Ryan by the hand and led her to the elevator.

On the way upstairs in the elevator a thousand thoughts flew through Ryan's mind. *I feel almost ready to take the plunge but there's just something holding me back. I know I'm phobic about commitment, but still ...*

By the time they were shown to a small table by the window, Ryan was so focused on her date that she completely failed to notice Jamie in a large group of lawyers and their wives. But Jamie most definitely noticed Ryan. *My God she looks great tonight*, she thought as she watched the supple leather stretch taut against her legs as she sat down. *And Tracy looks fantastic, too. But I wonder why they're here? I'd think Ryan would have her in a horizontal position by now.*

Ryan ordered her first real drink of the night. When the server brought their Scotches she lightly grasped Tracy's hand and said, "Are you really ready to make love?"

A slow nod accompanied by a sly grin was ample evidence of her readiness. "Are you?' she asked as she squeezed Ryan's hand.

"I ... I think so. I mean in one way I've been ready since the first time I saw you in class. I find you incredibly attractive and extremely desirable." She lifted Tracy's hand and gave it a gentle kiss. "But I made you a promise and I want to be sure we're both aware of where we stand. I feel close to being able to make a commitment, but I'm not quite there."

"I'm not very interested in standing tonight, or tomorrow for that matter," Tracy replied. "I want to take you home and not let you out until school starts."

"But that's two weeks!" Ryan squeaked.

"I know," she whispered. "It'll take me that long to love every part of that long, luscious body."

"But I have to be home for the football games tomorrow," Ryan replied lightly, in a partial tease, just trying to break the sultry mood.

"There's plenty of time for football some other time. But just to keep you happy I promise I'll have you screaming about my illegal use of hands." She slid her hand up Ryan's leather-clad thigh, creeping dangerously close to her inseam.

"And I'd love to get my hands on your tight end," Ryan growled, shivering from the touch. She shook her head to clear it and said, "I'm losing focus here. I was serious about needing to be home for football tomorrow, though. I thought it would be a good time to introduce you to the whole family."

"But I've met your family," she said. "We had dinner right before I left for Christmas."

"That was just my father and brothers. Now you need to pass inspection from my uncles, aunts and cousins."

"How many are there?" she asked, looking less than comfortable.

"About twenty-five. They'll all be at the house tomorrow."

"I … I … I'll let you know if I can make it. I have some things I need to get done tomorrow."

On New Year's Day? What could you possibly have to do on New Years Day? Just to test the theory that was slowly forming in her head, Ryan asked, "If I decide to skip the family party, could I come over?"

"Sure," she said. "Anytime. Or you could just avoid putting all those miles on your father's car and stay over."

"I don't think I'm ready yet, Tracy. I made a promise, and until I'm ready to commit to you I don't feel right about it."

Tracy's hand was wandering up her thigh in the most alluring manner that Ryan had ever felt. "I release you from your promise," she purred. "Turn your vigilant little conscience off and follow your desire. It's okay if you don't love me yet—or ever. I just want you to take me home and love every little inch of me—slowly."

"Oh, God," Ryan moaned weakly as she felt her resolve float away in a cloud of erotic thoughts.

Jamie spent a solid ten minutes of staring at Ryan, and Jack finally turned his eyes to follow hers. "Isn't that …?" he started to say, but Jamie faced him again and leaned in for a kiss.

"Take me home," she begged. "I want to feel you inside me."

His eyes opened as wide as they were capable of opening and he completely lost his prior train of thought. *God he's easy*, Jamie thought to herself as Jack immediately leaned over to ask Jim if he was ready to leave.

Just as they were getting ready to leave the bar, a couple that Tracy knew came in. "Don't even bother trying to get your car," they informed them. "There's a half hour wait."

Ryan hopped up and said, "I'll go wait in line. Why don't you all have another drink and come down in a half hour?"

Tracy's friends handed Ryan their valet ticket and gratefully accepted her offer.

As she stood in the bracing cold wind, Ryan felt some of her determination return. *I'm really not ready yet. I have to get to the bottom of this family thing. It might be my imagination, but I get the impression that she's not interested in meeting and getting to know my family. And there's no way in the world I'll get seriously involved with anyone who doesn't like my family.*

The last drink was obviously the kicker, since Tracy was sound asleep with her face pressed against the window of the truck by the time they reached the Marina. She was lucid enough to get into her apartment, but as soon as they hit the door she was on Ryan like a hungry dog on a bone. However, once Ryan made up her mind, the erotic temptation was quite a bit less than it had been in the bar. She lovingly undressed her friend with only a momentary desire to jump on top of her. After waiting for Tracy to finish in the bathroom, Ryan guided her back to the bed. "Aren't you going to undress?" Tracy asked hazily.

"I think these leather pants will feel really good against your skin," Ryan said softly. "Let's try it and see."

Tracy was obviously in the mood for a little experiment, since she dropped face forward onto the bed. Ryan climbed on top of her thighs and forced herself to concentrate when Tracy let out a sexy, low moan. God she has a gorgeous body, she thought as she fought to keep her desire at a manageable level. Ryan began to massage that gorgeous naked body; starting at her shoulders and slowly working her way down. By the time she reached her waist she heard the soft, deep breathing that signaled sleep. Leaning over her prone body, she kissed her cheek and slid off her hips, then covered her with the sheet and duvet and carefully removed all of the pins that held her hair up. When she finished, she ran her fingers through the silky tresses and thought, *I'd love to have that hair trailing over my breasts right about now. But a promise is a promise!*

As the days of winter break passed, Jamie felt so close to leaving so many times that she lost count. The most frustrating thing was that her parents were absolutely no different than they had ever been. She realized that she felt like a blind person who had been given the gift of sight. Things that she had never noticed before were blatantly clear now … the interactions between her parents; the way they treated her; even the way they treated the staff. The insight was driving her crazy however, and she yearned to go back home to Berkeley. Seeing Ryan on Monday, Wednesday and Friday afternoons was the only thing that kept her sane.

She worked out with a frenzy in order to keep her mind off her family, putting in two or three hours of riding every day except Friday, since she trained her legs that day. She had seen the nutritionist a few times, but she was so tense during this time that she continued to lose weight. She knew she was down lower than she had been when she fainted at the talk line, and she began to wear more modest work out clothes so that Ryan wouldn't notice.

She had to admit that Ryan was truly going out of her way to help cheer her up. After her workouts, she took her over to the big empty parking lot of the local high school and patiently explained more of the intricacies of the motorcycle, allowing Jamie to ride the big bike for at least an hour each time. A week before break was over she surprised her by driving her over to the Department of Motor Vehicles and announcing that Jamie had an appointment to take her driver's test for her motorcycle license.

To her shock, she passed the test easily and after breezing through the written test, she proudly displayed the temporary license to her beaming friend. "I'm proud of you," Ryan said fondly as she enveloped her in a generous hug.

"This was a wonderful gift, Ryan," Jamie said. "Spending your time with me and being so patient has really made me feel special."

"You are special," she insisted as she leaned over and kissed her lightly on her blushing cheek.

As she got ready for her ride on the Thursday before she was to leave Hillsborough, she heard a knock on the door. Before she could reply, her mother opened the door and came into the room. Jamie was only wearing her underwear and her mother dropped her jaw in pure shock. "My God, what have you done to your body?"

"What do you mean?" she replied defensively as she grabbed her jersey and yanked it over her head.

"You know perfectly well what I mean. You look so … different."

"I've lost some weight, but I'll put it back on soon," she said, feeling very uncomfortable at this invasion of her privacy.

"That's not what I mean. Your weight is fine. It's those … muscles. You've obviously changed your body on purpose. Why?"

Now she's interested in me? "I've been working out quite a bit, Mother. I'm going to participate in a big charity bike ride, and I need to get in shape to complete it."

"That makes no sense at all, Jamie. What does riding a bike have to do with looking like this? I've never seen you look so … I don't even know what to call it," she said, clearly flustered. "You've lost all of your softness."

"I need to be in good shape to be strong enough to ride five hundred miles. I look a lot more muscular than normal because of the weight that I've lost."

"Do you mean to tell me that you plan on riding that bicycle of yours over five hundred miles?" She stared at her child, having trouble comprehending her statement. Before she could stop herself, she adopted a very stern tone—one she'd never used on her daughter. "I'll not have it! That's a ridiculous feat to even attempt. There's no reason on earth for you to do that, and I forbid you to even try."

Jamie was absolutely dumbfounded. She stared at her mother for a few long moments. Neither woman spoke as the gulf between them widened perceptibly. Finally, she simply turned and removed her jersey, folded it and put on a T-shirt. When she was dressed, she began to pack up her clothes in silence.

Her mother stared at her back for a few minutes. "Jamie, I want your word that you'll stop this nonsense right now."

"I can't do that. I refuse to lie to you just to make you happy. I make my own choices in life and this is a choice I've made that I intend to pursue. I'd prefer that you support me, but I don't require it."

"Don't forget that we do support you. Quite well, if I do say so myself. I believe we *do* have a right to express our opinions about your choices so long as you're our dependent."

Jamie picked up her heavy suitcase and dragged it towards the door. "Mother, I appreciate your financial support, but we both know that I don't need it." She continued down the stairs, leaving her mother to stare at her in shocked silence from the doorway of the bedroom.

As soon as she was in her car she dialed Ryan's pager. Moments later she heard the reassuring tones over her cell phone. "Hi, are you going to be at home for a while?"

"Yeah, until six or so. I'm having dinner with Tracy. Why, do you want to come over?"

"Yeah, if you don't mind, that is. I just had a really bad fight with my mother and I need to talk about it," she replied shakily.

"I'll be waiting for you."

When Jamie arrived an hour later, she saw Ryan rollerblading down the street at breakneck speed. *I can't believe she can blade up these hills. I have trouble walking up them! Boy, I bet my mother would love her body*, she thought, taking some satisfaction from imagining her mother fainting from shock.

"I think I understand why your father had to take you to the emergency room all the time, if this is the kind of stuff you used to do," Jamie said when Ryan approached.

"Not really. Most of my injuries were from skateboarding," she said. "I used to go down to the financial district and zoom down all those cool plazas and walkways. He'd have to come get me from the security guard's office and take me straight to the E.R."

"Did you ever seriously hurt yourself?"

"Not really. Just broken bones."

"Boy, my parents think I'm tough to handle," she shook her head in dismay at her cavalier friend.

They went down to Ryan's room, the house actually being empty for a change. Ryan took a quick shower, while Jamie looked at the pictures on the walls. She particularly loved the pictures of Ryan when she was a little girl. There were at least a dozen framed shots taken at various stages of her youth. Her favorite was one of Ryan as a toddler, no more than two years old. She had the cutest round face, and with that shock of black hair and crystal blue eyes she looked like a beautiful little china doll.

When Ryan came out, wearing a long-sleeved, red T-shirt and faded navy blue sweats, Jamie crossed the room and asked for a hug. Ryan wrapped her arms around her friend, and Jamie just stood in the embrace for a very long time. "You're the only person I feel safe with anymore," she mumbled into the strong chest.

"Come over here and relax," Ryan said, as she tugged her over to the bed. Ryan lay down first, scooting to the middle of the big bed. She pulled a couple of pillows behind her back to elevate herself, then she held out her arm in invitation. Jamie gratefully accepted the offer and climbed right up next to her. Ryan wrapped her arm around Jamie's back, resting her hand on her hip.

"Tell me what happened."

"My mother came into my room and saw me in my underwear," Jamie said, as though that explained everything.

"I didn't convert you to boxers, did I?" Ryan asked with a hint of levity in her voice.

"It wasn't the underwear—it was my body. Specifically, my muscles."

"I remember we talked about this at the beginning. I asked how Jack would feel about your changing body, but we didn't discuss your parents."

"She was unbelievably proprietary about how I looked. She forbade me to participate in the AIDS Ride, and she threatened to cut off my support," Jamie muttered, still shocked by the events of the afternoon.

"Can you survive if they cut you off financially?"

"Yeah, I've got a good chunk of money in my personal account, and I get part of my inheritance on my birthday. I'm certain they can't do anything about that … unless they try to have me declared incompetent."

"Is it enough to live on?" Ryan asked.

"Yeah." Jamie finally smiled. "It's enough for your extended family to live on, including the ones still in Ireland."

"Does that mean you're finally gonna start paying me to be your best friend?" she asked as she began to tickle Jamie's waist.

The smaller woman began to giggle uncontrollably at the attack. "How did you know I was ticklish?" she howled.

"You just look like the sort who would be," Ryan said, beginning another round of the assault.

After Jamie recovered her breath, Ryan got serious again. "What can I do to help? You know I'll do anything I can."

"Just knowing you're here and that I can count on you makes a huge difference."

When she returned to Berkeley, there were four messages from her father and two from Jack.

Bad news travels fast. I wonder who'll be less supportive? She decided to call Jack first. He was very upset that she'd left the Peninsula without calling him, and he didn't understand why she'd upset her parents like this. "Jamie, don't you care enough about their feelings to give up this stupid ride?" he finally asked out of exasperation.

She fought to control her temper, and was finally able to speak in a normal tone of voice. "Why is it that in every one of my relationships I'm expected to be the one to give in?"

"I assume we're talking about us now. And I've been more than understanding about all of your changes and your new friends. Don't think I haven't noticed all of the muscle you've begun to put on. I like you to look like a woman, Jamie. I like your softness. But you didn't ask me what I thought before you decided to change the way you looked. Just like you didn't ask my opinion before you cut your hair off. I keep hoping that you'll have your little rebellious phase, then things will get back to normal."

"Keep dreaming, Jack. It's not gonna happen."

The conversation with her father went just as well as the one with Jack. Her father didn't understand what had come over her. He thought her new friends were responsible for the changes to both her body and her personality. He said that he and her mother thought that she should live at home for a while and commute. She thanked him for his concern and said she'd think about it. *February Eleventh cannot come soon enough. I'll be twenty-one, and legally responsible for myself in every way.*

On the first Sunday morning of spring term, Jamie drove into the city at seven. After receiving permission, she stopped at her father's city apartment to trade the Boxster for the larger Range Rover. When she reached Ryan's house, she was pleased to find that Martin was at home. He made a big breakfast for the three of them which she ate with gusto. After the meal, she and Ryan thoroughly cleaned the kitchen. "Whose job do I have?" Jamie asked.

"You're Brendan and Conor. I'm me and Rory."

"Well, I certainly feel like part of the family." She added after a pause, "More like two parts, actually."

By eight-thirty everything was in order, and Ryan drove the very short distance to her Aunt Maeve's home.

Maeve's son Tommy was a fireman, and he generally had two or three days off in any given week. His wife, Annie, was a nurse anesthetist at San Francisco General. She worked second shift so she could be with Caitlin during her most active hours. When Tommy was at work, the baby slept at Maeve's, an arrangement that worked out beautifully. They tried to arrange their days off so that one of them was home, but one or two days every week Maeve took over. "You know, Ryan," she chided her niece, "I shouldn't let you have my precious little one for a whole day. I only saw her once last week."

"I know, I know. If only all babies could have it so good."

Caitlin was as delighted as a four-month-old could be to be in her big cousin's arms. They took the carrier for the baby, the stroller, the car seat and the huge diaper bag out to the car and struggled to load it all securely, then hooked the car seat into the rear passenger side so the baby could see the driver, who for a change was Jamie. She had offered to drive so that Ryan could sit next to the little passenger to keep her entertained.

After a short drive, they arrived at their destination—Golden Gate Park. Jamie loved the big old park, but she hadn't visited it since she was on a field trip with her fourth grade class. They strapped Caitlin into the infant carrier, and Ryan stood patiently while Jamie attached the giggling baby onto her big cousin's back. The stroller came out next, and they put the diaper bag on the shelf of the bottom of the sturdy vehicle. Jamie had a feeling that the stroller would be used as a carryall more than a carry-Caitlin. Ryan seemed to have almost a primal need to have the baby attached to her body, and Caitlin seemed to be much happier when she was able to feel Ryan's sturdy body moving against her own.

They walked around the park for a long time, pausing to watch people play tennis, ride horses and bikes and generally enjoy all that the park had to offer. Leaving the stroller at the gate, they carried the now-dozing baby into the gravel-lined paths of the Japanese Tea Garden while they walked along chatting companionably.

After a diaper change, and a snack from the Italian deli that Jamie had snuck into the diaper bag, they continued to walk rather aimlessly around the park. After several hours of walking, stopping, and being carried, Caitlin began to get cranky. Ryan had Jamie remove her from the carrier and she patiently swooped her up and held her securely in her strong arms until she gave up the fight and fell asleep on her shoulder.

"You sure do have a way with her," Jamie said. "Have you spent a lot of time with babies?"

"No, not really. I think about what I'd want, and I try to give that to her," she said. "I think every person wants to be understood, no matter what age she is. It's tough when she's this young, because she can only communicate through her cries. But when you really pay attention you begin to notice that her cries each mean something different. I think the trick is to listen to her and try to understand, even when she makes it hard."

"That's the truth," Jamie said, linking her arm with Ryan's. "Everyone wants to be understood."

They found a peaceful, grassy area near the large windmills that dotted the grounds. Jamie spread out a thick blanket on the dry ground, and Ryan gently placed Caitlin down. She artfully constructed a tiny little tent out of another small blanket and some rigid toys to keep the sun from the baby's body. They sat quietly, eating sandwiches from Jamie's secret stash. "You sure do know how to throw a good picnic," Ryan said.

"I come from a family of football tailgaters, remember? You're lucky I didn't bring a grill and a bag of charcoal."

They relaxed on the grass for a while, then Ryan turned to Jamie and asked, "Are you in the mood to offer some advice?"

"Sure, what is it?"

"I need some advice about sex."

"You need my advice about sex? What's your question? 'How do I have less sex?' or 'How do I make sex feel worse?'"

"I know this is hard to believe, but Tracy and I haven't had sex yet."

"What!" Jamie said with alarm. "I thought your record for abstinence was two weeks! You've been seeing her for almost two months!"

"I know, I know. But when I first asked her out, I promised that I'd be serious about our relationship. To me, that meant being sure about her before we started having sex. I didn't want her to be just another sex partner. I wanted this to matter." She paused, and looked at Jamie with wide blue eyes. "Do you understand? I don't want to have sex with her until I'm sure there's a future for us. I don't want to hurt her if it doesn't work out."

"Has it been hard for you?"

"It really has. It's been very hard, and Tracy hasn't made things easy for me, either. She's so attractive, and she turns me on so much that it's a constant battle when we're together. To tell you the truth, she's angry with me about New Year's.

She really wanted to sleep together, but I stuck to my promise. I mean, this probably sounds stupid to you, but I've always looked at sex as purely fun. I never really let it effect me emotionally. This is really new territory for me, and it confuses me a little."

"What confuses you about it?" Jamie asked gently, reading the fragile look in her friend's eyes.

"How do you know if you're falling in love with someone?" she asked, with the sweetest, most innocent look that Jamie had ever seen on her face.

Jamie reached over and patted her friend's thigh, stroking her for a moment. "That's a very big question. I know you were in love with Sara. How did you know that?"

"Sara felt like a part of me," she said. "But that still confuses me How could I love someone who didn't love me back?"

"I think Sara did love you, Ryan. I can't believe that your feelings for her were one-sided. I think it's possible that she wasn't a lesbian. That wouldn't mean she didn't love you, just that she couldn't be your lover."

"I guess that could be right," she said as she thought for a minute. "But she sure did find a cruel way to tell me she was straight."

"No argument there," Jamie said. "But kids do stupid, hurtful things, and sometimes they don't know how to make things right."

"Yeah," Ryan said. "I've done my share." She was pensive for a few moments, then said, "I guess I'm confused about Tracy because I don't know how to separate my feelings for her from my desire. I'm afraid that my need to have sex with her is obscuring my feelings. That's why I'm trying to hold off. I want this to be about love rather than sex."

"I really admire your restraint, Ryan. I know it's not easy for you. But I can empathize. That's why I waited so long with Jack. I wanted to be sure of my feelings before I let sex confuse the issue."

"How did you know that you loved Jack?"

"I felt right with him. I admired him, I respected his moral sense, and I trusted him completely. I could really picture being with him for the rest of my life and sharing everything together." She shook her head at the memory. "But maybe I'm not the right person to answer that question right now."

"I'm really sorry things are so tough for you. Have you made up from your last fight?"

"I guess we have," she said. "We've talked on the phone several times, and things seems pretty much back to normal. But normal doesn't satisfy me anymore," she said. "I want to be closer, Ryan. I just wish he'd spend as much time trying to understand me as you do Caitlin."

"I wish that too, Jamie," she said. "I can't tell you how happy that would make me."

"So ... what will you do about Tracy?"

"I think I have to keep putting her off," Ryan said. "I'm not sure I love her, even though there are things about her that I love. I'm not gonna have sex with her until I know she's the one. Or at least a one," she said, laughing softly.

After a long while spent talking and listening to the birds fly overhead, Jamie finally said, "I really envy Caitlin. She can curl up and go to sleep whenever she wants to." She shook her head with envy at the sleeping infant.

"You can too, if you have the right equipment," Ryan said as she scooted up next to a sturdy eucalyptus tree. She rested her back against the trunk, then stretched her legs out and patted a strong thigh. "C'mon, catch a little nap. I don't want to have to carry both of you."

Jamie smiled shyly, crinkling up her nose, but did as she was told. She crawled over to Ryan and placed her head on a firmly muscled thigh. Ryan gently ruffled her hair for a few moments, and within minutes Jamie was sound asleep.

Caitlin was the first to wake. She began to fuss a little, and Ryan carefully lifted Jamie's head and placed it on the blanket. She crawled back to the baby, and expertly changed her diaper and fed her a bottle. She had a diaper over her shoulder and was burping her little charge when Jamie awoke. She smiled over at Ryan who returned the grin. After a stretch Jamie began to get up, but she stopped abruptly when she saw Ryan's face freeze in fear. The next sensation was that of a strong hand against her mouth and another arm sliding under her left arm, crossing over her chest to drag her to her feet.

"Don't say a word. Don't fight and don't scream," said a man, hissing right behind her ear.

Jamie could see Ryan's face grow unnaturally calm and heard her utter slowly, "Don't you dare hurt her."

"Oh, I'm not gonna hurt her," the low voice rumbled. "She's gonna like what I do to her, aren't ya blondie?" Jamie could feel his hot breath on her neck, and she felt the all too familiar sensation of total blackness overcome her. The last thing she felt was the heaviness in the legs that could no longer support her.

Minutes later she woke, lying in Ryan's arms. She gathered her wits and finally focused enough to see Caitlin giggling from atop a very tall horse, in the arms of an even taller mounted policewoman. She shook her head to clear the cobwebs, and saw an unconscious man lying on the ground, bleeding from his nose, with his right arm at an unnatural angle. Several other people stood around them offering statements to another officer, this one on foot.

"What happened?" Jamie asked, her mind foggy.

"Hey, are you all right?" Ryan asked as she looked carefully at her eyes.

"Yeah, I think so. But what happened?"

"This poor excuse of a human," Ryan said, indicating the prone man, "tried to abduct you."

"And I fainted?" she pressed for details.

"Like a champ," Ryan said, smiling at her with pride.

"Why's that a good thing?"

"It gave me the chance to stop him," Ryan said, again skimping on the details.

"How did you stop him, Ryan?" Jamie struggled to sit up, then put her hand on her friend's shoulder and squeezed it tightly. "Will you please tell me everything that happened?"

"Your girlfriend is being modest, ma'am," the mounted officer interrupted. "After this perp tried to drag you into those bushes," she indicated a deep stand of camellias right behind them, "she laid your baby down and executed the most perfect flying kick I've ever seen." The officer beamed at Ryan, who blushed thoroughly. "He didn't let go of you fast enough for her, though, even though I think he was unconscious already, so she dislocated the arm that he held the weapon with." She shot Ryan another big smile. "We don't encourage citizens to go up against armed attackers, but I've gotta tell ya, that was a thing of beauty."

"H ... h ... h ... he was armed?" Jamie stuttered.

"Yes, ma'am. He had a knife that he was holding to your neck," she said, over Ryan's scowl and fiercely shaking head.

When Jamie woke from her second unplanned nap, Ryan was again cradling her in her arms. "Don't you get enough sleep at night?"

Jamie shook her head and stared at her friend for a moment. "Once again, Ryan, you're a lifesaver." She shuddered a bit, "Although this time I mean it literally."

She again struggled to sit up with Ryan's assistance, then threw her arms around her neck and sobbed. Ryan stroked her back murmuring soft words of comfort. The mounted officer still held Caitlin securely, and she turned her big horse so the baby didn't see Jamie cry. After a long while Jamie composed herself enough to stand on shaking legs, Ryan supporting her firmly until she felt confident enough to walk unaided.

The officer handed Caitlin back to Ryan, and said to Jamie, "You're a lucky woman, ma'am. I have a child at home just a little older than yours. I know how you must feel."

Jamie was too tired to argue about the details. She simply said, "I know how lucky I am," as she grasped Ryan's available hand.

After assuring the officers that they'd return to make their statements, they bundled the baby up and returned her to her grandmother. They decided to downplay the incident to avoid upsetting the family, so they merely said that there had been a small incident at the park, and they needed to return to make a statement. Since everyone seemed fine, Maeve left it at that as she made over the baby and her big adventure at the park.

Hours later, the pair finished up at the police station. The perpetrator had been booked into the hospital ward for treatment of his various injuries, and he'd be charged with his crimes when he was released. Jamie was still very shaky when Ryan drove them over to Jamie's father's apartment to exchange cars. She hadn't asked Ryan for any more details, and Ryan was concerned that she was still in shock. After they had retrieved the Boxster, Ryan drove them back to her home. Because of her concern for her friend, she decided to tell her father the whole story. He looked at Jamie's still face for just a moment before he called his station. Within minutes, a paramedic was at the house. She examined Jamie thoroughly, and agreed that she was in a mild state of psychological shock. The woman was concerned with Jamie's low blood pressure, but Ryan assured her that this was normal for her friend.

Jamie insisted that she was all right, but no one believed her. Martin thought that they should call Jamie's parents or her boyfriend, but Jamie was adamant that they not be involved. Ryan decided to cancel her date with Tracy but Jamie insisted that she keep it. She agreed to keep the date only if Jamie would agree to stay at the house that night, and Jamie reluctantly complied.

Before Ryan left for her early date she bundled Jamie up in a pair of large sweatpants and a soft fleece pullover, then put her on the big bed in Martin's room and turned on the television for her. Jamie refused her offer to go rent some movies, being content to just channel surf for a while.

After Ryan was gone, Martin made dinner for the two of them. Conor was out on a date, and to avoid any more stress, Martin didn't tell the boys what happened. Jamie didn't have much of an appetite, so after he removed her plate, Martin tried to tempt her with ice cream or cookies. That finally got a laugh out of her. "You're just like Ryan," she said. "She's always trying to get me to eat."

"Someone has to try, darlin'," he said affectionately. "A good stiff wind would whip you right into the bay."

Martin sat down in his favorite chair to read the paper and curse the poor light in the room, angling the paper until he could make out the small print. Jamie half-heartedly watched a few shows, shifting from channel to channel. After a while she broke the silence. "I owe her my life, you know."

"You don't know that, Jamie, and it's best not to dwell on what could have happened. But I thank the good Lord that she was with you," he said as he shook his head. "I've never been so happy that she decided to get involved in martial arts."

"Has she ever had to use it before?"

"Not that I know of, but she could have been involved in a lot of things that I don't know about," he said, laughing wryly. "She's a tough one to keep out of trouble."

"You know how special she is, don't you?" she finally asked.

"Jamie, there's no man on earth who's more proud of his daughter than I am. She has been an extraordinary person since the day she was born."

"Was it hard for you when she told you she was gay?" she asked, somehow knowing that Martin wouldn't mind discussing his feelings.

"I can't say that it would have been my choice for her, but it certainly doesn't bother me," he said. "I do wish she'd find a nice woman who she could really love, but that will come in time, I suppose."

"Maybe it'll be Tracy."

"Perhaps," he said shortly, and without elaboration.

"How would her mother feel about her being gay?"

"You know, Fionnuala was a very insightful woman. When Maeve told her about Michael, she claimed she had always known the lad was gay. She made her sister see that it was the same Michael we had always known and loved. We didn't find out about his illness until my poor Fionnuala was just about gone, but she summoned every ounce of strength she had to stick up for that boy." He grew quiet for a while, but finally continued. "She couldn't make a dent in old Charlie though. His rejection of Michael weighed very heavily on her heart. About six months before she died, we were talking one night and she made me promise that if any of the kids turned out to be gay, I'd love them just the same. I looked at her and made that promise without hesitation." His eyes filled with tears as he acknowledged, "I think she knew that Siobhán would be the one. There was something about her that was different from the other little girls," he reflected. "And I don't mean her activity level or her athleticism. It's hard to describe, but there was something different about her spirit. And she has that same confident spirit today." After a long pause he continued with a quavering voice, "When I think of making that promise to my Fionnuala, I realize that it was the easiest promise in the world to keep. I wouldn't change one thing about my Siobhán for all the riches in the world."

"I think she's a very lucky woman to have a father like you," she said, tears escaping from her eyes.

"The lads and I were the lucky ones. I think it was our love for her that kept us all so close. She was such a small child when her mother died, that we all had to join together to make sure we could do our best for her."

"You've done a marvelous job, Martin. And I know your wife would be proud of you all."

Ryan was home early, around ten o'clock. She found them both in the bedroom, her father asleep in his chair, Jamie in the bed. She quietly went to the bed and slipped her arms under her friend, and gingerly carried her down to her own room. *I've never met an adult who conked out like this*, she thought as she struggled down the stairs with her burden. After wrestling her limp body under the covers, she went back upstairs to turn off the TV and wake her father. He gave her a smile when he saw her, pulling her down for a kiss to both cheeks. "I love you, baby," he said as he released her.

"I love you too, Da. Thanks for watching over Jamie for me tonight."

"Did you have a good time on your date?" he asked as he neatened up the newspaper.

"Yeah, I did. I like Tracy a lot."

"Do you think she's the one, darlin'?"

"I don't know, Da," she said as she sank to the bed. "But I'm doing my best to find out." She shot him a grin, and he ruffled her hair in an affectionate gesture.

"Why don't you bring her around more often?"

"I think I will," she said as she got up to return to her room. "That's the only way I'll know if she's right for me. If she fits in as well as Jamie does—I think she might be the one."

Back in her room, she changed out of her clothes and put on a pair of flannel pajama bottoms. Then she removed her bra and blouse and slipped on a long-sleeved T-shirt. After she brushed her teeth, she got on top of the covers, unfurling a blanket over herself. She spent a long time reviewing the day, shuddering each time she saw the terror in Jamie's eyes when those evil hands had grabbed her. Finally she offered up her prayers of thanksgiving finishing with an audible, "Thank you, Mama," as she closed her eyes and fell asleep.

Jamie sat bolt upright when the panic caused her chest to tighten. Ryan flew up a second later, and wrapped her in her arms, holding on tight as Jamie struggled to breathe. "Calm down, it's all right. I've got you. You're all right. I'm here," Ryan repeated in a soothing cadence as she rocked her gently.

When she was able to breathe normally, Jamie pulled back and asked, "How did you get here?" Looking around in confusion, she added, "How did I get here?"

"We're in my room. I carried you down here about four hours ago," she said as she glanced at the bedside clock.

"You had to carry me again?"

"Yep. I think I'm gonna train you to sleep walk. It'll be easier on my back."

After a while Jamie said, "I'm afraid to go to sleep again. That nightmare really scared me."

"C'mere," her friend replied as she slid under the covers and opened her arm in invitation. Jamie accepted the offer and cuddled up next to her warmth. Ryan wrapped her arm around Jamie's back and gently rubbed her side. She brought her other hand around to softly tousle her hair back and forth in a slow rhythm. Within a few minutes, she could feel Jamie's breathing even out and felt her relax in sleep. She followed moments later.

Just as dawn broke Jamie woke, still nestled in Ryan's powerful embrace. *I don't think there's any safer place*, she sighed, as she closed her eyes and let her friends' steady heartbeat lull her back to sleep.

Later that morning, they drove back to Berkeley in the Boxster. Ryan tentatively suggested that Jamie visit the student health service for a few sessions with a counselor.

"I don't really want to talk about this to anyone, Ryan," she said. "The sooner I can put this out of my head, the better."

"I'm afraid that's not how the mind works, Jamie," she said after a moment. "If you don't process this it'll just stay in the back of your mind. And the chances are that it'll come up again and again."

"But it scares me to think about it," she finally admitted, her voice wavering slightly.

"Of course it does. But your mind will make you think about it either when you're awake or asleep. I'll make you a deal," she offered. "I'm really upset about the whole thing, too. I'll go with you, and maybe they'll let us talk about it together."

Jamie finally agreed, and promised to go over that afternoon if Ryan went with her.

As promised, Ryan showed up on time for their joint session with the counselor. The young Ph.D. candidate was a bit uncomfortable seeing them together, but she agreed to one joint session before she made a decision on further treatment.

As usual, Ryan was right. Jamie felt significantly better after just forty-five minutes of facing her fears. She was surprised by how much the incident had affected Ryan, however. Ryan admitted to having had nightmares the night before, and she said that she felt panic overtake her once or twice during the day. They both agreed to see the counselor for another session or two alone.

As they walked along the tree lined path outside of the student health center, Jamie pensively looked up at her friend. "What bothers you most about yesterday?"

She thought about the question for a long time. "I go over it in my mind, again and again. What really bothers me is that I didn't have a plan for what to do if you hadn't passed out." She shook her head to clear the image from her brain. "I was holding the baby, and he had a knife to your neck. If you'd been able to walk, I'm afraid you'd have been gone by the time I could do anything." She looked at Jamie with the most pain-filled eyes that the smaller woman had ever seen. "I don't think I could have saved you," she choked out as Jamie threw her arms around her and let her sob into her neck.

"But you did, Ryan, you did save me," she murmured. "You'd have thought of something. I know you would have. You wouldn't have let him have me," she whispered fiercely.

Ryan looked up with those beautiful blue eyes clouded by tears. "You really trust me, don't you?"

"With my life," Jamie uttered right into her ear as she once again held her close.

Jamie considered her decision not to tell Jack about the attack. *I can try to convince myself that I did it to protect him from worry. But there's a part of me that wanted to see if he noticed that anything was wrong. How could he not have noticed?* But Jack hadn't noticed. The first weekend after the attack she had cried inconsolably when he approached her from behind and put his hands on her. He was clearly puzzled, but he didn't pursue the issue after she told him not to worry about it.

As she drove back down to Palo Alto on the first Friday in February, Jamie thought about the upcoming week. She and Ryan were due to meet with an assistant district attorney to go over their testimony regarding her assault, and she was quite worried about the meeting since she was afraid that it would rekindle her nightmares.

Ryan reassured her that the dreams might come back, but they'd be less severe and stay with her for a shorter time period. She stressed that the best thing they could do was continue to talk about the attack and all of their fears and projections.

Friday night with Jack went pretty well. They had a pleasant, if not earth shattering sexual encounter, and she was almost successful in convincing herself that it wasn't harmful to have to picture Ryan sweating in the gym in order to become aroused. *They're fantasies because you don't act them out*, she patiently explained to her conscience.

On Saturday morning, Jack went to school to work with his law review partner, while Jamie went on a long ride. He returned in time for lunch and actually helped Jamie clean up the kitchen as part of his new campaign to be more connected.

After they cleaned up, they went out for a walk to the bookstore so he could pick up some notebooks. The day was warm and clear as they walked along holding hands. They decided to stop at Palo Alto Espresso for a latte, and sat outside watching the constant traffic on University Avenue for a few minutes.

"You're moving funny," Jamie commented as she gently ran her fingers down his back. "Is your neck stiff?"

"Yeah, you know how it tightens up when I'm concentrating for too long. I wish I could remind myself to get up and move every half hour or so, but I get too absorbed."

She moved her chair behind his, and worked on his tense neck and shoulder muscles for a few minutes. His head was hanging loosely by the time she was finished, and he let out a deep, relaxed sigh as her fingers left his body. He turned his chair to face her, moving as close as he could. Smiling gently, he lifted his hand and tenderly traced the planes of her face. "It makes me feel so good to have you notice when something's wrong with me. It shows me how much you love me," he said softly, gazing steadily into her eyes.

"I do love you, Jack," she whispered. Turning her head slightly she placed a kiss on his large, warm palm. "Even when we're fighting, I still love you."

He leaned over even closer, and placed a gentle kiss on her lips. He kept his head right where it was, staring into her eyes for a few moments. She slid her arms around his neck, and she felt her desire for him begin to stir. As she lifted her head, his dropped a bit until their mouths met for several slow kisses. "Make love to me," she said softly as he began to pull away.

He didn't reply with words, but he quickly stood up and took her hand again. As they walked home, she considered that even though she didn't like the way she'd been reaching orgasm, those few seconds of pleasure dramatically cut the tension between them. He was more playful and lighthearted when she was sexually satisfied, and his playfulness made her feel more relaxed. When she was relaxed she was able to be more physically affectionate, which led to better sex. It was all interconnected, but she was glad for the increase in affection.

As soon as they got into the apartment, he began to strip her clothing off. She realized that she wouldn't make it through their lovemaking without a quick trip to the bathroom, so she pulled herself away with the admonition, "Don't move a muscle. I'll be right back."

She thought she heard her cell phone ring, but she assumed whoever it was would call back. But when she came back, he was staring at her with an unreadable expression on his face. He held the phone out and said, "It's Assistant District Attorney Mendez."

She felt all of the color drain from her face as she accepted the phone. It was obviously too late to try and hide the issue any longer, so she flopped down in the closest chair and dropped her head into her left hand as she answered the phone. "Hello."

"Ms. Evans? Sorry to call you on Saturday, but I'm just getting caught up on my paperwork. I need to reschedule our meeting for this week. Can you make it at two on Monday?"

"Yes, I can," she replied, feeling drained and slow.

"Good. I can't find the name of the other witness right now. What was it again?"

"O'Flaherty," she said. "Ryan O'Flaherty."

"Right … here it is. Can you let Mr. O'Flaherty know about the time change?"

"Ms. O'Flaherty. She's a woman," she corrected.

"Okay, sorry about that. See you on Monday."

She switched off the phone and gently placed it on the table, but the silence in the room made the soft tap sound like a gunshot. "Jack, something happened that I didn't tell you about. Please try not to get angry until I can explain," she begged.

He was sitting on the couch with his legs splayed out, looking like she had punched him in the stomach. "What?" he asked, his voice filled with fatigue. "What now?"

"Just after the beginning of Spring Term, Ryan and I were in the park with her little cousin. A man tried to abduct me," she said as an involuntary shudder ran down her spine. "I assume he was going to rape me," she continued, "but I passed out before he could force me to go with him. Ryan stopped him, and now we need to go to court to testify."

He blinked at her slowly, trying to take all of this information in. He said nothing, but his eyes relayed his fear.

"Nothing happened to either of us," she said. "Ryan knocked him out before he could do anything. I just got a few bruises from when he dropped me. But I didn't tell you or anyone else because the whole thing upset me too much. I saw a counselor at school, and she helped me see that I did need to talk about it. I wanted to tell you, but I knew you'd be mad and hurt that I hadn't told you originally, so I just … didn't."

He got up in total silence, walked over to his books and calmly picked out two that he needed. Placing them in his book bag, he slung it over his shoulder, letting out a tired sigh as the relatively light weight hit his strong back. Glancing around the room, he found his keys and his sunglasses and walked out of the room, closing the door behind him.

Jamie spent the rest of the day and all of the evening in a state of panic. A heavy weight had settled in her stomach as she came to grips with the knowledge that she had probably torn their foundation of trust from its moorings. Jack didn't call, and he didn't wear a pager or a cell phone, so she had no way to get in touch with him. At around eight, she got in her car and drove to the law library, but a thorough search of every cubicle failed to find him. The next hour was spent in a dazed inspection of every possible place that he could have hidden himself on the campus, with every library and every student lounge being thoroughly investigated. Next, she got back in her car and parked on University, just outside the gates of the school. She walked from one end of the long street to the next, looking carefully in every restaurant and bookstore. But her hour-long search proved fruitless. Even though she knew it was probably pointless, she preferred to walk around aimlessly to the terror she felt when she was alone in the apartment.

Eventually she had no more ideas, so she returned to the apartment and flopped down on the couch. She fell asleep in the same position that she had collapsed in, exhausted and depressed. Around midnight, she woke with a start to the sound of Jack's key in the lock. She dashed to the door before he was even in the room and tried to speak to him, but he brushed her aside as he placed his book bag on the floor and walked into the bathroom.

She was waiting right outside the door, but again he walked past her like he didn't know she was in the room. He stripped down to his boxers and got in bed, turning his back to the door as he turned off the bedside light. "Aren't you even going to speak to me?" she asked, dumbfounded.

Silence was his only reply. She considered getting in her car and going home, but she didn't think it was wise to further escalate the issue. The sofa was big enough for her, but she thought her physical closeness might thaw him out at some point. So she got ready for bed, and slid in next to him, being careful not to touch him.

She lay awake for hours, going over the events that she had clearly set in motion. *I'm so angry with myself for not telling him! How would I feel if he withheld something so big? I'd feel utterly betrayed. I just don't know how he'll ever be able to forgive me for this.*

Some time during the early morning hours she drifted off into a fitful sleep. She woke every half hour, with the fear of the incident burning in her chest. Around four, she let out a startled gasp as she turned to find Jack's intense gaze fixed upon her, the moonlight glinting off his steely blue eyes. "Did you ever love me?" he asked with a flat, emotionless voice.

"Of course I do!" She lifted her hand to stroke his face, but he caught it and held it tightly, actually causing her a slight bit of pain. "Please, Jack, please let me touch you. Let me hold you."

He closed his eyes and let go of her hand. She took that as a sign of acceptance, so she quickly moved closer and wrapped her arms around his body. She pulled him to her as tightly as she could, and murmured into his ear, "I'm so sorry. I know I hurt you, and it's all my fault. It's all my fault, Jack. Please forgive me."

Tears were streaming down her face as she began to kiss his rigid body. She started at his neck and breathed in his musky scent as she worked her way down to his collarbones. His scent became a vital need as her lungs filled with the fragrance, and she sought to increase their capacity just to satiate her craving. Licking and kissing down his body, more for sustenance than to arouse, she continued on her slow, torturous path. When she finally began to nibble around the waistband of his shorts, she grasped them by the legs and pulled them halfway from his body, then lifted them to slide over his erection.

She kissed and sucked her way down his belly, and found to her amazement that she had an overpowering need to take him into her mouth. She was an inch from her goal when he pushed her onto her back and quickly entered her, completely without warning. The combination of her need and the fear of losing him combined with his raw aggression to make her more aroused than she had ever been. She moved with him, urging him on more vocally than she had ever done. Feeling completely out of control, her climax swept over her like a tidal wave, washing some of the pain and dread from her soul. Her release pushed him over, and he finished quickly, panting and sweating until he collapsed on her body.

Recovering quickly, and emotionally unsatisfied, he started the same intense examination of her body. He kissed and sucked and bit his way from her face to her toes, needing the constant stimulus of her flesh vibrating against his mouth. She was fully ready for him when he climbed on top for another connection. Every muscle ached for rest, but she managed to merge with him for another debilitating climax. He couldn't be satisfied for a long while, but he finally groaned out his release. Sliding down her body as he withdrew, he collapsed with his head against her breast. His weight was mostly on the bed, but even the small portion that rested on her was terribly heavy. But she would not, could not bear to move him. They fell asleep in that same awkward position, and remained nearly motionless until morning.

When they woke, they struggled through an hour or so of embarrassed silence. But as the day went on, things got more familiar and settled back into a relatively normal day. Before dinner he turned to her again, and while she knew the encounter would be painful, she willingly gave herself to him, trying to maintain their connection. She couldn't overcome the discomfort, and she knew that he wouldn't be satisfied unless she reached climax, so for the first time in their relationship she successfully faked an orgasm. Her performance must have been Oscar caliber, because it pushed him over immediately. He nuzzled against her breasts tenderly for a long while before he relaxed and fell asleep against her in much the same position as the night before.

She woke at ten that night, disoriented and disheveled. It was such a pain to drive to Berkeley in the morning that she decided to get into her clothes and go right then. *Well, we settled absolutely nothing*, she thought as she settled into the Boxster for the long ride home. *We never talked about what happened or how either of us felt about it. God, what if I had been raped? Would he still refuse to talk about it? Is this really the way it'll be for our entire relationship? Fight, have sex, fight, have sex … all the while ignoring the huge issues that are bearing down on us?*

"Jamie?" the deep voice reverberated through the phone on Sunday night, just minutes after she arrived home.

"Hi, Daddy," she said with a mental rolling of her eyes. She had conversed with her parents infrequently since their last argument, and each of the conversations had been rather stilted, if not contentious. Her father hadn't again brought up his ridiculous idea about her moving back home, though, and for that she was grateful.

"Jamie," he began again, clearing his throat, "I don't like the distance that seems to have developed between us. What can I do to make things right?"

Wow! Someone noticed! "Well, uhm … first of all, I'm really glad that it's important to you to stay close," she said. "That means a lot to me, Daddy."

"Of course it's important to me. My relationship with you is the most important one in my life! You mean the world to me, and I want you to know that I'll do whatever I can to work on this. I mean … I know we've each said things that we regret, and I want you to know that I'm sorry for upsetting you."

"I'm sorry too, Daddy," she murmured as her voice caught. "I don't want you and Mother to be angry with me, but I have to learn how to be my own person."

"I know, dear," he soothed. "That's part of growing up. We'll try to be more supportive of your choices. It's just … well, I guess it's just hard to have your baby become independent."

"Thanks, Daddy," she said. "Sometimes it's hard for me too. But I guess growing up is never easy."

"Well, another reason for my call is to discuss your official growing up," he said with a small chuckle. "You know that you're entitled to your first major distribution from the Smith trusts on your birthday. Have you given much thought to that?"

"Uhm … well, I knew it was happening, but I haven't really spent much time thinking about it. What do I need to do?"

"There are hundreds of decisions to make, Jamie. We're talking about a massive amount of money here," he reminded her. "Do you want to keep the money managers I've hired? Do you want to sell off the securities and take a cash distribution? Who do you want to represent you?"

"Wait … wait," she begged. "I don't know what I want to do! Do I have to make all of these decisions immediately?"

"Well … yes," he said slowly. "If you want the distribution, you need to be prepared to handle it."

"What do you mean, 'If I want it'?" she asked.

"The trust makes the first two distributions discretionary," he said. "I thought you knew that."

"Okay … back up a bit, Daddy," she said. "Give me the whole story."

He took in a deep breath and slowly let it out. "All right, dear," he said. "Here's the story. The bulk of your inheritance will come from the Dunlops, and other than the discretionary income that has been used on your behalf, you get nothing from that trust until you're thirty. But the Smith money can be distributed in several ways. Your mother and I are the trustees for your funds, and we can make three distributions to you—twenty-five percent at age twenty-one, twenty-five percent at age twenty-five and the remainder at thirty. The first two distributions are entirely at our discretion—if you don't want the money or we don't think you're ready for it, we can wait. And as I'm sure you remember, the entire trust is due to be distributed when you marry."

"Yeah, I do remember that," she mused. "I guess I thought I'd just take it all at once and Jack could help me figure out what to do with it."

"There's no reason we can't do it that way, Jamie," he assured her. "There are many, many decisions that you have to be prepared to make if you want the money now. If you don't feel up to it, there's no reason to force it."

"Maybe that would be best."

"Are you happy with the way things are now?"

"Yeah … I guess I am," she admitted.

"Then let's hold off," he suggested gently. "Or do you want to discuss this with Jack first?"

"No," she said. "This isn't really Jack's concern."

"Well, it will be, honey," he reminded her. "He's going to be a very, very wealthy man when you marry."

"No …" she explained, "he's going to be married to a very wealthy woman … there's a difference, Daddy.

Her father's wry chuckle surprised her a bit, but when he said, "I'm well acquainted with the difference," she blushed at her unintentional gaffe.

"I'm … I'm sorry, Daddy, that came out all wrong."

"No offense taken, Jamie," he said. "You're absolutely right, of course. And believe me when I tell you that it's vital for you to work out an agreement about how you'll handle your money before you marry. Otherwise it will be a constant source of contention."

Oh boy! Another constant source of contention! Just what we need!

Chapter Thirteen

Ryan had been pestering Jamie for a week, trying to get her to decide what she wanted to do to celebrate her birthday. Since the day fell on a Thursday, Jamie wasn't going to see Jack or her parents. Her parents had invited her down for a celebration on Saturday, the thirteenth, and Jack had decided that they should celebrate both her birthday and Valentine's Day at the same time. Ryan found this arrangement more than odd, but she kept her comments to herself. *The jerk lives twenty-five minutes from here! He can't drag his ass up here for a couple of hours to celebrate her twenty-first birthday? And who wants to lump her birthday in with Valentine's Day? That's beyond cheap!*

It took Jamie until the day before the event to finally decide that she wanted to go to a bar to have a legal drink. This was fine with Ryan, but the next problem was finding an acceptable bar. "Where do you normally go?" Jamie asked.

"I don't go to a lot of bars. I don't drink much, and I'm not crazy about crowded places. But when I do go to one in the East Bay, I usually choose a lesbian bar right on Telegraph. I don't think that's what you had in mind though. Maybe we should ask Mia, I'm sure she knows every hot spot in the bay area."

"I don't care about the atmosphere. I just want to have a drink without fake IDs."

"Would you be comfortable in a lesbian bar?"

"Yeah, I would if I was with you. Besides, we'd be bothered less at a gay place."

"Hey, speak for yourself," Ryan said haughtily, as she ineffectively hid a grin.

"You know what I mean, silly. The men there won't want us, and you've said that lesbians aren't very aggressive, so I thought we'd be left alone."

"That's probably true. It's fine with me if that's what you want to do. How about dinner first?"

"Sure. You pick where we go. Why don't you come over at six or so to pick me up?"

As promised, Ryan showed up slightly before six o'clock. She was dressed in her black silk T-shirt, and a new pair of black, lightweight wool slacks with deep pleats. The pants were held up by a thin black belt, and they draped attractively over her long legs. Her black leather jacket was draped casually over her shoulder and she looked tall and lean and strikingly sexy. "We need to get going, Jamie. I made reservations for dinner at six sharp."

"Reservations? We're going somewhere that you need reservations?"

"It's your birthday, knucklehead. I thought it'd be nice to take you somewhere where the biggest question isn't 'You want fries with that?'"

Jamie looked down at her jeans and golf shirt. "You wait right here, I'm going to change. I need to keep up with my escort. You look so … so …"

"Evil?" Ryan supplied helpfully, her face breaking into a crooked grin.

"No, I'd say you look sleek."

"Sleek, I think I like that."

Five minutes later, Jamie came down the stairs in an outfit that clearly rivaled her escort's in terms of sleekness. She had changed into a black, crepe, tube dress that followed the curves of her slim body. The dress was covered by a supple, black leather bolero jacket that gleamed dully in the light, with small black flats finishing the look. "I've decided that we should both be PIBS."

"PIBS?" Ryan inquired as she slowly walked around her friend, looking at her outfit with open appreciation.

"People in black. It's very L.A."

"If this is how they look in L.A., I'm moving tomorrow."

"You're such a tease, Ms. O'Flaherty."

"Oh, I'm not teasing," she said with mock sobriety. "You just look so … so … so …"

"Sleek?" Jamie inquired.

"Yeah, but more than that." She pondered her image again. "Sophisticated, glamorous, sexy … somewhere in there," Ryan said, waving her hands in the air.

"That's probably because my mother bought this for me. She forced me to attend an art exhibit down in SOMA, and she insisted that all of my clothes were either too mainstream, or juvenile."

"Well, I'd say that's one of the least juvenile outfits I've ever seen."

As they left the house, Ryan dashed ahead and opened the passenger door, waiting until Jamie was settled before she gently shut it. *Jack could learn some manners from her,* she thought. Ryan drove, of course, and they pulled up to the valet at Chez Laurent at six sharp.

"Ryan, you're so sweet! I told you I liked this place months ago. It's adorable that you remembered."

Ryan gave her a curious look. "If it's important enough for you to tell me, it's important enough for me to remember. I couldn't get reservations downstairs, but I thought we'd be more comfortable upstairs anyway. It's more casual."

"I actually prefer the upstairs. It's not filled with stuffy businessmen trying to impress clients. People from the neighborhood eat upstairs."

Jamie ordered her favorite meal, a small steak with French fries. Ryan had rack of lamb with some delectable oil-roasted rosemary potatoes. She insisted on ordering a bottle of wine, but made Jamie pick out the vintage since she was wholly ignorant on the subject. Jamie was just a bit disappointed that the server didn't ask for her I.D., but she had to admit that she was glad she looked over twenty-one.

Jamie was impressed that Ryan seemed very comfortable in this atmosphere, even though she was certain that she didn't dine out much. They had a leisurely dinner, and both saved room for dessert. After they had savored cups of cappuccino and a delightful piece of chocolate silk cake, they headed home. The bar was close to Jamie's, so they had decided to park back at the house and walk.

After parking the car, Ryan dashed over to her bike and removed something large that was lashed to the seat. She carried the big box into the house with a wide grin on her face.

Jamie tried to wrestle the box from her hands, but Ryan held it securely, finally holding it above the laughing woman's head. "What makes you think this is for you anyway?"

"Because it's my birthday and you're too sweet not to give me a present, even though you don't need to."

"Well, you've got me there. This is for you." She presented the box to Jamie with a flourish.

Jamie proceeded to rip off the wrapping paper and tear the heavy cardboard in a matter of seconds. She was delighted to pull out a brand new, bright yellow, motorcycle helmet. "Ryan, this is so cool! I absolutely love it!"

"I've been worried about your wearing my spare. It's fairly large so that anyone can wear it. But I wanted to get you one that would fit properly. Your head is mighty important to me, you know." The fit was perfect, and Jamie decided she wanted to take the bike to the bar. Ryan agreed, but suggested that Jamie might want to change first. "Have you ever ridden a motorcycle in a short tight skirt?"

"Oh, good point. Should I change, or should we drive my car?"

"I'm very content to have you stay in that outfit … forever. But you get to choose. It's your birthday."

"Can I drive?" Jamie begged as her face scrunched into an adorable little pout.

Ryan pursed her lips as though deep in thought. But she quickly let her face slide into a grin, as she said, "You know I'm powerless against that puppy dog face. Of course you can."

Jamie was running up the stairs to change before Ryan finished her sentence. "Be right back!"

A surprisingly short time later, Jamie jogged back downstairs, still looking lovely, but much more equipped to drive a motorcycle. The short, black leather jacket remained, but now it covered a white turtleneck. Neat black jeans topped shiny black boots, now firmly placing Jamie into the sleek category. "Do you often warn your dates not to wear skirts?" she teased as they made their way to the driveway.

"Well, no. I encourage my dates to wear short skirts."

Jamie was concentrating on getting onto the bike, and she hadn't noticed Ryan's leering grin. "Why would you …" she started to say but the answer came to her quickly. "Ryan!" she cried as she slapped her friend in the stomach. "You're such a …"

"Letch?" she once again helpfully supplied.

"At least!"

Moments later they pulled up to a rare, legal parking space near the bar. It was still early, and there weren't many people in the establishment. The place was dark and smelled of smoke, even with the ordinance that banned smoking in bars. Jamie figured that years of smoke had permeated the walls and floors.

"Well, well, well," said bartender. "The class factor in here just went up a hundred percent." She reached over the bar and shook Ryan's hand. "Haven't seen you for a while. I'd ask what you've been up to, but it's pretty obvious," she teased as she regarded Jamie with a long look.

"You're incorrigible, Sandy. This is Jamie. Tonight's her twenty-first birthday, so treat her right."

"You certainly look like you're used to being treated right," Sandy said as she leaned over the bar and moved her head close. "I guarantee that I'll continue that tradition," she purred.

Jamie unconsciously moved closer to Ryan, and meekly ordered a white wine spritzer. Ryan asked for the same, but without the wine. After Sandy had placed their drinks before them Jamie whispered with a laugh, "I thought you said women didn't come on so strong."

"Sandy would be the most surprised person in the world if anyone ever took her up on one of her propositions. She's been in a committed relationship for years, but she loves to joke around."

They found two stools near the rear of the bar. The jukebox was on, and the volume was a little higher than Jamie would have preferred but they could hear each other if they leaned close. "So what do you think?" Ryan asked. "Is it what you expected?"

Jamie looked around carefully. "I haven't been to a lot of neighborhood bars, but from the few I've seen, this one looks pretty typical. If you looked in quickly you wouldn't notice it was a gay place at all. Are most gay bars like this?"

"No, this is more like your typical, middle-class lesbian place. Some of the weekend clubs are very glitzy and appeal more to the lipstick lesbians. I don't know why, but I feel more comfortable here. There are tons of good-looking women at the weekend places, but I hate the noise level. I like the more laid back atmosphere of this place."

"Why do you call them weekend places?"

"Some promoters have a traveling club that's only open one night a month or one night a week. You'll see signs up advertising where the party will be. It's a lot cheaper to just rent a place for one night, then they don't have the upkeep of keeping a place open on the slow nights."

"But you don't like them?"

"No, it's not that. Sometimes they're a lot of fun. But they're real high energy and uhm … well, let's just say that I wouldn't take a date to one."

"Why not?"

"It's hard to uhm … well, I tend to uhm …"

"You get hit on a lot don't you?" she asked with a big grin.

Ryan's chagrined look was a clearly affirmative answer. "A lot of people I know go to those, and it gets kind of embarrassing."

"You can't help it that you're irresistible."

"It's hardly that. I've just dated so darned many women that it seems like half of the city knows me when I go to one of those big parties."

"Well, I think it's because you're so darned cute," she said as she tweaked her nose. "I've got to use the rest room. Is it right there?"

"Yep. It's just behind that wall. I'll keep your seat warm."

There were about five women in line, and she waited patiently while watching a spirited game of pool. When she emerged from behind the partition, she was surprised, and a bit peeved to see someone on her stool. *I don't get any respect in this community. Hitting on her when I go to the bathroom! Unacceptable!*

She marched right over and slid in between Ryan and the stranger. Ryan's legs were splayed wide apart, and she nestled herself right between them as she leaned back against her. When she received a rather wide eyed look from the visitor, she smiled sweetly and said, "Hi, I'm Jamie, Ryan's date. Who are you?"

"Just leaving," she said quickly as she did just that.

Ryan's head moved forward to rest on Jamie's shoulder. Her deep chuckle rumbled across Jamie's back as she said, "I guess I could take you to one of those weekend clubs. You'd just open a can of whupass on anyone who got near me."

"It's all about respect. You've got to let them know they can't mess with you."

After Jamie had reclaimed her stool, they sat and chatted amiably while they people watched. After a while, Jamie ordered another drink, which surprised Ryan a bit. "Are you sure you're up to another?"

"Yes, Mom. I may have just turned twenty-one, but I've been drinking for years. I've spent a lot of time in Europe, and wine is part of every dinner there."

"I just want you to be careful. Alcohol will hit you harder because of your weight loss. You won't be insulted if I drive home, will you?"

"Nope. I'm a big fan of the designated driver. But since you're driving it won't kill me to get buzzed on my birthday."

Around ten o'clock Jamie decided that she needed to dance. The small dance floor was nearly filled as she pulled Ryan to her feet and led her to a spot near the jukebox. A current song that Jamie particularly liked was playing as they began to move to the beat. *My God, I assumed that she could dance, but this is ridiculous!* she thought as Ryan became one with the music. Every part of her body reflected the strong beat of the thrumming bass. She moved her hips and shoulders in a teasingly seductive way that had every pair of eyes on her. *I'm sure she isn't conscious of how sexy she is. Every woman in this bar wants her*, she marveled. They continued to dance as three more good songs came on.

Jamie was no slouch as a dancer herself, and by the time they finished, most of the women in the bar were deciding which one of them they'd choose if given a chance.

The exertion of their dancing and the closeness of the room made Jamie feel a bit tipsier than she normally would after two drinks. Ryan actually felt a little light headed herself, due to the lingering effects of the wine from dinner. They went back to the bar for a few minutes, and Jamie signaled Sandy for another round. When her spritzer was delivered, she drank it quickly, mostly to get hydrated. She knew she was getting buzzed, but she was having such a good time that she let herself go for a change, ignoring the inner voice that normally kept a tight watch on her actions and her emotions.

It was too loud to talk, so they just sat back on their stools and watched people dance for a few minutes. After a while Jamie felt cool again, and as soon as another favorite came on she rose and took Ryan's hand. The song was very slow and sensual and Ryan cocked her head as she gazed down at her friend. She leaned over a little and asked, "Are you sure?"

Jamie's answer was to guide her to the dance floor without a word. As she slipped her arms around Ryan's waist, she felt her partner's strong arms slide around behind her shoulders and drape loosely behind her neck.

As they moved to the slow, insistent beat of the music, Jamie drew imperceptibly closer to her friend. There was still a respectable distance between them, but she could occasionally feel Ryan's thigh brush against hers. A warm tingle passed down her body when Ryan's breasts touched hers slightly. They continued this soft and gentle connection when the song changed and another soft melody began.

There may have been other people on the dance floor, but only one person existed for Jamie at that moment. The connection between them was both soothing and electric. Each small touch, each warm breath that passed by her ear, made her feel more and more deeply bonded. The next song was considerably faster, but neither woman made a move to break the connection. They continued to hold one another as they moved at half time to the quick beat.

When the next song began, Jamie found herself drawn inexorably closer to Ryan's body. The slow love song thrummed in the background, but Jamie felt so connected that she swore they were moving to the merged beat of their hearts. The song was over much too soon, and as it wound down, they stood back slightly with their arms still gently holding each other. They silently regarded each other for a few long moments, both feeling the electricity in the air. Ryan leaned down slightly to speak, but Jamie misinterpreted the movement. She slowly closed her eyes and slid her hands up the powerful back to rest behind her neck, then she placed her lips gently on Ryan's and let the warmth wash over her like a summer rain shower. The kiss was gentle and tender and relatively chaste, but it lasted considerably longer than she had intended. Ryan didn't make any move to separate, so Jamie eventually pulled back. Ryan's crystal blue eyes locked onto hers, freezing her in place for a moment. There was a hint of a question in those deep blue eyes, but Jamie simply wrapped her arms around her neck and held her in a tender embrace for a few seconds. Ryan returned the affection, and when they broke apart, Jamie found that she held Ryan's hand in hers.

Ryan's gaze had gentled as she looked down at Jamie and asked, "Are you ready to leave? It's getting late." Her face broke into a sweet smile, and she added, "And I think we're both a little drunk."

Jamie returned the smile and acknowledged the truth of both statements. "Yeah, we probably should go," she said as she leaned against her for another full body hug. "It's nearly midnight, so my special day's almost over."

"That's where you're wrong." Ryan leaned over and hugged her tightly, whispering softly into her ear. "The day doesn't make you special. It's the other way around."

Jamie dropped her head against Ryan's shoulder, and held onto her for as long as she could. *How does she do that? She makes me feel so precious with just a few words.*

When they emerged from the bar, they followed their previous agreement to have Ryan drive. It was just a few short blocks to the house, but as Jamie hopped off, the skies opened up as a heavy rain began to pelt them. They both made a mad dash for the door, making the front porch relatively unscathed. Both Cassie and Mia were obviously at home, but the house was quiet. Jamie beckoned Ryan to follow her into the kitchen where they could speak normally without waking anyone.

"I don't want you to ride home in this weather, Ryan."

"This is one of those nights I told you about. You know, fifty degrees and raining like heck."

"Take my car home tonight. You can return it tomorrow."

"I don't feel comfortable driving your car alone, especially in the rain. I'm not on the title or the registration, and my motorcycle insurance wouldn't cover me if I wrecked it. I'm a careful driver, but not everyone else is, and I don't want you to have to explain an accident to your father."

"Then call home and tell them you're staying here. I won't be able to sleep if you drive home in this."

"Okay, you win. I can ride in the rain, but it isn't the safest thing to do." She looked a bit shy as she asked, "Where should I sleep?"

"It looks like everyone's home, so you're stuck with me," she said with a crooked grin. "Unless you want to sneak into Cassie's room and make a woman out of her."

"I think that's beyond even my considerable skills."

Jamie took her clothes into the bathroom to change, while Ryan called home to tell her father she was taking refuge from the rain. A few minutes later, Jamie emerged in glen plaid flannel pajamas, with her face scrubbed and her teeth brushed. She offered Ryan a new toothbrush and showed her where the clean towels were. Finally she asked, "What do you normally sleep in?"

"Uhm, my normal outfit's a little casual for a sleep over."

"It's okay if you like to sleep in your underwear," Jamie reassured her. "Your underwear covers a lot more than mine does."

"My normal attire is quite a bit more casual than that."

"Ooh, that would be a touch casual. I'll find something for you." Jamie rummaged through her dresser, finally coming up with an old pair of sweats and a T-shirt that Jack had left with her during the summer. "He's taller than you are, but these should fit."

Ryan followed Jamie's lead, and went into the bathroom to change. As she brushed her teeth she reflected on the events of the evening. *God, I don't know what happened at the bar, but it felt all together too good. I know the alcohol got to her a little bit, but there was more to it than that.* Rinsing her mouth, she gazed at herself in the mirror for a moment, and admitted the truth. *I know she feels close to me ... or maybe more than just close ... but I have to keep my head. The last thing she needs is to make her life more complicated right now. When she kissed me I didn't want to encourage her, but I also didn't want to hurt her feelings by pulling away. I'm not sure I did the right thing, but it honestly felt too good to stop. Boy, this is one of those days when it's a real bitch to have morals!*

As she slipped into Jack's clothes, she thought, *I don't know if it's a good idea to sleep in her bed tonight. I wish there was another place to crash, but it would really be insulting to curl up on that little loveseat when she has a king-sized bed. I just have to remind myself that she's a wonderful, attractive, sexy, straight woman, who's engaged to be married to an idiot.* She shook her head, angry with herself. *Don't focus on the idiot part! That'll confuse you. Focus on the engaged part. She made the decision, and you need to help her honor it.*

After a few minutes, she emerged with her hair in a simple braid and Jack's clothes covering her body. Jamie marveled at her appearance for a moment. "You and Jack couldn't look more different, but those are exactly your size."

"Yeah, we just fill them out in different places."

I'll say, thought Jamie silently. She climbed into bed and turned the covers down for both of them.

Ryan looked at the bed and hesitated. After Jamie was settled, Ryan attempted to pull the covers back up on her side and lie down on top of them. "What are you doing?"

"I just thought I should sleep outside the covers."

"Afraid I'll bite?" Jamie replied, a bit cross at the insinuation.

"No, not at all," although that was exactly what she was afraid of. "I just don't want to put you in a bad position. I know Jack isn't wild about me, and I don't want you to have to explain anything that might make him mad."

"It'll make me mad if I'm trapped by these covers all night," she said. "Get in here!"

Ryan complied, despite her reservations. "I do kind of hate to sleep on top. It's lots cozier inside."

They kept a respectful distance as they shifted and adjusted their positions for a few moments. As they both settled down, Ryan quietly said, "Happy birthday, Jamie."

Jamie smiled at her friend in the dark and replied, "You made it happy, Ryan. Thank you."

Several hours later a loud clap of thunder woke Jamie from a deep sleep. She had been having a vaguely arousing dream, and as she struggled into consciousness she realized with alarm why the dream had seemed so real. She was plastered up next to Ryan, touching her with her body from her shoulders all the way down to her feet. Her right hand was slowly tracing gentle patterns on her friend, starting at her waist and traveling down her hip to the inside of her thigh. She nearly gasped in shock at what she had been doing, but when she pulled the offending appendage away she heard Ryan softly mumble, "Please ... please don't stop."

Jamie felt as though she was in a trance, as she felt Ryan's strong hand grasp hers and place it on her breast. She felt those sensuous hips move against her as they began a slow, steady beat. She wasn't sure what propelled her to respond, but she did so enthusiastically. Her hand touched, and rubbed and teased both of those perfect breasts until Ryan's hips began to grind into her lap insistently.

Suddenly, she felt herself being rolled onto her back. Ryan appeared on top of her, bracing her body with her forearms, blue eyes dark with desire. She dipped her head and stared intently for a moment, gauging Jamie's receptivity. The vivid green eyes that gazed up at her unblinkingly were a clear signal, so she locked her warm mouth onto Jamie's waiting lips. The smaller woman felt her mouth open just a bit and seconds later that warm, wet tongue slid in.

Jamie felt her head begin to spin as the sensations became overpowering. Ryan's tongue moved slowly in her mouth as her own tongue joined in the sensual dance. Jamie felt her body respond in a way that she had never imagined possible—feeling a connection with this woman that was bone deep.

Ryan lowered her torso onto Jamie's and began to move slowly against her body. Every part of Jamie's body was rubbed softly by its counterpart. Breasts glided against breasts, firm bellies and strong thighs slid sensually against each other. Every nerve ending tingled in anticipation. As the touch became overwhelming, Jamie growled as she wrapped Ryan in her arms and rolled her onto her back. She felt Ryan's legs open in invitation and she slid in between them, settling her hips in the warm furrow. Those long, strong thighs wrapped around her hips as she pressed herself against the apex of Ryan's desire, the heat radiating from her as Jamie groaned into her mouth, claiming her with her lips again and again.

Ryan's hands slid under her top and moved slowly up her sides until they found their target. Soft, warm fingers teased the taut nipples as Jamie felt the contact deep in her groin. She moaned again and again as those fingers continued to torment her aching breasts. She reached down and grabbed the hem of her top, pulling it over her head in one swift move as she pulled herself up towards that inviting mouth. Ryan didn't relinquish the firm hold that her thighs had claimed as she moved as one with her.

Jamie lowered herself over Ryan's mouth and let out a low growl as that warm mouth captured a throbbing breast. She raised and lowered herself repeatedly as each breast was loved in turn. Ryan's hips were nearly off the bed, but she clung desperately to her.

Jamie felt herself nearing climax as Ryan bit down on a tender breast. She threw her head back and felt herself release as wave after wave of sensation coursed down her body. Unable to support herself on her shaking arms, she felt herself collapse onto Ryan's powerful chest.

A loud thunderclap rumbled through the house. Jamie sat bolt upright in bed and whipped her head around trying to make sense of where she was. She focused her senses and found that she was fully clothed. She looked to her left and found a peacefully sleeping Ryan. *Oh my God, was that a dream?*

She lay back down and let the dream wash over her again. *I've never felt anything so real! Touching her and being touched felt so completely erotic. I don't think I've ever been that aroused.*

Thoughts and sensations fought for space in her overtaxed brain. *Why did I dream about Ryan like that? Is it just because I'm a little high and she's lying so close to me? I mean, every woman at that bar wanted her. If I'm going to fantasize about a woman, why not choose Ryan?*

I'd give anything to be able to respond to Jack like that. Why can't I just accept what he's able to give me and get on with my life? It's not like there's anything wrong with him. He's really a lovely man. I just wish he could excite me half as much as I was in that dream.

The alarm sounded at six-thirty Jamie stuck an arm out of the covers and slapped it with her hand, then groaned as she opened her eyes and saw the time. She turned and saw Ryan gazing over at her with a big smile on her alert face. "You're not a morning person, are you?"

Jamie merely responded by covering her head with the pillow. She felt Ryan hop out of bed and found herself falling back to sleep when she heard the shower running. When Ryan was finished in the bathroom, she came over and perched on the side of the bed. She was wrapped in a huge bath sheet, and she debated whether to put her nice clothes back on, or try to get away with wearing Jack's sweats. While she debated her wardrobe choices, she decided to wake Jamie. She looked down at her friend, so peaceful and serene in sleep. She considered a gentle way to wake her, finally letting her evil side win. She threw the covers back as she climbed onto the bed and began to tickle her mercilessly. Jamie giggled and thrashed about on the bed as Ryan refused to let her go. There was a very brief knock on the door that occurred almost simultaneously to it being thrown open.

Cassie opened the door a bit and stuck her head in. Ryan was mostly covered by the bath sheet, but she was straddling a wildly twitching Jamie. Their hands were locked together as they fought, but the open door caused them both to freeze in place. Both women caught the expression on Cassie's face that was a mixture of glee and revulsion. "Jack's on the phone," she said as she ignored Ryan's presence and their very compromised position. "He said he called you yesterday to wish you a happy birthday, but you were obviously … out. Do you want to speak to him … or are you too … busy?"

"Of course I'll speak to him. Just give me a second," Jamie said as she hopped up and dashed to the bathroom.

Cassie went back downstairs and was speaking with Jack when Jamie picked up the upstairs extension. "You can hang up now, Cassie. I've got it." Cassie signed off and Jamie greeted him. "Hi honey, thanks for calling. Sorry I missed you last night."

"Isn't it a little early to have visitors, Jamie?" he inquired softly.

She sighed deeply as her hopes were dashed that Cassie had been discrete. "Do you want me to answer that, or was that a rhetorical question?"

"I suppose it might as well be rhetorical. I don't feel that I ever get the whole truth out of you anymore."

"If you want to know why Ryan is here you can ask me. I don't lie to you Jack, and if you don't know that we've really got problems."

"I'm not sure that I do know that, but I'd agree that we most definitely have problems. I hope you had a nice birthday, Jamie. I'll see you tonight if you're still planning on coming down." He hung up before she could form a reply.

This is a big deal. You can't continue to ignore the fact that Cassie is making him nuts about this. Look at it from his perspective. To him, Ryan is the same as a guy. All he knows is that you were in bed with someone who he believes is sexually interested in you. Cassie probably made it sound even worse than it was … which wouldn't have been hard to do.

But even though she knew that the last two weeks had been very damaging to her relationship, and that she should be concentrating on that, she couldn't help thinking about Ryan. *I cannot believe that I kissed her like that! God, I can't believe how incredibly soft her lips were. So much different than kissing a man. It was just like melting into the softest thing I can imagine. And what in the hell must she have been thinking? She wasn't as buzzed as I was, and she's always in such control. Did she enjoy it too? I know I should bring it up or apologize or something, but I don't think I can.*

Her stomach was in such turmoil that she was only able to get down a diet 7-up for breakfast. Ryan bought her story about being a bit hung over, so she didn't give her too hard a time about not eating. Now lunch was coming up, but there was no way she could even think of eating.

I've got to talk to Jack. Obviously I can't concentrate today anyway; maybe I'll drive down to Stanford and look for him. What the hell. I'll take my bike and ride around campus for a couple of hours to get rid of some of this stress.

An hour later, she was furiously pedaling around the campus. She knew he had a long class on Friday afternoon, and she thought she remembered that it was over at three. *I think that's his last class of the day so I should be able to find him.*

At 2:45 she was riding up and down the street where most of the law buildings were housed. *Oh, there's his law review partner. She'll know where he is.* "Hey, Natalie!" she called out.

"Oh, hi Jamie," she replied with less warmth that she usually exhibited. "Looking for Jack?"

"Yeah. Do you know where he is?"

"He's just getting out of his Secured Transactions class. I'm supposed to meet him here to go over some things. But … uhm … I'll just go to the law review office. Ask him to come over there when you're done talking." She looked uncomfortable as she added, "Good luck."

A few minutes later he came around the corner with a neutral expression on his face. But the moment he saw Jamie his eyes narrowed and his entire demeanor became rigid. "I saw Natalie and asked her if I could talk to you for a few minutes before you get together. She said she'll meet you in the law review office. Can we please go somewhere quiet for a little while?"

"Sure. Let's go over to one of those benches," he said, pointing to a quiet picnic bench in a grove of pine trees.

She walked her bike as he walked beside her in silence. She climbed up to sit on the table and he sat on the bench so that her head was a little higher than his. "Will you talk to me about how you're feeling?"

He stared straight ahead for a few moments until he finally said, "I'm confused. I'm more confused than I've ever been. Were things really so bad for you before? I really thought we were happy, but maybe I was deluding myself."

"No, Jack, that's not true. I was happy before, we were happy before. And we still have really good times together. I know this is a hard period of adjustment for both of us, but I promise it can be even better when we get through it. I know it seems like I've changed an awful lot, but deep down inside I don't think I've changed at all. I think I was just afraid to let my real self out before. I was trying to be the woman that my father and mother wanted me to be. Then I wanted to be the woman you wanted. Now I'm just trying to be who I am. I know it's difficult, but I think I'm getting to the real me. And in the long run, I think that's the only way you and I can be happy together. We both have to have the freedom to be ourselves."

"I'm not really sure what you mean by freedom," he said slowly. "Have I been stopping you from doing what you want?"

"No, not really. But you're not always as supportive as I'd like. The AIDS Ride is really important to me, and you just don't seem to have any interest in how my training is going. And you don't seem interested in my schoolwork. You used to ask me questions about my classes, but you don't anymore."

He looked down at the ground for a few moments as he pondered this. "You're right. I haven't been supportive. It's just that since Ryan is so intrinsically involved in the ride I try to steer clear of the topic. I don't think we've ever discussed her without a fight, so I guess I do avoid asking you about it just to keep the peace."

"But we can't live like that, Jack. You have to be able to tell me when things bother you. It doesn't help to avoid topics."

He looked at her for a moment and nodded his head slowly. "Okay, I think that Ryan's continued influence is harming our relationship. I'd feel much better and more secure if you'd stop seeing her."

She took in a deep breath before she replied. "That's not talking about your feelings, Jack. That's just telling me what to do! I want you to talk about how my friendship with Ryan affects you. But I can't stop seeing her just because it bothers you. What if it bothered you that I was in college? Should I drop out?"

"If you chose to go to college in New Zealand or Japan, and we could never see each other, and I couldn't afford to talk to you on the phone? Yes, you should drop out if it was harming our relationship. I'm not asking you to get my approval over all of your friends. I'm just telling you that this particular friend is a real threat."

"But she's not! That's the point. She's only harming our relationship because you perceive that she does." She reached down and rested her hand on his shoulder as she looked into his eyes. "This is just the type of issue that we're going to have again and again in our relationship. There are going to be choices we make that the other isn't going to be happy with. But this is me. I have needs just like you do. And one of my primary needs is the freedom to choose my friends and my activities."

He looked up at her in reflective silence for a few minutes. He gazed at her face carefully, starting with her eyes. She felt like she was on display, but she allowed the discomfort since he seemed to need to do this. "Okay, I think I'm finally starting to understand. This isn't just some temporary thing. You're showing me for the first time who you really are. And it seems that one of the things that's most different is your independence. You want to be able to make your own decisions without regard for how it affects me or your parents. Right?"

"Well, I wouldn't say without regard, but that's essentially true. I need to do the things that are important to me even if the people I love aren't that crazy about them."

"Like when you told Stephanie that you weren't going to have children for several years," he said by way of another example.

"Exactly," she said, happy that he was finally beginning to understand. "I know that's something that we haven't really talked about, but I want to go to grad school, or spend a few years writing. I don't think I'll be ready to have kids for at least five years."

"I see. Well, it's your body, so I guess the decision rests with you."

"Well, no, not completely, Jack. Your opinion matters too. Either of us has veto power over something like that. We both have to say yes at the same time. I wouldn't get pregnant if you didn't think you were ready yet."

"Okay," he said. "I think I understand. I need to go see Natalie now, so …"

"Are we okay?" she asked tentatively.

"I'm glad you came down. I appreciate that you went out of your way to clear some things up," he said as he reached up to kiss her lightly. "I'll see you later." He got up and strode away.

Did that go well? He seemed so flat, but he did sound like he finally understood my point. I guess time will tell.

When he arrived home, they discussed neither Jamie's birthday nor their subsequent fight. *As usual, we ignore the things that cause the most strain in our relationship. It amazes me that he still hasn't asked why she was in my bed. If another man slept with him I'd like to know why!* They spent their evening as they usually did. Jamie made dinner and later watched a movie while Jack read. When they went to bed he made love to her, but she could tell that he wasn't very emotionally connected. Normally he spent a lot of time looking into her eyes while they touched. But this time he broke off eye contact just a few moments after he entered her. He buried his head in her shoulder and just pumped away, almost like he was forcing himself to finish. She didn't have an orgasm, and for the first time that she could remember, he wasn't concerned about that fact. When he was finished, he merely kissed her on the cheek and wrapped his arms around her. He was asleep in moments, but she was awake for hours, feeling partially aroused and rather lonely even in his embrace.

On Saturday night they went to her parents' home together. Jack looked very handsome in a navy blue, double-breasted blazer over a white, long-sleeved golf shirt. Gray flannel pleated slacks finished his look. Jamie was dressed in a short, sleek silk dress in a deep, burnt umber. The deep earth color complimented her golden hair and showed off the tan she had obtained from her frequent bike rides.

Catherine greeted them at the door. She was obviously over her pique at Jamie, as she kissed both of her cheeks and gave her a firm hug. Jim came down the stairs moments later, giving Jamie a hug and a kiss as well.

They chatted about law review and Jack's recently completed finals. Jim was working on a case that had been in the news, and he and Jack discussed it in detail. After a while, Catherine asked what Jamie had done on her actual birthday. She casually replied that she had gone out for a drink with friends, noticing Jack's discomfort at the topic. She didn't elaborate and they didn't pursue the topic.

After a delicious dinner, Catherine brought out several small boxes as Marta presented a lovely white cake with coconut frosting, Jamie's favorite. Her mother had purchased a lovely pair of emerald earrings, the stones fashioned in a brilliant cut, nestled in simple gold collars. The earrings were lovely, and they looked fantastic when Jamie put them on.

Her father gave her the thinnest watch that she had ever seen. Its solid gold case was no more than one-eighth inch thick. It was waterproof and shock resistant which made her happy as she thought about wearing it while working out and riding. It had a woven gold bracelet that hung loosely on her small wrist. Engraved on the back was "Happy 21st, Love, Daddy."

Jamie was very pleased with the gifts, and she thanked both of her parents profusely. They told her of their travails and different choices available to them in deciding on the gifts. After a little while Catherine handed Jamie an envelope. Inside was a first class ticket to Milan via Air Italia. "I want to take you to a wonderful new exhibit at the Ufizzi," Catherine said with excitement in her voice. "I've seen so little of you this year I thought it would be a great way to reconnect."

Jamie's pleasure turned to dismay when she noted the departure and return dates. "Oh, Mother, this is so thoughtful, but I'm not free during these weeks."

"Of course you're free. School will be out by then, I checked myself."

"Mother, I told you about the bike ride I'm participating in. My ride is right in the middle of this trip."

"Jamie, I thought I made it clear that I didn't want you to do that ride," Catherine said slowly.

At this point Jim interrupted, looking confused. "I don't know anything about a bike ride."

"As I told Mother, I committed to riding in the California AIDS ride this year, Daddy. It begins on June sixth and ends on the twelfth."

"Where are you riding, New York?"

"No, it's from San Francisco to Los Angeles. This year almost 3,000 people are going to participate."

Catherine interrupted, "Jim have you ever heard of anything more dangerous or foolhardy? You know what Highway 1 is like. I'm afraid she'll be killed!"

Jim regarded his daughter for a long while. He cast a glance at Jack who seemed to be studying the pattern of the Oriental rug. "Is this something you're preparing for properly?"

"Yes, Daddy. I bought the right kind of bike, I've been working out in a gym with a trainer, and I'm riding about a hundred miles a week now."

"What do you think of this, Jack?"

"Jamie makes her own decisions, Jim," he said without much enthusiasm.

"Catherine, I think that Jamie is old enough to decide to do this. I trust her judgment, and this seems like a good character building experience." He smiled at his now grinning daughter, "How does this benefit people with AIDS?"

"Every rider pledges to raise at least $2,500. The money I raise will go to the San Francisco AIDS Foundation. People who live in Southern California donate their pledges to the Los Angeles Gay and Lesbian Community Center. Both of those groups give direct care to people living with AIDS."

"Catherine, I think you should allow Jamie to decide if she wants to go to Europe with you this summer. If she chooses not to go, perhaps she can turn that ticket in and donate the money to her ride."

Jamie jumped off her chair and raced over to her father. She wrapped her arms around his neck and whispered into his ear, "I knew you'd understand. Thank you, Daddy."

As she pulled back, he lay his hand on her cheek and smiled up at her with admiration. "I'm proud of you, Cupcake," he said as he used a favored childhood nickname. He turned to Jack and beamed, "This one has a ton of determination, doesn't she, Jack?"

"Yes, sir, she certainly does," he replied somewhat stiffly.

Catherine finally relented and agreed that Jamie could use the ticket however she chose. She was firm in her resolve to worry as much as she wanted, however. "I still think of you as my little girl, Jamie. I suppose I'm having a hard time letting go."

Jamie walked over to her mother and kissed her cheek. "I don't want you to let me go completely. Just let me make my own decisions."

"It's so hard for me to believe that you'll be married in a little over a year. But I suppose you can decide to ride a bike if you can decide to get married," Catherine said, smiling.

Jack had been nearly silent during this whole interchange. He finally spoke up to tell Jamie that he had a present for her back at his apartment. She found that a bit odd, but nodded her assent.

At around ten o'clock the young couple was on their way back to Palo Alto. Jack was silent on the ride home. Jamie noticed that he looked very tired, and that his movements weren't as smooth and graceful as usual.

When they arrived at the apartment Jamie was surprised that Jack didn't immediately change into his sleepwear. He sat down on the couch and looked at her with a blank expression on his face. She was very uncomfortable with his attitude, and she sat next to him on the couch as she took his limp hand in hers. "Honey, are you all right?"

In a flat voice, he responded "Don't you want your gift?"

"Uhm, sure, if you want to give it to me," she said unsteadily, as her heart started to pound strongly in her chest.

"I'm giving you what you want. I'm giving you your freedom." He stared at her with emotionless blue eyes.

"H... h ... how are you giving me freedom?"

"I'm giving you the freedom to live your life exactly like you want. You don't have to answer to me. You don't have to be concerned with my feelings. You're officially a free woman, Jamie. Congratulations."

A wave of panic hit her like a tsunami. "Jack, please don't do this," she begged. "It doesn't have to be like this!"

"Yes it does. I don't feel the way I used to feel about you. You've become a different person." He slowly looked at her right in her eyes as he delivered the knock out punch, enunciating clearly. "I don't like that person."

Jamie rose on shaking legs to stare at him, as she backed away from the couch. "Is there anything I can do to make you change your mind?"

"No. Last night, when we were having sex, I realized that I wasn't in love with you any more. There's no way to change that."

She could feel her ire rise as her eyes narrowed dangerously. She spat out angrily, "Did you realize that before, during or after we had sex, Jack?"

"During," he said, through gritted teeth. "I tried to connect with you, but as usual you looked like you'd just as soon have been riding your bike as making love."

Jamie used every bit of control that she had left in her shaking body to refrain from hurling an insult back at him. She knew from the look in his eyes that his love for her was gone. She felt her control start to take over as she slowly, sadly, and thoughtfully removed his grandmother's engagement ring from her left hand and handed it to him.

"You're right" she said. "You do deserve someone who can please you. I'm just sorry that it couldn't be me." With that, she turned and went to the bedroom to pack her bag.

When she returned to the living room he was sitting right where she had left him, tears running down his cheeks. His eyes stared at the floor, unfocused. She stood by the couch and looked down at his face, then touched his cheek with her palm. After a moment she leaned over and kissed him one last time, whispering as she rose, "I'm sorry, Jack. I'm truly sorry."

She didn't want to do it, she really didn't. But she had no other option. It was nearly midnight, but it was Saturday night and there was a good chance that she was still out. But she had to call her. She dialed the pager number from memory.

Minutes later the smooth, deep voice came through the little phone. "What's wrong?" Ryan asked in more of a statement than a question.

"Are you busy right now?"

"No, I'm just trying to get to sleep after a very frustrating evening with Tracy."

"Did you have a fight?"

"Not that kind of frustrating," Ryan's voice rumbled out a full octave lower.

"Oh, I'm sorry. I … I … I didn't mean to disturb you," Jamie muttered.

"Jamie, I'm teasing you. Now please tell me what's wrong."

"Jack just … broke up with me," she sobbed in reply.

"Oh God, Jamie, I'm so sorry! Where are you?"

"I'm in Palo Alto, sitting in my car."

"It's not a good idea to drive when you're upset. I can come get you wherever you are."

"No, I can drive. It just hurts so much," she wailed as she pulled over to the curb. She was overcome by wracking, deep sobs that felt like they were being pulled from her body. She continued to cry without a pause for several minutes. Ryan was panicking since she didn't really know where she was or what her mental state was. She couldn't hear much background noise, so she was obviously not on the freeway, which reassured her.

"Jamie, Jamie," she said. "Where are you?"

"I'm just about to get on the freeway."

"No! I'm going to come get you. I don't want you to drive!"

"I'll be okay. I don't want to just sit here and wait for you."

"Could you go to your parents?"

"No, that's the last place I want to be tonight. I just want to go home," she said as the sobs began again.

"Please let me come get you. I'll be crazy with worry if you drive."

"How about if I drive, but stay on the phone. Would you feel better then?"

"Call me back in five minutes. I want to get dressed in case you can't make it," she said as she switched off. *Damn him, damn him to hell! He breaks up with her at midnight and then lets her get into her car and drive all the way home!*

Ryan was sitting on the front stairs of her house when Jamie pulled up thirty minutes later. She was emotionally exhausted from trying to keep her friend focused on the long drive, and her constant pacing made her feel like she had made the trip by foot. As Jamie killed the engine, Ryan approached the car and squatted down by the driver's door. "You can stay here tonight or I'll drive you home. I want you to think about where you'd feel more comfortable."

"Can I stay here with you?" she uttered through her tears.

"Absolutely, for as long as you like." She stood and offered her hand to Jamie. When her friend was firmly on her feet, Ryan slipped her arms around her and hugged her close. They stood like that for many long minutes. Finally, Ryan pulled back and guided the distraught woman up the stairs.

Ryan was the only one home. She led Jamie into the kitchen, and sat her down on a stool. "I'm gonna make you some hot cocoa, then we can talk, okay?"

The blonde nodded, her face the color of the milk.

"Do you have any other clothes with you?"

"Yeah. I have my bag in the car."

"Watch the milk for me," Ryan said. "I'll go get your stuff."

She was back in a few minutes, dismayed to find Jamie's head resting on the Formica countertop.

"Do you want to go downstairs and change while I finish our drinks?"

Without comment, Jamie took the bag and walked downstairs. Ryan followed her minutes later, and settled herself on the bed with the two steaming mugs of cocoa.

Minutes later Jamie emerged from the bathroom, still in her dress, crying inconsolably. "I only have one of Jack's T-shirts. I can't bear to smell him," she sobbed violently as she bent over, wrapping her arms around her stomach.

Ryan had learned this early warning signal, and she jumped up to steady her friend. "Are you going to be sick?"

A silent bobbing head was her answer. She came up behind Jamie and quickly unzipped her dress, then she slid it down her slim body and helped her step out of it. Guiding her over to the toilet, Ryan supported her as she fell to her knees and began to retch violently. Ryan knelt down right next to her, with reassuring hands around her heaving waist. When all of the contents of her stomach had been expelled, Jamie was stark white and sweating. Ryan dropped the lid and maneuvered her so she was sitting on the seat, then she grabbed a washcloth and ran cold water over it for a moment, squatting down in front of her friend to wipe her face and neck with the cool cloth. When she was fairly certain that the nausea had subsided, she guided her to the bed and sat her down.

She dashed over to her dresser and pulled out a long-sleeved, white, T-shirt, and gathered the garment in her hands. She reached behind her back and unhooked her bra, slipping the delicate lace off her shoulders, and in nearly a single move managed to slide Jamie's limp arms into the long sleeves and pull the hem down.

Jamie looked a bit better now. Her color was returning and Ryan was relieved at the thought that she probably wouldn't pass out. Ryan pulled her up onto the bed, and placed a few pillows behind her head. She debated whether to offer her the cocoa at this point. She had slipped a healthy shot of Bailey's into the drink, and she was concerned that the alcohol would further irritate her friend's delicate stomach.

Nonetheless, she held up the mug in front of Jamie's eyes. "What do you think?"

Jamie reached for the still steaming mug and swallowed a mouthful. "I think it'll be okay," she said as she savored the steaming concoction. They sat in companionable silence as they sipped their drinks. Ryan didn't want to rush her, so she allowed her friend to go at her own pace. After a good half-hour of reflective silence, Jamie was ready.

"You know, I'm mostly sad, but there's a part of me that's so angry at him that I can hardly see straight. I think that's the part that's making my stomach hurt."

"Why are you angry?"

"I think he said something just to hurt me," she said. "I've never known him to do that, and it made me question what kind of man he is."

"Do you want to tell me about it?"

"Yeah, I guess so," she said. "He told me that he realized that he didn't love me anymore while we were having sex on Friday night." She blushed deeply at revealing this intimacy. "I asked him when this dawned on him. You know—before, during or after." She sighed deeply, "He said during! During! He realized he didn't love me, but he kept fucking me, just so he could have an orgasm!"

Ryan wrapped her arms around her sobbing friend and began to rock her gently. After long minutes she was able to continue. "It made me feel so violated! I thought we were making love, but he was planning on breaking up with me." She heaved a few more deep sighs, "Could you continue having sex if you felt like that?"

Fuck no! she wanted to scream. *I'd never have sex just to satisfy myself!* But instead, she soothed, "I don't know that I can answer that, Jamie. Except for Sara, I've never had sex with someone I love. It's impossible for me to be able to put myself in his place. But I can empathize with how that made you feel," she said as she continued to rock her softly. "I'm certainly not on Jack's side here, but there's a chance that he was just lashing out at you for hurting him. You might feel better if you don't try to understand his motivations, and just let yourself feel the hurt."

Jamie nodded her agreement as she tried to let go of her anger. But she quickly realized that the anger was helping her stay afloat. As she felt it ebb, she was overcome with sadness. She rested her head on Ryan's chest and let herself reflect on the three years they had together. Images of Jack flooded her mind. His smile, the way he cocked his head when he was interested in something, his quick mind, his long lean body, the way he smiled at her in pleasure after she climaxed. There were so many sweet and loving things he had done for her, it became impossible to focus on this one betrayal. But the sorrow was so overpowering that she felt too weak to bear it. Only Ryan's strong arms and powerful body kept her grounded.

It was nearly two in the morning when she began to feel more in control. For the past ten minutes or so Ryan had been softly humming into her ear. The melody was gentle and smooth as the vibrations rumbled through her body. Finally she asked, "What are you humming?"

Ryan paused for so long that Jamie was unsure if she was going to answer. "A song that my mother used to sing to me," she finally said, in just above a whisper.

"And you remember it after so long?"

"Yeah, it's the only one I really remember. She sang it as a lullaby. I'm sure I heard it hundreds of times." After a very long pause she finally asked, "Would you like me to sing it for you? It always worked to make me feel better."

"I'd love it. I've never had anyone sing me to sleep."

"Then we're even, because I've never sung this for anyone."

Ryan pulled down the covers and got Jamie snuggled in. She slipped off her own sweats and nestled close. Fluffing the pillows, she had her friend adjust them to her taste. When she was in her favorite sleep position, lying on her left side, Ryan snuggled up against her back, wrapped an arm around her and began to sing the tune.

Sleep my love, and peace attend thee
All through the night;
Guardian angels God will lend thee,
All through the night,
Soft the drowsy hours are creeping,
Hill and vale in slumber steeping,
I my loving vigil keeping,
All through the night.

Angels watching ever round thee,
All through the night,
In thy slumbers close surround thee,
All through the night,
They should of all fears disarm thee,
No forebodings should alarm thee,
They will let no peril harm thee,
All through the night.

As Ryan began the refrain again, Jamie was soothed into slumber. Her last conscious thought as she drifted off was of the profound connection she felt for this woman. *There's no safer place on earth than in her arms.*

She felt Ryan slip out of bed just after the sun came up. Not one molecule in her body wanted to follow her friend, so she slipped back into sleep easily. At around nine her body demanded that she answer its call, and she slowly stirred. She heard a soft chuckle from behind, and she sleepily turned and saw a smiling Ryan, sitting at her desk, in her underwear, pouring over her books. "I didn't wake you, did I?"

"No, I didn't hear a thing. How long have you been up?" she asked through a yawn.

"About three hours," Ryan replied after checking her watch. "Duffy and I went on a run, then I made breakfast for the boys, and I've been studying for about an hour."

"What time is it?" Jamie inquired, shaking the fog from her brain.

"It's just after nine. What can I make you for breakfast? You name it."

"Something bland would be good. I'm still a little queasy. I think I'm going to go to Mass at ten-thirty." She stretched languidly and asked, "Do you want to go with me?"

"Uhm … I will if you need me to," Ryan replied after a brief hesitation. "I have plans to have brunch with Tracy, but I'm sure she wouldn't mind if we shifted it to a late lunch. Actually, let me call her and cancel. I think I need to stay close to you today."

"No, Ryan, really. I'm fine going alone. I'll call my grandfather, and see if he can spend some time with me after the service. You go meet your girlfriend." She climbed out of bed and patted Ryan on the shoulder, then walked a step or two before turning back and wrapping her arms around Ryan's neck. "I can't thank you enough for last night. I honestly don't know what I'd have done without you."

Ryan leaned her head down to rest on Jamie's entwined arms and gave her a gentle pat. "I'm glad you called me. Now go get ready while I get you breakfast."

Jamie was amazed at the array of items in front of her place at the table. There was a large bowl of slow cooked oatmeal, a small pitcher of cream, bowls of brown and white sugar, a bowl of raisins, a cut up banana and a tiny bowl of blueberries. "I wasn't sure what you liked on your oatmeal, so I brought out everything."

"I usually have what Mr. Quaker gives me. I'm unfamiliar with all of these options. What do you recommend?"

"I am a fan of cream, brown sugar, banana and blueberries. May I," she asked as she picked up the bowl of oatmeal.

Jamie nodded her assent, ands Ryan got to work mixing the ingredients one by one until the dish had the proper consistency. She presented it with a flourish and was very pleased by Jamie's compliments.

"I don't think I've ever had oatmeal before," she mumbled through a large mouthful of the delicious cereal.

Conor came in just then and sniffed appreciatively. "Ooh, oatmeal. Is there any more?" He walked over to Jamie and kissed the top of her head and he gave her a firm hug. She leaned back against him from her position on the kitchen stool as he maintained the contact. It was obvious that Ryan had told him what happened, but equally obvious that he was more comfortable giving her physical comfort than verbal. She patted his hands as he drew away.

Ryan came back with two more bowls filled with the warm dish. She placed one in front of Conor, and the other in front of an empty stool. Moments later, Rory poked his head in inquiring, "Oatmeal?" as all three laughed.

As Jamie was leaving, Ryan asked, "What are you doing after you speak with your grandfather?"

"I guess I'll just go home," was her sad reply. "I've got some reading to do for school."

Ryan moved around so that she was facing her friend. She squatted down a bit so that she could look directly into her sad, green eyes. "I'd feel better if you came back here. You've got your books with you, don't you?"

When Jamie admitted that she did indeed, Ryan persisted. "I want to see you again today. My date will be over by three at the latest. Why don't you come back here and study?"

"I don't know. I might feel uncomfortable with you not here."

"Let me ask Conor if he'll be home. If you're lonely, he can keep you company or you can go to my room and read." When Jamie hesitated, Ryan played her trump card, "Will you do it as a favor to me? If you won't come over, I'll have to come to your house to check on you. This will save me a lot of driving."

"Like I could refuse to do you a favor, huh? Very sneaky Ms. O'Flaherty, very sneaky indeed."

As they had arranged, Rev. Evans waited for Jamie in the Sacristy after Mass. He was in very good spirits, and was happy to see his only granddaughter, but one look at her forlorn face immediately alerted him that something major was amiss. "Do you want to tell me what's wrong now, or over lunch?" he asked as he gave her a hug.

"Over lunch, I think. It's gonna take a while." They walked next door to the small house that the church provided. The housekeeper had made them a nice lunch before she left for the day, and as they sat down at the kitchen table Rev. Evans placed his hand on Jamie's and said, "Tell me what's wrong, sweetheart."

Before she could even attempt to stop them, the tears started to flow. Jamie couldn't remember crying like this in front of her grandfather, but he patiently waited until she was able to speak. Finally, she was able to say, "Jack broke off our engagement, Poppa."

"Oh, Jamie, I'm so sorry! What a sad thing for both of you. Tell me what happened."

"Well, we haven't been getting along great since the school year started. We just fight about little things, and we'd never done that before."

"I must admit that surprises me. I honestly never saw any tension between you two."

"Maybe that's part of the problem. Neither one of us is very good at showing how we feel. Anyway, it's been getting worse lately. He's gotten very jealous, and he hates one of my friends."

When Rev. Evans looked confused Jamie explained, "Remember Ryan, who's training me for the ride?" At his nod, she continued, "Jack didn't want me to see her, and it had become a big issue. I don't think the issue is really Ryan, though. I just don't think he liked the fact that I did something against his wishes."

"Do you really think he called off your marriage just because he didn't like your friend? That doesn't seem like Jack."

"That's part of it, but another part was that I was spending lots of time with Ryan, even though it didn't interfere with our time together. He didn't like the fact that I was doing this ride, and he didn't like the changes in my body." She blushed when she said this.

"Still, Jamie, that's a drastic action over some minor issues. Is this really everything? What specifically doesn't he like about Ryan?"

"I think it's mostly that she's a lesbian. He thinks that hanging out with a lesbian is exactly like hanging out with another man. I've got to admit, I've been disappointed in his attitudes about gay people, Poppa."

"That's not an uncommon reaction, honey." He paused to look at her carefully. "Do your parents know your friend?"

"Uhm … no, I've never taken her home."

"But you've been at her home. Quite often, if I recall."

"Yes, her family has just about adopted me."

"Why haven't you introduced her to your family?"

"Mainly because Daddy agrees that I should stop seeing Ryan. He's on Jack's side on this. He doesn't understand why I'd make Jack unhappy over a friend."

He leaned back in his chair and nodded briefly. "Do your friends like Ryan?"

"Well, Cassie hates her. She's part of the reason this got so bad with Jack. She's been trying to get him upset about Ryan, and she's been very successful," she said. "But Mia likes her a lot. She's even hired her to train with."

"I want you to think about the next question carefully, Jamie. You tell me that your fiancé has broken up with you over her, your father agrees with him, and one of your closest friends hates this woman. Is there something about her that creates this level of dislike, or are they all narrow-minded?"

Jamie did as he suggested. She was deep in thought for several minutes. Finally she replied, "I think Ryan is the sweetest, most thoughtful, kindest person I've ever met. I swear there's nothing about her that isn't a positive force in my life. I really think they've jumped to conclusions because she's gay, Poppa."

He let out a breath, and rubbed the bridge of his nose in a frustrated gesture. "Well, it wouldn't be the first time that people had an irrational reaction to a lesbian." He shook his head and turned to gaze thoughtfully at his granddaughter. "How do you feel about her, Jamie?"

Jamie began to turn red as she realized that she had to tell everything. "I feel safe with her. She's my best friend, and I treasure every moment we share. She's the most extraordinary person I've ever met."

Rev. Evans leaned over and gently grasped Jamie's hand. He gave her a small smile, as he said, "Seeing how your face lights up when you talk about her could be part of the issue. Maybe Jack felt he had to compete against her. And maybe he thought he'd lose."

She nearly gasped. "What do you mean?"

"Describing her as the most extraordinary person you've ever met doesn't leave much room at the top for Jack, does it?"

A deep sigh preceded her answer. "No, I suppose not. But she really is remarkable, Poppa. She's helped me change and grow in so many ways. And I just couldn't give her up. Not for Jack—not for anyone!"

After a moment spent gazing at her face, he asked, "Do you have romantic feelings for her, honey?"

The blush that flew to every exposed inch of her skin was a dead giveaway. "Uhm, I … I … I guess the thought has crossed my mind," she said. "She's incredibly attractive and I've had a … romantic dream about her. But that's really recent. I haven't had any thought about leaving Jack for her, I swear! I love her, Poppa, but just because I love her doesn't mean I'm in love with her does it?"

"Of course not. It's entirely possible to form a very close and loving attachment to a friend. But you say that you've recently been thinking about her in a different way. Tell me more about that."

"I guess it's snuck up on me," she said. "I … I actually kissed her on my birthday," she said with a furious blush. "But it was just one kiss, and we didn't even talk about it afterwards. We've slept in the same bed twice since then and nothing has happened, so I think it was just kind of a fluke."

"Do you think it's within the realm of possibility that Jack could have picked up on your changing feelings?"

"What? That I kissed her?"

"No, honey. Could he have picked up on the fact that your feelings for her are beginning to deepen?"

"I'm not sure that they've deepened, Poppa. I'm just so confused," she moaned. "I suppose it's possible that Jack noticed something. But he disliked her from the very beginning, long before I knew her well at all."

"Besides this thing with Ryan, how are you getting along with your parents?"

"Not great. Mother is very unhappy about my involvement with the AIDS Ride. Daddy actually defended me last night—that really made me feel better, but I just don't think the issue is dead. And I'm worried about their reaction to Jack's breaking up with me. I'm sure they'll blame me."

"Anything else?"

"I feel like I'm growing up all at once, Poppa. I'm making decisions for myself and no one is supporting me. They still think of me as a child, and I think Jack did too."

"How have you been feeling, honey? Is this all bothering you a lot?"

"Yeah, it really has. My sleep has been way off, and I can't seem to keep my weight up. You know how I get my nervous stomach? It's been a lot more nervous than normal and that contributes to the weight loss," she said. "I'm down to less than I weighed when I entered high school."

"Have you ever considered seeing a counselor? I think this would be a great time to get some professional help with these issues."

"Can't you help me? You always have before," she asked with a look that reflected both fear and surprise.

"No, honey, I'm too involved. I don't think you have any terrible secrets just waiting to jump out at you. But I do think you're going through a tough time dealing with some very adult matters, and I think you could use some help. What do you think?"

"I guess that's a good idea. Can you help me find someone?"

"Sure, I have a couple of referrals. I really think this will help, Jamie. Give it time, and I guarantee you'll feel better. Now let's try to get some of this lunch into you."

Chapter Fourteen

At around two-thirty, Jamie pulled up in front of the house in Noe Valley. After knocking on the door, Conor and Duffy came to answer. "Hi. How was church?" Conor asked.

"It was good. What have you been up to?"

"Rory and I are watching the Warriors on TV. Ryan just got home. Go on down."

She started down the stairs, but paused when she reached her friend's open door. Jamie stood in open-mouthed shock at the scene in front of her. Ryan was lying half on the bed, with her new slacks around her ankles. She had on her standard knit boxers, this pair bright white. Tracy was straddling her waist, and was bent over her prey, kissing her in a thoroughly erotic manner. Ryan's wrists were pinned down securely by Tracy's hands, and the smaller woman was slowly undulating her hips. Ryan seemed to be struggling a bit, but just as Jamie turned to go back upstairs she heard her friend utter a long, low moan that turned her knees to rubber.

She had to place her hand on the wall to steady herself, but she was able to climb the stairs and reach the safety of the living room.

A few minutes later, Martin entered the front door and spoke to Rory and Conor. A shaking Jamie was standing in the kitchen, trying to compose herself.

Doing her best to look normal, she went out to greet him. "Hi, Martin."

"Ah, Jamie. I hoped that was your little car I spotted out in front." He walked over to give her a hug. "What are you girls up to today?"

"Nothing much. I just got here. I went to church this morning, and Ryan went to brunch with Tracy. I think she's downstairs changing or something."

"Does she know you're here? Go on down if you like."

"No, no," she said. "I'll wait until she's finished."

"Let me get you a drink or something to eat," he said as he regarded her thoughtfully. "You look like you're losing weight, darlin'. Are you still troubled by the attack?"

"No, it's not that. I've been having a hard time, and I have trouble with my stomach when I'm upset."

"What's troubling you, lass?" he inquired as he brushed her cheek with his palm. He was thirty years older, and a man, but his touch was so like Ryan's that Jamie found herself opening up to him.

"My fiancé broke off our engagement last night," she said shakily, as a few tears started to stream down her face.

"You poor little thing," he said soothingly. He wrapped her in his arms, and Jamie felt completely comfortable resting her head on his chest and letting out her feelings. "That man must be daft to let a prize like you get away."

"Thanks, Martin," she said softly, pulling away. "That makes me feel better."

At that moment, Ryan and Tracy came in to the kitchen hand in hand. Martin greeted them both as Jamie struggled to erase the image burned into her brain. Finally, she was able to say hello in a fairly normal tone of voice.

Ryan looked at her quizzically, as she asked, "Have you been here long?"

"No, just a few minutes. I was chatting with Martin here," she said as she smiled at him.

He smiled back and replied, "I'm going to go change out of my uniform. Try to get this one to eat a bite or two will you, darlin'?"

"I try, Da. I really do," she said as she grinned at her friend.

Tracy came over to Jamie as Martin left the room. She placed her hand on her shoulder, and looked directly into her eyes. "I'm really sorry to hear about your breakup, Jamie. How are you doing?"

"Thanks, Tracy," she replied, still shaky. "I'll be okay, but I'm not doing very well today."

"You stay close to blue eyes. She'll take care of you."

Jamie smiled at her friend. "I know she will."

Tracy went back to Ryan's side and smiled up at her. "I've got to go study, sweetie. I had a very good time at brunch."

Ryan placed two fingers on Tracy's chin, slowly lifted her head, then softly touched her lips with her own. Both kept their eyes open, and Tracy's mouth broke into a grin as Ryan pulled away. The kiss was completely chaste, no more than a light touch. But Jamie felt like she had witnessed a terribly private moment. Her chest ached with emotion at the tenderness of the contact. And somehow, right at that moment, she knew. She was as sure as she had ever been about anything in her life. No qualms, no doubts. She wanted Ryan. She wanted to be with her, to touch her, to love her. She felt herself begin to become aroused thinking about how she wanted to touch her and be touched. Her dream came back to her, and she had to close her eyes to concentrate on remaining centered.

She heard herself say goodbye to Tracy, and she knew that she was now alone with Ryan. She wasn't sure who moved first, but in seconds she was wrapped in Ryan's arms, holding on tight. But this hug felt different from all of the other hugs she had received from her friend. This time she let herself really feel Ryan's body, rather than trying to block out the sensations when they touched. She inhaled deeply to imprint her scent, she felt her warm breath tickle the side of her face. She focused on the soft firmness of her breasts as they pressed against her chest. *This is what I want! I want this woman!*

Hours passed, but Jamie was in such a fog she couldn't specifically account for any of the time. She knew they had all eaten dinner together, and she knew they spent the evening in Ryan's room, studying. Rather, Ryan studied as she tried to force herself to look at her books, instead of daydreaming about the beautiful creature sitting mere feet from her, clad only in her underwear.

As the evening wore on, Jamie watched Ryan repeatedly shove her dark hair behind her ears in an irritated gesture. Since her entire focus was on her lovely friend, she automatically found herself standing behind her and gently pulling the dark tresses back into a ponytail. But the silky hair felt so fabulous in her hands that she unconsciously began to run her fingers through it, starting at the scalp and extending all along the length. A deeply contented murmur of satisfaction greeted her ministrations, which only served to encourage her. She continued her stroking until Ryan sleepily mumbled, "Two more minutes and I'm out."

Her eyes flew open, and she stared down at her hands in amazement. She was fully conscious, but she had no memory of getting off the bed and beginning to rub her friend's beautiful head. She stood there with her fingers entwined in the dark hair, not able to reply in any fashion. Slowly, Ryan turned her head and Jamie felt the silky threads fall gently from her hands, one lock at a time. Ryan gave her a warm smile and asked, "Are you having a tough time concentrating tonight?"

Jamie tried to control the blush that was rapidly traveling up her neck. "Yeah, I guess I am. It's … hard."

"Is there a lot you need to do for tomorrow's classes?"

"No, I'm actually pretty caught up. I'm just trying to stay ahead."

"Why don't we go for a walk? I'm about to go cross-eyed from looking at these chem problems. If you feel up to it, we could walk over to the Castro and get some ice cream."

"How far is that?" Jamie asked suspiciously, knowing that Ryan's athletic capacity far exceeded hers.

"It's about a twenty minute walk at a leisurely pace," she replied. "I guarantee it's not too far for you."

They got dressed and stepped out into the foggy, damp evening. There wasn't another person in sight, and no cars passed by to disturb the silence. The fog seemed to muffle every sound from the neighborhood, and Jamie felt like they were all alone even though they were in the middle of a very large city. Ryan slipped her arm around her shoulders and said, "I'm so sorry for you, buddy. I know this is a horrible time you're going through."

Jamie smiled up at her friend, happy for the closeness. She reached up and held onto Ryan's dangling hand, pressing it into her shoulder. They walked for another few minutes before Jamie asked, "You seem to get along with Tracy really well. How do you think it's going?"

"We don't need to make small talk. I know you're not up to it."

"No, really, I'm interested."

Ryan's eyebrows gathered in concentration. After a moment, she cocked her head slightly and said, "I'm not sure, to tell you the truth. I thought a long walk might clear my head." She pursed her lips together and allowed her forehead to crease into a little frown. "I'm not sure I'm up for talking about her right now. Let's talk about you."

"Ugh," she grunted in obvious disgust. "I thought a walk might take my mind off my stuff." Looking up at Ryan, she quirked her mouth into a grin and observed, "So both of us have things on our minds that are obviously bothering us but neither wants to talk about it. That's a switch."

"Yeah, I guess it is," she agreed with a nod, not rising to the bait.

"Well, let's talk about where we're going. I've never been to the Castro, you know."

Ryan stopped short and stared at her. "You haven't? I thought they brought bus loads of straight children up here to observe the natives in their habitat!"

Jamie laughed at her exaggerated antics. "Nope. I missed this on the cultural tour. I never had a reason to come here. There's no museum, gallery, symphony, or outstanding restaurant here, is there?"

"Nope. Although I think Hot 'n Hunky Hamburgers is worth a trip."

"Riiiight. Sounds just like my mother's kind of place. No, for living so close to the city, we didn't come up for anything other than restaurants, sporting events, or culture. We actually didn't do a lot of investigating the Bay Area. I've spent much more time sniffing around Tuscany than I have San Francisco."

"Well, stick with me, pal, and I'll introduce you to every dark alley in this town."

"Did you go to many places with your family?"

"No, not really," she admitted. "Because there's six years between Brendan and me, he was involved in sports and school things by the time I was old enough to go out in civilized society. So it was hard to do things that appealed to all of us. We stuck pretty close to home. Our lives centered around our extended family, our parish and our sports teams."

"Then how do you know so much about the back alleys?" she teased.

"'Cause as soon as I was old enough to ride my skateboard over these hills I was gone," she said with satisfaction. "I still remember the first time I had the guts … or the stupidity to ride down Castro."

Through the fog, Jamie saw the steep terrain that they had to descend to reach the main business area of Castro Street. "You … you rode down this?"

"Yep. I strapped my little helmet on as tight as I could, and let 'er rip! My heart was in my throat the whole time, and my legs were shaking so badly I almost fell off, but I did it. When I got to the bottom, I actually spent a minute feeling my body to make sure I was still in one piece. I was tingling so much that I couldn't really tell!"

"So once you crossed the Rubicon there was no stopping you, huh?"

"Nope," she said. "I had some buddies from the neighborhood, boys of course, who had to do it since I could. Once we all had our wings we just started ranging farther and farther from home. We had MUNI passes, so we'd go over to Castro and Market and jump on the first train. We'd ride until we got tired of it, then get off and ride around on our boards until we got bored. Then we'd get back on and head home."

"My God!" she cried. "I had to get advance permission to go to a friend's house, and she lived three doors down!"

"Well, Da didn't know a tenth of what I did, and it's better that way. But I remember the first time I got pinched for trespassing down in the Embarcadero."

"The Embarcadero! That's miles and miles from here. How old were you?"

"Probably ten or so," she said. "Anyway, we were skateboarding down some really cool handicapped ramps some of the big buildings have. The big clothes trend had just barely started, and we were all dressed up in our big skateboarding pants and those huge parkas. It was winter and really cold, so I had on a stocking cap, too. Da wouldn't buy me the big pants of course, so I'd swipe Rory's pants when Da was at work, and roll them up so I didn't break my neck. Anyway, the pants were too big, even for my purposes, and they started to fall down just when the guards started running. My buddies blew out of there, but I caught the rolled up hem in a wheel and took a header. One of the guards caught me and started treating me pretty rough, just to teach me a lesson."

"Did he hit you?" Jamie asked in horror.

"No, he was just dragging me by my coat and screaming at me. Anyway, he drags me into the security office, and they start to give me the third degree. But I clam up and refuse to talk. I figure they'll let me go 'cause I'm just a little girl, right?"

"Wrong?" she asked tentatively.

"Wrong indeed! They searched me, and found my MUNI pass. It was in my name, but they didn't know that Ryan was a girl's name. I had to sit in that office with these goons threatening me for hours! They left a message on the machine at home, since the number was on my pass. Da finally called at around six o'clock. Listening to their end of the conversation was pretty funny," she recalled. "I heard them say, 'Mr. O'Flaherty, we have your son down at Number Three Embarcadero. He was caught illegally skateboarding, and we're holding him prior to sending him to the Youth Authority.'"

Jamie was horrified at the rough treatment that her friend had been subjected to. "Weren't you terrified?" she cried.

"Not of them or the Youth Authority," she admitted. "Actually the Youth Authority sounded pretty good compared to facing my father. The guy on the phone started insisting that I was Da's son, and I could just imagine him telling the boys to line up and count off," she laughed. "But then the guard's eyes got big and he turned to me and yanked off my stocking cap and all of this long hair came tumbling out. He about croaked! They got real nice to me after that—brought me a soda and some cookies. That really pissed me off," she grumbled.

"What? It pissed you off that he was nice to you?"

"Yeah, since it was only because I was a girl. If he was going to be a jerk 'cause I was a boy, he should have been a jerk when I turned out to be a girl."

"You're something else, Ryan," she laughed. "So then what happened?"

"Oh, I had to sit there until Da came to get me."

"Was he mad?"

"He was more mad about the parking fee than anything else," she laughed. "But I had to pay him back for that out of my allowance. Since I only got two dollars a week, it took me a month!"

"Was that your only punishment?" she asked, not imagining that Martin would ever hit a child.

"Yeah, plus a very long lecture that I really deserved about using a handicapped ramp for play. We learned our lesson that day. From then on we always kept one kid near the ramp to warn us if a real handicapped person was coming."

"You're incorrigible, Ryan O'Flaherty."

"Yeah, well hanging out on my skateboard was nothing compared to the trouble I got into down here," she smirked, as they entered the business district of Castro Street.

"It looks so … ordinary," Jamie remarked as she looked around.

"You expected what? Dungeons … transvestites in every window?"

"No … I don't know what I expected, but it hardly looks gay at all," she said as she turned in a complete circle.

"Yeah, it's pretty hard to tell," Ryan dryly remarked as they stopped in front of a small housewares store. "Do you like those towel bars?"

Jamie squinted at the very small towel racks that were displayed. The bars were actually cast concrete replicas of massively engorged penises, all extra large. The towels were embroidered for guests. One read "Cum Towel," and other "Trick Towel," and a pair that hung together read "His and His." She stood in slack-jawed shock, finally turning to her grinning friend as she muttered, "I don't know what a trick towel is, and I don't think I want to!"

A video store had a display celebrating the upcoming Academy Awards. Cute Oscar replicas lined the display window, but each Oscar was sporting a massive gold erection. Jamie gazed up at her smirking friend and asked, "Is the other side of the street all vaginas?"

"No," Ryan laughed. "It's pretty much all about the penis in the Castro."

Now Jamie's sense of equality was insulted. "That hardly seems fair," she demanded with hands on her hips. "Lesbians need love too!"

"I couldn't agree more," Ryan soothed as she wrapped her arm around her feisty friend to continue their walk.

When they reached Ryan's favorite ice cream shop, Ryan insisted that Jamie get two scoops of the double chocolate flavor. Because it was cold out, they ate in the small shop. Ryan ordered a hot fudge sundae, and Jamie watched her eat with obvious pleasure.

"Are you sure you like kissing better than eating?" she teased.

"I'm positive," she replied with a little eyebrow wiggle.

"Then you must really like kissing." Jamie said this slowly, while watching Ryan's lips and tongue caress the ice cream.

"You have no idea," Ryan intoned solemnly as she slowly shook her head.

Oh God, but I want to know. I really want to know!

Back on the street, they decided to return via the opposite side just in case there were hidden vaginas that Ryan hadn't previously noticed. "It really seems unfair to me," Jamie insisted as they confirmed that the street was clearly focused on gay men and their equipment. "I mean, the Castro is supposed to be this big gay mecca, and it's all about men. I mean, lesbians are the least interested group in the world when it comes to penises."

"Well," Ryan drawled, "ones with feeling in them at least."

"Huh?" she asked as she turned to face her friend, cocking her head slightly as she did so.

"Sorry," Ryan said quickly. "I was just making a joke. I was only referring to lesbians interest in non-human penises."

Jamie gazed down at the ground for a moment, and Ryan thought she had offended her by the little joke. But she was obviously considering the matter because she finally looked up and said, "Is that really a thing? I mean, I thought that was a bad joke that guys always make."

Ryan's color rose dramatically as she pursed her lips and tried to decide how much to reveal. "Uhm … well, it's kind of a … do you really … uhm … should I give you my personal response or do you want a lesbian-wide answer?"

Jamie immediately grasped her arm and assured her, "I'm sorry. I don't mean to make you uncomfortable. I've just heard snide little comments about lesbians and their fake penises for years. I guess I want to know if there's any truth to it."

"Well, you did see the assortment at Good Vibrations," she reminded her.

"Yeah, but I thought the vibrators would be the lesbian thing. I kinda thought the penises were for gay men."

"Uhm … well … I guess it depends on the uhm … person …" she stammered.

"You don't have to answer," Jamie insisted. "I just … I guess I'm surprised this bothers you, since nothing else has seemed to."

Ryan considered this as they started to walk again. "Hmm, you're right about that. Maybe it's because I know you a lot better now. I don't know, Jamie," she said slowly. "Maybe I don't want you to think badly of me. Your opinion of me means an awful lot."

"Ryan," she said, "why would something like this change my opinion of you?"

"I don't know," she mumbled, looking oddly adolescent. "You've been so conservative with your sexual expression, I guess I worry that you'll think my experiences make me kinda … I don't know … uhm, maybe slutty?" She gazed down at Jamie through the long bangs that had fallen into her eyes, adding to her adolescent demeanor.

"Ryan, you're a totally honorable woman! I'd never think any such thing about you! But I also have no desire to make you uncomfortable. Let's just drop the whole topic, okay?"

"'Kay," she agreed, happy that Jamie respected her privacy. She slung her arm around her friend's shoulders and said, "I'd like to talk about Tracy now. Are you up to it?"

"Definitely," she said, as she turned slightly and Ryan's arm dropped from her shoulder. She wasn't ready to relinquish the contact, so she reached over and grasped Ryan's hand. She threaded their fingers together as they walked along, hand in hand, as Ryan gathered her thoughts.

"Okay," she finally began. "I've told you that I don't want to have sex with her until I'm sure we have some permanence." She looked to Jamie for acknowledgment.

When she got it, she continued, "When we first discussed this, she agreed completely." She gave her friend a sheepish look. "She seems to have changed the rules on me, and I'm not sure what to do."

"We discussed this briefly before," Jamie said. "Is she putting more pressure on you now?"

"Yeah, it's getting more intense. If I'm gonna stay focused, I need to stop going to her apartment. God! We went out to dinner last night, and she put on this little camisole and a thin silk robe when we got back. In no time at all my hands were inside that robe, and she felt better than naked in that thin, soft silk." They had been making steady progress on their walk, but this thought made Ryan stand stock still for several moments. She looked positively transported by her memories, and Jamie actually had to give her hand a squeeze to bring her back. "Wow!" she blushed. "I'm sorry for zoning out like that. It's just ..." she mumbled as she shook her head.

"I know," Jamie said gently. "She's obviously decided that she's ready to sleep with you. Women don't put on clothes like that just to stay cool."

"Right," Ryan nodded. Then as if she had just heard her friend's statement, she looked at her and laughed as she gently shook her head. "Well, last night was bad enough, but today I went downstairs to change. I thought she'd stay upstairs, but I had my pants half off when she came down and she literally threw herself at me. I had to fight her off!" she said with a bewildered expression. "It's hard enough to hold my own lust in check. There's no way I can keep a handle on hers at the same time!"

"Do you want to be with her ... like that?" Jamie inquired.

"Yes ... yes ... God, yes! I want her so much my teeth ache," she moaned. "I've never in my life turned down sex from someone that I wanted like this."

"So ... what's the problem? She wants you, you want her ..."

"I feel like I want her like I normally want women. I'm used to having sex, Jamie. A lot of sex!" she said. "I think Tracy is beautiful, and very sweet. She's smart and quick and funny. And if she makes love as good as she kisses, I bet she's tremendous in bed."

"And those are bad things?" Jamie asked, thoroughly confused.

"No, those are good things. But I have a hard time imagining that she's the last woman in my life. I don't know if I'm in love with her," she said thoughtfully. "And since I made this pledge to her and to myself, I don't feel right about breaking it."

"I can't tell you how much I admire your self control, Ryan. I know how hard this is for you."

"I guess you probably do know, given how long you waited to be sexual with Jack," she said. "How did you deal with the frustration?"

"Well, besides the obvious ways of releasing pressure, I knew it was the right thing for me. And to be honest, I enjoyed those days a lot more than I enjoyed having sex."

Ryan stopped dead in her tracks, mouth gaping open. "You did?" she squeaked out.

"Yeah, I did," she replied as she looked down at the pavement. "I guess that should've been a clue that things weren't going well in the relationship, huh?"

"That must have been awful for you. What do you think changed?"

"Mia tells me that this is what to expect from a lot of guys," she said. "She says that they like kissing and touching, but that once you have sex they focus on that instead of foreplay."

"Conor always teases me that lesbian sex is all foreplay," Ryan laughed. "Obviously it's not, but I'm not sure if it would bother me that much if it were. There's nothing on earth that I enjoy more than kissing a woman." She closed her eyes in pleasure, and Jamie felt her own close as well. "I guess that having a penis just changes the focus of sex."

"From my limited experience, I'd tend to agree," Jamie said, her voice straining a bit as they climbed the aptly named Hill Street. "With Jack, sex was all about intercourse and orgasm," she said. "I'd just be getting into it, and he'd be done."

"Ouch," said Ryan as she visibly grimaced. "You've told me about him not liking oral sex after intercourse, but I guess I didn't realize how pervasive the problem was. Were things ever good?"

"Yes, sometimes we'd be on the same wavelength. But usually I felt like I had to have an orgasm by the time he did or it wouldn't happen. It made me feel under pressure to finish, and that doesn't work for me."

"That doesn't work for anyone. I know it doesn't seem like it now, but maybe it's best that Jack broke it off. If you were really in love with him don't you think sex would've been great?"

"I always thought so," Jamie said. "I just assumed there was just something wrong with me—that I wasn't responsive enough or something."

"I rather doubt that," Ryan said with a grin. "I bet you'd be a little firecracker with the right person." She bumped Jamie with her hip and slid her arm around her shoulders again.

And you're the one I want to light my fuse, she silently replied.

Ryan finally turned to her and asked, "What do you think I should I do about Tracy?"

Don't ask me that, please! I want you to drop her like a hot rock and kiss me until I pass out! But she stoically quieted her inner conflict and responded thoughtfully, "Tell me how you feel about her."

"I like her a lot," she said. "She's got all the attributes that I want in a woman. But there's one thing that really bothers me."

"What's that?"

"I don't think she likes my family much," she said thoughtfully.

"How could that be?" Jamie asked. "You've got the nicest family on earth!"

"Obviously, she's always been complimentary, but she has very good manners, so I'd expect that. She's from a wealthy family in Los Angeles." After a beat, she added, "No offense," with a little grin.

"None taken," Jamie said.

"She doesn't complain about her own family, she just wouldn't do that, but I don't sense any real love there. She doesn't like to visit them, and she never mentions talking to them on the phone." She shook her head. "I can't imagine that."

"God, Ryan, I can't imagine not loving your family. I miss them when I haven't seen them for a few days! Maybe she just hasn't had enough time with them."

"No, that's not it. I've had her over for dinner at least six times. After it became clear that I was trying to get close to her, Da encouraged me to have her over more often. She always says she's had a nice time, but she always seems to prefer getting me alone." She looked at her friend thoughtfully and said, "I don't think Da's crazy about her either. He's friendly and polite, but he's never hugged her. I think he hugged you the first time you came over."

"Yeah, it seemed like the most natural thing in the world."

"He'd never tell me if he didn't like her, of course, but there's just no enthusiasm there. Not from the boys, either."

"I can see that would concern you, but maybe she wants to spend her time getting to know you. Maybe she thinks you'll have time later for the extended family," Jamie offered.

"You may be right," she said slowly. "But I suggested that we take the baby for the day, and she was decidedly unenthusiastic."

"Well, that seems very odd. Caitlin is the most precious thing on earth. But again, maybe she just wants to be alone with you."

"Maybe," Ryan said. "But when I talk about my desire to have children she always changes the subject or tries to distract me. The other day I asked her flat out if she wanted children, and she just laughed and said she hadn't spent much time thinking about it."

"Well, she's young," Jamie reminded her. "Lots of women don't make up their minds about that until they're in their thirties."

"True. And if you both agree that's just fine. But I don't want to wait that long. Having kids is one of the biggest reasons that I want to be in a stable relationship. And I want to have them before I get too involved in my career. If Tracy and I are gonna be a couple, she has to be enthusiastic about having kids in the next couple of years, and I sure don't get the idea she's on that wavelength."

"I guess you have to be more blunt with her, Ryan. Tell her what your plans are, and see if she shares them. She might surprise you."

"Well, there's one other thing," Ryan added. "And it could be the deal breaker."

"What's that?"

"She doesn't believe in God," she said quietly.

"Do you mean she's agnostic?"

"Nope. She's a card carrying atheist. I don't think I ever considered that I'd need my girlfriend to have some spiritual belief, but I think I do." She added thoughtfully, "It wouldn't even bother me if she were agnostic, you know, like she didn't believe in God, but she allowed that there was a possibility of a God. But we've talked about this several times. She believes in nothing. No God, no creator, no karma, no afterlife. She thinks we're here by some cosmic accident, and she thinks every bit of our energy dies and is put in a box. She has actually referred to spirituality as a fairy tale."

They were approaching the crest of the hill that led them back to Noe Valley, and Jamie had to concentrate just to keep her breathing even. But the pause let her collect her thoughts for a moment. "I think I know what you mean. My faith is such a part of my life that I'd hate to not be able to share it with someone I loved."

"Exactly!" Ryan replied. "I mean it's clear that I have issues … big issues … with the Catholic Church. I go back and forth between being really connected and really disconnected. I'm in a disconnected period right now, as a matter of fact. But my belief in what I call 'God,' for want of a better word, as the source of love and goodness and peace is unwavering. I just don't know if I can love someone who doesn't believe in what I trust to be the source of love."

"I get it, Ryan, I really do. I mean, I love to go to church. It's often the highlight of my week, but I could love someone who didn't go. I could love someone with an entirely different view of the world, like a Buddhist or a Hindu. But I'd hate to have my lover think I was wasting my time, or doing something foolish."

"That's precisely the problem with Tracy. It's not just that she doesn't believe—she equates my search for meaning in life with believing in the Easter Bunny or Santa Claus. She seems to think it's kind of a cute little phase that I'll grow out of when I mature. I mean, I like her so much, but if I'm going to be committed to her we have to have a similar moral framework. My spirituality and my family are so integral to me, it's almost like she can't know me if she can't understand and respect that."

"It sounds to me like you've already made up your mind."

"Yeah," she glumly replied as she let out a breath. "I suppose I have. I've just been trying to convince myself that it can work. I mean, it's hard to find everything you want in one person, and she seems so close." She held her hand up and spread her thumb and index finger just a tiny bit apart.

"What will you do?"

"I guess I could tell her I'm not interested in a committed relationship and see if she just wants to play around," she replied with a leer. "Or I could just tell her I'm not ready to go any further, and stop seeing her." She gave her friend a scowl. "I don't like option number two, but that's probably what I'll do."

"I think you'll feel better about yourself if you do that. Although you could tell her the total truth and see if she's open to changing her opinions."

"I think the Spanish Inquisition showed that you can't force faith on someone, Jamie."

"I don't mean that, goofy. I mean, tell her the whole truth and see if she wants to just fool around for a while. Maybe she wants to hop on the O'Flaherty Express now."

"I'm not certain what I'll do. But I guess she deserves total honesty for putting up with me for almost four months."

"That's a lot for one poor woman to bear," Jamie said, laughing. "Gosh, we're home already!" she said as she looked up and noticed they had turned onto Noe. "That went fast."

"Yeah, it did. But time always flies when I'm with you."

Jamie looked over at her grinning friend's guileless face and gave her hand a gentle squeeze. "You can say that again, pal."

Ryan let her smaller friend precede her as they climbed the short flight of stairs up to the front door. When they were nearly at the top, she leaned in close and whispered, "Just for the record, I've been on both ends of artificial penises. As Martha Stewart would say, 'It's a good thing!'"

Both ends? What in the hell does she mean by that? she wondered, unable to get the images of Ryan and artificial penises out of her mind.

When they were back downstairs, Ryan walked over to her bookshelf and pulled out a neatly labeled photo album. Idly turning the pages, she found the photo she was looking for and called Jamie over. Turning the book and handing it to her, she pointed at the photo in the center of the page without comment. Jamie barked out a laugh, slapping her hand over her mouth and staring up at Ryan in shock. There, memorialized for all to see, was the little street urchin that Ryan had described earlier in the evening. "My God!" Jamie finally got out, now able to control her laughter. "Is this really you?"

Ryan walked around to stand next to her friend. Taking the book in her hands, she smiled fondly at the image of her young self and nodded briefly. The photo showed five little ragamuffins, all of a similar age. They were posing on Maeve's front steps, and each child tried to appear older and tougher for the camera. The other four were boys, but all five were dressed nearly identically. Ryan was in the front, standing on the ground in front of the stairs. She was so extraordinarily tall that she was the same height as the two boys standing on the stair behind her. Jamie guessed that she was rail thin, but it was very difficult to tell for sure because of her laughably large clothes.

She had on a canvas barn jacket, tan in color, with a darker brown corduroy collar. The hood of a dark green sweatshirt peeked out past the collar, but the jacket was so huge she could have easily fit another sweatshirt on and still have had room. Stiff looking, dark blue jeans covered her long legs, the cuffs rolled up at least five inches. The pants were so large it was impossible to see where one leg started and the other stopped—it just looked like a big mass of fabric. She also sported flat, black, thick soled tennis shoes that looked to be about size eight. A black baseball cap rested on her long black hair in its usual backwards position. Her trusty skateboard was resting on its tail, held upright by her long, slender fingers.

Every child bore a scowl with varying degrees of success. Ryan was the least successful of all, her dancing blue eyes and microscopic smile giving her away.

Jamie stared at the picture for so long that her eyes became dry. "I don't think I've ever seen anything more precious," she finally said, looking up into Ryan's bemused eyes.

"Precious?" she squawked. "I look like a … I don't even know what I look like!"

"You look like a tiny little seed of who you've become. Look at yourself!" she urged excitedly. "You look so confident and strong! Those boys weren't leading that little group—you were! That's completely obvious. And even though you were trying to look tough, you still have that gentle spirit just pouring out of those blue eyes. See it?"

Ryan gazed at the picture and then turned back to her friend. "Are we looking at the same picture? I just look like a little hoodlum!"

"Not at all!" Jamie cried. "I'd have killed to be able to hang out with you for just a day! I bet you guys had more fun in an afternoon than I did in a year! This is what being a kid should be, Ryan. Testing your own capabilities, learning to interact with other kids, trying to look outrageous! That's the essence of youth!"

"I guess I see your point," she said slowly. "Da let me test myself constantly when I was little. I don't think I ever got in trouble for trying something stupid. He only got mad when I did something that could hurt someone else, like taking over those handicapped ramps. He really let me be who I was, even though I'm sure he was constantly worried about me. That really was a gift," she reflected. 'I hope I can do the same for my kids."

Jamie wrapped her arm around her friend's sturdy waist. "You'll probably be completely overprotective," she teased.

"Hmm, maybe," she said reflectively. "But I don't think so. I want my kids to experience the freedom that I had. It's what allowed me to dream," she added with a small smile. She closed the book and replaced it on the shelf, then turned to her friend and announced; "Now it's time for you to dream, pal. To bed with ya."

The walk, or the climb, as she referred to it, had really relaxed Jamie and she felt ready to sleep. She went to the bathroom to put on her pajamas and when she returned she was pleasantly surprised to see a grinning Ryan, sitting on the bed, holding the bottle of massage lotion.

Jamie flung herself onto the bed, pulling her shirt up as she fell.

"I don't want to force you …" Ryan teased.

As the strong, cool hands began to work their magic, Jamie closed her eyes and silently wished that one day those hands would know her completely.

When Jamie got home on Monday night, she spent the better part of the evening telling her roommates about the breakup. Both of them seemed shocked, and had insisted on a long recitation of the events leading up to it. Jamie was tired of talking about it, but after the whole story was out, Mia was very supportive. Cassie was less so, but Jamie had a feeling that even she felt guilty about the role she had played in the scenario.

She decided to tell her parents in person. On Tuesday afternoon she drove down to the Peninsula, arriving just after her father had returned home. She had never driven down on a weekday, and when she thought about it, she had never visited unannounced. Her parents were obviously quite surprised to see her, and they both seemed anxious, so she immediately launched into the reason for her visit. She told them most of the story, omitting the role that Ryan had played. She talked more about the difficulty of being apart during the week, of Jack's intense schedule, and of her own doubts about her commitment.

To her amazement, her parents were completely sympathetic. It was obvious that her father was saddened by the news, since he had grown quite fond of Jack. But she had tried her best to remove any animus towards Jack when she described the reasons for the breakup. They both seemed to agree that even though he was a wonderful young man, Jamie was probably not really ready to make a permanent commitment. Catherine in particular seemed relieved that Jamie wouldn't be tied down at such a young age.

As she was leaving, her father walked her to the car. "Was part of this because of your friend?" he inquired with a touch of hesitation.

"Yes, Daddy, it was partly that."

"It seems odd to me that Jack would be so bothered by that, but maybe that was just a sign that he wasn't ready either."

"I'm so happy that you and Mother are so supportive of me, Daddy. I can't thank you enough."

"I love you very much, Jamie. I've always been proud of you, and the way you've handled this makes me that much prouder."

"I want you to promise me that you won't treat Jack any differently, Daddy. I don't want this to interfere with his job opportunities."

"I don't mix business with emotions, honey. Jack will be a good lawyer, and we'll be lucky to land him. Don't worry about that."

On Wednesday morning, Jamie sat in a long hallway waiting for Linda Levy's office hours to begin. The professor came strolling down the hall, and waved a friendly greeting. "Hi Jamie," she said. "Sorry I couldn't see you earlier in the week. Come on in and tell me what's on your mind."

"I need a referral for a therapist, and I thought you might be able to refer me to someone good."

"Sure, I know a lot of therapists in the area. Would you feel comfortable telling me what types of issues you need to deal with?"

"I'm having some general growing up issues, and a little trouble with my parents," she said as she stalled for time. "And I think I might have some issues with my sexual orientation." She fidgeted in her chair, looking everywhere but at her professor's face.

"Okay, I know a lot of people who could probably help you. Is cost a factor?"

"No, not really."

"Do you have a preference for any particular type of therapist, like a psychiatrist or a psychologist?"

"No. I just want someone I can relate to."

"Do you care if it's a man or a woman?"

"I think I'd like a woman." She blushed as she heard her double entendre.

Linda grinned back at her, and looked through her address book, finally jotting down three different names. "I'm going to refer you to a psychiatrist, a psychologist and a clinical social worker. They're all good, and I think you'd like each of them. You can set up an appointment with each if you'd like to interview them, or you can just pick one. Do whatever feels comfortable, Jamie."

"Is there one of these women that you'd recommend more highly than the others?"

"I know the psychologist pretty well, and she's a very warm, empathic person. I suppose she'd be my pick."

"Thanks a lot, Linda. I really appreciate your input."

"Any time, Jamie. If you ever need to chat on a non-therapeutic basis, I'd be happy to. I hope things work out well for you." Jamie reached for the note but Linda held onto it tightly, drawing Jamie's eyes to hers. "One piece of advice," she said quietly. "You can never make a mistake by being who you really are, no matter how scary the truth might seem."

Jamie nodded briefly, and took the names from the professor They shared a quick smile, then Jamie left the office.

On Tuesday evening, Ryan finished preparing the simple dinner that she and Conor were going to share. He finished setting the table and came back into the kitchen to help carry their plates to the dining room. "Boy, Tracy sure looked good on Sunday," he said. "She looks fabulous in that dark brown color. You should have her wear that more often."

"I don't think I get to have input any more," she said as she carried the last of the dishes into the room. "We broke up this afternoon."

"What? I thought you were serious about her." He had stopped in the center of the room, a big plate of pasta held in one strong hand.

"I was. But I finally realized that she wasn't the one. So rather than wasting her time, I told her the truth."

"How did she take it?" he asked, remembering some of his more disastrous break ups.

"Fine. Actually a little too fine," she admitted with a smirk. "She told me she loved me on New Year's Eve, so I thought this would be hard on her, but she took it like a trooper."

"That's kind of weird. But why did you break up with her? She was pretty, smart, funny and very sexy. Well, she looked sexy," he grinned. "But you'd know best."

"She was all that. But she didn't really like the amount of time I spend with the family. She said she loved me, but she wasn't ready to love my whole family."

"What is she, some kind of psycho? What's not to love?"

"That's how I feel," she agreed with a smile. "But she was pretty reserved. I think we were a little overpowering for her when we were all together. And she doesn't like to be teased. You can't get through a dinner here without being teased ten times."

"Gee, Ryan, if you'd told us we would have laid off the teasing."

"Nope. That's not the kind of woman I want. I can't be with someone that I have to be so careful with. If she'd told me that she wanted to work on being more comfortable around you guys I'd have made some concessions. But she just wanted to maneuver me into spending less time at home. And that was not going to happen."

Conor gave her a smile and said, "Even though she was hot, I'm glad you broke up. She didn't seem to fit in at all. Too stiff."

"Yeah, I think she had a hard time being comfortable with us working class folks. Her family's pretty wealthy."

"They can't be richer than Jamie is," Conor said. "And she's one of the gang." He looked at her for another moment and said, "It's too bad Jamie's straight. She'd be perfect for you."

"Really? I thought she was perfect for you," she dryly observed.

"Yeah, but I've never gotten any vibes from her. She treats me like an older brother. How about you? Any vibes?" he asked, mostly because he was interested, but partly to protect his $50 bet with Rory.

"Uhm," she started to say but her cheeks were rapidly blushing.

"I thought so," he said slowly. "You two were acting awfully friendly when we went bowling together. So what are you gonna do about it?"

"Well, she did something about it last week. But it was nothing huge," she said defensively. "She got a little tipsy on her birthday, and she kissed me. But we both just acted like it didn't happen."

"Again, what are you gonna do about it?"

"Nothing," she said quickly. "I have a firm policy not to date good friends, and Jamie is the best friend I have. I couldn't stand to lose her."

"You know, Ryan, I'm not the best person to give relationship advice, but maybe you should change that policy."

"Why do you say that?"

"Well, you claim you're ready to find a real girlfriend. Why not get rid of six months of work and date someone you already know? You were with Tracy for four months before you found out she didn't have the goods. If you tried to make it work with a friend, you could concentrate on the love and sex parts instead of having to get to know one another."

"That might be a good idea in theory, but given my record, all I'd do is lose her as a friend as well as a lover."

"That's not being fair to yourself," he admonished her. "You haven't tried to have many steady girlfriends."

"That's true, but I don't think it's wise to even consider Jamie. She's ostensibly straight, she just broke up with her fiancé, and she's my best friend. That's an awful lot to overcome."

"But you *are* into her, aren't you?"

"I'm not blind Conor," she laughed.

"So you'd try to date her if you weren't friends, right?"

"I'd be on her like green on grass," she said with a sly grin.

"Well, I still think you should consider what I said."

"I'll give that some thought, Conor, but right now I've got to go make up for lost time."

"Hi, Ally," she said. "It's Ryan."

"Hey, gorgeous. Long time no see."

"I've been out of circulation for a few months. Do you have any interest in helping me get back in the saddle?"

"I'll be home by eight."

"Should I bring anything?"

"Just a hearty appetite," she purred.

The next morning Jamie was waiting for Ryan after her eight o'clock class. "I was going to ask you if you wanted to go get coffee, but I can see I'm too late," she said as she eyed the empty twenty-four ounce cup in her friend's hand.

"I can use more."

"Are you okay? I know you were planning on talking to Tracy, and I was worried that it might be hard for you."

"No, actually we had lunch yesterday and we talked it all out. She admitted that she didn't really have an interest in being part of my extended family. She said that she wanted to have a relationship with me, but that she wasn't really ready for a big commitment thing. She said she probably doesn't want kids either, so my suspicions were correct."

"So how did you leave it?"

"Well," she blushed a little, "she was more than willing to have a little fling, but for some weird reason it didn't feel right to me."

"Really?" *Maybe she's getting this serial dating out of her system. Oh please, oh please.*

"Yeah, it was really weird. Once I decided that I wanted a committed relationship with her, just having sex didn't seem that appealing. It felt like I'd have been settling for something inferior."

"Wow," Jamie said. "Maybe you've really changed how you feel about sex. Maybe you won't be satisfied without some substance in your encounters."

"I think that's a rush to judgment," she admitted with another blush.

"Why? Are you already planning for your next victim?"

"Uhm … I had a date last night."

"Jeez, Ryan! You didn't break up with her until noon. How did you find someone to go out with in an afternoon?"

"I didn't really go out," she said. "I called my friend Ally and she uhm … helped me … ahh … make up for lost time."

"God, I bet Tracy would love to hear that!"

"She was really okay with breaking up, Jamie. As a matter of fact, I got the impression that she was mainly interested in me to see if she could get me to be faithful. She was hardly broken up about it. It just made me realize that I can't merely look at a checklist of what I want in a woman. There has to be some chemistry there, and I don't think Tracy and I ever had that. We had sexual chemistry, but we didn't click emotionally. We both wanted different things from a relationship."

"I didn't mean to sound judgmental," Jamie said, wincing. "I think I'm just projecting how I'd feel if Jack had a date on Sunday."

"I understand. But believe me, Tracy didn't cry herself to sleep last night."

"And you obviously didn't either," she said as she gave her a mock scowl.

"Oh, I cried," she teased. "I cried for mercy!"

Just after eight on the following Saturday morning, Jamie and Ryan pulled into a parking space in Golden Gate Park. Jamie was riding in the back seat of Conor's big crew cab, playing with a giggling Caitlin. Ryan hopped out and came around to the rear passenger door, and began to busily unstrap the baby from her car seat. When the infant was released, Jamie held her while Ryan climbed into the bed of the truck by holding on to the top rail, stepping on the top of the big tire and throwing her leg over. She picked up one bike at a time, lowering each to the ground to rest against the truck. Then she picked up the lime green baby carrier and did the same.

She spent a few minutes attaching the carrier to her bike, after playfully attempting to stick it onto Jamie's. When everything was set, they all put on their helmets. Jamie and Ryan laughed for a long while when Caitlin kept trying to see what was on her head by looking straight up. She finally satisfied her curiosity by reaching for the helmet repeatedly with her little hands. The baby had just celebrated her six-month birthday and she was going to be put to the test. She had been in the carrier many times, but the last time she was quite a bit younger, and Ryan was certain she didn't remember the experience.

Caitlin wasn't at all sure that she wanted to get into the carrier by herself. She made some very serious baby faces, but finally began to smile when Ryan started to pedal. The wind whipped by her little head, and she giggled from the sensation of the movement and the gentle bouncing of the carrier on the pavement. Jamie stayed behind for a while to make sure that the baby was enjoying the experience.

"She's loving it, Ryan!" she said as she came up alongside her companion. She continued this little switch for a long time. A few minutes behind or next to Caitlin, chatting with the happy infant and laughing at her joyous face, then a few minutes next to Ryan, excitedly describing the baby's antics.

After a good hour, they both needed a rest. They left the park and rode a short distance to a coffee house. Although they had eaten breakfast, they were both hungry now that it was after nine. Jamie offered to buy, and she waited in line while Ryan took the baby to the restroom to check her diaper. When they returned, changed and happy, Jamie was waiting for them at a sidewalk table. Since Jamie had been left to her own devices, she had purchased two cranberry scones, a poppy seed muffin and a big cinnamon roll. Two very large lattes waited alongside the food. "You're finally starting to catch on," Ryan said. "You can never order too much."

While Jamie ate her scone, Ryan polished off the remaining three items, while Caitlin sucked on her bottle and observed the other patrons from her resting place on Ryan's lap. Ryan looked at Jamie thoughtfully and asked, "How did it feel to be back in the park?"

"It felt okay," she replied after a minute to think. "I'm not sure how I'd feel if we were sitting down like we were then. And I don't think I could relax enough to sleep," she admitted. "But it was okay."

"How do you feel about testifying? It's coming up pretty soon."

Jamie was well aware that they were scheduled to testify at the trial of her attacker in two weeks. "It's kind of weird for me. I mean I didn't see him until after it was over, and he was unconscious, thanks to you." She shivered a bit as she said, "I'm not nervous about the actual trial or anything, but I don't like to have to talk about the whole thing."

"I know what you mean. It's not my favorite thing to think about either."

"Does it still bother you, Ryan? I mean, I know you had trouble sleeping for a while. Are you okay now?" She reached out and gently touched Ryan's hand.

"I'm mostly fine. Every once in a while I have a flashback, though. It still scares me more than I'd like."

"Tell me what bothers you," Jamie asked, coaxing her friend.

"I flash back to the helpless feeling that I had when I thought he was going to drag you into the woods. I knew I couldn't put the baby down in case he was working with someone. It might have been a ruse to steal Caitlin," she smiled down at the gurgling baby on her lap. "But I also knew that I couldn't take her with me if I had to run after you. I couldn't risk her getting hurt." She shook her head at the memory. "It was just the most awful feeling of powerlessness. I knew I could stop that guy in a second, but I couldn't risk it. I don't think I could have lived with myself if he had hurt you," she said softly.

Jamie smiled at her in sympathy. "Sometimes I forget that this whole thing is probably harder on you than it is on me. You saw everything, and you had to make the hard decisions." She gripped Ryan's hand. "If anything had happened, it wouldn't have been your fault. You did everything perfectly. When you're trusted with the care of a child, she has to come first. I'd have been very angry with you if you hadn't protected Caitlin."

Ryan looked like she wanted to speak, but she pursed her lips and looked down at the baby, deep in thought.

Jamie could tell her friend was troubled, and she tried to lighten the mood. "You know, I'm still impressed by the hurt you put on that creep. Tell me about your training."

Looking up at her, Ryan's mouth curled into the gentle smile that Jamie loved. "Okay. When I was about twelve, I started taking martial arts. Da was worried about me, justifiably, as it turns out. I ran around all over the city on my skateboard, and I had many opportunities to get into trouble. I studied for about six years, and I was pretty good," she reflected. "I haven't had to use it in a while, but I did teach a kick boxing class at my old gym."

"You know, I might feel more confident if I learned some self-defense. What do you think?"

"I think anything that empowers a person is a good idea," Ryan said. "Learning some self-defense would make you feel more confident physically. But what about the emotional fallout from the attack? Have you considered talking about it with anyone else?"

"Funny you should ask that," Jamie replied. "I had my first appointment with a therapist yesterday morning."

"To talk about the attack?"

"Uhm … yeah, that's a part of it. I need to talk about Jack and my parents and a bunch of stuff that's been on my mind."

'When did you decide to do this?"

"My grandfather persuaded me. He was worried about my weight loss, and he thought that a therapist could help calm me down."

"Did he recommend someone?"

"Uhm … I asked Professor Levy for a referral. I mean, I know she knows people in Berkeley, so I thought it would be easier."

"So, what did you think? Did you like him or her?"

"Yeah, I did like her. Her name is Anna Fleming, and she seems pretty cool. She's down on Telegraph, right across from that Ethiopian place you like."

"Cool. I hope she can help you get rid of some of your stress." Just then Caitlin let out a yell that made them both jump. "I think Caitlin's been still long enough. Ready to go?"

"Yep, let's go."

As they rode along, Jamie brought her bike alongside Ryan for a little while since Caitlin was sound asleep in her carrier. "Have you ever been in therapy?"

"Yeah. I've had short term counseling a couple of times to get me through some rough periods. After my cousin Michael died, I had a really hard time. He and I had always been close, but we got a lot closer during his illness. I tried to go see him every day after school and help out in any way that I could. I think I believed that if I worked hard enough, and we all did everything possible, that we could save him. In retrospect, I think I was re-experiencing the trauma of my mother's death." She looked over at Jamie with her big blue eyes clouded over with grief. "I had a hard time eating or sleeping for a long time. Da didn't know what to do, but luckily someone from the S.F. Aids Foundation referred us to a grief workshop for kids. I went for almost a year. I can't tell you how helpful it was to talk to other kids who had lost someone to AIDS. Most of the others had lost a parent, and some of them had lost both parents."

"God, I can't imagine how horrible that would be. To watch your parents just waste away," Jamie said. "Wasn't it tough to listen to that?"

"Yeah, it was really hard. But some weeks the only peace I got was at that meeting. It was one of the most worthwhile things I've ever participated in."

"I'm really glad it was available to you," Jamie said. "I hope therapy works for me, but I guess it'll take a while to adjust to it."

"I'm glad you've decided to do it, Jamie. You've had an incredibly stressful year, and it makes sense that you might need some help to get through it."

"You've helped me more that I can say, Ryan. You've really been my rock, and I thank God every day that I have your friendship."

"I do that too," Ryan admitted.

"What?"

"I thank God for your friendship every day. You're part of my roster now."

Jamie beamed over at her for a moment as she said, "Best team I've ever been on."

Two weeks later, they emerged from the rather stately entrance to the Superior Court of San Francisco. The entire day had been consumed by the hurry up and wait atmosphere of the trial, and for reasons they couldn't understand, the prosecutor called the policewoman to testify in between them, forcing Ryan to hang around for an additional four hours to wait for Jamie.

"Well, at least we're done with it," Ryan observed, as she filled her lungs with the cool, moist fresh air.

"I don't know what you're planning on doing for a living, but you should consider becoming an expert witness in whatever it is," Jamie told her. "You were just phenomenal."

"Thanks," Ryan said, looking embarrassed. "I wrote down a very detailed description of what happened that day, right after we got home. It helped me sort things out. I've reviewed it a couple of times when I was having problems sleeping—in a odd way it calmed me down—so the details were pretty well set in my mind."

"I sounded like the village idiot compared to you," Jamie laughed. "The jury must have thought I had brain damage."

"I think they understood that it's hard to remember details when you're unconscious," Ryan teased. "I think you did great."

"I guess we just have to hope we convinced them," she said. "I want him to be put away for a very long time."

"Well, we should know within a couple of days. The prosecutor thinks they'll have a verdict by tomorrow or the next day. Do you want to know what the outcome is?"

Jamie thought for a moment as she leaned against the large base of a statue near the front steps. "No, I don't. I don't think they can put him away long enough to suit me, so I think I'd rather assume the best. How about you?"

"I'm interested, but only so I don't have to worry about him for a while. I see him enough in my dreams, without being worried about seeing him on the street."

"I'm so sorry that you're still bothered by it," she said softly as she leaned in to wrap Ryan in a gentle hug. "I hardly think about it anymore, thanks to you."

"I'd trade a lifetime of nightmares for your safety," Ryan said right into her ear.

Jamie had been seeing her therapist for three weeks when she finally had the nerve to bring up her sexuality. Since cost wasn't an issue, they had decided that twice a week sessions were a good idea, at least until Jamie felt some relief. After only four sessions, she actually felt significantly better. But she had spent nearly all of those sessions talking about Jack and her distress over the breakup. Now it was time to open up fully.

She finally broached the subject on a bright, cool, Tuesday morning. "There's something that's bothering me, Anna," she said. "Something I've been afraid to talk about."

"Tell me, Jamie," she said, looking at her with interest.

The younger woman stared at the pattern on the rug, unable to force herself to look Anna in the eyes. "I think that I might be gay." It was the first time that she'd ever said the words aloud, and she expected the ceiling to fall onto her head.

"What makes you think so?" Anna asked.

Jamie met her eyes, stunned to see nothing but passive interest. She found her voice and said, "I'm incredibly attracted to my closest friend, Ryan." She shifted in her seat, knowing that she had intentionally left out a lot of information in the sessions they'd had. "I haven't told you the whole story about why Jack and I broke up," she said, trying not to look as embarrassed as she felt.

Anna's soft voice said, "You don't have to tell me everything at once, Jamie. Talk about things when you're ready."

Jamie looked at her and saw the empathy in her eyes. "I'm ready to talk about this," she said, and for the first time in her life—she really was.

It took most of her session, but Jamie told Anna the whole story. After hearing her out, the therapist asked, "Have you ever acted on your feelings for Ryan?"

"Sort of. On my birthday I gave her a kiss on the lips."

"How did she react?"

"We both acted like everything was normal. But right after that, she said she thought we should leave because we were both a little drunk." After a moment she added, "Maybe it made her uncomfortable."

"Did she act any differently towards you after the kiss?"

"No, not really. She's pretty much the same."

"It must not have bothered her too much—if at all," she observed.

"Yeah, I guess you're right," Jamie said, showing a smile for the first time. "She's very honest about her feelings. If she was upset, she would have told me."

"So, what would you like to do? Do you want to try to have a sexual relationship with her?"

"I think I do, Anna. But I feel so overwhelmed by everything that's happened. I'm afraid of what I'll do if she isn't interested."

"You don't have to jump to conclusions. You don't have any idea of whether Ryan would be receptive or not. So try to think this through logically."

"Okay," Jamie said, trying to stop her heart from beating so loudly.

"Is there any reason that you have to do something right now? Or could you wait a while until you feel more grounded?"

"I guess I'm not in a rush," she said, considering this for the first time. "She just broke up with someone, and I don't think she wants to get into another relationship right away. You know, it makes me feel better to think that I don't have to hurry."

"You might feel better if you resolved some of your feelings about Jack before you put all of your energies into connecting with another person. And I think you'd be clearer on what to do about Ryan if we spent some time exploring your feelings for her."

"So you'd recommend waiting to talk to Ryan?"

"My recommendation is that you keep your life as simple as possible until you're sleeping better and able to eat. If expressing your feelings for Ryan would cause more stress, I'd advise against it for the time being."

"Well, given that I feel one hundred percent better already, I guess that's good advice," Jamie said, her smile now full and wide.

Ryan was finally able to fulfill her long-standing promise to take Jamie to hear Rory's band play. On that Friday evening Jamie drove over to the O'Flaherty house at six p.m. Everyone was there, and dinner was a boisterous affair with lots of teasing and boasting from the boys.

At eight o'clock they left in several cars to hear the band play at Kildare's Public House, a local pub where they appeared frequently.

Shortly after they all arrived, the band began their first set. Jamie was charmed by the very accomplished musicians. Most of the melodies were light and melodic, although the lyrics to nearly every song were sad or downright tragic. All of the band members sang, but Rory handled most of the lead vocals. He had a rich, mellow tenor which carried beautifully through the small room.

Jamie had been with Rory on numerous occasions, but she never would have guessed how much emotion he packed into his music. She was nearly brought to tears on several occasions by the expressiveness of his voice. After playing around fifteen songs, the band took a long break. Rory came over to the table, while the other musicians went outside to smoke.

"Rory, you were fantastic!" Jamie said. "I was so moved by your songs!"

"Thanks," he said, his fair complexion turning rosy. "Which songs did you like the best?"

"That's a hard one," she said. "I guess I liked the more poignant ones."

Everyone at the table laughed, and Jamie cast a quizzical look around. "What?"

"Which ones were happy?" Ryan asked.

"Well … there was the one about …" Her eyebrows knit and she looked up at the ceiling, trying to recall all of the songs.

Conor tried to help. "There was that happy one about losing the family farm."

"Don't forget losing your only son to a terrorist bomb," Brendan piped in.

"I like the one about the young woman who kills herself rather than marry for money," Martin teased. "That one's quite a laugh."

"How about the guy whose lover broke up with him because his family wasn't high enough on the social ladder?" Rory asked, his green eyes dancing. "It's pretty lighthearted when he throws himself off the cliff."

"Fine," Jamie said, giving them all a mock scowl. "I liked the song about the woman who lost her lover at sea, and now she's pregnant and trying to decide if she should live or die."

"I'm betting she dies," Martin said. "They always die."

"Jesus, Rory, you're making Jamie think we don't have one happy song in our whole culture," Conor complained. "Ryan, why don't you go sing a cheery one?"

Jamie stared at her friend. "I didn't know you sang in public!"

Rory replied for his sister, "She could make a good living with music if she wanted to, Jamie. She's probably the most talented of all of us."

Ryan shrugged her shoulders. "I like to sing, and I don't mind singing in public once in a while, but it's not something that I love enough to do every day."

"I'd love to hear you Ryan," Jamie begged. "Please?"

"Okay, okay. You know I can't turn you down," she grinned. Since the band was still on their break, Brendan agreed to accompany her on the guitar. They discussed what songs to play and finally settled on two favorites. "You asked for it, Jamie," she said with a smile as she got up.

She was wearing her deep red, Angora turtleneck, and a pair of soft, black slacks. Her hair was loose around her shoulders, and she had just a few wispy bangs touching her forehead. Brendan grabbed an acoustic guitar, and adjusted the strap. When he was ready, Brendan said, "We're not on the program, but the band has agreed to let us do a couple of numbers. I'm Brendan, and this is Ryan, the most lovely and talented member of the O'Flaherty family." There was a single spotlight shining on Ryan, and she beamed a smile back at him as he began the first chords to the song they had chosen.

The spotlight highlighted the mahogany and gold tones in her raven hair. Her cheeks were pink from the warmth of the room, and her eyes sparkled and danced in the bright white light. She looked entirely at ease, as she sat on a tall stool with the heels of her loafers hooked over a rung. Her posture was upright and poised but very casual, and to Jamie's appreciative eyes she looked as though she was singing in front of very close friends at her home.

In her smooth, clear alto, Ryan began to sing,

The warbler in the morning, she rises from her nest
And flies above the trees so high, the dew upon her breast
And with my ploughboy, Johnny, she'll whistle and she'll sing
And then at night, the workday done, she finds her nest again.

Several things impressed Jamie immediately. First, of course, was the sheer beauty of Ryan's voice. The music seemed to flow from her so effortlessly that she almost seemed to be talking, rather than singing. The second thing was the girlish smile and body language that Ryan had appropriated to sing the song. This was clearly a song about a young heterosexual girl, and Ryan had the ability to adopt that demeanor to sell the lyrics. The final impressive element was Ryan's ability to just have fun.

When his workday's over, I know what he will do
Into the town he'll head around, conspired to see me, too
My sweetheart he will hold me, we'll dance and we will sing
When night is done, my heart still won,
He'll leave me by the spring.

His spirits high from courting, he strolls all through the town
He'll mow the meadow and the grass until it is cut down
The nightingale she whistles, above the salt sea spray
The new moon shines and lights the way for ploughboys come they may
I love my darling Johnny, and mine he'll always be

He'll take my hand and pull me round to sit upon his knee
And with a jug of porter, we'll whistle and we'll sing
When I'm upon my ploughboy's knee he's happy as a king.

Jamie was easily able to believe that Ryan could be Johnny's lassie. But for a genetic difference, she could easily be the girl that boys fought over. She could be sitting in her house on a Saturday night waiting for her Johnny. With an internal smirk, Jamie mused that she was never so glad that homosexuality existed. It gave her a fighting chance to one day know the love of this woman.

Conor and Rory sat behind Jamie, casually watching both their sister and her friend. Conor had told Rory of his conversation with Ryan, and they decided to use this opportunity to see if there was any mutual interest on Jamie's part.

Even though Conor doubted that he'd win the bet, he offered to double it, but Rory held firm. At the end of the song, they both looked at the expression on Jamie's face. It was a mixture of love and desire, with a good measure of pure worship thrown in. Rory smiled knowingly at Conor as he held out his hand, and his older brother reached into his wallet, pulled out two twenty's and a ten, and slapped them hard onto the table.

Later that night, Ryan walked her friend out to her car. Jamie lavished praise upon Ryan, for both her singing voice and her stage presence. After discussing the band and the various members for a long while, she could tell that Ryan was beat, so she bid her goodnight.

As Jamie got into the car, Ryan asked, "What are you doing tomorrow?"

"Uhm … nothing. Why?"

"It's Saint Patrick's Day, lassie!" she announced in her lilting Irish accent.

"Okay … what are you doing?"

"I'm the barmaid at the Dublin Pub, of course!"

"Since when do you work in a bar?"

"I do it every St. Patrick's day," she explained in her normal voice. "If you're free, come over and have a pint. Conor and some of the cousins will be there to harass me, of course, so it should be fun."

"Is that the place right on 24th Street?"

"Yeah, but if you come, be prepared for a huge crowd. It's quite a zoo!"

Jamie didn't want to be at the bar alone, so she waited until eight to head over. She had to park so far away, that she wound up a block past Ryan's house. *My God, it's never been this congested over here! I guess everyone is out celebrating St. Patrick's Day.*

Her suspicions were confirmed when she tried to wedge into the bar. The rowdy patrons were packed in so tight she knew they were violating several city ordinances, but she assumed the local police turned a blind eye on St. Paddy's Day. It took a great deal of patience, and a few well placed elbows, but she finally made her way near the large wooden bar. She lucked out, and found that the crowd had deposited her right next to a happy little group that featured Brendan, Conor, Niall, Kieran and Frank. "Jamie!" they cried, nearly as one.

The overly exuberant tone to their call indicated the advanced level of their inebriation, but she gamely allowed each of the men to offer a hug, and didn't even complain about Conor's rather sloppy kiss on her cheek. "How long have you boys been here?" she shouted over the din.

"We walked Ryan over at five," Brendan said. "What time is it now?"

"Almost nine," she yelled in reply.

"No wonder I can't feel me feet!" he said in his own Irish accent.

Just then Jamie spotted her favorite barmaid. Ryan looked extremely attractive this evening, not that that was a news flash. But there was something about her that looked very different. It took Jamie a moment to realize that Ryan looked straight! It wasn't just that her hair was held back with a braided green and white ribbon, it wasn't that she was dressed in a form fitting emerald green, knit vest, sans blouse, it wasn't even the fact that she wore a touch of makeup. No, it was the fact that she was acting straight, and that, to Jamie's keen eye, was a first. Ryan spotted her, and gave a demure little wave along with a toss of her jet-black hair. Jamie grinned and shook her head at the display, but when Ryan approached the man to her left, she nearly fell from the stool that Brendan insisted she occupy.

"Evening darlin'," she announced in a rather dramatic, thick Irish accent, as she graced him with her most winning smile and a girlish batting of her eyes. "How can I help ya?"

The tongue-tied man seemed as flabbergasted by the raven-haired beauty as Jamie was, but he managed to choke out, "Are you new around here?"

"Aye!" she cried. "Just over from Killala in Mayo!" She said this with such joy that it appeared she expected the man to be a relative from the old sod, or at least a fellow Kilallan.

"Welcome to America," he said dreamily. "Can I have a pint of Guinness and your phone number?"

"Ahh, go on with ya!" she cried. "You lads are all so friendly! I've had more good wishes and offers to show me around than I can count. Such a friendly place!" she said as she turned to draw his pint. Jamie noticed that her friend bent over just enough to show her best assets as she drew his stout, smiling that unnerving smile the entire time. She placed the pint in front of him, and said coyly, "I'm not sure how long I'll be stayin', luv. It costs a pretty pence to stay in your lovely city."

He nodded as if in a trance, pulling out a five-dollar bill for the three-dollar pint, and thanking Ryan profusely as he walked back to his mates, happy to leave the gorgeous woman a sixty-six percent tip. Ryan dashed to the register and rang up the three dollars, sticking two singles into her bulging back pocket, then she dashed back and signaled to Jamie, "Meet me at the end of the bar!"

It was a tough trip, but she made the short distance not too long after her grinning friend. Ryan dug into her straining pocket, and handed the gob of slightly damp bills to her friend. "Keep my tips, will you?" she said right into Jamie's ear in order to be heard. "I don't want to look like I'm doing too well."

"Geez Ryan!" she cried. "How did you make all this?"

"An Irish accent, a tight sweater and a Wonder bra!" she laughed. "How else?"

"So you put on this act just to make money?" she asked, slightly incredulous.

"Mighty!" she agreed as she pinched Jamie's cheek and trotted back to her post.

By the time Jamie made it back, Conor had procured a perfectly poured pint of Guinness for her as well as another round for his drinking buddies. She had never seen any of the boys in their cups—had never in fact seen them drink at all except for bowling night. But she had to admit that they were a fun group of drunks. Conor especially was twice as charming, if a little sloppy. He tossed an arm around Jamie, and held on to her for the duration of the evening. But after a while it became clear that he did so to maintain his balance as much as to show his affection.

The boys had been teasing and taunting each other mercilessly all night, and Jamie found herself on the end of a few pointed barbs herself. But she didn't mind a bit—in fact it made her feel like one of the group, and she did her best to give as good as she got. She limited herself to two pints, but that was more than enough to give her a very pleasant buzz. Her mind reeled at the thought of how the boys must be feeling, since she had personally seen them each have three in the two hours she had occupied her stool.

When one patron got a little too enamored of Ryan, she watched all of the boys give him a long, stern look, but they didn't make an obvious move to deter him. Ryan took his wandering hands in stride, stepping quickly out of the way when he tried to grab a handful of her shapely butt. "I'm amazed you didn't flatten him," Jamie chuckled into Conor's ear.

"Ahh, you can't blame them, Jamie," he explained rather expansively. "She looks like she wants them to grab her, she flirts with them constantly … hell, I'm half tempted to make a play for her!" He laughed at his own joke, and nearly passed out in hysterics when he caught the look on Jamie's stunned face. "I'm kidding!" he howled. She slapped him lightly on the side and rolled her eyes in exasperation at his antics. But he leaned over as he pulled her tightly against his side. "How about you?" he purred rather seductively.

Her mouth grew bone dry as she stammered, "M … M … Me what?"

"Do you have an interest in my baby sister?" he asked in the same seductive growl.

"W … W … Why would I have an interest?" she stuttered weakly.

"I asked first," he reminded her. "Come on now, you can tell Uncle Conor," he crooned. "I promise I won't tell."

"I … I … I uhm …" she muttered, annoyed at her own inarticulateness.

"Uhm-hmm," he murmured, "Just as I thought." Her rapidly blushing face and weakening knees caused him to pat her shoulder comfortingly and hold on a bit tighter. "There, there," he assured her. "You could do worse than to fall for my sister, you know. And personally, I think she'd be a fool to let you get away." He tilted his dark head down and rested it against Jamie's for a moment. "You're quite a woman."

She closed her eyes tightly, and accepted the truth of his statement But a relatively soft object, hurled at her head at close range, broke the moment. Turning faster than her slightly blurry eyes appreciated, she whirled around to find a grinning Ryan tossing peanuts at her from a dish on the bar. "Don't encourage him, Jamie," she warned. "He'll follow you home like a lost puppy."

Jamie tried to look normal, but she was afraid that Ryan had, through some miracle, heard her conversation with Conor. But her friend was gazing at her with her usual, happy smile. "No problem. I've always wanted a puppy," she said affectionately as she teasingly petted Conor's dark head.

"Well, don't blame me if he starts humpin' your leg," she warned, accent firmly in place as she dashed down the bar to pour another pint.

Even though she valiantly tried to leave several times, Jamie found herself still in place as Ryan called out, "Last call, lads! Final pints!"

She lifted her arm to gaze at her watch in amazement, finding it did, in fact, read 1:45 a.m. "My God," she muttered. "How did it get to be so late?"

"And how did I get to be so drunk?" Brendan moaned, dropping his head into his hands.

"You are drunk," Frank agreed, shaking his head and clucking in distain.

"Can't hold his liquor," said Kieran, who was clearly as drunk as the rest of the boys.

"I've only had two, and I can hardly talk!" Jamie moaned. "How will I get home?"

"Yer comin' wit us," Conor insisted in his own Irish accent. "As soon as we help da wee one wit her chores."

Jamie watched in awe as the drunken O'Flahertys got to their wobbly feet and gamely bussed the tables around the still-crowded bar. "Drink up, drink up," Niall insisted as he walked from patron to patron, trying to retrieve their still-full glasses.

She hopped to her feet, held onto the bar for a moment to get her balance, then went behind the bar to aid Ryan and the other two women in their daunting task of washing each glass. But many hands made short work of it, and by the time Frank and Brendan forcibly ushered the last patron out at two-fifteen, the bar was clean enough for the professional cleaning crew that would arrive soon.

Ryan walked, and the others stumbled, the few short blocks—first to Frank's home, then another few to Kieran and Niall's. They arrived at the O'Flaherty house at 2:45, grateful for the fact that Martin was at work. Ryan guided Brendan to her father's room, and gave him a kiss on the cheek as he fell to the bed. Conor was able to make it all the way up to his room, but he accomplished the feat by holding on to the banister for dear life.

Ryan tossed an arm around Jamie, and guided her down to her bedroom. "So, did ya have fun?" she asked, back in her Gaelic persona.

"Yeah, very much so. Your family's really a blast to hang out with. And it was worth the trip to see you playing the coquettish straight girl," she teased as she playfully backhanded her in the belly.

Ryan looked thoughtful for a moment. "It's fun for me to act like that once in a while," she said. "But I can't imagine having to do it every day! I don't know how some straight women keep that act up." She held out her hands as Jamie started unburdening her pockets of the plethora of bills she carried. "Like you," Ryan said as she started to sort the money. "You're a straight girl, and you don't hardly ever seem like you're putting on that 'Oh you're so cool, and I'm such a helpless creature' routine." She looked up at Jamie, who was choosing a T-shirt from the massive selection in Ryan's neatly labeled drawers.

"Hardly ever?" Jamie asked.

"Well, I saw you do it with Jack that time I was in Palo Alto," she said. "But that's the only time."

"Hmm, I guess I don't do it much," she admitted. "But Cassie does it constantly. She acts like she's got a brain stem injury when her boyfriend's around."

"Well, it's nice that you don't do it much," Ryan observed. "It must be demeaning."

"Well, you do some manipulative things to get women too, Ryan. Don't act like you don't."

Ryan looked up at her with a completely guileless look on her handsome face. "I don't think I do. Oh, I flirt, and act a little more forceful than normal, but I don't think I try to alter who I am, or what my capabilities are. I just try to show my assets to the best of my ability," she said with a wicked glare as she shook her shoulders and jiggled her breasts in an entirely provocative manner. "That kind of stuff is too easy," she muttered disdainfully. "Women don't go for it."

Some women do, Jamie thought as she quickly scrambled to the bed to avoid falling down.

After Ryan had methodically counted her booty, they got ready for bed and hopped in together. "What's up?" Jamie finally asked after she felt Ryan toss and turn for long minutes.

"I don't know. I guess I'm worked up after tonight. I'm having a hard time relaxing."

"Let me help you out for a change," Jamie said. She found the massage lotion on the bedside table and shook it provocatively.

Ryan smiled in the darkness, and rolled over onto her stomach. Jamie began to push her T-shirt up, but Ryan just reached down and yanked it off. There was no moon, and the light in the room was too dim to make out anything but rough shapes, but Jamie was still a bit excited at the thought of Ryan's half naked form lying right before her.

When Ryan rubbed Jamie's back, she usually straddled her waist. But she had always had sweats on. Jamie was only wearing a long T-shirt and her underwear. She considered her options—get up and put sweats on, sit next to Ryan on the bed, or jump on and hope for the best. She threw caution to the wind and hopped on. Thankfully, Ryan was still wearing her sweatpants, so when Jamie straddled her hips there was an adequate layer of fabric between them. Nonetheless, she found herself feeling a bit weak at the sensation of sitting on those softly muscled buttocks.

She hadn't given many massages, but she had received hundreds during her travels in Europe. She knew what she liked, and she assumed that Ryan would like a similar touch. Focusing her attention, she did her best to rub the strong back in a clinical, professional manner—but she failed miserably. She found that her hands were guided by an unseen force. They lightly and gently touched and rubbed and prodded the tense muscles. Her hands began to dig deeper into the tissue, eliciting a hiss of pleasure from Ryan. After that sensuous verbal cue, she really got into the experience. After a while she had a difficult time feeling where her hands ended and Ryan's back began, so close was her connection to her friend.

She was rewarded with occasional grunts of satisfaction when she hit a particularly tense spot, but her toes nearly curled when she touched a spot low on her back and Ryan let out a low, pleasure filled moan. *Focus, damn it*, she shouted to herself. After working for a long while, the muscles felt smooth and pliable under her fingers. Ryan hadn't made a sound for several minutes, and her body was still and loose. Jamie finished up by touching her entire back lightly with just the tips of her fingers. She slid off the strong hips and was surprised when she felt no movement from her friend. She leaned over and heard rhythmic, deep breathing and realized that she was sound asleep.

Oh, this isn't good. Definitely not good. I don't want to wake her to get dressed, but I can't sleep next to her naked chest.

She fretted about the situation for a few minutes, finally deciding to be brave and try to get to sleep. She lay right next to her deeply sleeping friend, occasionally trailing her fingers down her lovely bare back. When her fingers strayed too far to the side she could make out a very sexy bulge where Ryan's generous breasts had compressed. Try as she might, she had a very tough time keeping that hand away from that gentle curve. Every nerve in her hand itched in anticipation, but she clamped down on her raging impulses and forced herself to close her eyes. Eventually she succeeded, and she fell into a deep, sound sleep

Ryan woke just before seven, puzzled by several sensations. One was that she was in exactly the same position that she had been in for her massage. *I never sleep on my stomach,* she thought. Secondly, she was naked from the waist up. *Did I take off my shirt? Oh, yeah, I took it off for my massage. Ooh, what a massage. I had no idea Jamie was that good*. Thirdly was the warm hand of her masseuse resting low on her back, with a couple of fingers under the waistband of her sweats. *God, this is a pleasant way to wake up. She wanted to just lie there and feel the connection. Why does it feel so good to have her touch me in such an innocent way? Geez! I don't know if I can keep my wits about me this morning.*

Finally, her good sense got in the way and she slowly extricated herself from the contact. As she rolled over, she pulled the shirt on over her head.

Jamie was still just inches away. Ryan lay back and regarded her sleeping face in the morning light. The sun was just beginning to touch the pillow where her head rested, and her golden hair was mussed from sleep, tumbled in an attractive fashion around her face. The tips of her long, dark blonde eyelashes were lightly brushed by the sun's rays. Her smooth skin was beginning to take on a golden tone from all of the outdoor activity, and a few freckles dusted her nose. It was all that Ryan could do not to lean over and kiss each of those cute little freckles.

God, I wish she were a lesbian! It's so frustrating to feel this way about her and not be able to do anything about it! But she knew that she could never do anything about it. It was one thing to take a lesbian friend and try to make her into a lover. But it was quite another to take a straight friend and try to turn her into a lesbian. *Thanks Conor, thanks a lot! I've never thought of the possibility, but you had to put the idea in my head!* She shifted a bit in frustration, as she gazed at the peaceful face resting so close to her. *God, I'd love to touch her. She looks so delectable lying there, all soft and smooth. And she smells so good*, she thought. *It can't hurt to take a little sniff can it?* She leaned over to inhale—

And was greeted by sleepy green eyes, half-open and dull. "Is it time to get up?" Jamie asked, sounding very unhappy at the idea.

Ryan was having a hard time ordering her thoughts, but she finally replied, "Only if you want to. We're not in a rush today." With that she tousled the golden hair a bit and hopped out of bed. *Definitely time for a cold shower thanks to you Conor*, she muttered to herself as she closed the bathroom door.

After going for a brisk run with Duffy, she stopped at her favorite coffee shop, Megan & Brothers, for a pair of giant lattes. She didn't expect Jamie to be up for a while, but knew that her friend would be in a much better mood if she had a big cup of coffee waiting for her.

As expected, the house was completely still when she entered. Since the morning was cool and her pace had been slower than usual, she didn't really need another shower. Sneaking back down to her room, she grabbed a pair of sweat pants and a hooded sweatshirt and tiptoed back upstairs. She had to get dressed in the kitchen, since every room was occupied, but when she was finished, she briskly towel dried her hair and went out to the front deck.

The fog showed no sign of dissipating, but that didn't bother her in the least. She actually had to admit that she preferred a cool, gray morning, a nice soft day as her Granny would say, to a bright, sunny dawn. Given her habit of running nearly every morning, she welcomed the heavy damp air that the fog brought, and she always found that her times were better and she was more rested after a run in the fog. Her coffee was nearly finished, and her perusal of San Francisco's joke of a daily newspaper was just about complete, when a still-sleepy, tousled blonde head poked out of the front door.

"It's freezing out here!" the grumpy little mole face groused.

Oh-oh, Ryan privately thought. *Somebody's hung over.* "It's not too bad," Ryan said as she rose to greet her friend. "Sit down and I'll bring you a nice cup of latte and a blanket."

Jamie didn't reply to this thoughtful offer, she merely flopped down on Ryan's now-empty chair and waited for her delivery.

Well, I've become pretty adept at getting Caitlin out of her cranky moods. Now I'll see how my skills work with a bigger baby. She dashed into the linen closet next to her father's room, and got out a soft, cotton quilt that her grandmother's sewing circle had made for her when she was a baby. Even though she had been tiny, the women had let practicality dictate, and they had made the quilt fit a full sized bed.

Trotting back to her charge, she gently tucked the blanket around the shivering woman, receiving only a grunt of thanks.

Next came the coffee, which she warmed in the microwave while she took out a big earthenware mug and ran some hot water through it. By the time she returned, Jamie looked warmer but even grumpier, as she waited for her caffeine boost. *Hmm, this calls for drastic action*.

Ryan sat down on the roomy, padded chaise lounge and said, "If you come sit by me I can make your headache go away."

"Who said I have a headache?" she muttered, staring into her cup.

"No one," Ryan said. "But sometimes I get one when I'm up late at night." *Especially when I've had too much Guinness.*

"Where do you want me?" she replied none too happily, as she tried to hold onto both her coffee and her blanket.

Ryan spread her legs wide, placing her feet on the floor. She patted the seat in front of her and said, "Come sit between my legs. I'll hold your coffee until you're settled."

Jamie handed her the cup and climbed onto the chaise with her back to her friend, then she settled the comforter over her body and held her hand out silently, indicating that she wished the return of her beverage. When Ryan was sure she was settled, she brought her hands up and began a very light massage of her shoulders. "Tell me where it hurts," she cooed into the nearby pink ear. "Here?" she asked as her fingers climbed the throbbing head and settled just above the neck. "Here?" she asked again as her hands moved to the area just behind her ears. "Or here?" as they moved to her temples.

"Yes," her patient replied with a sigh. "Everywhere."

"Okay. First I'm going to massage your shoulders and neck to get the blood flowing. Then, when you're nice and loose, I'm going to apply some acupressure points on your head. I guarantee that you'll feel better in no time."

"Prove it," the grouchy skeptic demanded.

Wow, tough crowd, Ryan mused with a smirk as she set to work. But she enjoyed few things more than a good challenge, and she was determined to make her friend happy before the morning was up. She started off nice and slow and gentle, allowing time for deep sips of the steaming latte. When she could see that the cup was nearly drained she got a bit more aggressive, and within minutes Jamie's head was rolling around on her shoulders like a limp rag doll's. When she had thoroughly relaxed her, she started on the acupressure points.

Working gently but firmly, she applied pressure to all of the spots that she knew might be causing her friend pain, compressing each of the major blood vessels for a few seconds, smiling to herself as the limp woman in her lap sighed with each release.

It took almost a half hour of determined work, but she was amply rewarded when a very satisfied voice purred, "God, that felt divine. Thank you, Ryan. You're the best."

The brunette replied by beginning a very gentle head rub of the adorably mussed golden hair, and within minutes Jamie was curled up against her chest, purring audibly. Watching her friend relax so thoroughly brought a wave of sleepiness over Ryan, and before she knew it she felt her eyes begin to slowly close.

At ten o'clock Conor stumbled onto the deck, stopping dead in his tracks at the sight before him. His sister and Jamie were sharing the same chaise; Ryan in the back with Jamie nestled between her legs. The smaller woman was slightly on her side with her knees drawn up, and her head pillowed nicely on a plump breast. Ryan's baby quilt covered them both and Ryan's arms were loosely draped around her body in a protective embrace. Sweet smiles graced both sets of lips. *That's about the cutest damn thing I've ever seen*, he thought, through his own splitting headache. *Call me narrow minded, but I'd be out of my mind if my straight girlfriend was curled up like that on her lesbian best friend's lap!*

Chapter Fifteen

On the next Friday night, Ryan pulled Martin's truck up a fire road on Mt. Tamalpais, looking forward to joining her friends for their regular monthly mountain bike ride. Jamie was more apprehensive about this ride than she wanted to admit, and she hadn't had the nerve to share her fears with Ryan.

It wasn't that she felt unprepared. Ryan had spent long hours showing her how to shift her weight to climb curbs and small rocks and tree stumps. And she had spent quite some time learning how to position herself in the saddle to go down a steep incline. In all honesty, she was beginning to feel pretty confident, and she wouldn't have had any qualms about doing the ride alone.

But she was a rank amateur compared to these women, and she desperately wanted to fit in. She knew she wouldn't be as adept as anyone in the crowd, but she was loath to make herself look foolish in front of Ryan or her friends.

Ryan instructed Jamie to purchase a halogen lamp for her bike, and as an extra precaution, she had insisted that Jamie wear a light on her helmet, too.

Jamie was dressed in long bike pants, heavy, off-road bike shoes, and a light nylon jacket over her jersey. Ryan had on similar attire, plus a pair of clear, polycarbonate wraparound glasses. When Jamie had inquired about their purpose, Ryan had merely answered, "mud."

Jamie left it at that, figuring she'd find out soon enough.

Ryan's bike was a serious off-road machine. She had outfitted it with a very aggressive tire, just made for dirt, and had systematically beefed up components as her finances allowed. The bike was forced to endure a tremendous pounding from its owner, and she did her best to make sure it would never let her down.

Ryan waved a greeting to the other women as they drove up in their trucks, jeeps and sport utility vehicles, but the group was there for action, not socializing. When about twenty of them had gathered, they took off. It was a fairly normal ride at first, and Jamie felt her confidence growing until they reached a small peak. Ryan turned around and showed the wild grin on her face. "Don't follow me," she told Jamie. She and another woman took off, pedaling furiously until they stood on the top of a set of very large boulders. Each rock was at least twenty feet tall, and they sat atop one another to form an outcropping almost 100 feet high.

When they reached the peak, she and her partner gave each other demonic smiles just as Jamie wondered what on earth they were going to do. She found out a split second later, as Ryan hurled her bike straight down the rock face. Jamie was too shocked to scream, or she surely would have. Ryan and her friend catapulted down the sheer face at incredible speeds. They crossed paths as they came down in a zigzag pattern, much the way a skier descends a steep slope.

When they reached the bottom, Ryan threw her head back and howled like a wild dog. She slapped hands in the air with her friend, and as they rode back to the group they were laughing uproariously. When Ryan pulled up next to Jamie, she smiled an enormous grin and proclaimed, "Sweet Jesus, that rocked!"

Jamie caught her infectious happiness as they sped along down the trail, but she didn't catch Ryan's recklessness—being very careful and prudent the entire time.

They came to a small rocky creek that still had a decent amount of water flowing after the winter rains. The descent at this point wasn't too steep, but some of the rocks were rather large. Another woman came up to Ryan and slapped her hard on the ass. "Tag!" she shouted as she pedaled away right down the middle of the creek.

Within a heartbeat, Ryan was on her tail. The creek curved down the mountain in such a way that it was possible to stand at the top and see the path of the water for a good half mile, so Jamie scrambled over to the edge to watch the pursuit.

Ryan flew down the hill, seemingly with no regard for her safety. Jamie's heart nearly stopped beating when Ryan slipped dangerously at one point, but her incredible athleticism kept her from flying over the handlebars. She caught her assailant near the bottom of the creek, slapping her equally hard on the butt as she yanked her bike 180 degrees and began to climb back up the creek bed.

The woman tried to keep up, but Ryan had a good ten yards on her by the time they reached the top of the hill. She beamed with pride at having won the impromptu game ... getting a great deal of pleasure out of winning any contest, no matter how contrived.

Jamie was shocked when she saw her, dripping wet from head to toe. Mud covered her legs and ran halfway up her back, but she wore the most blissful smile that Jamie had ever seen on a human being. "I won," she said, looking spent and satisfied.

The rest of the ride was more sedate. Since it was now fully dark, they stayed on the trail, although the dust from the dry earth stuck to Ryan's wet body like glue. This last portion of the ride was entirely uphill, and by the time they made it back to the car they were all sweating heavily. Jamie had never felt so grimy, and she could only imagine how Ryan felt—her entire body covered with mud and dust.

One of the riders called Ryan over, and Jamie surreptitiously watched them speak. For a moment, Jamie wasn't sure which of the women this was, since it was so dark. But as some of the other cars turned their headlights on, the pair was illuminated for a few seconds. The woman was a particularly striking Latina that Jamie had noticed immediately upon their arrival.

She was very dark skinned, and had gorgeous jet-black hair that went half way down her back. She had put it into a loose braid for the ride, but she shook it loose while they spoke, and it now attractively framed her beautiful face. She and Ryan were obviously well acquainted, and they stood very close together as they spoke. The woman put her hand on Ryan's cheek, and the taller woman turned her head slightly and kissed her palm. It was unclear what the woman was asking, but Ryan was gently shaking her head. She reached into the woman's SUV, and pulled out a couple of wet wipes, quickly wiped her face and then delicately cleaned all around the woman's mouth, trying to remove the caked on mud and dirt. When she was satisfied, she leaned in for a few very friendly kisses. As she pulled away she started to turn, but whirled around for another passionate kiss. Reaching up, she gently touched the woman's cheek, and then she turned and crossed back over the road to the truck where Jamie waited.

Most of the women were going out for a few beers, but Ryan said, "If you want to go out I won't argue, but I'd much rather have a shower."

"No, I wouldn't think of going out in public like this." She looked at her friend and said, "Not to mention my fear of being seen with you!"

Ryan laughed, and waved to her friends, putting up with a few taunts as the women drove away.

After their bikes were secure, they got in and pulled onto the fire road. "I don't know why I always forget to bring clean clothes," Ryan said. "Although I guess it would look just as stupid to have clean clothes on and a mud-caked face."

"Yeah. That's a look that would never catch on. By the way, who was that lovely woman you were talking to?"

"One of my friends. I should have introduced you."

"That's okay."

When Ryan didn't elaborate, Jamie persisted. "Are you close friends?"

"Yeah. Pretty close."

Jamie couldn't take any more of this cat and mouse game, so she blurted out, "Who in the hell was she?"

Ryan let out a deep laugh that rumbled through the cab of the truck. "I'm sorry. I'm just playing with you. That was Alisa Guerra. She's an assistant district attorney in the city. I've known her for about three years."

"Were you an item?"

"We still are. Or at least as much an item as we ever have been. She's one of my long-term ... what did we agree to call them?" she asked. "Oh, right ... fuck buddies."

"Oh! I'm not stopping you from seeing her, am I? I can easily head on home if you want to go out."

"Nope. She wanted me to come over, but I'm not in the mood. I'm really too tired for anything other than a warm shower and a soft bed."

"Well, I should think so." Jamie studied her filthy form for a few minutes, noting that Ryan still had an energized glow about her that she found mesmerizing. "I don't think I've ever seen you act so wild."

"I don't do it very often, but every once in a while I need to blow off some steam. Riding up here's the easiest way I know to really clean out the pipes."

"You just seem so full of joy when you're doing something crazy like that sprint down that huge hill. Aren't you afraid to try something like that?"

"That's the whole point. It's the fear that makes it hot. If you knew you were safe, you wouldn't get off on it."

"Get off on it ..." she repeated, unconvinced of the sentiment. "Do you need that kind of excitement?"

Ryan only hesitated a second. "Yeah, I guess I do. I've always been an adrenaline junkie. I was like this almost every day when I was a kid. If some other kid dared me to do something, I did it, no matter the consequences."

"Is that what you mean by blowing off steam? Do you need to do this kind of thing or else something builds up until you can release it?"

"Yeah, I guess it does. I've never thought of it in that way, but that's a good analogy. If I don't have some excitement in my life, I get kind of anxious and I have to find an outlet. It's almost like a sexual release. As a matter of fact, this is the first time I've been on a ride that I didn't go home with Alisa. We don't see each other a lot, but we both get hot after a really good ride."

Jamie was afraid to ask the next question, but she had a pressing need to hear her friend's answer. "Do you think your need for excitement is why you like to ... date lots of different women?"

"I guess that's part of it. I get bored easily, and I need to have a different kind of stimulation, if you'll excuse the double entendre."

There was a long silence before Jamie screwed up her courage, and asked, "Do I ever bore you?"

Ryan immediately pulled the car over to the side of the road, then turned fully in the big bench seat and looked directly into Jamie's eyes. "Never! I don't know what it is about you, but every time I'm with you it feels fresh. Sara was the only other person I've ever felt that way about."

"Really?" Jamie hoped that her face hadn't lit up like a child's at Christmas, but she knew it was unlikely.

"Yeah. Absolutely," Ryan said, nodding her head. "It's funny, but I was with Ally for a few days a couple of weeks ago. She's the most amazing lover." Ryan looked a little wistful. "I mean truly amazing," just in case Jamie missed it the first time. "But after being with her for three days in one week I'd had enough. It's not that I don't like her, I really do—and she's so totally hot in bed!"

"You mentioned that," Jamie said dryly.

"Oh, right, anyway, I was thinking about her since I had just broken up with Tracy. I thought, maybe I could make it work with Ally. Conor had just given me this big talk about how he thought I should date a friend rather than a stranger, and I mulled that over when we were together. But it's the sex that makes her appeal to me. We don't have enough in common to fill the other four or five hours in a day." She shot Jamie an impish look, and wrinkled up her nose.

"Funny, O'Flaherty. But knowing you, you might not be exaggerating."

"I am," Ryan said, her grin starting to fade. She gazed at her friend for another few moments, then said, "I've never gotten tired of being with you. Never. Other than my family, you're the only person I don't get tired of."

Jamie gave her friend a smile and patted her leg as she said, "I've never gotten bored with you around either, you wild woman."

When they arrived home, Martin came out to the deck to greet them. He laughed at the sight of his muddy daughter, and told Jamie, "She's just lucky you're here. I used to take her out in the back yard and hit her with the garden hose to clean her off before I'd let her in the house."

After a short lecture about contracting pneumonia, Martin ordered them to enter the house through the door next to the garage, to avoid tracking mud through the living room. Once inside, Jamie was so exhausted that she gladly accepted Ryan's invitation to sleep over.

After two long showers, they relaxed on the bed. "Thanks for showing me your wild child, Ryan."

"Anytime, Jamie, anytime."

As they settled down, Jamie heard a sharp grunt as Ryan rolled onto her side. "What's wrong?" she asked.

"When I was going down that creek I almost lost it. I yanked it out at the last second, but I felt something pop in my leg. It just pulls a little when I roll over."

"Let me see," Jamie switched on the bedside light. Ryan was wearing thin, Royal Stewart plaid, flannel pajama bottoms and a dark blue T-shirt.

Turning her face to gaze at her friend for a moment, Ryan said. "I think it'll be okay, you don't have to do anything."

Jamie leaned over just a bit until she was able to face Ryan fully. She placed her hand on her shoulder and asked, "Why won't you let me help if I can? You're always so eager to help me, and I've got to tell you, it feels great to be pampered a little."

"I know it does," she admitted. For some reason she obviously found it difficult to maintain eye contact, and Jamie was completely puzzled by her demeanor. "It's just that you might be uncomfortable with the location of the problem." She quirked her mouth into a lopsided grin, and rolled her big blue eyes when Jamie looked stumped.

Ryan was lying on her side facing her friend, who was mimicking her pose. She reached over and gently took Jamie's hand, bringing it behind herself and placing it on the abrupt swell of her right buttock. "It's my hamstring," she needlessly informed her. "And it's really high, almost in my glute."

Smacking her lips together to increase the flow of saliva, the smaller woman took a deep breath and found the courage to say, "The offer still holds. A sore muscle is a sore muscle, no matter where it is. If it would help, I'd be glad to work on it for you."

With a dubious tilt of her head, Ryan decided to take her friend at her word. She rolled over in the other direction until she was fully on her belly, arms stretched out above her head.

Jamie was eternally grateful that Ryan couldn't see her face, but she sucked it up and allowed her hand to explore the area. As she probed gently, she heard a sharp intake of air pass through Ryan's lips when she touched the spot. "Does it hurt a lot?" she asked, gingerly touching the swollen muscle.

"It's just tweaked a bit. I'm sure it's nothing serious. Start a few inches below the swelling and slowly work up to actually touching the sore muscle, okay?"

"Okay, I can do that," Jamie replied, as she tried to figure out how to position herself. She straddled the injured leg, and went to work on the hamstring. The pants were going to be an impediment, but Ryan made no move to remove them, to Jamie's concurrent relief and disappointment, so she did her best despite the obstacles.

She decided to draw an imaginary circle around the injury, and attack it from all sides before actually touching the sore spot. Regrettably, this called for a large amount of actually rubbing her friend's smoothly muscled buttock. But she had made the offer, and she felt obligated to perform the task without allowing herself to become sexually excited.

Working as gently as possible, she began to knead all around the injury, never drawing closer to the actual spot. Her plan was to sneak up on it after relaxing all of the surrounding muscles. And her plan would have worked if the muscle was right on the surface. But it wasn't only high on Ryan's leg—it was deep. In order to reach the surrounding muscles she had to exert a lot of pressure, and after a few minutes Ryan mumbled, "You're rubbing my skin raw." She lifted up onto her elbows and said, "It's okay. It's a tough one to reach."

"We can do this," Jamie insisted as she placed a hand on the small of Ryan's back to hold her in place. "Lotion would help," she suggested after she gave the issue some thought, but when she thought of how the lotion would have to be applied, she began to regret her idea.

Ryan seemingly sensed her hesitation and turned her head to gaze at her friend. "You sure?"

Now feeling trapped, Jamie felt her head move up and down, but it was obvious to Ryan that she was struggling with the concept. She scrambled off the bed, wincing when she put weight on the leg. "I think an equipment change is in order." She was standing in front of her underwear drawer when she made this declaration. After rummaging through the neat stacks for a moment, she found what she was looking for. "Better access," she said, and Jamie saw her holding a tiny piece of black fabric when she dashed into the bathroom to change.

Jamie could feel her heart thumping in her chest so hard that she feared Ryan could hear it in the bath. *Please God, don't let that be a thong!* Alas, her prayers weren't answered. When Ryan emerged, revealing a high cut black thong in a satiny material, Jamie could feel every bit of moisture leave her mouth and travel straight down to her groin. The look of terror mixed with lust must have been evident, because Ryan stopped in her tracks and asked, "Is this okay? It's all right if you don't want to do this."

"*No!* No, really. I just didn't want to get anything on those," she fumbled. "They look really ... uhm ... nice."

"Oh," Ryan said as she looked down at herself. "Thanks. I never wear them for long," she laughed. "They're more of a prop than anything."

"A prop?" she asked, her mind not firing crisply, due to her anxiety.

"Yeah, Ally likes things like this, although she never lets me leave them on for long." Ryan found this quite humorous, but Jamie couldn't loosen up enough to find humor in anything right then since she needed every bit of her strength and concentration just to stop her hands from shaking.

Ryan climbed back onto the bed, once again face down. This position did nothing, however, to alleviate Jamie's discomfort. She hadn't realized it with such clarity until just that moment, but she discovered with a gut-clenching jolt that she was inordinately fond of Ryan's ass. Ryan's rounded, incredibly firm, finely muscled, smooth, creamy white ass, that is. And to have that perfectly shaped derriere placed right in front of her eyes for her shaking hands to massage was too much for her racing heart.

She nearly stumbled when she got to her feet, but she managed to right herself as she said, "That ride really dehydrated me. I'm going upstairs for a drink. Need anything?"

One foot was on the lowest step by the time Ryan could reply, but she managed to respond, "Uhm, sure, some water would be good. You sure you don't want me to go?"

"No, no, I know my way around." She scampered up the stairs, trying to put as much space between herself and her friend as possible.

Luckily she was dressed in the roomy top to Ryan's pajamas along with her own panties, because she ran into Conor sitting on a stool in the kitchen, reading the paper.

"Hello, there," he rumbled, looking her up and down briefly. "Nice outfit, by the way. You should wear that type of thing more often."

"Thanks," she blushed, suddenly feeling very exposed even though the top covered her body to mid-thigh. "It's your sister's. We went on a ride up on Mt. Tam, and I was too tired and dirty to go home."

"Oh, riding with the big girls, were you?"

"Yeah, and I did pretty well, if I do say so myself. Of course, I could never keep up with Ryan. She's amazing." She walked over to the refrigerator and peeked at the contents. "What are you doing down here?"

"Oh, I had a long meeting with some thick-headed clients. Ruined my whole evening. So I thought I'd at least have a beer and read the paper before I went to bed."

She turned and eyed his dark, creamy-looking beer, held in a pint glass. "What's that? It looks delicious."

"Murphy's stout," he said as he held the glass out. "Have a sip."

All of a sudden, the thought of alcohol was very, very attractive. She reached for the heavy glass and took a long gulp. Wiping her mouth with the back of her hand, she pronounced, "Now that's a beer!"

"Have one with me. Ryan won't miss you."

"I'd like to. But Ryan hurt her leg, and I promised I'd give her a massage after I got something to drink."

"Well, if you had a wee one with me you'd still be getting something to drink," he said in his most seductive voice.

"You know, a little alcohol might make her leg relax. Would you pour one for us to share?"

"Geez," he grumbled as he got to his feet and retrieved another pint glass from the cabinet. "Even when you're single you won't give me a chance!"

Jamie read his teasing as just that, and as he finished pouring the big can into the heavy glass, she stood on her tiptoes and kissed him on the cheek. "You're irresistible, and you know it, Conor O'Flaherty."

He graced her with a big smile and a gentle one-armed hug as he handed her the glass. "Go take care of your patient," he ordered. As she started from the room, he asked, "She's not hurt badly, is she?"

Looking over her shoulder, she gave him a grin and reminded him, "It takes more than old Mt. Tam to get the best of your little sister."

She was a good bit more relaxed when she made the turn to descend the stairs, but just for good measure, she slugged down at least a quarter of the pint on the short trip. Ryan was just where she had left her, lying on her tummy with her arms extended. She was obviously very relaxed, but Jamie could still see the muscular tension in her powerful thighs and butt. "Where've you been? I was about to come looking for you."

"Oh, Conor was upstairs, and he talked me into having a short one with him," she said. "I brought a pint down for us to share. I thought a little alcohol might help relax your leg."

"Hmm," she rolled onto her side and supported her head with her hand. "That might be the key to increasing my massage business. Have a pint and a rub."

"I think they already have that in the Tenderloin," she scoffed, mentioning the city's notorious sin district.

Ryan held out her free hand and grasped the glass, giving first it, then Jamie, a speculative look. But she didn't comment about the large missing portion, easily matching the amount Jamie had siphoned off with one enthusiastic gulp. "Ahh, that's smooth," she murmured.

Jamie got up on the bed and took another hearty swallow. They passed the glass back and forth, drinking quickly and in silence, until it was drained. "I guess we were thirsty," Jamie observed as she eyed the empty glass. "Care for another?"

Ryan shook her head. "I'll be pissed if I have more on an empty stomach."

"Why would you be angry?"

"No, pissed. One of the many, many terms the Irish use for inebriation." She rolled over onto her belly and turned her head to maintain eye contact. "Still interested?" she asked with one raised eyebrow.

"Yep," Jamie bravely agreed as she resumed her former position. The stout had helped a bit, she was pleased to note, and her hands were hardly shaking as she poured a generous amount of massage lotion onto them. She delicately began to implement her former plan, again working around the perimeter of the swollen muscle. Once again Ryan relaxed into the touch, controlling her breathing with deep, steady breaths, evidently to control the pain.

Jamie imagined that the distended muscle must be very painful for her friend to admit to it, but Ryan stoically allowed her to work, never even flinching at her touch.

As she got into her work, she carelessly allowed her mind to wander, a very bad decision as it turned out. She allowed herself to actually realize that she was straddling her friend's firm thigh with only her satin panties between them. And the movement that she needed to press deep into the muscle caused that firm thigh to rub in a most delicious fashion against her throbbing vulva. At this point her only option was to distract herself.

She tried everything. She thought of car crashes, world hunger, tornadoes, and pestilence. Nothing helped. She was only able to carry on by trying one of Ryan's tricks. She focused her mind totally on Ryan's leg. She rubbed, kneaded, stroked, tapped, fondled and petted that sinewy muscle all the way to the middle of her buttock. She had never been so focused on any task, and her concentration carried the day, letting her work without distraction.

When she had done as much as she could for the injured muscle, she spent a few minutes working on its twin. Small, satisfied grunts greeted her touch, but she was so focused that she didn't need feedback. When both hamstrings were loose, she slid off and instructed, "Roll over for me."

Ryan didn't question her plan, meekly complying with the edict. She began to work on the stressed quads, making both legs as pliable as possible. After a very long time of very loving connection she realized that she hadn't heard a sound out of Ryan for a long while. She abruptly lifted her head and she saw it—an unguarded look of sexual desire on that beautiful face.

Ryan knew from the look on Jamie's face that she had been caught. Nonetheless, she tried her best to adopt a neutral expression as Jamie slid off her leg and lay down next to her. Without allowing herself to form a conscious thought, Jamie placed her hand on Ryan's soft cheek and turned her head until they were breathing the same charged air. As though guided by a magnetic force, she dipped her head, closed her eyes and began to place delicate kisses on her forehead, across her cheeks, her chin and even the tip of her nose.

She pulled back for a moment to gather her thoughts, and to her horror, saw not the desire of moments before, but wide-eyed fear clouding that beautiful face. She shot upright and leapt to her feet in a panic. "Oh, God Ryan, I'm sorry, I'm so sorry. I thought …"

In the next instant Ryan was on her feet, wrapping Jamie in a strong embrace, cooing into her ear, "It's okay Jamie, it's all right." She rubbed her back and ran a hand through her hair as she continued to reassure her shaken friend.

Jamie was crying softly against her chest. "I'm so ashamed. I don't know why I did that. I promised myself I wouldn't …"

Ryan pulled back and stared at her trembling friend for a long minute, "What do you mean, you promised yourself that you wouldn't?"

This brought on a new flood of tears as Jamie shook from head to toe. Ryan guided her to the bed and urged her onto her side, then got in right behind her and wrapped her arms around her quivering body, murmuring comforting words the entire time. After a few minutes Jamie finally had the ability to speak. "I am so sorry, Ryan. I just assumed that you might feel the same way," she murmured, her voice filled with grief.

"Is this something that you've felt before tonight?" Ryan asked softly, gently rubbing her body as she spoke.

"Yeah," she said softly. "It's one of the reasons that I started seeing Anna. I was so confused about how I felt about you, that I needed to talk to someone about it. She told me she didn't think I was ready to act on my feelings. I guess I should have listened, huh?"

Ryan turned her friend over so they were face to face. "Jamie, I want you to hear me carefully. You're the most desirable woman I've ever been near. If we weren't such close friends, you'd be on the way to your third orgasm right now." She gave her a seductive smile, "At least."

This brought a little chuckle from Jamie as Ryan continued. "You just broke up with your fiancé four weeks ago, and it wasn't your idea. You're under an incredible amount of stress, you're not eating well, you're not sleeping well, and you're very anxious. Anna's right. You need some time to know what you want. To bring sex into our relationship could destroy it, and I'm not willing to take that risk," she said. She grasped Jamie's chin in her hand and stared directly into her eyes, "You're far too precious to me to risk losing you over a passing urge," adding after a pause, "even if it is the most tempting urge I've ever resisted."

Jamie tried to clear her mind so she could concentrate on Ryan's words, as well as her meaning. "Are you saying that you might be interested in me if I were sure that this was what I wanted?"

"Uhm … didn't you see the look on my face when you were rubbing my legs?" she asked, an adorable blush covering her cheeks. "I was about to … I don't even know what I was gonna do!"

"Of course I saw it," she replied softly. "I just thought maybe I'd misread it."

"No … you didn't misread it. If I could make you my lover, without losing you as a friend, there isn't a doubt in my mind that I'd leap at the chance." Ryan leaned closer and gently kissed her forehead.

"So what do we do now?" Jamie asked, afraid that the revelation alone might affect their friendship.

Ryan sighed, wishing she could kiss her friend and forget about caution. "We stay just like we are," she soothed, gently stroking her face. "You continue in therapy. You take as long as you need to figure out what you want. When you make up your mind, you just let me know. If you want me, I'll be waiting for you. But if you don't, I want you to feel like you can tell me. I want what's best for you, Jamie. If you're a lesbian, I would love to build a relationship with you. But if you're not, I want to be your best friend for as long as you can stand me."

"You'd really be okay if I told you that I was straight?"

Ryan chuckled at the question. "I thought you were straight fifteen minutes ago. I think I've been getting by all right."

She blushed furiously as she realized how her question had sounded. "No, that's not what I meant. I meant do you think we could go back to how we've been? Wouldn't it change things too much now that I've told you how I feel?"

"Not for me. I love you, Jamie," she said as tears formed in her eyes. "Whether I ever get to love you sexually is a separate issue. No matter what, I love *you*. And if you're straight, I want you to find a man who will love you like you deserve to be loved."

"I love you too, Ryan. Very, very much," she said as she closed her eyes and sank into a welcome hug. The hug turned into a full body cuddle, and after a few minutes Jamie felt herself begin to relax fully. All of the sexual tension between them had dissipated, and she felt herself drift off into a contented sleep just minutes later, relishing the feeling of being wrapped in that comforting embrace.

The following Friday afternoon, Ryan returned a page between clients at the gym. "Hey, Ally."

"Do you have my phone number memorized?"

"Yep. I tend to remember things that I associate with pleasure."

"I know this is late to ask, but would you like to have dinner with me tonight?"

"Dinner?" Ryan asked, a bit surprised.

"Yeah, dinner. I know that's not normally how we use our mouths, but I wanna talk to you about something."

"Uhm, yeah, I can do dinner. But I have something to talk to you about, too. I'm not able to stay over tonight."

"That's okay. I'm actually not calling for sex this time. I really want to talk."

"Okay, what time should I come by? I'm off work at five."

"Just come over when you can. We'll decide where to go when you get here."

"Okay, see you then." *That's weird. Neither one of us wants to have sex. That's a first!*

At six-fifteen they were seated at a casual little place in the Castro. The restaurant was small, rather dark, and very quiet. Ally was obviously a regular since she was greeted by nearly every employee.

They were shown to a small table in the back of the room, where they could speak in private. After they placed their orders, Ally cleared her throat and started to speak. "I … ahh … I want to talk a little bit about some changes I'm making," she finally got out. She looked very nervous, and Ryan reached up to cover Ally's cold hand with her warm one. She gave her an encouraging look, but didn't respond verbally.

"I've decided to try to change some of my sexual uhm … phobias." She looked down at the table. "Uhm I have … some … issues that I … uhm." She looked at Ryan helplessly as she was unable to find the words to express herself.

"It's okay, Ally," she said gently. "I know you've got some things that get in the way. Tell me as much as you want to."

"Okay. I don't know why I feel so nervous talking to you about this. You obviously know I have some hang ups."

"Everyone has some."

Ally looked up at her with a quizzical glance. "Even you?"

"Yep. Most of mine don't come up when I'm with you, but I've got my share. My big issue is being in control. I normally can't let anyone be in charge—it really freaks me out if someone is too aggressive."

"Uhm, Ryan," she said gently. "That's exactly what I do to you."

"I know! But I swear you're the only one! I'll have you know that most people think I'm a total top!"

"You? You're the biggest bottom I've ever been with!" Ally howled with laughter.

"Hey! Keep it quiet! I've got a reputation in this town."

Ally laughed long and hard at this revelation from her friend, but it seemed to relax her quite a bit, and when she resumed her story she was much calmer. "I know you're pretty perceptive, Ryan. So I guess you've figured out that I was sexually abused."

Ryan gave her a small nod, and Ally continued. "My oldest brother raped me when I was eleven," she said softly. "He continued to molest me until I was thirteen. That's when he left home to get married.

"Anyway, there were all sorts of reasons why I couldn't go to my parents or anyone, but that's not important right now. What's important is that I'm going to try to open myself up to be with one person. And because of that, I'm not going to have casual sex any more." She looked over at Ryan and gave her a shy smile. "Even though I don't want to stop, especially with you."

Ryan gave her a smile in return and squeezed her hand. "I'm so glad that you're trying to feel more comfortable with yourself. I think you'd be a wonderful person to be in a relationship with, and please don't feel bad about us. I … uhm … I wanted to tell you that you were right about Jamie, my straight friend. Seems she might not be quite as straight as I thought," she said with a deep blush.

"Ah ha!" Ally crowed. "I knew it! So are you two an item?"

"Not really. She made an overture, but I don't want to get involved until she works out some issues in therapy. She's too important to me to ruin our friendship before she's sure this is what she wants."

"Anyone in her right mind would want you, Ryan. You're one perfect little prize."

"I don't know about that," she said. "But thanks for the compliment."

"So do you think we could still see each other once in a while? I like you a lot, even outside of bed."

"I'd love that," Ryan said sincerely. "And I'm really honored that you called to talk about this."

"Well," Ally blushed deeply. "I do like you a lot and I trust you. I knew you'd be safe to talk with. But uhm … the other reason was that I didn't want you to call me to have sex. I feel confident about this now, but I was afraid that an invitation from you would blow my resolve to hell!"

Through an unspoken, but mutual, agreement Ryan and Jamie didn't speak about therapy. Ryan didn't want to intrude, and Jamie didn't want to burden her friend any more than she already had.

Things had settled down, and they were treating each other just like they had before. What impressed Jamie the most was how honorable Ryan had been about the whole episode. She loved her all the more for her fortitude in being able to rebuff her advances to preserve their friendship. *Even if we never become lovers, I know I'll never have a better friend.*

Just as March was winding down, Jamie asked Ryan how she felt about baseball. "I'd have to say that baseball was my first love," she reflected thoughtfully. "Conor was a big fan, and since I did everything he did, I became one too. How about you?"

"Football is a much bigger deal for me but I like baseball a lot. How would you like to go to opening day next week?"

"Do you have tickets?" At Jamie's sly nod she enthusiastically accepted.

Jamie did indeed have tickets. Her father was a big supporter of the group that had bought the Giants from the Stoneham family years earlier. When the team was struggling just to draw 8,000 fans he had purchased four sets of box seats for the law firm, and a set for himself. He didn't go to a lot of games, preferring to give the tickets to young associates and their friends, but he was always willing to let Jamie use them when she wished.

Since they had four seats, it was obvious that they had to invite Conor, but they weren't sure who the fourth should be. Martin had to work, and he would never take a day off just for pleasure. Brendan was in trial all week, and Rory was out of town. Jamie asked Conor if he had a friend he'd like to bring. "Sure, I've got dozens of friends and cousins who'd love to come. But it's hard to choose just one. Don't you have any great looking friends you could bring, Jamie?"

Jamie and Ryan looked at one another and laughed. "I've got one, Conor, but she's a handful," Jamie said.

"Bring her on. I'm up to the challenge."

The game was on a Tuesday afternoon. Conor was going to work in the morning, and Mia needed her car for an appointment in the city, so Jamie and Ryan agreed to meet them in front of Gate A at one o'clock. The day was perfect for baseball, seventy-five degrees with a crystal blue sky and a light breeze off the bay.

Jamie drove the Boxster down into the underground parking garage of her father's law firm at noon then hopped into the elevator that led to the main reception area where she patiently waited for him to come down. After a few minutes he arrived, with a big smile and a hug as a greeting. "I'm glad you wanted the tickets today, honey. I like to think of you at the park on a beautiful day like this, playing hooky," he teased. "It reminds me of my own misspent youth."

"I really appreciate the tickets, Daddy. Thanks for saving them for me."

"It's my pleasure, Cupcake. Hey, I've got Mother's new car here. Do you want to see it?"

They went back down in the elevator together. He led Jamie to a brand new, brilliant red Mercedes CLK320 convertible. She whistled appreciatively at the sexy car as she walked all around it, admiring it from all angles. "I didn't know you were such a fan of cars, Jamie," he said with a grin.

She blushed as she said, "I'm really not, but I'm taking Ryan and her brother to the game, and they're both fanatics. I was just thinking of how much they'd like this one."

He reached into his pocket and handed her the keys. "Take it, honey. I'll be here until at least ten o'clock tonight. Bring it back on your way back to Berkeley."

"Are you sure, Daddy? Would mother mind?"

"She barely knows which car is hers, you know that. Now go have fun. Feel free to let your friends drive, Jamie. I know the lure of a hot car."

As Jamie pulled up in front of Ryan's home, she looked up to see her on the deck, as usual. "Hey little girl, want a ride?" she said as Ryan trotted down the stairs.

Ryan's mouth gaped open as she slowly walked around the car. She lightly touched the paint with loving hands as she made three complete circuits before she uttered a word. "Is this yours?"

"No. It's Mother's. Daddy's driving it while she's out of town this week." She turned off the car and got out to stand next to Ryan. "Wanna drive?"

"You're kidding, right?" she gazed longingly at the keys dangling from Jamie's extended hand.

"I would never kid you about something as serious as a car."

"Is it okay? I mean, this is your mom's."

"It's fine. Daddy insisted that I take it, and he insisted that you drive it."

That caught Ryan by surprise. "Did you tell him I was going?" she asked, realizing at that instant that it was important to her that Jamie not be ashamed of their friendship.

"Yes, I told him that you and Conor were going, and that you were both car nuts. That's when he told me to take the car."

"You know Jamie ..." she began, but stopped short. "Never mind," she added quickly.

"What were you going to say?"

"Uhm ... I was going to make a joke about being your best friend again, but I decided that our friendship means too much to me to joke about."

Jamie gazed over at her with respect and admiration, "You're just about the sweetest woman I've ever known."

"Oh yeah?" she grinned as she snagged the keys from her outstretched hand and hopped into the convertible, Laughing maniacally, she said, "Let's see how sweet you think I am after I peel the rubber off these tires."

Ryan pulled into the line for valet parking as they approached the stadium. "I think I'm beginning to have a small appreciation for why rich people don't give all of their money away. Having money really does make life easier in terms of creature comforts. I don't think I ever realized the seductive nature of it."

"It really is seductive. It's so easy to forget how little most people have when you have a lot. You can be so insulated that you never get in touch with normal people." After a moment she added, "I hope that never happens to me."

"I'll give you a dose of reality anytime, kiddo. I'll show you my bank statement if you really want a shock."

After their car was taken, they had a short walk to the front gates where they saw Conor waiting. He was wearing faded blue jeans, a white golf shirt and an authentic Giants warm up jacket—black wool with black leather raglan sleeves, with "Giants" across the chest in bright orange script. "Boy, Conor, you really do look like a fan," Jamie said, giving him a hug.

"I am a fan. I know the opening day roster of every team back to 1976," he said. "Did you have a hard time parking? It's really a zoo."

"No, we didn't have any trouble at all, did we Jamie?" Ryan replied innocently.

"Spill it, Ryan. You never could keep a secret," he said as he wrapped his arm around her waist and began to tickle her.

Through her giggles she admitted that they had driven the new Mercedes to the game. Conor was crestfallen. "I've never been in a CLK. Could I come to the parking lot with you after the game to drool on it?"

Ryan took pity on her big brother and generously offered, "I'll take your truck home, and you can go with Jamie. I know how insidious the addiction is, and I empathize with you."

He gave her a big kiss on the cheek and hugged her soundly. "You're my absolutely favorite sister."

"Wow!" they heard from behind. They turned to see a startled Mia staring at them in shock. "There's two of her!" she said to Jamie as she walked around the still linked siblings.

"I prefer to think there's two of me," Conor said smoothly as he released his sister and grasped Mia's hand. "You must be Mia. I'm Conor," he said as he shook her hand. Within seconds he was guiding her to their seats, with a strong arm loosely around her shoulders. "Keep up, you two," he said as he turned around slightly to wink at Ryan.

Jamie shook her head at a smirking Ryan. "Boy, are you two ever related."

Their seats were directly behind the Giants dugout, just four rows back. Neither O'Flaherty had ever had seats that came close to the quality of these. Ryan and Jamie sat in front, with Conor and Mia right behind, but Ryan was turned around for most of the game, kibitzing with Conor about a particular player or a dubious strategy.

Jamie was impressed with Ryan's knowledge of the game. She seemed to understand the small details that made the sport interesting. "I don't see half of the things you notice," she admitted when Ryan correctly predicted that the Dodger first baseman would get a hit.

"Well, I used to follow the game very carefully. I could teach you a few things if you're interested."

"I'm very interested. Teach away."

Ryan spent the better part of two innings showing Jamie some of the finer points of baseball. "When I see a team that I don't know, I always spend some time watching the catcher. I see how he calls the pitches to each hitter and see where he positions himself behind the plate. You can learn a lot just by watching the catcher for an entire inning."

They proceeded to do just that. Jamie had never really noticed how much in control the catcher was. "I never realized he has to run down to first base on a ground ball. He's all over the place."

"Yeah, and he has to cover third base also. It's funny, catchers are usually slow guys with bad knees, but they have to run their tails off during a game."

After the sixth inning, Mia and Jamie went to find a restroom. Ryan and Conor went with them to wait in line for more food. When they reached the privacy of the women's room, Mia slapped Jamie hard on the shoulder. "Where have you been hiding him?"

"Hey, knock it off," Jamie said, rubbing her shoulder as she laughed. "I haven't been hiding him anywhere. He's just Ryan's brother."

"Are you sure he's not why you broke up with Jack?"

"I'm sure I didn't break up with Jack at all, Mia. And if I had it wouldn't have been because of Conor. He's a doll and a real sweetheart, but I'm not interested in him."

"Why wouldn't you be?" she asked incredulously. "He's a total babe!"

"I'm just not. Besides she has two other brothers who are just as cute, and about a dozen cousins, all good looking, and all unmarried. I wouldn't know where to start."

"Well, I do," Mia replied. "I'm starting with Mr. Muscle out there."

"I wish you the best, Mia. But aren't you forgetting someone?"

Mia looked at her blankly. "Who's that?"

"Jason … your boyfriend?"

"Jason who?" Mia asked innocently as she entered a stall and closed the door behind her.

As promised, Ryan drove the big Ram truck back to the house to allow Conor the pleasure of chauffeuring Jamie in the Mercedes. "This is one sweet ride," he said through his wide smile. Of course, he was taking them home via side streets to make the ride last as long as possible. "And speaking of sweet, your friend is quite the little prize. Is she dating anyone seriously?"

"Mia doesn't ever date seriously."

"Ooh, a girl after my own heart," he said with a leer. "Would you mind if I asked her out?"

"No, not at all. You'd be a definite improvement over her normal choices," she said with a grin. After a pause she asked thoughtfully, "Have you ever been serious about anyone?"

"Yeah, I have," he responded quietly. "I had a very serious girlfriend for almost two years. We were on the verge of moving in together, but Da talked me out of it."

"Really, why?" she asked, a bit surprised that Martin would get involved.

"He convinced me that if I loved her, I should marry her. I'm only going to get married once, Jamie, and after I thought about it for a long time, I realized that I didn't love Melissa enough to commit to her forever." He looked at Jamie, "Da made me see that living with her just took her off the market and prevented her from finding someone who really did love her enough to marry her. I can't tell you how hard it was for me, but he was right. As usual," he added with a laugh. "That was three years ago, and she got married last year, and is gonna have a baby soon."

"Do you want to settle down soon, or are you still enjoying your freedom too much?"

"If I could find the right woman, I don't think I'd hesitate. But I'm damned picky, so I don't know how soon that'll be. Maybe Mia will be the one."

"I think Mia is a long way from settling down, Conor. But you two could have a lot of fun together in the meantime."

Jamie was leaving her last class on the first Friday afternoon in April when her cell phone rang. "Hello," she mumbled as she tried to balance the little phone against her ear while struggling with her textbooks.

"Jamie?" the familiar voice asked.

"Jack," she breathed, amazed to hear from him. "Uhm … hi."

"Uhm … " he stumbled a bit, obviously unsure of himself. "Would you … uhm … what I wanted to know was … uhm … if you'd have any interest in talking to me."

"Talking to you?" she was rather confused by his tone and his request.

"Yeah," he said with more confidence. "I've been doing a lot of thinking, and I have some things to say to you."

"Uhm, well, sure Jack, I'd be happy to talk to you," she agreed even though her stomach was clenching. "What's good for you?"

"If you're free tonight I could come take you to dinner."

"Uhm … okay. I'm free after seven."

"Great," he said happily, sounding very much like himself now. "I'll call and make reservations. Any place new you'd like to try?"

Is this Jack Townsend? she wondered warily. "Well, there's a nice little Northern Italian place called Andiamo in North Berkeley. I don't know the number though."

"That's okay. I'll make a reservation and come get you at seven." He paused a moment and asked, "You aren't seeing anyone are you?"

"Uhm, no … no, I'm not," she replied, unwilling to reveal her feelings for Ryan.

"Great! See you then."

"Okay," she said slowly as she clicked the cancel button. *What in the holy hell was that all about?*

She felt a bit off kilter during her workout, and several times she glanced up at Ryan to find her looking at her with concern in her eyes. The hour passed quickly though, and at the end of the session Ryan asked, "Thai?"

"Pardon me?" Jamie replied, looking confused.

"Wanna go out for some Thai food after therapy?" They had been spending every Friday evening together, and it had become an unspoken date. Jamie went to therapy while Ryan worked out, then Ryan rode over to her house and took a shower before they went to dinner. It all worked out beautifully, even though they had never formally discussed it.

"Uhm … well, I uhm … can't do it tonight," she said, as she nervously scratched the side of her face. "Uhm … something came up and I uhm … "

"It's okay, Jamie," Ryan assured her as she lightly squeezed her shoulder. "We don't have to have dinner together every Friday night." She smiled broadly, but Jamie could see a tiny bit of disappointment on her handsome face.

"I know. We just … "

"It's okay," Ryan said again. "Call you tomorrow?"

"Yeah," she said with a smile as she went to the locker to pull her things out. As she walked out the door, she could feel Ryan's piercing blue eyes follow her out to the parking lot. *Why do I feel like I'm lying to her?*

Since Jamie was ready to deal with her sexual orientation, and needed all the support she could get, she and Anna had decided to see each other three times a week since.

After settling down and briefly telling Anna what had happened, the therapist smiled neutrally, encouraging Jamie to explain her feelings about the issue. "I don't know what I think about seeing Jack. I'm just trying to be polite."

"Hmm," Anna mused. "Do you normally feel like you're doing something wrong when you're just being polite?" Jamie once more felt like Anna could see right into her soul.

"Oh crap! I don't know what in the hell I'm doing! He sounded like he just wanted to chat, but then he offered to buy me dinner—in a real restaurant, no less! And right before he hung up he asked me if I was seeing someone." Her last sentence was quieter than the previous ones had been, and she was looking at the floor when her last word fell from her mouth.

"And that makes you feel … ?"

She threw her hands up in frustration, amazed that Anna couldn't see the problem. "I feel like I'm cheating on Ryan!"

"Cheating? How exactly are you cheating?"

"I told Ryan I loved her! Now I'm going to have dinner with my ex-fiancé, and I didn't tell her about it."

"I think you're getting ahead of yourself here. Yes, you told Ryan that you were attracted to her, but she told you to take the time to figure out what you wanted. If what you told me is accurate, you didn't make an agreement to be her lover."

Jamie nodded her head slowly, her brow creased. "I told you the truth. But we've been spending all of our time together. If she's dating anyone else it's very late at night because she's with me most of the weekend. It seems like we're slipping into a dating relationship, even though we don't touch each other sexually."

"Oh, I see," Anna said. "You think your actions have sent a message that your words have not."

"Kinda." She shook her head roughly, causing her thick blonde hair to bounce all around her face. With an annoyed move, she shoved her hand through her hair, brushing it out of her eyes and settling it in its normal, casual style. "I was just starting to feel like I was getting close to making a move, Anna. I really felt like I was on a path. Do you know what I mean?"

"I think so, but tell me more."

"I know it's been a tortured path, but it felt like a path. I feel like since I met Ryan I've made consistent baby steps towards being with her. This is the first time I've felt my desire waver."

"What's the pull with Jack?"

"Oh, I don't know," she said after a deep breath. "I did love him, you know." She stared at Anna with a defiant look on her face. "And I didn't break up with him. He dumped me. It feels good to have him make overtures to getting me back."

"Well, he did have a little help with the breakup," she reminded her gently.

"What do you mean by that?" Jamie asked, her hackles obviously rising.

"Only that Jack was worried about your relationship with Ryan. He told you he was threatened by her, but you refused to let her go."

"He was trying to control me, Anna!"

"Maybe he was. But he was right about Ryan. She was a threat and she did take your focus away from him."

Jamie stared at the woman in amazement. "Are you saying it was my fault that we broke up?"

"Fault isn't the correct word to use. All I'm saying is that I think you had a hand in causing your breakup. And it's possible that you feel guilty about that now."

"So what should I do?" she asked her head dropping into her hands.

"I can't tell you what to do, and you wouldn't want me to if I would."

Jamie looked at her and nodded.

"You have a hot button about anyone controlling you. But you also have to be careful not to try to control yourself where your feelings are concerned."

"Do you think I should see Jack?"

"I want you to do what you want to do. You made the date, Jamie, you must have wanted to see him."

"I do," she admitted. "But I don't know why!"

"Try to stay open tonight and see how you feel. Don't worry about Ryan, or even about Jack. Just stay open to your feelings."

She barely had time to shower and wash her hair, but she got both tasks accomplished before the doorbell rang. "Mia!" she cried out.

"Yeah?" she asked as she ducked her head into the door of Jamie's room.

"I'm running late," she needlessly explained as she stood in nothing but a towel. "Would you go downstairs and keep Jack company?"

"Jack?"

"Don't ask," she urged, as she rolled her eyes.

Mia gave her a puzzled look, but ran downstairs and did as Jamie asked. The blonde stood in front of her closet with a critical eye, finally choosing an outfit that she was certain Jack hadn't seen her in—a deep salmon dress in a fine linen, just short enough to be sexy, but demure enough in cut and style to look sophisticated. The rich color showed off her golden tan and made her already sun bleached hair even paler. She dabbed on just a touch of makeup and found herself automatically putting on a dash of perfume, adding the fragrance to all of her pulse points. *It's just dinner*, she reminded herself sternly as she found herself dabbing the perfume between her breasts.

She slipped on a pair of black pumps and ran down the stairs, pausing in alarm when she got a glimpse of his lean body perched on the edge of the table by the front door, and felt her pulse begin to quicken. *What's that about?* But she quickly remembered Anna's advice, and she let herself just feel. She took a deep breath and let her eyes roam over his sandy blonde hair and his very attractive profile as he chatted amiably with Mia. Inexplicably, she felt just like she had when they had first started to go out. She was excited and a little nervous … wondering what the night would bring.

She descended the last few stairs slowly, taking him in the whole while. When she got to the bottom stair, he turned and met her gaze. His bright blue eyes gentled into a warm smile as he walked over and gently took her hand, giving it a slight squeeze. *Yipes!* she cried in alarm as a jolt of sensation hit her deep in the groin. *Where did that come from?*

But she knew exactly where it had come from. Jack was being his most attentive, engaging self, and she had always found him extremely attractive when he acted that way. He had the ability to focus on her completely, making her feel like he could see deep within her. It was a little unnerving, but also completely arousing.

"You look great," he said, his eyes slowly moving up and down her body, taking her in.

"So do you." He wore crisply pressed, charcoal gray slacks, and a white oxford cloth shirt, with thin navy blue and yellow lines running through it, creating a wide plaid. "Thanks for coming down, Mia," she said as she forced her eyes away from him to glance at her smirking friend.

"Anytime," she replied lightly as she leaned over to kiss her friend's cheek on the way back upstairs. "Have fun, you two."

They watched her go and looked back at each other a little awkwardly. "Did you get reservations?" she asked to break the tension.

"They were booked. But I remembered that nice place in the city that we went to with your parents a couple of years ago. So I made reservations for eight o'clock at Café Lucerne."

Jamie was stunned by this development. Café Lucerne was a lovely place, but it was most definitely a romantic setting. The restaurant could only handle around fifty people, but the tables were set well apart to allow for quiet, intimate conversation in the intimately lit space. "O … Okay. I guess we'd better go then."

He helped her on with her coat and grabbed his navy blazer, shrugging into it with casual, graceful movements. When he led her to his little sedan, he held the door open for her, waiting until she was safely inside to close it.

As he got in, he looked over at her, once more locking eyes. "Thanks for seeing me," he said softly. "I can't tell you how good it's to see you again." He blinked slowly, and she allowed the sensations that buffeted her to fully enter her brain. He was just a foot or so away, and she could see the smoothness of his cheek where he had obviously recently shaved. He smelled of a subtle after-shave, likely one of the ones she had bought for him. His dark blonde eyelashes framed his blue eyes attractively, giving him an almost delicate, boyish look. But the intense gaze he fixed her with was anything but childlike.

Oh boy, I'm in trouble here, she thought, as he smiled and started the car.

They relaxed at the small table, waiting for the waiter to bring them the bottle of wine that Jack had confidently ordered. *He seems more mature, more sure of himself,* she thought when he placed both of their orders with the attentive server.

After their wine was delivered, Jack touched the rim of her glass with his own as he toasted, "To self awareness." He took a deep sip of the golden colored Chardonnay and said, "I've given more thought to our relationship and the problems that we had than I can ever remember devoting to any topic. And do you know what I've decided?"

She shook her head rather dully, her eyes never leaving his lips.

He leaned over slightly and enunciated each word. "You … were … right," he said simply. As she blinked slowly he quickly followed up. "You were right about how I took you for granted. You were right about how unfair it was for me to be jealous of your friendships. You were right about my failing to see who you were, and how you had changed." His voice lowered and he blushed adorably as he added, "You were even right about how one-sided our sex life had been." He lifted his head quickly, as a cascade of sandy blonde hair tumbled into his eyes. "You were right about everything, Jamie. And I'm here tonight to ask for a second chance."

His eyes hadn't wavered from hers and hers hadn't wavered from his lips. Her heart heard his sincere apology, but her head couldn't process the information. He was validating all of those months of struggle—agreeing with every point she had ever made—and it was too much. Her hand reached blindly for her wine glass, grasping it firmly and lifting it to her lips to swallow a great deal of the contents down in one gulp. "I … I'm," she tried to get out. "I'm … amazed."

"I don't doubt it," he said gently, as he tenderly pried her hand from her glass and grasped it in his own warm one. "I never gave you much reason to think I was a reflective kinda guy."

"But why —?" she began but he immediately answered.

"You're too valuable to let you get away without fighting for. It's like throwing away a fistful of diamonds because you don't like the cut." He sat back in his chair, still gazing deeply into her eyes.

She let his words sink in for a moment, relishing the sincere compliment with a gentle smile on her face. It was exactly what she had wanted to hear him say for the past year. To acknowledge that she had been a very willing and receptive partner and that it was he who had the problem … it was he who had been wrong … it was he who caused her to look to Ryan for emotional sustenance. *Yes! Dear God, yes! I didn't try to find someone else. He pushed me into it!*

She gazed up at his sincere, warm blue eyes and said, "That means so much to me." She was struggling with her emotions, but he just held her hand more firmly and maintained his smile.

"Will you give me another chance?" he asked softly, still holding her gaze.

She blinked slowly and took a deep breath. Anna's words came back to her and she paused for a moment, letting herself feel the deep sense of relief and joy that his words caused. "Yes," she said. "Yes, I will."

On the way back to Berkeley, she found her hand automatically drift over to rest upon his lean thigh. He gazed over at her and gave her an encouraging grin, reaching down to gently pat her hand. She could hear the deep breath that he took, smiling to herself when he said, "That feels so absolutely right."

And she had to admit that it did feel right. This was exactly where twenty-one years of conditioning had led her. To the strong, secure embrace of a young professional who would love her and the children they'd have together. Someone her parents and her grandfather would be proud of. Someone that she could build a life with, along with the full approval of society at large.

She'd never have to learn those painful lessons Ryan had told her about. She'd never have to face the glares and snickers that they had suffered at the Tea Room. She'd never have to explain to her children that mommy loves mommy and that the other children just don't understand. *Wow, that was a big one*, she thought, as she blew out a breath. She actually felt a moment of compassion for Ryan. *She has no choice*, she thought. *But I do. I really do! And if I can love and be loved by a man, I'm sure she'd rather have that for me. She wants what's best for me, doesn't she? I'm sure she'd want me to live with society's approval if I can.*

But even though she reasoned that her friend would support her, she didn't want to see her this weekend. "Jack? I think I'll go down to my parents tonight. Would you like to spend some time together this weekend?"

"Absolutely," he replied without hesitation. "I've done a lot of thinking about school too. I'm not going to let it run my life any longer. I've already got a job and a clerkship lined up. What am I trying to prove at this point?"

"Wow," she said slowly. "You have changed."

"I have," he said. "In many, many ways." He placed his hand atop hers and squeezed it affectionately. "And I'll change in any other way that you need. I'll do anything to make this work."

He insisted on waiting for her to pack a few things so he could follow her down to Hillsborough. She found it odd, but also touching that he was so concerned with her safety, so she graciously allowed him the honor of escorting her.

She could see his headlights right behind her on the whole trip and she found that it was, in fact, reassuring to see him there. She called her parents from the road but there was no answer—not an unusual result given their active lives. But when she rang the bell, Marta informed her that her father was down in L.A. for business and that her mother had decided to go with him at the last minute. Marta was surprised and appeared pleased to see Jack with her, but she followed protocol and quickly disappeared after offering to bring them a drink. They both accepted her offer and sat on the large sofas in the living room, nervously sipping cognac.

After a few minutes, Jack looked at her and asked, "Do you mind if I sit next to you?"

She patted the cushion next to herself and smiled at him as he stood and switched places. They spoke casually about their respective school terms, and he pointedly asked her about the ride in great detail.

Ryan wasn't even off topic as he asked Jamie about Ryan's training and how they were working together. She bent to place her nearly empty glass on the table, and when she sat back up his arm was around her shoulders. She found that she liked the sensation, and leaned against him, letting out a sigh that seemed to have been building for ages. He turned his head and gently kissed the top of her head in a friendly, affectionate manner. Almost unconsciously she found her head turning and then tilting upwards as she opened her mouth to accept his warm lips. *Oh God*, she moaned to herself. *I forgot how good it feels to kiss him. God! I've missed this!* She had in fact missed the tender intimacies with a lover. She had missed the casual way they had grown to know each other's bodies, and the natural way they meshed together when they kissed. It was a heady, thrilling discovery as her hormones kicked in fully and she felt herself growing aroused. The deep, intense kisses were having an identical effect on Jack. One that she could feel as he gently pulled her into his lap to continue his passionate assault. *What could it hurt?* she asked herself as her vulva began to throb. *It will just be like picking up where we left off.* But there was a tiny part of her that wanted some time to reflect before she dove right back into this relationship. She knew this was a momentous decision, and she felt that she needed more time.

Obviously Jack had improved in his psychic abilities, because moments before she was going to halt the embrace he gently guided her back to an upright position. "I'm about to lose control," he whispered as he leaned his forehead against hers. "And I'm sure that you don't want to move this fast."

She nodded demurely, now feeling that maybe she did want to go further just to show she could change, too. But he placed another soft kiss on her lips and stood with some difficulty. "I'll call you tomorrow," he promised as he stole one more kiss and quickly walked to the door, leaving her throbbing and frustrated.

"Wow," was all that she could get out.

The next morning, she lay in bed for a very long while, just trying to be open to her feelings. She thought she was doing a pretty good job of it, but she found that she was really only able to concentrate on how she felt being with Jack again. Every time she tried to force herself to think of Ryan she felt her brain shut down and immediately turn to Jack again. But that didn't seem that odd to her at this point. It's been nearly a month since I've let myself think about him. *I have an awful lot of feelings to process.*

After a leisurely breakfast, she spent some time in the living room, idly looking through the plethora of neatly labeled photo albums that chronicled her childhood.

Mother sure wasn't very good at being involved in my life, but she was great at memorializing it, she thought wryly as she perused the books.

The first book was labeled "1978" and showed several photos of her mother and father looking very happy together as they anticipated the birth of their child. Catherine was a very small woman, and she obviously didn't gain much weight during her pregnancy. Her belly was very protuberant, but she looked like she was wearing a balloon under her clothing, since the rest of her body looked exactly like it had before she was pregnant.

There were a number of shots of the shower that her mother's sorority sisters had thrown for her, the happy-looking young women joining in the traditional rite of passage into motherhood. Jamie thought ahead to the future, picturing herself in a few years, surrounded by friends from high school and college, preparing to welcome her child into the world. *It would be a far different experience if I were with Ryan*, she thought wryly. *For one thing, I'd have to get a whole new set of friends. Different parents wouldn't hurt either.*

Jesus! she thought grumpily. *It's easy for her with that fabulous family! They'd probably think it was great that she was going to have a baby with a woman! No matter how society treats her, she always has her family to remind her of how special she is. But most of us don't get that. And I don't want to have to lose my family if I don't have to!* she thought defiantly. *And if Jack is serious about the changes he's made, I don't have to!*

Jack called a little after ten, obviously trying to be considerate if she wanted to sleep in. "Hi," he said. "What would you like to do today?"

"Do?" she asked slowly, trying to understand his exact meaning.

"Yeah … do," he said with a chuckle. "You know, like normal people. I've actually heard that some people venture outside during daylight hours."

"You don't have to study?"

"Whether or not I have to isn't the issue. I'm not going to, so it's a moot point. Now, where would you like to go? The Giants are in town, we could drive down to Santa Cruz and hang out on the beach, we could even drive over to Napa for the day. If we did that, we could have an early dinner and still get home at a decent hour."

She was silent for a minute, letting his words sink in. "You really have changed," she finally got out.

His voice deepened as he replied, "I've changed a lot, Jamie. Our breakup made me look at my life in a very critical way. And I didn't like what I'd become."

Her heart picked up a beat as she considered what this all meant. "Let's go to Napa. Come on over and we'll take one of my parents' cars."

"I'll be there in thirty minutes," he promised. "Wear something that you'll be comfortable in at a nice restaurant."

She hung up the phone and stared at it for a moment before she placed it on the table. *Is it possible to do a brain transplant? That sure as hell didn't sound like Jack!*

She decided on a casual print dress, short enough to show off her legs, but long enough to allow them to go to a nice place for dinner. The day was warm, and she knew it would be warmer in Napa, so she also brought a white knit wrap to keep her warm against the usually chilly evening.

Jack was right on time, and he happily accepted the keys to Catherine's new Mercedes. They left the top up while they were on the freeway, but as soon as they crossed over into Marin, Jack pulled over and lowered it. They had been chatting about his law review duties on the way over, and even though he seemed interested in his topic he didn't seem as obsessed by it as he had before. As they neared Napa, he gazed at her briefly and said, "I've been thinking a lot about my decision to clerk for a federal judge next year. It'd be good for my career, but if we're back together I don't think I can tolerate being too far from home. I'm going to do my best to find a spot in Northern California, but if I can't, I think I may just go directly to Morris, Foster."

Jamie nearly swallowed her tongue at this pronouncement. From the day she'd met him, Jack had stated clear plans for his future, and clerking had been the keystone of those plans. To hear him casually dismiss this important step was absolutely stunning to her. "But why would you do that?"

He glanced at her briefly, and then pulled over onto a little-used access road. He turned in his seat and reached over and grasped her hand as he gazed into her eyes. "I explained to you last night that my priorities have changed. Being away from you for a year is not acceptable." He chuckled as he admitted, "I've been away from you for seven weeks and it almost drove me crazy."

She sniffed back her tears as she leaned against him, relishing the feel of his muscular torso, the spicy scent of his after-shave and the rough starch in his crisp, sky blue, oxford cloth shirt. "That means so much to me."

He lifted her chin and leaned over to place a gentle kiss on her lips. "You mean a lot to me. Much more than I knew."

She had been to Napa many times, but never with Jack. This was only his second trip, his first being when he was a young boy. He was very interested in the wine making process, so they went on a tour of the Christian Brothers winery, the largest big-production winery in the valley.

It was so nice to walk along the tour, holding his large, warm hand. As usual, he was focused on the details of the operation, something which didn't interest Jamie much. But she got a lot of enjoyment out of watching him try to digest the vast array of information that was fed to them. He asked several perceptive questions of their guide, and she found herself smiling up at him as he spoke, admiring the clean, sharp planes of his face, and the bright, perceptive look in his eyes.

Their tour group was a mix of ages, but she noticed that the older women continually gave them appreciative glances. One elderly woman in particular stole a glance repeatedly, and Jamie realized that her interest wouldn't be so benign if she were here with Ryan, holding hands and whispering into each other's ears. *This is just so easy*, she thought to herself. *I won't have to endure the sharp glances and whispered taunts that have followed Ryan her whole life. She's so confident and self assured that those things don't seem to bother her. But I'm not like that! I want people to like me and smile at me when I go places. I really like that people look at Jack and me with appreciative glances, rather than hostility. Is that so wrong?*

Their next stop was to the Schilling Winery for a tour of their champagne caves. The winery was very cute and quaint, and the tour they were part of was very small, only two other couples. The storage area for the filled bottles was quite cool since it was deep in the ground. Jack wrapped his long arm around Jamie's shoulders and she snuggled up against his body for the rest of the tour. She felt so warm and safe when he touched her like this, and she breathed in his scent with a lazy, contented feeling permeating her bones.

By five o'clock they were both famished, and she was a bit tipsy from consuming the wine samples on an empty stomach. They decided to go to Tavolo in St. Helena for dinner, and since it was so early they had no trouble getting a table.

They were shown to a nice spot and presented with the extensive wine list. Jack handed the list to her, always content to have her exercise the skills that he lacked. The server presented the bottle of Merlot that she had picked out, and Jack indicated that Jamie would be the one to taste the wine. After pronouncing it acceptable, they relaxed and waited for their appetizers to be delivered.

"Can we talk about Ryan, Jack?"

To her relief he didn't tense up or look uncomfortable at the topic. He just tilted his head a bit to encourage her to continue. "I know that you said last night that you accepted full responsibility for our breakup, but that's not really accurate." He furrowed his brow a bit as he stared at her intently, but still didn't speak. "You were right about Ryan."

His eyes widened perceptibly, and she realized how that must have sounded. "No, no, not like that! You were right that she was part of the problem."

"How?" he finally asked, swallowing hard.

"She was part of the problem because I turned to her for the emotional support that I didn't feel from you. Ryan is very available emotionally, and she was always there for me when something was bothering me. Like when I had that pregnancy scare," she reminded him. "It wasn't that I didn't want you involved. I just thought you'd be upset with me for not making sure we used a condom. I felt like she'd be there for me without judging me. And I didn't feel that from you."

"But that sounds like a good thing, Jamie. It's nice to have friends who you can count on like that."

"Yes it is," she agreed quickly. "And I want Ryan in my life permanently. The problem isn't with her. It's with me. Rather than trying to work out my issues with you, I took the easy way out and got the support that I needed from her. That was unfair to all of us, Jack. It didn't let you know what I needed, it got her involved in things that weren't appropriate for a friend to be involved in, and it let me take the easy way out. In a way, I used her, and I feel really bad about that."

He nodded briefly and gazed at the wine in his glass as he lifted it and swirled the deep red liquid around. "I'm glad that you admit that I wasn't imagining that she was interfering with our relationship," he said quietly. "And I'm sorry that I assumed it was sexual. It was narrow-minded of me to assume she was actively trying to interfere. I guess I owe her an apology."

"No, you don't," she said quickly. "I never told her any of the comments you made about her. I'm sure she doesn't know how you really feel."

He smiled gently and said, "Thank you. It makes me feel good to know you don't talk about me behind my back."

She rubbed the bridge of her nose nervously as she conceded, "I wouldn't exactly say that." A small chuckle bubbled up from her chest and she added, "I talked about how I felt about you, and how hurt I was by you. I'm not sure she thinks you're a fabulous guy. I just never spoke about what you said about her. And I've never told my parents anything bad about you. I only said that we had some issues we couldn't get over."

"That's still pretty good. If I only have to repair my reputation with Ryan, I think I'm in good shape."

She looked at him and asked directly, "So you won't mind if she and I stay close? She really means a lot to me, Jack."

"Jamie," he said confidently as he grasped her hand. "She can be your personal trainer, your biking partner, the maid of honor at our wedding, heck, she can be the godmother to our children! I just want you back!"

It was late when they finally arrived back in the South Bay. He walked her in, and they spent several minutes sitting on the couch and kissing rather innocently. But she could tell he was very tired, so she suggested, "Why don't you stay over … in the guest room?"

He sighed deeply and stretched before he nodded his head. "That's a good idea. I'm really beat."

"Come on, sweetie," she urged as she got to her feet and tugged his hand. "Time for bed."

She got him settled in the guest room right next to hers. After a few tame kisses, she walked to her room and got ready for bed. Just before she slid into the sheets, she glanced at her cell phone that she had inadvertently left at home. There were three messages from Ryan on voice mail, each one sounding a little more concerned. *God Ryan,* she thought, *don't be so possessive! Can't I have a day without my cell phone?*

She woke at six, still very tired, but in dire need of the bathroom. After she had relieved herself, she got a sly grin on her face and snuck next door and slipped soundlessly into Jack's room.

He was sprawled out across the bed, consuming nearly all of the king-sized mattress. He was sporting a cute pair of navy blue and white checked boxers … and an erection. *Oh-oh*, she thought, as she reconsidered her plan. *I don't want to have sex just yet, but I would like to be close. Well, maybe he'd be willing to just cuddle*, she thought, deciding to go for it. She slipped in next to him, and his body curled up on his side in immediate reaction. She snuggled up against his strong back, taking in his slightly musky scent and the smooth, lightly tanned skin that her cheek rested against. *God I missed this*, she thought, as sleep claimed her almost immediately.

As her eyes blinked open, a deep voice whispered, "Good morning."

"Oh, hi," she said with a shy grin. "I hope you don't mind that I snuck in here this morning." He was lying on his back, and she was curled up against his chest with her head resting on his muscular shoulder. His arm was securely wrapped around her shoulders, and his large hand rested on her hip.

"Best surprise I've had in weeks," he replied as he placed a tiny kiss on her head. "But I need my arm back for a minute." She released him and watched his cute butt twitch as he padded into the bath. A few minutes later he emerged, with his face washed and a toothbrush sticking out of his mouth. "What do you want to do?" he asked through a mouth full of toothpaste. "Ready to get up or would you like a little cuddling?"

She was a bit surprised by that offer since cuddling was never his forte. "I'd love to cuddle if you really don't mind."

He gave her a grin that lit up his whole face. He dashed back into the bath, spitting noisily, then ran a few steps toward the bed and launched himself at her with a wild look in his eyes. She laughed heartily at his antics, trying to remember the last time he had been so playful. He grabbed her roughly and plastered his toothpaste smeared mouth against hers, making her giggle uncontrollably. She calmed down after a minute, and he braced himself on one arm, leaning over her and saying in a very serious voice, "I missed cuddling with you. After we broke up I would lie in bed in the morning and just ache to feel your body next to mine."

She gazed up at him in amazement, both at the sentiment and his very successful attempts at emotional openness. Her face curled into a welcoming smile and he lowered his head to place a few delicate kisses on her lips. But true to his word, he immediately flopped down next to her and wrapped her in a warm embrace. She turned onto her side and scooted up against his lap, relieved to find him flaccid. *I don't think we've ever cuddled in the morning without him getting an erection,* she thought. *Maybe he really is serious about just being close*. They were both still tired, and after a few minutes of the tender embrace she slipped back into a contented slumber.

They cycled through sleep and hugs for another half hour or so, turning from one side to the other several times.

At around eight she woke on her left side, cuddled up against his back. She now felt rested and content and found herself start to nibble on his neck and shoulders. He stayed right where he was but he woke also, tugging her arm close against his chest as he relaxed and let her kiss him at her own pace. "Jack? Can we talk about sex a little bit?"

"Sure. What do you want to talk about?"

"Uhm … I've done a lot of thinking about how sex was between us, and I think we need to make a few changes … "

"Oh, I agree," he said without hesitation. "I know you weren't very satisfied, Jamie, and I take full responsibility for that."

"You do?"

"Yeah, I do. I was the more experienced partner, and I should have made your pleasure my priority."

"Well you did … at first."

"I know," he admitted quietly. "But that was another of my insecurities. I started to feel shut out and I reacted by trying to care less. Towards the end I admit that I was a total asshole! I still can't believe I acted that way. Your pleasure is very important to me, and I swear I'll work harder to focus on you."

"It's not that you didn't work hard enough, Jack, it's almost the opposite. I think we both have to loosen up and be more experimental if we're going to make this work."

He rolled over onto his back and gazed over at her with a very serious look on his face. "Tell me what you liked and didn't like," he asked, his gaze never wavering.

"Gosh," she said as her eyes blinked slowly. "Uhm … I loved the way we were before we started having sex."

"Why? What exactly did you love about that?"

"You used to turn me on," she gave him a wistful smile. "God! Some nights I could hardly walk when I left your apartment. Your kisses and your soft little caresses just drove me wild! But when we started to have intercourse, a lot of that stopped."

"You're right," he said immediately. "I admit that I was having a great time, and I didn't spend enough time making sure you were, too."

"Sometimes I did enjoy intercourse, Jack. But our schedules weren't the same. Like in the mornings, for instance, you'd wake up most mornings and be ready for action, but you seemed to just want to have a quick orgasm. That will never work for me. I can get aroused in the morning, but it takes a while. And it's painful when you enter me before I'm fully aroused."

"It's painful?" Jack asked, a hurt look on his face.

"Yes, honey, it's actually painful. And when you cause me pain, it just makes me tense up the next time, so it becomes kind of a vicious cycle."

"I swear I didn't know that. I guess I figured that you'd get aroused from having me inside of you."

"No, that doesn't work for me. It might for some women, but not me. I need slow, soft kisses and touches to get aroused in the morning, but that's obviously not what you need."

"No," he admitted as he blushed deeply. "I wake up horny, and I just want to have an orgasm. But there's no reason that you have to satisfy all my needs. We can reserve our lovemaking for when we're both in the mood and we have some time."

"That's not necessary. This is where we have to get creative. I'm more than happy to help you have an orgasm whenever you need it. I'm just not willing to have intercourse all the time."

"Oh," he said as he nodded slowly. "You really don't mind fooling around when I'm aroused?"

"No, I not only don't mind, I think it would be fun," she said, with an impish grin on her face. "Can you be satisfied with other kinds of stimulation?"

"Of course. Any assistance you can offer would be appreciated," he said with a grin as he leaned up for a kiss.

She turned him over onto his side and cuddled up against his back. "Would you like a little help now?" she whispered into his ear.

"Well, uhm … I'm not really arou … oops! Check that," he laughed as he felt his shorts grow snug. "Sure, I'd love a little help. What do you have in mind?"

"Well," she purred. "I could kiss you while you touched yourself …"

He tensed up at that suggestion, but gallantly agreed. "Okay … we could try that if that's what you want."

"No, Jack … it's not what I want, it's what pleases you."

"All right." He guided her hand, helping her to understand how he liked to be touched. His eyes closed and he shivered from head to toe. "Ohh, that's nice," he growled.

She gazed at him for a moment as a slow smile crept across her face. There was something so obvious about his genitals that was oddly appealing. If his penis was hard, he was aroused. Once he had an orgasm, it became flaccid and he was satisfied. The simple, straightforward nature of his needs was reassuring to her, as she tried to throw off some of her restraint and get more fully involved.

"How does this feel," she whispered.

He hissed out a moan of pleasure that effectively answered her question. It took a few minutes, but she satisfied him, smiling to herself when he groaned softly and finished. He turned his head languidly and gazed at her with a bemused smirk. "Are you sure you didn't date anybody while we were broken up?"

"Nope. Not a one. I was obviously waiting for you," she whispered as she leaned over him and kissed him tenderly.

To her extreme pleasure, they lay in bed for another hour, their soft, stroking caresses interspersed with tender kisses. "This is exactly … and I do mean exactly, what I needed," Jamie mumbled into his chest. "I love touching you and kissing and hugging in the morning, and I really enjoyed helping you have an orgasm. But if I had my way, we wouldn't have intercourse in the morning."

"This is a perfectly acceptable alternative," he agreed as he snuggled up against her back and nuzzled her neck.

This is what I thought marriage would be like, she thought as his hand ran slowly up and down her leg. *Nice long cuddles, lots of kissing and hugging, and when problems happen you just talk about them.*

Marta was very surprised to see Jack saunter downstairs, hand in hand with Jamie, but she made no comment other than to ask what they wanted for breakfast. It was after ten when they finally got out of bed, and a quick check of her cell phone while Jack was showering showed that Ryan had called at eight *God, I don't want to have to go into everything with her right now*, Jamie thought. *I think I'll just call her house and leave a message on the machine*. Her message was truthful as far as it went, but she knew that Ryan would be concerned. She merely said that she had unexpectedly decided to come down to her parent's home, and that she'd see Ryan at their appointment on Monday afternoon. *Oh shit,* she thought as she hung up. *She probably waited for me to take our long ride today.* She gamely tried to put the image of Ryan's disappointed face out of her mind, but she found that was easier said than done.

"You're being terribly generous with your time, but I know you have things to do," she said as she tried to keep her train of thought. They were sitting on a double chaise out by the pool after a lavish brunch, and Jack couldn't refrain from kissing her on every exposed millimeter of skin.

"I don't want to let you out of my sight ... or my touch," he whispered as he pinned her against the cushions with his chest and leisurely explored her mouth with his tongue. "Are you sure you don't want to go back upstairs and let me show you how experimental I can be?"

She pushed him away slightly by placing her hands flat on his chest. "I need some time to process this, honey. I really feel overwhelmed right now. And besides, I don't have any condoms in the house, and if you have one in your pocket I'll be terribly insulted."

He smiled back and stuck his hands in his pockets, pulling them inside out to show that they were devoid of birth control devices. "I understand. I just want to make sure you're satisfied if you need some attention."

She kissed him gently and stayed very close, whispering right into his lips, "Oh, I need it, alright. You've been driving me wild with those kisses. But I can wait for what I want. And I think you need to go get your work done, sweetheart."

"I won't be able to think of a thing other than your face," he pledged as he kissed all around her smiling face.

"You're too sweet," she said as she kissed him back. "But I've got work to do, too, so I'd better go." She got to her feet and extended both of her hands to pull his lean body from the chaise. But instead of going along willingly, he gave a sharp tug and pulled her right onto his lap.

"Just a few more kisses," he begged with his eyes closed.

She smiled at his dramatics, but granted his wish, now more than ever regretting her decision not to go back upstairs … condoms be damned.

She arrived back in Berkeley at two o'clock, emotionally exhausted but very energized physically. A quick check of the list of messages in Mia's handwriting showed that Ryan had called twice. The stab of regret hit her again, and only Ryan's clear instructions to do what was right for her allowed her to banish the feeling.

Chapter Sixteen

Monday afternoon found Ryan patiently waiting in the gym at four o'clock. Jamie made light of the weekend, mentioning that she had decided to go to Hillsborough at the last minute, and that she had forgotten to wear her phone.

"Did you have a good time?" Ryan asked behind slightly hooded eyes.

"Yeah, pretty good," she said absently. "Hey, let's work extra hard on my legs since I didn't ride this weekend."

Ryan just nodded, never asking why Jamie didn't give her prior notice that she'd skip their Sunday ride. She was pretty much her normal self, but when they were done she just gazed at Jamie with an absolutely neutral expression on her face. They had been having dinner together at least three nights a week, usually on Monday, Wednesday and Friday. But she made no mention of that as she shoved her hands in the pockets of her warm ups, and continued with that penetrating gaze.

The last thing Jamie wanted to do was talk about Jack at this point, and she knew she couldn't avoid it if she was with Ryan alone, so she just smiled and said, "See you Wednesday, okay?"

"Sounds good," Ryan said as her normally open face shut like a steel door.

"I've never been so surprised by anything in my whole life!" Jamie cried with elation as she recounted the events of the weekend to Anna.

"Tell me about how you felt when he made the overture," Anna urged.

"Just like I told you before," Jamie said with a touch of irritation. "I felt great! It was so validating to have him admit that he was in the wrong about so many things! It made me feel great!"

"And you accepted his offer immediately," Anna said, stating the obvious.

"Well, yes! Why wouldn't I? He apologized for everything, Anna! I must not be making myself clear! He took away every issue that bothered me in our relationship. And he showed me in very concrete terms how willing he was to change. That's what really made me believe him."

"He didn't take away every issue, Jamie," Anna reminded her. "He didn't take away Ryan."

Jamie had to bite back a sharp retort. Anna obviously didn't understand the gravity of Jack's actions, but her slowness was beginning to irritate. "Anna," she said as patiently as she could, "he forced me to seek comfort and understanding from another person. I wouldn't have even noticed that I was attracted to her if she hadn't been such a good listener." Jamie moved to the end of the couch, closing the space between herself and her therapist. "This is important to understand, Anna. I'm not in any way accusing Ryan of being opportunistic, but I was in a really vulnerable space during all of this. I allowed her to fill a void that Jack shouldn't have created!"

"So you believe that your attraction to women was just a reaction?" she asked with one raised eyebrow.

"I'm not attracted to women!" Jamie shouted. "I was attracted to Ryan. Just Ryan. But if I can have a normal relationship, there's no reason to even explore those feelings." She scooted back into her seat and stared at a colorful print on the wall for a few moments, trying to order her thoughts. "What if Jack and I were married, and I met a guy who I thought was just a tiny bit more compatible with me. I wouldn't explore that possibility … no matter how tempting it was. I'd be committed to Jack, and by its very nature that commitment precludes me from doing that. It's the same with Ryan," she insisted. "I might be more compatible with her than I am with Jack, and I might be able to have a fulfilling sexual relationship with her, but I was committed to Jack when this started to develop. Isn't it morally wrong of me to try to start something with her if Jack's willing to fix the problems we had?" Her tone had become nearly pleading, as if she was trying desperately to convince Anna that she was doing the right thing … the only thing possible given the circumstances.

"I see your point," the older woman said. "But your scenario assumes that Jack is fully in control of the success or failure of your relationship. I think you're being disingenuous if you look at it that way."

The blonde head nodded slowly as she acknowledged the truth of Anna's statement. "I know that we both contributed," she said quietly. "But things were really good before Ryan showed up. I think they can be good again."

Her eyes were filled with such hope that Anna had a hard time forcing herself to say, "I didn't know you then, but it seems odd that a woman could show up on the scene and destroy a perfectly good relationship. Surely there were issues that made you seek out her closeness."

Again, Jamie nodded, forcing herself to remember the lack of spark and the loneliness that she often felt when she was alone with Jack. "Yes, of course we had problems. What I'm trying to tell you is that many of those problems were because we weren't communicating well. One thing Ryan's done for me is show me how vitally important it is to tell Jack what's bothering me. He seems really receptive, Anna. I swear we can make a go of this if we both try hard enough."

"So, you're confident that you can put your feelings for Ryan aside?" the therapist asked gently.

"It'll be hard," Jamie said, staring at her feet. "But what's vital is our friendship. As long as I can keep her in my life I'm sure I can put my attraction aside." She shook her head and said, "Ryan is a wonderful woman, but I can't let myself forget that she's never shown an ability to be committed to one woman. I can't imagine anything worse than turning down this opportunity to be with Jack, and then have her find that she can't be monogamous! God, I'd kill myself!" She threw her head back against the cushions and shivered at the thought of having Ryan break her heart—knowing at that moment that she could never allow herself to risk it.

"Well, our time is about up," Anna said as she stared directly into her eyes. "Try to remember that your life doesn't have to come down to a decision between these two people. Try thinking in terms of what you want from a person rather than Jack versus Ryan. Think of your attractions in general—the men and the women that you've been attracted to throughout your life."

"I can save the time," Jamie said softly. "I've never been attracted to another woman. Ryan's the only temptation I've ever had, and if I can keep her as a friend I think I'd have everything I want."

Just before she got into bed, Jamie's cell phone rang. "Hello," she said as she fumbled with the flip-up cover.

"Hi," Jack's deep voice replied. "I wanted to make sure I got home in time to catch you before bed. How did I do?"

"I was half in," she admitted. "So I'd say you did well. How was your day?"

"Slow … very slow in fact. I was counting the hours until Friday when you come down." He paused a second and quickly said, "God! That was presumptuous of me! Do you want to see me this weekend?"

"Yes, of course I do," she replied, laughing gently at his question.

"Okay, would you like me to come up to Berkeley? I'd be happy to."

"You would?" she asked, her mouth hanging open in shock.

"Sure. Your house is much nicer than my apartment. I'd be happy to stay with you. I don't even know how we got into the rut of your coming down here, anyway."

"I'm not sure myself," she said slowly. "But I like to get away from my roommates for a while. So I'll come down there."

"I still don't think I can wait until Friday," he said. "How about dinner on Wednesday?"

"Okay," she said, completely charmed by his neediness. "I'm busy until six-thirty. Meet me here?"

"Deal. I'll call you tomorrow," he said. "I love you, Jamie."

"I love you too, Jack." I really do, she thought as the happiness welled up in her chest.

Wednesday afternoon was a replay of Monday, except that Jamie kept up a constant dialog during their training session. At the end, she smiled at Ryan and said, "Gotta go, don't wanna be late for therapy."

This time Ryan didn't even reply. She nodded almost imperceptibly, and turned to start her own workout, leaving Jamie standing in the middle of the gym, alone.

Her frustration was at the boiling point as she unloaded on Anna. "She acts like I owe her an explanation for my whereabouts! Just because we've had dinner together a lot doesn't mean that I'm obligated, does it?"

Anna recognized that this question was rhetorical, so she kept her opinion to herself.

"She clearly told me that if I wanted to find a man, she'd support me totally! But now she acts so possessive! You should have seen her, Anna. She barely made eye contact with me!"

"Tell me again what she told you when you made that overture to her," Anna urged.

With a heavy sigh, Jamie recounted the conversation once again. In a nearly mechanical voice, she said, "She told me that if I wanted to be with men, all I had to do was tell her and she'd understand."

"You haven't upheld your end of the bargain, Jamie," the older woman gently reminded her.

"What?"

"You haven't told her anything. You're rolling along as usual, and all of a sudden you don't go on your bike ride, you don't answer your phone and you don't keep your normal dinner plans. You've told me how perceptive she is. Don't you think she knows something is going on?"

Crossing her arms over her chest, Jamie grumbled, "I shouldn't have to report every little thing."

"Do you think this is a little thing? You can obviously make your own choice, but if you want to retain Ryan's trust I think you should at least tell her that you need some space. That would be much more generous than just ignoring her."

Jamie took in a deep breath as she shook her head and groused, "This is why I've never had many close friends. It's so hard to keep everyone happy!"

Jack showed up at seven on the dot, carrying a big paper bag that emitted a delicious aroma. "I thought you'd be tired after running around all day. I remembered that you liked that dim sum place down by me, so I stopped and picked up dinner."

"That's so sweet!" she cried as she tossed her arms around his neck. "Kitchen or dining room?" she asked as she led him into the kitchen to get plates.

"How about your room? We can be a little more casual up there."

She gave him a knowing grin, but quickly acceded to his wishes.

An hour and a half later, they were sprawled across the loveseat. She wasn't ready to have intercourse with him yet, and to her amazement he didn't press the issue in the least. Unsure of how it even began, both of their jeans wound up on the floor, as they touched each other with their hands, managing to have a surprisingly satisfying, albeit very casual, sexual encounter.

Afterwards, resting in each other's arms, she lazily commented, "That's the kind of thing I should have been doing in high school."

"Pardon?" he asked, not sure he had heard her correctly.

"I wish I had played around like that a little bit in high school," she reiterated. "It put a lot of pressure on you to help me figure out everything about my sexual response. Going slow like this and making it seem more lighthearted feels very good to me."

He chuckled and said, "Well, this is exactly what I did in high school, but I like it a lot more since I'm doing it with you. Going slow is helping me remember how great it felt to get to know someone sexually. This feels good to me too, and I promise we can go just as slow as you need to. I want to build a good foundation for our future life."

She cuddled close, feeling completely understood and very content.

She knew that Ryan was generally free on Thursday evenings, so after her last class she paged her. It only took a few minutes for the return call. "Hi," Ryan said rather neutrally. "What's up?"

"Can we have dinner tonight?" Jamie asked hesitantly.

"Uhm … let me think about that for a moment," Ryan replied. "Okay," she finally said, "I can do it."

"If it's not convenient …"

"No, I was just trying to remember what we were having, since I'll have to eat it for lunch tomorrow," she said with a chuckle.

"Are you sure?"

"Yeah. You're worth cold pork chops. I'll be there in fifteen minutes."

"So …" Ryan said after they were seated at her favorite Chinese restaurant on Telegraph. "Why did you want to see me?"

"Gosh, can't I just want to have dinner with you?" she asked, giving her a sharp look.

"Sure you can, you just haven't seemed to want to lately," Ryan replied as she leveled her gaze and stared right into Jamie's shifting green eyes.

She knew she sounded defensive, but she couldn't stop herself. "I've uhm … I've had some things to do. I didn't know we had any plans that I was breaking."

"We didn't," Ryan assured her as she reached over and covered her small hand with her own. "You just seem like something's bothering you, and I've been concerned."

"No, nothing's bothering me," Jamie assured her. "But I do have some interesting news to report." Ryan didn't reply verbally, but her eyebrows lifted in question. "Uhm ... I've re-established contact with Jack," she said quickly, afraid of the look she'd see in Ryan's eyes. But her friend either didn't have a reaction, or she was very good at hiding it. Ryan just tilted her head slightly and nodded, encouraging Jamie to continue.

Ryan still held her hand while she maintained her gaze. A couple of guys, obviously students, walked by the table. The one in the lead muttered, "Dykes!" as they passed, much to the enjoyment of his friend. Jamie yanked her hand back roughly, shocking Ryan in the process. A look of quiet sorrow flashed across her handsome features, but she composed herself almost immediately without commenting on the men.

Jamie couldn't bring herself to mention it either, so she jumped into her reason for the dinner. "I'm ah ... not sure where this will lead, but he seems very sincere about changing the things that bothered me about our relationship."

"That's encouraging," Ryan said absently as their food was delivered. She dug in immediately, savoring the spicy tastes as her attention was fully occupied. After several bites of everything, she said, "Tell me more if you want to." Her voice was flat, and reflected no interest.

For the first time in their relationship, Jamie didn't feel safe with her friend. It was clear that Ryan had a barrier up, and Jamie didn't have the energy to try to break it down. "There's not much else. I'll let you know how it goes."

"Do that," she agreed with a ten-watt smile.

The rest of the dinner was filled with periods of stilted silence, and Ryan slowly drove her crazy as she fixed her with a penetrating stare every time Jamie looked up. But the dark, enigmatic woman had nothing to say. Jamie had to carry the entire conversation, and by the time they were done she was really ready to go home.

"Let me get the check, Ryan," she said, as she tried to tug the bill from her friend's hand.

"Not necessary," Ryan assured her briskly. "Your portion is $11.26," she added after a quick glance. She pulled her neatly folded bills from her side pocket and tossed them on the table.

Jamie threw $15 at her, and quickly got to her feet. "Keep the rest for tip," she mumbled as she stumbled out the door, trying to stop her tears from flowing.

Ryan quickly settled the bill, and chased her down the street, having to grab Jamie's shoulder to slow her down.

"Jamie, please stop and talk to me," she begged. But Jamie was resolute in her determination to hide her face from her friend. No matter how Ryan approached, she turned her back quickly, brushing her aside with finality.

"I tried to talk to you … that's why I asked you here tonight. I … I thought you'd be happy for me," she sniffed, still unable to face her. "You said …" she sobbed, "you said you wanted me to be happy."

Ryan came up behind her back and silently wrapped her arms around her small waist. She leaned in close and closed her eyes as she felt Jamie's stiff body start to relax into the hug. "Jamie, I am happy for you if this is what you want," Ryan whispered. "It just hurt my feelings that you've been so distant. I swear I support your decision, no matter what you choose, but I don't want to lose you as a friend. You've been avoiding me for a week, and it's killing me," she said, whispering feverishly. "I'm sorry that I didn't hide that better."

"You don't have to hide anything," she tearfully assured her. She slowly turned in her embrace and rested her head on Ryan's chest. "I'm sorry," she sniffed. "I didn't mean to avoid you, but I've been feeling overwhelmed. I wasn't sure what you'd think, and I felt like I needed to have a better handle on things before I talked to you. I'm sorry I shut you out."

"That's what makes me your friend," Ryan insisted. "I want to be there for you when you feel overwhelmed. I want to be there for you when you're hurting or confused. I swear I do, Jamie." She looked down at her friend with pain-infused eyes and the smaller woman immediately felt disgusted with herself for avoiding her.

"I … I was afraid that you'd …"

Ryan gripped her chin with her fingers and tilted her head up so she had to look into her eyes. "I want you to have what you want … what you need … I'm your friend. I meant what I told you. If you want to be with men, I just want you to have the man who makes you happy. If that's Jack, I say good for him." Her eyes gave credence to her sincerity, but there was a hint of sadness that was impossible for Jamie to ignore.

She dropped her head again and nestled against Ryan's broad chest. "Thank you," she whispered. "Thank you for being my friend. I just wish that I deserved you."

Friday afternoon found Jamie once again in Anna's office, talking about her relationship with Ryan. "Thank God I was right about her," she said with relief. "She was very supportive and I really believe she wants what's best for me."

"She has been an extraordinary friend."

"Yeah, I haven't shown I'm worthy of her more times that I care to admit, but she always welcomes me back." She hesitated a moment, and then told Anna, "I think I'm going to sleep with Jack this weekend."

She just nodded non-committally.

"Do you think that's a good idea?" Jamie asked, searching Anna's eyes.

"Do you really want me to make those decisions for you, Jamie?" she asked her, cocking her head in question.

"I guess not," she replied glumly. "I just wish I knew if I was doing the right thing."

"Right thing?"

"Yeah. Am I sure I want to be back with him? Should I be certain before I sleep with him? All that stuff."

"Have you tried to stay present and let yourself feel your feelings?"

"Yeah, I think I have, but sometimes it's hard for me to stop analyzing things."

"That's hard. But it's the best advice I can give you. Just open your heart and let your emotions guide you."

Just to be safe, she carried a box of condoms in her overnight bag. She knew she was overreacting since she was still on the pill, but she wasn't sure if Jack hadn't been with anyone else during their hiatus, and she didn't want to know if he had. So she thought it was best to make him think the condoms were a necessity. She also hadn't told her parents she was coming down, reasoning that she'd just show up if she didn't feel comfortable sleeping with him.

When she arrived, Jack had carry-outs waiting, and he was filling their plates. "I hate to see you spend your Friday evenings cooking for me," he said, grinning broadly. "I know you have a long week too, and it just seems unfair."

"You," she said as she tapped his nose, "are making a lot of brownie points with me, mister."

"I'm not trying to make brownie points," he said with a sincere look on his face. "I'm just trying to be considerate."

After dinner, he proposed a walk in the neighborhood, or even a movie. "No, I'd rather stay in and concentrate on you," she said with a smile.

They relaxed together on the sofa, talking about their respective weeks. The time flew by as they sipped several glasses of cabernet, their bodies getting closer and closer until they were fully entwined. Jack placed their glasses on the coffee table and started to kiss and caress Jamie with a relentless intensity. He kissed her more and more passionately until she was squirming against his weight. "Let's go to bed," she murmured into his ear. He was on his feet in a nanosecond, tugging her up with him.

When they reached the bedroom, he tenderly undressed her, slowly running his hands over each part of her body as it was revealed. "You look so awesome, Jamie," he said in a nearly reverent voice. "Your body is so firm and sleek. The muscles really make you look hot," he whispered as he nibbled her neck.

She spent a long time undressing him, gazing at his long, lean body with complete approval. She crossed the room and retrieved her bag, pulling the box of condoms from it with a flourish. "A whole box?" he asked with a rakish look.

"Don't be a glutton," she chided with a toss of her head. She went into the bath and got ready for bed, stopping to stare at herself in the mirror for a moment. *I want this*, she said firmly to her suspicious conscience.

When Jack had finished brushing his teeth, she was lying on the bed with the covers pushed back. He slid in next to her and started to kiss and touch her again. It didn't take long to draw her right back up to her previous heights of arousal, and a few minutes later she whispered, "I'm ready for you, Jack."

But instead of entering her immediately, he started to lightly touch her just as he had at her house on Wednesday. This surprised her, but it felt divine, so she didn't complain. Automatically her hand went to his groin and she began to touch him in a similar fashion. They began to kiss again as their hands worked away and the dual sensations caused her to be swept away to a delightful orgasm surprisingly quickly. He followed close behind, uttering soft moans of pleasure as he climaxed.

They rested for a brief time, and she finally broke the silence when she murmured, "We didn't get to use a condom."

"No big deal," he assured her. "I had a great time."

"That was exactly what I've wanted sex to be like," she murmured slowly as she sank into a peaceful, satisfied sleep.

He woke up on Saturday ready to go again, but very happily settled for a little manual assistance. Jamie got all of the cuddling she wanted, so they both started the day in an ebullient mood. They both had studying to do, so they spent the better part of the day in front of their respective books.

At around six, he suggested they take a walk and have dinner in the neighborhood. When they returned at nine, she was beat and she found that she had no interest in sex. He accepted her choice without complaint, cuddling against her after a few chaste kisses.

Sunday was another day of surprises. "How about brunch?" he asked with a sunny smile as she woke from a nice dream.

"Brunch?"

"Sure. We can go somewhere in the neighborhood, or we could go to the club if you want to go with your parents."

"Hmm, I'd rather be with just you," she said, not mentioning that she didn't want her parents to know of the reconciliation attempt quite yet.

"Great, you pick the place and we're there."

They had a great time together, and he even let her pick up the check, smiling sedately as she whipped out her American Express card.

Heading back to his apartment, they each spent a few hours reading. She had already decided that she needed to be home early so she could work on a paper on her computer. At around three, she looked up to see him eyeing her hungrily. *He's been such a darling,* she thought to herself. *Come on and make the first move*. She didn't say a word as she got up from the sofa. Rather, she extended her hand and led him into the bedroom. He smiled shyly at her as she started to undress him, but he happily allowed her to continue. After he had returned the favor he picked her up and carried her the short distance to the bed.

Jack spent the next fifteen minutes driving her absolutely wild. He placed her on her stomach and started at her heels, slowly kissing and licking and sucking every bit of skin that he could reach. She just hummed with pleasure, murmuring small words of encouragement. Then he rolled her over onto her back and started at the bottom again. Unable to hold back her question any longer, she lifted up onto an arm and asked, "Where did you learn all of this?"

He chuckled deep in his chest and released her foot from his grasp. "I … uhm … read some books," he said with an adorable blush that covered him from his chest to his hairline.

"You read books?" she asked in amazement.

"Yeah, that's how I learn everything else," he explained. "Why not this?"

She flopped back down on the bed and spread her arms out in surrender. "Those were some very, very good books," she murmured compliantly as he continued his quest.

He moved up her body an inch at a time, smiling at her encouraging entreaties, but not moving any faster than his current torturous pace. When he reached her breasts, he worshiped them for long minutes, ignoring Jamie's small, soft moans and her invitingly spread legs.

She felt more turned on than she had ever been before, finally feeling safe to abandon some of her inhibitions and show him exactly how she felt. He seemed to be enjoying himself as much as she was which increased her arousal even more. But try as she might, she began to grow tense as he tentatively moved between her legs and gingerly spread her lips apart. She could actually feel her heart thumping in her chest and she tried to breathe deeply to relax. A quick glance down showed a look on Jack's face that mirrored that of an anxious father trying to assemble an intricate bike on Christmas Eve. His brow was furrowed, and he looked very hesitant, but he took a deep breath and moved forward.

"Oh my God!" she cried aloud when his soft, smooth tongue glided across her aching flesh. Her legs spread even further open in an unconsciously automatic gesture. His forehead was still knotted in concentration, but he began to move his head slowly, like a cat lapping milk from a saucer. *How can anything that feels this good make me this anxious?* But she was anxious, very anxious in fact, and her anxiety was compounded by the fact that she knew this was a seminal event in their sexual relationship. She desperately wanted to be able to enjoy oral sex if she was going to be with Jack for the next fifty or sixty years, but she knew that he wouldn't have the confidence to try again if she wasn't receptive.

But he looked so tense and rigid lying between her legs, that she fought with the instinct to tap him on the shoulder and pull him up.

You have to concentrate on the feeling! she reminded herself over and over. *The feeling is fabulous! Don't look at his face, that's throwing you off!* She closed her eyes tightly and tried to concentrate fully on the sensations flooding her body, but it was rough going.

She realized that the only way to enjoy this experience was to shut off her conscious mind, something that she found difficult to do in the best of situations. She desperately tried to force herself to think of calming thoughts and experiences but something kept creeping into the corners of her mind.

Her unconscious mind knew the truth, though, and it kept reminding her that the most relaxed she ever felt was when she was with a certain dark haired beauty. She tried to keep those images out of her head, but eventually she grew tired of fighting and just succumbed. Jack's rigid body was immediately replaced in her mind's eye by the long, smooth body with the soft, sensual curves. His tense face gave way to the dark flowing hair, so silky and smooth as it trailed over her sensitive thighs. The dark head lifted just a touch, and those clear blue eyes, so confident and experienced, twinkled up at her as one brow lifted rakishly. The crystal blue eyes stayed locked on her own as that soft pink tongue dipped down to take another taste. A look of indescribable pleasure settled onto her beautiful features and her eyelids fluttered heavily as she dropped her head to lustily consume the tortured flesh. Suddenly, nothing existed except those few precious inches of real estate. Every sensation in her body went to and came from her vulva. Before she was even conscious of her actions, she grabbed a handful of sandy blonde hair and thrust herself hard against his face, moaning deeply as her orgasm permeated every nerve and muscle in her body.

Jack had obviously taken her comments about intercourse seriously, since once again he placed her hand on himself rather than even try to enter her. Her body was still so completely enervated that she hardly knew what she was doing, but he didn't seem to mind, finishing quickly. She knew something was bothering her, but she was too exhausted to think of it, instead just wrapping her arms around Jack's heavy body and drifting off into a dreamless sleep.

Soft lips nuzzled her neck, and she shifted slightly to increase the sensation. *Oh, God, Ryan, you're so good,* she mused from her sensual haze. She turned to kiss those rose-tinted lips, but as she turned and met Jack's twinkling eyes she nearly screamed in shock.

"What's wrong, honey?" he asked quickly upon seeing her jerk.

"Oh, nothing, nothing," she insisted. "I was just dreaming … I must not have been fully awake." She shook her head roughly, trying to focus on who she was, where she was, and why she was in bed with Jack, since Ryan had just made love to her.

Oh shit, not this again, she moaned to herself as she became fully conscious. *Why did I have to use her again? Jesus! He's doing everything I ever wanted him to do! Get out of my god damned bed, Ryan!* But even though her emotions blamed Ryan, she knew in her soul that it wasn't her fault. She couldn't help that she was gorgeous and sexy and alluring and so smooth and warm and soft when Jamie was wrapped in her strong arms. Stop it! Just stop it right now! she ordered her mind. *You're in bed with Jack, and he's being the sweetest man on earth! Concentrate, damn it!*

"Are you really okay, Jamie?" he asked rather tentatively, trying to connect with her far away look.

"Yeah, yeah, I'm fine," she said as she tried to shake the image of that beautiful face from her brain. She smiled up at Jack and said, "I think you sent me into another world with that orgasm."

He smiled down at her, beaming proudly at his accomplishments. "Should I send in a reader's review to Amazon.com on the books I bought?"

"Definitely," she said with a matching smile. *While you're on there see if you can find me something on self-hypnosis, will ya?*

She had to head home and work on her paper, so she left Palo Alto around six. Even though her mind urged her to go home, she found her little Porsche heading north on 101, winding up in Noe Valley. Her fingers automatically dialed the pager, waiting patiently for her friend to return the call. As usual it took mere minutes. "Hi," Ryan said, in a reasonable facsimile of her normal tone.

"Finished with dinner?" Jamie asked.

"Yep. I just finished being me and Brendan," she said with a chuckle, referring to their clean-up regimen.

"Any plans for tonight?" Jamie asked.

"I was going to spend the evening with a few thousand pairs of chromosomes, but I could easily be persuaded to put my biology homework aside. What do you have in mind?"

"How would you like me to buy you dessert?"

"Sure. When will you be here?"

"About thirty seconds? I'm in front of your house."

"Get in here, you loon!"

They decided to do the Hot Fudge Sundae Death March, as Jamie affectionately called it. The walk wasn't only long, it was very hilly, but it allowed her to gather her thoughts. They spoke of their respective weekends, and Ryan regaled her with a hilarious description of a frazzled ride leader who got over fifty people completely lost in the Berkeley hills that afternoon.

Ryan could clearly tell that something was bothering Jamie, but she tried to keep the conversation light and let her go at her own pace. By the time they reached the ice cream shop, Ryan was out of interesting stories about her weekend with Caitlin and

Duffy's latest exploits. They got their ice cream and started trudging back, the silence descending upon them until Jamie finally broke it.

"Can we talk about sex?"

"Uhm, sure," Ryan said carefully. "What do you want to talk about?"

"I want to talk about some pretty graphic stuff. Are you sure you're okay with that?"

"Hit me with your best shot," Ryan said with a confident smile, her eyes slightly hooded.

"Well, you know I'm trying to work out some issues with Jack to see if we should get back together permanently."

A nod urged her to continue. "Since one of our biggest problems is sex, I decided to sleep with him this weekend." She wasn't sure, but she thought she caught just a glimmer of pain flash across that beautiful face, but Ryan turned slightly and smiled at her, still not commenting. "Something really bothered me about it and I don't know who else to talk to."

"Go ahead," she urged stoically. "I can take it."

"Okay," she said as she took a breath. "Uhm … do you ever … ahh … fantasize while you're having sex?"

Ryan nodded just a tiny bit and said, "I think that's a very common thing for women to do. Some women do it once in a while, some do it every time. But I don't think it's necessarily anything that should concern you."

"You didn't really answer my question," Jamie said.

"I didn't?"

"No. I asked if you ever fantasized."

"Oh … I guess you did, didn't you. Well, uhm … sure I have. I think everyone does."

"When do you do it?" she persisted.

"When? Like specifically when?" she asked lamely.

"This bothers you," Jamie said firmly. "We don't have to talk about it any more."

"No, no, it's not that it bothers me. I'm just worried about why you want the information. I'm afraid of saying something that you'll misinterpret as the norm."

"Huh?"

"I don't want you to assume that the way I have sex is the right way, Jamie. I'm happy to tell you anything you want to know, but I don't want you to over-interpret."

"Okay. I promise I'll view your opinion as a sample of one," she smirked.

Ryan shot her a quirky grin and finally answered her question fully. "I've fantasized in order to have an orgasm, but it's not something I do routinely. I'd have to say it's a last resort."

"Last resort?"

"Yeah, if I can't come any other way, I'll fantasize to get there."

"But it doesn't happen often?"

"No. And it never happens with anyone I know well. I'm all about connection when I have sex. I'm really into experiencing my partner. You know … like on every plane. I love to taste and smell and feel her … let her in as much as possible. If I'm having sex with someone I really like, that feeling just gets more intense. I try to open myself up even more with people I trust so I can experience everything she has to give. A fantasy is something I use to be less connected to my partner … like if I misjudged someone."

"What do you mean by that?" Jamie asked, her brow wrinkling up in question.

"Well, I don't know if I've mentioned this, but if I don't know the person I'm with, I usually don't let her touch me … genitally at least," she added with a smirk. "But once in a while I let someone I don't know touch me, and sometimes I misjudge her and find that she doesn't arouse me, or her technique doesn't work for me. Rather than hurting her feelings and telling her to stop, I'll fantasize so I can have an orgasm and get out of there." Her lips quirked up in a grin as she added, "Pretty romantic, huh?"

"The first part was," Jamie said wistfully as she let out a heavy sigh.

They were back at the house by now, and after a few minutes of small talk with Martin they walked down to Ryan's room. Jamie sat on the loveseat and Ryan pulled her desk chair over, climbing onto it back wards and leaning forward to face her friend. "Tell me what's really going on. It's clear that something's bothering you."

"God, I really want to talk about it with you, but I don't want to make you uncomfortable."

"You won't," she said sincerely. "I really can take it, Jamie."

She nodded briefly as she bit her lip in a nervous gesture. "Okay," she finally said. "We had some of the best sex we've ever had this weekend. He was like a different guy, Ryan. He was gentle and very loving and he tried really hard to be experimental. And things went great! They really did," she said emphatically.

Ryan continued to gaze at her with a penetrating stare. "But …" she said softly.

"But, this afternoon bothered me … a lot," she admitted. "He went down on me, and even though it felt fabulous, I had a lot of trouble concentrating and staying connected to him. I mean, he was really doing a good job!"

Ryan just nodded, not saying a word.

"I had to … fantasize to have an orgasm and it really bothered me," she said as tears welled up in her eyes.

"Why did it bother you?" Ryan asked softly, her deep voice surrounding Jamie's senses like a dense fog.

"Because I had to think about … you," she sniffed as she broke into tears. Immediately, Ryan was next to her, cradling her in her wonderfully warm and comforting embrace. She rocked her slowly, making soft shushing sounds to calm her.

"I … I don't know what to do," she sniffed. "Part of me only wants to be with you and no one else for the rest of my life. But another part knows that Jack is safe and reassuring and … and …"

"Normal," Ryan finished for her quietly.

Jamie lifted her tear streaked face and gazed at her pathetically "Is it so wrong to want to be like everybody else?"

"No, it's not wrong," she said softly. "But it won't work if it's not right for you."

"But how do I know, Ryan? I'm so afraid …"

"I know, Jamie. I really do know," she said with her voice full of emotion and empathy.

"I just wish there were some way that I could … you know … kind of experiment before I had to make a decision." She looked up a Ryan with the barest hint of a question in her green eyes.

"What exactly do you mean?" Ryan asked carefully as she sat up slightly.

"I don't know. I mean I know what it's like with Jack, but I don't know if I'd really be happy with a woman. I wish I could … you know … experiment a little before I had to jump in."

"And you'd like to experiment with me?" she asked in that same calm tone of voice.

"Well, yeah," Jamie laughed with an embarrassed giggle. "I'm not attracted to any other woman."

"Oh," Ryan said as she released her hold and stood. "You want me to make love to you so you can make sure I really do turn you on." She was obviously getting angry and Jamie tried to stop her to explain, but Ryan was on a roll. "So if I fuck you well enough I win, but if your orgasm doesn't reach a certain height you put me back in friendville, and go marry Jack, right? Now correct me if I got any part of this wrong," she said with biting sarcasm. "Do I get two out of three tries? Do I immediately go to oral sex, or can I pull out a big dildo to help me out?" She was towering over Jamie's now shaking body, glaring at her with an intensity that was terrifying to the smaller woman. "I'd tell you where you can stick your idea, but that might be another area I might be expected to satisfy!" She turned and ran up the stairs, yanking the front door open violently and shutting it with a glass-rattling slam.

She wasn't sure of many things right then. But she was most definitely sure that she had never been more bereft. She was as sure as she had ever been that she had destroyed her friendship with the closest friend she had ever dreamed of having, and she was equally certain that Ryan would never have her as a lover.

She hovered over the commode, heaving every morsel of food and acid from her clenching stomach, hoping fervently that she didn't pass out, since that would only make a worse mess for Ryan to clean. She was crying so violently that she didn't hear her come back into the room, but soft, warm hands lifted her gently from her kneeling position and scooped her up into a warm, comforting embrace.

Ryan carried her back to the loveseat and gently placed her on the cushions, but Jamie's fragmented brain could hardly accept the generous gesture. Seconds later, a warm cloth whisked the tears from her face and wiped her mouth gently. Then the cushions compressed as Ryan sat down right next to her and pulled her onto her lap.

The dark head leaned forward and planted tiny, soft kisses all over her face, reassuring Jamie with her physical intimacies. When the great, heaving sobs calmed she tugged the smaller woman even closer and whispered, "I'm so sorry, Jamie. I'm so very sorry."

She accepted the apology even though she didn't believe that Ryan had anything to apologize for. "I'm the one who should apologize," she murmured against her damp neck.

"No," Ryan said firmly. "I told you to tell me what was on your mind, and when you did I blasted you for it. That was wrong of me, and I'm very sorry for doing that."

"I hurt your feelings, Ryan," she mumbled softly.

"Yeah, you hurt me. But you didn't mean to. You're just trying to find a way to make this whole thing less frightening for yourself, and I should have realized that."

"Are you still my friend?" she asked tentatively.

"Always," Ryan replied confidently. "I'll always be your friend." After a second she explained, "But if we slept together on a whim I don't think I could be your friend. You mean too much to me to cheapen what I feel for you. I can't, and I won't, reduce my feelings for you to mere sex."

"I'm so sorry I made you feel that way, Ryan. I don't know where that even came from," she said as she shook her head. "I find myself saying and doing things that are just not me! I hardly recognize the woman who propositioned you just to try out lesbian sex."

Ryan's gentle chuckle caused her to look up. "It wasn't that bad."

"Yes it was," Jamie said. "That's not who I am. I don't even know where that thought came from, but it's not how I think of you."

"Thank you," she murmured as she gave her a gentle squeeze. "That makes me feel better."

Jamie uttered a deep sigh and moaned, holding her stomach. "I should get home. I need to get something in my stomach."

Ryan sat back and regarded her carefully. Jamie was still terribly pale, her face nearly ashen. Her hands were clammy and shaking a little, whether from nerves or vomiting, Ryan wasn't sure. She was, however, sure that she wouldn't allow Jamie to drive in this condition. "Two options," she said. "You stay here, or I drive you home. Your choice."

She knew that nothing could budge Ryan when she had that determined look on her face, so she pursed her lips and said, "I'll stay."

Ryan got her a pair of flannel pajamas, but she couldn't keep the pants up, so she decided to sleep in the roomy top and her panties. The brunette tucked her into bed and went back to her desk to study for a while, but it was clear from the tossing and turning that Jamie couldn't sleep.

Without even asking if she wanted comfort, Ryan took her book and got into bed, lying in the center of the king sized surface. She urged Jamie to rest her head in her sweatpants-covered lap, and began to slowly run her fingers through her short blonde locks. As expected, the smaller woman's breathing evened out and deepened almost immediately as Ryan smiled down at the gently dozing woman nestled up against her body. *Come on, Jamie,* she urged in silent prayer. *Face the truth! We could be so good together, if you'll only take the chance!*

"I understand that the dream upset you, Jamie, but maybe we can make some sense out of it if you'll talk about it," Anna urged. They were sitting in Anna's office, trying to make sense of the dream that had woken her early in the morning, panting and sweating.

"All right," Jamie begrudgingly agreed. "I was swimming in my parents' pool at home. Everything was fine, nice day and all that, but the water was chilly, so I had to keep moving. All of a sudden I was in the ocean. It was weird because I couldn't see land, but the water was so calm and still that it was just like the pool had been. Nice and calm, but still a little cold. But it was definitely the ocean, and I knew that it was really deep, so I had to keep floating. There were all sorts of things floating right by me, a life preserver, a thick pool float, even one of those floating chairs. But I didn't want any of them for some reason. I just kept on trying to swim. It went fine for a while, but eventually I got tired of trying to just stay afloat. But here's the weird part. Instead of grasping on to one of the life rafts, I started to swim towards the choppy, rough water that I could see in the distance.

"I don't know why I did it," she marveled. "The place I was in was so much calmer and safer, but I had to reach that turbulent water. The closer I got, the more energized I felt," she said, shaking her head in wonder. "It was really rough going, but I had to continue farther and farther out. Even though the water was wild and rough, it was much warmer and clearer. I could actually see all of the marine life surrounding me and that made it very exciting. The water was so blue and clear it was like I was in the Caribbean, rather than California. But again, the waves continued to grow. The chop must have been two feet, and I felt like I'd never make it. But out of nowhere Ryan appeared. She swam right up to me so confidently that I immediately started to relax. I really needed her help, but she didn't grab me like I thought she would. Instead, she gave me a beautiful smile, and turned so that she was lying on her back. She started to kick and move farther out into even rougher weather. Her eyes were on me the whole time, and seeing her encouraged me, but she wasn't giving me the kind of help I needed. She just smiled and kept kicking. I knew that I had to follow her, because she was my only chance at survival, but I soon found that she wasn't going towards shore. Now I could see the shore and the calm waters, but I was inexorably drawn to follow her. It made no sense to me!" she said in a frustrated tone. "The shore was the other way! All of those things that could keep me afloat were in the other direction. But I followed her into those deep, treacherous waters."

"Is that all you remember?" Anna asked.

"Yeah, that's it."

"Have any ideas about the meaning?"

"Yeah, that choosing Ryan's going to be the death of me," she grumbled. "I mean, I had that nice pool, I had the nice calm ocean, but I just had to let her lead me into the depths."

"Maybe," Anna mused slowly. "Or maybe she wasn't leading you at all. Maybe she was supporting you on a journey that you were determined to take."

"Journey?"

"Yes. A journey of discovery, Jamie. Tell me again about the water."

"Well, the water in the pool was nice. A little cold, but nice. Then the calm ocean water was about the same. But as I went into the rough water it became warm, almost my body temperature. Wait a minute!" she said excitedly. "It was my body temperature! The farther out I got, the less I could even feel the water. It must have been exactly my temperature."

"What else?"

"It was warm and very, very clear. The water in the calm part had been like regular ocean water. You could only see a few inches. But the rough water was so clear you could see everything around you. It was really exciting," she related. "Kinda like scuba diving."

"Were you afraid to follow Ryan?"

"Yes! I was scared to death!"

"But you chose to, even though you could see the shore and the nice calm water."

"Yes, I did," she said quietly.

"Why do you think you chose to follow her into dangerous waters, rather than go back to safety?" Anna asked.

Jamie was quiet for a long while. She had closed her eyes to allow herself to think more clearly. The silence continued until she lifted her head and opened her eyes, focusing on Anna with a defiant look in her eyes. "Because the calm water was going to kill me," she said firmly. "The only chance I had was to risk the turbulence."

"Was it Ryan's decision to lead you out there?" she asked gently.

"No." Jamie shook her head forcefully and took a deep breath. "She came out to the turbulence for me. She was risking her own security to help me save myself."

Anna nodded briefly, and asked the critical question. "What does the dream tell you, Jamie?"

She closed her eyes and involuntarily shivered from head to toe. Her eyes blinked open slowly and her voice grew quiet but determined, "It tells me to say goodbye to Jack."

She considered every permutation of plan. Should she have him come to Berkeley? Should she go to his apartment? Over the phone? In a letter? But none of the options seemed right. She had never broken up with anyone special before, and she truly hated that Jack had to be the one. Finally deciding that she had to get it over with, she called his apartment at seven o'clock.

"Jamie, hi," he said warmly. "I didn't expect to hear from you so soon."

"I need to talk to you, Jack. Can I come down?"

"Tonight?" he asked in surprise. "What is it? Is something wrong?"

"Yes, something is wrong, but I need to tell you in person."

"No," he said firmly. "I don't want to wait an hour. Don't hold me in suspense, please," he begged.

She drew in a breath and let it out slowly, trying to steel her nerves. "It's about us," she said with a tremulous voice.

"I assumed that, Jamie," he said calmly. "What about us exactly?"

"We … we can't be together," she whispered as the tears began.

"Why?" he asked so softly that she could barely hear him. "I thought that I had—"

"You did nothing wrong, Jack. You were absolutely perfect," she said as the sobs shook her body. "It's not you … it's me."

"What's you?" he asked, again in a barely perceptible voice.

"I'm not able to commit to you, Jack. I … I … I have sexual feelings for other women," she mumbled, refusing to make Ryan be the villain.

"So do I, Jamie," he said with as light a tone as he could muster. "But I don't act on them because I love you. Don't you love me enough to put those feelings aside?"

She was shaking her head even though he couldn't see her. "It's not like that, Jack. It would always interfere between us. You're too wonderful a person to settle for someone who wasn't able to give you all of her love."

"Shouldn't I be the one who decides that?" he asked. "Please don't try to make my decisions for me."

"This isn't just for you. I've tried to focus on you, but I haven't been able to. This is something I have to experience. It will haunt me forever if I don't. I swear, the pull is just too strong."

"Stronger than your love for me?" he asked quietly.

"It must be," she admitted as her voice broke. "God! I wish it weren't, Jack!" she sobbed. "I want to be with you, and have a bunch of kids and close this part of myself off. But I can't. I just can't," she added weakly. "It would be unfair to both of us and our children; because someday the pull would be too great and I'd ruin all that we'd built together."

A long silence developed since she had nothing more to add. Finally, he asked, "Are you absolutely certain?"

"Yes," she said quietly. "I'm certain."

He blew out a long breath and quietly said, "I love you, Jamie." Then the phone went dead.

The phone rang again at ten, and she was tempted not to answer, but she stumbled to the handset and picked it up. "Hello?" she said with her stuffy nose and raspy voice.

"Jamie?" Ryan asked, unsure if it was her.

"Yeah."

"What's wrong?" Ryan asked amid the noise of wherever she was.

"I had a tough evening."

"Well, you looked upset while we were working out. That's why I called. I was getting ready to go home and I wanted to make sure you were all right."

"I'm all right," she said, very unconvincingly.

"Jamie, we talked about this last week," she reminded her. "You can tell me what's bothering you. That's what friends do."

"I can't," she muttered as she started to cry. "I've been crying for three hours, and I don't want to start again!"

"I'll be there in five," Ryan said decisively as she hung up.

True to her word, Ryan knocked softly on the door mere minutes later. Cassie poked her head out, but she nodded when she saw Jamie open her door to go answer the knock. Her eyes were swollen from crying, and red blotches covered her face and neck, her hair was seriously askew from trying to sleep, and her nose was running continually. But Ryan gently placed her hand on her back, and led her upstairs. When they reached the room, she put a calming CD in the changer and turned it on to disguise their voices from prying roommates. "You don't have to tell me anything," she promised. "Just let me hold you and comfort you."

Even though she didn't speak, the tears started again. Jamie stood in the middle of the room looking lost and small and frightened. Her shoulders shook from crying, and she was sobbing so hysterically that she couldn't have been understood if she had tried to speak. But she nodded her head at Ryan's offer and closed her eyes as the warm embrace enveloped her. "Bed or loveseat?" the taller woman asked gently.

Rather than respond, Jamie started moving towards the bed, and Ryan released her tight hold to drape an arm around her shoulders. She half fell onto the mattress and Ryan kicked off her shoes and climbed right up next to her, snuggling behind her and stroking her arm. She asked no questions and Jamie offered no explanations, but after a few minutes she felt the aching sadness begin to lift a little bit. She knew she was close to collapsing from exhaustion, so she asked, "Stay with me?"

"Of course," Ryan murmured. She got up and removed her jeans and slithered out of her bra, a difficult feat when one doesn't take off the T-shirt covering it. But she quickly returned to the bed, and cuddled up behind her friend, wrapping her arm around her waist.

Jamie was almost asleep, but just before she drifted off she mumbled, "I broke up with Jack tonight. Permanently," she added.

Ryan felt a huge amount of empathy for her friend, but the tiny glimmer of hope in her heart that had nearly been extinguished flickered and grew warmer, causing a small smile to grace her lips as she tilted her head up to gently kiss Jamie's tear-streaked cheek.

On a cloudy, damp afternoon Jamie sat in Anna's warm office and declared, "I think I'm ready to move forward with Ryan—if she's still interested after my meltdown," she added with a smirk.

"Have you spoken to her about your relationship since that little incident?"

"No. We've become strangely silent about the whole thing. But we seem to be even closer than we were before," she said. "She hovers over me like a hawk, always making sure that I'm doing all right. We're together almost constantly, and when I don't see her she calls me right before she goes to sleep."

"That sounds encouraging. What makes you think you're ready?"

"My feelings for her get stronger all the time. I feel so good when we're together. It's like she's so complementary to me. I can honestly say that she helps bring out the best parts in me," she said thoughtfully.

"Do you have any doubts about moving forward?"

"Yeah, oh yeah!" she laughed. "I'm scared spitless, to be honest. I know in my heart that this is right for me, but I'm terrified of so many things."

"Tell me about them," Anna urged.

"Well, I'm afraid to tell my parents, and my friends. I'm worried about how I'll deal with the rejection that I'm bound to receive from some people," she said thoughtfully. "And I'm really, really scared about sex," she admitted, a bit embarrassed.

"What is it that scares you?" Anna asked gently.

"It's just that I've never been with a woman, and she's been with … let's just say that she's been with a lot of women. I worry that I won't be able to please her, or that she'll get frustrated with my inexperience."

"Would you feel comfortable talking to her about your fears?"

"I think I would. I mean I tell her everything else. I may as well own up to this too," she laughed. "It's funny, but I dated boys for almost six years before I had intercourse. I just wish I could spend a little time exploring with Ryan before it got too intense. I wish I could get a lesbian learner's permit. But that didn't go over very well the last time I brought it up," she added with a noticeable shiver.

"That was a completely different situation, Jamie. You're asking for something very different now. There's nothing compelling you to do things that you're not ready for. If you want to go slow and just explore, there's no reason that you can't do that."

"I'm just afraid that Ryan wouldn't be able to do that," she added shyly. "She has needs that she's not used to denying."

"If she's the person that you think she is, you might be surprised at what she'd do to make you comfortable. I think you owe it to yourself to make this experience as safe as you need it to be. I think you need to talk to Ryan," she said firmly.

They met at the Ferry Building, in the foggy chill of a late April morning. Both had several layers of clothing on to guard against the stiff breeze that constantly fluttered through the Golden Gate. They loaded their mountain bikes onto the first ferry to Sausalito and found places on the rail to watch the panorama unfold before them.

"You really can talk me into anything, can't you?" Ryan said as she smiled down at her companion.

"Don't you think the ferry is fun?"

"I haven't been on one since my fourth grade class went to Alcatraz," she recalled. "All I remember is that Shelly Blake got sick, and spent the whole time hanging over the rail. We thought that was pretty cool, so I guess I do think ferries are fun."

"Well, I like them a lot, so you have to, too," Jamie said. "I can't remember the last time I was in Sausalito, though. I think it's fun to do touristy things once in a while, don't you?"

"I'm learning that I do," Ryan said. "We didn't do a lot of touristy things when I was growing up, so a lot of this is new for me. Actually, I'm not sure I've ever really been to Sausalito. I mean, I've gone through it on the way to someplace else, but I don't think I've ever explored it. I'm really looking forward to it. Thanks for taking me."

The trip was almost too short for Ryan. She loved the feeling of the fresh breeze in her face, loved the smell of the sea and the feeling of the heavy air as she drew it into her lungs. Jamie just stood back and watched all of Ryan's senses enjoy the trip.

When they arrived in Sausalito, they unloaded the bikes and took off. It was around ten o'clock and Ryan was hungry as usual, even though she had consumed a rather large breakfast. They found an outdoor coffee shop right on the water, and sat outside in the damp mist while they drank their hot lattes and ate warm muffins.

Ryan looked particularly adorable. Several weeks ago Jamie accompanied her to the Patagonia store near Fisherman's Wharf to buy some new bike clothes. Ryan was making enough money now that she was able to bring her savings up to a comfortable level for the first time in years. With fewer worries about money, she decided to splurge and buy several items that she had been lusting after for a long time.

Due to her fitness level, Ryan sweated a ton when she rode her bike. She hated wearing cotton T-shirts, because the sweat just stuck to her body. She had always liked the silk weight underwear from Patagonia, but had never had the money to buy it. Now that she was slightly flush she was ready to shop.

She bought three, silk weight, T-shirts that would pull moisture away from her body. She also bought two bike jerseys, one short sleeved and one sleeveless that would also wick her sweat away. She had a number of jerseys in her wardrobe, but they were all from various races that she had entered, and were covered with logos. Since she absolutely hated to be a walking billboard, the sedate little logo on the Patagonia tops was very welcome. But her favorite purchase was the fluffy fleece jacket that she had on. It was electric blue and kept her toasty warm on this cool day. Under the jacket she wore a thin nylon vest in a brilliant yellow. This cut the wind, and would be handy for wearing later in the day when the weather warmed up.

Jamie had purchased a fleece jacket in a bright blue and green print, as well as a new jersey, both of which she had on this morning. Both women also wore long black bike pants and their heavy, off-road shoes.

After watching the morning harbor traffic for a while, Jamie asked as casually as she could, "So, have you been dating anybody lately?"

"No, I haven't," Ryan said as she removed her gaze from the harbor and fixed it upon Jamie. "What do you think I do? Leave your house at ten or eleven and go trolling for my nightly fix?"

Smiling at her flippant reply, Jamie teased, "What about all those girls I've seen you around campus with?"

Ryan raised an eyebrow and said curtly, "I'm polite. Just because I'm talking to women doesn't mean I'm sleeping with them." She picked up her trash and walked to the nearest bin to toss it away. When she returned, her smile was back in place, and she held a hand out to help Jamie to her feet.

As they got on their bikes, Jamie asked gently, "Did I hurt your feelings?"

"No. It's nothing. I'm a little sensitive today. I'm in the throes of PMS, and sometimes my mouth has a will of its own." As she rode away, she turned to Jamie, "Thanks for asking though," she said with a sweet smile.

They rode for a long while in companionable silence. The trip to Muir Woods was rather arduous, but well worth the effort. The scenery was breathtaking, as bit by bit the morning fog lifted and more of the scenery was revealed. Finally they reached their destination. Both women had doffed their jackets due to the exertion. Jamie had hers tied around her waist, but Ryan's was stowed in the pack that was securely attached to her bike. The packs also held a delicious picnic lunch they had purchased at a deli in Sausalito. Ryan had the honor of carrying all the food and drink since she was both the stronger rider and the bigger eater.

As they rode around Muir Woods, Jamie had to put her jacket back on. The path they were traveling was densely populated by some of the oldest and tallest coast redwoods in the state. The tall trees obscured the weak sun and made the path rather dark. It was still and quiet in the forest, the only sounds those made by the two women.

As they drew near Redwood Creek, they got off their bikes and stood on the bank of the quick running stream. The sun was stronger now as it neared noon. It poked through the tall canopy of trees, and cast deep shadows on the glistening creek. They decided to eat lunch, so Ryan went to her packs and removed their purchases.

She had brought a neatly folded, reflective space blanket which she spread on the ground, and the shiny metallic surface gathered what sun there was to warm them.

They sat and ate, mostly in silence, content to listen to the stream and the birds and the wildlife that surrounded them. After the remains of their meal were cleaned up and placed back in the pack, Jamie looked up at Ryan with a little smile and said, "Guess what I want?"

"Hmm, let's see," she reflected as she tiled her head up. "What would a pleasure hound want after a long ride and a big lunch? I'd guess that you want either a leg massage or a nap." She glanced over at her companion as she asked, "How did I do?"

"Pretty good," she admitted. "I choose the second option."

Ryan just shook her head, and grinned at her friend as she scooted over to the nearest tree and patted her thigh, "Come on, sleeping beauty, it's time for your nap."

Jamie happily complied by crawling over to Ryan and lying down parallel to her stretched out legs. She laid her head on the Lycra-covered thighs and moved around until she was comfortable. Ryan's hand dropped to rest on her golden hair, and she began to run her fingers through the soft locks. "I don't think it's possible to feel more content than I do right now," Jamie murmured as she heard Ryan begin to hum a slow, soft tune.

She awoke after a short, but very restful nap. She heard Ryan's rhythmic breathing and turned her head just enough to see her friend's head resting against the redwood bark, sound asleep. *Oh, she looks so pretty, I want to scoot up there and kiss that beautiful mouth awake*, she thought longingly. In lieu of that she let the peaceful feeling wash over her as she lay there on Ryan's lap. She let herself drift off again and eventually woke as a blade of grass was drawn over her eyelids and lips. "Hey, no fair tickling me awake," she complained.

"How would you prefer to be woken up, princess?" Ryan asked.

I can think of a hundred different ways, but they all involve your mouth and some level of nudity, she thought wryly. "I'll consider that and get back to you," she said with a grin as she sat up and stretched. "Ooh, my thighs didn't appreciate that last hill." She turned to Ryan and smiled coquettishly, "Is it too late to order option one?"

"I hope you brought me here for more than my thighs and my hands," she playfully groused as she began to massage the stiff legs.

Well, those are two of the biggest reasons, but it's too early to talk about that.

When the massage was complete, they hopped back on the bikes and began the ride to Mount Tamalpais. Jamie had been here numerous times, but she had never experienced it in quite the way she did today. The feeling of slowly climbing the 2,200 foot hill was completely exhilarating. It allowed her to test her aerobic capacity, as well as the strength in her legs and her overall fitness. To her surprise, she was quite pleased with the results. While the ride was clearly not easy, she managed it with very little serious trouble.

The climb was made even more pleasant by the profusion of wildflowers that sprouted from every meadow and glen. This was a particularly spectacular year for the wildflower crop, and she offered up a silent prayer of thanks that they had come to this place on this beautiful day.

They stopped frequently on the ride. At one point they spotted a family of deer in the distance, and they stopped for a long while to watch them graze peacefully, seemingly unconcerned by the presence of humans. It was nearly four o'clock by the time they reached the peak. Daylight savings time would begin that night, but today the sun was scheduled to set at around six.

"I'm worried that we're going to have trouble making it back while it's still light out," Ryan said as they paused to drink a bottle of water. "Are you up to starting back right away?"

"That wasn't really what I had in mind. I really wanted to stay up here for a while—maybe watch the sun set." She thought about the problem for a minute, and then extracted her cell phone from her seat pack. "Let me see if I can resolve our little problem," she said mysteriously.

Moments later, Jamie had booked the last remaining room at the Osprey Inn. The small inn was near where Redwood Creek emptied into Muir Beach, and it would take no more than a half hour to ride there. Ryan was a little reticent to allow Jamie to pay for the room, but she was finally convinced when Jamie insisted that she was staying over whether Ryan did or not. Of course she didn't mention that only the largest, most expensive room was still available, and she had no plans to reveal that information, either.

They stood on the peak, alone in the waning sunlight. There were several large boulders and they climbed onto the biggest one to talk and watch the sunset. The view was stupendous, with the huge panorama spread out in front of them. They could see for miles in all directions on this clear afternoon. The fog was still off in the distance, and the sun beat down, warming them on their rock.

Ryan was half reclining on the large stone, her torso supported by her forearms. Jamie gathered up her courage and did her best to calm her racing heart. She crawled around until she was sitting right next to her, facing her directly. "You're missing the beautiful view, Jamie," Ryan chided her.

"No, I'm not," she said. "I'm looking at the most beautiful view I ever hope to see."

Her eyes locked onto Ryan's, and that clearly got the brunette's attention. Ryan sat up carefully, keeping her eyes on Jamie's, her expression open and very interested. She cocked her head a tiny bit in question as she continued to stare into sea green eyes.

Jamie reached out and took each of Ryan's hands in hers. They sat directly in front of one another, crossed legs just touching at the knees. "I've given a lot of thought to how I feel about you," she said in a very quiet voice. "I know that I hurt you when I tried to go back to Jack, but I hope you understand that I did that out of pure fear. I never wavered in my desire for you. Never," she insisted, gazing deeply into the cool blue depths of Ryan's eyes. "I was just too afraid to express how I felt. I know it was hard, but in a strange way that finally knocked some sense into me and made me face my true self." She took in a deep breath and gathered her courage, saying in a quiet, but determined voice. "You're the person I love." She dropped one of Ryan's hands, and reached out to touch an even softer pink cheek that began to tremble slightly under her fingertips.

She leaned in closer, as her eyes bore into Ryan's with a fierce intensity. "I'm absolutely certain about this, and I want to move forward and build a life with you."

The pupils in the blue eyes grew larger, and the trembling increased slightly as Jamie added, "Our friendship means more to me than anything on earth, and if that's all you can offer, I can live with that. I want so much more, but I swear that I'll accept whatever you can give."

Ryan squeezed her hands tightly and tried to speak, her voice failing her at first. She took a deep breath and tried again, whispering, "I've prayed to hear those words every night since you first told me that you were attracted to me." She closed her eyes and took several rapid breaths, trying to calm her racing heart enough to speak. "I know I told you that I'd be fine if you decided that you were still in love with Jack, but I was lying—to myself and to you. I don't know how I'd have survived if you'd decided to marry him, Jamie. Your friendship means everything to me, and I'd have figured out how to stay close, but I swear it was ripping my heart out." She let herself shed the tears that she had been forced to conceal from her friend, relishing the tender embrace that Jamie now offered. They held each other for a long while, as Ryan let it all out, weeks of bottled up feelings pouring from her in a steady stream.

She sniffed as she continued, "Every night when I say my prayers I ask for the chance to love you like you deserve to be loved." A shiver ran down her body as she took in a deep breath, closed her eyes tightly and pledged, "I offer much more than my friendship, Jamie. I offer you everything that I am and everything that I can become. I want to give myself to you, totally … completely … eternally."

Jamie gazed at her with every tender emotion she felt clearly displayed in her eyes. "I love you completely, Ryan, and I want to be with you." She leaned close and said even more quietly, "Emotionally, spiritually …" Leaning over until she was right next to Ryan's ear she whispered, "physically."

Ryan's heart was pounding so loudly that she was certain Jamie could hear it. Removing the graceful hand that covered her cheek, she slowly turned it until it was right before her lips, then closed her eyes and kissed the palm reverently. She placed kiss after kiss on the small hand, as she slowly nodded her head in acceptance of the offer placed before her. Her eyes remained closed the whole while, and Jamie could see another tear slide down that beautiful face as she rose to her knees and felt Ryan do the same.

She lifted her hands to rest on the smooth planes of Ryan's face, using her thumbs to tenderly trace over the dark brows, across the prominent cheekbones, down the strong line of her jaw, finally finding the soft, warm lips. One lucky thumb continued the task, softly moving over her moist lips, as they slowly opened to envelope it in their warm wetness.

A jolt of sensation shot up and down Jamie's spine with a force so great that she felt dizzy. But Ryan stayed right where she was, waiting for Jamie to proceed as she felt comfortable. It took her a few seconds to gather herself, but she finally was able to move forward. She took in as deep a breath as she could manage, and cradled Ryan's face in both of her hands, trying to memorize the achingly tender, loving expression on the woman's face. Tilting her head just an inch, she leaned forward and captured those incredibly soft lips without hesitation, losing herself fully in the long-denied sensation.

A tiny moan escaped from Ryan as Jamie's mouth sealed hers with the promise of her love. Their arms slid around one another's waists as their lips came together again. The kisses were slow and soft and gentle—but unceasing. There was a great depth of emotion behind each tender kiss, but they didn't vary in their intensity. These weren't the passionate kisses of lovers about to consummate their union; rather, this was the first stirring of promises to come. Knowing there would be plenty of time to explore in depth, they reveled in the first tender meeting of warm mouths.

Jamie placed her hands on either side of Ryan's face and delicately kissed each closed eyelid, chasing each tear away. "I love you, Ryan. I love you so much," she said as she kissed the tender lips again and again.

Ryan's eyes fluttered open and she gazed at Jamie with a depth of emotion that she had never before felt. "I love you too. I do, I swear I do," she whispered fiercely as she drew her into a forceful hug.

They remained just as they were for a seemingly endless time. They alternated soft kisses with warm tender embraces, occasionally shedding a tear or two at the overpowering feeling generated by their nascent bond. As the sun began to slip into the sea, the boulder provided warmth to their entwined bodies, but as the chill in the air began to overtake even this heat, they reluctantly parted. "I don't ever want to lose this feeling," Jamie whispered as they gripped each other tightly one last time.

"We can't lose this feeling," Ryan said firmly. "This feeling is just the cornerstone of a lifetime of wonderful moments. It will always be with us, reminding us of how we began. I promise you this, Jamie," she said fiercely as she locked onto her sea green eyes, "this is just the first step of a journey that will take our entire lives to complete. We've just barely begun."

"I'll follow you anywhere, Ryan," she pledged, as she lifted her head for several more loving kisses.

Ryan pulled her head away and gazed at her with a look of pure devotion. "No, I don't lead you. We go together," she promised. "Always together."

The End